# Dr. Sharma's Fantabulous Fantasies

*Dr. Sharma's Fantabulous Fantasies*

Published by The Conrad Press Ltd. in the United Kingdom 2021

Tel: +44(0)1227 472 874
www.theconradpress.com
info@theconradpress.com

ISBN 978-1-914913-45-7



Printed and bound in Great Britain by Clays Ltd, Elcograf S.p.A

Typesetting and Cover Design by The Book Typesetters
www.thebooktypesetters.com

The Conrad Press logo was designed by Maria Priestley.

# Dr. Sharma's Fantabulous Fantasies

Kris Mulliah

# Preface

*Dr. Sharma's Fantabulous Fantasies* started as a collection of surreal short stories. The idea was to write them as a fun way to exercise my creative muscles after too long atrophying at an unfulfilling office job in South London.

I had always wanted to write something that would be somewhat unhinged yet somehow hopeful too. Little did I know when I began that collection of short stories that this was where it was heading.

In writing *Dr. Sharma's Fantabulous Fantasies*, I found myself writing topics I never thought I would even approach. These topics pulled the short stories into a single narrative that went far beyond my original simple aim.

Gradually a more relevant and personal story broke the surface and tied all the themes together. A story connected to my own experience growing up across different countries, amongst different cultures.

I worked periodically on this novel over several years, each new draft changing the makeup of the story and the narrative structure. As a result, it has tried on various titles along the way. These have included: *Destroyed Room, The One Who Weighed The World, A Curious Descent,* and *Amina On A Bridge.*

Writing *Dr. Sharma's Fantabulous Fantasies* has been mostly a labour of love, sometimes of bewilderment and often of anxiety, but never one of boredom. It has reminded me (yet again) that it is in writing that I find a greater capacity to understand others. And myself.

Kris Mulliah November 2021

# 1. The end

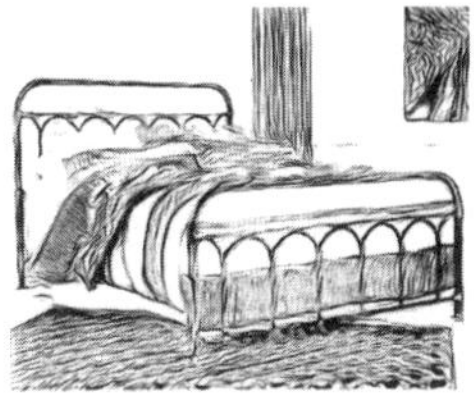

His latest death finds him face down on a bed.

Belt around his neck, he struggles to breathe.

Short sharp breaths.

An unusual position to find oneself in, but the doctor does not let that distract him from his last gasps of life.

'But wasn't that the point?'

*Yes, but not to actually die… I should be free… should have read the instructions… Will that be my dying thought? How disappointing.*

The circumstances are far from ideal, but let's take a better look at him. This grimacing, sweating, grunting individual is named Dev Sharma. Friends and family call him Dev. To his patients, he is known as Dr. Sharma.

Let's try them out:

'Dr. Sharma. It's my trapped nerve again. Every winter…'

'Dr. Sharma, could you quickly sign this prescription? Mrs Bradshaw's cortisone again.'

'Dr. Sharma! Nice to see you… That last prescription really

did the trick. Can I have another one?'

'Oh. Can you peel and chop two onions for me? That'd be a big help, Dev.'

Nearing forty, Dr. Sharma is pleased that he still enjoys an even coverage of fine, wavy black hair that he combs back. Some curly wisps peek from behind his ears as if peeping around a curtain, with a keen interest in what is happening elsewhere. He keeps his hair at a length of roughly two to three inches, believing this to be long enough to serve as evidence to friends and family of a relaxed attitude to life. To patients and colleagues, he hopes this will show he is far too busy with work to tend to trivialities like haircuts.

Dr. Sharma isn't vain, but he is sometimes preoccupied with looking effortlessly inconspicuous.

His typically south-east Asian deep brown eyes give him perfect vision, despite needing glasses when he was five. As he grew older, Dev's vision improved until he no longer needed visual aids. Dr. Sharma can still remember his reaction when the ophthalmologist first told him his eyesight was improving.

'But things always get worse, not better,' argued six-year-old Dev sitting in the elevated chair and stretching the teal sleeves of his jumper to bring the cuffs to cover his hands completely. He wouldn't reconcile the news without posing a few choice questions.

'Who says that? Try to stay still,' replied the elderly optometrist as he peered into Dev's eyes through the lens of the mobile unit he had brought to the school library.

'My dad,' replied Dev, as one of the elasticated cuffs escaped his grip and pinged back to his wrist.

'That's true of a lot of things, but not in this case,' replied the optometrist, leaning back with a smile, a smile that made Dev focus on the hairs of the moustache facing him. It was patchy and all the yellowy hairs seemed intent on worming away from one another; additionally, the optometrist smelt of cigarettes. Both factors made Dev wrinkle his nose a little.

'But you get better with medicine, and I haven't been taking any medicine. So how did I get better?'

'You're still growing,' explained the optometrist vacantly, as his chair swivelled to point him and his attention to the bank of lenses to the side where he replaced the ones he had been using.

'So that's why my eyes are getting better?' asked Dev. 'The more I grow, the better I'll be?'

'Yes. Right behind your eyes is your brain. It helps you see everything the right way up and recognise things. So it is probably doing a lot more things than we know about.'

This incident may have been one of the key catalysts behind Dev Sharma becoming *Doctor* Dev Sharma. That, and the fact that his father, and most of his family who already worked in the medical profession, encouraged him throughout his childhood and adolescence.

What brings Dev to be lying face down on a bed, legs flailing frantically, kicking the air, arm swinging for the cord that could loosen the belt around his neck, is a little more difficult to track.

It could stem from a magazine thirteen-year-old Dev picked up whilst waiting his turn for a haircut. (His hair at that time was a lot less *tame*, as one barber once put it.) Upon the coffee table, in the middle of the waiting area, lay the usual collection of ragged and dog-eared car periodicals, do-it-yourself guides and sports magazines.

'Next!' called the barber, before a man in his twenties wearing dirty jeans got up from his chair and dropped the magazine he had been thumbing down onto his now empty chair.

Until recently, Dr. Sharma has naively, and somewhat lazily, believed that his interest in the thoughts of others might have had something to do with this chance encounter whilst waiting for a haircut.

The magazine's glossy cover, which screamed for Dev's attention with its explosion of lurid, saturated colours, almost gave the impression it was expelling from its being the entirely alien, shiny, silver print that depicted the magazine's title and stretched across its width. *ICE*. It glinted under the autumn sunlight on this particularly bright day. The magazine was clearly one of the newer additions to the barbershop library, and as such was highly prized. A couple of seats away a middle-aged overweight man surreptitiously eyed Dev, evaluating his level of interest in *ICE*, weighing up whether he should bother moving for it. With Dev on the edge of his seat, the man thought better of it and continued to content himself with his ragged car magazine. A moment later, Dev was flicking through the pages about blandly good looking, well-dressed men decorated with conventionally attractive women. Most of the articles revolved around expensive wishlist cars, drinking games, interviews with beery stand-up comedians, worn depictions of the rock star lifestyles of… well, rock stars. It wasn't long before Dev's flipping brought him to the obligatory letters that readers had sent in. Or that an intern had created. Most of the letters, each sporting its own subheading and frame, recounted a sexual experience, a tale, or sought input on an issue.

'WHAT DO WHITE SPOTS MEAN?'

'HOW CAN I TELL HER?'

'BUSHED!'

'I LIKE TO BE BLINDFOLDED.'

'COULDN'T GO BACK.'

'IT WAS ALL OVER ME!'

'TRAMPLED WITH HIGH HEELS!'

'THE DOG LICKED IT.'

'WISH I COULDN'T HEAR HIM.'

'SHE TRIES TOO HARD.'

'MONSTER LIPS!'

Years later, the only letter that Dr. Sharma could vaguely remember read as follows:

'Me and my bird was in bed and sumfin appened wen we was doin it. when i came i took of the rubber and lickd the outside. I likd her of the condom. she smild took it of me an likd the inside. Its bin weeks now and we keep doin it. Is this reely wierd or is this sumfin peepl do'

'Next! Who's next?' called the barber as Dev stared quizzically at the combination of words he had just read and didn't move from his seat. The poor spelling was a prominent issue, but the words left him with little understanding of... anything, even when reconstituted. He understood the actions, but not what lay behind them.

Poking his head around the wall, the barber called: 'Come on then, young man. You here for a haircut or to read?'

'Sorry,' apologised Dev, placing the magazine neatly atop the pile on the table before getting up and moving towards the waiting chair. 'Short back and sides, please. Thank you.'

Sitting there, as his haircut happened around him, Dev stared at the magazine reflected in the mirror that stretched across the wall before him. He ran the letters through his mind over again, wondering if they were authentic, or cooked up by the magazine.

*Where would the physical pleasure come from in licking a used condom?* he asked himself. *Who would do that? It has to be made up. But if it's made up, then obviously someone thought of it, and if they thought of it... why did they?* To Dev, it no longer mattered whether the letters were genuine or not. It was enough that someone had thought of the actions. What piqued his interest was *why* they had thought of it.

Dev imagined the comments he would receive if at school he mentioned the letters. They would be quick to see the funny side of the topic.

*Dev, you been looking at pornos?*
*Supposed to look at the pictures, not the words.*
*Was it a gay one, Dev?*
*Did you get the pages stuck together?*
*What magazine was it?*
*Who reads the articles?*
*You had a good weekend!*
*D'you use up a whole box of tissues?'*

Once the novelty had worn off, the opportunistic passers-by, desperately looking to break up the monotony of the school day, would fall away to seek amusement elsewhere. Even Tim, someone who had become a good friend since Dev had started at their school and wouldn't make fun of Dev in front of others, would have some fun on the way home.

Being a year into his time at this latest school, Dev knew better than to leave himself vulnerable to cheap jokes when something genuinely interested him.

Thought.

Twenty-one grams.

A study published in 1907 by Duncan MacDougall detailed his twenty-one grams experiment. Dev's history teacher had briefly used it to introduce to his class the idea of selective reporting before discussing wartime propaganda and modern election campaigns. To Dev, it was fascinating that someone would take it upon themself to prove the existence of souls by obtaining incontrovertible evidence. In MacDougall's case, his evidence was far from convincing.

MacDougall used only six test subjects. Nursing home patients close to death and too weak to move. Patients finding themselves on the cusp of death also found themselves on MacDougall's industrial-sized scale as he and his team scurried around, calibrating the equipment to obtain accurate, up-to-the-second readings before and in the moments immediately after death. Of the six subjects, only one registered a significant difference in weight. A single patient's loss of twenty-one grams led MacDougall to believe he had determined that the human soul has weight. The idea of proving the existence of something so *ethereal* had captivated Dev, and this is what he had in mind as he skimmed the submissions in the magazine.

After that, Dev hardly thought of the letters. However, the thread had already been woven, perhaps even long before the barbershop episode. It was inevitable that the patterns and paths of thought would fascinate and entice Dr. Sharma, drawing him into a dance that would lead him to marvel at the sheer power of human thought, but also its delicate nature. He would grow to appreciate its fragility, potential and beauty, and the unforgivable monstrousness of which some people are capable. It is rarely one powerful moment that leads one toward a particular career, lifestyle or taste. Impulses, thoughts and ideas are fed by other impulses, thoughts, ideas and experiences. So it was for Dev for whom these threads would form a different pattern years later.

Adolescence, adulthood, relationships, university, medical school... These all sparked disparate ideas that, had he thought to link them, may have led him to begin his research much sooner. Undoubtedly, Dev's studies at medical school brought up other things which would have added to the foundations of his interest. A short course on counselling here, a workshop on psychological triggers there. Or just watching a horror movie at a friend's house after precisely three and a half pints of thin lager and wondering: *who is it that thinks up this stuff?*

In any case, it was years later, as a general practitioner, that Dr. Sharma sat in a doctor's office – not his own, one he was using as a locum – and pressed the little button that sent a signal along the wire that ran through the walls to light up the little bulb beside his name – written on masking tape and applied over the regular doctor's name – in the waiting room, calling forth the next patient. On one occasion, the next patient was Mr Kenneth Stanton. The episode occasionally occurred to Dr. Sharma because it was the first time he had felt deliberately antagonised by a patient. Unsurprisingly, it was also the first time a patient had left his office more agitated than when they had arrived.

# 2. 'And I was like: 'Oh my God!''

## Dr sharma

Mr Stanton was a man struggling with his sexuality. Dr. Sharma believed that sexual orientation was not a matter of choice. He did not believe any amount of *praying the gay away* would work. However, specific details from Mr Stanton's story provided a spark that ignited another flame of thought for Dr. Sharma.

'Doctor,' said Ken flatly in greeting as he stepped into the room.

'Mr Stanton?' asked Dr. Sharma, looking up from his notes.

'Yeh,' confirmed the man, in his fifties with greying blonde hair combed with a left side-parting. Wearing a plain black jumper, blue jeans and black work boots, he stepped into the room and pressed his hand against the door until they both heard the *click*.

'Hello,' greeted Dr. Sharma, 'take a seat and tell me what I can do for you.'

'It's a little difficult to explain,' warned Ken as he lowered himself into a chair, held together by tubular metal with faded green fabric over the seat and backrest padding.

'Okay,' said Dr. Sharma, continuing to scan through Ken's notes. 'Take a deep breath, count to three and then tell me. Agreed?'

Ken took up his option of a deep breath but skipped the counting. 'Can you give me something to stop me getting a stiffy?'

Dr. Sharma was braced for most things, but he still couldn't help showing a little surprise now and then. A quizzically angled head was how he now expressed that surprise. For clarification, he asked: 'By *stiffy*, you mean… an erection?'

'Yeh,' replied Ken, a note of annoyance creeping into his voice.

'So, I'm guessing, you're developing erections when it's less than convenient?'

'You can say that again, feel like a teenager,' muttered Ken, with a little laugh. It was the first time Dr. Sharma had seen him smile, let alone laugh.

'Do you know what might be causing it?'

'Do we have to talk about it? Can't you just give me something?'

'I need to understand what it's all about so I can identify… the right course of action. Tell me. What is it?'

For a while, Ken's gaze ricocheted from one surface to another behind Dr. Sharma before he finally answered. 'It happens at work. When I'm driving.'

'What do you drive?'

'A van. I fetch car wash supplies to garages.'

'I see. So do you know what's causing this?'

'No.'

'Is there ever anyone else in the van with you?'

Ken helped himself to another deep breath before replying. 'My mate. The driver does the driving, the mate, mine's Glenn, checks off the delivery spots, unloads the stock, takes payment, and does invoices and receipts. That sort of thing.'

'What's your relationship with Glenn like?' asked Dr. Sharma gingerly.

'I know what you're thinking,' laughed Stanton again. 'Look, I ain't gay for Glenn, or anybody. No offence to anyone, but that's just not me. I like women. I'm not… against *the gays*. Y'know, what they do in private is… y'know. But… That's all, that ain't me,' stated Mr Stanton.

Dr. Sharma stiffened at this, and Stanton instantly picked up on it. 'No offence to anyone, like. Are *you* one of 'em?'

'That's… um. I'm here to talk about you,' Dr. Sharma replied tactfully, lowering his face to the notes on the desk.

'Oh, right. That's how you lot are, isn't it?'

'I'm sorry?' asked Dr. Sharma without raising his head, the blood instantly rushing to his neck. He found Stanton difficult to read, but he could feel the conversation getting away from him.

'Doctors. You need to ask all the questions, don't you? So you can have the answers. And when you don't have the answers, you just pretend. You use some jargon and throw us a prescription. You're all in league with the pharmaceuticals. I know all about it. We're not stupid, we know when we're being fed a story. I read things, I know what happens.' His words suggested anger or resentment, but his tone was calm.

Dr. Sharma understood that Stanton was anxious. Something was happening to him, and he didn't know what it was. His body was surprising him with unexpected reactions, and he didn't know how to control it.

'Well,' began Dr. Sharma, 'you're right. For now, I don't know what is causing this reaction. It could be a number of things. It happens when you're in an enclosed space with Glenn? Do you know if there is something in the cab that triggers things?'

'In the cab, all I can smell is him. His clothes, his hair, soap, aftershave, shampoo.' Ken cleared his throat and re-crossed his arms. 'Look, all I want is something to stop me getting a semi.'

'Says in your notes that you're married.' Dr. Sharma felt compelled to ask: were he able to prescribe some magic pill to stop his erections altogether, how his wife would feel about it. In the moment, he couldn't find a way to approach the question.

'Have been for more than twenty years,' he replied before pausing. 'I don't need this, don't want it.'

'Have you told your wife?' asked Dr. Sharma.

'What do you think?' replied Ken, not bothering to conceal the scorn.

'The important thing is not to do anything hasty. I suggest seeing the nurse to test your blood for allergies. There may be something in the cab causing this, some aftershave or shampoo that Glenn uses. Also,' continued Dr. Sharma, as he reached for the neat stack of metal drawers behind him, 'take this leaflet and use the number. Make an appointment to speak with a counsellor to talk things through. You might need to talk through some issues with someone more specialised in the field than I am.'

'Shampoo?'

'Yes, you mentioned scents. Something different could be triggering…' Dr. Sharma trailed off as the look of disbelief crawled across Ken's face.

'Look, I don't think a smell is giving me erections. Otherwise, blokes would be using potpourri instead of little blue pills, y'know what I mean?'

'Yes, but you are an individual, and something could be provoking this response in just you.'

Ken ignored him. 'Is there something you can give me for the erections?'

'Well, if it's not a reaction to external stimuli, the erections could be a physical manifestation of some other malaise that is best discussed with the counsellor.'

Ignoring words he didn't understand, Mr Stanton continued with his original thought. 'What about something that has the side effect of, y'know, easing erections?'

'I strongly recommend that you avoid thinking along those lines. Instead, try to think of other things when you're in the cab. Concentrate on just your driving. Take this counselling information, and let's get some blood work done. Okay?'

That evening, upon leaving the practice, Dr. Sharma caught sight of the maroon colouring of the counselling leaflet. It had been crumpled and tossed away, the breeze eventually blowing it to some tall weeds where it had become snagged.

He ate dinner alone that night and thought about Kenneth Stanton. That he may be gay was neither here nor there for

Dr. Sharma. He was interested in the details that Mr Stanton had mentioned. Dr. Sharma wondered why he had mentioned those in particular. *Perhaps he was gay, but were the mentioned details part of an unacknowledged fetish that was only just surfacing?* For Dr. Sharma, the episode led to questions like this.

He considered Stanton's insistence that he was neither homosexual nor homophobic. Stanton wanted something to stop his erections or something with the side effect of quelling his erections, but he didn't appear to have considered how that would impact relations with his wife. His wife aside, Stanton didn't seem to care about an inability to achieve an erection. Apparently, all that was important to Ken Stanton was his own sense of self, holding on to his identity as a heterosexual male. It appeared he would willingly sacrifice what made him a virile male to preserve his sense of self and remain secure in knowing that he was not attracted to other men. The possibility that he could be gay was one that Stanton seemingly refused to entertain. He may have laughed about it, but it was an uneasy laughter.

As the late summer sunlight filtered through the kitchen window, Dr. Sharma picked at his sweet and sour chicken. It wasn't often that he saw patients with sexual concerns of this type. However, it did remind him of another patient he saw some years ago. Lucy Rawlings. Lucy was seventeen and had booked an appointment to see her regular doctor, Dr. Susan Gregson. Dr. Gregson had become unavailable at short notice, and Dr. Sharma was taking on some of her appointments as that evening's locum.

'I thought I was seeing a woman doctor.' Lucy Rawlings

wore a pink jacket over a white top with black jeans that looked a size too small for her.

'Dr. Gregson is unavailable. Didn't they explain at reception?' asked Dr. Sharma, exasperated at the lack of cohesion amongst the reception staff.

'Yeah, but I thought Sharma was a woman's name,' Lucy muttered, annoyed.

'It's my surname,' huffed Dr. Sharma, turning his head back down to the notes on Dr. Gregson's desk. 'Dr. Gregson isn't here, so her appointments have been reallocated.'

'But the receptionist told me she'd put me in to see another woman doctor,' persisted Lucy with a faint whine creeping into her voice.

'There must have been some miscommunication,' he replied, covering for the staff. It was at least the fourth time since his shift started. 'This evening there are only two doctors. Myself and Dr. *Joel* Mattheson.'

'What's the point of booking an appointment two weeks away to see a woman doctor and then get there and find she couldn't be bothered to turn up?' grumbled Lucy.

'Can you talk to me?'

'I ain't comfortable. I wouldn't be startin' if I could talk to you.'

'Why don't you shut the door, sit down and try me?'

With a swish of her thin brown hair, Lucy sighed theatrically and shut the door before dumping herself in the chair facing Dr. Sharma.

'All right,' she said as she sat down, 'but I ain't happy.'

'Who is?' deadpanned Dr. Sharma. 'How can I help?'

'This is delicate. It's *sensitive*. D'you understand? I need you to really listen. A lot of doctors, especially blokes, don't bloody listen, so you *need* to listen and don't act like you know everything before I've said nothing.'

Smartly clicking the top of his pen and setting it down, Dr. Sharma assured her: 'I'm listening.'

'My boyfriend. He's been getting ideas. He thinks… He says he wants me to do stuff with him. Porn stuff'

Lucy stared down at her hands in her lap. Her pink nail varnish was chipped. Her mousy brown hair was unkempt and tied back lazily. Looking at her, Dr. Sharma was suddenly awash with the realisation that he was talking to someone's little girl. Maybe her mother taught her to ride a bike. Perhaps she held Dad's hand at the ice cream van. Dr. Sharma suddenly regretted asking her to give him a try. He no longer wanted to hear her story.

On the other hand, patients are patients.

'So, you're unsure of this thing that your boyfriend has proposed,' suggested Dr. Sharma.

'I don't need you to tell me what to do. I just needed to tell somebody.' The hardness in her voice was reflected in her eyes as they nailed him where he sat.

'Do you not talk to your friends about this sort of thing?'

'There's no one I really trust. If I tell any of my mates… Well, we're not really mates. You don't understand. It'll get around, then what gets around won't be the truth anymore. It'll be something else. D'you know what I mean? Besides, if I don't do it, somebody else will. I just want to hear what I already know. I want to hear it from someone else.'

Dr. Sharma studied Lucy. He rarely had the instincts for the correct thing to say to anyone. Here he searched the makeup around her eyes and tried to pull from within himself what he imagined she wanted to hear.

'Lucy, you're an adult, capable of your own decisions, and you should not let anyone else take advantage of you, um, push you into doing something you don't want. If your boyfriend truly respects you, he will accept that you need to do what is right for you. Sex should be right for you both, and he needs to understand that.' Dr. Sharma finished with a hopeful look on his face that asked: 'How did I do?'

'Yeh,' assessed Lucy concisely. 'Thanks.' With that, Lucy got up and left the room.

Dr. Sharma didn't see Lucy Rawlings again, but through his mind her shadow now slips as his body twists on the bed, struggling against the belt around his neck.

*Why is this not working? Why can't I use these cords to get myself out of this? When is Katie coming back? Doesn't she know I'm dying here? How long does it take to smoke a fucking cigarette? Oh my God, what if she's smoking two? What if she got chatting to a neighbour? I'm not going to last.*

The more he thinks, the quicker the panic sets in, and the faster he fades. Dr. Sharma's face is turning blue fast as he speeds through these thoughts, and his mind races for a solution to his predicament. The fibres should have relaxed when he pulled the cord. His fingers find no purchase as the black material continues to tighten around his neck. He desperately wants to pry himself free to return to his safe life before all this began. If only he could go back. Ten minutes ago, and he wouldn't have slipped the belt over his head. Twenty minutes ago, and he wouldn't even be there. Now he is twitching uncontrollably on the bed, fingers scrabbling at his neck. If he could have his life back, he thinks to himself: *I would do so much more... I would use my time more wisely...* the usual things people think just before they die.

His eyes bulging, Dr. Sharma's clothes are drenched with sweat. Slowly, and with great effort, straining for every pitiful gulp of air, he manages to roll onto his back, hoping he can grab at the cord, whatever it is he seeks. On his back, Dr. Sharma now sees the rest of the room. Having been face down on the hideous bedspread, the light from the afternoon sun streaming through the window comes as a surprise to his eyes and seems to transfix them. As the light oozes patterns through the net curtain and over his brown skin, his contorted mouth seems set in his sweat-drenched face. Dr. Sharma's eyes open wide against the light as his lips slowly wrap around words. Stolen words, audible only to him.

And I.

# 3. Modus Operandi

Even now, in his last few moments, Dr. Sharma's mind is ablaze with thought.

*What am I doing here? Looking for… ? What was it all for? To end here? In Katie's bed? Belt around my neck. They'll think it's breath-play gone wrong. This belt is made for that. Auto-erotic asphyxiation. They won't believe it was for anything else. They'll believe I wanted to feel a high. Is this what they're thinking, what they are pursuing? Pleasure at all costs? A calculated risk?*

*Or is it more than that?* asks Dr. Sharma to himself. *Danger? The thrill of doing something so dangerous for something so fleeting, so intangible as pleasure? Heightened pleasure through combining sexual stimulation with hypoxia that induces ultra-lucid hallucinations.*

*All the senses, resulting in an experience that draws one back, again and again, providing one survives the first attempt, to feel something more. It feeds the human impulse to go beyond what everyone else does.* Dr. Sharma can't help asking about this impulse to go further.

*What leaps and connections the brain would have to make to wind up prioritising pleasure above all else, placing it above other needs? What must it leave behind? What must happen in a brain for it to tease and ultimately compromise its own survival?*

*What is this boundary we continually need to cross?* He asks himself. *The obscuring of some line, invisible yet apparent to everyone. The filling of a space between one thing and another. Things that we think have nothing to do with one another are what we bring together in the name of pleasure.*

*Entertainment. Pleasure and asphyxiation. Elephant on a stool wearing a top hat. Bear, muzzled and forced to dance on hot metal plates. Until it associates music with movement and dances from one paw to another upon hearing it.*

*Like the subject of a fetish,* he theorised, *something transcending its typical presentation, taking on a new significance. A new way to view something relatively mundane. Does this drive towards the new suggest a conquered fear that now amuses us? Is erotic asphyxiation the most naked expression of that idea? Complete control of one's own body. Mastery over its limits. So much so that one would take said body to the knife-edge where control meets assured death. The arrogance of the absolute certitude that they will not die, convinced of the total ownership of their body that they would risk relinquishing that ownership altogether. Should we be repulsed by the idea, or awed?*

As he asks all these questions, Dr. Sharma's mind drifts. *Willing to go that extra step in the pursuit of pleasure. Willing to alter something irrevocably to see it in a different context, making it different, making us different in relation. The thrill of being a different person reaching for an unknown. You but not you. A hidden version of yourself, with longer arms, sharper fingers, grasping and exploring the textures of those things you had forgotten.*

*But that wasn't my intention! So, what if I die like this? On Katie's bed with this belt around my neck? This stupid belt. Stupid lesions around my neck. Contact Urticaria from this stupid belt. I should know my body. How could I not know I'm allergic? But I'm not allergic to the fibres, or the leather edging. What could I be allergic to?*

As Dr. Sharma's thoughts return to his current state, he tries again for the cause of his condition. *Red, weeping lesions all over my neck. I can feel them against my fingers. I don't have allergies! What fucking allergy? Panicked… belt beyond safety. Something… leather.*

*Dimethyl Fumarate… panicking… tightening… struggling… leather treated with Dimethyl Fumarate… lesions… acute... weeping… tightening… grasping… open-mouthed… gasping… pulling… kicking… DMF... permeates leather.*

*What shitty fucking luck? To research and buy something with fail-safes. Only to be surprised and defeated by acute contact dermatitis.*

Eager to distract himself from his predicament, here, Dr. Sharma's thoughts get a little… unusual as he begins to play a game with himself. *'B for burial. C for cremation. Seems like there should be an A for something. What could A be for? A… Astral projection? No, you need to be alive for that. Asphyxiation? No, that's what you're doing now, Dev. Stop thinking of your own problems. You're so selfish. Hey, if you can't have a laugh when you're dying, when can you?*

Dr. Sharma tries to laugh. Instead, 'he-lthsquegrrr,' is the only sound he can produce.

*Okay, so I'm not going to die with a laugh on my lips. That much is evident. Maybe A could be for absinthe. They could douse your body in absinthe, then set it on fire. No, that's too close to cremation. Maybe they could combine the absinthe and the ceremony to make a brand new game show with an element of social responsibility to discourage alcohol abuse. The heart in a corpse is stimulated into pumping absinthe all around the body.*

*Homeless alcoholics are then brought into the studio on the promise of free alcohol, but then it is revealed that to get at the booze, they will need to rip the body apart with their bare hands and drink it out of the corpse any way they can. Of course, they will score bonus units of alcohol for every major artery they gnaw through. They could freshen up the format every other week by introducing other addictions.*

*Perhaps, for a Christmas Special, they could have alcoholics and addicts form tag-teams. Fun for all the family. I'm getting light-headed, not in control of my own mind. I'm dying, so kill me! He-he. I'm not dying yet, so long as I'm struggling, I'm not dying. That's right, I'm not suffocating. My face is just turning all different shades to find one to suit this hideous bedspread. See? So long as I'm joking, I'm not dying.*

*So A could be, 'er, maybe they pickle you in absinthe, stuff you in a barrel and roll you out off a liner in the middle of the ocean, like some kind of weird boozy offering to all the sea monsters. Or A could be for ash cloud. All recent corpses could be skewered up and laid across a volcano in anticipation of its eruption. There would be the mischievous satisfaction of knowing that when the volcano does blow, your loved one will be helping to ruin the holiday plans of thousands of complete strangers. Ha-ha. Eh? What is that light through the window? Can't be the sun. It isn't sunshine season, it's shunsine season. The town is out there. The people going about their business while I lie here making colours with my face.*

*Tomorrow they'll awaken to the news that someone in their town died like this. They'll think I was hanging from a door handle and having a wank. No doubt I'll be called a pervert. When they find out I'm Asian or a doctor, will they be even more disgusted? A doctor? Supposed to be able to trust a doctor.*

*Can you trust people and their impulses? People who do the things they do, whether for some obscure reason or a bunch of reasons. That's what I was trying to get to, I remember now. The reasons. Yes, their reasons, but my reason for wanting their reasons. The thoughts behind the thoughts.*

*Surely, if we can accept that there is a complex web that influences our thoughts, we can reconcile that others have different beliefs and traditions. Wouldn't that lead to greater understanding and compassion for other people, and wouldn't that eventually lead to us not doing the terrible things that we do to each other?*

*They say things will change, but change comes ever so slowly, and I am dying ever so quickly. So many of us seem resigned to this reality because that's the way it is. What if the reality of our everyday lives was to suddenly change? Wouldn't we suddenly forget our grievances, our differences? I'm not sure what makes sense in this light of day, this light that presses through the window and then disperses, like dandelion seeds on the breeze. I see the individual dust particles in the room, and each one is a tiny pinprick of light floating before the crack in the curtains.*

*Beyond that, the town, the people.*

*If their lives, their safe lives, in this safe little town they all know so well, started coming apart, what would they do? If their version of reality began coming apart at the seams, would they not forget all about petty grievances and prejudice? We would all just be people together dealing with the new reality of an immediate crisis.*

*Religion, sex, regrets, memories, they would all count for nothing in the face of a shifting reality. Bending, refracting like light. Photons, unconcerned with the political, religious, or sexual, persuasions of this world's various organisms, travelling millions of miles through the black, empty, vast nothingness of space to light up this town. This world.*

What if the light burnt out?
What if the light shone brighter than ever?
What if the light refracted?
What if the light dispersed?

What if the light became solid?

What if light shattered?

What if light turned to dust?

What if…

# 4. Delta waving, not drowning

Michael Monroe awakes in darkness. In the middle of the black night, he is immediately alert to everything. It is as though he has not even been asleep. He has not awoken so in tune with his surroundings since Christmas Day when he was nine. That was the last year he had allowed himself to believe in Father Christmas. After that, he was ten, and it was "time to grow up, you're becoming a young man," as his father used to say. The last time he had heard his father say something similar was seven years ago in the hospital. 'It's time to grow up,' were the exact last words his father spoke to him. It seems to Michael that he has spent his whole life growing up, and no matter how grown he is, it will never be enough for his father. There is always more growing to be done.

Now aged thirty-nine, he wonders how long it will be before he, in turn, will absentmindedly let the phrase slip out to his children. The way parents do, without really considering the implication of their words. Robin is five. Heather is three. Still lying in bed, Michael looks around him. His wife, Karen, is thirty-seven. The wardrobe, pine, is seven, and the alarm clock, digital, had been in situ for two weeks. Since then, Michael has concluded that it is too bright. In the dark, Michael can feel the light permeate his eyelids. He fancies he can even make out the numbers, as though the clock is forcing him to face each passing minute. Each second. He has often toyed with this notion. It would be a good party trick.

Michael had spent considerable time exploring the different models of alarm clocks available and had even looked up whether a green display would be more conducive to a good sleeping environment than a red display. In the end, despite his research, they had settled on this model. Because Karen had liked the purple buttons.

'But you're not going to see the purple buttons in the dark,' Michael protested, minded to bring up his findings, despite already being warned against such action.

'I'm not going to see anything in the dark, so why does it matter about red versus green?' asked Karen. She has blonde hair and a perpetually rosy glow to her cheeks. In recent years she has begun to feel more and more comfortable in her work attire, sometimes more relaxed than in her casual clothes.

'You'll see the digits,' argued Michael.

'No, I won't.'

'Why not?'

'Because I'll be asleep, Michael. So will you. It's on sale. Half price. Let's just get it,' said Karen, losing patience.

'Maybe it's half price for a reason. What if it's too bright?'

'Then we'll put something in front of it. Or we'll put masking tape on it.'

'But then I won't see the clock.'

'I thought that was what you wanted.'

'Yes, but I want to see the time *sometimes.*'

'Michael, I don't know if you've noticed, but we have two small children to raise. This is exactly the sort of thing I was talking about in session the other day. I need your support. We can't fixate and waste time on trivialities like this anymore.' With that, Karen grabbed a boxful of purple-buttoned alarm clock and stalked away, leaving Michael to slope past a smirking eavesdropping sales assistant.

Karen continues to sleep, breathing gently as Michael quietly picks up his clothes and slips out of the room. Now dressed, his hand is steady as it pushes further open the door of the room where his children sleep, dead to the world. They sleep deeply and hardly protest as he bundles up each child and takes them out to the car.

Michael is not surprised to see them both fit snugly in sleeping positions on the car's back seat wrapped in their blankets. He silently administers and accepts for himself a mental pat on the back, acknowledging his diligent research leading to the purchase of this model for their growing family. He takes the driver seat and looks back at them in the mirror before smiling and thinking: *if they were in an alien supermarket or something, they'd be labelled: human children, individually hand-wrapped and reared to perfection on our award-winning farming outposts. Kids in Blankets.* Michael runs his tongue over his lips to wet them and starts the car.

It's not long at all, feels almost like seconds before they arrive at their destination, the woods just beyond the town. Michael is surprised that neither of the children has woken up, but relieved as it would have made for an uncomfortable journey.

Robin, small and warm, breathes softly as Michael lifts him from the car's back seat, still wrapped in his blankets. Supporting the boy against his chest with his right arm, he uses his left hand to gently close the car door.

Michael leaves the engine running. For two reasons:

1. The headlights to illuminate the area.
2. The gentle rhythm of the engine to encourage little Heather to sleep.

A dozen or so metres from the car, Michael deems a spot by a tree suitable and lays Robin down on the ground with his face to the sky, still swaddled in his blankets. Michael straddles the boy, kneeling either side of him on the blanket, watching him sleep, waiting for him to awaken. Curious about what the child will see when he opens his eyes, Michael twists around to have a look above him.

Out here, the low light pollution allows the blue night sky to make silhouettes of the bare autumn branches. They look like the red veins against the whites of Michael's eyes after a day spent swilling coffee before his computer screen, but the branches are black and between them shine teeny tiny stars. Michael turns back to Robin, who is still asleep. *Robin wouldn't think the branches look like veins. His eyes are just milky whites, pupils surrounded by clear irises.*

Tiring of waiting, and remembering he no longer has time to ponder things like this, Michael decides to wake Robin up gently. He brushes Robin's forehead lightly with his little finger. The little boy continues to sleep soundly. Undeterred, Michael again uses his little finger to playfully tickle his son's forehead. Again, no response. Quickly growing impatient, Michael taps Robin gently on the forehead with his middle finger. This time, Robin stirs a little but continues to sleep. Michael taps harder this time and is rewarded with a nonsensical but clearly indignant '*marh*'. This level of consciousness will do for Michael.

Bracing himself over Robin, his left hand on the damp ground supporting his upper body weight, Michael's right hand reaches as far back as it can go before he grimaces. He holds for a moment, letting the muscle burn in protest at the unusual movement, before swinging at the little face with a stinging open-palmed slap that cracks the silence of the forest. With this, the child is immediately awake, but with the side of his face slapped against the ground, the first thing he sees is not black veins against a starry sky but the dirty tail of a grey squirrel. The smack echoing around the trees sends the animal scurrying amongst the dead leaves towards the nearest tree trunk.

It's a startling awakening. The environment is entirely unexpected. The slap is a shock, but Robin does not initially feel the pain. He turns his head, and after a few moments, he recognises his father before finally feeling the rush of pain as his brain registers the slap and the disorientation from this unfamiliar landscape. He cries out, softly at first, and Michael lets him have his moment. As Robin gets to the end of his breath and inhales for another wave, Michael takes another swing, exercising his other hand.

Little Robin does not know what is happening. Having no

baseline against which to compare his current situation, he is at a loss. *Even if he had experienced this before, he wouldn't think of it because children live in the moment. That's the beautiful thing about them. They don't consider the past unless they're prompted to,* thinks Michael, as he feels Robin struggling under the blanket pinned down by Michael's legs.

*That's another thing I like about this strategy. The blanket performs two functions. One. It keeps the child warm during transportation. Two. When necessary, it acts as an excellent restraint to prevent them from fidgeting.*

'Mummy!'

Michael lands another slap and decides to get serious.

'Mummeee!'

Closing his legs tighter and higher around Robin's small frame to plant himself firmly, Michael now curls his fingers to form a fist before bringing his knuckles crunching into the child's face.

'Mummeee!'

Punching.

'Mummeee!'

Punching him.

'Mummeee!'

Punching the child.

All the while, observed only by a squirrel and two mice.

It isn't long before the squeals and cries cease, and Robin's small head is a swollen, bloody mess. Split lips. Gashed skin. Matted hair. Loose jaw. Eyelids slightly parted. Damp soil in his ear. Michael can't say which happened first: the cessation of the squeals or the bloody mess. In the frenzied excitement of the moment, he hasn't paid attention to this.

The nose is unrecognisable as such. The eyes are caked with blood. The lower jaw hangs unnaturally limp, dislodged from its usual setting. The skin, greased with blood and saliva, is tight and swollen in some places, loose in others, mashed into the collapsed bone underneath. It is as if the boy is wearing a Halloween mask several sizes too big for him.

Michael sits back, feeling as though an hour has passed, but it has only been a few minutes. Robin's body is still warm as he rises to his feet and ambles back to the car, turning his thoughts to Heather. He had thought he would mix things up, maybe force her face into a bucket of water, maybe give her a few options and let her choose. The three-year-old would have no idea what she was choosing. Eventually, Michael decides it is only fair on Robin if she receives the same.

The only difference: he doesn't wake her for it. And no woodland creatures are in attendance this time.

Michael sits under the tree with the two children and watches the sun come up. He imagines what his wife's reaction will be to find him and her children gone. Will her mind immediately imagine the worst, or will she begin making up plausible stories to explain their absence? Will the vaunted mothering instinct kick in?

Michael imagines what he will say.

*I found them like this. Like that when I got here.*

That sort of excuse would work for a child, so what changes between childhood and adulthood? If they don't believe him, he'll ask for his mum and dad. They'll believe him. If the worst comes, he'll say he is sorry and stand facing the corner for a bit, like he did at school. Under his tree, Michael rolls a dead leaf by its broken stem between his thumb and index finger, watching as the morning sunlight shows its frailty, silhouetting the veins like a skeleton through the brown surface.

*Who do they think they are, the police? If I broke a knick-knack at home, Mum and Dad wouldn't break out a forensic kit, dust for fingerprints and collect DNA. I'd apologise, promise to be more careful and that would be the end of it. No one else would be involved.*

With that, Michael lets the leaf drop and promptly falls asleep, holding Heather's limp little hand.

When Michael awakes, he pulls his hand back to his nose. He can smell that earthy, peaty smell from the woods. He turns it over slowly and draws his knuckles close to his eyes. No trace of the soil and dead leaf particles that had become stuck to the blood on his knuckles in the woods. Now, both hands are clean. The radio blathers about traffic queuing up behind an accident. The accident, at a roundabout, is impeding access to the dual carriageway. The very dual carriageway that Michael takes to work each day. He slowly pushes one hand out from under the duvet and silences the alarm clock.

The plan had been to wait to be found. Michael had been very clear in his mind about this. His mother always told him that if he should ever become lost, he should sit still and wait for her to find him.

So what is he doing here, listening to his wife starting the day in the kitchen? He should be back in the woods with his children. With the dewy grass… twittering birds… rough bark of the tree… smell of the damp ground…

That peaty scent that he could clearly detect when he first awoke is now complemented by the aroma of freshly filtered coffee before it is altogether spirited away on the air. He searches his hands again, certain that he can still feel the texture of blood caked in the creases, but there is no sign of it. Certain also that he is still wearing the sweaty clothes from last night, he kicks away the duvet in one swift move.

Underwear.

Nothing more.

Michael sits up in bed and examines his knees. He can still feel the inside of his jeans as his knees ground against them during the exertions of the night, but there aren't any bruises, no redness.

*I should be back in the woods*, thinks Michael. *Perhaps I can get out of the house without being noticed and get back over there.*

Now, from the corner of his eye, Michael sees the bedroom door move silently open. His head swivels and his eyes goggle, but from his position on the bed, he sees no one. At the bottom of the bed is a solid wood bedstead. Perhaps the cat had pushed the door open and is now lurking around, tail twitching, wondering why the children weren't around to annoy her.

'Daddy?'

Michael's heart passes a sliver of ice going in the opposite direction as the organ races to his throat, where it joins the rest of his body in freezing. The only part of him left unaffected are his eyeballs, which now track Robin as he scampers up and joins Daddy in bed.

It is a rare treat for Robin to find Daddy in bed at this time.

And so alert! Normally Daddy is grumpy and sleepy in the morning and would tell Robin to lay still and sleep if he got into bed with him, which would be not at all to Robin's liking since he had arrived to bounce, not *sleep*.

This morning, however, Robin has remembered the dream he had had during the night, and he is as eager to bounce as he is to tell his father about it, especially since the dream featured him.

'Daddy, I had a dream last night, and you were in it.'

Michael, still in shock, can only stare slack-jawed as this little boy snuggles under the duvet next to him, oblivious to his inner turmoil and the tsunami of guilt that is engulfing him.

'Do you want me to tell you?' asks Robin.

Michael eventually manages to nod.

'We were at the funfair, you and me, and we were in the queue for the big loop-the-loop,' explains Robin, making appropriate swirling motions with his hands to fully illustrate the fundamental concept of loop-the-loop to Daddy. 'We were in the queue, and it was a long queue, but we got to the front. Then the man told us I was too little to go on it. You were very angry with the man, and you were telling him I was not too little, and we had been waiting a long time, but he wouldn't let me go. We were going away when I just… got bigger. I *magicked* myself bigger, and then I was big enough. Everyone put their hands over their mouths because they didn't know what was happening, but I ignored them because the man was letting us go on the loop-the-loop.

'We went on,' continued Robin, 'and we went round and round and round. When we came back, the people still had their hands over their mouths because they were still surprised. There were other children crying because they were still too little to go on the loop-the-loop, and they didn't know how to magic themselves bigger. So I *magicked* them bigger too so they could go on the loop-the-loop and everyone was happy with me. The other children all wanted to be my friends, and they wanted me to go to their school, but I couldn't because I already go to my school. Can I jump on you now?'

Having given fair warning, and knowing when to grab at an open opportunity for bouncing, Robin does not wait for an answer. Despite his son proving himself to be very much alive, Michael is still surprised at the warmth of the little body clambering on top of his.

Six days later, Michael has still not come to terms with what he is calling his *experience*. Far too vivid to have been an average dream, his stomach turns as he tries to make sense of bludgeoning his children with his bare fists. It is the weekend, and the children are with grandma for the day, so Michael and Karen are free to discuss things.

They have not had a good week, and Karen is keen not to

let it pass unaddressed.

Setting coffee cups down on the table, Karen asks: 'what is going on?'

'Truthfully, I don't know,' answers Michael, truthfully indeed.

'You have hardly been here this week, and when you are, your mind is somewhere else.' Karen takes a deep breath. 'Be honest with me here. Are you having an affair?'

'What? No.'

'Do you want a divorce?'

'No.'

'You didn't turn up to our session this week. You're the one who wanted to try therapy in the first place. When you did answer your phone, your excuse was that you'd forgotten. We both know that's bullshit! You never forget anything. So when you can't even do me the courtesy of thinking up a half-decent lie that I can persuade myself to believe, it makes me think you have finally given up, which is fine. It really is. I just need to know what we're doing and what steps we need to take.'

'I don't want a divorce.'

'Then what do you want?' asks Karen, as she sips coffee, only to cover her emotions, not really tasting anything.

Turning his own mug around on the table, Michael replies, 'I just need some time alone.'

'So you want a separation?'

'No, I just want a day on my own, or even just an afternoon where I don't need to feel the pressure of work or family.'

'Family isn't supposed to be pressure. It's supposed to be

enjoyable, to ease the pressure of work.'

'I know, and it *is* enjoyable, but a bit of it is still pressure.'

Karen exhales loudly, puffing out her cheeks. 'Okay, well, it's mid-morning now. Why don't you take the rest of the day and I'll see you at dinner tonight. We'll talk more when the kids are asleep. I'll want your input and suggestions,' she finally manages with a firmer edge to her voice. Karen gets up from the table with her coffee and moves toward the door before turning back. 'You know, I do love our family, Michael.' With that, Karen turns and disappears to another room.

Having told his dear wife he needs solitude for the day, Michael inevitably cannot bear to be alone with his thoughts. Instead, he phones a friend to meet that afternoon. A friend in whom he could confide and trust to be completely untrustworthy, as far as the general public was concerned. Should Si (Simon) blab about what Michael was about to tell him, he would be summarily ignored.

Simon and Michael had been at college together, but while Michael had leaned toward business, Si had careened towards Theatre Studies. Leaving college early, Si had joined one of those companies that scrabbled along by specialising in murder mystery nights. He was by no means a talented actor, but he made up for it with enthusiasm and quick wit. He was perfect for improv and loved being the centre of attention. Some years later, tiring of murder mystery nights and the sporadic nature of his income, he had decided to seek solid employment. Si completed the necessary studies and training to become a liaison officer placing young offenders with supportive foster families.

Si enjoyed this work, and his caseload of young teenagers enjoyed his easy-going nature and the non-authoritarian, jokey banter he exchanged with them. All was well until one day, Si finally stopped resisting and gave in to temptation when he let one of his young charges, fifteen-year-old Tracy, tuck her hair behind her ears, lean over from the passenger seat in his car and put her tongue to his exposed penis. After that day, this incident would have been safe with Tracy had Si not felt a shiver of fear grip the back of his neck every time he saw her. Unlike any other man she had encountered, Tracy actually liked Si and would not have posed a threat. The real problem came into being when Si persuaded himself that an envelope stuffed with cash would ensure her silence.

The money was a nasty surprise to Tracy, who was hurt at Si's apparent suspicion she might do something to harm him. Seeing him as someone she had grown close to, she still trusted him after the fellatio, but it was clear to her that he did not feel the same way. On the other hand, she did have some cash to splash, and perhaps this was something she could try on someone she didn't like so much. She did. She tried it on her new foster father, who wasted no time getting to the truth of the matter.

Before long, Si was off the job, on the Sex Offenders Register and out of favour with the town that now regards him as a notorious local scumbag. Si's sick mother is the only reason he remains there.

Outside in the beer garden behind the pub, and away from eager ears, Michael exchanges cordialities with Si before getting his story off his chest. Si is dressed, as always, in his comfy tracksuit bottoms, an oversized T-shirt and a light jacket. His long but receding brown hair is tied back in a ponytail, while his nose twitches under his spectacles as he listens attentively and absorbs Michael's information. Time has changed him, and he no longer has to fight the urge to interrupt others, using the dead time whilst others are talking to plan what he will say next. Instead, Si considers Michael's words until he finishes speaking before offering his suggestion. He picks up his pint of lager and drains half of it while Michael waits for his response. Eventually, Si puts down his glass, wipes his mouth and says: 'You should go to the press.'

'What? Si, you're crazy. That's not what I'm talking about. It was just so vivid, so real. I haven't been able to shake it off since it happened.'

'But it didn't happen, it was a dream.'

'Yeah, but it was, like, more than a dream, it was like it was being projected through some mega-techno-vision, high intensity, magnified sensory, hyper-reality sort of thing.'

'Would you be surprised if I told you you're not the only one who has had this type of experience this week?'

'I'm not?' asks Michael, his eyes widening. 'Other people are dreaming they're going to kill Robin and Heather?'

'No, idiot! They're dreaming their own stuff. Look, you're just the latest one I've spoken to. Something is happening. People all over town are having that *experience* and are convinced that sooner or later they will actually do those things.'

'Like a premonition?'

'Exactly. It's so intense, so real, that people don't want to go anywhere near the ones they have seen themselves hurt. You're the fourth person I've spoken with, and the other three have all spoken to one or two other people who have had a similar experience. They, in turn, have heard from other people and so on and so on. Get the picture? This isn't just a few people having a nightmare after too much cheese. This is something.' Si gulps down some more of his beer while Michael stares at him, incredulous. 'Haven't you heard from anyone? Hasn't anyone told you?'

'No, my world's been turned upside down. I've been trying to keep myself to myself, put it out of my mind, but it's not working.'

'People are petrified,' continues Si, 'they're convinced they are going to hurt other people, or themselves. The people I've spoken to have tried turning themselves in to the police, but the cops are turning them away. Even though they're certain they're going to do something bad.'

'Why?'

At this, Si glances around before answering: 'Too many people coming forward. They don't know what to do, so they're being told not to worry. But there are far too many people to ignore. Now we need to see what the authorities will do.'

'How do we do that?'

'The press. We contact them. We go to the fuzz, all of us. Together. *And*, we take megaphones.'

It is the evening, and Karen is not surprised that Michael has failed to turn up in time for dinner. She had asked him for input, for a decision, and she believes that Michael's absence is his way of avoiding this request, an indication of his feelings, and perhaps his intentions. It is irrefutable that he has struggled since they had had children, and firm decisions on any topic are difficult to elicit from him.

Karen runs cold water over the contents of her salad spinner, drowning out the sound of the news on the small kitchen TV, but she glances over at it anyway. The newscaster hands over to the local reporter whose mouth makes the sound of cold water over lettuce. Karen turns back to the sink and turns off the tap. Shaking the drops from the colander, she can now hear the reporter.

'… taken completely by surprise here as these concerned citizens demand action be taken to stop them from harming other people. These are people from all walks of life, the vast majority of them are people with no previous history of violence or violent acts, but here they are tonight making themselves heard to anyone who will listen.'

'Bunch of nutballs,' mutters Karen.

'Who, Mummy? Who's a nutball?' asks Robin as he plays with his stuffed *Jodie-the-Giraffe* toy.

'People on TV, darling,' replies Karen.

'… and now we can speak with Simon Johnson and Michael Monroe,' babbles the reporter in the kitchen.

'Michael?'

'Daddeee, yay!'

'Mr Johnson, you are listed on the Sex Offenders Register, are you not?'

‘That’s right,’ says Si.

‘Are you convinced you will re-offend?’ asks the reporter.

‘N-no, I already told you, this isn’t about me. I’m here to support these other people who want action from the authorities.’

‘I see. And Mr Monroe, you say you are afraid you will hurt your family?’

‘That’s right, Penny! We are turning ourselves in, but they don’t want to listen to us.’

‘Have you hurt your family?’

‘No, I thought I had, but I hadn’t. Coming here is the best thing I can do for them.’

‘So you intend to hurt your family?’

‘I don’t want to, but it was so powerful. I just want to turn myself in, keep myself away from them.’

‘Well, that’s input, I suppose,’ mutters Karen to her lettuce.

‘Thank you both for speaking with us,’ dismisses Penny as she turns her attention back to the camera. ‘Clearly, this town has been rocked by something bizarre, and the authorities need a plan to address these high emotions. Back to you in the studio,’ she beams.

Karen shakes the colander over the sink one last time and looks over at her small boy, who has suddenly grown quiet.

# 5. Airy fairy, la di da

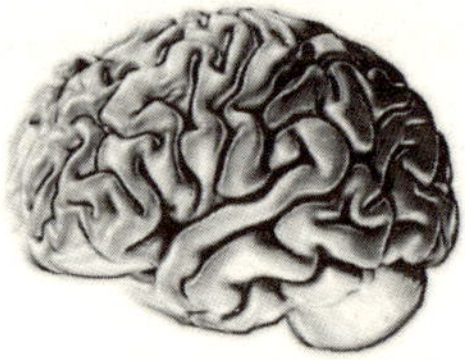

Eight-year-old Dev was quiet as his parents sat down with him and his elder sister, Amina, at the table. First, his father took some salad from the bowl, then his mother. He knew it would be his mother who would spot that anything was amiss.

'How did all this fluff get all over our salad?' asked his mother, as expected.

'What fluff?' asked Raju, his father.

'Look, there's fluff and stuff in the salad.'

They both turned to Dev while twelve-year-old Amina leaned over to peer into the salad bowl and inspect the evidence with her wide brown eyes. A lock of her shiny black hair escaped from behind an ear as she pursed her lips inquisitively. Having had her own history of clumsiness, she felt bad for Dev and showed this by not adding her voice to the conversation. Instead, she sat back in her seat and looked out of the French windows thoughtfully, wondering about all the other houses around them.

Raju's devoutly Hindu family had thought the name Amina cute, until they realised it was Arabic in origin. It had been Serena's suggestion. Serena had also been raised as a Hindu in Mauritius, but not nearly with the same burden of conservatism. Instead, she had grown up in a more multicultural part of the island and was generally more open-minded. To Serena, Amina was a name she liked, and she disregarded any cultural baggage that came with it, other than its Arabic meaning: honest.

When it came to their new baby boy, Raju suggested selecting a traditional Hindu name to placate his ultra-Hindu family. Serena, not the type to compromise to appease others, suggested Dev. In her time in France, she had come across and liked the name Devin. For Raju and her, Dev would be short for Devin. If Raju's family came to the misguided notion that it was a truncated form of the Hindu name Devendra, then so be it.

'Dev? Did you drop the salad when you were bringing it to the table?' asked his father.

'No,' replied Dev.

'Then how did this fluff get in the salad from the kitchen to the dining table?'

'Yes. I dropped the salad.'

'Then why did you lie about it?' asked his mother, Serena.

'I don't know.'

'Never mind,' interjected his father, sensing a small thing was about to become a big thing when all he wanted was a quiet dinner. 'Let's just forget about the salad.'

'You have to stop dropping things,' continued his mother.

'Sorry,' said Dev.

'And why did you lie?' asked his father.

'Lying won't make anything easier,' stated Tim, years later as he dumped himself in Raju's armchair by the window in the living room. 'They want you to practice, they want the whole… cliché for you,' he concluded matter-of-factly. 'Raju is never going to go for this. He won't understand why you need to research *this*. I've been listening to you for years, and *I* don't understand it.'

'I know,' replied Dev, leaning against the painted wood door separating the living room from the dining room. He stared down at the old-fashioned carpet with its faded pattern of flowers. *Who thought it would be a good thing to print flower designs onto carpet?* 'Research means less actual contact with sick people,' he eventually offered. 'What do you think? Think that argument would work?'

Tim had been Dev's friend since secondary school. They had begun college together, but Tim had opted to leave after just a year. Classrooms are not for everyone, and they were never for him. Instead, Tim wanted to leave, not just college, but everything. The area, the country, the people.

Tim wasn't as tall as Dev, almost a foot shorter at five feet and some change. The gay community would refer to him as a *cub*, and it was a term that Tim happily self-ascribed. When he and Dev first met in secondary school, he had chubby cheeks that were almost always a rosy hue, as if he had just finished a workout. Tim had lost the chubby cheeks and the redness by now, revealing a light sprinkling of freckles under his bright grey eyes with their blonde lashes. When Tim has been away for a while, Dev misses seeing his ever-fresh and curious eyes. He misses Tim's skewed views, and, in his absence, he imagines how those eyes see the world. Except, he is always too busy to realise it. It is only when his friend returns that Dev understands the impact his friend has.

Here Tim is about to embark upon his second trip to travel the United States, and Dev has agreed to drive him to Heathrow. Even when he was in the UK, he didn't linger long, always zipping around with something to do and people with whom to do it. Dev and Tim had this in common, the need to stay busy. The friends differed in that Dev was happy to focus on one activity and follow it to its conclusion. Tim's lust for change didn't allow him to concentrate on one thing for too long. It wasn't uncommon for him to grandiosely declare a small Greek village the most glorious place on earth and then claim to have tired of it by the following morning.

At secondary school, Tim had no choice but to turn up, but once at college, he and Dev were of an age that they could do as they pleased. Dev committed to his studies, as was expected of him. There had never been any question over him following through to attend university and later medical school. Tim had tried college, but not with any conviction. It was a year before the lure of adventure and vistas-new inspired him to submit the paperwork for a passport before booking the first flight of his life, to a three day holiday in Majorca. That was six years ago. The travelling bug had bitten him hard, and Tim hadn't stopped moving since.

Dev had expected to pick up Tim from his parents' house, but with so little luggage, just a large backpack, Tim had decided not to wait and had walked over that morning. Now, occupying Raju's armchair, he crossed his legs, his lips pursed in scepticism. 'I just don't think there is any way Raju and Serena are going to be okay with you researching… thought.'

Tim hated to be the one to pour cold water on anyone's ideas, particularly Dev's. Whenever they discussed it, Tim asked Dev to explain it to him again. Not because he didn't understand or couldn't remember, but because he secretly hoped that Dev would find the right combination of words to explain it in a way that convinced him of his sincerity. Or that Dev would finally realise that his theory was unworkable.

Despite having discussed this several times, it was apparent to Dev that he had failed to successfully communicate the aim of his proposed study. He had never thought of himself as being particularly bad at explaining concepts to others. So, the way Dev saw it was that Tim was deliberately obtuse, failing to visualise what he was outlining.

'It just seems far-fetched,' Tim blurted, Dev's frustration feeding his own before he strategically conceded: 'Perhaps, I'm getting confused on the wider aspects and implications.'

'It's an idea. All ideas are far-fetched until they are explored further. Then they get, well, deeper,' tried Dev.

'It just seems impossible to prove. Too *huge*. What would

you even get out of it?' asked Tim, getting up from the armchair and turning to the window behind it.

'I don't need to actually prove anything to make progress,' argued Dev plaintively. 'Thomas Edison said he successfully proved how not to make a lightbulb 10,000 ways before proving how it should be made. Human thought. Consciousness. It's a huge web, and in that web are lies, hubris, dead ends, contradictions and paradoxes. It goes on and on, all of it influenced by the thoughts of others, hormones, genetics, experiences, the passage of life. It's massive and somewhere in between all that are thin slivers of truth.'

'Yeah,' agreed Tim vaguely. 'It's a riddle wrapped in a mystery. And surrounded by… a… what is it?'

'Enigma. And I think you messed up the order.' At this, Tim flicked Dev a middle finger. 'Seriously, what do you think my dad would say if I told him I wanted to switch to research?'

Tim thought a moment before an opportunity for fun lit up his face. 'You wanna roleplay it?'

'Go on then,' agreed Dev.

'Would it be racist if I did the accent?' Tim asked with a grin.

'Just don't. *Hi Dad!*'

'What is it?' asked Raju, in the adjoining room, six years later. Nothing much about the house had changed in the intervening years, except that the flowery carpet had been replaced with an unremarkable plain one, necessitating no further remarks.

'So… I want to go into research,' said Dev to his father across the dining table. Dev, Raju, Serena and Tim had finished dinner and were drinking tea when it seemed like a good moment to bring up the topic.

'Hm. What kind of research?' asked Dev's father.

'Uh…' trailed Dev.

'This is –'

'Yeah,' Dev quickly cut in.

A moment passed as Raju reconsidered the timbre of his voice and adjusted accordingly. Somehow mothers appear to do it effortlessly, while fathers need a pause. 'We talked about this.'

'Yes.'

'Why is this so important? You keep bringing it up. Last time was a year ago. You want to talk about this again? With Tim here?' asked Raju.

Raju, like most fathers, had his own version of the stern dad look that he deployed when necessary. However, in his case, the stern look was ready to slip away from the moment it appeared. His wavy hair still covered the top of his head, but it was not as thick as when Dev was a child. Neither was it as black. He had a wide nose which made it tricky for him to find glasses that settled comfortably, so he usually used contact lenses. Raju had recently discovered that his eyebrows were thinning out, a development that bothered him more than he felt it should.

All in all, he was an active man at this point, but one who was beginning to feel tired more often. Dev's enthusiasm was refreshing, but he wished Dev would turn that energy towards something more worthwhile. Raju loved his children and could even honestly say that he liked his son, but that didn't mean that he often felt close to Dev.

With a quick breath, Dev launched his latest pitch. 'Thoughts, ideas, that's what we all have in common,' explained Dev, 'it makes us all equal. If we all think, then we should all understand more about it. How we think, that is. Thoughts. All of us. Not just psychiatrists and… neuroscientists. There are so many ways that people think, the ideas they have. Where do they come from? Haven't you ever wondered?'

'No,' replied his father, 'I haven't.'

'What about you, Mum?'

'I don't want to know anything about this. You're old enough, do what you think is best,' replied Serena, collecting her mug of tea from the table and leaving the room.

Dev had started, and so he continued. 'Some things that people do are so *out there* that it's impossible not to wonder how it first came to them. How did one idea start, and how did it lead to another? I want to research this and… see where it goes.'

'To save humanity,' added Tim, theatrically waving his teaspoon like a wand, mangling a key phrase from an early pitch several years before. In the last six years, little had changed about him, except that he had stopped applying gel to his blonde hair and had let it grow long and soft, down to his neck.

'*Benefit.* Not save,' clarified Dev. 'Just think, we all do things that are so basic and common to everyone on the planet. If we can all understand how different thoughts are formed and become part of what we accept as true in the world, doesn't it follow that we will be more open to different cultures and beliefs? Suppose we can understand how people form their ideas. In that case, cultural differences can't be so insurmountable, can they?' asked Dev, hoping his father would see the broader implications as he saw them. Or, at least humour him and give his blessing so Dev could commence formal enquiries about his research.

As immigrants, Raju and Serena had had no choice but to work hard and fight to save every coin in their pockets, no matter how black it was. They knew they needed to work twice as hard as the rest because the society they lived in was not set up to make things easier for them. Raju wondered if this was something that was lost on Dev. He wondered if being born in England and having things *easier* had left Dev with a rose-tinted view of the world. Raju sometimes feared that he had somehow failed in his duty as a father to fully prepare Dev for how indifferent the world can be to one's dreams, and how cruel it can be in all other regards. He would always worry for his son, but he sometimes felt that Dev deliberately made him feel uncertain.

As for myself, I can see what Dev is going for, but, like a child, he simply expects more than this world will offer. Raju and Tim both love Dev, but, like me, they find his theory ill-conceived and his suppositions naive. However, unlike me, they do not have any other explanation for his interest in this topic. With nothing else to go on, they simply indulge him with the expectation that this fascination will pass. I know that there is more to Dev's interest than even he knows. His interest in thought, he has put down to the magazine at the barbershop, as well as other episodes. His interest in opening people up to different cultures, he attributes to his own challenges. Somewhere along the way, the two have become connected. Dev may believe that he wants to help people become more open and accepting of other cultures, and perhaps that is genuinely a reason for his interest, but that is not the only reason. He just doesn't realise it yet. Let's indulge Dev with a little more of his utopian outlook.

'We're constantly told how what other people believe in is different from what the rest believe in. What if we took what it means to be human and boiled it right down? We think, consume, procreate and sleep,' continued Dev.

'Usually in that order too,' joked Tim.

'I am interested in locating exactly where an impulse comes from to do a specific thing that we have never done before. If we can accept that each idea is the result of a thought process, conscious or otherwise, we should accept that people don't easily fall into single, easily defined categories.'

'So there'll be *more* categories?' asked Tim.

'No, there'll be just one. People. We'll just accept that we're all people. Not scary. Just people. All with different thought processes, but just people. That's why I need to research. That's what I want to do. I don't want to go straight to practice medicine. I want to research. Write papers. Does that make sense?'

After a pause, Raju slowly answered. 'Frankly, yes and no. Yes, we do all think, and it would be lovely if we could teach the world to sing, and all get along, but we're all already told this. That we all need to forget our differences and get along?'

'Yes, but the message isn't getting through to everyone,' helped Tim.

'Exactly, how do you explain suicide bombers?' asked Dev.

'It's not that simple, Dev,' said Raju.

'I'm not saying it is. Look, it wouldn't come in your lifetime or mine but just think of the difference it would make to later generations if they could accept that people do things differently, but they're still people. They're not less than, and those people are not in a far-off place. They're next door. A study would not only map out the thought process but also reveal the backstories, so everyone can see that people different to themselves are not degenerates to be cast out. We are people. Wouldn't it be great if in the future people looked back and said, *wow, look how closed-minded we were, glad we're not like that now? Hey, maybe we should apply that same open-minded attitude to religion or something.* We're not only allowed to be different, we should be expected to be different because we're individuals with unique ideas and identities all stemming from this thing that we all do. We're not billions of separate people.'

'We're not?' asked Tim.

'Well, we are,' conceded Dev, 'but we're also conduits for streams of information running all over the world, regardless of national borders, or race, or religion. Each of us is a tangle of different thoughts, and if we can figure that out, then we can work on belief systems, faiths, religions. Why is one thing more pleasurable to a particular person than another? Why is one thing more acceptable than another?'

'And what about the rapists? What about the paedophiles?' asked Raju. 'Are you going to try to explain where their thoughts come from?'

'We're getting away from the main thing. That's sex. I'm interested in thought.'

'But sex is connected to thought. They feed each other. You can't ignore it,' argued Tim.

'Well,' began Dev hesitantly, 'eventually, if the study got to that stage. Like any others with a specific sexual... predilection, they would need to be interviewed and studied... It's not black and white. That's the whole point.'

The three men were silent for a while, each nursing his private thoughts. Raju wondered how his son had become so attached to this idea, while Tim wondered if he should tell his friend how he truly felt, in front of Raju. Tim didn't want to undermine Dev in front of his father, but he didn't know that he would be able to tell him how he felt if he waited. It was natural that Tim would see Dev's ideas in terms of what it meant for him or anyone whose needs diverged from what was generally termed *socially acceptable*.

Dev wondered how better he could explain what he was thinking. His mind drifted as it was wont to do. He thought about the patients he had seen as a trainee and wondered if they genuinely were happy to be seen by a trainee. *What were they thinking? Were they thinking: another Asian doctor using our resources to train. Resources that should be going to an English lad. It's no wonder I can never see a proper English doctor. There's all this lot taking their jobs.* They smiled for the prescription or the medical certificate signing them off work for another week. They were happy to reach out to take it.

They always were. Would they still smile if they didn't want something? Perhaps some feel reassured by the cliche of the Indian doctor. It's comfortable and makes them feel safe. What are they honestly thinking when they are sitting across from him? To have some insight into what was going on in their minds would be to have some sense of control, wouldn't it? *Some will show their hate, but many more will hate behind their smiles, even if they do not realise it.*

'Y'know, I've been listening to you bring this up from time to time over the years.' It was difficult, but Tim had to tell his friend what he truly thought. 'The thing that always strikes me is the same thing that stops me from fully understanding you.'

'What?' asked Dev.

'Dude. You know I'm bi. Doesn't it occur to you that what you're saying is a little like you're trying to find out why people are… not straight? Is that what you're saying? That it's a thought that can be changed. Do you know how insulting that is, not to mention depressing? Same as you can't… pray away the gay, you can't think yourself out of it. People feel what they feel.'

Dev was hurt that his friend believed that he thought this way, in the same way that he had been all those years ago when Tim asked if being gay would affect their friendship. However, Dev was more upset that Tim had clearly struggled with conflicting feelings every time he had spoken of his project. It was clear to him that he had failed to explain himself.

'The received wisdom is that we should all be more open, understanding and accepting of the cultural convictions and religious beliefs of others,' Dev tried. 'I'm just saying that that can be difficult because one person can believe something that strikes another as entirely alien. If we can understand why someone enjoys… getting wet in the rain, then would we not think to ourselves, *hey, if I can understand the thought process there, then accepting other cultures and beliefs should also be possible*? It's about getting people into the mindset of being open-minded and seeing a train of thought. Accepting that people have different ways isn't difficult. It's about having the ability to accept. Ultimately wouldn't it be amazing if we could move the world forward as one, so we are all more open and accepting?'

The whole time Dev spoke, Tim couldn't look at him, which only spurred Dev on more. He was upset that Tim, doubting his sincerity, thought he wanted to find a *cure* for homosexuality.

'Tim, I'm not talking about finding out why people are gay. You're my friend, I love you, and I would never knowingly suggest that we could intellectualise sexual orientation and trace when it was in someone's life that they *became* gay. I know sexual orientation is not something someone actively chooses. I'm talking about thought and how external and internal factors can influence it. I don't consider homosexuality any more a choice than heterosexuality.'

Buoyed as Tim looked up to make eye contact with him, Dev continued. 'If I got to the stage of researching sex, it would be about the things we discover we have a taste for. Fetishes. Something that appeals to us, but why that thing in particular appeals to us. Why does… I don't know… why does one person enjoy dressing in PVC? Why does another enjoy watching machinery operate? I wouldn't mock these people. I wouldn't hold them up to the light, analysing them like unnamed specimens, cross-sections, anonymous samples. I'd love how open those people are to new experiences. I'd love how committed they are. I'd want to know these people, hear their stories. In many cases, it would have been scary for them to pursue the thing that gave them pleasure, to open up that box and then keep it open, but they did it anyway. And in doing so, they opened up themselves to a new way of thinking. They opened up themselves to understand more about themselves, but also about other people.

Even the most indulgent parents tire of their children, and Raju decided to bring the conversation back to something he was more comfortable with. 'Dev, I thought you were going to talk to me about medical specialities. Surgery.' Dev looked directly at his father, knowing he had lost his attention. 'Look, you're young. You think you're going to change the world. You're not. Why don't you look into surgical specialities?'

'I just think it's important to know how people think,' struggled Dev.

'Why? Where's the reward? Where's the future? You know, the world always needs more surgeons.'

'I'm sure advertisers would like to know what we're all thinking,' Dev tried.

'Great, let someone else take the risk and do the research. You pursue this, you publish anything, it will follow you around your entire career,' said Dev's father with a look that signalled that the conversation was over as far as he was concerned. Having made his feelings clear, Raju decided to call it a night. 'That's enough for me. Goodnight, both of you.'

'Goodnight, Dad.'

'G'night, Raju.'

'Dev, I'll see you at the weekend. Don't forget to lock the door when you leave. Tim, I'll see you when I see you.'

Dev and Tim listened as Raju plodded up the stairs. A moment or two passed after they heard him close the bedroom door. Dev valued his friendship with Tim and was desperate to know what his oldest friend was thinking. Dev would never be able to fully convey to Tim how sorry he felt that, despite his efforts, it had appeared to Tim that Dev was trying to explain homosexuality.

Helping homophobes to *cure* homosexuality wasn't Dev's aim, but he could understand Tim's perspective. Dev wished he had slowed down to see it that way himself. He would have been more sensitive. Instead, remorse enveloped him as his mind naturally set to wondering what Tim had been thinking of him all this time. The familiar anxiety washed over him as all the most negative thoughts rose and engulfed him. Just as Tim didn't want to think of Dev as enabling homophobes, Dev didn't want to imagine Tim thinking the worst of him. Dev looked to Tim as his mind ran through all the possibilities that his imagination could invent. They all seemingly hit him at once.

Dev pushed back the imagined thoughts before Tim jolted him from his reverie. 'It was always going to be a hard sell,' consoled Tim as he got up from the table.

'I shouldn't have tried all that *good for humanity* stuff,' conceded Dev.

'We always expect more from the people we love.' Tim knew, for whatever reason, this was important to his friend who was struggling to make himself understood. 'Do you even know *why* you're into this?'

'The brain, our thoughts. It's… huge,' Dev trailed away.

'Eloquent,' smirked Tim sarcastically.

'Think about our instincts, our *primal* instincts. Eat, drink, fight and fuck. Right?' asked Dev.

'Sleep. I like to sleep,' informed Tim helpfully.

'We don't have to worry about eating anymore. Food and drink are everywhere. All that's left is sex and violence. If we could figure out how we all think, we could figure everything out about everything and everyone. It would all just unravel.'

'Unravel?' exhaled Tim heavily.

'Half the world's population is being encouraged to daydream about sex and possessions. The other half is riddled with poverty, disease and injustice. It's all of it, stuff that's been going on for ages. The child soldiers, the terrorist bombers, the immigrants crammed into camps at borders, the sex trafficking, the modern slavery. We used to think it was somewhere else, places that everyone could ignore, but it's everywhere. No one can ignore it anymore. We need to know what *they're* thinking.'

'You're sounding a little paranoid, Dev.'

'If we can unravel it all, we could know what they're thinking. Eventually, future generations could eliminate violence, dictatorships. All the negative stuff.'

'But Dev, that's not going to happen.'

'I know, I sound earnest, but it doesn't make it any less

true. We've become so inured to hearing it, but people *are* complex. We need to catalogue and connect their thoughts, unravel who they are and know what they are thinking.'

'It's a cool idea, maybe for a sci-fi movie or an episode of *Trek*, but it's completely… unworkable, and I think you know that. Do you keep bringing it up to needle your dad?'

Feeling belittled and misunderstood, Dev didn't answer. Even then, with it being just the two of them, he still couldn't admit his real reasons, or at least what he believed was the real driving force behind this little project of his. Maybe he was embarrassed. Perhaps he didn't want his father to feel that he failed in some way. Perhaps if he admitted it to Tim, it would be like putting a distance between them.

'Have you thought about how your parents would explain what you do to their family? Back home, in Mauritius? From what you've told me, they won't get it. He'd be embarrassed. My dad's the same. I know what I'm talking about. He's embarrassed about me. Things like *this* are universal. You've told me yourself before. You told me, as far as they're concerned, in Mauritius, when you're brought up in England, you're supposed to have a good education, go to university, then have this amazing job and live a charmed life full of nothing but beautiful things. We can't all be exactly what everyone wants us to be. It's like you said, we're not one thing or another. We're not all winners or losers. Some of us are dreamers and –'

'That's not something that Mauritians understand,' interrupted Dev.

'And, for some of us,' continued Tim, 'our parents are fucking ashamed of us. So are you going to do what you want or worry about your parents being ashamed?'

'You heard him. He won't want me to do it. All this study, all the money, I've got to start paying it back. I've student debts the size of a small mountain. He's right. It won't be a good use of my time.' Dev still felt unsettled that he hadn't made himself clear to his friend. 'Tim. You know –'

'I know,' Tim interrupted.

'Sexual orientation –'

'*I know*,' Tim insisted.

'I believe it's as immovable as gender identification. You know I wouldn't dream of suggesting anyone could change how they identify or who they're attracted to.'

'I know you don't think that, but it just feels sometimes like you're talking about finding an event, or a bunch of influences, that makes someone gay, for example. Like you're saying that by thinking the right thoughts, people can change significant, fundamental things about themselves.'

'I don't see it that way,' pressed Dev. 'I see sexual orientation and gender identification as... *firmware*,' Dev explained, with an anxious chuckle that Tim did not reciprocate. 'I see that as unchangeable. My idea is about identifying the influences that lead people to ideas that most others wouldn't ordinarily think of. If that helps minorities not be seen as second-class citizens, LGBTQ+ people as deviants, or women as property, then that's a good thing.'

'Okay, setting aside that you could be making the homophobic case for *curing* gays, don't you feel like it would be robbing life of the romance? The mystery?' Dev didn't reply. Instead, he looked away, unable to find a suitable response. 'You know,' began Tim again, looking to re-establish his support, 'if you want to understand how these people think you're going to have to get under their skin. Maybe you're not meant to be a GP. Maybe, like Florence Nightingale, your real strength is as an analyst.'

Dev hears Tim but looks past him through the living room window to the tree branches dancing outside with the wind. At that moment, Dev feels a rumble beneath his feet, but then he thinks he must be mistaken since there is no traffic in the street outside the window. Dev glances back at Tim, but he is no longer there. Through the window, there is nothing much to see. The road, the flickering street lamps, a few trees, the houses across –

# 6. In praise of water

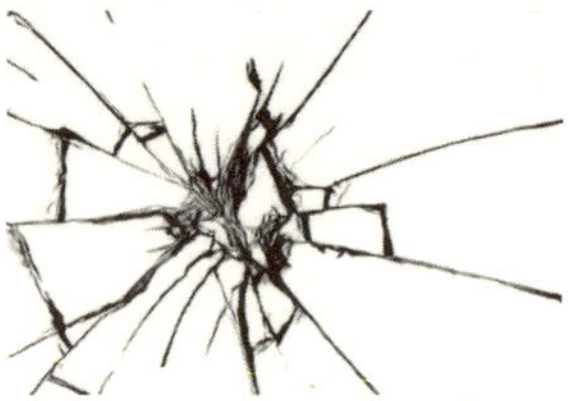

CRUNCH of the windows as it cracks and shatters into countless particles, all rushing towards him like a shoal of fish in the water that crushes through the frame and blasts through the living room, into the dining room, slamming Dev against the metal frame of the French windows that also shatter. The water keeps coming through, pinning Dev against the frame of the French windows like something left behind in a sieve.

Dev can't hold his breath much longer. Bubbles of carbon dioxide, and other gases, leave his mouth. Past the floating furniture, he can see light through the living room window. A streetlamp. Through the gloom of the water, it looks like a diving torch.

Diving tank would be useful.

Oxygen.

Breathe.

The streetlamp goes out.

Breathe.

The water is a thick, black cream.
Breathe.
Constant push against the body.
Breathe.
Breathe.
Celia breathes.
Breathe.
Celia breathes.
Remember.
Celia remembers.
Remember.

Celia remembers the streetlamp falling away as she drops backwards, away from the bridge.

Celia remembers the cold, black night *whooshing* around her ears.

Celia remembers the underside of the bridge coming into view.

Celia remembers hitting the water.

Celia remembers sinking through the icy depths and feeling everything grow heavier and slower around her until the darkness closed in and the thoughts dissolved.

Celia coughs up river water and feels it gush over her chin.

She is awake.

She is alive.

She has no idea how.

Celia blinks rapidly, about a dozen times to bat away the water from her eyes and allows them to adjust to the light. Finally opening her eyes fully, Celia finds herself on the riverbank. *Clearly yet another epic failure in my life,* she thinks, *jumping from a bridge into deep, icy, murky river water. I wanted to die, right? So why am I still alive? I really can't do anything right. I'm a catastrophe,* she moans to herself as she gets up and trudges away in the direction of home, too depressed for another suicide attempt.

By this time of night, the buses have stopped. The trains have stopped. No taxi driver will take her anywhere in her sopping wet clothes, and even if they would, she has no money to pay. She has left everything in her flat, including her door keys. Thinking she would never need them again, she had supposed to leave them behind helpfully rather than take them along to the silty depths of the river. Now this good intention, like seemingly everything she did in life, is coming back to bite her.

Unable to get into her flat without her keys, she knocks on Jeff's door.

'Jeff, I know you're in there, open the door. It's Celia.'

'Celia, do you know what time it is?' asks Jeff, rubbing the sleep out of his face as he opens the door.

'Yeah, time you were probably playing video games, as usual. I need my spare key.'

'Your spare key?'

'Yeah, I gave it to you so you could water my plants.'

'Water your plants?'

'When I went on holiday.'

'You went on holiday?'

'Yes, I asked you for it when I got back and you said you couldn't find it.'

'Right, right,' remembers Jeff, moving away from the door and going into the flat to begin rummaging around a desk in the living room. 'How long ago was that?'

'About three weeks.'

'Tell me, if I couldn't find it three weeks ago, what makes you think I'm going to be able to find it now and at four in the morning?'

'Because I actually need it now, so look harder than you did three weeks ago.'

'Okay, I'm looking. Come on in, shut the door. So how was your holiday?'

Celia closes the door behind her, her mousey brown hair still lank with river water. 'I told you before. It was hell. Me and twelve other women.'

'Sounds pretty good to me. Listen, um, since you're here… d'you wanna….' Jeff trails off, arching his eyebrows hopefully.

'Look at me,' Celia replied, gesturing with both hands to her sodden clothes hanging off her narrow shoulders and clinging to the rest of her petite frame.

'So…?'

'So, no.'

'Why don't you stay here tonight, and we'll look for it in the morning? We can share my bed if you want. Wait, why are you wet?'

'Jeff, I think it's best if we leave that in the past now. I'll be fine here on the sofa. Do you have any spare sheets?'

A few minutes later, Celia is out of her wet clothes and amongst dry, warm blankets on the lumpy sofa. She has had some horrendous days in her thirty-two years, but this one tops them all: the day she tried to top herself. The day she failed, wet, cold, shivering and having locked herself out of her own flat in the process. Celia can describe how her best intentions and plans have gone awry on almost any random day of the calendar. Of that, at least, she is confident. Each day seems to bring her some new humiliation, some unforeseen catastrophe that leaves everyone looking at her with even less respect than ever.

In the cramped living room where Celia lies, the only light comes from electrical appliances. The small lights indicate that they are dormant but receiving their lifeblood of electric current, ready to spring into action at the touch of a rubber button. The TV, the DVD player, the games consoles, the laptop computer, the surround sound speaker system. All items with a single purpose. Zero or one. Little LED lights piercing the darkness. Proud, obstinate little torches. Somewhere in the corner, Jeff even has an old VCR. Celia remembers her father's cassettes stacked up. Seemingly at random, one would be selected to have its memory recorded over with another. Another show. Another documentary. Another movie.

For reasons unknown to her, it is this thought that brings the hot tears rolling from her eyes down over her cheeks, making their way until they dry up and become nothing in the dark.

The following morning, in the comfort of her own surroundings, Celia runs herself a warm bath and is sure to include her favourite bubbles. She finally feels the river wash off her skin. This is a familiar pattern for Celia, the need to wash off another lousy day or night or a bad week as in the case of her holiday. Yes, the last time Celia had sought out the comfort of bubbles was roughly two weeks ago upon returning from the week in Spain.

Celia had thought it would be good, mainly for her, to round up some of her most loyal friends from university to take a holiday together and reconnect. Although she didn't realise it, Celia had also hoped that being amongst the people that she identified with her more carefree days at university would stoke the embers of her youthful optimism. She would feel good again, stimulated and reassured by seeing her own intelligence and ideas reflected in her old friends' understanding, recognition, and esteem. Celia had wanted to feel substantial again. Significant, whole and solid, instead of how she felt then, like an empty shopping trolley abandoned at the far end of the supermarket car park.

What Celia had not anticipated was that Vicky would invite one or two other friends that she was close to, Ellie and Sarah. Ellie would go on to mention this to her brother, who suggested they use his holiday home in Spain. Sarah reached out and, not expecting any results, asked if any of her friends would be in that part of Spain in that week, suggesting they could meet up. By sheer coincidence, two of her friends whom she had not seen for years were visiting that region but staying at a hotel, thus turning idle speculation into an entirely doable scenario.

Meanwhile, upon receiving news of the exact week Ellie and her friends had settled upon, her brother was sad to inform her that the house would be occupied. However, if Ellie wouldn't mind changing their arrival date to a couple of days later, his girlfriend and her two sisters would be the only occupants. Everyone would be welcome to share the large house with several ensuite bedrooms and communal pool.

So Celia's original plans for a quiet, meditative, and

vaguely intellectual break away with some dear, old friends had been liberated, like a freedom-seeking Slinky making its escape down a flight of steep steps. When it had returned to her… the plan had not been broken by someone she hadn't even invited, but it had begun a metamorphosis into a rowdy, chaotic week-long ladies exodus from the mundanities of their daily lives.

Which, except for Celia, is what everyone had truly wanted anyway.

Having had the dates, venue and nature of the holiday entirely hijacked by someone with whom she was barely acquainted at university, Celia felt her position had been usurped. All communication pertaining to the event was now flowing via thirteen conduits, with Ellie now installed as Coordinator In Chief following the coup of securing a rent-free house and pool. Whilst feeling slightly put out by this in the weeks leading to the holiday, Celia chose not to dwell on it for long and refocused on the positives of having a larger number of people to make up a happy, bustling household. Like a large family.

Or a tiny cult.

Flying to Malaga alone, Celia was determined to make a good early impression on the other twelve. Unfortunately, she had opted to save money by taking the night flight, meaning she landed later than everybody else. To save some more money, Celia chose to take the bus instead of a taxi. She was further away from the house than when she set off when Celia realised she was on the wrong bus. By the time she arrived in a taxi, she was both later than intended and lighter of pocket, both annoying things to her.

Standing at the gate, Celia was already exhausted. Not only had she endured an unexpectedly long journey, but she had risen extra early that morning to rehearse how she would present herself to everybody in the best possible light. Keen to fit into the new programme and prove her fun-time credentials, Celia had also thought up a new drinking game. However, she was disappointed to walk through the front door and find that she was too late to be the one to kick off the revelry for them. Empty bottles were collecting, the music was turned up, and the atmosphere oozed with ambience as the group partied without her.

It was a few moments before anyone noticed her standing in the doorway, and it was Vicky who eventually spotted her.

'Hey, Celia! Hey everybody, it's Celia! Hey, turn the music down. It's Celia!'

Gemma, another of Celia's friends, turned the music not only down but down to zero, taking Ellie, her brother's girlfriend and her two sisters by surprise. They hadn't noticed Celia's arrival and were busying themselves with the business of teaching one another the delicate art of the *slut-drop*. The sudden break in the music froze them mid-drop, and all attention was suddenly focussed on Celia as they stared at her expectantly.

Between the unexpected scene she had walked in on, her abject fatigue, and then finding herself the centre of attention, Celia momentarily misplaced the quirky, fun demeanour she had practised that morning and simply squeaked: 'Hi.'

'Hiii,' they all responded, some slurring their speech less than others. Vicky, Gemma and Charlie went over to group hug.

After gathering names from faces around the room, Celia excused herself to have a swift shower and change her clothes. Twenty minutes later, she was back in the living room with the other twelve.

'Let's get this party started!' roared Celia, with a grimace on her face which she thought looked like a theatrical rock star-like snarl, but to everyone else looked like an aborted sneeze.

'It was already started,' replied Ellie, 'until the music got switched off.'

'Well, we can get the music back on,' asserted Celia.

'The button on the player is jammed now. My brother filled this house with cheap tat for rentals. We'll have to get a new one tomorrow.'

'Okay, well, I have a brilliant drinking game for us all to play.'

'Actually, it's pretty late,' said Charlie, 'I was thinking of bed.'

'Yeah,' agreed Jo, 'I think we've had enough drinking for one night. Maybe bed isn't a bad idea.'

'Maybe we could play your game tomorrow,' suggested Ellie.

'Oh no, come on, ladies, it has to be tonight. If we wait until tomorrow night, it won't work,' pleaded Celia. 'It's based on us not knowing a lot about each other. So, you see, if we wait until tomorrow night, it won't make sense.'

'I'm up for it,' piped up Suze, one of the younger sisters.

'Yeah, let's give it a go. Maybe let's not make the drinks too stiff, eh?' said Vicky.

'Cool, I'll make the drinks,' cried Celia, thankfully. 'I have one that I'm going to make. It's called a Black Lagoon.

Anybody ever had a Black Lagoon?' asked Celia.

'What's in it?' inquired Sarah.

'Milk, port, vodka and coffee liqueur.'

'Milk?'

'Yeah, it's fun because the milk turns black.'

'What? That… sounds awful. Why does the milk turn black?'

'The milk itself doesn't turn black. The drink turns black because of the dark coloured ingredients.'

'Yeah, I get that it has dark drinks in it. Shouldn't it turn grey or something?'

'I don't think a grey drink sounds very appealing, Celia,' doubted Ellie.

'It won't turn grey. It'll turn black,'

'We've all had a fair bit to drink already, and your drink sounds a little rich. Why don't we just have little shot glasses with vodka, cola?' compromised Sarah.

'Okay.'

'Good. What's your game?'

'It's based on us not knowing each other very well yet. So we spin the bottle to pick someone, and while that person is making the drinks, the other twelve write down on a piece of paper one word that best encapsulates what they think of that person so far. When the person comes back with the drinks, the others reveal what they wrote. Any two or more people with a similar word, or a derivative, have to drink.'

'I don't get drinking games. Is the aim to drink or not to drink? Which one means you're winning?' asked Lauren, the brother's girlfriend.

'Well, the aim is to not drink, so you don't get drunk and

behave like an imbecile,' answered Celia, smiling but growing testy at how her game was already facing a threat to its existence. 'If the aim was to drink, we'd forget about the game and just drink.' Celia took a breath. 'The spirit of the game is to encourage us all to notice something different about each other and not just focus on first impressions, the surface.'

'Boring,' called out Suze, Lauren's younger sister, 'sounds like school.'

'You used to drink alcohol at school?'

Suze cocked her head to one side thoughtfully, then answered: 'sometimes.'

'What if everyone has something different?' asked Ellie.

'Then the person we're describing has to drink all the drinks,' concluded Celia, triumph shining in her eyes. She believed it was a good game that she had devised all herself.

'Okay,' said Ellie, 'I'm guessing you brought paper and twelve pens as well.'

'I have,'

'Then let's play.'

Celia wasted no time distributing paper and pens amongst the other women before going to the kitchen to pour the mini-drinks. There were only six shot glasses, so she had to wash out some regular glasses and make do with those. Making her way back to the living room with the drinks on a large tray Celia was sure to take care. It would have been typical of her to trip over one of those shoulder bags dumped in the corridor or a careless sandal and send the entire tray crashing to the tiled floor.

As she entered the living room, still concentrating on the tray, she was aware of being the centre of attention once more as the ladies' chatter suddenly died away.

Setting down the tray and taking a seat with a pad and pen, Celia noticed that some of the women who had been less enthusiastic about the game were now wearing bright smiles, which she took to be a good sign. On the other hand, her friends seemed uncomfortable, choosing to pay attention to the tray, the table, the floor, the light fittings. Anything but Celia.

Charlie broke the silence. 'Perhaps we should save this for another night? If we get some sleep now, we can be ready to go out bright and early tomorrow.'

'No, Charlene,' shot Ellie, 'Celia was clear that she wanted to play this today to help us get to know each other. So who wants to go first?'

'Let's go around the room,' started Celia brightly. 'Charlie, why don't you go first?'

'Okay, Celia,' began Charlie, 'if I was meeting you today, for the first time, I would say... I would describe you as *late*.' Charlie passed Celia her scrap of paper showing the word she had written. On the paper were other words that had been crossed out beyond recognition. Celia was surprised at her friend. She had intended her friends to describe her as they knew her rather than what their first impression would be if they met her today.

Suze was the next to flip over her piece of paper. In capital letters written over several times, presumably for emphasis. "BOSSEY."

'Ah,' said Celia tightly. 'Bossy.'

Suze smiled thinly at Celia, who suddenly saw what she had walked into and began to wish she had tripped over the sandal after all. Once again, she had been the chief architect of her own public fall, and this was only the beginning. She would have to endure another ten words specially selected to bring her down and shut her out.

They must have collectively decided this while she was making the drinks. This had been the flaw in her game that she had failed to spot. *You need to trust strangers you just met to not hatch plots,* she thought. On the faces of the strangers, Celia could see that they were enjoying seeing the realisation sink in. Not just that a cruel joke was being played on her, but that this humiliation before the entire group would effectively cut her off at the knees for the whole week.

They may not have known her favourite novel or music tastes, but they had all sensed the desperation, and they all knew that she would be irrelevant for the rest of the week, unable to engineer a way to recover any standing within the group. *Why would anyone want to do such a thing?* She asked herself. *Easy,* she answered, *because they saw an opportunity for fun at my expense. One or two of them were drunk and took the others with them. Now I will have to sit here and take it.* Despite this, she still couldn't help looking on the bright side. It was her nature. *They might not know anything about me, but I've learnt something about all of them.*

Vicky had written, "lost." 'Because you got lost on the bus, right?' she explained apologetically.

Dana revealed the word "grey." Also feeling the need to apologise to her friend, she explained, 'because you were wearing a grey hoodie when you arrived. And your luggage was grey. It was a lot of grey.'

'I see,' replied Celia.

'Sweaty,' offered Sarah, 'because you were sweaty.'

'Thanks. Yeah. I understood.'

'Sorry, I thought we had to explain as well.'

"Tired" was written on Gemma's paper.

'School teacher,' suggested Lauren, 'because you seem quite knit-picky. In fact, I thought you might knit-pick that school teacher is two words and not one.' Everyone laughed, glad for a break in the tension. 'But then I thought, I don't fuckin' care,' finished Lauren as she reached for the nearest shot glass, lifted it and poured the contents down her throat.

'Hey, don't,' admonished Ellie, 'you're ruining Celia's game. She might need that later,'

'Again,' replied Lauren, 'I don't fuckin' care. I'm going to bed now. G'night all.'

All replied, 'goodnight,' then turned back to the slow, relentless grind of this *game*.

Sameera was next, and she held up: "unbalanced."

Another of Celia's friends, Willow, brought "tight" to the collection. 'As in tightly wound. From the long journey. Probably.'

Jo contributed: "boorish." The word which finally saw Celia's shoulders slump forwards and her fixed smile fade. 'I am not boorish,' thought Celia, 'I am the most non-boorish person I know.'

Sitting on the floor, Sophia had fallen asleep with her head resting against the sofa seat. However, this proved no obstacle as Ellie picked the paper out of Sophia's dozing hand and read, 'trapped. No idea what she meant by that. As for me, I have the word: invisible. Did any of us have the same word, Celia?'

'No,' replied Celia.

'Any derivatives? Perhaps you should read them out and make sure.'

'No.'

'Oh, then I suppose all the drinks are yours. I'd love to watch you enjoy them all, but we're all ready for bed.'

They all got up stiffly and began wishing each other a good night as Celia remained seated, her feet frozen to the living room floor as she contemplated the remaining eleven drinks.

'You don't have to drink them,' said Gemma to Celia. 'We'll see you in the room.'

Celia listened to the household prepare for bed until all was still and silent before she turned out the living room lights and went through to the back door in the kitchen to look out over the garden. It was a large communal garden that linked another four large houses. Strategically placed garden lights lit up beads of water arching from the timed water sprinkler irrigating the garden.

The atmosphere inside the house was so warm and stifling, while the water flitting through the night air looked so cool and inviting that Celia couldn't help herself. She unlocked the back door and stepped out into the warm night air. It surprised her to find it was warmer outside than it was inside the house. Although the house was equipped with air conditioning units, they had been disabled since Ellie's brother did not want visitors racking up huge electricity bills for him. Celia turned, stepped back in and walked through the kitchen.

When she returned, Celia was bearing her tray of drinks.

Flicking off her flip-flops, she stepped out of the house and into the soft light thrown from the various garden fittings. The bushes outside thronged with the sound of busy crickets and happy frogs delighting in the irrigation system. She soon identified a spot of dry grass where the tray could rest with its eleven little loads and not be bothered by drops of water from the sprinkler. Adjacent was an area just within reach of the irrigation system where beads of water could reach Celia, pleasantly cooling her skin without making her too wet and uncomfortable. Celia lay on the grass with her knees arched, trying to grasp blades of grass with her toes and pull them from the ground.

After a while, she rose, reached out to the tray and picked up a glass. 'Cheers,' she said to no one in particular before gulping the drink. 'Bossy with an extra *e*.' She put down the empty glass and picked up another from the round tray as though she was plucking petals from a flower. 'Tight. Tightly wound. Or tight with my taxi money. Or both.' She shut her eyes and swallowed. The black liquid burned its way down the back of her throat. Celia wasn't great with vodka, she was more of a wine drinker, but of course, she hadn't anticipated that she would be drinking. Plus, keen to not be accused of being *a pussy* in making weak drinks, she had been generous to appease her audience. Opening her watery eyes, the softly illuminated garden was a blobby mess of colours.

Another glass. 'Knit-picker. Or school-teacher. Something.'

Between arriving, showering, changing clothes and making drinks, the snatched conversations she had had with the women had revealed they were all married to one thing or another, and they were all keen to point it out. Husbands.

Children. Jobs. Important jobs. Husbands with important jobs. Creative outlets. Standing in their community. Application. Promotion. Contribution. Recognition. Appreciation.

'Grey.' Swallow. 'Agh.'

Celia had achieved none of these things in the eleven years since leaving university. Whilst there, she had felt that she had purpose, and knew her aim in life. However, since joining the working world, this anchor had slowly eroded and left her without a harbour to call home.

'Late.' Swallow. 'Hmm.' Celia had drunk so many shots that they were beginning to taste unexpectedly good.

She had trouble keeping any kind of job. Even the lousiest office jobs would be so dull that she could not stand being there any longer than eight or nine months. So she drifted from one meaningless job to another, sometimes moving town to explain at interviews why she had left her previous position after so little time. 'Tired. Sweaty.' Swallow. Watery eyes.

Celia looked around, blinking the water out of her eyes, and that was when she noticed the communal pool. She could just see the sliver of blue, past the rear of the house and to the side of the next one. From where she was sitting, the thin slice of pool enticed her. Celia glanced at the tray of drinks beside her. There were still some shot glasses left, but they would fit into one large glass.

Celia got up and tottered to the kitchen through the spray. Before long, she was back with a tumbler into which she took great care to transfer the remaining drinks as though she was pouring the very elixir of life. Eyeing the water, Celia sipped from the glass and slowly made her way towards the pool through the refreshing jets. The blue rectangle stretching wider and wider as she approached, Celia felt herself lit up from head to toe as she came to the edge of the pool.

Wobbling to a crouch, Celia tasted the water with her fingers. She was surprised to find it still warm from the sun's rays that day. She sat on the edge of the pool, dangling her legs in the water and drank from the tumbler. The water itself was illuminated from below by lights also illuminating the sheet of moths, dragonflies, butterflies and, well, regular flies that had flown too close to the surface.

Celia was now facing a week as the invisible – swallow – hanger-on. She could, of course, do her own thing and see very little of them, but that would mean hiding, admitting defeat. Plus, then what would have been the purpose of staying in the house with them if Celia was to have nothing further to do with them? She could get a hotel room, but without having pre-booked, it would be expensive. Money she didn't have. She could fly home and never see these people again, except for her university friends, and that had been the whole point of this trip, to spend quality time with her old friends from uni.

Celia didn't know what to do. Heavy headed, she felt sleepy. *Maybe the water would wake me up*, she thought, unsteadily slipping fully clothed amongst the dead wings, legs, abdomens and exo-skeletons. Up to her neck, she hesitated for moment before plunging her head under the surface of the warm water. Below the surface, Celia opened her eyes to the new blue world all around her as she sank to the bottom.

Looking up above her, beyond the bodies of dead insects, apparently attracted to the sparkling water before it claimed their lives, the sky was the blackest she had ever seen. Or perhaps it only seemed that way from the brightness of the five bright blue walls of the pool. On the floor, Celia uncurled herself, lay back and opened her mouth a little, slowly letting in the pool water. She watched the bubbles leave her lips and travel up and away towards the black sky. *Never mind astronauts and science*, thought Celia, *maybe that's what stars really are. Bubbles floating away and away.* With that, Celia finally closed her eyes and fell asleep.

When she awoke, Celia could not tell for how long she had been at the bottom of the pool, only that it now had six matching sides with the sun showing off a cloudless and beautiful early morning sky. In a panic at the sudden thought of drowning, Celia desperately started waving her limbs, tearing frantically at the water and scrambling for the surface. Heart pounding, Celia burst from the water and grabbed at the side of the pool.

Later that day, Celia took the first available flight home. She had been rocked to her core by the event and didn't care how her early departure appeared to the others.

Once home, and having ascertained from Jeff that he couldn't find her spare key, Celia took every opportunity she could to test her newly discovered skill.

She held her head down in a bucket of water until her neck hurt. She swam laps around the bottom of the local pool until she could no longer stand the sight of lost pennies and abandoned plasters. She walked into the sea and swam until she was tired. Celia felt amazing. With this new skill (talent, gift?), she suddenly felt strong. She felt able. Able to do anything. Able to breathe underwater, seemingly for hours at a time.

This amazing gift had surely been given to her by God, Him or Herself. What else could explain things? With this conclusion, Celia was determined that she should use her new gift in her everyday life.

Like Marie Curie.

Frida Kahlo.

Or some type of superhero.

Celia looked up relevant persons in the maritime industry and reached out to them, telling of her extraordinary power and offering her services in any way that might be of use to them.

The way she saw things, she could be of use to deep-sea treasure hunters… globetrotting geologists… marine insurance claim handlers… navy investigators… nature documentary filmmakers, to name just a few.

Celia waited a day, two days, then three days. Finally, it was a week before Celia received word from anyone, and what she read did not please her.

> Dear Miss Croft,
>
> Thank you for your interest in joining the team.
>
> The skill you described in your email is indeed one of significant curiosity, and I briefly discussed your case with a colleague. She would be interested in meeting you at her research institute to witness the basis of

your claim first-hand, run some tests, take some blood samples and so forth.

As for joining my particular team, I am sure you will understand that Oceanography is a field that, out of necessity, has had to develop specialist tools and equipment relevant to the challenges we face.

In short, while yours appears to be a remarkable ability on the face of it, it is a little too late to be of use to us. Technology does an accurate job with less risk to human life. In my experience, it would be tricky and/or prohibitively costly for any industry to find an insurer willing to provide the necessary cover for the type of work you are proposing to take on.

If your ability is what you say it is, I would suggest that the scientific community benefit from studying your ability. Or head to Hollywood! Surely a career as a stunt person would be very exciting!

Please let me know if I can pass your contact details to my colleague.

Yours,
Prof. D. Cook

Celia had already considered stunt work. For that, one needs to train. To train, one needs money. For that, one needs to work. Could she seriously be expected to go back to stuffing envelopes in an office while her unique new gift went unused?

*This is typical Celia. I'm finally given something, only to find it's too late for it to be of any actual use to anyone, about a hundred years too late. I was so sure that I finally had something special and unique that people would want. For a week, I was exciting. My life was exciting and hopeful again. Now it's gone, my holiday time is over, and I have to return to the shitty fucking office.*

Resigned to her fate, Celia packed a lunch for her first day back at work. Tuna mayonnaise with sweetcorn on wholegrain. Throughout the day, she shredded and photocopied before returning home to feed a frozen meal into her microwave.

Packed lunch.

Shred.

Photocopy.

Frozen meal.

Microwave.

Ding.

The pattern continued for three weeks until the night Celia first attempted to kill herself. It was too much for her, like some kind of cosmic joke. Not only was she a punchline to people on Earth, but also apparently to any beings beyond. This beautiful gift was going to waste within her while laughter echoed amongst the stars and planets.

*Well, what if I killed myself? How hard would you laugh then?* Reasoned Celia as she jumped from the bridge.

*Apparently, they're still laughing,* thinks Celia the morning after the night before, as she watches the foam on the surface of the water from the bottom of her bathtub. *Must have thrown up the pills before they had an effect.* Celia continues watching the foam slowly dissolve in the warm water bubble by bubble.

Foam.

The sea.

The crashing waves.

The beautiful deep ocean.

This is how she wants to go. Not some shitty river.

Celia had once read somewhere that more is known to humans about space than some of the world's oceans and the different species that live down in the murky depths. That idea has always fascinated her.

Suddenly Celia knows what she must do, and every moment is precious. She jumps out of the bathtub and quickly dresses, not bothering to dry herself. Stuffing her shoes with feet, she grabs her purse and heads out through her door without even bothering to shut it.

Twenty minutes later, it is almost one o'clock in the afternoon when Celia arrives at the beach where people are walking their dogs, their friends, or just themselves along the promenade. Very few people there pay any attention to anyone on the beach, and fewer are actually on the beach on such a windy day. So no one notices as Celia drops her purse on the pebbles and proceeds to remove every stitch of clothing from her soft, delicate human body.

Pulling the scrunchie from her hair, still wet from the bottom of the bath, Celia walks into the waves until she is up to her waist. Sinking to her knees, the waves soon cover her head and her loose hair swirls around her face. On her knees, Celia puts her hands together silently beneath the waves, among the detritus thrown up by an excitable sea, launches herself by pushing against the pebbles with her feet, and begins to swim.

Celia's head breaks the surface of the water again, and she takes another look at the grey, cloudy sky before ducking back under and heading further and further away from shore. She swims away from everything she knows. She forgets her family, she forgets her friends, she forgets her life. Her name. Herself.

She swims until the only thing that matters is that she swims deeper and deeper. She passes rocks, small and large. Boats. Vessels. She passes shoals of fish. Crabs. Plankton. Driftwood. Seaweed. Celia crosses the paths of ships, wrecks, human remains, animal remains, debris, metal barrels, parts of aircraft. Celia dodges crashing containers and swims through water so cold she can no longer feel her skin, no longer feel the debris hitting her. Celia swims until she feels nothing and disappears amongst this collection of objects. This giant jumble of seafloor monuments and structures, beings, lifeforms and remains. Until she becomes just another object in a dark, briny world of unclaimed objects.

# 7. Time

The light glints in his eyes. *How long have I been like this now?* Wonders Dr. Sharma. *Can't be long.* In fact, it has been roughly four and a half seconds since he flipped over onto his back, his fingers still scrabbling uselessly at the leather, the buckles, his skin. Like his thoughts, they seem to reach for everything at once. Like his memories, they are so impotent now. Nonetheless, the images keep coming.

*What do blind people see when they're dying? People blind from birth. Do they see their lives laid out before them, or do they just hear, or is it a feeling? Or do they see things as they imagined them? Why didn't I ask about this stuff before? Because I was too busy to consider that I might die.*

*He's gone,* thought Dev. At the funeral, he kept hearing strangers muttering to each other about the "waste of a young life," and then the strangers would turn a hard stare towards Dev and the group. This happened a few times, and Dev struggled to understand whether he and his friends were being somehow blamed for Alan's death or whether they were being reproached in Alan's absence for him apparently wasting his youth. In the way that a parent might point out another child's failings in a deliberately *wondering aloud* kind of way, hoping their own child will pay heed to the tip-off. In the end, the group wordlessly decided to accept that, in this particular instance, they were being used to illustrate a point that one stranger was making to the other.

At the house, there were photos of Alan everywhere. His blue eyes peeking out from his oval face, under a mop of brown hair in each of them. The photographs had not recorded any change in hairstyle throughout the years, which was strange. *Everyone changes their hairstyle at some point,* thought Dev (whose own hair was styled much shorter than it is right now in Katie's bedroom). Stranger still was the presence of at least one dog in almost every photograph, regardless of whether it was a family shot or not. Dogs of various breeds, colours, sizes. Older dogs, younger dogs taking the place of their dead predecessors as newer photographs showed older Alans.

'You wondering about the dogs too, Dev. Or are you weighing up how much you could get for the silver frame?'

Momentarily forgetting he was at a wake, Dev chuckled and then guiltily stifled it before replacing the frame on the piano and turning to Michelle. 'Yeah, I was wondering how to smuggle it out of here without getting caught.'

'Forget that,' said Lindy, taking a sip of coffee, 'I'd go for the painting in the hallway. Roll it up and sneak it out up your coat sleeve or something.'

‘Why?’ asked Dev, ‘is it valuable?’

‘Probably. *Everything* here looks valuable. What’s with the dogs?’

‘I don’t know. Did Alan ever talk about dogs? I don’t remember him saying anything about liking dogs so much. Or that he grew up with a pack of them,’ queried Michelle, turning and surveying the crowd behind them before another nibble of her ham and cucumber sandwich.

‘Yeah, but who knew his family was so filthy rich either?’ Lindy blurted and then immediately covered her mouth as she was met with pursed lips and a disapproving glare from a woman passing by. ‘Sorry,’ she muttered under her breath, then to Dev and Michelle: ‘Clearly that was *bad form, old girl*,’ she continued in a mock-haughty voice.

‘Does make you wonder what he was doing hanging around with us,’ whispered Michelle.

‘Forget us. Makes you wonder why he wasn’t going to a better school altogether.’ Lindy took another sip of her coffee. ‘I mean, all these pictures of Alan, that house there, this house here, this holiday, that trip, that amazing country. One vintage car, then a different one. Then another. Alan may as well be a prop for what they really wanted to photograph.’

‘Or maybe it just seems that way to us,’ replied Dev.

‘Yeah, maybe. Maybe they’re just normal family photos, and all these other people here are seeing just that, and I’m the only one seeing a wealth of… wealth.’

‘Would it have changed anything if you’d known?’

‘I’d have made him get the drinks in more often,’ laughed Lindy. ‘Did you know he’d been to Mauritius?’

‘No.’

'See, why wouldn't he mention that to you? Your family is from Mauritius. There's a picture of him and his sister by some statue. Says Port Louis. That's the capital, right? It's over here,' she stated, pulling Dev by the arm across the room.

'Hey, don't just leave me,' whined Michelle before following. 'Do you think the thing about the dogs is that they're like seasonal pets?'

'Seasonal pets,' repeated Lindy to Michelle, a scornful look already beginning at the corners of her eyes.

'Yeah, like rich people have homes they use for different seasons, and cars they only use in summer? This lot are so rich they have dogs they trot out for different seasons,' laughed Michelle. 'At the end of the season, the summer dogs go back to their kennels and have to bide their time until the following year, when it will be their time to shine again as the family pets. Meanwhile, the winter pets are back on duty.' Lindy ignored her, but Dev chuckled his support as they approached the photo on the bookshelf. Sure enough, Alan and Patricia were standing by a statue of Sir Seewoosagur Ramgoolam, Mauritius' first Prime Minister. He didn't recognise where precisely in Port Louis the statue was. It had been a very long time since he had been on the island. Over ten years.

Glancing away from the photo towards the entrance, Lindy spotted Richard loitering at the threshold. He had just arrived and his face wore the same wide-eyed look that theirs had when they first arrived, as though he had accidentally wandered into the wrong place. 'I know,' mouthed Lindy across the room to him as she and Michelle left Dev with the photograph.

Seeing Alan with all those dogs, Dev suddenly remembered an afternoon in Mauritius with his mother when he was a child. They had been at the beach with her family. It was turning to early evening, and everything was being packed up for the journey home. Mauritians, back then, tended to take almost an entire kitchen to the beach. They did not often go, so when they did, it was treated as an opportunity for a full-on picnic, and for real Mauritians, cold sandwiches and a juice box would not satisfy.

Amina floated in the sea while seven-year-old Dev sat on a tree stump watching her, staying out of the way of the bustle all around him. He listened to the sound the waves made as they lapped gently upon the golden sand when, as if out of nowhere, a collection of stray dogs suddenly arrived on the scene. They seemed to have invaded from all directions, all at once. Like they had been waiting for the sun to abate before the group of ten or twelve emerged to go from family to family, scavenging for food. Eating tossed away leftovers, sand and all, they would jostle one another in the search for food.

In the melee, one or two of them would forget they were looking for food and become distracted by other impulses. Dev watched a female stare blankly ahead, only shaking her head to shoo a fly from mucus that had collected in the corner of an eye. There was no way of assessing whether she was enjoying the attention of the male firmly planted over her hindquarters or discerning her thoughts on the event.

*Surely, if there was no pleasure to be had, then what was the point? Why didn't she just shake him off and go back to scavenging? Eating should have been the main priority for her body, and he wouldn't be bringing her any food*, thought Dev, years later as a teenager. *Didn't she know that she'd soon be pregnant? Did she connect the act with becoming pregnant? If she survived giving birth at the beach, she'd then have puppies to feed until they went off on their own. Wasn't her life tough enough, searching for scraps in the sand? Or was she obeying a deeper instruction, from within herself, to breed? Blindly following a preprogrammed set of rules.* Teenage Dev couldn't help asking these questions whenever this memory passed into his thoughts.

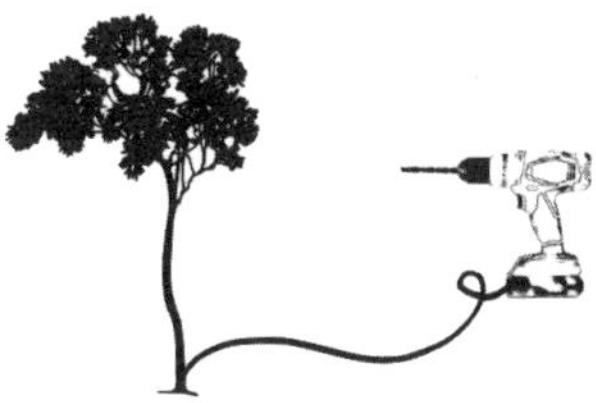

The jar.

The tube.

The coloured earth.

It all came back to Dev as he, Lindy, Richard, Michelle and Jerome gazed down at Richard's hand holding the little pill bottle, filled to the brim with a scoop of Alan's ashes. Dev, Michelle and Jerome were already a few drinks in at a homely local pub they had found in a visitor's guide, but Lindy and Richard had only just made it to the agreed rendezvous point. Having gathered around a table to plan the next day, the group had come to an impasse in their debate with Jerome.

'Dunno what you're complaining about,' said Richard. 'Mission was to get some of the ashes, and we completed it.'

'It's like we're dividing up the body. It doesn't feel right. It feels like the whole body should be together, wherever it goes,' said Jerome.

'Did you think we were getting *all* his ashes? Don't you think his parents would notice if suddenly all the ashes were gone? You're being... overly sensitive about this,' replied Lindy.

'That's probably why I dropped out of med school, Lindy. I actually care about people. I have a heart. Not like you… *ghouls*!' Jerome snarled, clunking his pint glass down on their table. After a few drinks, he was beginning to make a little noise, and the rest of the group noticed the looks being shot at the tourists by the local patrons.

'That's *not* why you dropped out of med school,' stated Lindy.

'It was because you kept imagining you had whatever condition you happened to be studying, you know it, and we know it,' corrected Richard, only to receive an eye roll from Jerome.

'Do you have any idea how difficult it was to get this?' asked Lindy. 'Even getting into the house? We had to sit there for an hour making small talk with his mum and dad before we could even get to the ashes.'

'Small talk? What small talk?' asked Jerome irritably.

'What do you think? Alan. All Alan-related topics. What he was like, our memories of him, their memories, blah.'

'That's not exactly small talk, is it? Small talk is the weather or the price of fucking stamps. You were talking about Alan. They were talking about their son who just died.'

'He didn't *just* die, Jerome,' said Lindy, 'it was six months ago. Frankly, they were surprised they were seeing us again, and we knew how they felt. You're complaining, but you didn't do any of the hard work.'

'Oh, hard work? This was hard work?' Jerome asked, his voice rising in volume and pitch. 'I'm sorry you found it such a chore,' he continued sarcastically, 'to do something to make sure our friend is laid to rest as he would have wanted, and not in some jar on a shelf, gathering dust like some… some moose head on a wall.' At this, Dev and Richard forgot themselves and giggled. 'I'm glad you two are finding this funny,' reprimanded Jerome, as Lindy and Michelle also aimed glares their way.

'I'm sorry,' apologised Dev.

'Why are you sorry?' asked Richard. 'It was funny. *Moose head*,' he repeated, starting to laugh again.

'I'm not trying to be fucking funny,' spat Jerome.

'I know, it's just that it's a funny situation. If Alan was here, he'd see the funny side, and really isn't that what this is all about?' attempted Dev.

'Yeah, but which part of him *is* here?' asked Jerome.

Lindy put up her hands in defeat and turned away, only for Richard to step in. 'They're ashes, Jer,' There isn't one molecule that belongs to one part of the body. They've been ground down and mixed up. Nothing belongs to anything anymore. In fact, his remains are mixed up with the remains of other people cremated before him.'

'I know that,' said Jerome.

'Okay then, so it doesn't matter.'

'Yes, it does.'

‘Well, I think you’re drunk, and if you don’t quieten down, they’re going to kick us out.’

‘I’m not drunk. If the whole point of the exercise is to satisfy his wishes, then we should satisfy the whole body, not just part of it.’

‘Drunk,’ echoed Richard.

‘At least if we knew for certain we had the brain, we could say, ‘well, at least the brains are happy’. For all we know, we’ve got a foot.’

‘So the foot will be happy,’ tried Michelle.

‘No, it won’t. It’s a foot.’

‘It’s ashes. It’s symbolic,’ reminded Richard.

‘It doesn’t know what’s going on,’ continued Jerome. ‘If we were only going to get part of the body, then it should have been the head, the brain.’

‘But it’s all mixed up, Jerome. There’s no way to tell what is what,’ offered Lindy.

‘I know. Exactly my point. So we should have got all of him, all the ashes like I said.’

‘Jerome!’ Richard snapped firmly, suddenly tiring of the entire exchange.

‘Richard!’ Jerome snapped back, feeling the same way.

‘In this pill bottle, we have enough of Alan to give him what we think he really would have wanted. To be scattered out here in the wide-open space where he loved to walk.’

‘Shut up, Richard, you don’t understand. None of you fucking does,’ Jerome spat at them.

‘Hey, he was our friend too, Jerome. You weren’t the only one who knew him,’ said Lindy.

‘Yeah, but you weren’t the one sharing his life,’ blurted

Jerome, swept up in the emotion of the moment. 'We lived together. We shared a life. That has to count for something. His family didn't know him anymore. They didn't know who he really was, and yet they have all of him and all we have is this fucking pill bottle.'

The next day the group woke up calmer and sober enough to set about the five hour round walk up to Kinder Scout from Edale in the Peak District. Most of them had wanted to do one of the shorter walks, such as Minninglow with its Neolithic burial chambers or the beauty spot of Longstone Edge, but Jerome and Lindsay had convinced the others that Kinder Scout would be the best spot for Alan. He had walked the shorter routes but had always wanted to walk to Kinder Scout. The friends would make the journey for him.

It was two hours before they got to the higher ground of Kinder Scout. Standing side by side on the high ridge, the friends looked out over the carpet of green land that stretched away from them. Silently they thought their thoughts and stared out at the landscape. It looked like an elaborate and highly detailed hand-painted set of ornaments, all brought together in a special museum exhibition for their satisfaction.

Luckily the rain had held off, but the sky was a murky grey as it hung over the vista.

The green of the grass and moss.

The grey of the stone and exposed rock.

At Kinder Downfall, they carefully made their way over enormous rocks that looked like giant steps the size of double beds. From there, they stepped gingerly onto the damp grass on the slope, and this was where they stopped again to finally leave their friend at this place of exquisite natural beauty.

Jerome pulled the pill bottle from the inner pocket of his jacket and twisted the cap. It clicked. Frowning, he twisted some more. To everyone's consternation, the cap continued to click but refused to come free from the bottle.

'There's a problem,' announced Jerome needlessly.

'It's childproof,' explained Michelle. 'You have to push and twist.'

'I know that. You think I don't know that? I'm pushing, I'm twisting,' Jerome insisted, grappling with the small container. 'It's still not coming fucking loose.'

'It's clicking, so you can't be doing it right. Give it here, let me try,' bossed Lindsay. She spent a minute pushing and twisting before trying pulling and twisting. Finally, she resorted to just pulling. 'Fucker won't open,' she eventually conceded, red-faced from her exertions.

'Told you. What now?' asked Jerome.

'Maybe crack the bottle on a rock,' suggested Dev.

'It's plastic, not glass,' Lindsay huffed, 'it's not going to just crack.'

'If we had a drill, we could drill into it,' said Richard.

'Oh, that's a great idea, Richard. Do you happen to have a

drill handy?' asked Lindsay, her tongue slick with sarcasm. 'Have you had a moment to notice where we are? Have you taken in your surroundings? We're in the middle of fucking nowhere, up a fucking hill and two and a half fucking hours away from the nearest electrical fucking appliance. Even if you had a drill here, where would you plug the fucker in?'

'Cordless,' retorted Richard, 'and I was only thinking out loud. No need to get so angry.'

'Wait a minute,' said Jerome. 'Richard, what about your Swiss army knife?'

The friends turned towards Richard, eyes boggling at him, daring him to say he'd left it behind. Richard instantly threw his rucksack from his back onto the ground, and his hands set to ferreting around in it.

'Or,' said Richard as he pulled the tool from a side pocket, 'we could use my Swiss army knife.'

Twenty minutes later, the group began their return journey down the hill, along the ridge to Kinder Low, in silence. Dev brought up the rear, behind Jerome and, looking back at Kinder Reservoir, he thought of a rare instance when Alan had shared something personal with him. While Dev had liked Alan, he had never been close to him, a sentiment shared by everyone in the group, except Jerome. There was much about himself Alan had kept from them, including, it seemed, the nature of his relationship with Jerome. Jerome was gay, but it had never occurred to them that Alan might share that with him. Perhaps, with the exception of Jerome, none of them had known him very well at all.

The incident Dev recalled as they walked back to the inn happened a year ago at med school. Alan and Dev sat together at a table on the second floor of the library one evening. No longer able to concentrate on studying, and with the entire floor to themselves, they instead took the time to chat. About nothing in particular, just this and that. About nothing in particular, but it was a welcome distraction from the pressure of exams and decisions. As he followed Jerome along the path, Dev cast his mind back to the funeral.

The cremation.

The body, burning.

All that made them who they were.

All thoughts, feelings, emotions, ideas, desires were bound up within this small package of tissue, and within moments it was all gone. Dev tried to imagine the flames licking at the body, but he just could not do it. Instead, all he could picture were scenes from movies. Particularly, *Scrooged*. Dev couldn't bring himself to imagine the body lying there. Burning. Smouldering. The fats hissing and popping.

Thinking about Alan, for some reason, the clearest image Dev could conjure up was from one night when they were waiting to buy drinks at a nightclub. The lighting effects bounced off Alan's skin, lighting up his eyes and glinting from the metal frame of his glasses. So this is how Dev imagined his friend in the furnace, lit up by flashing and swirling nightclub lights, waiting for a drink while his body dissolved into the smoke.

*Seems somehow nonsensical,* thought Dev, *that everything that makes us us should be carted about on top of our bodies, behind our eyes in this fragile container, with no backup at all. Or maybe that's what children are supposed to be. The backup. A copy of a copy that is inevitably corrupted and distorted along the way until it changes into something else entirely. Another person.*

*Everything that made up the Alan that we knew has been transformed into ashes. A completely unrecognisable state. Like when you're small, and you first learn of caterpillars turning into butterflies, but you're unable to reconcile this into something that fits into your worldview. Now it's like Alan is frozen in time, like a stand-alone computer having been disconnected from the network and sent to the company basement to gather dust.*

As a medical student, Dev knew he shouldn't, but he did find it surreal that they had taken someone once alive with thoughts and idiosyncrasies peculiar to that person and reduced them to almost nothing. It felt to Dev that everyone living and dead should fit together perfectly, like some unimaginably immense puzzle that spanned all time, and that removing something should not be possible. That Alan, one cog, had been removed should have meant that the entire global network made up of every single person on the planet should somehow cease to operate correctly.

*If Da Gama looked up at the sky to find that one or two stars were missing from each constellation, wouldn't he be unable to recognise where he was? To Jerome, Alan was one of the stars in his constellation, and his sudden death has left Jerome lost and alone.* To Dev, a package of thoughts, quirks, dreams and memories had simply been removed from existence.

Descending from Pennine Way and finally reaching Edale, just over three hours after they set off from the ridge where they left Alan, the group stopped for a final look. Dev put up his hands to shield his eyes against the sudden spark of afternoon sun that was now beginning to break through and whisper over the landscape. Sucking in deep lungfuls of fresh, clean air, he thought he could hear that newscaster again on the TV. He turned to his friends to see if they shared his surprise at hearing TV sounds scrawling along the air towards them, but they were no longer there.

Their friends are no longer there. Instead, Zaeen turns to find the image of the human female, on the *television* device, in the corner of the recreation room, whom they had spotted earlier that day talking with the one that called himself the prison governor. Now she was talking about the situation in progress within the prison. Presumably, they thought, the building behind her was what the prison they and their friends currently occupied looked like from the outside.

'… are angry today, and prison officials have spoken anonymously about the authorities suspecting the inmates of pure fabrication. Meanwhile, it is the overwhelming belief amongst the friends and family of the inmates that they have been used in human experiments that have gone awry. While prison authorities have denied this, the inmates involved maintain their story that their individual consciousnesses have essentially beamed into the prison inmates' bodies and that the personalities of the actual inmates have been suppressed. Meanwhile, friends and family of the inmates want answers, fast.' Meanwhile friends and family of the inmates want answers, fast.'

Zaeen listens to the woman and contemplates the irony that they and their friends had schemed for so long to escape Extor 4 by dispersing and taking over bodies of people on another planet, only to discover that those bodies belonged to prisoners. It seemed that whatever they tried, they would always be a prisoner and would always lose. Now they and their friends have lost even their own bodies. Zaeen can't bear to look at themself. Even though the security at this facility is primitive compared to what they are used to, it is designed for this body that apparently cannot accommodate, or replicate, the actions they know their previous body could. Actions that would allow them to escape this latest cage. From here to where, though? In any case, they and their friends would not be seeing the outside of this place for some time.

With hindsight, it had probably been a mistake to tell the warden their story. However, the warden had provoked them, saying that their behaviour was not at all *normal.* By "normal", Zaeen, and their three hundred and forty-six fellow escapees that had reconstituted in the new bodies, understood that they were not behaving according to what was expected of those people who previously controlled these bodies. Telling their story seemed like the right thing to do at the time. They had no way of knowing it would cause this much... consternation.

At first, they had been discussed by the officials in charge, which was fine, except that some of Zaeen's colleagues were growing increasingly dissatisfied with their new lives. The drab environment. The bland food. Their awful new bodies. They were making a fuss, demanding to be heard, and incensed they were not being believed. Instead, they were being punished for telling the truth. They refused to meet with the beings who had come to this place to speak with the previous controllers of these bodies and see faces they recognised.

Mothers
Husbands
Sons
Daughters
Wives
Fathers
Girlfriends
Boyfriends
Cousins
Friends
Uncles
Aunts
Nieces
Nephews
Religious representatives
Legal representatives
Law and Order representatives

Eventually, a small group of the worst offenders had been taken away and questioned. Then more. Then still more. Until all the inmates had been questioned and all were found to be telling the same story.

Zaeen now watches the angry faces on the *television device* as they demand to know what has become of the people they once knew. Even if Zaeen could explain it to them, they doubt their capacity, or willingness, to understand.

On the *TV*, the focus returns to the woman. 'This is the latest in a spate of incidents around the world to upset the foundations of society. The people are once again in an uproar. This time they accuse the government of playing Dr. Frankenstein with the inmates. This town is demanding the central government to step in and bring the inmates back from wherever they have gone.'

Zaeen wants to use all five puny senses this body could offer to see, hear, smell, taste, and feel the world outside. They want to know the secrets the planet has to share. The fresh air, the hills, the trees, the mountains, the birds, the caves, the seas. Zaeen wants to know these people. All of them, if possible. They want to know these minds that these people seemed to value so highly that they were moved to such anger over their loss. *Indeed, the minds of these inmates must be great, they think. On this planet, their minds must hold great worth, great beauty.*

Zaeen wants to connect with that which is frustratingly hidden from them. They reach out to the woman's image and press their fingers against what they see, but all they feel is the smooth flat glass.

# 8. Shopping

The woman's face slides from her head. Not exactly. Features from the woman's face slide about the front of her head. As though her skin has acquired some gelatinous quality. Attributes such as her nose, eyebrows, various wrinkles have been liberated from their original locations and allowed to roam free over the surface, taking on new contours. There is nothing the woman can do to control it, and why would she want to? Such a thing would only make one more interesting, wouldn't it?

Dev has no idea why he is thinking this, laid on Katie's bed, his own face a contorted mess of struggling features. *What an odd thing to see at this point*, he thinks. *Certainly not a memory flashing before my eyes, just another bleed of weirdness from my brain.* He doesn't recognise the woman's assortment of features, but the ears, eyebrows, lips, teeth and eyelashes hanging over him reminds him of what parents suspend over cribs to help their babies to sleep. Despite the absence of soft lights and lullabies, the display is oddly soothing.

Now, as the eye comes into view again, Dev can see it silently forming words. Now the other eye also comes into view, the same motions, but on its side. Hypnotised by how the eyes bunch and stretch around the words, Dev drinks in all the different hues and shades. Mesmerised, he has been unconcerned about how close the eyes are getting to him, but now he focuses and draws everything in.

Before he knows it, Dev is sitting in the chair facing the bed, which had been made up neatly. It is in the exact same room he had been struggling in, but it's different. The sheets are back in place, and the pillows have been collected from the floor. Dev turns to his right to see a silhouetted woman in a short, close-fitting dress settle in another chair by the window. As his eyes adjust to the light behind her, the shadows and colours fall into place. The first of these is the woman's dark hair and healthy, pink complexion. With a start, Dev realises the woman is Katie. Struggling against the belt, he almost forgot about her but is now relieved beyond belief that she is here to help him.

'Katie! Help me! Please!' Dr. Sharma hears himself say, but not with the sense of urgency that he had anticipated. He wants to scream out to Katie, but they aren't his lips to scream from anymore. Instead, he hears himself continue.

'Katie, help me, please. I… I want to understand what people are experiencing when they engage in… alternative sexual practices. I'm looking for somewhere I can begin to gain some insight.' Dr. Sharma idly fingered the edges of his notebook as he waited for Katie's response.

'So, Dr. *Sharma*, you want to know about weird stuff that

you can try at home,' replied Katie, her typically friendly smile playing on her lips. They were in the bedroom she used for work, the same room Dr. Sharma is currently dying in. Katie's room, with its soft textures, was not what Dr. Sharma had anticipated. If he was honest, he'd admit that he didn't know what he should expect. Katie was a prostitute. Or, as she preferred it, an escort.

Not that she often escorted anyone anywhere. With most of her time spent in her bedroom, Katie had paid a lot of attention to the furnishings to make the room welcoming to clients and comfortable for herself.

This was Dr. Sharma's first time visiting Katie, and he had already taken some time to attempt a succinct explanation of his project without flooding her with too much information. So far, she had surprised him by not only proving herself a good listener but also being open to sharing her story and experiences.

Katie was thirty-two and had been working as an escort since her teens. Her mother did it before her, 'so it's like a family business, really,' she had joked, with a practised smile. To Dr. Sharma, Katie looked younger than her thirty-two years, but not significantly so. Her straight, chestnut brown hair, cut into a playful bob, amplified her youthful looks as she sat on the edge of the bed with one leg crossed over the other, dressed in suggestive but not overtly sexual satin shorts and matching sleeveless top.

'*Weird* wouldn't be my word, but... yes,' answered Dr. Sharma.

'Look, I do what I do, but that doesn't make me an expert on sex or on what people get up to in private. You know what I mean?'

'Yes. I want to understand the gratification they receive, the pleasure and why they find it satisfying.'

'But, whatever other people do is not necessarily going to be what you're into, is it?' Katie clarified, trying to understand how this would help him.

'I don't know. You don't know you like something until you try it,' replied Dr. Sharma with a smile.

'We're not talking about Mexican food. We're talking about sex. You want to experience what someone else does when they... I don't know, shove stuff up their arse, right?' asked Katie. 'But if you're not into it, you won't understand the… result that other people get.'

'Hopefully, I'll be able to see their point of view and understand where they are deriving their pleasure, understand what they thought would be a turn-on about it in the first place.'

'Maybe they were just like you. They heard of something and thought they would give it a go.'

'Okay, but there must have been something about it that spoke to them in the first place. Not just that it was something new, but something that stimulated them. Why did it stimulate them?'

'Why don't you ask them, then?'

'I'm hoping you will ask them for me,' explained Dr. Sharma. 'Are there any special requests amongst your clients that you can suggest as a starting point?'

'That's private. You have doctor-patient confidentiality. I have escort-client confidentiality,' came Katie's playful response.

'I'm not asking you for names. Just a run-down of things

that people do. What do you say?'

Katie mulled this over for a few seconds, teasing the stitching in the duvet cover. 'A few things come to mind, but I don't think you'd like them.'

'It's not about liking it. It's about getting the point of view. Connecting and trying to understand for myself, instead of just reading about it.'

'Okay, okay, but I think you should also talk to someone who specialises a little more in the fetish stuff. Because I don't really do that.'

'I'm already working on that. So, if I see you on a regular basis, how can you help me?'

'Me? I feel like I'm at a job interview. I do *this* to stay away from that.'

'I want to establish a relationship with someone who can give me insight.'

'You're going to need a few relationships then. It's such a wide… thing. There isn't one person who can tell you everything.'

'I know. I just want to know of your experience so I can cultivate… additional relevant relationships.' He was beginning to lose Katie's understanding.

'Doctor –'

'Just call me Dev.'

'*Dev*,' began Katie, 'I work from home. Clients find my number, and they give me a call. For every bloke that turns into a client, there's another ten that are a waste of time. Out of the ones that do visit, some just want sex. Some want to chat. Some want both. Sometimes they want a couple of hours at a time. Some want only twenty minutes. Those are generally the ones who just want a quick blowie.'

'Okay. The ones who want to talk, what do they normally want to talk about?'

'Some regulars I have like to feel like we're friends, like I'm pleased to see them and that I enjoy being with them. Obviously, on a quickie, there's not much talking, just not practical.'

'But, it's not always about simple sexual gratification.'

'Well,' began Katie, beginning to feel slightly annoyed by Dr. Sharma seemingly explaining her job to her, 'it is, on the surface, and most of the time I only deal with what they say they need. There are different types of gratification, aren't there? Different people, different wants. Some want a mate. Some want to be seduced. Some want a treat. They want to leave feeling better than they did when they arrived. That's what I try to keep in mind. Everybody wants to feel better than they do.'

'Why don't you tell me about some of the men that come to see you?' asked Dr. Sharma, looking to dig deeper.

'I thought that was what I was already doing.'

'I mean specifics. Some case studies. Maybe let's focus on one client in particular and tell me his story.'

'Okay, where shall I start?'

'How about your first time?'

'I was asking *myself*, not you. I'll tell you about the last person I saw. He's a lorry driver. Or that's what he tells me. He's away from home a lot, and when he's 'round this way, he comes to see me.'

'And what's special about you?'

'Charming,' Katie commented sarcastically, with a

surprised smile on her lips.

'Sorry, I didn't mean to be rude. What I meant is, what is it that attracts him to you in particular?'

'The first time, he told me that I reminded him of his wife. Actually, we don't really talk that much. He's got an accent. He's difficult to understand.'

'Where's he from?'

'Um, Germany. That's where his family is. He was telling me once how they have all these massive brothels in Germany. *Mega brothels*. I'd hate that. I like working for myself.'

'Is that the only objection you have?' asked Dr. Sharma.

'I don't know what the rest of it is like. Maybe it'd feel like more of a job. So, if I wouldn't be able to set my own schedule, that would annoy me too. I like my freedom. I don't like to feel like a… factory.'

'This German client,' re-focussed Dr. Sharma, 'what does he like?'

'Nothing unusual. Missionary. Doggy. Some oral. He seems to like hearing me talk. Well, he keeps coming back for more, so he must like it.'

'And you think when he leaves, he feels better than when he arrived?'

'Yeah, I think so. Otherwise, why would he keep coming?'

'Because he's *hoping* to feel better?'

'That's what everyone's doing. Hoping for better. There's always better. I'm his idea of *better*. It's nice to believe I make him feel better.' Here Katie paused a moment before continuing. 'What else?'

'Hm. I don't know. What other firsts do you want to tell

me about?'

'I don't really have strong memories of the first times I did this or that. Listen,' said Katie, eager to clarify the agenda for the rest of their meeting, 'did you want to get up to anything, or are we just chatting?'

'Er,' began Dr. Sharma, his eyes meeting hers, 'just chatting. Thank you.'

'Okay, wait there.' With that, she hopped off the bed to leave the room. A moment later, Katie returned carrying in a padded chair from the kitchen. She put it down facing Dev and reached for her warm dressing gown, pulling it over her before sitting. 'I did find my first threesome interesting. A client wanted a threesome with him and his wife. It was fine. It was my first time, but it was fun. Different. After they'd finished, we were chatting, and the wife was talking about how she really enjoyed giving oral. She'd spent most of the night with her mouth either between my legs or on his dick.

'What she liked most was going down on her husband while I sat on his face and watched her suck him. But this is the bit that I'd never heard before. She said she loved using her mouth, her lips, for pure sexual pleasure. The same face that was on show to everyone every day. At work, on the train, at the shops. It was like she was getting a thrill even when she was telling me. I suppose, to her, her mouth was like another sexual organ. But one that wasn't hidden behind clothes. Just out for all to see.'

Dr. Sharma watched Katie as she spoke. He observed her mannerisms, movements, vocal inflections and wondered what it was to be her. Not just another person, but to be a specific person other than oneself. Wake up with different creases in your skin, a different taste in your mouth, a different texture to your hair. What would it be to look at events through a different filter of past experiences? He wondered how exciting it would be to switch to another backstory and have a different feeling about the same event, directly informed by that alternate history.

It was something he often wondered about his sister, Amina. If he shut his eyes tight and tried hard, could he see the world from her point of view?

Perhaps a particular memory?

Perhaps with a little push…

Dev was four years old and struggling to sleep one night when his eight-year-old sister, Amina, entered the bedroom they shared.

'Aren't you asleep yet?' she asked.

'No,' came the muffled response from beneath Dev's *Ninja Turtle* covers.

'Aren't you sleepy?' Amina asked.

'No,' came the reply, with a playful tone.

'Why not?' asked Amina as she closed the bedroom door.

'Just not. Do you want to play a game?'

‘We’re supposed to be sleeping. It’s bedtime, not playtime. Do you get that?’ asked Amina with unnecessary sass, something she’d seen on TV and was trying out on herself.

‘Why?’ asked Dev, as he pulled the sheet from over his head and peeked at his sister.

‘Because it just is.’ Amina stepped between the flower patterns in the carpet on her way to her bed. It was a habit of theirs. Dev had spotted Amina doing it and had begun copying her. Amina found his copying of her annoying and pleasing in equal measure. She was annoyed that he had begun copying her habits but secretly a little bit pleased that it meant he was looking up to her.

Since Dev’s birth, Amina had felt protective about him, but he was getting to the age where trying on and adopting the habits of others was becoming a habit. Serena had had a chat with Amina about some of her peculiarities, such as avoiding the flower design on the carpet to step only on the blank patches. Serena didn’t want Dev to pick up the same habit.

‘Before you know it, he’ll be avoiding cracks in the pavement and only using particular cutlery. Wherever we go, he’ll have to travel with his own knife, fork and spoon set,’ Serena had said.

So Amina found herself having to curtail the habits that she had conceived and nurtured through the years. She wasn’t particular about cutlery, but she did insist on bedding of specific colours (yellow and/or green) and socks (of any colour) with spots (again of any colour, but preferably pink).

‘If Mum comes up and finds us awake, she’ll be cross.’

‘I know, but I can’t sleep.’

'What will help you sleep then?' asked Amina, waiting for the inevitable answer, which she was also always secretly pleased with.

'Hmm,' Dev wondered aloud, theatrically. 'Well, hmm, maybe you could do something like… tell me a story?'

'A story, Dev?' repeated Amina feigning annoyance, the way she always did, as she got into bed and pulled the covers up to her neck.

'Please,' pleaded Dev.

'Okay, but you have to promise.'

'All right. I promise I will fall asleep straight after.'

'Not good enough,' countered Amina. 'Storytelling at this time of night is high-risk. I'll need a *double-wubble* promise.'

'Okay then. I double-wubble promise,' promised Dev again, wiggling his toes under the covers with anticipation.

'Double-wubble is really serious, Dev,' warned Amina.

'I know,' replied Dev, in a tone with a level of gravitas commensurate with the occasion, satisfying Amina that her little brother was taking the mysterious consequences of a broken double-wubble promise seriously.

'Where's your storybook then?'

'Make one up. Tell me a new one.'

'Please,' reminded Amina.

'Please,' agreed Dev.

'Okay. Where shall I start?'

'Once upon a time!'

'Shh, not so loud.'

'Sorry,' he whispered, 'once upon a time.

'Okay. Once upon a time… there was… what was there?'

'I don't know.'

Amina thought for a few moments before beginning again.

'Once upon a time, there was a little ripple.'

'A little ripple?' asked Dev.

'Yes, a little ripple. It lived in the middle of the ocean.'

'What's an ocean?'

'Er, the sea. You've been to the sea, haven't you?'

'Yes.'

'Well, far, far away, way way back where you can't even see, there are lots of little ripples of water, and they live in the sea far far away from land. Far away from where we live. This little ripple lived with its mummy and daddy.'

'What was it called?'

'Oh. It was called… Mario.'

'Mario? That's a funny name.'

'Well, it's Italian. Mario, the little ripple, wanted to know what it was like on land.'

'So what did he do?'

'Well, he thought about it a lot, and after a while, he decided to find land. Mario's journey towards land would be long for him, so he had to begin as quickly as possible. He said goodbye to his mum and dad, knowing he might never see them again.'

'Oh. Why not?'

'Because the ocean is a big place, and he might get lost forever.'

'Oh. Where did he go? Was he going to England?'

'No. Mario wanted to go somewhere warm. He decided to go to Mauritius. You know what Mauritius is, don't you?'

'It's where Mum and Dad are from. Far away. Mum says we'll go one day, on holiday.'

'That's right. So Mario, the ripple, said goodbye to his family and friends and set off on his journey through the sea, rippling along with all the other little ripples. From time to time, he would get a lift from the bigger waves. At other times currents would take him the wrong way, but Mario wouldn't give up. He kept going. It was months later that he finally got a glimpse of land.'

'What was it like?' asked Dev, momentarily forgetting that he lived on land himself.

'Well, you've been to the beach, haven't you? Well, it looked like that but from far away.'

'Oh.'

'At his first sight of land, Mario became very excited and used all his might to get there even quicker. The closer he got, the bigger the land looked and the more excited he was to get there. Mario surged forward quicker and quicker, but what he hadn't realised was that he was no longer a little ripple. Mario had grown up, and now he was a big wave, and as he picked up speed, he also picked up a lot of the other little ripples along the way,' explained Amina.

'Together, they didn't just make a wave. They made a humongous, *ginormous* wave. A wave like that is called a *Sue-Mammy*. As Mario got closer to the beach, he could see the people running away. They were scared and very worried because he was so big and rushing towards them. Mario realised he would crash all over the land and destroy the things he had been in such a rush to see, but he couldn't stop himself. It was too late!

'Everybody was running away. Everybody was scared, and as he loomed so wide and tall, Mario could see the shadow he cast over the whole island. He had been travelling for so long because he wanted to see land and Mauritius and be somewhere warmer, but now that he was there, he couldn't stop himself from crushing it!' As she spoke, Amina waved her hands to emphasise the jeopardy of Mario's situation.

'Mario wondered what he could do to avoid this. He thought hard and, just before it was too late, he came up with a plan. Mario pushed on and continued to gather pace, and collected all the little ripples and smaller waves around him to help. With them, he surged faster and faster with more and more strength until he got to the beach. Just before Mario got to all the deck chairs and ice cream vans, he jumped into the air with all the ripples and other waves. They all jumped their best, and they flew through the air chasing birds out of the way.

'People came out of their houses and saw all this water whooshing through the air far above their heads. Mario and his friends blocked out the sky and the sun. All the people could see was water flying over the trees and mountains. '*Whooooooosh!*' the water screamed through the air over their heads. Mario and his friends carried on whooshing through the air as quickly as they could so they wouldn't harm anyone or anything below.

'Meanwhile, on the island, the people began to cheer as they realised what Mario and his friends were doing. 'Yay. Hip hip hooray,' they all shouted as the last of the water fell from the sky and landed on the beach on the other side of the island. That day Mario and his friends became the first waves since records began to jump over an entire island. They became so famous that even Mario's parents far away heard the news, and they were very happy and proud of him. After that day, Mario relaxed around the warm beaches of Mauritius and kept his promise not to surge or whoosh ever again. Everyone lived happily ever after. The end.'

'That was good,' said Dev, momentarily satiated. 'Tell another!'

# 9. Approaching by moon

It was late in the night when Raju entered four-year-old Amina's bedroom. She had been having nightmares recently, and it hadn't been long since she had begun sleeping alone in her room again. Now, with her father silhouetted in the doorway, Amina rubbed at her fading dreams and wondered if it was already time for school. It didn't feel to her as though she had been asleep for long. 'Dad?'

'Amina? You have to wake up,' Raju said as he entered his daughter's bedroom. His nerves were getting the better of him.

'I'm still sleepy, Daddy.'

'Don't be difficult,' urged Raju as he approached her bed.

'What's going on?' the little girl asked, still rubbing sleep away from her face.

'I need you,' began Raju, his words catching in his throat. 'I need you to get up. Take off your pyjamas, just like we practised. Get dressed. It's time to go.'

'Really?' beamed Amina, the sleep instantly vanishing.

'He's here?'

'Not yet, but soon,' replied Raju as he picked up her pre-packed backpack from atop the chest of drawers. 'Come along, into the car.'

'Does Mum need help? I want to help,' she stated, pulling off and on her clothes.

'You can help her by hurrying down and waiting by the back door. Wait for us, we'll go to the car together.'

Minutes later, the trio was in the car and en route to the hospital. Seatbelt on, Amina felt sleepy once again, but the flutters in her chest each time she heard Serena take a deep breath stopped her from drifting away. Serena and Raju had tried for some time without success for another baby and had eventually resolved to be content with their small family. Yet there they were, driving to the hospital, eight months after confirming Serena's suspicions, without even having been trying.

Amina had been aware for months that she should expect a new baby brother. She had been asked her thoughts countless times by various people, often by strangers when she was at the shops with her mother. The strangers seemed to enjoy asking whether they were expecting a boy or a girl. They asked when the baby was due to arrive, or one of the other convenient euphemisms to avoid the less than elegant reality. As if they had purchased a ticket and were waiting for their gate to be called.

They would also ask Amina how she felt about the impending change, not realising the change had already started. Most of all, Amina noticed, they enjoyed rubbing Serena's tummy. Their faces appeared a mixture of happiness and envy. To Amina, it seemed that the more they chatted about the coming arrival, the more they wanted to know, as though they could pretend it was happening to them.

As the car rumbled along towards the hospital and Raju tried to find the balance between speed and bumping Serena around as little as possible, Amina tried to sort through her feelings in her sleepy state. As she had told those countless strangers, she was excited. However, Amina was also very aware that this was something that could not be undone, and that she had already had the last day of her life as she knew it. She hadn't done anything special, it had been a school day. They had taken a quick spin around the park after school before setting off for home because Serena's feet were hurting. Because of the baby. Because of this baby that had already changed everything and would change everything once more.

That night they had eaten curried fish and butter beans with rice. A typical Mauritian dish that her parents would have had as children in Mauritius. It was part of them, a simple meal that reminded them of home. Not a special dish, not elegant or complicated, just comforting to Serena and Raju. Aged four, Amina did not know the difference between Mauritian dishes and anything else. At that age, they were all just meals, and that evening's meal had been just another one. Although they didn't have curried fish and butter beans very often, that evening's meal didn't feel like a special one. It didn't feel like a birthday meal to Amina. It didn't feel like something special was about to happen.

The more Amina thought of what was about to happen to Serena, the more bizarre she found it. The idea of one person coming out of another. She couldn't imagine why anyone would want that for themself. She could reconcile the concept of, for instance, a cow giving birth to a calf. But those were animals. It didn't seem reasonable that the same process should apply to people. Amina could even reconcile the reproductive process of the Tarantula Hawk. She had seen it on television. The narrator, whom she had no reason to mistrust, claimed it was the only creature that had ever led Charles Darwin to question the existence of God. Amina had no idea who Charles Darwin was, but she was impressed nonetheless.

Darwin's wonder was inspired by a wasp that deliberately hunts, stings and temporarily paralyses tarantula spiders to lay an egg. The egg eventually yields a maggot that lives within the tarantula, feeding off its flesh. According to the narrator (if you can call him that, personally, I found him haughty and full of himself), the part that troubled Darwin was how the maggot has the instinct to avoid the tarantula's vital organs. It consumes the flesh around them so it doesn't kill the tarantula and can continue feeding on fresh flesh as it grows back, without its host being any the wiser.

Wasps and their maggots couldn't speak. Tarantulas and their guests couldn't speak. Cows couldn't speak. People *could* speak. A fundamental difference, as far as Amina was concerned. It was difficult for her to wrap her mind around one person bringing another, smaller person out of themself, equally capable of thought, sight and sound. The whole thing sounded like an unseemly story, like something from her favourite anthology, *Fanciful Tales For Fantastic Dreams*.

It was clear from a young age that Amina was a very average

pupil when it came to school activities involving numbers. However, she loved to read, and her creativity invariably delighted Raju and Serena. The corkboard in her classroom, designated for outstanding work, was typically graced by a story Amina had written, a picture she had drawn, or something she had painted. Amina had a fertile imagination, and she took every opportunity to exercise it. Raju and Serena just wished she would apply herself to mathematics with the same vigour.

They didn't want to stop her creative pursuits, but they wanted to influence her from an early age to hone skills that employers would want. This started from the moment Amina entered school. It didn't matter to her parents that Amina, still a small child making potato prints, had yet to discover her own identity. They were already looking at her career prospects and pushing for her to focus on more academic strengths.

As typical parents, they desired for Amina a stable and more comfortable life than they had had. They wanted to put her in the best position to achieve that, and the future for an Asian woman, as far as they were concerned, was very dubious if she relied solely on creative skills to make a living in the UK. Then, there weren't any Asian women represented in the media. Asian men might occasionally pop up in TV shows, but always as a source of comedy. A figure of ridicule. A bumbling, ignorant immigrant to be pitied. But not too much, as that would detract from their primary purpose. A tool to make the audience feel relieved. Glad for their exalted position as Caucasians entitled to confidence and a sense of belonging as part of their birthright. A deserved reward for their accomplishment of having been born white.

Amina's parents wanted her to succeed on her own terms. Not to be appropriated to serve as a tool to distract others from the crippling, combined pain of high unemployment and rising taxes inflamed by an arrogant Conservative government seemingly indifferent to the crushing struggle it had inflicted upon the people. The only representations of non-Caucasians Raju and Serena saw in the media were designed to reinforce the perceived superiority of Caucasians by denigrating all other races and establishing them as inferior.

However, Raju and Serena saw it as a small price to pay for the opportunity to earn a better living and make a better life for themselves and their children, an opportunity they always appreciated and never took for granted. Raju and Serena had the steely determination typical of immigrants. People who had left their families, knowing they would not see them again for several years, if at all, and travelled far away to make a new life for themselves, a home in a country suffering a dearth of medical professionals. A country that needed their compassion, empathy, knowledge, and work ethic, but that did not always value anything else about them.

Anyone looking to make a new life in a foreign country far from home must have the ability to grit their teeth, keep their head down and grind daily to achieve their dreams. Every milestone comes at a price, and nothing they have comes easily to them. The Sharmas were working class, but Raju and Serena wanted to strive for more. They wanted their children in professions where they would be respected and valued as members of English society, equals to all other citizens, with the protections, confidence and sense of belonging commensurate with that membership. Securities they would still need to work for. They would not come by simply being born in the country. They would need to earn it, and even that would not be enough to overcome the perception that their skin was the wrong colour.

As Amina and her artistic aptitude grew, her parents continued to take pleasure from her successes. However, it was not an area where they felt confident. They needed to measure how well she was doing, something that is easy when it comes to arithmetic, or science, for instance. When it came to her creative endeavours, they had no way of knowing for themselves. They were entirely dependent upon parents' evenings to learn how she was developing, another factor that they found alienating.

Creativity was not part of Raju's and Serena's education in Mauritius. It was not valued there. At the weekend, they would encourage Amina's math skills by setting her problems to solve. This wouldn't last the whole weekend, but it would be enough to affect her mood for the rest of it after Serena had lost her patience explaining the theory yet again. Sometimes one or two of Amina's school friends would come to play, but this wouldn't put Serena off. She would set them all math tasks. Amina feared that they wouldn't want to come again, but they did. Children like to compete and prove themselves, especially for an easy win against a weaker child.

Amina could see that her friends were eager for Serena's approval, in the way that all small children seek the love of adults. They're conditioned for it, and the conditioning works up to a certain age. Amina herself had behaved like that, seeking the gentle smiles and easy reassurance of people who would congratulate her warmly for the most minor victory. What Amina couldn't reconcile was how much her mother seemed to welcome the attention of these other girls. She basked in it and gave the girls exactly the encouragement they needed to continue seeking her affection. Little Dev could see it too.

It is only now, as an adult, that Dev can rationalise Serena's eagerness to be the centre of the attention of a willing and easily pleased audience. Having struggled, as one child amongst many in a large family, to gain the love of her father, it was natural for Serena to grab at the light when it shone on her, trying to keep it as it slipped between her fingers. Trying to keep the affection of those whose love she didn't already have. Dev can understand it now as an adult, but the memory is still bitter.

The way she made jokes to make other children laugh. At his expense. At Amina's expense. It stung, the betrayal. He didn't have the word for it when it happened. Betrayal. It was a word on a movie poster. It was a twist in a TV show or a book. At that time, it wasn't something he associated with their mother and the few words she needed to take Amina's friends away and leave her on the outside, the butt of the joke.

Neither Amina nor Dev would ever bring up with Serena how she would turn on them when it suited her. Amina preferred to pretend it hadn't happened. By the time Dev realised the importance of the event, he was of an age where he knew it would have sounded a triviality. And it would be, to an adult.

Dev remembers an incident where one of Amina's friends had come to play. Serena decided to set them some time-based tasks. He and Amina had a chalkboard with two sides, so two could use it at once. Amina and her friend, Sandy, readied themselves on opposing sides, waiting for the nod from Serena as Dev watched from the sofa. A teasing pause, and then the signal came. Both girls set to applying their chalk to the board in a flurry of lines, shapes and shading. Sandy was the first to put down her chalk.

'Finished,' she announced awkwardly as Amina kept working.

'Stop, Amina. You lost,' said Serena, in a tone that the siblings recognised as displeasure. Amina put down her chalk.

'Chocolate milk for the big winner. Come with me to the kitchen, Sandy.'

Sandy skipped after Serena, and they both disappeared through the doorway. Dev watched Amina, but she didn't meet his eyes. Instead, she stepped to the other side of the board. The picture was a simple square with a few rectangles inset and a triangle on top. Dev could see Amina's effort from the sofa, with a smoking chimney, a doorknob and curtains in the window. The upstairs window was unfinished.

Push and risk snapping a child's self-confidence. Or press for a victory with the potential to boost their sense of self-worth. A delicate dilemma.

Despite occasionally annoying Amina, she and Dev were pals and always played together, even when her friends came for a sleepover. On one such occasion, nine-year-old Amina left little Dev alone with her friends while she padded downstairs to petition Serena for treats. Returning to her bedroom laden with the snacks her mother had prepared, Amina was surprised to find five-year-old Dev pinned to the bed by her friends and having makeup applied to his face and nail varnish to his fingers by her friends who were splitting their sides with laughter. Amina wasted no time in ordering her classmates out of her bedroom, down the stairs and out of the front door, barefoot and clad in only their pyjamas.

'But it's cold outside!' Raju could hear the girls complain as Amina unceremoniously shoved the last one out of the door.

'Amina, what's going on? Who were you opening the front door to? Haven't I told you not to open the front door to anyone? It's dangerous.'

'I wasn't letting anyone in. I was saying goodbye.'

'Goodbye?' asked Raju, confused. He looked over at the coat rack where seven little coats awaited their owners. 'What happened?'

'They put makeup on Dev.'

'Well, you can't just chuck them out! It's nighttime. It's dark out there, darling. They must be freezing.'

At that moment came a timid little knock at the front door. Raju quickly answered it as Amina folded her arms. The sight that greeted Raju was five little girls in pyjamas shivering in the biting cold wind. Three of them were sobbing while another appeared to be in genuine shock at the swift turn of events, staring blankly into the middle distance. The fifth that had knocked at the door was clearly upset but holding her nerve admirably despite the tell-tale tremble in her voice.

'We're really sorry. Please, can we come in?'

'Of course! Get back in and get warm. *We're* sorry.'

'No, we're not,' chirped Amina, as little Dev stumbled down the stairs, tears ruining his mascara.

'Yes, we are, Amina,' corrected Raju over the heads of the girls as they filed in, cold and bedraggled, and made their way to the living room floor where they sat by the fire.

'But they made Dev wear Mum's makeup,' complained Amina. 'Look at him.'

'So? You do it all the time.'

'Yeah… but… he's my brother.'

For years, every weekend, Amina would dutifully attend swimming lessons at the local pool. By the age of ten, Amina was a competent swimmer and took on the responsibility of teaching six-year-old Dev under the watchful eyes of Raju and Serena. Amina would encourage Dev to take a deep breath and dip beneath the surface to swim underwater. Dev avoided this at every opportunity. It wasn't that he didn't want to do it. He felt simply unable to stop himself from panicking whilst underwater. Amina would show him how easy it was and then ask him to do it.

'Like this,' Amina would say before taking a deep breath and then submerging her head under the water, bubbles floating to the surface. A few seconds later, she would re-emerge, wiping water from her face. 'See?'

Dev did see, but this was one thing he didn't think he could copy. After weeks had turned into months of trying, he still couldn't explain his fear.

'What about snorkelling one day when we go to Mauritius?' asked his father. 'Won't you come with us? Or will you stay behind?'

'Maybe I'll stay behind,' Dev forlornly conceded.

It was only when Amina suggested that they do it together that Dev made progress. The first and second times, he managed to put his head under the water but wouldn't open his eyes. The third time Dev opened his eyes a crack and glimpsed Amina's legs under the water. Seeing that she was there for him gave him the confidence to open his eyes fully. She smiled broadly, and bubbles left her mouth as her black hair swirled around her against the aquamarine blue of the pool. It was as though he was seeing her for the first time. That would be the image of Amina that would remain with Dev for the rest of his life.

Once Dev gained greater confidence, he and Amina would chase each other underwater. Swimming amongst the bodies and limbs of the other pool users, playing tag and seeking each other out.

# 10. Something revealing

On his back, Dev watches from Katie's bed at the bottom of the blue pool. He watches himself with Rachel. He can smell the chlorine and see the bubbles bumbling from the filter as he watches everything from the bottom of the pool. Dev can also see the other people splashing about, but they are distant and vague, so he focuses on his younger self, with Rachel.

They are eighteen and have taken a break from a music festival to shower and swim at the town's public pool. Rachel's long brown hair fans out in the water around her head as Dev hugs her from behind and edges her closer to the side of the pool before clandestinely cupping a breast. Rachel turns her head to smile at him and then tugs lightly at his shorts in response.

Eighteen, their behaviour feels inappropriate and risque as parents teach their children to swim nearby. Nobody has come to admonish them – nobody has seen – but they feel daring, believing the lifeguard could come along at any moment to remind them of the pool's family-friendly ethos. It amuses them to behave this way here.

Dev remembers and watches as the smell of chlorine suddenly becomes so overwhelming that he can't take it anymore and screws his eyes shut against the burning sensation. Under the water, he can't hear properly. Under the water, he can't hear properly. With all senses blocked, he can no longer feel any part of himself. On the bright side, the water means he's no longer suffocating from the belt. A few precious moments of respite.

Dev opens his eyes to find he is still underwater, surrounded by the overbearing blue, but it is no longer the synthetic blue of swimming pool tiles. This is the natural blue of the sea. The tiles on the floor and walls have been replaced with sand and small rocks. The sunlight succeeds in penetrating and illuminating the shallow water. Further away, he sees what he assumes are people occupying the water near the beach and splashing about with their inflatable beach toys.

It's peaceful here, and Dev is about to close his eyes again, grateful for the respite from the belt and the chlorine, when two people come into view, much closer. It's him again but with a different woman this time. *Oh, this would have been Italy*, he thinks. *Some beach there. So that would be… Elise.*

There in the Italian sea, Elise's eyes shone with the sunlight. They had only arrived in the country the previous night, but already her skin had absorbed the sun's rays, exuding health and vitality.

Suddenly, Dev wanted Elise right there and then in the sea. Despite the cold of the water, he could feel his penis become engorged. Hugging Elise close to him, Dev lifted her in the water. Her legs encircled his body, and her elbows brushed his back as she caressed him and coaxed his head closer to hers before they kissed salty water into one another's mouths where it became part of them. Pressed to one another, they kissed until Dev brought a hand from behind her and slipped it between her legs.

He thought Elise might object at a public beach and was encouraged when she opened her eyes and smiled her desire as he stimulated her under the water. They were far away enough for it to look like they were just hugging in the sea, their bodies below the surface indiscernible. Her breathing quickened and matched the anticipation in her eyes.

With her legs clasped around him, Dev let go of her and pulled at his shorts before returning to Elise's embrace. It was a moment or two before she felt the tip of his erect penis against her skin. Their breathing quickened again, almost matching one another as Dev's fingers pressed the fabric of her bikini bottom between her legs. Through the cold water, she could feel his warm fingers ease the flimsy material aside to tease and arouse her. Kissing her neck, Dev wrapped his arm around her, bringing her in tighter against him as his penis rubbed against her labia.

His fingers pressed harder against Elise's clitoris to elicit a quiet moan from her. Urge building in them both, Dev wanted her, and as he held Elise close, she grabbed at his shoulder and nape with little anticipatory gasps, waiting for him. As Dev pressed and moved with her, Elise's warmth felt incongruous, alien, conflicting with the cold water.

Gasping together, the waves of sensation intensified as Dev

shifted and grabbed at Elise's breast, yanking the fabric away to expose an aroused nipple before licking it, then further teasing it with his lips. They pushed at each other and tasted the sea again as they kissed.

Moving faster, they agitated the otherwise calm water as Elise's hot breath from shallow gasps hit Dev's ear and she climaxed quietly, to not draw attention. 'Don't come inside me!' she urged Dev as he pressed with purpose.

'No,' was all Dev managed in reply.

They continued gasping, rocking and disturbing the water until Dev buried his face in Elise's neck and lifted her from him, surprised by the sudden cold of the water after her warmth. He still climaxed, but the result had been less than expected as he ejaculated, releasing into the enormity of the sea.

Later that afternoon, Dr. Sharma looked up at the sky as he floated while Elise lay on a towel upon the smooth sand. He felt at peace as the sunlight began to fade on their first full day on holiday together. Dr. Sharma thought of Elise's newly sun-kissed skin and hoped it wouldn't progress to the blotchy, red state it often did. He opened his eyes and squinted at the horizon before him. All he could see was the blue of the water as it disappeared into the distance with no sign of waves crashing, just tranquillity. Peace. Freedom. Almost no line on the horizon as the sky took up the rest of his field of vision. A perfectly cloudless, blue sky.

It occurred to Dr. Sharma that he had not felt this satisfied and peaceful since Christmas during his second year of college, twenty-two years ago. Alone in the family house, while his parents were out completing their Christmas shopping, Dev was also making a concerted effort to complete all his coursework before Christmas Eve. Such was his zeal that the quality of the coursework was admittedly questionable. But it was Christmas, and he no longer cared.

Dev was just glad that it was done, out of the way, and he had nothing left to consider except what would be most relaxing for him. Mince pies and cream with a cup of coffee and a little TV. A documentary on McCarthyism, then another on Ancient Rome. After that, he enjoyed more mince pies with a repeat of Palin travelling the world in eighty days. The one where he was on the *dhow*.

It was dark and cold outside, but inside it was warm with the Christmas tree up and festooned with lights. One of the kitchen cupboards was stocked up with mince pies. There was plenty of cream in the fridge and ground coffee in the machine. It was indeed a satisfying Christmas Eve for Dev.

Floating on his back in the sea with ripples of happiness lapping at him, Dev didn't yet realise it, but he was to experience one of those curious coincidences in life. Twenty-two years ago, feeling happy and satisfied at Christmas, Dev soon learned Tim's important secret. This time, upon his return to England, he would again find Tim with some news.

Just after that Christmas twenty-two years ago, at the age of seventeen, Dev was due to see his old school friend who had returned from an adventure abroad. They had arranged to meet at Tim's house in the next town over before walking to the cinema, and Dev reached his house at two o'clock in the afternoon.

Dev hadn't seen Tim for over six months and was surprised that he had started applying gel to his blonde hair. It wasn't quite twisted up into punky little tufts, just a look Tim was either half-heartedly toying with or taking up but trying to make his own. He was still not ready, so Dev waited in the living room. It appeared to Dev that Tim was ready, but he took a seat in an armchair anyway and listened to Tim scuttling around upstairs from the bathroom to the bedroom and back again.

Returning from the bathroom to the bedroom for the last time, Tim sat on the bed in his check shirt and black jeans, collecting his courage. Tim, much like Dev at that age, never looked entirely relaxed in his clothes. Being not much more than five feet in height made shopping for clothes he liked more difficult. Tim would always be wearing something that fitted him perfectly but wasn't his style or something that was fashionable at the time but looked a size too big on him.

'So are we going?' Dev finally called up the stairs.

'I've something to say,' Tim called back.

Folding his arms, Dev patiently waited for the punchline. Tim was constantly repeating jokes he had picked up from stand-up acts or was reciting carefully memorised dialogue from sitcoms.

'I have something to tell you,' Tim repeated as he slowly descended the stairs to reach the foot where Dev was waiting.

'Okay,' said Dev, 'but you better spit it out so we can get going. You don't like to miss the trailers.'

'This is difficult for me, so… it doesn't matter about trailers.'

'I'm all ears.'

'Dev,' Tim began as he fiddled with the edging on the stairway bannister, 'Dev, er. You're my friend. We've known each other a long time… I…' he trailed off.

Dev sniggered, 'are we breaking up?'

'What?' asked Tim, with a look that mixed annoyance with confusion.

'Nothing, nothing. It just sounded, for a moment, like we were a couple… breaking up.'

'Dev,' Tim took a deep breath and pushed the words out of himself. 'I think I'm gay. I mean… I'm gay.'

Dev's instant reaction was to humour him and chuckle at Tim's quotes. 'That one's a little generic. What's that from? *Friends*?' For some reason, Tim was always doing *Friends*.

'I'm not doing a sitcom.'

'Oh. I'm sorry. Seriously?'

'Seriously. I'm gay. Or bisexual, perhaps.'

'When did you decide this?'

'I didn't *decide* it, Dev. It… it's how I am.'

'Of course, yeah, sorry, I didn't mean it like that,' waffled Dev as he moved aside for Tim to leave the staircase. 'You're just… I'm just caught by surprise. Okay, so, what does this mean?'

'It means I like men,' Tim answered sarcastically.

'I know *that*. I mean, how are things changing for you? Have you told your family?'

'No, and you're not to tell them. Or anybody else.'

'Nobody else knows?'

'Nobody except you. And Malcolm.'

'So how will things change?' asked Dev with a smile. 'Will you start being fabulous?'

Tim grinned. 'Hey, I've always been fabulous!'

Dev glanced down at his watch. 'Yes, you have. The film starts in twenty minutes. Do you still want to go or stay and chat about this?'

'Do *you* still want to go?' asked Tim, pushing his hands into his pockets.

'Yeah, why?' answered Dev.

'You know why,' replied Tim with a look that suggested his question was entirely reasonable.

'Tim, you don't need to ask me that.'

'Yeah, I do, Dev. I can't take anything or anyone for granted.'

Dev felt slightly hurt but ignored it. Clearly, Tim feared revealing his true self would put distance between him and his friend, something that couldn't be further from the truth. Dev mused that ancient Romans would have looked upon homosexuality with more compassion than modern society. He wondered how a myriad of factors had since coerced society into demonising those following their nature.

Dev could see Tim's typical cheeky glow drained from his face, replaced with apprehension and insecurity. This was a moment that Tim had already lived through with Malcolm, maybe with others whom he hadn't mentioned but who had not reacted as well to the news. This was a moment that Tim would have to live out again and again as he would finally express his truth to all the others he cared about. His friends, his family.

Not all would be understanding. Tim had a difficult time ahead of him. He may have been nervous about Dev's reaction, but he wouldn't have been scared. He would have been hurt to lose Dev's friendship. It would have been a significant blow to his already faltering sense of security, but it wouldn't be as scary as losing actual family, a prospect that Tim was still facing.

He feared their anger, their resentment. He feared their perceived sense of betrayal. Whatever their reaction, he worried that his family would no longer treat him like one of their own. There was no way of knowing what any of them genuinely thought, even if they did profess to accept him. Tim still lived at home. Like many others in the same position, he faced leaving if his family responded with prejudice instead of love. He feared knowing how they truly felt but needed to know nonetheless.

'Tim, nothing is different between us. I'm happy to go to the movies with you. You're my friend,' Dev stated simply.

It rained as Dev and Tim scurried to the cinema, and by the time they arrived, their clothes squelched with each movement. Taking his seat, Dev could feel the water roll from his hair down his forehead, along his nose and fall from the tip onto his T-shirt.

On the last day of their holiday in Southern Italy, Dev and

Elise felt the water drip from their bodies as they stepped out of the sea before leaving for the airport. Later, in their plane seats, regular travel clothes over their swimwear, they watched as the lights of the cities and towns pulled away from them. Those lights, the final mental snapshot of thoughts and feelings bound to the tiny Tuscan village they had visited, would always be with them. It had been a good break, and they had enjoyed each other.

Dr. Sharma had been prepared for the end of their relationship since it began. This is how he is in all his romantic relationships. Prepared to disconnect. Prepared to never see the other again. He doesn't see it as an issue. In fact, he doesn't even see it going on. Whether he realises it or not, he is always prepared for a cessation of familiarities. That is not to say that he dislikes being alone. He merely anticipates.

What he thought as the town disappeared from view was: *Whatever happens, weeks from now, years from now, wherever we are and whomever we're with, we can think back to this week and remember how happy we were.*

Back from Italy, Dr. Sharma thought of this moment as he drove to meet Tim.

# 11. Modern daze

After seeing his last patient of the day, Dr. Sharma drove fifteen minutes to the pub by the pier that he and Tim frequented during the off-season. In the summer, they preferred to visit a quiet bar near the town centre than this pub, which would typically be jammed with tourists. Since it was autumn, the pair felt free to reclaim their space.

The pub was part of a chain and, as such, was reassuringly characterless to Dr. Sharma and Tim. Its bland bar and functional furnishings were illuminated by soft, forgiving lighting. In the summer, the pub was the perfect refuge for tourists seeking the comfort of a non-threatening, family-friendly environment. Outside of summer, it was perfect for Dev and Tim, wanting only to chat, watch the twenty-four-hour sports news channel and not be annoyed after the day at work.

Dr. Sharma and Tim sat with their respective beer and coffee before the large screen TV hanging from the wall.

'Why?' asked Tim, not shifting his gaze from the TV.

'I don't know, Tim,' replied Dr. Sharma. 'It's your hypothetical scenario. Why would she?'

'I don't know. I just asked you that.'

'Are we sure she's happy? How do we know? I mean, what if there's something else?'

'Something else? If I came to you and told you that my wife was having an affair, you'd *want* there to be more bad news?'

Tim disliked the cliche of promiscuity that had been thrust upon those from the LGBTQ+ community. He didn't feel it necessarily applicable, but he did believe it was an easy way for homophobes to get away with voicing narrow-minded judgements. Since it was no longer acceptable or fashionable to say that genders should only have sexual relations with one another and not their own kind, they would point to promiscuity as somehow being an undesirable fact of LGBTQ+ life. They would highlight how it jarred with the idea of *traditional family values.*

Like when racists rant about "different values" to justify their hatred of legal and/or illegal immigrants. Tim wondered what exactly they meant by values. *That word is thrown about so often*, he would think to himself, *but what does it actually mean? The principles by which lives are lived? When you get right down to it, surely values are universal. Surely, when you boil it right down, values are achieving and spreading love and happiness without harming others for it, right?*

As far as Tim was concerned, promiscuity in the LGBTQ+ community was a stereotype and not one that he felt applied to everyone within it. Tim did not think that he had had more than the average number of sexual partners despite his hedonist past.

'Something *else*. Otherwise, why is she seeing another man?' asked Dr. Sharma before a glug of his beer.

'She's not seeing him,' corrected Tim. 'She's…' he trailed off, unable to finish. 'I thought maybe it wouldn't be so bad if it was just feelings, but actually, feelings would be worse.'

'Explain.'

'I don't… Dev, this is my hypothetical scenario. I wanted your input, not you to make me work harder by thinking about it. I'm just exhausted by the whole thing. What am I going to do?'

'Are *you* happy in this scenario?'

'Not anymore. No.'

'But were you happy before you started screwing this other man?'

'I suppose. Yes.'

'Can't you go back to that, forget about all this?'

'Are we still doing my hypothetical? You want me to just sweep it under the rug that she's been screwing someone else?'

'Your alternative would be to ask her about it.'

'Confront her? I don't do confrontations very well.'

'No, *ask* her. If you weren't having an affair of your own, then you could confront her. As things stand, you have given up all rights to moral outrage.'

'But *she* doesn't know that,' reminded Tim.

'Oh, in your hypothetical, she doesn't know that you're having sex with someone else?'

'Why would anyone have an affair when things are good? Just kicks? To feel good? Emotional support? When everything is fine? Maybe it's just about sex?'

'Why are you torturing yourself with this?' asked Dev.

‘Ruth isn’t having an affair. You are. She’s not going to know about it unless you tell her. Those are the facts of the situation.’

‘Why do you call it torture? I thought you would find this interesting.’

‘Okay then, it’s not torture. It’s fantasy. You’re fantasising about your wife having an affair, but you keep saying that, in this scenario, she’s happy with her life, happy at the firm. The only motive left is pure pleasure.’

‘No, that’s not why she’d do it.’

‘Oh, why? Because you can’t reconcile that women like sex as much as men do? For a bisexual, you are surprisingly closed about some things. If things are so *fine*, then why did you start an affair?’

From a young age, Tim had known that he was attracted to other boys, even though he could not quite understand in what way he was drawn to them. It wasn’t until his early twenties, when he found himself sharing a bed in a dormitory in Australia with Nancy, another traveller who had agreed to bunk with him to save money, that Tim found his sexuality being challenged again. Hitherto he had reconciled his homosexuality with the help of friends and trusted cousins. Eventually, he had come out to his parents and siblings and faced their judgements, scorn, questions and, finally, acceptance.

‘Hey, I know Ruth likes sex. I know she likes sex with me. I just like to think that I’m the only one she enjoys sex with. I like to think that even if she had never met me, she would refuse sex with someone else for the basic reason that that person isn't me.'

'Even if she didn't know you existed?'

'I'd be a feeling. An instinct. Some faint... glimmer in the back of her mind telling her to wait for me,' Tim whispered theatrically.

'Maybe the other bloke does something better than you?'

'Do you *want* to get punched?'

It was one warm night in Adelaide that Tim found himself with a newfound appreciation of the female form, and that feminine fragrance that Nancy exuded as she climbed into bed with him. Believing Tim to be gay, she had not suspected the thoughts that had suddenly seized him. He knew it, and that made him feel guilty, as though he had betrayed her confidence, but it wasn't something that he had anticipated. It hadn't happened before. For months afterwards, Tim applied himself to dismiss the episode as something brought on by the fatigue of travelling. However, he eventually reluctantly conceded that, aged twenty-one, he was still surprising himself and that his sexuality was very much still a work in progress.

As a result, Tim had begun seeing women as well as men, bringing himself to appreciate much more than simply a woman's fragrance. Prior to meeting Ruth, when asked by friends or family about commitment, Tim had always answered cagily. A New Year's Eve in London had brought Tim and Ruth together, leading to his thoughts on the topic being broadened.

To Tim, that he had married Ruth was not at all an

indicator of stronger sexual attraction to women or a step towards fulfilling the desire for a more traditional family unit. He had committed himself to a person, not a gender. Having dated Ruth for a year, he refused to entertain facile conclusions that his family, and some friends, drew. That he had made a choice and had chosen women over men. The idea was ridiculous.

'Why so touchy?' asked Dev. 'I thought this was a fantasy.'

'But it's *my* fantasy. People fantasise about things that aren't going to happen.'

'Wow, you're not arrogant at all, are you?' Dr. Sharma asked sarcastically. 'It's inconceivable that she could screw somebody else who does it better than you?' Dr. Sharma looked over at Tim, who tried to grin back at him, but it quickly faded.

'I think I want to feel bad… about….' Tim shrugged. 'But I just don't. I don't know what I feel anymore.'

'Maybe you like thinking of yourself as a victim. Blameless. The only possible victim in your hypothetical scenario is you. Everyone else is a perpetrator,' mused Dr. Sharma.

When Tim asked Ruth to marry him, she had agreed. Eventually. She had always planned to say yes, but, the way she saw it, there was nothing wrong with making him sweat a little, making his mind work. She charitably saw it as part of her mischievous sense of humour, just one of the qualities that had drawn Tim to her in the first place. Others would call it manipulative. Others still would say that this was her way of establishing control.

Yes, Ruth liked control, but she also enjoyed the pinpricks at her heart whenever she lost it. She relished the way her breath would catch in her throat when Tim would suddenly grab her by the wrists and use his weight to pin her to the mattress. Ruth knew these snatches of pleasure would only retain their impact if she retained overall control. Ruth and Tim both needed something the other provided. Some would call this a sound basis for a relationship.

A week later, Ruth gave Tim the answer that would set their wedding preparations in motion. For the first time in a long while, Tim had begun to feel complete. The feeling continued throughout their wedding preparations. It was a few years into the marriage that, like spots of rain on a windshield, like a thousand eyes looking in, the doubts began to shine their lights.

'It's okay for you. You can joke. How do I sleep in the same bed? How do I go home?' asked Tim.

'Easy. I'll drive you,' offered Dr. Sharma.

Later that night, having deposited Tim near his front door, Dr. Sharma drove home to his flat. As the car glided through the rain, he pushed away thoughts of his conversation with Tim and focussed on enjoying the drive. He loved driving at night. It made him feel invisible. Impervious. Calm. He particularly enjoyed driving through town, his car seemingly gliding along the road, the engine barely audible to him above the rumbling of Primal Scream's *Vanishing Point*.

The illuminated shop window displays floated past, around his car, their reflections contorted over the body of the vehicle. There was hardly anyone around, few other vehicles, barely any pedestrians, just the scent of the night through the open sunroof, filling his nostrils as the world slid past him. When the street lights would blink into life, he would glance at his watch and mentally note the time. For no particular reason.

Having parked, Dev kicked at the dried out brown autumn leaves as he walked away from his car. Carried by the light breeze, the brown leaves bustled along like spooked Jersey cattle running together, seeking comfort. Dev liked to hear their rustle as he walked and then feel the silence as the wind died in the empty car park.

Arriving at home, Dev tossed his keys and wallet aside and hung up his coat before moving through to the kitchen, where he filled the kettle and boiled some water. Into a mug, he threw a tea bag and waited for the steam to rise at the other end of the counter. He loved these quiet moments where he could lose himself in the pleasure of something as simple as watching the change as the cold water warmed, simmered and boiled, releasing into the air delicate wisps of vapour.

Once the kettle clicked off, he allowed the boiling water to settle for a few seconds before slowly pouring over the tea bag in the mug until it floated to the lip. Dev left it for a few moments, allowing the leaves to colour the water before pressing the milk carton against the rim of the mug and tilting it, so the white liquid hugged the side on its way down into the rich brown infusion. As he leaned the carton back, the heavier liquid settled at the bottom of the mug, leaving only a faint trace on the surface. He smiled, satisfied that the milk hadn't yet dispersed and discoloured the tea, anticipating the fleeting satisfaction to come.

Taking a teaspoon, he delicately broke the surface with the steel and silently slipped it past the floating tea bag into the depths. Ever so slowly and with the utmost care, he made tiny circular motions with the teaspoon to agitate the milk, so it billowed upwards, swirling and clouding through the water for a few seconds before mixing, diluting the rich brown of the tea, turning it the colour of a sandy beach.

He found preparing a typical English cup of tea to be the perfect relaxing activity before sleep. Leaning over the mug, the aroma of the tea wafted up to Dev's face. Straightening, he took the cup by the handle and tipped it into the sink.

He didn't like tea.

After the day at work, and in the wake of the apparent revelation that Tim's life was disappearing around him and that his world no longer made any sense, Dr. Sharma was ready to wash it all away. Tim insisted that it was hypothetical, but it was pitifully obvious that it wasn't. Ruth was finding pleasure elsewhere, and Tim couldn't reconcile his wife's apparent faithlessness with the happy home life he thought they shared, despite his own infidelity.

*If Tim's life fell apart even further, in a more radical way,* thought Dr. Sharma, *wouldn't he forget all about his differences with his wife?* Tossing his clothes in the hamper, Dev stepped under the shower before setting the water free. Under the jets, Dr. Sharma washed the day out of his pores and calmly dissolved into the warm water.

Mitch stands in his bathroom, stunned into silence.

The E train brings him home every day after work. Every

day, he comes into this room and speaks to no one in particular about his day, about his work, about his progressing hair loss.

About the vitamin supplements he is taking.

About the woman at work who is perfect in every way.

About having to work Christmas Eve. Again.

For the first time since Mitch moved into his tiny New York apartment, he stands in his bathroom, uttering not a single syllable. As he stands at the sink, he swears he heard a voice behind him. Spinning around, all Mitch can see is the door closed behind him and the drawn shower curtain at his side in the cramped space. There is nothing he can use as a practical weapon, so he balls a fist.

Having absolutely no previous experience of successfully defending himself, Mitch casts a strange silhouette against the curtain as he holds his fist aloft, as though readying a spear. With his eyes wide open, and a tremble at his lips, Mitch tells himself he is ready for anything and yanks the curtain aside sharply with his other hand.

'Argh!' he cries as the plastic flurries past.

No one.

Is he cracking? Mitch is sure he heard a voice. Was it someone next door or in the apartment above his? The walls are pretty thin, but this sounded like someone in the room with him, the voice ricochetting from the hard surfaces.

*I'm imagining things*, thinks Mitch. *Great. What next?* he asks himself as he leaves the curtain and turns back to the sink. Picking up his toothbrush, the last thing he hears before he turns, passes out and hits his head on the towel rack is the surly, bullying voice: 'Don't forget those back teeth. Your dentist warned you.'

Mitch opens his eyes to the pipework beneath his sink, his mouth wet. His tongue pokes out, and feels the wetness on his bottom lip. *Was I drooling?* He is on the floor, his pyjamas heavy with water. *How much drool did I drool? Where's water from? Water from the shower?*

The showerhead.

The shower head was spraying him with water.

The showerhead with, apparently, the voice of an impatient cabbie.

'Hey hey,' says Shower Head, suddenly narrowing the water flow into a sharp dart of water, aiming directly at Mitch's right eye.

'Ow,' Mitch shrieks, urgently shielding his face with his hands.

'Don't be such a fuckin' baby. I've seen that look before, don't you go fainting on me again,' says Shower Head, still shooting water at Mitch's hands.

'But this can't… I'm going crazy,' Mitch eventually manages, tentatively getting up from the floor, using the wall to support himself as he edges closer to the shower.

'Whoa, fella! What you doin' there?' asks Shower Head.

Mitch freezes, not knowing how to respond. Eventually, 'turning off the water?' fumbles out of his mouth.

'Allow me,' replies Shower Head before the jet slows a trickle and then just drips.

'You're, you're just the showerhead. How did you do that?'

'I'm a showerhead. It's water. It's all linked, Kid. Don't worry about it.'

'But I'm dreaming, or crazy, or something.'

'You're not dreaming. You're not crazy. But you are somethin', and that somethin' is a guy talkin' to his showerhead. Get used to it.'

'But –' Mitch begins to protest.

'Now,' interrupts Shower Head commandingly.

'Okay,' Mitch acquiesces, suddenly feeling intimidated by the moulded white plastic.

The showerhead itself is nothing to get excited about. It is, after all, a simple conduit that allows a user to direct water in a particular direction, at an adjustable rate, to its final destination. It had cost Mitch $14.99 at a nearby store because he couldn't bring himself to use the mouldy, cracked, yellow one that had come pre-installed, courtesy of the previous tenant. The new shower head is white. It is plastic. It has little grey rubber nodules. That's what the rubberised holes are called on the box it came in. Nodules. Mitch liked the way the word sounded, so he had said it aloud to himself several times as he unboxed the contents.

As Mitch recalls, there are five different spray settings, but he had only ever used one of them: moderate.

'I been watchin' you,' says Shower Head. 'I been listenin' to you all this while. Siddown. On the edge of the tub.

Siddown.' Mitch gets in the bathtub and perches on the edge. 'Get closer. Whatcha 'fraid of? Get closer!' Mitch obediently moves closer. Shower Head continues. 'Mitch. What do you *want*?'

Mitch looks up at the showerhead, not knowing quite how to answer, unable to decide whether he is hallucinating or whether this is really happening. 'You mean right now?'

'I mean in life.'

'Well, I guess I want to be happy?'

'Of course, you wanna be happy. I know that. Nobody wants to be fuckin' sad,' spits Shower Head, their voice bouncing off the hard surfaces. 'I wanna hear you say what would make you fuckin' happy,' explains Shower Head with a tremor of impatience creeping into their voice.

'Um. Well, okay. Um… let me think.' Mitch had completed an undergraduate degree in business, but somehow it hadn't led anywhere. Three years after graduating, he is still driving around, delivering water cooler tanks all over his old university campus. Mitch always wants to prove himself, so he feels the need to answer all questions directed at him to the fullest degree. So he thinks hard before answering any of Shower Head's questions, wanting to give the answer he thinks they want.

'Knowin' what will make you happy. Knowin' how to get there. And what is knowin'?' asks Shower Head to prompt Mitch.

'Knowing is… knowing.'

'But what must you need to have to know?'

'Knowledge?'

'Right. Information. It's all around you, Kid. It's

everywhere. Everything you want to know. You can access it.'

'Everything? Like what? How?'

'The information, all information, any information that you need is right there in the water, in the air. It's knowledge. You just need to reach out and touch it. Access it. Why else do you think water is so important on this damn rock?'

'So why is it that we can't access it? This information? I mean us, humans, who presumably would be the ones with most to gain from it. Why put all this information in the air, in the water and then not give us the necessary ability to access it?'

'That's a fair question. Hmm, how to answer with the necessary tact? If I told you you are all still too fuckin' stupid, would you be able to leave it there?

'What do you mean we're too stupid?' Mitch asks blankly.

'Clearly not,' Shower Head mutters. 'What I mean is that you have simply not proved yourselves.'

'Well, hold on there just a second. All due respect,' Mitch begins to Shower Head, 'I don't wish to cause you any offence, sir, but you do have quite a blunt way of expressing yourself. When you say that we have not yet proved ourselves and are too stupid, is that your way of saying we have not yet sufficiently evolved?'

'No. It means you're too fuckin' stupid.'

'So, to clarify, we have evolved, but some higher authority simply believes that we haven't proved ourselves,' Mitch summarises.

'Right. And you're too stupid,' answers Shower Head.

'But we can't be that stupid if we managed to evolve, right? I mean, we crawled out of the slime, grew legs, started walking and –'

'And began chuckin' bombs around. Yes, of course, you're brilliant,' interrupts Shower Head.

'Look, we don't all… *do* bombs. Besides, what I'm trying to say is that we've clearly come some way from the primordial soup, so we've made our way quite well.'

'That was pretty much all nature. Yeah, what you call *Mother* Nature, the thing you all keep pissin' on, she could have wiped you all out with a few deft touches at any point in your *evolution*. She still can. A few tsunamis here, a couple of earthquakes there, some well-placed forest fires. Or perhaps just an exotic new virus to rain down from the sky. I told you, it's all in the water.'

'So we have the potential to access all the answers to the greatest mysteries that have puzzled humankind. We just don't have the ability to access them.'

'I see you still got to get your head around this. Look, you guys were making good progress, and everything was going well, according to schedule, until… Well, I suppose our Mother Nature fumbled the ball a little, and she let you all get a little too far too soon.'

'What happened?'

'You all decided to begin developing your own quirky little personalities. Along with your quirky little ideas.'

'What was wrong with that?'

'Nothing, except it was clearly too much too soon. Before long, you got ideas that were, shall we say, beyond your station.'

'Above,' corrects Mitch.

'You don't know what's above. Better to say *beyond*.'

'Okay, whatever,' snaps Mitch, tiring of being constantly wrong. 'What were those good ideas we had?'

'You're not going to like it.'

'Tell me.'

'You won't understand.'

'Try me.'

'Plumbing.'

'What?'

'Plumbing.'

'What?'

'Are you deaf now? You heard me.'

'You're telling me that we lost the privilege of one of the greatest resources known to humankind, or *unknown*, rather, because of plumbing?'

'More or less.'

'What's wrong with plumbing? Or, what aspect of it? The waste? Is that the offence?'

'Not exactly.'

'Then what? What is so objectionable about water in your home?'

'No, water in your houses wasn't the problem.'

'So, what was the problem?'

'The problem came when you all decided that the water should come to you.'

'What?'

'Don't you get it? It is an amazing privilege to have water in your life. Not only because you're seventy per cent water and you need it to survive, but because of how greatly it contributes to the quality of your life. The amazing drinks you make with it; jumping into a cool pool on a hot summer day; water-based lubricants for those *special*, intimate times, to name but a meagre few. That is without the added benefits that you're only now becoming aware of.'

Mitch turns his head away from Shower Head and looks up to the tiny window above him, rubbing his chin thoughtfully.

'Don't you see?' continues Mitch's showerhead. 'You should all have been worshipping this thing and visiting the nearest source at regular intervals to appreciate how blessed you clearly were to have this in your lives. Instead, you forced it to come to you. You drew up plans and built systems to have this beautiful, and I don't use that word lightly, beautiful resource brought to you because you guys were clearly too busy killing each other, or shooting off into space, or whatever you were doing.'

'I think it's the Romans who really rolled out plumbing like they meant business. So yeah, probably they *were* busy killing and conquering.'

'I don't know what you guys were thinking. It is something to be worshipped. Instead, you put it in bottles and sell it to one another, like it was yours to sell in the first place. Who goes around selling stuff that should be worshipped?'

Not realising the question is rhetorical, Mitch launches into, what he considers, a well-considered answer. 'Well, we can probably safely say that religion, as an industry, has been pretty big for some time. Lots of people buying Torahs, Bibles, Qur'ans, the Vedas and loads of others. Lots of likenesses of Jesus are sold. All those saints that the Mexican cartels worship. How about all those Hindu Gods?'

'I didn't want an actual answer, you doofus. Besides, you

don't see Hindus with a direct pipeline to the temple, sucking in all the blessings, or whatever, do you?'

'Actually, they do seem to have a lot of little statues wearing garlands in a dark room or cupboard in their houses. The zipper on my suitcase broke earlier this year when I was packing for Maui. My brother's wedding. So I went next door to borrow Vikram's, and in his spare room, where he keeps his suitcase, there is a little shelf with lots of little statues of gods and a few framed posters of them on the wall. And incense smoke all over.'

'Who's telling this story? Me or you?'

'I'm just saying I agree. Worship, belief becomes a commodity, marketed and managed. But we don't worship anything as much as we worship ourselves. Humans, our wants, needs and desires are the biggest industry. For certain things, we can't seem to build enough humans. Or,' continued Mitch, warming to his train of thought, 'perhaps the problem was that there were too many humans, more than we know what to do with. So we find new purposes for those too weak to resist or too strong to die. They're turned into slaves of one sort or another. Women pay traffickers for the chance of a better life in another country, only to be gang-raped and forced into prostitution. Others make it here only to become slaves, conditioned to believe that their life will be worse if they run away.'

'Jeez, who asked about all that shit?' mutters Shower Head. 'Anyway, you understand about trade.'

'Yes. Look,' began Mitch, edging closer along the tub, believing that he had figured out the reason for this tête-à-tête and warming to his own theory, 'this might be the bang on my head talking, but I think you want my help. I think that's why you're talking to me. You want me to stop this… trade. You want to help me fight human trafficking. What do you want me to do?'

'We want you to kidnap someone and make a deal.'

'Ah. Oh. Huh? Who?'

'You deliver water to some important people. I have to explain some stuff to one of them. So you have to kidnap them and bring them here.'

'Why don't you just tell me, and I'll pass along the message.'

'It doesn't work like that. I need information from them too.'

'Well, explain to me how exactly I'm supposed to entice someone here for a meeting of minds… with a showerhead? I mean, I hardly believe it myself.'

'Let me ask you a question. You're talking to your showerhead, or you're talking to your therapist. Really, what's the difference?'

'What do you mean?'

'Every day, you step in here, and you talk to me. You have no one else in your life. You tell me about your day, your hopes, your fears. Who knows you better than me? Why is it less plausible that you should be having a conversation with me than with a psychiatrist? Why did it never occur to you that one day I might talk back? That's what you should really talk to a psychiatrist about.'

'Well, when you put it like that, it does make a kind of sense.'

'Sure it does, Kid. Anyway, I said kidnap, not invite.'

'Kidnapping is not something I know about.'

'But isn't that something you can find out about?'

'Probably, but reading about kidnapping and doing it are different things, and kidnapping is just not something I have the stomach for.'

'But you said you understood about trade. Trade of information, that's how you guys work, right? This is what you all understand, so we're working within a framework that you guys could find relatable.'

'Who do you even want me to get for you?'

'The Dean, at the university where you work.'

'He's not important. I mean, he's important, but not *important* important. He's just the Dean.'

'No, but we're in this for the long haul. He will eventually get us the Deans at Stanford, Yale, Harvard, who will eventually get us the relevant professors at universities worldwide. In turn, they will lead us to governments and then to world leaders.'

'Are you… are you terrorists?'

'Hey, nobody's perfect.'

# 12. Hiding behind a window

'Isn't it fascinating?' asked Dr. Sharma from the edge of the bed, across the room. 'You must think about it. Don't you?'

Dr. Sharma could feel he was losing the woman's attention as she lightly clicked her fingers to a song only she could hear and stared through the net curtain at the world outside. Dr. Sharma noted the tensed posture as she stood by the window in her underwear and a purple basque, one thigh-booted leg crossed in front of another.

'I do,' Dr. Sharma continued, despite Mira's studied indifference, 'I have, and that's why I'm here, to talk to you. I think you can really help me with this. Of course, I'm going to talk to other people too and… so forth,' he nervously added. 'I just think that with your background, you'll be able to give real insight. Do you see?'

At this, the woman turned her gaze from the window to fix Dr. Sharma with a glare.

Mira was in her thirties. Her natural hair colour was

brown, but she had dyed it black with subtle purple streaks. It was a look that she had long ago adopted. When Mira looked in the mirror, she could barely remember looking any other way as an adult. If she tried to remember another look, all she could picture was herself as a child or a teenager. Old photos of her as an adult presented only a stranger.

As she glared, the clicking continued, and so did the doctor.

'I've read a lot. A lot of studies, and nowhere in any of them does it mention speaking to people like you to any great degree. I mean people in your field. Yes… as a performer in sex films, a successful performer at that, I understand you are relatively famous. As a performer in staged, if you will, pre-scripted films exhibiting explicit sexual acts taking place between yourself and… others.'

Mira had been afforded enough time during Dr. Sharma's babbling to formulate a response, but that was forgotten as her annoyance surfaced to interrupt him.

'Why do you talk like that?' Mira asked, the words slowly crawled from her mouth.

'Like… like what?' asked Dr. Sharma.

'Pornstar… is what everyone says. Why don't you just say that?'

'Well, I didn't want to presume that you'd be okay with that. I thought something more neutral,' stumbled the doctor.

'That's what I do. I make porn. I am the *star*. Therefore, I am a pornstar. Not a big one, not *really* famous or anything. But I shift product.'

'But you're not only a performer, with other such

professional performers. Men can also book you, um, privately.'

'Like you did. Problem?'

'No. Look, I'm not here to… to… I'm here to talk to you about what you think about what you do. I'm interested in hearing what you think about the acts you perform.'

'You make it sound like I'm a magician.'

'I'm sorry, I didn't mean to make it sound like that.'

'You're falling over your own words. You don't know how to make anything sound the way you want because you don't know what you want to say. How many others did you try to talk to?'

'What do you mean? No one, you're the only person I've contacted,' Dr. Sharma lied.

'I bet a lot of people said no to you, just like I did.'

'I haven't –'

Mira interrupted. 'About a month ago, I got an email from someone saying they wanted to meet with me and hear my story. As if I have a story to tell. That was you, wasn't it?'

'No.'

'Yeah, that's what *I* said. *No*. And so you ignored that and booked me for two hours today, and you want me to talk. You want to listen. You want to make notes. You want to sit over there and tell me to repeat things. Maybe you even have a microphone recording the whole thing.' Mira moved from the window and sat in an old armchair across from Dr. Sharma. 'I said no a month ago,' she said, looking away from him.

'Let's say, for instance, I did email you a month ago saying I wanted to hear your side of things,' pressed Dr. Sharma. 'I'm here now. I've paid you for your time. All I want is for you to talk to me.'

'And now you're getting frustrated,' replied Mira, leaning forward in her armchair. 'You feel like you should be getting what you want because you paid for it.'

'It's not like that, it's really not,' answered Dr. Sharma, feeling he was being misunderstood.

Mira uncrossed and re-crossed her legs and turned her head a little to look at him. 'The way you talk, it's just like your email, that's why I remembered it. I didn't want to talk to you about my story, but even if I did want to talk about it, why would I want to talk to *you*? Why would anyone?'

'What's wrong with how I talk?'

'You sound like a lawyer, or like you're afraid of getting sued, so you talk in a way that you think can't be misunderstood, won't cause offence. Or like you're talking to a victim, and you don't want to commit yourself by saying it's all going to be okay. So it's like there's a space between what you say and what you mean. There's no victims in here. I'm sure there's loads of victims out there but I ain't one of them.'

'I never meant to talk to you like you are a victim –'

'Of course not,' Mira interrupted sarcastically. 'You wouldn't presume, would you? You came in here and started this whole thing off by talking about understanding where different people are coming from and what they're into. But you came in here already thinking that I was some victim. Some damaged person.'

'Okay. I'm sorry. I understand you're not a victim, not damaged.'

'I don't think you do. The punters that come in here to see

*me* don't want a victim. The men that pay good money to see *me* don't come to treat me like nothing. They know they won't get that opportunity. They come to *me* because they want their equal. I don't speak for other girls, but when they're with me, they're with a woman they can fuck and who will fuck 'em back, that will climb 'em, pin 'em down, sit on 'em and fuck 'em.

'Because of how I am, they feel free to say what they want. A lot of it is vile, nasty stuff.' Mira paused, and when she spoke again, her tone had softened, almost imperceptibly. 'The first-timers usually say *sorry* afterwards. They say they didn't mean it. "Don't know where that came from. It was just heat of the moment," they say. But I make 'em feel they don't have to apologise, I give back as good as I get, I make 'em think I'm enjoying it. And sometimes, I am. The next time they come around, they don't apologise. I've trained 'em.'

'Why shouldn't they apologise?' asked Dr. Sharma, sensing that her anger at him had actually led to a finger hold in the conversation.

'Maybe they should, but not to me. As far as I'm concerned, you shouldn't apologise for saying what you want to say. You want to talk about 'em. *Them.* As if you're better than 'em, but you can't say what you want to say. So what do you want to do? Do you want to sit and talk about the men that fuck me, or do you want to come over here and do it?'

'That's not what I came here for,' replied Dr. Sharma.

'Yeah, right. You know what I think? I think you're fucking already.'

'I'm sorry?'

'This is how you get off, isn't it? Talking about it. Look,' her attitude softening again, 'I like to be the focus of attention in the room, so I don't do this... talking. While the bloke beats off into a tissue. A lot of girls do, but I don't. That's just me. I like to be part of the action. I like control. But even if I did do that, I wouldn't do it with you.' Her voice hardened again. 'You're a liar. You couldn't just come in here and say you want to listen to me talk about other men while you have a wank. You had to make up a whole story around it to pass it off like a noble thing. Here, gather 'round everyone,' she invited, beckoning to imaginary onlookers, 'come witness the noblest wank ever.'

'That's not what I'm into. It's not why I'm here,' replied Dr. Sharma, beginning to feel the situation was getting away from him again.

'Then why don't you show me?' she suggested, uncrossing her legs and standing on her high heels again. You've paid what other men pay to fuck, but all you want to do is talk. I told you I like action, so are you here to fuck or not? Because if not, then you can take your money and fuck off.'

Dr. Sharma sat silently as Mira glowered at him. He could see that she was angry, but he wanted to salvage the situation. Her attitude and aggression were fascinating to him, but, shifting on the bed, Dr. Sharma realised he would have to make a concession if they were to progress. He slowly got up from the foot of the bed and moved a little further up. Like those of a wary animal, Mira's eyes tracked his progress as Dr. Sharma moved closer. He hovered for a moment before lowering himself to sit on the edge of the mattress.

Softening her tone slightly, Mira asked: 'you ready to fuck

now then?'

Dr. Sharma wondered about the bubble in which she lived and ached to directly ask her about it. Was everything in her life inevitably linked to sex? Could she conceive of a life without such clients? A life that didn't involve selling sex? Was she as strong and in control as she told him, or was she trapped within a labyrinth of her own creation? Did her rhetoric mean she had no choice but to follow through with this life? To Mira, if she made a significant change, would that mean admitting she was wrong? Would it be too much for her to be wrong? Would she even want a change in her life?

*She is so adamant that she loves what she does. Who am I to doubt her? So many possibilities, ideas and thoughts. Would I be able to explain my project to her? Would she understand me like I'm trying to understand her? If the rules of the world were suddenly pulled from under her, would she be able to change with them? Or would she be lost?* 'What do your clients normally ask of you?' he asked.

'Another question,' replied Mira, frustrated. 'I told you. Fuck me. Or fuck off.'

'Mira –' Dr. Sharma began before stopping as Mira rose abruptly from her armchair.

'What do you think you're going to achieve by doing this?' Mira asked as she slowly stalked over to Dr. Sharma and looked down at him.

'I've tried to explain to you,' he managed to get out with a slight shake of his head.

'If you are doing this, are you talking to anyone else?'

'Yes, another woman. Look, I have nothing to hide from you. I'm being honest. Work with me.'

'No,' spat Mira, before turning away from him to face the window again. 'I don't want to. Go *work* with someone who wants to.' A moment or two passed before she continued. 'Tell me something,' she started before spinning to face him again. 'Why are you only talking to women?'

'I have to start somewhere.'

'So you've started with two women. Why not one woman and one man?'

'I did start with a couple, Alex and Roisin, they led me to you. I particularly want to focus first on the points of view of women. The other woman I'm speaking to isn't quite on your, shall we say, level?'

'And then you'll move on to men? Gays, bisexuals. What about transgender people? Will you talk to them too?'

'I'll add them as part of a wider… consultation.'

'I think it stinks. I don't trust you,' Mira concluded.

Dr. Sharma was stunned. 'I'm the one person paying you, who doesn't want to fuck you, and you don't trust *me*?'

'Don't… talk as if you're better than them,' Mira shot back, pointing a fake nailed finger at him. They're clear about what they want from the beginning.'

'I think I've been clear about what I want.'

'I know you want to fuck me. Why the charade?'

Exasperated, Dr. Sharma asked, 'would it make you feel better? Would it make you trust me if I said it?' The conversation was taking a lot more out of him than he had anticipated. 'I'll say it if it will make a difference.'

'You're a liar,' declared Mira, coming close to him again. Her face leaned in close to his. 'Everybody wants to fuck me. While they fuck I watch. I look in their eyes, and I see the truth. Men are only ever true when they're fucking and when they're crying. I only get to see when they're fucking.' She straightened but didn't step back. Instead, she lingered before Dr. Sharma. He could feel the warmth from her barely clothed body.

'You'll trust me if I fuck you? Is that it?'

'I don't know. Probably not.'

'Then I don't know what I'm supposed to do here, Mira,' he said, finally believing it to be fruitless to continue any further. He got up from the bed and retrieved his jacket. At this, Mira's attention was finally thoroughly piqued.

'You're getting angry,' she said, a playful smile at the corner of her mouth illuminating her eyes.

'I'm not angry,' replied Dr. Sharma, turning back. 'I thought you'd recognise that I'm being genuine,' he continued, his voice rising. 'I came to you openly. I didn't realise I'd have to pass tests and prove myself. I didn't realise it would be this difficult to convince you to spend an hour without a cock in your arse!' It wasn't often that Dr. Sharma lost his patience. A few moments passed before he continued. 'I'm sorry, that was wrong. I… don't want to offend, I just want to understand.'

Mira, outwardly the very definition of nonchalance, inwardly teeming with her own questions, flicked the hair away from her eyes. 'What's this other girl like then?' she asked, lowering herself back into her armchair.

'She's like you. Just not as… versatile,' answered Dr. Sharma, feeling like a small boy again, explaining himself, but pleased to answer any questions as long as it kept the conversation going.

'Why do you have to dance around it? Just say what you mean.'

'Okay. She doesn't let men piss or shit on her. She doesn't take it up the arse. She's… keen to roleplay.'

'Oh. She's one of those.'

'One of those… what?'

'She hasn't *fully embraced the lifestyle*, to use your flowery words.'

'What do you mean?'

'Exactly that. She's not open to doing everything.'

'She knows where her limits lie, and she knows what she's comfortable with.'

'You're defending her lack of scat. That's cute.'

'Her clients have different needs to yours,' She serves a different… demographic. I respect her choices. I respect yours.'

Satisfied, for now, Mira continued. 'What do you ask her then?'

'The same stuff I've been asking you. What do people want? Why does she think they want it?'

'And she just tells you?'

'She's open.'

'So you're finding me a challenge. That's good,' Mira admitted, beginning to see the opportunity for some fun. 'What else do you ask her?'

'I ask her what they say. I ask her about her experiences.'

'And she just tells you? How do you know she's not just making shit up?'

'Why would she?'

'Why did those kids on that island make stuff up? For a laugh.'

'What kids?'

'We learnt it at school. History. Or social studies. Margaret – something. She went to some old tribe to ask them questions, study them, and their kids fed her a load of shit. She wrote it into a book, and it was only years later that they found out it was all a load of rubbish.'

'You mean Margaret Mead?'

'Yeah. Probably.'

'I don't think Katie would make up stuff. I trust her.'

'Katie, eh? What makes you think you can trust me?'

'What reason would you have for lying?'

'Don't need a reason.'

'Well, in this case, I like to think that even lies would have value because any exaggeration must stem from some kind of truth. All I want is to trace the roots.' A few moments passed, and Dr. Sharma edged back to his spot on the bed while Mira played with her hair and looked out of the window from her seat.

Mira was unconvinced as she evaluated Dr. Sharma. She had been sitting in judgement from the moment he had begun talking and had decided that, ultimately, he was no different to any other man. 'You think we can fix you, don't you? Why do men always think a woman will solve all their problems? What sort of magical powers do you think we have? We're all just people muddling through as best we can.'

'I know that. I just want a woman's perspective.'

'You want a woman to tell you everything's going to be okay. Make you feel good. I don't do feelings, only what's between your legs. So, again, either fuck me or fuck off. Make a decision. Be quick.'

# 13. Hop, skip and a jump

Everything had moved so quickly that morning, loading the taxi with suitcases and making the drive to the airport. However, the afternoon had been long, so long, with all the waiting around. At least it seemed that way to Amina and Dev. At gate eleven, the children stood with Raju and Serena and all the other passengers as they waited to board the plane. It had already been a long day by this stage, and Amina, Dev, and the others were anxious to settle in for the twelve-hour flight.

Once on board the plane and in their respective seats, Raju encouraged the children to buckle up even though passengers were still boarding, and the plane was nowhere near ready for take-off. Once satisfied that the rest of his family was safely strapped in, Raju promptly fell asleep and began snoring loudly, signalling to Amina that it was safe to unbuckle again.

'Is he going to do that for the next twelve hours?' Amina asked, embarrassed and irritated.

'Don't start,' said Serena, equally irritated at having been in mum-mode for so long that day.

'I'm not *starting*. Do you think I'm starting?' Amina asked, turning to Dev, only to find him snoozing in the seat next to hers, next to the window.

'He's definitely your father's son,' smiled Serena to her daughter.

After an exhausting night, the morning brought them their airline breakfast served in convenient little plastic containers. Amina had heard her friends complain about airline food, so she felt she had to complain too, although she had found nothing to complain about her meals on the plane. Soon after breakfast, the aircraft landed with an almighty jolt prompting Dev to make his breakfast reappear in the little sick bag from the back of the seat in front, as Serena had predicted. 'Little children are always sick when they land in Mauritius. The runway here is still too short for these planes to make a gentle landing.'

Raju's relatives had come to collect them from the airport in two taxis and were waiting patiently outside when the family finally emerged from the dimly lit airport into the blazing sunshine. Raju quickly spotted his brother and his children, waving beaming smiles at them.

'There they are,' said Raju excitedly, struggling with their unruly airport luggage trolley as his brother quickly covered the distance, and his children ran along. The two families embraced, at which point, despite having bounded up to the travellers, the Mauritian children were suddenly overcome with shyness.

'Say hello to your cousins,' said Raju's brother. 'You've been talking about nothing else for months, and now you won't even say anything to them. Don't be shy,' he said in Creole. 'Amina, how are you?' he enunciated carefully in English.

'I'm fine, thank you,' Amina politely replied.

'Good. Dev, you must be happy to finally be in Mauritius,' continued the uncle.

Eschewing traditional greetings, Dev decided to impart vital information: 'I've been sick in a paper bag,' he informed his uncle.

'Raju and Serena looked at each other before smiling awkwardly at Raju's brother.

'Oh,' he replied, nonplussed. 'Well, welcome to Mauritius.'

The tiny tropical island, southeast of Madagascar in the Indian Ocean, is home to 1.3 million people. People who form a genuinely multicultural society where Hindus rub shoulders with Catholics, and Christians work alongside Muslims who frequent Catholics, who hang out with Christians who enjoy the colourful religious events of Hindus who share drinks and swap stories with Christians. A true melting pot of beliefs, cultures and cuisines, Mauritius is home to people who generally do not bat an eyelid at working or playing with those from other races or belief systems.

The families packed themselves into the two taxis before making their way to Raju's sister's house, where they would be staying for the first week of their trip. It was a short drive from Sir Seewoosagur Ramgoolam International Airport, and, having been incarcerated in the plane for so long, the children were excited to see the country they had only seen vicariously through their parents' memories.

There weren't many cars along the way, and those that they saw were white and markedly old. Dev could tell from a glance the make and model of the cars on the road in England, but he was at a loss in Mauritius. Seatbelts were apparently deemed optional, and their taxi driver had not bothered with such frivolities. Out of the windows, the children watched as the dusty roads breezed past, lined with trees they could not identify. Some were clearly palm trees, but others were alien to them, such as the bearded fig tree with its bizarre aerial roots that hung down serenely, minding their own business. It was a while before Amina noticed the pavements. Or lack thereof.

'There aren't any pavements.'

'Yes, there are,' replied Serena, before adding: 'sometimes.'

'Sometimes?'

'Along the edge of the road, there are these gutters. Storm drains. They're one to two feet deep, and they carry away the excess rainwater. Sometimes they're covered by huge paving slabs, but those usually crack with the heat, and they trip people up. Maybe that's why they don't bother with them. They usually only have slabs where necessary.'

‘The pavement trips people up?’ asked Amina, seeking clarification.

‘Yes.’

‘So they think it’s better to risk people falling over into two-foot deep storm drains?’ asked Amina, processing the contradiction.

‘That’s the thinking.’

‘But I see lots of garages without paving slabs in front of them. How do they get their cars over the gutters?’ Dev asked.

‘Garages?’ asked Serena. ‘Where have you seen garages?’

‘Garages, or maybe they’re sheds. They’re everywhere. We keep passing them.’

Serena wore a puzzled expression and looked out of the window until she realised what her son was talking about.

‘Those aren’t garages, Dev. Those are homes.’

‘Homes? But they have those wiggly metal roofs, like our garage.’

‘It’s called corrugated,’ Amina informed him.

‘Look,’ said Dev, as they passed another garage/home, ‘they have metal doors too.’

‘That’s what home is for a lot of people here,’ said Serena, stroking his hair.

‘Oh. Is that where we’re going to stay?’

‘No, your aunt has a house made from bricks.’

‘They must be cold in the winter,’ said Amina, tapping on the window as another wiggly roof whizzed by.

‘Yeah, especially on a tropical island. Freezing,’ joked Serena, rubbing her arms theatrically with a smile for her daughter.

'Yeah, but it must be windy sometimes, and we know it rains because of the huge gutters.'

'It's not so bad when you've grown up with it. In fact, it's quite nice to listen to the sound of rain on the roof at night when you're in bed. It's like God letting you know he's still there.'

Dev took a moment to consider this. Then: 'God should learn some manners and let them sleep.'

'We should go to the beach. Can we go to the beach, Dad?' Amina asked loud enough for her father to hear in the front passenger seat over the ancient Bollywood song vibrating the car's decrepit speakers.

'We'll go tomorrow, Amina.'

'Is the beach far away?'

'No, but we should go to my sister's place first. She's waiting to see us. She's probably prepared a meal for everybody.'

And so she had.

Later that day, they all sat around a dining table with other, extra dining tables tacked on to the end. There they had lunch with various family members and extended family that had come to welcome Raju, Serena, Amina and Dev on their first trip to Mauritius in ten years, Dev's first such trip.

As each new branch of family arrived, Raju, Serena, Amina and Dev were subjected to a barrage of gender and age-consistent greetings consisting of handshakes, kisses, hugs, back slaps, and shoulder squeezes. For Amina and Dev, there was also the added bonus greeting of cheek squeezes and head pats. Usually, Dev would also be at risk of hair-ruffling, but he wasn't handling the heat as well as others, and with his hair limp with sweat, many declined this option. All the while their cousins, joined by further children each time a new family arrived, continued to stare dumbly at Amina and Dev, as though in the presence of space aliens.

In all, there were seven families there, and Raju's alcoholic cousin, Das. Das was so thin and emaciated from decades of self-abuse that when he tried to kiss Amina and Dev in greeting, only his hard nose and stubbly chin made contact with their cheeks. Amina later remarked, 'it was like being kissed by the letter *C*.'

In Mauritius, it wasn't unusual for lunch to extend into dinner and beyond, and so it was on that day. To Mauritians, food was more than sustenance. A meal took on greater significance than mere fuel for the body. A dish prepared for another became a vessel delivering love, loyalty and care. While most Mauritians would not stop to consider what their cooking represented, it genuinely held great meaning, forming a significant part of almost any relationship between friends and family.

There, each spoonful of rice was a conduit for often unspoken feelings of affection. For Mauritians, it was an unparalleled pleasure to prepare a decadent meal for visiting family. An offering, not to show off, but to show care and strengthen bonds. This would even extend to those in the hospital when Mauritians visited friends and family there. They did not take the usual tokens of flowers and fruit. Instead, they prepared and took containers of favourite hearty meals. Patients could have hospital food, or opt for warm canisters from home, brought to their bedsides and opened to release into the air the flavourful aromas within, to the keen interest of fellow patients.

Whether preparing a weekday meal at their own home or changing out of their fancy finery to help cook at a *pooja* held elsewhere, Mauritians were acutely aware of the effect food had in their society. Even if they never actively considered the meaning of its significance.

That night almost everyone stayed the night, with some of them sleeping at Raju's brother's home who lived nearby. It seemed, to Amina and Dev, that Mauritians liked nothing better than a merry sleepover. Amina, Dev, Serena and Raju shared a room that night, with Amina and Dev sharing a bed. The two children were exhausted after the long journey and wanted nothing more than sleep to claim them for the night. However, they were both experiencing that close, stifling tropical heat for the first time. Despite taking cooling showers before bed, they were sweaty and uncomfortable. The incessant snoring coming from the slumbering Raju didn't help matters.

'I thought Daddy only snored on the settee,' said Dev to his sister. He knew Amina wasn't sleeping. He could feel the vibrations through the mattress they shared as she tapped on it in time to Raju's sonorous exhalations.

'He can't help it,' explained Amina.

'I can't sleep.'

'I know. Neither can I.'

'I'm bored.'

Don't ask me for a story.'

'I want a story, but I haven't got my book.'

'Too bad.'

'Go on.' When this was met with no reaction, 'go on,' he repeated.

'Amina exhaled heavily, adding to the warm air. 'Oh, all right then.'

'Yay!'

'But we have to be quiet, or we'll wake them up.'

'I'll be really quiet. Hey, isn't it weird that you can't hear traffic? I think I saw a cow in someone's garden earlier.'

'Did you want a story or not?'

'Yes.'

'Okay then. This story takes place in Sweden.'

'Sweden? Where's that?'

'Northern Europe, where it is cold. Colder than England. Bigger than England too, it's huge.'

'Is it bigger than Mauritius?'

'Much bigger. So, this is a story about Bjorn.'

'Bjorn? What kind of name is that?'

'It's a Swedish name. Bjorn has a brother named Benny and a neighbour named Anni-Frid. The story doesn't begin with Bjorn. It begins with Agnetha.'

'Is she Bjorn's sister?'

'No, she isn't. She isn't a relative. Agnetha is driving her car along the snowy road. There is a van driving too close to her, urging her to speed up. She does the thing that Mum does. She slows down even more. Unfortunately for Agnetha, she isn't paying enough attention to the traffic ahead, and she accidentally hits the car in front.'

'Ooh! Is she hurt?'

'No, she's fine, it is just a little bump, but her car is damaged, and now she needs to get it fixed. She can still drive it to a garage, and that's what she does. That's where she sees Bjorn, her regular mechanic. He's happy to see her.'

'Why?'

'Because he likes her. He *like* likes her.'

'Oh.'

'But normally, he doesn't have anything interesting to talk about with her. Normally all he can talk about is car stuff, and girls aren't usually interested in car stuff. It's difficult for him to find a way of working more into the conversation besides cars. He just doesn't know how to mix with Agnetha. Do you know what I mean?'

'I think so.'

'Sometimes he sees her at the supermarket, but he doesn't know what to say to her. He wonders if she would even talk to him if she didn't have to. Bjorn is not good at small talk. He can't easily fit it into conversations about cars. They're like oil and water. They don't mix.'

'Don't they?'

'That's what Dad says. Anyway, after working on fixing her car, Bjorn thinks: *Today, there will be small talk on a big scale. Or perhaps big talk on a small scale.*

'Why? What happened?'

'Bjorn dials Agnetha's number at work.'

'What is her job?'

'It doesn't matter. She's a teacher. Okay? Agnetha thinks nothing of it. She just wonders what the bill will be. A little while later, she makes her way to Bjorn's garage. He tells her that he has fixed the bumper and the radiator –'

'Cars have radiators? Is that to keep them warm? Like houses?'

'I don't know, something like that. Bjorn tells her that a few other things will need seeing to, in time, but her car has a bigger problem. One he doesn't know how to fix.'

'Oh, what is it?'

'That's exactly what Agnetha asks. "I didn't find any other damage, but I heard something," he said. "I thought there was a leak, but I couldn't see anything. So I listened and followed the noise." "What is it?" asked Agnetha. "I found something," replied Bjorn, "something unusual. I've never come across anything like it." "Oh God, this sounds expensive," said Agnetha. Usually, Bjorn didn't have much to tell Agnetha, but today he had news to deliver, so he decided to be a bit more dramatic. "I don't know how to say this... but you have a *fish* in your tank." "What?" asked Agnetha. "You have a fish in your petrol tank," repeated Bjorn. "I have a fish in my tank?" "You have a fish in your tank." "Is this a riddle? Because I don't have time for this, Bjorn." Agnetha took a step away and then turned back. "I really have a fish in my petrol tank? How did it get there?"

'Bjorn thought it would have gone much better and was hurt. He hadn't counted on her being angry or suspicious of him and had hoped she would react with wonder. "It's alive, with the engine on?" Agnetha asked. "How can it be swimming around and living happily in my petrol tank?" "I don't know," Bjorn answered. "So, what does that mean for me? I need my car." Bjorn is surprised by her question. He thought the meaning would be clear. He hadn't stopped to think about it. He just knew. 'Everything we know is changing. Nothing is fixed anymore. This little fish inside your petrol tank means everything is changing."'

Amina paused a moment before asking: 'Dev, what do you think it would be like? If everything changed? Like if everything you thought made sense didn't make sense anymore?'

# 14. Release

The following day, as promised, they all piled into a minibus and headed to the beach, along the narrow roads that divided the fields of tall, imposing sugarcane that rustled and waved at the vehicle as it sped past. Amina and Dev had been eager to leave the house that morning for new adventures. But Raju's sister fully intended to prepare another generous meal for the family to enjoy at the beach, as well as plenty of Mauritian rum.

Amina and Dev, watched in earnest by their cousins, in turn, watched with interest as the women scurried around, cooked food, fetched containers, and located beach mats. Meanwhile, the men wandered to the nearest *tabagie* to buy crates of beer, bottles of rum and exchange empty, clinking bottles for full bottles of fresh cola.

The food was soon reverently placed, in their saucepans, alongside the drinks in the minibus, to be warmed over a fire in the shade of a filao tree. The saucepans were placed on tea towels that were folded up and over the lids before being knotted tightly to prevent any of its tasty cargo from escaping.

Deep wicker baskets were filled with tin canisters full of different compotes, chutneys and pickles. Fresh flatbreads and baguettes, as well as the traditional Mauritian *du pain maison*, all made their way to the back of the bus. Rice was cooked and contained for the beach while jars of spicy pickled mango jiggled and clinked excitedly against jars of spicy pickled octopus. Together all the drinks, food and other accoutrements took up almost as much room as the minibus' passengers.

At the beach in England, Raju, Serena, Amina and Dev would usually just share a large bag of chips from the fish and chip shop. Maybe also an ice cream each.

In Mauritius, it was common to see and hear vendors coming and going on their bicycles or motorbikes. They would go by, calling out what they were selling, usually some type of food. Guavas with salt. Fried finger-food. With so much food already prepared and brought to the beach, they needed no further supplies. But one vendor caught Raju's attention, and he called out to do likewise. He asked Amina and Dev whether they would like something cool, and the pair followed, slack-jawed at the sight that greeted them.

'What's this?' asked Amina.

'A *Mauritian* slushie,' replied Raju with a rub of his daughter's shoulder.

Amina and Dev discovered that a Mauritian slushie was something sold by a man pushing a bicycle announcing himself by shouting *glaçon râpé* – grated ice – at the top of his lungs. Strapped to the back of his bike was a plastic box the size of a small microwave. In it sat a heavy block of ice. The man grabbed a small paper cone made from rolled-up newspaper, reinforced with several folds, before using a sharp metal scraper to grate the top of the block into a pile of ice chips.

He quickly scooped the ice shavings into the cone before they melted under the Mauritian sun. The man then proceeded to squirt a red-coloured sugary syrup, followed by a green version, over the shavings before concluding by impaling a tiny plastic spoon in the glistening, rapidly melting ice, like a Norwegian at the South pole.

'Thanks,' said Amina.

'It's nice,' added Dev, after a taste.

Together the three returned to their camp on the warm white sandy beach bearing *glaçon râpé* cones for everyone. The adults sat, chatted and watched the children play on the beach. The Mauritian and English child factions were still unsure of each other, lacking a common language but quickly finding common ground.

One of the Mauritian children had had the foresight to bring a small football, and two team captains were quickly appointed. Dev, who had never expressed any interest in football, was bemused to learn that each hastily assembled team considered him a prized asset and were hotly contesting which would have him. Since Dev was from England, they had all assumed him to be some kind of footballing prodigy. (Had Mauritians more access to England's televised international matches of the time, their children would have been swiftly disabused of that notion.)

While Dev played on the beach with the children, Amina

swam small circles in the sea. She couldn't remember sunshine like it on her skin before, as if it was warming her from within. Amina didn't just feel the warmth on her skin. She felt it emanating from her tummy to spread throughout her being and light up her limbs, all the way to her fingertips. There again, in the sea and the sunshine, Amina wished she could remember having been there as a toddler. How could she have forgotten something like this? Something so different. Before long, Serena joined her daughter, and they chatted while they swam.

'Remember to be careful of sea urchins,' warned Serena, 'step lightly.'

In Mauritius, Amina felt eyes upon her wherever she was, but at the beach, it was different. There in her brightly coloured one-piece swimming outfit, she could feel a gaze of a different kind. Amina felt she was a novelty, different to all the other girls. In the beginning, she found the lingering looks uncomfortable and squirmed under the gazes as she walked through town with her family, wanting to blend in and become invisible.

However, as the days went by, she became accustomed to the attention. She didn't relish it but became more comfortable with it. At the beach, where there were more tourists in equally new-looking, brightly-coloured clothes, she drew less attention. It felt to Amina that the beach, the sea, was the only place she could pass unnoticed.

# 15. Capture of sound

By the end of their first week at her aunt's house, Amina began to feel bored, unable to understand much of the conversation around her. Rather than English or French, Raju's family spoke Creole or Telugu, the language spoken all those years ago by their ancestors from the Indian state now known as Andhra Pradesh.

Dev's footballing skills had improved in the street with his new friends despite their lack of common language. This was not something Amina found she could replicate with the girls and young women around her. Her understanding of, and ability to use, the Creole language was limited. For most conversations, Serena would translate more accurately the questions posed to Amina and her responses. Serena herself was growing increasingly anxious to see her own family in the north of the island.

It didn't encourage Amina to make more effort when they, believing she could not understand them, talked about her as if she wasn't even in the room. On one occasion, a few of her young cousins, only a year or two older than her, openly talked about her, glancing at her from time to time. Amina didn't understand everything, but she pieced most of it together.

'Do you think *Appa* Serena teaches her to cook yet?' asked one girl about her auntie.

'What does she need to cook for? They all have maids in England,' the second girl would reply.

'No, they don't.'

'How do you know? They just tell you they don't.'

'What about cleaning? Do you think she cleans?'

'I haven't seen her do anything. She just wears nice clothes and looks pretty,' the second girl stated, letting off some resentful steam.

'She's only a child.'

'So are we. We don't go on holidays and relax.'

'They won't have a maid when she moves here,' predicted a third girl.

'Why would she move here?' asked the second girl, clearly the leader of the trio.

'When she gets married. She'll marry a Mauritian boy, learn Creole and French, won't she?'

'She'll go to university. It's all free over there for them. They get everything.'

'Won't they be worried that she gets in trouble with a boy over there?'

'It's the price of living over there. Everyone knows European girls are *putains*,' whispered the second girl, relishing the taste of the forbidden word on her tongue, glad for the opportunity to cement her position as the daring one.

'Especially the English,' she continued, eager to push her view, 'they can't wait to do it. You know how the tourists dress. They're like that all the time over there.'

'We shouldn't talk about her like that. She's only a child.'

'Not anymore. Over there, once they have periods, they're women.'

Amina was more than happy when they left for the north the next day. With their luggage packed in the taxi, Raju's family, including the three gossiping girls, waved at them as the car pulled away. Amina didn't wave. She just stared straight ahead.

'Mum, what does *putain* mean?' Amina asked.

'*Putain*? Where did you hear that word?'

'Over there. What does it mean?'

'It means… I'll tell you one day when you're older.'

'Mum?'

'What is it, Dev?'

'I need the toilet.'

'Really? Are you joking? We just left.'

A couple of hours later, the taxi pulled up at Serena's family home in the country's capital, Port Louis. Serena barely allowed the car to stop before leaping out, pushing past the white-painted metal gate and running up the steps to the front door like a little girl again.

'Mum, Dad, Sachin! We're here!' she shouted.

More greetings, kisses, hugs, handshakes and cheek squeezing ensued before their luggage was plucked from the car and the driver remunerated.

'Mum?' asked Amina, 'are we going to the beach today?'

'Not today. Maybe we'll go tomorrow.'

'*Maybe?*' Amina complained.

'We've been every day since we got off the plane. We need to spend some time with our family too.'

'What's the problem?' Uncle Sachin asked.

'Oh. She wants to go to the beach,' explained Serena.

'The beach? Why do you like the beach so much?' Uncle Sachin asked his niece. Amina stared at him dumbly, unable to process such a seemingly ridiculous question. The Mauritians did not understand the fascination that Amina and Dev had with the beach. They thought beaches were the same all around the world and could not understand it when they heard that some English beaches were covered with rocks and pebbles, with no soft, white sand leading to turquoise water. With the beautiful beaches of Mauritius as their birthright, the Mauritians took it for granted.

With so many equally good answers available to her, Amina struggled to pick the best one.

'What's the matter? Don't you speak English anymore either?' he asked sharply, in a way that was normal for him and for anyone who knew him. However, Amina could not think of another time she had been spoken to so abruptly by an adult and didn't know how to react.

'Mum?' Amina called uncertainly, but Serena was chatting with her mother and sister-in-law. Bored, Uncle Sachin, stalked away leaving Amina alone.

'Don't worry about him,' said her grandfather as he approached softly behind her. 'Tonight we're going to have a good meal and dance to some *sega*. Do you know what *sega* is?'

'I think so. Mum has cassettes you copied for her that she plays at the weekend.'

'Jean-Claude. Do you know Jean-Claude?'

Amina shook her head. 'Who is he?'

'He's a *sega* singer.'

'Oh, I don't know their names.'

'Well, tonight, you will find out.'

And so she did. After they had all had their fish dinner, and the adults had had a few glasses of Mauritian rum, Grandad loaded a cassette into the player. With the volume turned up, the sound of *sega* bounced from the hard, tiled surfaces and filled the entire house. The wicker furniture was quickly shunted aside, suggesting to the children that this was a regular occurrence. It didn't take much encouragement for Raju to join Serena and his in-laws on the makeshift dance floor with their arms aloft, hips swaying to the beat of the *ravanne*, laughing at the risqué lyrics of the singers.

Amina and Dev sat and observed a side of their parents they had never seen before. Intoxicated by the atmosphere, it was not long before they joined in and danced with their parents. Red-faced from their efforts, the grandparents soon bowed out and sat at the dining table to watch from a safe distance as the younger generations fanned their imaginary *sega* skirts.

The children hadn't yet seen the sega dancers in the flesh, but they had already seen them on TV. While the musicians played in the background, the male singer would cavort in between verses with the female dancers clad in tight-fitting bodices sewn together from brightly coloured light fabrics. The skirts would also be brightly coloured with exaggerated and frilly hemlines that the dancers would gather up to fan theatrically as they danced around on the balls of their feet.

Serena had long anticipated this evening. Giddy from the alcohol and the dancing, she hugged Raju tightly before demanding Sachin put on a sega song with a faster beat. Round and round, she swirled barefoot on the tiled floor, memories of her childhood flooding back. She felt light on her feet, lighter than she had felt in a long time, with nothing in her heart but love for her family. Serena asked herself how she had endured so long in England without seeing her family and tried to ignore the impending sadness at leaving them behind again.

A couple of days later, Raju left to visit family elsewhere on the island.

Unfortunately for Amina, her uncle Sachin had decided to make it his mission to keep up her education in Mauritius. Amina was terrible at maths, a fact that had not escaped Uncle Sachin, who proceeded to make almost the entirety of her time at their home one big maths lesson. Every day of their stay there, Amina was tested on what she had learnt while Uncle Sachin had been at work at his market stall.

When Uncle Sachin had a day off, he seemed to look for every opportunity to catch Amina daydreaming and not concentrating on her copybook. Being a highly skilled and prolific daydreamer, Amina would often let her attention wander beyond the window to the trees outside. 'I'm testing you in half an hour. Then we'll see how much the window will help you,' would jerk Amina's attention back to the book.

Dev felt sorry for his sister. It was more than their curtailed playtime together. He wasn't used to seeing her under pressure and being picked on, and it didn't sit well. He wondered why Mum didn't say anything to her brother and found it unsettling how Serena seemed to change when her brother and father were around. When they were in the room, Serena wasn't their mother anymore. She was another person. She seemed to agree with them on everything, including how Amina should be pushed to achieve more. Dev found it challenging to reconcile this with the mum that he knew and trusted.

By far and away, the biggest bugbear for Amina was the multiplications table. The back of her Mauritian copybook listed them from two to twelve. As a teenager thinking back to this incident, Dev could only conclude that it was a subconscious act of defiance from Amina. No matter how hard she tried and how blunt and overblown the accusations were that she was disappointing and shaming all her family, Amina persisted in failing to follow the pattern and memorise the numbers.

She could make head nor tail of the thing and might as well have been learning another language. To Amina, it was a mysterious jumble of numbers she was being forced to memorise in a particular order without recognising that they held a pattern.

One day, Amina, Dev, his mother, Grandfather and Uncle Sachin were preparing to visit a tourist attraction called *Chamarel: La Terre Sept Couleurs*. Getting in the car that morning, Uncle Sachin handed Amina her navy blue copybook with the mysterious numbers printed on the back in black. 'I'm going to test you when we get there,' he promised.

Throughout the car journey, Amina couldn't help but look out of the window at the tropical foliage brushing past. From time to time, she would look down at her copybook but was so worried about being tested at Chamarel, and apparently bringing shame upon herself and disappointing all her family, that she couldn't concentrate on the frayed book in her lap.

3 12 36 24 42 27 144 45 15 72 64 18 6

Dev couldn't enjoy any of the journey either and spent it in silence, not wanting to provoke a sharp comment from his uncle. When they reached their destination Amina, fearing the moment she would be tested, wouldn't enjoy the visit.

Chamarel's appeal to visitors lies in its ground, the beauty of which is entirely due to the island's volcanic origins. When Serena had tried to explain it to them at home, Amina and Dev had found it difficult to imagine. But as they approached on foot, her description made sense as the undulating land before them caught the clear sunlight to reveal its hidden beauty.

Like they were standing on a magic carpet, the ground before them shimmered and changed colour as they moved around. Naturally made up of different colours, the earth of this stretch of land bewitched all who set foot on it. Browns and reds would yield underfoot to shades of orange, purple, blue and everything in between. It was as though a giant prism had been placed before the sun to rain colours down from above.

The family members thoughtfully walked the perimeter of the visitor attraction, inspecting the earth from different angles and marvelling as the colours glowed under the Mauritian sun. The gift shop sold small test tube-like glass souvenirs with ground samples of each colour layered within, and Serena bought one showing the layers of earth, toned from lightest to darkest. Captured and held in place in a glass container, the earth didn't sparkle as it did under the sun and was a pale imitation of the real thing.

While Chamarel offered views of the earth in all its multi-tonal glory, Amina, fearing the test at the end of the visit, couldn't let herself enjoy the trip. However, it eventually passed without event as, satisfied with their visit, everyone piled into the car and made for home. Even on the way home, Amina feared the test would come when they arrived, but it didn't. Relieved, Amina continued to count down the days until they would leave Mauritius. Dev, glad that the threatened test didn't come that day, was also curious.

Had Uncle Sachin felt sorry for her?

Perhaps his work had left their uncle too tired for the effort involved in testing her?

Maybe their uncle had become bored with the whole thing?

Maybe he had simply forgotten?

That evening Dev lay on the bed, and between his fingers, he held the little trinket to the light from the bare bulb hanging from the ceiling. He wanted to see if the light could pass through, illuminating the different shades. It didn't. All he saw was a dark tube against the light.

It reminded Dev of when he was younger still, about five or six. Raju had a glass jar at their house, about a foot in height and layered with the different shades of the Chamarel earth. Unlike the little test tube trinket, the vessel had some space between the uppermost layer and the lid. Dev had thought it might be fun to shake the jar to see the different layers slide along and back. Unfortunately, that was not the case. Instead, all seven layers became intermingled, and the seven different shades became one. Every molecule had changed place with another, becoming indistinguishable in the process.

# 16. Shifting baseline syndrome

At the end of the week, Raju returned in a taxi to collect Amina, Dev and Serena for another week with his folks. Glad for her father's warm voice again, Amina hugged him tightly before they bundled into the car. Feeling finally able to breathe, Amina wound down her window and felt the breeze blow her hair around her face.

'How was your week, Dad?' asked Dev.

'Fine, Dev,' replied Raju from the front passenger seat. Then, recalling an incident, 'Mauritians will always sacrifice long-term gain for short-term profit,' he replied simply, shaking his head with a wry smile on his face. Dev didn't know what he meant, but he nodded sagely nonetheless.

Seemingly, wherever they went, Amina could detect the scent of burning wood drifting on the air, and she smelt it again as they drove away. She knew that it was from the wood-burning stoves that many people there still used at the time instead of gas cylinders, but she didn't understand why the smell seemed to cling to the atmosphere. It felt that wherever they went, something was burning. Even at a temple far away from any houses, they could smell it.

'Before we go to the beach, we're going to stop at a temple. It was your father's local temple when he was your age,' Serena reminded the children.

Getting out of the taxi, what immediately struck Amina and Dev was the sound from the fields of sugarcane that surrounded the temple as the leaves swayed and rustled in the breeze. The soft whispers only served to highlight the silence of the temple by contrast. Before entering the grounds, they all left their shoes and sandals at the threshold. Stepping through the white-painted stone archway, it felt like they had entered a place entirely separate from Mauritius. It was almost eerie to be somewhere in this country without the bustling of people and the jabber of voices. Other than the rustling sugarcane, the only sound was the blunt cry of the bell that each member of the family ahead of them sounded as they entered the main building.

Amina and Dev looked up at the intricately decorated domes of the temple. Neither of them had seen anything like this before. When their mother had mentioned visiting a temple, they had pictured something akin to a church, of which there were several near their home in England. But none of them looked like this. The buildings that made up the temple were predominantly painted white on the outside, and in the pure sunlight, they almost glistened. Precisely sculpted adornments, painted in joyful yellows, garish greens, and vivid pinks, lined the temple's domes, walls, and pillars.

Once through the archway and onto the stone path, the children instinctively instantly fell silent and stared at the immaculately manicured grounds. The grass was clipped, the bushes were pruned, and trees clung to their blossom as if afraid to besmirch the ground with them. The main building at the end of the path housed giant statues of various Hindu gods, but Parvati was the star of the show, with Saraswati and Lakshmi flanking her. Parvati held up one of her four hands, seemingly in greeting, as the *pandit* in his faded orange robes tended to the worshippers ahead of the Sharmas.

From them stepped forward one of the women to offer the *pandit* the silver platter she was holding. It held a bright green banana leaf upon which lay small *zinzli* bananas, their skins having been pierced with incense sticks. The bananas had been joined by coconut pieces, sweet cakes and flower petals. With those items was a tiny pile of camphor squares that were promptly lit by the *pandit* after he took the platter from them. Flames from the camphor lent the offering with a soft, warm glow, satisfying the worshippers that they had the attention of their gods. The *pandit* recited religious scripture in Sanskrit, a language that no one there understood, whilst flicking a cigarette lighter to ignite the camphor. Once this was done, he turned to the statue of Parvati holding the platter of items to be blessed.

Continuing to recite in his low, monotonous mumble, devoid of inflections or seemingly any recognisable sentence structure, the grey-haired *pandit* reached out holding the platter. With it, he circled the front of the statue, the smoke from the incense sticks wafting over Parvati's face, suggesting he was inviting the goddess to bless the items the platter held. The incense sticks gave off their pungent aroma while the accompanying smoke swirled around Parvati before making its way up to the blackened ceiling.

When it came to their turn, Amina and Dev followed the example of Raju and Serena. They put their hands together under their chins in prayer as the *pandit* took their platter and entreated the deity to bless them and their endeavours.

Before long, their blessing had reached its conclusion, with the results yet to be seen, and it was the turn of the following family in the queue. 'Remember not to turn your back on the goddess as you leave,' whispered Raju to the children. 'Walk backwards out of the door.'

'Why?' asked Dev.

'Because Hindu gods are real pranksters, so always keep your eyes on them,' joked Raju.

Leaving the main building, the children discovered other little huts to visit that offered likenesses of other deities, each with their own speciality subjects.

'What do they all do?' Dev asked.

'I don't know, but let's visit them anyway,' said Raju.

So they visited all the gods on offer in their little huts. A little like visiting different stages at a music festival to visit your favourite bands, eighteen-year-old Dev would later muse. The family stared at the gods and goddesses, seeking to understand their meaning. In turn, the gods and goddesses – different shapes, sizes, forms, colours, poses, expressions – stared back, offering silence.

Driving around Mauritius, Amina and Dev were fascinated by how each house they passed was entirely different from the other in terms of designs, colours, sizes, as well as construction material. Some were made from metal sheets.

Some were brick-built. Many of them would have a little concrete box with a tiny glass door sitting atop a pillar in the yard. Within the concrete boxes could be seen small likenesses of various deities, depending upon the household. Serena explained to the children that the people from the house would light incense sticks, camphor and bring other offerings for the deities when they visited for daily prayers.

'Like at the temple?' Amina asked.

'Yes,' said Serena.

'So it's like they have their very own little temple with their favourite god in their garden? What if it's raining? Why don't they just keep the god in their house?'

'Um, I'm not sure,' confessed Serena. 'Maybe it's something to do with not showing disrespect by sharing a house with the god.'

'But why would the god be upset at sharing a house?' asked Dev.

'Um, well, maybe...' began Serena, after some thought, 'maybe there are certain things people do at home, and they would rather not have their favourite god around as they do those things.'

'But I thought God was everywhere and saw everything?'

'I don't know, Dev. Raju? Help.'

'Don't ask me. I don't know.'

'But *your* family is the traditional one. You should know about all this.'

Later that day, Raju took Amina and Dev for an after-dinner stroll through the village surrounding his sister's house. The roads were narrow with no pavements, not even enough space for the drainage system, just enough room for one car to pass at a time. The sun glowered as it slowly crept below the horizon, its embers still providing adequate light for everyone to carry on about their business. Children played football or skipped rope in the streets. Dev recognised some of them from their previous stay and waved as the trio ambled along, taking in the evening. Outside houses, dogs barked at one another while spouses squabbled inside.

'You hear a lot more of everyone's private lives here than in England,' remarked Amina.

'It's because all their windows and doors are wide open,' replied Dev, unnecessarily.

From time to time, they would come across someone Raju knew from old times, and they would stop so Raju and the acquaintance could chat. The acquaintance would be an old friend, an old neighbour, a local shopkeeper, someone who once knew Raju's now-deceased parents. Eventually, the conversation would come to an end as the other person would have things to do: stray dogs to chase away, children to round-up, a wife with whom to bicker.

In the centre of the village, Raju showed them a playing field where he hung out as a child. It was more of a dustbowl now than a field, and in the absence of anyone else to use it, they wandered around kicking little stones across the brown dirt ground that constituted the surface. Looking up, Amina noticed something strange to her. At one end was a large, square concrete box the size of a chest freezer with one open side facing the field. The concrete box was supported roughly thirty feet in the air by four solid concrete pillars. She stared at it for a few moments trying to work out its purpose or significance. She wondered if it once held the likeness of a deity, whether the competitors paid their respects before playing their sports. *But then, being so high up, it would be a hassle to get incense sticks up there every time. Maybe it used to be some kind of scoreboard?*

'Dad? What's that?' asked Amina.

'Oh, that?' asked Raju, pointing at the unusual concrete structure. 'That was where they put the TV,' Raju replied nonchalantly.

'The TV?' Amina and Dev asked in unison.

'Yeah. A long time ago, people here couldn't afford a TV, but I suppose the government still wanted everyone to have access to the news and government announcements, so they had a communal TV put up there. There was an aerial, and they would run a generator to power the TV.'

'They had one TV that everyone would come here to watch?' Amina asked, seeking clarification.

'How did they all decide which channel to watch?' Dev asked.

Raju laughed. 'That wasn't a problem. There was only one channel back then. Until idiots threw rocks at it. Then there weren't any channels for a while.'

'What idiots?'

'People who didn't want change.'

Generally, Amina was more willing than Dev to try previously unencountered fruit, vegetables, drinks and dishes. She found the market fascinating with its array of bright colours provided by the unfamiliar items for sale. Beautiful, unblemished papayas plucked from the trees that very morning, fresh lychees still attached to their branches, *bouillon brede*, small *zinzli* bananas, raw sugarcane straight from the field, calabash, jackfruit, *goyaves*, spiky skinned *corossols*, *longan* fruit with its soft flesh, *jamblons*, *caramboles*, *alouda*. Amina and Dev tried everything, but it was Amina who would return for a second helping.

As street foods of all kinds passed their lips, they savoured all the aromas and tastes Mauritius could offer. *Dholl puris* was a delicate flatbread filled with ground split peas and then warmed through on a round, flat *tawa*. The resulting soft and moist bread would then be served in pairs to sufficiently hold a serving of curried butter beans and chutney without compromising structural integrity. *Gâteau patate* was a favourite of Amina's. This was a small fried snack consisting of a soft outer case made from sweet potato and flour and a filling of grated coconut and sugar. When she bit into a fresh one from the pan, the soft filling oozed with sugary syrup. A dentist's nightmare.

*Gâteau Vermicelle* was also in demand, with Amina taking pleasure in their dusting of desiccated coconut and the sweet raisins. By contrast, Dev preferred *napolitaine* cakes and *poutou*. *Napolitaine* consisted of two layered circular pieces of crumbly pastry with a raspberry jam filling. This was covered with a layer of pink icing that would harden to a shell that would shatter under his teeth, leaving pink shards on his tongue. The aroma from a fresh batch of *poutou* cakes was always enough to turn Dev's head as he walked past a street vendor, and Raju would inevitably end up buying up a batch for him and the rest of the family. The basic ingredients of rice, coconut, flour, sugar, butter and hot milk went through steaming, compression and drying. Warm from the press, the resulting cake would melt in Dev's mouth, delivering rice and coconut's subtle but distinctive flavour.

A week later, it was time to leave the island. On the plane, flying away from Mauritius, Amina examined the complimentary jigsaw puzzle the steward had given Dev. She had been expecting to receive one too, but the steward had seemingly decided that she was too old for it. Piecing together the picture of one of the airline's planes in flight on a bright sunny day, Amina thought back to the fields and fields of sugarcane and tea crops that spread as far as her eyes could see. She thought too of the gentle, warm water she had enjoyed swimming in as it lapped against the beach. Lastly, she thought of the temple they had visited in the first week and the tranquillity they had experienced there. It had been surprising. She hadn't expected to feel anything.

# 17. Thinking aloud

Dr. Sharma continues to feel the belt digging into his erupting skin. He is beginning to bleed from where his nails and the belt have clawed the skin of his neck. His blood mixes with sweat as his eyelids bulge open again, and Dr. Sharma hopes for his eyes to alight upon something, or someone, that can help. He thinks he has seen help arriving in the form of Katie, but he is apparently mistaken. It is almost as if someone, or thing, is toying with him. Instead of help, Dr. Sharma sees the room tremble around him. The thought occurs to him that it might be some sort of earthquake, but it is just his vision. Oxygen deprivation. Dr. Sharma wonders if everyone in his position experiences this, but he reasons that most people would be too busy panicking to notice such things or remember them afterwards.

For Dr. Sharma, the colours from the room bleed into one another like a photograph taken in a dimly lit space. A memory of another time and place and person that he has not thought of in years, or ever. Moments that he has just lived through without thinking of it, like most of us. *Why am I seeing these things?* wonders Dr. Sharma. It's a good question. Why not see himself aged eight, splashing about in the sea, or as a six-year-old approaching the tree to find that Father Christmas had visited? Why not feel that joy again? The joy of innocence, blind faith in something positive. Trust that Mum and Dad have all the answers and will always watch out for you.

No, that would be too easy. Too easy to see only what we want. Sometimes it's fun to push someone beyond their comfort. Let's find something that inspires discomfort in Dr. Sharma, shall we?

'People get bored. That's why they look beyond the immediately obvious. Beyond what's right in front of them,' explained Alex. He sat on a stool before a coffee shop window beside Dr. Sharma. 'I think we weren't really meant to have this much brainpower. It's more than we can handle, even if it is only ten per cent of our brain's capacity. Is it really our fault if we begin inventing things to keep ourselves busy? That's why we make up weird sex stuff. Or aliens. Or vampires, or whatever.'

Alex was dressed plainly. Jeans and a T-shirt. Although Dr. Sharma did not know what he had been expecting of a male prostitute. Alex was young, in his early twenties, a brown-haired, average-looking young man who was in demand amongst men and also available to women. Roisin, on the other hand, was tall with long blonde hair. She wore three-inch high heels, stockings, a knee-length skirt, a blouse and a jacket that gave her a business-like appearance. Thus far, she hadn't said much to Dr. Sharma, perhaps choosing the right time for her contribution. Alex had been doing all the talking. They worked as a duo when necessary, but Roisin no longer offered complete sexual services. Instead, she was now a professional Dominatrix.

'What are the things that kept us busy two hundred years ago?' Alex continued, warming to the topic, agitating his hands. 'Stories. Folk tales. TV and radio opened things up, but the internet has made the unimaginable the merely frowned upon. Can you imagine if the only available websites were limited to, say, the church? What a coup,' he exclaimed, slapping a fist into an open palm. 'What circularity to have the latest means of distraction pointing straight back to one of the original means of distraction we used, fantasising about some guy in the sky. Watching us. Judging and rating us.'

'Some would say it does that now,' answered Dr. Sharma, finally managing to get a word in.

'What? Sex? Yeah, but religion is so fucking organised. That's what's so sinister about it. Somebody has spent time thinking about what will get people motivated. They're so good that they're still managing to suck people in. The fucking Jihadists. The fucking Scientologists. All those fucks. Well, I suppose the paedos are pretty organised too, for a non-religious group. They know what to say, how to groom. They know how to manipulate. Hardly surprising that the same people who can convince people they're ambassadors for a guy in the sky can convince altar boys to keep their mouths shut after swallowing a load. Right?' asked Alex, rhetorically.

'So, you both see men, women, couples, from all walks of

life. What do you think is the difference between them?' asked Dr. Sharma, treading uncertain ground with Alex. He was dubious about talking with Alex and Roisin and had decided to proceed with caution, for now, making his questions fairly rudimentary.

'What do you think?' came Alex's sarcastic reply. 'You really think men and women are so different?'

'Men don't just see prostitutes for an orgasm,' interjected Roisin gently. 'Neither do women. We can handle that for ourselves. People see prostitutes, escorts, Mistresses, whatever you want to call us, for danger, excitement, the thrill, a connection.'

'Connection?' asked Dr. Sharma, again playing dumb to encourage them.

'Another person. Another mind,' continued Roisin, 'it's not just about bodies. Sure, a lot of it is to do with bodies, but it's not a hundred per cent about simple pleasure. It's about interaction. Some people just want to fuck and go, people who just want to use someone else's body. But most people want a connection. That goes for men and women.'

'But it's a transient connection,' observed Dr. Sharma.

'Not always. But usually, yeah.'

'What... connection can one make in such a short time?'

'You'd be surprised,' replied Roisin, pausing before continuing. 'You need to not be yourself. If you really want to understand, you need to put yourself where they are. See things the way they do.'

'How?'

'They're vulnerable,' said Alex simply before taking a sip of his cappuccino. 'They don't know it, but they're vulnerable people trying to connect with others who can understand what they need. Not just do what they want, but understand. You can't do it properly if you don't understand it.'

'What is there to understand about a blow job?' asked Dr. Sharma as he shifted on his stool.

'That's only one part of what we do.'

'*You* do,' corrected Roisin.

'Yeah. Besides, who's talking about BJs? Not me,' Alex answered his own question.

'Then what are you talking about?' fished Dr. Sharma.

'Forniphilia. Sploshing. BDSM. Clown sex. And so on.'

Roisin couldn't help a smile before adding a suggestion to Alex's list: 'How about some Pony Play?'

'What… is Pony Play?' asked Dr. Sharma tentatively, putting his cold coffee back down, distracted again.

'You can't understand any of these until you really see things,' replied Alex, 'and if you don't, you don't get it.'

A natural pause ensued as the three of them considered the exchange and sipped from their coffee cups. 'I need the loo. Back in a few,' said Alex as he hopped off his stool, leaving Dr. Sharma alone with Roisin. A couple of moments later, Dr. Sharma pursued the conversation from another angle.

'It's like blind trust, isn't it, Roisin? BDSM. The people who come to you for it, they don't know you.'

'They trust me,' answered Roisin after a sip of her coffee. 'That's the point. Look, people trust all sorts of things on blind faith. They trust prophylactics. They trust the pill. Most people don't know how it works, but they trust it. That goes for all sorts of medication. Doctors prescribe the drugs their patients get hooked on. We take it because someone we trust suggests it, despite the list of side-effects printed in black and white.'

'But this is different. It's more immediate, the risk of getting hurt.'

'That's the thrill. You're only seeing one side of things. Yes, there is risk,' Roisin's voice picking up in energy as she no longer needed to compete for the floor, 'the thrilling unpredictability of giving control to another, but on the other side of the same coin, there is trust, care. Love. It's not just about the power held by one dominating person. I feel it's about the power that the sub has. Their capacity to trust and confidence in themselves gives them a different kind of power than the control that they give away. It's about feeling the domme's care. It's having power in the first place in order to not have power. It's a weird contradiction. A paradox. It's letting go of yourself to serve with trust and trust unquestioningly. At least, that's the way I see it.'

'Care?'

'A sub needs to believe that care underpins everything. They are affected by the decisions of another. They need to believe that care will stop a domme from going too far. I think, for many people, it is the only way to once again feel that all-encompassing love they once took for granted.'

'From what I've seen, BDSM is also about letting go of yourself,' observed Dr. Sharma. 'Not just control. Being someone completely different.'

'Look, what you need to understand is that what you've seen in videos is only what the camera sees, not what the domme or the sub feels. There is a lot more going on than simply tying people up or giving orders. The domme needs the sub. After all, without the top, what is the bottom? *The Brain* needs *Pinky*. Without *Pinky*, is *The Brain* really *The Brain*?'

A few moments passed while Dr. Sharma digested this. 'I told Alex I attended one of Mira Cassavetes' events to observe her with her clients. It wasn't how I expected it to be. He suggested I talk with her. D'you know anything about her?'

'Not really. Only the type of films I know she's been in. Couldn't hurt to talk to her. What you need to understand about what I do, what Mira does… We're at the centre of what we're doing, whether it's with one person or more. We're the focus of attention, the theatre, we're performers. The theatre of an interrogation, the theatre of dressing up and playing a part, being someone else. Just like when you go to the theatre, you agree to suspend your disbelief, when someone is with me, they have entered into a verbal, sometimes a written, contract to suspend reality, their reality.'

Roisin took another sip of her coffee before delicately dabbing at her lips with a napkin before continuing. 'A client having a sploshing session with me needs to be able to invest themselves in it. They can't do that if I'm not fully committed to it too. A prostitute selling blow jobs doesn't need to understand the thrill someone gets from sensation play, how different foods, and their textures, feel on your skin. The texture, the consistency of a raw egg is very different from almost anything else. Imagine the hard shell giving way to the soft, viscous innards as it crushes against your skin. The little shards of shell prick your skin for that tiny second, then the soft yolk presses before it gently explodes. Imagine that for a moment. Picture it, feel it.'

Dr. Sharma did take a moment. He also took in a forkful of his chocolate cake as he pondered how to broach the next topic. Directly or delicately? He swallowed and decided.

'Roisin, please do not take this the wrong way. I'd like to ask how you, and Alex, got into this.'

'Well, for me, it was a friend who was doing it. We'd just finished our undergraduate degrees –'

'Um, no. Sorry, I meant how… er. What was your history, or sexual experience, before getting into this?'

'Oh, by that time, I suppose I'd had a bunch of boyfriends and girlfriends, but nothing really serious. Nothing that lasted past five months.'

'That's it?'

'Yeah.'

'Nothing else you want to share?'

'Why?'

Dr. Sharma inhaled deeply with a little shake of his head, not knowing the words that would next leave his lips. 'Roisin, studies have shown that those who work in the sex industry have a history of sexual abuse, in their childhood, and so forth.'

'Don't forget emotional abuse,' added Roisin, as Alex retook his stool.

'What are we talking about now?' he asked.

'Dev wants to know if we suffered sexual abuse. That's what you were getting at, right?'

'A little insulting,' responded Alex, 'but I suppose it's a fair question, under the circumstances.'

'I didn't mean to insult either of you.'

'Do you know why it's insulting?' asked Roisin.

'I can imagine,' answered Dr. Sharma.

'It's insulting when people assume that the only way a woman can do this kind of work is if she was raped or assaulted in some way.'

'It's just that the data –'

'I was never abused. I just enjoy what I enjoy. How about you, Alex?'

'No, Mate, not everybody in the sex industry has suffered abuse.'

'I wasn't assuming that,' assured Dr. Sharma, 'I just had to ask.'

'Did you?' asked Roisin.

'What you also need to bear in mind is that even if your *data* says that most people in the sex industry have had sexual abuse, that's not necessarily the reason they work in the sex industry,' clarified Alex. 'Not in all cases.'

An awkward silence ensued, which Dr. Sharma broke by redirecting the conversation to a less contentious topic for the two.

'How about BDSM?' tried Dr. Sharma.

'Which bit?' asked Alex. 'BDSM is a huge umbrella. Like wrestling? Wrestling is about feeling completely defeated, dejected. Out of control. I bet you mean being tied up. Being tied does not have to be a violent thing. It's a release. Trusting and connecting with the person who is holding you. You can be bound, unable to move, without fear. It's a release to surrender yourself like that. Can you imagine?'

# 18. Urban hymns

I *don't have to imagine*, thinks Dr. Sharma as he continues to sweat all over Katie's bed. *But why this? If I need to go back, can't I go back to something fun?* The colours bleed, and he instead takes us back to the night of Bellyana's twenty-sixth birthday party.

Besides Tim, Bellyana was the only person from college with whom Dr. Sharma had kept in touch. To him, Bellyana was a rarity. Funny, highly intelligent, charismatic, open to new ideas and experiences. She had what Dr. Sharma described to himself as a genuinely enquiring mind. Not only was she interested in theories and studies, but she was also interested in people. That she was actively pursuing a career in law and was already married was surprising to Dr. Sharma. He had always thought she would travel more.

Nevertheless, there they were in her kitchen, the beating heart of any good house party, exchanging stand-out stories from their respective professions, over mulled wine. Yes, mulled wine since Bellyana's birthday is on December 28th –

a fact she has always bemoaned since it is so close to Christmas – and they were using up her leftover Christmas booze.

'… So we're suing Jackson Gafferty,' continued Bellyana.

'Jackson Gafferty? But, Bell, wasn't he a one-hit-wonder? Why would anyone expect more hits from him, especially after fifty years?' asked Dr. Sharma, sitting with her on the floor, leant against the backdoor in her kitchen.

'That's what I thought when I first heard. But, no. Although he's mostly known for that one song, he had some other hits back in the day. It's just *that* one dwarfs all the rest. The others don't get played as much.'

'I'm confused. What does this guy want exactly? I must have missed something here because I don't see how you have a case.'

'Exactly, that's why we're still looking into it. We don't think anything like this has ever been done before. This guy, our biggest client, might I add, bought all Gafferty's records as a young man, went to all his gigs, followed him on tour, practically worshipped him. Total. Hero. Worship. He collected memorabilia, waited for hours in the rain for autographs, that sort of thing.'

'Sounds like a stalker.'

'Yes, but he went from being a poor, teenage stalker to a multi-millionaire, and now he wants us to do everything we can to get in Gafferty's face.'

'Why?'

'Jackson Gafferty was everything to this guy when he was a teenager. Seriously, you should see him talking about it. It was borderline creepy seeing this old guy in his chair with his oxygen tank getting excited about having seen Jackson Gafferty on stage forty-six times. He can tell you details from each and every show. It's amazing. I can't tell you what I had for dinner last Wednesday, but this guy remembers what he was wearing for each show, what Gafferty was wearing, what his hair looked like, what jokes Gafferty made, that there was a problem with the lighting rig at one of the shows. It goes on. How does someone remain so fixated on something? To the extent that they remember details like that, all these decades later.'

'He was a teenager. We all get fixated on stuff when we're teenagers and at any time in life. Helps us get through other things.'

'Anyway, Gafferty eventually got tired of the limelight and stopped performing on TV shows. Then he stopped touring. He still put out records but, without touring to support them, sales dwindled, and he soon drifted into obscurity until the record labels gave him a choice. Either get out on tour or get lost. So he got lost and only put out records under his own steam, as and when he felt like it. Even then, the records he released weren't anything like the hits he was known for. People loved his straight country rock. The new stuff was self-indulgent jazz noodling.'

'And your client has only just realised this now?'

'With no Jackson Gafferty tours, and the scarcity of releases, the client reluctantly gave up on Gafferty, ventured out into the world and set about making his fortune.'

'Just like that?' asked Dr. Sharma.

'Just like that,' answered Bellyana. 'It helped that an uncle left some money in his will for our client who was able to set some things up. He stumbled upon something that worked and didn't look back.'

'Until now.'

'He's sick. Worst case scenario, he's got five months, best case a year. He wants to hear some new Jackson Gafferty material before he dies.'

'If he's a multi-millionaire, can't he just pay Gafferty for a private session? And Gafferty must have some unused material lying about. Did he try that first instead of going through lawyers?'

'Apparently, he's not just doing this for himself, but all disgruntled Jackson Gafferty fans out there.'

'There's more than one?' laughed Dr. Sharma.

'He wants to use legal proceedings to force Jackson Gafferty into making new music. Specifically, music that will please him and that he thinks will please the other fans of, as he puts it, *genuine Jackson*.'

'But it sounds like if it wasn't for Gafferty ceasing operations, your client would have remained just going from gig to gig instead of starting up in business.'

'It doesn't matter to him. This must be what happens when power and self-pity combine. It's not about whether it makes sense. It's about what he wants.'

'But surely Gafferty could just say he's an artist and he has to, I don't know, *feel the vibe to deliver the groove, man*,' said Dr. Sharma with a smile. 'It's like using pressure and forcing someone to be creative. Surely that's why there are so many bad ads on TV.'

'We said that to him, and his words were,' at this point, Bellyana adopted an East End London accent. "I ain't asking for The Sistine bloody Chapel. All I bloody want is another Gafferty record before I pop me bleedin' clogs," before sipping her mulled wine and continuing in her normal voice. 'He feels that Gafferty supplied a legally available product that delivered emotional well-being and that users of this product were left to fend for themselves when Gafferty discontinued the line. As far as he can see, Gafferty was producing more than art. It was a service that Gafferty ceased to provide for no apparent physical reason. Gafferty has no ailments, and lives a life of moderate luxury. The client believes that the relevant materials should still be in place to allow Gafferty to continue making music.'

'Doesn't he get that this is music, not… I don't know, baby formula?' asked Dr. Sharma, as Bellyana laughed.

'Do you know how naive you sound?'

'I get that music is business, but from what you're saying about Gafferty, it sounds like he already made enough money and just wants to make music for his own pleasure. Doesn't your client understand that it's just about the music now for Gafferty? Would he be thinking like this if he was still a teenager?'

'Well, he's not a teenager. He's a music lover looking at things through the eyes of someone who has been in business for the last forty years.' Bellyana took another sip of her mulled wine which had now lost its heat. 'So, what's your weird story?'

'My story? Mine pales in comparison with yours.'

'Tell it.'

'Okay,' replied Dr. Sharma, adjusting himself on his kitchen stool. 'So, we have a patient, Ms Davies. Her son, Mr

Davies, always brings her in, helps her with medication and things like that.'

'How old is he?' asked Bellyana.

'Early forties. Anyway, everyone knows him. He's a bit of a character.'

'In what way?'

'Y'know, he gently flirts with the receptionists. He brings in chocolates, biscuits, fairy cakes for everyone when he comes in. That sort of person. Nice guy.'

'Okay.'

'So, as you know, I've only been at this practice for a few months, but apparently, every time he visits, he updates everyone on preparations for his wedding proposal .'

'He's asking someone to marry him,' surmised Bellyana.

'His girlfriend of the last ten years. They've had some problems, and he was worried that she might say no.'

'So what happened?' asked Bellyana, as someone stepped over their legs to get to the fridge.

'He'd always wanted to make the proposal as special and memorable as he could. Sounds like he spent a while working on it, plucking up the courage. So, in the last year, he's been putting his plans together.'

'What was his plan?'

'I'm getting to it. His plan was to propose in front of all their friends and family. Apparently, he worked his socks off coordinating everything so everyone would be in the same place at the same time. Las Vegas.'

'Vegas?' smiled Bellyana.

'Uh-huh. He booked the entire top floor of a hotel there for all friends and family. He hoped that she would say yes, and then, whilst on the emotional high, they would go for a shotgun wedding right there and then.'

'Wow.'

'Yeah, when you think about it, it's quite smart. The family and friends all paid for their own flights and hotel rooms. The bloke paid for him and his girlfriend's flight, their penthouse suite, and the relatively negligible wedding fee, so it was a wedding and honeymoon in one. As far as weddings go these days, it was a pretty cost-effective plan.'

'You had to do that, didn't you?' said Bellyana, with a knowing smile.

'What?' asked Dr. Sharma innocently.

'Take a charming idea and boil it down to the pounds and pence, or dollars and cents in this case.'

'Sorry. Anyway, they booked what she thought would be a straightforward holiday, and I imagine she was very happy and excited. According to the receptionists, the plan Davies outlined was that once they got to the hotel, they would check in, chill out and then go out to dinner. On their return, they would find their suite filled with family and friends. Once Mrs Davies-to-be had gotten over that particular shock, Mr Davies would then drop to his knee, pop out a ring and then pop the question right there in front of everyone.'

'So what actually happened?'

'Just that. They went to their room after dinner, found everyone there waiting for them. He led her through the crowd, out onto the balcony and asked her to marry him.'

'And? What did she say?'

'She said yes.'

'Okay. Nothing weird so far.'

'No. What is weird is what happened next.'

'What happened next?'

'I'm getting to it. Now, bear in mind that this guy was very worried about proposing to her in front of everyone they knew. He would always ask the receptionists: 'what if she says no in front of everyone? I'll be humiliated, and all these people will have come so far to see me humiliated."

'But if he was so worried, why ask in front of everyone?'

'Getting a no was a risk he was willing to take to make it special and more memorable than the average proposal. I imagine that's why he spent so long over it, plucking up the courage and making sure she would say yes. So he got down, she said yes, and he went wild with delight.'

'That's nice.'

'Brace yourself, Bell. What happened next, no one could have predicted. As far as we have gathered, he just went nuts with delight and sheer relief. He was on an emotional high, bouncing off the walls. Except that he was on a balcony.'

'Dev…'

'He was running around, hugging everyone, kissing his new fiancée, and then running around some more. What we think happened is that he was hit by the immense relief that came from having this huge weight of worry and expectation lifted from him, combined with the sheer joy that she said yes. The adrenaline of the situation sent him running round and round like a loon. He was jumping around, taking running jumps on to people, on to the outdoor furniture. People were starting to get anxious and, eventually, he took a running jump onto a chair, then onto the table, then off the balcony.'

Bellyana was stunned. 'He jumped off the balcony?'

'*Off* the balcony.'

'So…'

'He's dead.'

'Oh my God,' exclaimed Bellyana, bringing her hand to her mouth. 'But that's terrible.'

'I know, and now the travel insurance claims guys keep phoning up to ask us about his mental health, whether he was an alcoholic, and so forth.'

'I have no idea what to say to that.'

'Well, they can't figure out whether it's suicide or misadventure. I suppose it's bizarre to them because no one willingly jumps from a building unless it's a suicide, or maybe they were under the influence of something. Of course, everyone knew they were there for a marriage proposal, so people took photos and filmed the whole thing. According to the woman from the insurance company, it looks like he just took a running jump straight off the building.'

'No. I mean, I have no idea what to say to the whole story. It's so sad. Poor Mum. Who's going to take her to the doctor's now?'

'I know, but think of the girlfriend. She was someone's fiancée for all of five minutes before he went berserk and jumped off a building. What a story she has to tell.'

# 19. Anything, anywhere, anytime

'I remember when I was small, my father told me a story that he called Tearstones,' began Katie.

'Tear stones? That sounds like something that wouldn't be pleasant. Is that like trampling or something?' asked Dr. Sharma, playfully, settling into his usual chair and getting out his notebook.

'Not tear stones. *Tearstones.*'

'Are you going to tell me the story?' asked Dr. Sharma.

'I can if you want,' replied Katie, smiling sweetly. She was beginning to enjoy Dr. Sharma's visits and was intrigued by the directions their conversations would take. She usually kept her father to herself, but she found herself sharing this with Dr. Sharma, despite herself.

'Sure,' invited Dr. Sharma.

'Tearstones is the story of a man, or a woman if you like. Dad always told it to me with a man. So this man was very sad. He lived in a very sad town in a very sad country.'

'Why were they sad?' asked Dr. Sharma.

'I don't know, I was small. Dad didn't say. Maybe they were poor, maybe there weren't many jobs going. Maybe the weather was shit,' laughed Katie.

Dr. Sharma smiled. 'Okay.'

'So this man lives in a very sad place. Some of the people are not only sad, but they're frustrated and angry as well. They know that things are not good and that they should be better. Somehow, as sad as everyone is, this one man is more miserable than them all, or at least he is the only one that lets it out. Each night when he goes to bed, he cries alone. He lies flat on his back, and despite his eyes being shut tight, the tears slowly seep out and roll down the sides of his head.

'One morning, the man wakes up and feels something at the corners of each of his eyes. He feels around and finds these small bobbly marbles. The man gets up and looks in the mirror. He sees these cloudy blobs at the corners of his eyes. He touches them, and they feel firm. His tears have come together. Bonded. Like tiny drops of glue. One tear had rolled onto another, and they had all dried together into these concentrated little stones.

'The man goes about his days, and at night he thinks his sad thoughts and cries his tears. The days, nights, weeks and months go by and the stones grow and grow. Soon they were as big as plums. Spanish plums, not our weedy ones. They were clamped to the sides of his head, impossible for him to remove.

'In the street, people laugh and point at him. In the pubs, he's beaten up by other men and women, drinking to ignore their sadness. They don't want him reminding them how bad things are, and they... resent how he can show his true feelings so easily. He doesn't have to hide it. He couldn't even if he tried. They punch him, and kick him, and shout: "what makes you so special? Who do you think you are?"'

'Katie, this story is a real buzzkill,' teased Dr. Sharma, an apprehensive smile on his lips.

'Dev, it's only a story. Anyway, eventually the man moves away to another town, another country, wherever, it doesn't matter. What matters is that things aren't so sad anymore. He feels better. The sadness goes away. Maybe he meets someone, and they fall in love, get married, have a family. The sadness the man felt disappears completely, and it's replaced by happiness. It's been years since he last cried, but the tearstones remain to remind him of how sad he used to be and not to take happiness for granted.'

'Your dad used to tell you that story?' asked Dr. Sharma, with a look of disbelief.

'Yeah. I don't remember if he told me it loads of times, or just the once, but for some reason, I clearly remember him telling me the story.'

'Did he make it up, or did he hear it somewhere?'

'Dunno. Did your Dad ever tell you stories?'

'I only remember him telling me a story once.'

'Okay, let's hear it.'

'It wasn't even a story. It was more like… well, almost a superstition. At the time, I didn't know what he was talking about. I remember thinking I was too old for him to be telling me stories. Do you know what I mean? Especially this. And it wasn't even a typical storytelling type of situation. We were driving somewhere. I don't remember where, but we were driving, and I remember him suddenly starting to tell me about these ghosts or spirits or something.' Dr. Sharma stopped as he thought back to the story.

'Well? Go on then,' prompted Katie.

'He just started telling me about these malevolent spirits that can take over a person when they're not looking out. He told me that if someone you know starts acting strangely, out of character, doing things they wouldn't normally do, it's not always their fault. It's just that some outside force has taken over their body, mind, and thoughts.

'He kept telling me that the person was not to blame and that it happens to everyone at some point in their lives. Their mind and body fall under the influence of some other power, and that person we know can vanish for a while, but they come back. Dad told me that it might seem like a long time to us, but in the bigger picture, it was the blink of an eye that they were gone. A millisecond. So really, it wasn't such a big deal.'

'That's a weird story.'

'Like I said, I don't think it was a story. Probably just trying to scare me into being good. If not that, then I don't know why. Just a stupid story.'

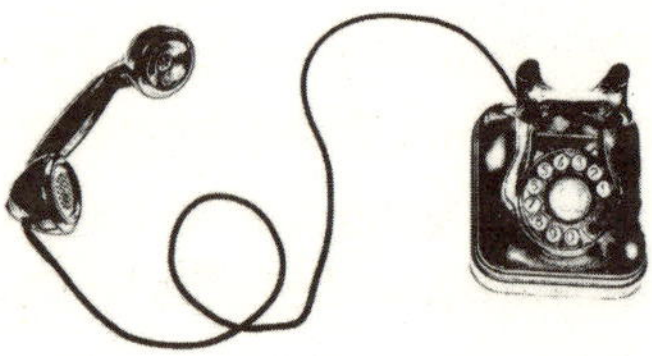

'But it's the story of my life,' pleads Luca, in his distinctive Argentinian accent, as he stares out of the dusty window.

'I don't care if it's the greatest story ever. If everyone already has it, they're not going to buy it. Are they?' asks the voice from the telephone in Luca's dining room, which also doubles as his office.

'But this… this is art,' tries Luca. He rises slightly from his seat as though leaning over to someone across the table. Luca has no idea what is going on anymore. Yes, he is an old man, but he doesn't remember his father dealing with such things. Then again, his father hadn't gone on to become a world-renowned chef who commanded astronomical fees to create dinners for the rich and powerful, the famous and infamous alike.

'They're the memoirs of a former celebrity chef. Not really art,' replies the voice of his literary agent.

'I am not former anything. I am still here. You weren't talking this way to me a week ago. A week ago, I had respect,' Luca spits at the phone.

'A week ago, we were publishing the previously *untold* story of the rise and rise of the great chef Luca Moretti, in his own words. This week we have nothing.'

'But I don't understand why we have nothing.'

'I've told you. Everyone knows the story. They didn't know it last week. This week they know it. Not just little bits, like where you were born or where you went to culinary school. They know the whole story. Inside out. They know exactly what you and your ghost-writer wrote, word for word. I know the whole thing, and I never even read the book. How did this happen?'

'You did read it. That's how it happened.'

'Are you kidding me? I can recite the whole thing word for word. Everyone can. People who haven't even read it can recite the whole thing. Now you tell me why would anyone buy a biography when they already have the entire manuscript lodged in their memory?'

'I will sue you,' wobbles Luca's voice as he steadies himself, placing a hand on the back of a chair as he shuffles around the table to begin pacing.

The voice laughs. 'What are you going to sue us for?'

'You let miscreants have my book, and now they've revealed it to everyone,' cries Luca, his pacing instinctively leading him to the kitchen. He seethes at the injustice of it all, his final shot at redemption cruelly snatched away from him and turned into a joke.

'And had everyone on the planet learn it word for word? How does that even happen? The world has gone insane. You're just another victim.' The man behind the voice decides to employ a gentler tone. 'Luca, I know you're upset, and I agree with you that this is clearly wrong, but we didn't do this. This is something weird. I'm telling you, you can pull anyone off the street, and they will be able to recite your autobiography in its entirety, down to the last word.'

In the cramped kitchen of his old family home, Luca sinks slowly onto a chair against the wall and leans his head back. His family had eventually moved there from the slum when he was ten. They had had the money to buy the small house, rarely the funds to fix anything that broke, never enough to refresh the fading and flaking paint. He feels the cool, hard wall against the back of his bald head and feels everything slipping away from him.

It was the same feeling he had when he realised that his career as a working chef was over. The voice comes back into focus. 'I sympathise with you, Luca. This is a terrible situation. I know how much you were counting on this, but as things stand, we cannot publish your memoirs. Fuck, if this keeps happening, no one will be publishing anything anymore. We'll all be out of a job, Luca.'

'This was not my fault,' states Luca quietly. 'These are my memoirs, my memories, this is my story, my life. This is *my* life. No two lives on the whole planet are the same, and this one is mine. Now you are telling me that you cannot help me because my life has no value?'

'At the moment, there is no way we can market your book and make it appeal to people in a way that they would spend money on it. Your story is already out there, and people know it. It's like it has been programmed into all our brains overnight. In that way, no, it has no value to me. Don't think of your memoirs as your life. Try to understand that it is like an album, or a computer game, or a movie. It has been leaked, and somehow everyone has a copy of it. I don't know why this has happened and, no offence, but I don't know why it would have happened to your memoirs. I mean, why not *War and Peace*? Or Shakespeare's sonnets? Luca? Mr Moretti, are you still there?'

'You said, "don't think of your memoirs as your life," but that is my life, my name, my memories are the only things of value that I still have. I have prepared dishes for the most powerful, important and wealthiest people on the planet. In my restaurants, I created flavours and textures that no one else had ever imagined. The aromas that disappear in the air, the sensations that linger on the tongue, and the beautiful desserts constructed with genuine love and designed to bring wonder and delight to people. People who couldn't possibly hope to do this themselves. Do you know what that is?'

'I don't understand.'

'I was born into very humble beginnings.'

'I know.'

'I was penniless growing up. Every day was an immense struggle. Such a struggle that I sometimes wondered whether any of it was actually worthwhile. In the end, what was I living for? One day I told my father this, and do you know what he did?'

'It's in your book, Luca. He slapped you.'

'He slapped me. Then he said, "all of life is a struggle. One hundred per cent a struggle. A lot of it is pain, but some of it is pleasure. You have to struggle through the pain so you can continue struggling towards the pleasure." So then I said, "which part of my life is pleasure then?" He replied, "you struggle through the pain of the day, don't you? Then in the evening, you eat. And when you eat, isn't that pleasure?" All I could do was nod because eating *was* pleasure. He said: "if there is no pain, there would be only pleasure and then how would you know that it was pleasure?"

'When people come to me, the aroma, the sight, the taste of what I have created changes their faces. For a little while, they are taken elsewhere. No matter how old they are, they instantly become small children at the fair again for the first time. They forget about everything else and focus only on what is on their plate and in their mouth. Do you know what it is for a Buenos Aires slum boy to give pleasure, that kind of pleasure that turns these important people, these politicians, these presidents, those beautiful movie stars, into small children again? Do you know what kind of power that is?'

'No. I don't,' comes the reply.

'But it all disappears. The ideas, the combinations, the balance of flavours, it all disappears in the end. It dissolves on the tongue, and nothing is left to show that it ever existed, that this pleasure was real. For once, I wanted to create something permanent, something that wouldn't be erased. I don't know what has happened. It doesn't matter to me. All I know is that another thing that I have created has disappeared. But in this case, I don't know if it gave them pleasure or not. People did not choose to go out and buy my memoirs. They just woke up with it. What does that mean? There is all this weird shit going on, and now this. Why has my life been given away like this? Like everyone has a right to it. Like water or air. What would you say to me if I told you that everyone suddenly knew everything about your life?'

Luca holds the receiver, waiting for a response, but the voice doesn't answer. Eventually, he hears the tone of the dead line as it stretches away from the earpiece into the space before him. Luca watches with old, watery eyes as the solid blue light of DeadTone flows away from him and ripples over to the closed window, wraps itself around the handle and jerks to reveal an opening to the world outside. Through the opening, DeadTone meanders beyond the confines of the building, beyond the telephone lines, beyond the hairy ears and frayed brains that translate its existence.

No connection.

Luca simply stares after DeadTone, unable to decide what to do next. What is it? Is it alive? Should he place the receiver back on the hook? Would that leave DeadTone dead? Or would that allow them to roam free like a homeless kite on the wind? At this point, the situation becomes more confusing to Luca as his phone cuts off DeadTone to emit its own tone, admonishing Luca for leaving it off the hook for too long. Frayed like the end of a rope, the back end of DeadTone wriggles through the window before ReceiverBeeper chases after them a few seconds later.

Luca stares after ReceiverBeeper for a few seconds before deciding: *enough*. Having had enough of everyone and everything, he wanders through to the living room and grabs the telephone base unit before yanking the phone line from the wall. Shuffling across the room to the window, Luca stares out after the two squiggles playfully chasing each other into the distance.

The two tones roam free across the land, through the polluted city, along the wind, out of the urban areas, to a rural region, amongst the trees, confusing people and animals alike as they breathlessly zoom by, emitting their squalls of sound and light. DeadTone and ReceiverBeeper wriggle after one another through parks and towns, around corners and under bridges, exploring and tasting everywhere they go. Nothing is too far or too high for them. Instead of baulking at challenging terrain, they thrive on it. Finally, free from their constraints, the pair want not to be bound. Not by space, not by time.

# 20. Glass feet

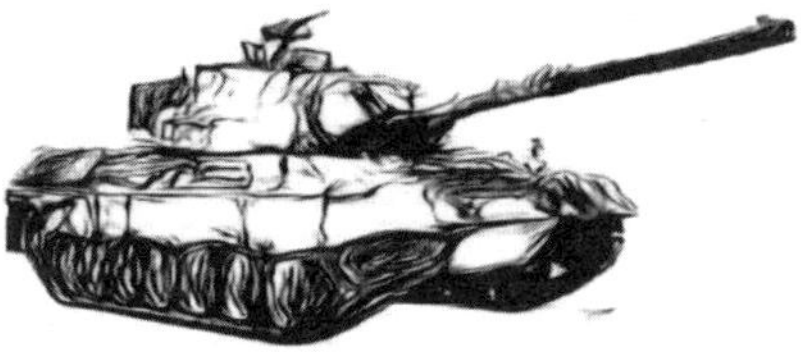

'What time are the Canadians going to arrive?' Amina asked.

'Around 5 pm,' replied Serena. 'And stop calling them *the Canadians*. Be nice to them. They're here for only a week before they go to visit Vijay's family.'

The Canadian lineup consisted of Serena's sister, Seeva, her husband, Vijay, and their daughters, Jessie and Abigail. Dev was excited because he didn't remember meeting them before. And because he generally found everything exciting. The last time they had visited was five years ago, and he was too young to remember the event.

Raju was the only one to fetch them from the airport so they and their luggage would all fit in the minivan he had borrowed from his friend, Henry. As the vehicle pulled up outside the house, at the kerb beyond the front garden, Dev jumped off the sofa by the window shouting, 'they're here!' He ran to the front door, where he came to a stop, hopping from foot to foot, unable to open it without permission.

'They're here, Mum, they're here!' He shouted up the stairs.

'Okay, okay, I'm coming,' called Serena, smoothing down her top and running a hand through her hair. 'Amina, open the door for your brother before he explodes, will you?'

'Okay,' called Amina, as she sauntered over to the door.

'Open the door, Mina,' implored Dev, jumping up and down.

'Can't open it if you don't move. Or do you want me to hit you with it?' replied Amina irritably.

Seeing her logic, Dev obediently stepped aside, and Amina opened the door on Raju and Vijay, lifting luggage from the back of the van while Seeva, Jessie and Abigail made their way along the short garden path.

'Hi, Amina! Gosh, you're growing into such a beauty,' said Seeva, leaning forward for a hug and kisses.

'Hi, Auntie Seeva. Nice to see you. How was your journey?'

'It was fine, thanks. Girls, say hello to your cousins. Oh, look at little Dev! He's grown up so much since the last time I saw him.'

'Hi Auntie,' said Dev, receiving a hug and a kiss.

'Hey,' said Jessie and Abigail airily.

'Hi,' said Amina, 'nice to see you all.'

That evening a lot of chatting went on as the adults caught up and discussed the successes, failures and general lives of other relatives. In particular, Serena and Seeva's sister, Saarika.

'I do feel bad that she is completely alone in Marseille now,' said Seeva.

'I think she should just be grateful there are no children involved,' said Vijay.

'You would say that.'

'But at least it's a clean break. She'll never have to see the guy again.'

'She doesn't have to stay in France either,' said Serena.

'That's right. She could go back to Mauritius,' added Raju.

'Or she could move to England and be near us,' suggested Serena.

Vijay and Seeva exchanged glances.

'Yeah,' Raju agreed, reluctantly.

'You don't sound convinced, Raju,' said Seeva with a smile. Vijay laughed in agreement with his wife, and also to break the tension.

'Well,' began Raju with a guilty smile, 'she is a little... needy.'

'Everyone is from time to time,' said Serena, 'you would be too if you just got divorced.'

'No, she's always been like that. She's always trying to convince everyone that she feels things more than anyone else, that what she is facing is somehow bigger.'

'But she's on her own,' insisted Serena.

'I think Raju is right. She has always been like that,' said Vijay.

'Anything new from Mauritius?' asked Seeva, tactfully changing the topic.

'No. I phoned last week. Sachin is still building the upper floor on his own, brick by brick,' replied Serena.

'He was building it when you were over there, wasn't he? When was that?'

'About... six months ago. He seems to spend ten minutes putting up three bricks and then spends an hour drinking three bottles of beer. By brick seven, the only thing he's good for is sleeping,' laughed Serena.

'Well, who wants to be building on a day off?' asked Raju. 'Work hard all week, and then you're still working when you should be relaxing. Especially in that heat.'

'Then he should have thought of that and not started it in the first place,' replied Serena. 'It's an eyesore.'

'It's an investment. He's trying to do the right thing,' said Vijay. 'Or maybe he's started something he doesn't know how to finish,' he wondered aloud.

'Well, never mind all that. What do you want to do tomorrow?' asked Serena.

Vijay looked at Seeva. 'What do you suggest?' she asked. 'We had a long journey, so maybe not too much?'

'Don't you want to do London? It's only an hour on the train from here. It's no trouble. We've taken the week off.'

'Oh, we're not staying for the whole week,' said Vijay.

'Really? I thought you were,' said Raju.

Vijay looked again to Seeva. 'We'll stay a few days if that's okay, but I think Jessie and Abigail are keen to head to Vijay's family in Liverpool,' he said.

'They've been listening to The Beatles a lot,' explained Seeva.

'Oh, really?' said Raju, turning his attention to the living room where the children were playing video games. 'Abigail? Jessie? Serena loves The Beatles. I was always more of a Stones fan. Which one is your favourite Beatle?' he asked.

'Um,' began Jessie, looking at her parents, before answering hopefully, 'the one from Liverpool?'

The next day everyone piled into Henry's minivan, and Raju drove them to the Warfare Museum where Dev, fascinated by everything he saw, touched and climbed on, ran around the displays as the families tracked the progress of weaponry from sticks and spears through to jump jets and stealth aircraft.

'So why are they going so soon?' Amina asked moodily.

'Oh, you know how those two girls are. They always think they're better than everyone else. I don't know how Seeva could have raised them that way.'

Amina was both disappointed and relieved that they were leaving so soon. She had always sought the approval of her older female cousins, but now she didn't want them to know it. Subconsciously she had hoped that it would simply happen organically, that Jessie and Abigail would one day visit and realise that she was an equal, worth being friends with. As teenagers, Amina feared they still held the impression she had given five years ago as a small child, desperate to form part of their clique.

As the visit to the museum continued, Jessie and Abigail seemed to loosen up, and their moodiness dissipated. They even joined Dev in clambering about on the old tanks while Amina watched from the ground, not knowing whether doing likewise would curry favour with Jessie and Abigail or if she would come across as childish as Dev.

A couple of days later, *the Canadians* left, and Amina went back to see her friends whom she had foregone out of politeness to the visitors.

# 21. Oh?

Yeah, my hair always looks this good!

After the visit from *the Canadians,* it was apparent that the shift in Amina's attitude was persisting. The moodiness Raju, Serena and Dev had perceived in Amina was extending beyond the departure of Seeva and her family. Raju and Serena explained it to themselves as *the teenage years* and thought little more of it.

ReceiverBeeper and DeadTone stopped when they got to the kitchen window, which looked out over the back garden. There they spent a few moments watching Raju and Serena washing the dishes.

'We weren't so moody when we were teenagers, were we?' Serena asked her husband.

'It's different here,' said Raju.

'But why? Everyone at work talks about the teenage years as if we should be expecting the apocalypse or something.'

'Discipline,' said Raju, simply. 'At home, they wouldn't tolerate the stuff teenagers here get up to. Over there, it's *all* about the family. Over here, they're encouraged to be individuals, see themselves outside of their family.'

'Do you think so?'

'I don't know. We need to find a way to communicate, blend our culture with theirs. We'll need to talk with them. Or at least we need to talk to Amina first.'

'We've already been letting her go out to that youth club, like all the other children.'

'She says that's what they all do.'

'That Ayesha and Sadie, they don't come here at all anymore.'

'I suppose they don't have to if they see her at the youth club. They don't want to be with parents. Parents are embarrassing here.'

'It was good when they came to eat.'

'It's not our job to feed them.'

'No, but we got a picture of who Mina is friends with and what's going on.'

'Maybe you should tell Amina to invite them.'

'Maybe.'

Aged twelve, Amina's priorities changed, as is usually the case with puberty. When she turned thirteen, she repeatedly tried to discuss and renegotiate the matter of Mauritian dinners with Raju and Serena.

'Maybe we could have more English meals?' she asked.

'We have plenty of those,' replied Serena.

'Then maybe we could reduce the spiciness of the Mauritian stuff.'

'Why? Don't you like it? You used to like it.'

'Some people at school said they could smell it,' admitted

Amina quietly.

'Which of your friends said that? It's that *Ayesha*, isn't it?' suspected Serena.

'It's not anyone you know.'

'I thought I knew all your friends.'

'They're not friends exactly.'

'If they're not friends, why do you care if they think you smell?'

'They didn't say I smell. They said I smell like Indian food. Spicy,' Amina clarified.

'Well, it's good to be yourself.'

'Smelling like Indian food all the time doesn't make me *me*.'

'I still like your food, mum,' chirped Dev.

Dev and his parents coped well with most of the changes that occurred. Serena and Raju privately discussed and openly adapted to the changes happening within Amina, her body, her mind. Their relationship with her was evolving, and her relationship with Dev was also going through some subtle adjustments. One of the changes he initially found difficult to reconcile was how she spent less time with him. Suddenly it seemed Amina had a third element to her life. In addition to her home and school life, she also had extra time with her friends from school that occurred at times that broke up their home life. From what Dev could gather, this now daily habit consisted solely of going out to the local youth club with other children of similar ages in the area.

Raju and Serena tried to be mindful of their daughter's developing needs, as well as their own instinct to provide her with the same boundary-ridden upbringing that they had had at her age in Mauritius. Despite their best intentions, the situation seemed to get away from Raju and Serena, leaving them without clearly enforced decisions. How to marry the values and priorities espoused by the upbringing in one culture to those of another culture?

Further complicating matters for Raju and Serena was the exclusive nature of the adolescent world, one of the oldest examples of a *catch-22* situation. Let's break it down:

No longer keyed into the latest adolescent mindset they wish to understand, the parents find it challenging to connect with and nurture their adolescent. Their only conduit to this would be the adolescent themself. Unfortunately, the one they seek to nurture will not openly communicate their thoughts due to the guarded nature of the adolescent mind. Surely this cycle of disappointment must have been represented on cave walls at one point or another. Right?

With no clear path to understanding how they might imbue Amina with the cultural beliefs they grew up with, without alienating her, Raju and Serena settled for the alternative approach. They waited for Amina to ask something of them or do something that they found unacceptable before adjusting or reinforcing a boundary, as necessary.

Knee-length skirts at school were acceptable.

Going out with her friends after school was allowed.

Makeup at school was unacceptable.

A little nail varnish when out with her friends was fine.

Boyfriends were generally acceptable under certain conditions but would be decided on a boy by boy basis.

Dressing, or acting a certain way, to attract boys was in no way, shape or form ever going to fly.

After much deliberation, it was eventually agreed that, in the summer holidays, 17:00 would be the time they would expect thirteen-year-old Amina home from being with her friends. Initially, Dev feared Amina had found other people she liked more than him. But after bringing up this slight with Amina, she convinced him he was the best company anyone could hope to have. Satisfied, he quickly resumed his spot on Team Amina and helped cover for her late arrivals: 'she called to say she'd be late. I forgot to give the message. Sorry.'

Dev was convinced his input worked every time, but the reality was it just gave his parents a convenient loophole for them to not have to admonish her for being late. It was a convenient lie they could all pretend to believe, and Raju and Serena wouldn't have to face the unpleasant task of finely judging the balance of their anger versus disappointment.

Anger could either: scare her into getting home on time.

Or: push her away, encouraging her to do worse.

Disappointment could either: shame her into getting home on time.

Or: … they could never think of an adverse effect of expressing disappointment, so they applied this liberally whenever in doubt.

Sometimes Amina's friends would come by, and they would all have dinner.

'Can you pass me the salad, please, Mum?' asked Amina on

one of these nights.

'Here you go, sweetie,' said Serena, passing the bowl. At the end of the table, Ayesha and Sadie exchanged glances and smirked at: '*sweetie*'.

'Why didn't you ask in Creole?' asked Dev in the blunt words typical for a nine-year-old.

'Never mind, Dev,' said Amina quickly.

'What did he say?' asked Ayesha.

'Nothing.'

'I said, why didn't she ask in Creole. She always speaks in Creole to Mum and Dad,' explained Dev.

'What's *Creole*?' asked Ayesha.

'That's our native language,' explained Raju.

'Oh. Aren't you all from Mauritius? Don't you speak Mauritian?' asked Ayesha, bemused.

'There is no formal language called Mauritian. The common language of Mauritius is Creole.'

'Or *Patois*,' chimed in Serena.

'Is that another language?' asked Sadie. 'How many languages do you speak, Amina?'

'Just English.'

'You speak Creole too,' corrected Dev.

'I understand a tiny bit, and Creole isn't even a language,' replied Amina.

'If that's what all Mauritians speak, how come it's not a language?' asked Ayesha.

'That's not the official language of Mauritius. The official language is English,' explained Amina, the blood rushing to her cheeks.

'I thought it was French,' said Serena. 'Everything is in

French in Mauritius. Except for English classes.'

'French!' blurted Ayesha, finding it incomprehensible that another language was throwing its hat into the conversation.

'Officially, it's English, but more people speak French,' explained Raju. 'Mauritius was once a French colony. Before that, it was Dutch, I think.'

'Before the British attacked the French and the island became a British colony,' added Serena.

'That's why the official language of Mauritius is *English*,' insisted Amina.

'Even though everyone speaks this… *Klingon*?' asked Sadie.

'Creole,' reminded Serena, 'or Patois.'

'Which is derived from French,' said Raju.

'Does everyone there speak English then?' asked Ayesha.

'No,' replied Raju.

'So more people there speak Creole than English?'

'More people there speak Creole than French, and more people speak French than English.'

'Then why isn't the official language Creole?'

'Because, I suppose, the language hasn't been… formalised.'

'What does that mean?' asked Ayesha.

Raju and Serena exchanged glances before Serena answered: 'It's not something you can really teach. For example, the spelling of words hasn't been settled, so there isn't a set way of writing it. That means it can't be used for official government papers and things like that.'

'So,' began Dev, apparently piqued that no one had answered his original question, 'why don't you speak Creole when your friends come?'

Everyone just looked at him in silence for a few moments until Raju spoke. 'Because, when in the company of others, it's rude to speak a language they do not understand, Dev.'

'Oh. Okay,' accepted Dev, satisfied.

Amina was discovering how the friends she had grown up with would digest the differences between them, now that they were getting older and understood that they were separated by more than skin colour. On the surface, at the dinner table, it didn't seem to make any difference to Ayesha and Sadie, but Amina and her friends were getting older, and puberty meant that relationships were changing. With this process came the evolving, complicated dynamics of inter-female relationships that coloured the way they perceived one another and the social hierarchy of their group. The need to successfully forge connections outside of immediate family and simultaneously express individuality while also belonging to a social group grew. So too, was the need to know themselves and establish their identity to take them through the imminent changes.

In short, status mattered.

Dev would never know the internal conflicts that Amina had battled. To him, her story would be forever incomplete. He could only guess what had happened.

He remembers her spending more time at the youth club.

He remembers her school work declining.

He remembers her staying out later and not hearing her voice as much when she was around.

He remembers hearing her crying in the night.

He remembers thinking she didn't want to be there

anymore, that she no longer wanted their Mauritian family. Wounded by the rejection, he didn't know what to say.

So he said nothing.

# 22. Now that's entertainment!

DeadTone and ReceiverBeeper couldn't contain themselves for long and were soon bounding away. Before long DeadTone and ReceiverBeeper came to the house of Mira Cassavetes. There they stopped for a while and keenly watched Dr. Sharma, through the window, talking to Mira in another session. They followed the to and fro for a short time but soon grew bored and set off again, chasing after one another. Meanwhile, inside the house, Dr. Sharma was still trying to bring Mira to offer her thoughts.

'Don't you get interviewed… for marketing and publicity, when you do the films?' asked Dr. Sharma.

'Not interviewed. More like reading a script. I know what they want to hear, and I just say it,' replied Mira coolly. This time, aware of Dr. Sharma's agenda, she was dressed a little more appropriately for his visit. The black jeans and top hugged tightly over her body while her bare toes tapped the carpet in front of her chair.

'I just want to hear what you think.'

‘I’m not the only one you’re talking to. Get what you need from one of them.’

‘There is just one other lady.’

‘Are you patronising me?’

‘What?’

‘Lady. Do you think saying *lady* will make me like you? Or are you having a laugh? I’m not a lady. I’m a whore. I let men piss inside my mouth for money. How does that make me a lady?’

‘Why are you always so angry? Isn’t it exhausting to always be so angry?’

‘I’m not always angry. I’m just always angry at you.’

‘There’s no reason for you to be angry with me. All I want is to hear from you in your own words.’

‘And I’m telling you I don’t talk about it.’

‘Why not?’

‘Because it’s… annoying. You’re annoying. Are we going to fuck or not?’

‘I’m not here to fuck.’

‘Well, I am, fucking is what I am here for. So how about it, this time?’

Dr. Sharma looked away from her to the framed painting on the wall. It was a watercolour of what appeared to be a wheatfield with trees in the distance and a church spire. He was not yet ready to admit his reasons for persisting with Mira, someone who was clearly unwilling to cooperate with him. He didn’t want to admit it to himself – perhaps he didn’t even realise – that he was drawn to unyielding women. However, there were other reasons for him to press on with Mira. He had unconsciously sensed something about her.

The seconds ticked by as Dr. Sharma stared at the painting, playing for time, probing his mind for a way to get her talking. *Keep talking, and something will happen, you'll find something*, he thought to himself.

'Okay. What shall we do?' he asked.

'Yeah?' asked Mira, seeking a solid commitment.

'I came to talk, but you don't want to, so I might as well make the most of my money and time. If we're not going to talk at all, let's fuck.'

'That's more like it. Anything. What are you in the mood for?'

'You'll do anything?'

'Within reason.'

Dr. Sharma smiled. 'Define *reason*.'

'Well, you know what I do. That's why you came to me, right?'

'That's when I was looking to talk. As you pointed out, talking and fucking are two different things. So why don't you tell me what's on the menu, and then I'll pick what I want to do.'

'Do you have your phone?'

'It's in my pocket.'

'Get it out.'

'Why?'

'So you can look it up and read what I do,' replied Mira, her smile instantly evaporating, 'because I am not talking to you about what I do. Did you think you were clever?'

Taking a deep mental breath, Dr. Sharma persevered. 'Pissing on you,' he ventured, with deliberate crudeness. 'What's the process involved there? If I wanted to take a piss on you, how do we do it?' These were not words that Dr. Sharma ever imagined he would say to another human being, but there he was. He wouldn't admit it, but something was refreshing and liberating, to put that crudeness into words and say them to another person.

'Firstly, if somebody wants to do that, they need to drink a fair amount of water. At least a litre. Have you done that? Because otherwise, there's no point continuing the conversation.'

'Let's say I have,' tried Dr. Sharma.

'You either have, or you haven't. I'm only talking to you about what you want to do right now.'

'Okay, I have. So what is the order of things?'

'That's up to you. You tell me what you want to do. We can have sex, then the pee. Or the other way around. Or we can stop for you to pee. It really depends on what you like about piss play. Why you're into it. The sensation of holding it in? Watching someone drink it? We can do it here. I just need to put some towels down.'

'When was your first time doing it?'

'Are you asking me as a punter or as a nosey-parker?' asked Mira.

'As someone who wants to know your thoughts on the whole thing.'

'Then what do you think my answer will be?'

'So, if I was asking as a punter, you'd give me a straight answer?'

'I would give you the answer you want to hear,' replied Mira knowingly.

'What does that mean?'

'Different people want different things. You know what already.'

'So you try to accommodate what you think the person at the time wants to hear?'

'Surely that's not a surprise, is it?' replied Mira in exasperation.

'Why do you do this?' asked Dr. Sharma finally.

'I've answered that already, haven't I?' Mira replied sharply.

Sensing he was making progress, Dr. Sharma pushed on. 'I don't think you have. You can do other things. Why do you choose this?'

'Because, with normal people,' Mira emphasised, 'not you,' she added for good measure, 'I enjoy it. What do you do that's so special?'

'It's not special, but I'm a doctor.'

'How can you enjoy that? Listening to everyone bitch and moan about their aches, pains and sniffles? Why do you do that? Is that what you want me to do? Tell you all about how I can't wait to get out of this work and that all the men I see use me up and then toss me aside?' Mira sat back in her armchair. 'They don't use me, *Doctor*. I use them. Maybe it sounds like a cliché, but, for me, it's true. Your question? Why do I do this? That's what I want to know about you.' Mira leaned forward, her eyes stabbing at Dr. Sharma's.

'Actually, I want to talk about what you think of the men that see you. Why do you think men pay to urinate on you? Why do you think groups of men, strangers to each other, pay for the opportunity to watch each other having sex with you and wait for their turn? What do you think they get out of it that they don't get through more conventional practices?

What's the difference between doing this with men off the street and the guys on the film set?'

'How about you?' Mira finally gave up the armchair altogether and got up to look down at Dr. Sharma. 'What is your problem that you need to know all this stuff? As if it's any of your business. It's not. People like what they like, and sometimes there are people, like me, who humour them just for the cash, or because we get a kick out of it too. I don't ask them why they enjoy it. I bet there isn't a girl out there that does ask. Fucking is fun. When you ask questions like that, it's not fun anymore. The more normal something becomes, the less exciting it is. Like shagging grannies, or something, it's something you're not supposed to do, and that makes people want to do it even more. It's not rocket science. Pissing on someone is not something you're supposed to do. That's what I think. Is that so difficult to understand?'

'It feels like there's more,' was all Dr. Sharma managed in return. He found Mira's sudden bursts of free-flowing speech unnerving, almost as unnerving as her curt answers.

'My theory, *Doctor*, is the more we know about what folks do behind closed doors, the more normal it all becomes, and some of us begin looking further for what's still taboo, still dangerous.'

'The danger, it's exciting?'

'I like different things. All the time. I can't let myself get bored. I always need something new, you know? A piercing or a tattoo. Next year I'm going to Germany for another boob job. Doing another few films while I'm there, having some time off too. Even when I'm making those films, it's always under the condition that we're doing something new for me.

Ten blokes instead of five, or a glory hole, something like that. As an escort, not knowing who you'll meet and what they'll want makes it exciting as well. When a group of blokes come to the hotel for a session, there's no real danger because Ed is there to take money and look out for trouble. *You* know that, don't you?' Mira shot, looking directly at Dr. Sharma. He didn't reply and instead looked back at her, impassively. 'That's where I first saw you, wasn't it?'

'You remember,' stated Dr. Sharma, genuinely surprised but not letting it show.

'Yeah. Around the kind of people normally there, you do stick out in the memory a bit.'

'I thought you'd have forgotten since you were so busy.'

'You just sat there watching, didn't you. You didn't even get your cock out, didn't come over to fuck, didn't even get a blowie. You sat at the back, watching everyone else. You waited for most of them to finish before you left. You waited even when some of them had already gone. Were you just there to see me in action before coming for a one on one?'

'I was there to watch everyone else,' replied Dr. Sharma.

'You could have bought one of my films. Would have been much cheaper.'

'It's not the same. That's a film set with pornstars. I wanted to watch regular people. I wanted to hear what they had to say to you, see how they treated you. I thought it would be like… like when you talk to a drunk person and they tell you how they really feel.'

'So?' asked Mira. 'How was it for you?'

'Surprising,' Dr Sharma answered simply.

'Yeah, it is that… I remember my first one.'

'I bet it's difficult to forget.'

'I was exhausted by the time the last one had finished. And then, to my surprise, I found the first one was ready to go again.'

Assiduous about his research, Dr. Sharma also kept a journal to document his personal thoughts. His entry for the experience reads like this:

> *The minder asked me a few questions, satisfying himself that i wasn't a troublemaker before he let me into the bedroom of the hotel suite where the action would be taking place. A few other blokes were already standing around, having a laugh amongst themselves. They eyeballed me as i walked in. Staring. Evaluating. Some were dressed casually in jeans and T-shirts, others in shirtsleeves and suit jackets. They all looked as though they had dropped in on the way home from work. Only instead of drinking a pint, they would be fucking a pornstar.*
>
> *i wondered if they were as nervous as i was. i don't even know why i was nervous. i knew i wouldn't be doing anything. i must have looked strange because one of the punters leant over to me and asked if the bouncer had given me hassle. He told me*

not to worry about it, that the minder always does that to newcomers and that i would soon be coming back for more of her. The others laughed in agreement when they heard this.

Mira charges £500 per person to meet at a four-star hotel in Central London. i was the fifth to arrive. We were soon joined by another two. One of the guys popped a pill as the minder came to say we were waiting for three more before starting. The event was due to begin at 7 pm and it was already 7:18 pm at that point.

The men were all different ages, different races. One or two of them – obviously the most seasoned of the lot – were already beginning to touch and rub themselves over their clothes in anticipation. i guess appearances and any semblance of decorum matter less with advancing years. Or maybe there's no place for decorum in a situation like this.

The hotel linen, blankets and pillows had been removed from the double bed. In their place, clear plastic sheeting covered the mattress. i could see it poking out at a corner where the black cotton sheet, clearly not in keeping with the room's décor, had not been tucked in properly over the plastic. Her thing, apparently, is semen. This pornstar, Mira, claims to like being showered with it, likes to see it. I suppose they use black sheets to show up the semen, like how white hospital linen shows up blood and dirt.

In the end, the other three didn't show up – a regular occurrence, it seems, with men losing their nerve. Maybe they were pacing the pavement outside the hotel, mustering the confidence to come up and go through with what must have been a fantasy for them. The minder left after announcing that we were no longer waiting for the others, then returned almost immediately with the pornstar striding into the room ahead of him.

Mira was all smiles as she made eye contact with us all and gave a special greeting to those who were regular visitors. It was almost like a sales strategy, the subtext being: become regulars, and I'll make a fuss of you too. She was dressed in knee-high boots and a matching underwear set. As she turned towards the bed, our collective gaze shifted to her back, covered in all sorts of different tattoos. So many of them that they melded into one from a distance. Jet black hair with a streak of violet. She wore piercings in her tongue, lower lip and nose, just like her photos. After greeting everyone, Mira climbed onto the bed, sat cross-legged in the centre of it and then leant back a little. The seconds went by as she surveyed us, her subjects. Of course, to her, I was one of them, but that didn't occur to me at the time. She didn't know I was to be just an observer. Stopping to take in the scene was, apparently, Mira's cue for her subjects to undress.

Two of them didn't even bother undressing. One of them just plodded over to her and unzipped. I didn't hear exactly what she said, but it was something like: "you don't waste any time." She smiled before leaning on her side and running her tongue piercing along the underside of his penis, from the tip to the base and back again, making the man's head lean back. Another one parted Mira's legs and began licking her clit.

Soon the other guys were also undressed

and ready. i turned to look for a chair. The only one in the room was in a corner by the door with the minder standing directly in front of it. i walked towards the minder and chair, but he must have thought i was heading for the door to leave the room.

'Where you off to?'

'Nowhere. i just want a chair.'

'What you want a chair for?'

'For sitting on.'

'What you sitting for? You got to go to her, Mate. She ain't gonna come to you.'

'i know. i'm just going to have a sit and watch for a bit.'

He stood still as though sizing up my true motive for wanting to sit on a chair. i decided to lie.

'i have... a heart condition.'

This seemed to appease him, and he left the room, allowing me access to what i joked to myself was the Royal Box. i sat watching the men gather around Mira, listening to her encourage them and goad them into fucking her harder or dripping their semen onto her.

She must just be telling them what she thinks they want to hear. Although her webpage says she does, it is difficult to understand how anyone could enjoy this, let alone some of the other activities she offers on a one to one basis. If anyone had a choice, why would they choose this? Why would anyone surround themselves with this week after week? Is it, on a level, natural to do this? i remember reading about a theory that women seek out gangbangs, not only for sexual pleasure. They may be driven by a powerful instinct that sex with all men of a tribe means she and the baby will be protected. Is Mira one of these people with a leftover primal instinct that means she leaves these events feeling comforted. Even if it's fleeting?

Or is it just human nature to constantly seek to subvert? But this is subversion in the interests of pure pleasure. Birth control means there is nothing to restrain us, no limit to the pleasure we seek. The only limits seem to be our imaginations and the constraints of our bodies.

They laughed, making jokes at their own expense, at each other's. Hers. But it's gentle, not malicious mocking. She takes it in good humour. She's one of them. Part of it. They're not doing this to her. She's an active participant, having as much fun as they are, or at least pretending to. There's a kind of relaxed tension. A contradiction, but that's the best way i can describe it. A forced casualness, like the situation is nothing special, harmless fun. Maybe, for them, it is. Perhaps she really is one of them. Maybe they all share an understanding, and her enthusiasm for her role makes her trusted. Accepted. One of them.

Sitting on the chair, i received the occasional glance from the men. Almost challenging. i wonder if they resented me just watching. They must have. i wouldn't be comfortable, waiting my turn, self-stimulating while someone watched from the corner. Perhaps i imagined it. After a while, i noticed their glances at me had softened a little. Less challenging, almost friendly. inviting.

For a few moments, Mira was almost facing me on all fours. For an instant, we locked eyes before another participant blocked her view. Her view. With the looks i got from the group, i momentarily questioned whether i was outside looking in, or being looked at. Was i getting what i came for, or were they getting off on watching me watching them? i was there to learn from them, their behaviour, but for a moment, it felt as though i was complicit, as though they were including me, but only for their own ends. Including me as long as i assumed my role.

i wondered how they would react if i suddenly joined them. Would the behaviour change momentarily throw them off? Would they then silently resent that i had retracted the thrill of being watched? Even if i wanted to, i wouldn't join them. The distance is familiar. Comfortable. To feel accepted would feel a pretence, the way a newly slim person struggles to see themself as anything other than overweight, struggles to see themself the way others now see them and have the confidence of someone who always felt like an equal.

These men were comfortable with each other, with themselves, certain in their right to exist, with the confidence that comes with the single-minded pursuit of pleasure. They were there to exert their will, to exhibit their potency, to feel real, to feel significant. But to whom did they want to matter? As far as they were concerned, I was participating by not participating. To them, I had become a prop to witness and validate.

Just like her. But with her, they also communicate. She was their equal, at least for some of them. She was in charge. They did not treat her as an unfeeling object. They joked with her. Most of them did. For the rest of them, perhaps they use her to measure themselves for their sense of self. Perhaps, for those few, she is a prop in that way.

We keep imagining new, weird and wonderful ways to pleasure ourselves, different fetishes, different impulses that suggest that some new thing might give more pleasure. And if such a thing doesn't exist, our impulse drives us to create it. Where does this impulse come from? Where does the thought come from that leads someone to put on a nappy, suck a dummy and pretend to be a baby, to be jerked off by a sex worker pretending to be their mother?

What will happen when our imaginations and impulses mean that the bodies we have are no longer fit for the purpose of pleasure beyond what was intended for them as they are. For extreme sports, we wear helmets, protective clothing, life vests to stop us from dying while doing this dangerous thing that we apparently enjoy. In the same way, condoms help us avoid catching infections, but will there be a time when the human body is deemed too frail for the pleasure we contrive for it? Extreme pleasure.

As a species, will we reach a point where the instinct to survive is matched or suppressed by an instinct for pleasure? Perhaps it has already happened. How many people die each year engaging in extreme sports?

Sports! That's what that room of men

reminded me of. For two hours, it was like they were a team that had come together for a specific goal. The goal was some sort of...

Wait! i need to write this down first: Beyond the obvious, what is the deeper connection between the mental and the physical? What are these thoughts that filter through our minds and dare us to push our bodies to their limits? As though we are constantly looking to redefine the way our bodies may bring us a sense of achievement, that new plane of pleasure.

Will there be a time when the only thing that will matter will be pleasure, whether through sex, eating, drinking, dreaming or sport? is that the Garden of Eden that we are all gradually working our way back to? Albeit via all the horrors we've cooked up so far, and those still to come. Maybe that's the biggest joke of all? That having made us how we are and given us impulses towards seeking out pleasure, whatever the form it might take, we are all constantly working towards some Eden. Working towards Total Global Bliss.

We stand on the shoulders of those who

came before us, and our children we will set upon our shoulders, imploring them to find their own bliss and be happier than we were. Maybe our descendants will arrive. We will be long forgotten, but perhaps they will get there, wherever there is.

... shared release. High emotions needing a release for there to be calm again, like at a riot. The burning of an effigy. A sacrifice to cleanse the palate. A lynching to satisfy the townsfolk. This was more like sport, with plenty of encouragement from all players, as well as pats on the bum, squeezing of each other's body parts, and sweat on the playing surface.

Was that what had prompted the impulse to engage in some kind of group sexual activity? The feeling that pleasure achieved as a team of people working together would be more satisfying than that experienced with just one other person?

Perhaps the impulse stemmed from wanting others to witness their deeds, wanting an audience to act as encouragement and support. Make them *feel they are part of the team. Like they've done their part when their semen splashes onto her skin.*

'Or maybe each man thought it would be fun to get together with another man to simulate what it would be like to dominate one woman and be all over her. Just totally use her, like an object,' Dr. Sharma suggested to Tim.

'Simulate?' asked Tim, half-heartedly. He was far more interested in hearing more about the actual event.

'Yeah, because she was definitely in total control. They knew she was in charge. If she had said back off, they would have asked how far. Maybe to them, it was an opportunity to simulate some kind of domination thing without hurting anyone, but from my third party point of view, it was more like a… team. And she was part of the team. They were all working together towards this goal. She was helping them, they were helping her, and together they all worked it out.'

'Well, yeah, it was a gangbang, not a gang rape.'

'I know, but I still find it difficult to reconcile. It was surreal even that these guys from different walks of life, different ages, could come together like disparate strands as if they had been *summoned* by some impulse to leave their normal life and meet in some hotel room for the sole act of fucking amongst strangers. And then they leave, probably never to see each other again, but this act will stay with them for the rest of their lives. Or until dementia sets in.'

'When you put it like that, it does kind of sound surreal,' admitted Tim.

'That's what it is when you boil it down.'

'But when you boil it down, you forget the pleasure part. When you add that, it doesn't seem as surreal anymore. We leave behind the people we love five days a week, or more, to spend eight hours a day, or more, with strangers at a job most of us dislike. Or hate. Most of our waking hours are spent with these strangers that none of us chose, and when we quit that job, we hope never to see them again. Isn't that surreal?'

'Ah, but *your* boiling down has meant you've forgotten the money part,' replied Dr. Sharma.

'What's money versus pleasure?' asked Tim, unwilling to concede the point.

'We need money for life, to support ourselves.'

'Then, money is an outmoded concept,' replied Tim, stretching his hands away from his body and yawning.

'Do you really think she can enjoy doing that?' asked Dr. Sharma as an octagenarian wearing a flat cap took a seat a few tables away.

'She's been doing it for some time. Sounds like she's making a lot of money. She says she enjoys it, but then people say a lot of things, right? No one's forcing her. She could do something else if she wanted. So I'll say that at least part of her must enjoy it.'

'But how can she?'

'Isn't that the whole point of your project? Understanding different people?'

'Yeah, but you weren't there.'

'I know,' said Tim, with a sip of his coffee.

'Imagine, week in, week out. The hotel rooms, the plastic sheets, the smells of different people in the room. Maybe the smell of smoke, drink. Maybe they're unwashed after a day at work. Then all these guys together, all over her, pointing dicks at every relevant orifice, shooting semen. The sweat of the room dripping from skin, her saliva dripping from dicks, semen dripping from her nipples, used condoms on the floor, soiled sheets.' Dr. Sharma finished, apparently exhausted, leaning back in his tub chair and bringing his pint to his lips as the old man's flat-capped head swivelled in their direction, finding their conversation more gripping than the TV.

'You said she was part of the *team*. The *gangbang* team,' said Tim with a grin. 'Many hands make light work.'

'Too many cooks spoil the broth,' joked Dr. Sharma.

'Seven dicks is better than one,' replied Tim.

'Especially for a gangbang.'

'*Especially* for a gangbang,' Tim agreed, staring into space. 'Can't believe you didn't tell me you were going.'

'You think it was easy for me? Besides, it would have been even weirder with both of us sitting and watching. You wouldn't have fucked her either. You already have your bit on the side.' Tim simply nodded, his face turned down to his coffee. 'How *did* that happen?' asked Dr. Sharma.

'How do these things normally happen?' deflected Tim.

'What about Ruth's affair?' asked Dr. Sharma.

'What affair? That was a hypothetical situation.'

'That was a feeble cover. Is she or not?'

'Not as far as I know. Besides, what actually makes an affair an affair?'

'Sex? Emotions, love?'

Tim paused a moment before responding. 'The person I'm having sex with… it's a man.'

'I know. You already said,' answered Dr. Sharma before

another glug.

'I know I did, but… I like him.' Tim paused before continuing. 'He ended it.'

'Who is he?' pressed Dr. Sharma, ignoring Tim's feelings for a moment, his curiosity piqued. 'What's his name?'

'I'm not telling you,' replied Tim.

'Why not?' asked Dr. Sharma petulantly.

'Because I don't want to,' Tim insisted.

'Are you going to tell me anything else?'

'There's nothing else to tell.'

'How long did it go on?'

'Not long. It didn't really make me happy.'

'Then why did you start?'

'I don't know. Maybe because the opportunity arose. Maybe, subconsciously, I don't want to be married anymore, and this is my way of forcing the issue?'

Reining himself in, Dr. Sharma gave his friend a little space before asking, 'what's happened with the two of you?'

'Ruth was seeing someone,' admitted Tim after a moment. 'Some bloke. That's over now too, she told me. She says she finished it.'

Tim felt silly telling Dev his true thoughts, so he didn't. He had been wondering about the man Ruth had been seeing. As unlikely as it seemed, to himself most of all, he empathised with him. They had both been ditched. The woman Tim truly wanted was Ruth, but it still hurt to be rejected by his fling. Tim wondered if Ruth's man felt the same way or whether he simply set it aside and refocus. Deeply hurt at his deteriorating relationship with Ruth, Tim had tried to evade his feelings by starting another relationship, but that too had ended in rejection, compounding the situation. Somewhere in the back of his mind, Tim had been vaguely aware of the childish and potentially destructive nature of his actions, but he couldn't help himself. He had wanted something that would feel good, someone to give him what he no longer had in Ruth.

'When you married Ruth, you must have had a special connection with her, right? A deeper bond than you had with anyone else. Isn't that when people marry one another?' asked Dr. Sharma.

'Of course,' began Tim. 'I… I don't know. I… think it just felt different back then. What's happened has made me reconsider things, question them.'

'And?' asked Dr. Sharma, after Tim came to a pause.

'And… this is difficult to say. Maybe…' Tim took a breath as he played with his coffee cup, idly rotating it on the table in front of him. 'Maybe I liked the idea of her. She had her life together. She… y'know?'

'Yeah. I know,' admitted Dev, his mind casting back to how Tim was when he had met Ruth, a drinking habit creeping up on him, unsure of who he wanted to be, or what he wanted from life. Back then, all Tim was sure of was where the next party was that evening. On the New Year's Eve they met, Ruth had entered Tim's life and given him something to work for. She hadn't any sizeable expectations. Her expectations of him were achievable, compared to those his mother and father had always held. Moreover, she was a reflection of the type of person he wanted to be. For Tim, Ruth was the person he needed, the one who inspired his change, the one for whom he wanted to change.

# 23. Go to sleep

One night, curled up in his little bed, Dev was awake when Amina came up to their room. Already in her pyjamas, she slowly climbed into bed. Everything seemed to cost her more effort than it used to, and she felt constantly tired. Amina couldn't remember whether this was normal behaviour for her or whether it was a new development. She had learnt in biology that cells are replaced every seven years, essentially resulting in a new human body, and she wondered if this was what it was like, to, every seven years, forget who you are. Amina could no longer remember where regular Amina ended, and the new stuff in her life began.

Her mind felt as full each morning as it did at the end of each evening, and Amina found it impossible to set aside any of her thoughts. Confusion and shame didn't just race through her mind. Their waves crashed through her thoughts, and the world didn't seem so bright anymore. Her family's company, which she used to anticipate at the end of the school day, now seemed oppressive as she sat silently at the dinner table, waiting for the minutes to tick past. The set of six small bulbs in the light fitting hanging from the ceiling appeared to mock her, and she could almost hear the electricity antagonising her senses.

'Are you okay, Amina?' asked Dev, getting out from under the covers and sitting on the edge of his bed.

'Yeah. Fine. Why?'

'Just asking.'

'How are you, Dev?' Amina asked, humouring him.

'I'm okay.'

'What did you do at school today?'

'Lots of maths and lots of spelling. What did you do?'

'Lots of maths, lots of science. Fractions. Fulcrums. Something.'

'You're very quiet. Are we going to play at the weekend?'

'I'm… yeah… I suppose not.'

'Don't you like me? Did I do something wrong?'

'Of course I do!' snapped Amina.

'Why are you so quiet now?'

'I don't know. I think. It's the lights. Do you ever feel like the lights are too bright?'

'The lights?'

'Yeah. I just… It… Everything seems too bright. I just want to… you know?'

'No, I don't know,' answered Dev. 'Dad says it's because you're a teenager. Mum says she's going to have a talk with you.' At this, Amina squeezed her eyes shut tight and brought her hands up to cover her face, despite the darkness of the room. 'Are you crying?' asked Dev.

'No. I just have a headache,' said Amina, trying to control

her voice.

'Would you tell me a story?' came the familiar request. Dev was tired and kept trying to push sleep away as it swirled around him, crowding out the rest of the world. However, this time he felt she needed to tell a story more than he needed to hear one.

Amina exhaled loudly, but other than that there was no response for a few moments while Dev rubbed his eyes. 'Okay. Just one. What kind would you like?'

'Anything. Just make one up. Tell me something like you used to.'

'This is a story about,' began Amina, as she rolled onto her side,' about… a building.'

'A building?'

'And a family. A family that visits a building. Olivia and Brian, and their little girl, Anna. From number 12, Gaumont street. 'I'm not doing anything,' said Olivia. 'Then why are you staring at me like that?' asked Brian. 'I'm not,' Olivia replied. 'What's the time?' asked Brian. They had been doing it for weeks. Not only Olivia and Brian but the rest of the town too. Each person visited the building. Olivia, Brian and their little girl, Anna, left their car and felt the cool air between their fingers. They passed another couple leaving the building with their small child. The adults nodded to each other politely.

'The building on the edge of town was an abandoned two-storey office block. The building was *ancient*, built in… like, the sixties. There had been talk of pulling it down and building a multi-storey car park in its place, but the building had found a new purpose, and nobody wanted it pulled down anymore.

'The family wandered into the building and breathed in the air. It was musty. Until a couple of months ago, the building had spent years as a home for vagrants. In fact, it was because of them, and the charity workers who had gone to help them, that the building's ability had been discovered.

'Anna didn't like being there, she stayed close to her mum. The council had wanted to at least renovate the building and convert it into offices, but people were worried that changes would make the building just a building again. Somebody had the idea of spreading the news about the building and inviting others, but that was also ignored.

'Brian wandered the ground floor and felt the painted concrete of the wall as he climbed the stairs to the first floor. Meanwhile, Olivia leant against a pillar on the ground floor, her head resting against the damp plaster. Anna skipped around her mother and the pillar. 'Mum, it smells here,' complained Anna. 'I know, darling, said Olivia. We'll go soon.'

'The building sensed the three of them within its frame. It didn't understand. People would come, stay a little while, and then would leave. One by one, they would pass through, flitting through as many thoughts as they could. Unkind thoughts. Bad. Violent and hateful. They would think up these thoughts and daydream about them, making up stories before forgetting them, and leaving.

'All the building could do was soak it all up. All the bad feelings, the guilt. The building didn't understand much about the people. It didn't understand their emotions. It was just a building. But it did understand that by thinking their thoughts and then forgetting them, the people left happier.

'Before long, Anna, Olivia, and Brian came together again. They were getting ready to leave the building when a young man went in. The family looked at him, but he quickly turned around and went back out as soon as he saw them.

'When they got back to their car Olivia put Anna in her car seat. 'How do you feel?' asked Brian, as she got behind the wheel and put on her seat belt. 'The same as always,' she replied. 'Foggy, like I've lost something that I was just holding. What about you?' she asked. 'I don't know,' replied Brian.

'Olivia started the car and drove the family away. On their journey through the town, they passed parents with pushchairs, elderly people with shopping trolleys, teenagers on skateboards, postmen with bicycles. Brian watched them go past like he was looking at a painting.'

Dev didn't understand the story, and he certainly didn't find it satisfying, but he knew better than to ask about it. He tried to encourage her to talk to him a little, but to no avail as he heard her breathe hard to control the sobs building in her chest. 'I didn't mean to upset you, Mina. I'm worried. You're different.'

'I know. Just go to sleep, Dev,' said Amina sharply as she rolled over. 'Let's all just go to sleep,' she pleaded into her pillow, no longer able to contain the tremors in her voice.

Upset and afraid of this unusual behaviour from the little bundle of shadow across the room, Dev quickly did as Amina asked and slid back under the covers to appease her, hoping this would stop her crying. Through the darkness, he listened to his sister's sobs but didn't tell anyone of them. Eventually, he fell into a deep sleep that muffled the events of that night while Amina also slept and dreamt. She dreamt of Mauritius and the way the sunshine had warmed her skin before she slipped into the clear, quiet water. In her dream, she once again felt the freedom and self-assuredness that comes with knowing oneself.

# 24. The weight

It was a sunny afternoon. It was that afternoon.

Dev played outside in the garden while Raju kept an eye on him through the French windows and pretended to read the newspaper. Like all parents, Raju liked to watch his children play, but Amina didn't play anymore, at least not when she could be observed. She was upstairs in Raju and Serena's bedroom, having the chat he and Serena had discussed. To keep Dev from becoming curious and interrupting them, Raju had encouraged him to play outside in the autumn sunshine.

He watched Dev create games for himself, and from them, he grew worlds, engaging their own peculiar logic. The logic behind why the goodies and the baddies always fight each other. The logic behind how the baddies exceed their limitations to surprise the goodies and initially gain the upper hand. Eventually, the goodies save the day with a bright idea reflecting the logic of the creator's world. Raju watched Dev, concerned about the chat progressing upstairs.

Amina sat on the bed beside her mother and dreaded what was to come. Deep down, Serena wanted to be better for her daughter, but the necessary response simply wasn't there.

'No, then everyone will know. I don't want everyone to know,' insisted Amina.

'I have to tell Raju,' Serena pressed on, speaking to herself more than Amina. 'We have to tell the police. How can this be happening? I have no idea how I'm going to tell Raju this. It'll break his heart. My God, what are we going to do?' Serena asked no one in particular, her eyes closed to her daughter as she began busying herself with thoughts of what was to come.

# 25. Spiders and flies

Her mother, gone from the bedroom, Amina was all cried out and exhausted by the effort she had expended. She stared at her parents' wardrobe facing her and wished she could walk into it and find that magical land at the back.

Instead, she looks over to the long wall mirror on the other side of the room. Amina gingerly lifts herself from the edge of her parent's bed. Tired and weak, her legs wobble as they take her weight, and she places one foot in front of another until she reaches the mirror. No, she can't disappear into the back of a wardrobe, so she has to make do with the mirror. Amina pauses for just a moment before pressing her hand to the hard surface of the cold mirror. Finger by finger, she pushes until the smooth surface gives way to reveal the gloopy textures beyond. Satisfyingly. Like the warm, sweet crust of a crème brûlée.

She pushes further and ignores the tiny shards of light that scratch at her skin, eventually piercing her and cutting at her flesh. Her entire hand disappears, and before long, she is up to her elbow. Face to face with her reflection, she screws up her eyes and pushes herself through the frame, ignoring the little tears in her skin and breaking the light of the surface to disappear within the viscous darkness of the world beyond. Behind her, the surface quickly becomes still and hardens again, but Amina no longer cares.

The reflective surfaces of the world are now hers for the choosing, but Amina isn't picky. She just wants to be elsewhere. Anywhere. The first option she sees is a television screen. A lone man is staring at it, with his hand up to the screen. From her side, she can tell that he is watching the news. It looks like he is in some kind of common room, but it doesn't look inviting. Amina presses on and holds out for the next option, a glass partition in a radio studio. She has never been to a radio station before and now seems as good a time as any. Quickly, she reaches out and pushes through.

Her knee is the first part of her body to make it through. She breathes heavily with effort and kicks her foot through. Clunk! Her trainer stamps onto the control desk, and she almost slips as the little sound level sliders give way under her weight which pulls the rest of her body through.

Safely through, Amina looks up to see if she has been spotted. Luckily the producer is on the phone, screening callers, with her back to Amina. On the other side of the partition, some men, and a woman, are busy at their respective microphones, talking animatedly. Quietly getting down from the desk, Amina slinks over to the door and lets herself out. *It is time to do some exploring!*

Meanwhile, on the other side of the glass, the group in the booth continues to argue.

'This is not some subconscious plea for help or something. People are not harming themselves and then waiting for attention. Something truly bizarre is going on, and we have got to work out how to deal with it.'

'Thank you, Dr. Franklyn. I now want to hear what the MP for Newcastle Central has to say about this.'

'Thank you, Jeremy. It is clear that this government does not have a single credible idea for tackling this crisis. It refused to take this seriously and is now playing catch-up. On the other hand, it is not surprising. This is this government's preferred operating method, no matter the circumstances.'

'Jeremy, it is only now becoming apparent that there is an issue to address. It is true that previously these people were deemed trouble-makers and they were disregarded – '

'Is that what we do now under this government? We disregard the people bringing up issues, the people openly asking for help? Is this how a modern government treats its citizens?'

'If the lady would allow me to finish. Until recently, these had been local matters under the care of local authorities – '

'In other words, you didn't care so long as it wasn't anywhere near you. You don't know the names of the towns, do you? Jeremy, I think the gentleman needs to be reminded that the UK does not begin and end with London.'

'I'm sure he is aware. Please carry on, Minister,' replies Jeremy.

'Thank you, Jeremy. What seemed restricted to a few towns is now appearing across the rest of the UK and the world. What we are seeing is like nothing that we have encountered previously.'

'I'm sure we all understand that, Minister, but what is the government doing about it? How are we contributing to the international effort?'

'Jeremy, what we are seeing is –.'

'You keep going on about what we're seeing, but not what you're doing.'

'Miss Adler,' begins Jeremy, 'I'm sure the Minister is secretly thanking you for all the interruptions, allowing him time to formulate his responses, but please leave the interruptions to me.'

'Sorry, Jeremy, it's just that this government has systematically isolated the very people it is meant to serve. This debacle is just the latest example of that.'

'Okay, let's hear from the MP now, shall we?'

'Thank you, Jeremy. There is no set template in place. The drills we run and the procedures we have, established with COBRA, for dealing with disasters, contagions, and the like, do not apply here. There are no precedents that have prepared us, but we are working tirelessly with the information we have at hand to lay down relevant plans and safeguards.'

'But will that be enough, Minister?' asks Jeremy, huffily. 'This does not appear to be a pattern of anomalies, but rather events mushrooming at any given moment and without warning. The world has simply ceased to make sense.'

'Jeremy, we can only work with the information we have at hand. The information thus far leads us to understand there are known unknowns that we can only address as their true nature becomes apparent.'

'Minister, tell us this. Is there any suspicion that any of this is due to terrorist activity?'

'The belief is that the effects we are seeing are far too advanced to be the work of terrorists.'

'Advanced?' asks Jeremy from behind his microphone.

'Yes, advanced, but also too inefficient for terrorists.'

'How so?'

'Terrorists want you to know that they are the cause, that it is directly by their hand that you are fearful. They want those they are attacking to know their agenda and ideology, so it can be more effectively imposed. But here we are, grasping at straws as to the cause.'

'But, Minister, might not the absence of information be the ideology?'

'I'm sorry, I don't follow you.'

'That there is no way of knowing anything truly. That despite all the scientific foundations we take for granted as our basis for understanding the world, there may be no way of predicting events that have no scientific basis.'

'Jeremy, you seem bent on arguing this is all the work of terrorists, but what you are describing is simply not possible. Everything has a scientific basis.'

'Thank you, Minister. At this point, I'd like to turn to Bishop Walton. Bishop, good evening. What is the official view of the church on all this? Is this the work of God?'

'Good evening, Jeremy. This has been the explanation that many have turned to. I would like to make it clear that the church is working with the government and other organisations to understand what is happening in our world and redress the chao -… disorder. I am sure that calm heads will prevail to find a cause and a solution in an atmosphere of cooperation. There is no need to panic. We just need to work together now.'

'Yes, but is it the church's view that this is the work of God?'

'It is consistently the church's view that everything is always the work of God, only by placing our faith in Him can we overcome any obstacle with which He chooses to test us.'

'So, in your opinion, is God the ultimate terrorist?'

'I… I beg your pardon?' asks Bishop Walton after a double-take.

'Is God the ultimate terrorist?' repeats Jeremy.

'Jeremy, I fail to see… Is it your intention to provoke? I am appalled that you should ask me such a question.'

'Bishop, the minister has just told us that there is so far an absence of scientific fact regarding these anomalies. In fact, that seems to be the only commonality amongst all these events. Might that not lead us to consider other possibilities? Such as a direct act of God sparking fear around the world. So, again, I ask you, what is the church's view?'

'Jeremy,' begins Dr. Franklyn, 'I'm sorry, but I feel I have to come in again here. The lack of traditional, scientific explanation does not mean we should abandon science altogether and resort to speculation bordering on fear-mongering.'

'Quite quite, Jeremy, I agree with Dr. Franklyn,' says Bishop Walton, 'it is irresponsible to jump to conclusions like this.'

'Ladies, gentlemen, I am simply reflecting what the public appears to want us to address, and it would appear that an increasing number fear this is divine retribution. End of days. Apocalypse. What you will. In light of that, the question would appear valid: is God the ultimate terrorist?'

'*If* this is God's work,' mutters Bishop Walton.

'You now suspect some other entity, Bishop?' asks Jeremy.

'I don't suspect anything. All I have is the same information as the other people on this panel. We have to decipher what is going on and what plans are in store for us using that information. The best we can do right now is to try to cope with things as they happen.'

'You mentioned chaos earlier, Bishop.'

'I fear I misspoke.'

'Nevertheless, you mentioned chaos.'

'Yes.'

'Many listeners are suggesting that chaos is the new order of the world, whether we know it or not. I quote one such believer: "In light of our continued actions of brutality, this chaos will lead us to abandon our harmful diversions and distractions to focus solely on making sense of this new world as it changes day by day."'

'What are they talking about?' asks Bishop Walton.

'Well, we have one of them on the phone. Hello, you're on the air. What's your name, and where are you from?'

'None of that really matters anymore.'

'Well, we have to call you something,' explains Jeremy, tetchily.

'Scott,' the caller states.

'All right then, Scott. What is this all about?'

'It's about how we have chosen not to evolve and progress as a species capable of thinking things through clearly.'

'What brings you and your fellow believers to that conclusion, Scott?'

'It's simple, Jeremy. Ours is the only species on this planet truly capable of advanced thought, learning from history and seeing the consequences of our actions. Right?'

'Please continue.'

'Despite our huge advances in industry, science, technology, biology, when it suits us, we still behave like savages. How can we reconcile our high-level intelligence and ability with how we continue to mistreat the vulnerable in our society. For example, why are there homeless and malnourished citizens when there is enough food and enough homes for us all? How is rape still a weapon of war? How are suicide bombers still killing the innocent? Why are rebel soldiers still forcing mothers to march away from their homes carrying the severed heads of their children? Why do we continue to kill the planet for profit? That already sounds like chaos, so maybe, since we like it so much, somebody is giving us all we want. It doesn't matter anymore how much money you have. Maybe this will finally make us all equal, make us all afraid of the world, make us all question what we can trust.' With that, the line goes dead.

'So again, Minister,' begins Jeremy, 'we turn to you. What is to be done? What is the official advice you wish to impart to our listeners tonight?'

'Vigilance, Jeremy. We recommend vigilance and reporting anything that appears unusual. Eyes akimbo at all times. Strangers and loved ones alike, we need to be on the lookout.'

'Thank you, Minister, and thanks to our panel tonight for their input. We hope to be back tomorrow. Until then, Goodnight.'

*Good... grief,* thinks Dev on Katie's bed. *Why is it so difficult to focus on one thing that means something to me?* All these thoughts and images running through his mind. As distinct as the beads of sweat on his face. He struggles to sort through the mess of pictures and sounds spilling through his mind to cling to anything that means something to him.

By this stage, Dev is not looking good at all. He's in horrible shape. In the struggle, his shoes have pulled up the bedsheets beneath him. For the first time, he genuinely wonders if this is how he will die, on this bed, in this room. How will Katie react upon finding him? Aside from the obvious, will she keep the bed? Will she get a new one? She'll probably get a new one.

Dev feels guilty that she will have to spend money on a new bed when there would be nothing wrong with this one were it not that he had died there. Except that upon dying, he might also release his bowels and soil the bed. This realisation stops his mind from drifting, and the messy business of death finally hits him.

From my point of view, the number of thoughts, ideas, memories suddenly gushing through Dev's mind in these last moments of his life is not particularly remarkable. Most people in his position experience the same. Like him, they too desperately struggle to focus on one memory, voice, or image, to hold on to through their last moments, that will give meaning to their life, to their death. Some purpose to help them make sense, some enlightenment they can hold onto. Like a shield, or a trophy, to evidence that they have gleaned some higher understanding in their field. Their field being: being a person on planet Earth.

So it is not entirely his fault that he is so scatterbrained at the moment that he no longer has command over his mind and eyes to frame one memory or image on the air before him. Something pleasant that he can go out on, to which he can breathe his last and slip away.

I almost feel sorry for him.

Almost.

What if we gave him a helping hand?

What if we whisper something in his ear? Would that set his mind on a different track? Would one word at the right time send him in another direction, give him something on which to focus his energies?

Let's try it. Let's poke the bear in the cage, whisper at him and see what the good doctor does next. They say the most pleasing sound is that of one's name. Let's see what he'll make of it.

'Dev!'

*My grandfather on my father's side. They say he really liked my name, but I never knew him. He died before I met him.*

'My dad always told me that it was a shame since he would have really loved me. Dad would tell me of his dedication. He worked hard every day to rear livestock and harvest sugarcane from the fields, but he always had time for his children. My grandfather struggled to make ends meet, but his family was happy, living simply. His children had fun growing up together, playing in the rivers, forests, and sugar cane fields near where they lived. My father told me how they would eat oysters straight from the river and how they would catch giant shrimp there that were fatter and juicier than at any seafood market he had been to since. No doubt, he remembers things being better than they actually were. Everyone remembers things being better or worse than the reality.

'One thing he told me has always stuck with me. I can see my father sitting at the table in the kitchen, a smile on his face and a glass of whiskey in hand. He would laugh as he told me how when he, or any of his siblings, had done anything naughty, his father would chase after them, intending to land a disciplinary smack on a backside or two. Of course, they would do their best to avoid this, and before long, Granddad would be chasing his children around the kitchen table. With no hope of catching them and presumably realising how ridiculous the situation was, out of breath and bent over, my grandfather would suddenly burst out laughing. Then his children would also start laughing as he knelt on the bare, red floor. Instead of disciplining them, he would end up hugging them all close and tight.

'What I took from this was that the entire family was united with the same love, kindness, and the aim of being good people, making progress towards a better life. Everyone around them, their friends and neighbours, were of the same mind, doing what they could. They all fitted into their community, never pondering how. They were just part of it, part of the pattern.

'From when I was little, my father would always tell me, "there was no one better than him," my grandfather,' clarified Dr. Sharma to Katie. He was sitting in a rickety desk chair that felt incongruous in the kitchen, where Katie had thought they would be more comfortable to talk than in the bedroom. '"There was no one better than him,"' He hadn't considered it before. 'A small collection of words, but it stuck with me, and I often wondered why I should bother with anyone else when they would always be runner-up to whom my Dad called *the best person*.'

'That's a terrible way to think,' Katie playfully tittered, suggesting her mischievous side agreed with his point. She sauntered over from the kettle with two coffees and sat on her kitchen chair in jeans and a T-shirt, her brown hair haphazardly tied back in a ponytail. 'It means you'll never give anyone else a chance.'

'I know, but I was small, and I thought, 'if I can't have the best, why bother with the rest?''

'How old were you?'

'Five or six.'

'It's funny that you were already thinking like that. I'm trying to imagine a five-year-old you.'

'I tried to have as little to do with my extended family as possible. When we would visit them or when they visited us, I would observe them and analyse, wondering what it was about them that made my grandfather the best.'

'How *they* made him the best?'

'Yeah. I didn't have him around to analyse, I just had my father's assertion that he was the best, and because I was a child, I just wholeheartedly believed him, the way children do. So I would watch those other people and try to figure out what they lacked and why they weren't as good. My grandfather had been built as a kind of saint, and so that's what he became to me. I used to imagine that from heaven, or wherever, he was always watching me doing good things, bad things.'

'What bad things do *you* do?' asked Katie disbelievingly.

'I wonder if he wouldn't think this was a bad thing.'

'What? Being here with me?'

'Doing this. Trying to find… some truth. I'm not sure he would approve. I think he was very much a: *live a simple life, don't go looking for trouble*, kind of man.'

'I think it's interesting what you're doing. It's unusual.'

Dr. Sharma leant back in the chair and pulled his notebook from the inner pocket of his coat hanging from the backrest. 'Have you had the opportunity to find out anything from your clients since last week? Or has anything occurred to you that you can tell me about?'

'No, Dev,' confessed Katie, a pained look on her face, 'I didn't get to asking anyone anything. To be honest, I'm finding it a bit difficult. It's not an easy, natural thing to work into a chat. But I did have an unusual client this week.'

'Tell me about it. Had you seen him before?'

'No.'

'Did he tell you his name?'

'Well, yes and no,' began Katie, 'he told me his name was Patrick, but that's just what he told me. Anyway, this guy was super-secret about himself.'

'Isn't that normal?'

'He made me switch off the lights before he came in.'

'Were you okay with that?'

'Not really,' Katie answered, 'but it's been a slow week. Besides, I spoke to him on the phone, and he sounded okay.

That was when he told me the flat had to be dark when he came in. I asked him why, but he said he would tell me when he got here, that it wouldn't make sense over the phone.'

'So what happened?'

'So we arranged for him to come over on Wednesday night at eight o'clock. I didn't think he'd turn up, but he did. Knocked on the door, and I let him in,' Katie continued with a little shrug of her shoulders.

'Weren't you a little concerned at this bloke wanting to be shrouded in darkness?' asked Dr. Sharma.

'Well, it was on the condition that he would have to come into the flat in the light so I could get a look at him, count his cash and check him out. Then we'd do the rest with the lights *dimmed*.'

'And?'

'So, he told me why he preferred for me not to see too much of him or know too much about him.'

'What's the story?'

'His story, or what I understood of it,' clarified Katie, 'was that he had lived alone with his mum after his dad left when he was three or four. Growing up, they moved around a lot, which he hated because it meant they would never settle down anywhere and become close to anyone. Eventually, when he got to eighteen, he decided he would remain in one town. His mother also decided to stop moving around and stay. Eventually, through his job, he made friends and felt he was getting to know people. He became close to them. Then, he met more people through them, and he started to feel he was part of a... well, like an extended family.

'One day, he found out that one of his friends had cancer.

It was a year before she died, but almost everybody he knew either died suddenly or became ill in that year. The only ones of his new family that weren't affected had moved away and were not in contact anymore.'

'What about his mother?'

'She was fine. Still is.'

'Everyone he knew died? Everyone?'

'They either died or got ill.'

'That must have really screwed up his social life,' muttered Dr. Sharma with a wry smile.

'It's not funny, Dev. He was serious,' empathised Katie, hurt on behalf of Patrick.

'It can't have been everyone. He was exaggerating.'

'I don't know, that's what he said, and that's why he doesn't want to get close to anyone. He said he felt it was all his fault, like he was cursed or something. He said maybe that was why his dad left. Because he could feel that his son was this… black hole of doom.'

'What kind of person comes up with a story like that?'

'How do you know it was a story?'

'For someone who didn't want to tell you much about himself, he kind of told you a lot about himself. Maybe he wanted you to feel sorry for him?'

'I did, but I still took his money. Anyway, he now goes through life avoiding knowing anyone and trying not to let anyone know anything about him.'

'But he told *you* his story.'

'Yeah, but that's the only thing I know.'

'So now he tries not to form any meaningful relationships with anyone for fear that he will hurt them, with only his mum for company?'

'Yeah.'

'And presumably, you're never going to see him again because familiarity would lead to a relationship of sorts.'

'Right.'

'So for that human contact, physical… warmth he sees only… um.'

'*Experts*,' reminded Katie.

'Right. Do a lot of the men tell you a story to try to explain themselves?'

'Well, it happens, but I don't think this was a story.'

'But it's not very likely, is it?'

'Look, you asked me to tell you stuff, and when I do, you tell me you don't believe me. How do you think that makes me feel?' asked Katie, her brow crinkled in a hurt look.

'I believe you. I just don't believe this bloke's story.'

'You weren't here. He really meant it.'

'Okay, well, I can believe that he believed his own story.'

'That's what I meant.'

'But as a doctor, in fact, as a sane person, I don't think you can kill people by association. Seriously, you can't have felt comfortable after he told you that story. It doesn't sound like something you would tell someone just before you have sex with them.'

'It's not always about *comfort*. It's about customer service. It's a service industry. People come here, to my home, and they want me to make them comfortable. It's not always pleasant, and I'm not always in the mood, but it's what I do, and I always count my blessings that I'm not working in worse conditions. I have things better than a lot of others.'

'So what did you go on to do with this guy? Any special requests?'

'We started with a BJ. Standard. Then he asked me for anal, which was fine, except I don't think he'd done it before because he tried to stick it straight in, which was never going to work. Some lube and a finger or two later, and it was fine.'

'I suppose, when you think about it, bigger picture, maybe that bloke's story isn't so strange compared to all the other stuff we want to do to each other.'

'Anal's pretty common. Lots of people do it.'

'I wasn't talking about anal.'

Changing the subject, Katie asked with a mischievous smile: 'Do you remember how old you were when you found out about kissing with tongues?'

'No, but I do remember how I felt when I found out about oral sex.'

'How old were you?'

'I don't remember exactly, but I clearly remember my feelings at the time.'

'Were you turned on?'

'No. It was a mixture of disbelief and fascination. It just seemed so bizarre that this thing that you use to urinate could also be something someone would lick. It felt like two things that should be entirely alien coming together in a way that didn't make sense but would apparently bring pleasure, so it makes perfect sense.'

'And do you think that led to your interest in this?'

'No, um, it wasn't that,' scrabbled Dr. Sharma, 'I don't know. How about you?'

'I found out about oral when I found out my mother did

this for a living.'

'Is that how you got into this yourself?' asked Dr. Sharma, glad for the turn the conversation was taking.

'Not really. I got into this properly… maybe because my mum had been doing it. It's difficult to remember. I'd sort of done it a handful of times. I left home when I was young. I suppose it's the usual story. I got mixed up with the wrong people, hooked on the wrong things.'

Katie grew silent at this point. However, Dr. Sharma could sense that he was on the verge of making progress, getting what he needed. Getting the story first-hand. He just needed to give her a little push. Not too hard, just enough to encourage her. He had done everything he could to let her know she could speak candidly with him. That she could trust him.

'And that's how you started doing this yourself?' he tried.

'No. Like I said, I'd done it before, but not much, before I got together with Jen, my girlfriend.'

'I see…' Dev invited her to continue. 'Hey, if you don't want to talk about it, that's fine.'

'No. I want to tell you.' Katie paused. She took a breath before adding: 'I don't tell people this.' Dr. Sharma maintained his silence, affording her the space to open up. 'I hadn't had any… I was in a bad way. My *credit* had dried up with my usual bloke. He was a mate, but I owed him money, and he wouldn't give me any more until I'd paid him. In the end, once you owe them money, you're not mates with your dealer, even if you start as mates. I didn't have a job. No money. Jen wasn't… using. She was too smart for that.' Katie closed her eyes a few moments before opening them and continuing.

'She went with me to keep an eye on me as I went shop to shop looking for quick work, late at night. Cash in hand, on the night. Anything, just to get some money. It was my idea. I was going out of my mind. I just really needed to get some. Jen told me not to go, that I was too ill, but I didn't listen. I was too far gone. All I wanted was some money to buy a hit. Jen just wanted to look out for me, take me home after I'd given up, and then see me through the night. It was my idea to go out, try to get some money. That time of night, the only places still open were pubs, petrol stations, and takeaways.

'Jen had to tell me about it afterwards. I only remember bits and pieces. We'd come across a kebab shop, and I'd gone in, with Jen looking out for me. I asked these two guys behind the counter if they had any work going. Jen said I told them I was desperate for work. They said they'd be closing in half an hour, so there was no counter work. They said we could peel spuds down in the storeroom to make chips for the next day while they closed up and cleaned the kitchen. I suppose most places get them in already peeled and chopped, ready for frying, but this place didn't.

'Jen said it felt like we were down there for ages peeling those potatoes and throwing them in buckets of water before they came down. They said they were going to pay us. They took us by surprise, although it wouldn't have been hard with me in that condition. They took us by surprise and hit us. I vaguely remember being punched in my stomach and then the side of my head. Jen must have put up much more of a fight because she had bruises all over. And cuts. She must have had the leader of the pair because the one on me… the one on me didn't spend too much time before going over to his friend and Jen. They must have thought she was the good looking one. Either that, or maybe they find it a bigger thrill if you fight back.

'I vaguely remember being desperate to help her, but I was too weak. I was out of it. I could hear them on her. Taking turns. Spitting on her. Hitting her. I remember her shouting and shouting at them to get off her. Crying. Begging them to let her go. Begging for my help. That's something I remember, what I'll always remember. Her crying out for my help. Again and again. But I couldn't help her. I was too weak. Later, when she asked if I remembered anything, I lied. I said no.

'They kicked us out when they were done, and we made our way home. That was the end of me and drugs. And it was the end of me and Jen. We're still friends. But it was too much. I went back home to Mum's soon after. We had rent to pay. There was no reason not to really go for it. It's not an ideal job, but it's normally straightforward. That's how I ended up following in Mum's footsteps.'

'Katie. I don't know what to say,' confessed Dr. Sharma. 'I'm… That's…'

'I didn't start escorting because I was raped, Dev. I want you to know that. One thing has nothing to do with the other. I had a choice. I do it on my terms. It's my choice.'

'How long ago was this?'

'About ten years ago.'

Dr. Sharma wanted to reach out to her, to hold her. 'I'm just so sorry you went through that. I'm surprised that you can even be in a room with men.'

'Well, not all men are like that. Otherwise, I'd miss out on a lot of nice people.'

'Including the bloke who says he kills everyone he gets close to?'

'Including him,' smiled Katie.

Katie was adamant that being raped had nothing to do with her decision to earn her living as an escort. She never used the word *prostitute*. She even inwardly winced at the term: *professional*. She preferred: *expert* or *temporary girlfriend*. That was her rationale to distinguish what she did from prostitution. Dr. Sharma thought of Katie at home that night and pondered whether she was as empowered as she suggested. Of course, she was vulnerable on a physical level, but perhaps also on an emotional one that she didn't want to admit.

In any case, he hadn't gotten from her what he needed. Her story, harrowing as it was, hadn't delivered the impact he sought. She was too calm and controlled. He needed a more visceral of emotions, one he felt he couldn't push Katie for.

# 26. I want to take these hands

Statements
    Witnesses
Words
Serena's wailing.
Shock and incomprehension scrawled all over Raju's face.

'Is there someone you can leave him with while you come to the station?' WPC Young asked. 'We'll also need you at the hospital.'

'The neighbour. Number 12. He's retired. And grumpy. But harmless. Um, I'll explain to him. Should be fine,' finished Raju, getting up from the armchair he had been frozen in since the visitors had delivered the news.

'That's okay, love, you stay there. We'll sort it. What's the neighbour's name?' WPC Young asked, putting her hand on Raju's shoulder, easing him back to his armchair.

'Dudley. Mr Dudley. Oh my God, are you really sure?' he asked, his eyes pleading with hers for the slightest hint of hope.

‘Martin, can you find Mr Dudley, please, at number 12?’ instructed WPC Young. PC Woodford nodded and left the room. ‘Raju, we’ll need you to come to the hospital.’ Raju silently stared into space. ‘What’s your son’s name, Raju?’

‘What? Um… Dev.’

‘Dev?’

‘Dev.’

‘Dev? Okay, shall we go and get Dev, then? You can explain to him what’s happened, later, in your own way. For now, let’s just get him ready to go next door. Shall we do that?’

‘Yes.’

‘Okay. Where is he?’

‘Um. Upstairs. I think.’

‘All right, let’s go call him down then, shall we?’ They both got up from their seats, and WPC Young led Raju, in a daze, to the foot of the stairs.

Dev had already heard his mother’s cry. He knew something serious had happened, but he was afraid to leave the safety of the upstairs.

‘Dev,’ Raju croaked. That was as far as he got before his mind lost the power to push words out of his mouth.

WPC Young took over. ‘Dev, can you come downstairs please, luvvie?’

It was the first time a complete stranger had called him “Dev”. It was also the first time anyone had called him “luvvie.”

# 27. Everlasting love

'They had better shut up, or they'll all be going to the hospital, including her,' thinks Rooble as he leaves the building. 'Even though Shamso will maybe be my mother-in-law one day.'

Things had been going well between him and Naaleeye, Shamso's daughter. They had been seeing each other for five blissful months and were deeply in love, still experiencing that curious sensation known as *heart skipping a beat*, each time they thought of or saw one another. Yet to have a single argument or even a disagreement, Rooble was convinced that he and Naaleeye were destined for one another. In fact, he had even been considering asking her to marry him. Until that morning.

Rooble had persuaded Naaleeye that it would be best to keep their relationship from her mother, Shamso. Whilst Shamso was not technically Rooble's superior at work, she had been there for five years compared to Rooble's one year. With that came a level of assumed seniority that the other staff respected by laughing at her various quips and comments. Rooble knew that once Shamso caught wind of his relationship with Naaleeye, there would be no end to the fun she would have at his expense. So, with Naaleeye's reluctant compliance, they had kept their relationship from her mother.

When Naaleeye would come to the factory to see her mother, she would be sure to walk past Rooble, ignoring him completely, as though he were part of the building. Whenever a conversation arose at work concerning Shamso's family, Rooble would go about his work and avoid being drawn into it for fear of letting something slip, but also in case he heard something about Naaleeye that he did not want to know just yet. Such as any previous boyfriends. Or that she might have poor dental health.

The deception had been so complete that, needless to say, Rooble was shocked to be greeted at work on Tuesday morning, two weeks ago, by all his colleagues shouting such choice lines as:

'Hey, here comes the big lover-man.'

'Rooble, how you been getting on with Shamso's girl then?'

'All right, Roo-meo?'

'Shamso, here comes your future son-in-law!'

Coming face to face with Shamso, Rooble realised that Naaleeye had spilt the beans and told her mother everything. For the rest of the day, Rooble braced himself for the cutting jibes that Shamso would inflict, but they never came. Instead, he had simply to endure the essentially well-meaning ribbing from the rest of his colleagues, and he knew this would soon fade away when they had tired of the topic.

At lunch that day, Rooble texted Naaleeye. He was due to see her at the end of his shift so he waited until she turned up at their usual place, Snack Bar.

'What happened?' asks Rooble, not bothering with greetings.

'I know. I'm sorry, I should have given you some warning,' replies Naaleeye, putting her bag down on a chair.

'What happened?' he repeats.

'Look, it just got too much for me. It's been five months, and I still couldn't tell my mother.'

'Apparently, you could and did!'

'My mother is my best friend. I couldn't *not* tell her anymore. I woke up this morning around two, and I couldn't sleep. I had to tell her.'

'So what did you tell her?'

'Well, you should know, didn't she tell you?'

'No, I haven't heard anything out of her all day.'

'So, how did you know?'

'She told everyone else, they're the ones who have been teasing me.'

'I told her not to give you any trouble, can't believe it actually worked.'

'Yeah, we'll see.'

What Rooble does not tell Naaleeye is that today, for the first time since their relationship had begun, he has seen Shamso as his future mother-in-law instead of just some woman at work. Although Rooble has always felt bad asking Naaleeye not to confide in her mother and friend, he is now beginning to regret having kept the whole thing from Shamso. He had been afraid that Shamso would poke fun at him, cheapening what he had with Naaleeye and tainting it in the process, but she hasn't mentioned it to him at all.

'Shall we go? The film starts in fifteen minutes, and we still have to get our tickets.'

'Yeah, good idea,' says Rooble, finishing his drink before the pair leave Snack Bar for the small cinema. There, as the lights go down and the music goes up, Rooble decides to try to somehow make amends to Shamso.

The following day Rooble arrives to find his co-workers' well of knowledge of his dates with Naaleeye has deepened.

'Heard you went to the zoo on your first date, Ray,' comments Suleeko.

Gabeyre jokes, 'did you show her the monkeys, mate? Show her what you're like after a drink?'

'Or did you get over to the pandas to get her in the mood? D'you know what I mean?' asks Sahal with a wink. Everyone knows what Sahal means.

Suddenly Rooble realises what is happening. Unable to let her daughter down by breaking her word, Shamso is letting everyone else do the job for her, fuelling interest by leaking fresh intelligence every day. Outraged, any thoughts of remorse and redemption are forgotten by Rooble as he seeks out Shamso in the break room later in the day.

'Shamso.'

'Good afternoon, Roo,' greets Shamso, her back to him as she faces the vending machine.

'Shamso, we need to talk.'

'What about?' asks Shamso as she slots a coin into the machine.

'Do you have a problem with me seeing Naaleeye?'

'No, why would I?'

'Then why are you telling everyone everything about me and Naaleeye?'

'I'm not telling them about you. I'm telling them about Naaleeye, my daughter.'

'But that involves me directly.'

'Well, that's not something I can help, is it?'

'You could stop telling them things.'

'Why would I do that? They're my friends. I always tell them about my life, and that includes Naaleeye. What does it have to do with you?'

'They're spending all day teasing me and mocking me, and you know it.'

'That's unfortunate, but they're kids.'

'But you could stop it. You could tell them to stop it.'

'I'm not *their* mother. I'm Naaleeye's mother.'

'Okay then,' says Rooble, trying a different approach. 'Maybe you could stop telling them so many things?'

'Roo, as I've said, it's my life, and I'll tell them as much as I like about it. I'm sorry if that doesn't suit you, but maybe you should have thought of that before you asked my daughter to keep things from me.'

'Is that what this is really about?'

'You have to admit it doesn't look good for you, does it?'

'We just didn't want to say anything until we knew it was going somewhere.'

'That's not how Naaleeye tells it. Maybe if you had both been open, we could have avoided this. Naaleeye has told me a lot about the last five months and the man she has feelings for. I'm very happy for her, and I shall enjoy telling everyone these little tidbits. As they come to my mind. Every day.'

'Shamso, is there any way we can make some kind of deal?'

'I don't make deals with people I can't trust, and I don't think I can ever trust you after you tried to make Naaleeye keep things from me.'

With that, Shamso collects her snack from the vending machine and leaves the room.

Throughout the following days and weeks, Rooble

considers reasoning with Shamso with talk of a possible proposal to encourage her to look upon him more favourably. However, deep in his heart Rooble knows this would be to no avail, so he doesn't bother. His co-workers continue to tease him, fuelled every day by new secondhand accounts of dates and events from his and Naaleeye's relationship so far.

Rooble has saved some money whilst working at the factory, but he begins to wonder if continuing to work there is worth this daily aggravation. Although he doesn't like to admit it, he is wondering the same about Naaleeye, but whenever this thought occurs, Rooble forces himself to remember that Naaleeye is not the problem. It's the mother.

'So you just need the mum to disappear, right?' asks Ciise at Snack Bar the next day.

'That would be ideal,' answers Rooble, playing distractedly with a flyer.

'Just leave it with me. I'll make it all happen,' says Ciise, bringing his glass to his lips.

'Ciise, I just need you to be a good listener, not make jokes about assassinating Naaleeye's mother.'

'I wasn't going to say *assassinate*.'

'All right then, *take out*, *whack*… whatever. I'm not in the mood.'

'Not doing any of that.'

'Then what?'

'You're going out with the daughter of someone called Shamso, right?'

'Yeah.'

'And this Shamso works with you at the textile factory across town, right?'

'Right.'

'And you just wish she'd shut up?'

'Ideally.'

'All right.'

'Okay, whatever, let's just talk about something else.'

And so they do, and Rooble thinks no more about his work troubles for the rest of the evening.

Today is Friday, and Rooble returns to the factory where he continues to endure the latest jibes. For the briefest of moments, he considers taking Ciise up on having Shamso *offed*. Unbeknownst to Rooble, however, Ciise is already working on it, but not in a way that Rooble anticipates.

The weekend passes without incident as Rooble and Naaleeye spend the Saturday together attending his cousin's wedding. As usual, Rooble finds it pleasant to be amongst so many of his own people. There in each other's company, they can forget that they aren't in Somalia. They can forget that the South Africans would rather they weren't there. Naaleeye is in her element at the event, dancing and smiling, and Rooble is swept along with her easy enthusiasm.

That evening Rooble takes Naaleeye back to her mother's house, where Rooble exchanges tense niceties with Shamso in the kitchen, politely declining the offer of tea before saying goodbye to Naaleeye and setting off for home. The only thing Rooble can imagine Shamso has against him is that he is not from a good enough family for her daughter. Either that or she doesn't want her daughter to be happy, to have her own life.

After leaving, Rooble considers his career and realises that he doesn't have one. In fact, he has never had one. He had thought moving from Somalia to South Africa would mean he could concentrate on a job that could lead somewhere and become important to him. In Somalia, all he had ever had was a series of jobs that meant nothing to him. Despite his intentions in Johannesburg, the trend had continued. A means to earn money to pay for what constituted his life.

Taking a pen, Rooble begins to list the jobs he has had. Two minutes later, staring down at the list, he realises that it is time to use the current negative situation at work as an impetus for change. Rooble feels good about this and feels even better once he decides he will begin seeking out contacts in Little Mogadishu to help him towards something better.

Over the last few years, a cynicism has crept into Rooble's thinking that is weighing him down. It has been a long time since he has been genuinely happy for himself, but Naaleeye is changing all that, and he is beginning to see her as more than a girl he likes. He sees her as a positive element effecting change elsewhere in his life. Tonight Rooble settles on his foam mattress, knowing he is taking steps towards a happier life.

It's Monday, and as Rooble makes his way towards the factory, he has forgotten the ridicule he will walk into, excited for the imminent brightening of his future. In fact, as caught up as he is in his thoughts, he doesn't notice the flat atmosphere amongst his colleagues until he is finishing his lunch. There are no jibes or jokes coming his way.

*Has everyone suddenly tired of the topic? Or has Shamso run out of gossip about his relationship with her daughter? Come to think of it, where is she?* wonders Rooble.

'Don't know, she just hasn't come in today,' answers

Gabeyre when Rooble asks him.

That night, at Snack Bar, Rooble asks Naaleeye, expecting her to say her mother has been ill.

'Oh, I don't know. I had a cup of tea with her last night before going to bed. She seemed fine then. I didn't see her this morning. I thought she had left already. I was late getting up,' replies Naaleeye. 'I'll let you know later. It's nice that you're asking after her.'

The following day there is still no further news of Shamso, and her absence from the factory continues. At lunchtime, Rooble checks his phone and finds a text message from Naaleeye.

*Mother isn't home. Haven't seen her. No one's seen her. Is she at work today?*

A little black sliver of ice drops through Rooble's chest at this news.

'Ciise!'

Straight after work, Rooble weaves his way amongst the noisy cars and hurries to the cigarette shop where Ciise works.

'What did you do to her?' whispers Rooble angrily at Ciise over the counter.

'Her, who? Who her?' jokes Ciise.

'You know who. Shamso!'

'Oh yeah, the funny mummy. I didn't do anything to her.'

'Then who did?'

'Someone else?'

'Who? What's happened? Tell me. Now!'

'Let's talk later.'

When later comes, Ciise buys Rooble a drink and explains

as much as he can.

'It wasn't me. I'll tell you that much,' states Ciise, setting the drinks down on the table and setting himself down on a blue painted chair.

'Just tell me what's happened,' says Rooble.

'What happened, Rooble, is that you've had a terrible time lately, and your friend saw that the ray of happiness that had entered your life was being shut out by some heartless hag who couldn't keep her mouth shut.'

'And?' presses Rooble.

'And someone owes me a favour. I gave that person the info, and they said they would get rid of Shamso,' replies Ciise, pushing away from the table and folding his arms in front of him with a self-satisfied grin, as though awaiting applause.

'What do you mean? Get rid? Does that mean kill?'

'No. It definitely does not mean kill. She's alive. She is not dead. She is very much alive.'

'Then where is she?'

'A wall.'

'A war? What?'

'No. A *wall*,' enunciates Ciise.

'What do you mean?'

'I don't expect you to understand. *I* don't even understand. Let's say she has been *transferred*. Look, the person who does this normally doesn't tell what becomes of the people they make disappear. Usually, the people involved don't want to know, but it is a special situation since you didn't ask for this. So I thought you'd probably want to know, and I found out. You're welcome, by the way. This person has told me that

Shamso… has been transferred. Into a wall.'

'Transferred? What do you mean? I don't understand.'

'Look, I don't understand it myself, but what I know is that Shamso is now a brick wall. You wanted her shut up and, as far as I know, walls don't talk.'

'So she's dead?'

'She's not dead. She's a wall.'

'So she's dead?' Rooble repeats.

'She's… in between. She's a wall. They're tearing down the slums, Rooble. They're building real walls. They need strong people for that.'

'Well, where is she? How do we get her back?'

'My friend –'

'The one who did this?' interrupts Rooble.

'Yes. He told me you could get her back by going to the wall and apologising.'

'That's it? That's all I have to do? Go to the wall and apologise? And she'll come back?'

'That's all you have to do.'

'Okay, let's go. Where's the wall?'

'That's the other thing. You have to find it. Her. It. Them. Whatever.'

'Where? How do I do that?' Ciise simply shrugs. 'This is a joke, right? This is all a big joke. What is happening? *How* is this happening?' asks Rooble with his fingers at his temples.

'Look at it this way. Do you want to find her? What has she given your life so far?'

'She's Naaleeye's mother. How can I have anything more to do with Naaleeye knowing that her mother is a wall somewhere and it is my fault? Can I even tell her Shamso is now a wall?'

'Can't see why not, but I can't see why you'd want to either.'

'You stopped making sense some time ago. You should shut up now.'

Rooble heads to Naaleeye's apartment, fully intending to tell her what has happened to spare her any pain and give her closure, no matter the consequences. Walking there, he has figured out a way to approach it.

'Your mother, Shamso, is part of an amazing new experiment that will be of major significance. She has been selected, seemingly at random, to participate in a study showing how truly open-minded individuals can successfully make the transition from one state to another. Like a fish out of water thing. Oh, or like that fish they found in that woman's petrol tank happily splashing about. It's just this crazy stuff now. The world, we have to find our place in it. Does that make sense?' ... is the speech he has thought up thus far.

However, upon arriving, he finds the police in attendance and Naaleeye telling them all she knows about her mother, who has been missing for over twenty-four hours. Seeing the uniforms sitting in the small room on the lumpy couch, with Naaleeye crumpled in a worn-out armchair, suddenly makes it all real to Rooble. Despite the absurdity of what had happened to Shamso, there could be grave consequences for him if they find he had a hand in making her disappear.

With all the strange happenings of late, does anything in their world make sense anymore? Does anything really matter anymore? So what if he doesn't have a job he likes? So what if Shamso is a wall? Can anything or anyone be trusted? Is there any law and/or order to uphold? If so, how much longer will it last?

'Maybe,' thinks Rooble conclusively, 'the best thing I can do is to keep quiet.' And so he kneels next to Naaleeye and, resting her head against his shoulder, she cries into his shirt. The tears sink into the material and merge with Rooble's skin, sealing his silence forever.

Silence was not an option as far as Raju was concerned. They had to talk. He and Serena. But what is there to say that is truly constructive when a child has been hurt? The words don't come easily. And for some, they don't come at all. I watched as Raju and Serena blindly felt their way towards and away from each other. Each making sense of their feelings, the circumstances, everything that may have led up to this point. Their actions, their words, their failures.

'What do we do?' asked one.

'I don't know. What have I done for this to happen?' asked the other.

'It's not you.'

'What happened?'

'I don't know. I don't know.'

'Did... did someone do this?'

'I don't know.'

'Why don't you know? Where were you?'

'I don't know. I know as much as you. Serena, this isn't our fault.'

'Why not? Whose fault is it then?'

'I... maybe no one.'

'How can this happen to our little girl, and it's not anyone's fault? It's not possible. Something is damaged somewhere. This isn't… reality. This is not really happening.'

'I don't know what to say.'

'Why won't they let me see her? How can seeing her hurt? How could this get any worse? Amina is gone. Amina is *gone*. What are we going to tell everyone? What are we going to tell Dev?'

'Somehow we have to tell him the truth. We have to tell him what has happened.'

'I don't understand what has happened. How are we going to explain it to Dev? To everyone?'

'I don't know what you want me to say.'

'Nothing, Raju. Nothing. As usual. You have nothing to say.'

'Listen, Serena. We need to stay together right now. We need to… we can't fall apart.'

'I can't think right now,' said Serena, her voice rising in a vain attempt to cut through Raju's noise. She was too exhausted to cry anymore, although she wanted to. She wanted to cry for her daughter. 'I just can't keep it all in my head. We have a little boy. What is going to happen? If I couldn't keep *her* safe, what can I do for him?'

'I'm here too. We're still a family.'

'What was she doing there?'

'I don't know.'

'Why don't you know? What kind of father are you?'

'You're upset. I know. So am I. Attacking me won't help.'

'Something has to. There must be an explanation. You let her go too far.'

'That's not fair.'

'It's true.'

'It's not true. She didn't have more freedom than anyone else her age.'

'Her age,' spat Serena at his response, '*here!*' she cried to make her point.

'It was an accident. These things happen,' tried Raju, weakly.

'They don't happen at home.'

'They happen everywhere.'

'Not to girls her age, not in Mauritius. She wouldn't have been… like that if she was in Mauritius. Raju, we failed.'

Serena and Raju weren't the only ones I watched that day. Later, I looked in as Dev tried to understand his new world order.

'Dev, we have something to tell you. We need you to listen. Okay?' started his father. Dev nodded as he sat on the sofa with his favourite *He-Man* action figure, Skeletor, whom he also made nod to his father. The way Skeletor's plastic muscles were moulded meant he could get a better view of the elastic within that held the limbs to the torso and made the toy work. 'It's about Amina,' continued his father.

'Where's Amina?' asked Dev.

'There's been an accident. She's at the hospital. Do you understand?' asked Raju.

'An accident? What's wrong with her?' asked Dev. Raju remained silent. 'Is she going to be okay?'

'We don't know, Dev. Um… we have to wait and see.'

'Wait and see?' echoed Serena, incredulously, snapping away from the window.

'Yes,' confirmed Raju firmly.

Serena turned back to the window as Dev asked, 'shall we go and see her?'

'No,' Raju answered gingerly.

'Why not?' asked Dev. 'That's what people do. They visit people in the hospital. We can take flowers,' he stated brightly.

'Well, Mum and I will go to see her.'

'But I want to see her.'

'You're not old enough.'

'Dev,' interjected Serena, pulling away from the window, but still forming a silhouette, stray strands of hair escaping her ponytail. 'Amina isn't coming back.'

'Serena!' cried Raju, afraid of what she would say next.

'What's wrong with her?' asked Dev again.

'She had an accident, Dev,' Raju quickly said to ward off another of Serena's outbursts. After a moment, he continued, hardly able to get the next words out. 'This is difficult, and I'm sorry. Really sorry,' he finally managed, the tears springing to his eyes again. He got up and walked away to hide them from Dev.

'Mum?' asked Dev.

'Mina… Amina isn't coming back. She's dead, Dev, she's dead. She's not coming back. She's left us,' whispered Serena.

Dev didn't know what to say. The little boy was stunned and silent as his mother crossed the room to hug him tightly, letting her tears fall on his head.

It was the first time Dev had really thought about death. He didn't know the word *surreal* at the time but, had he known it, that would have been how he would have described it.

Surreal.

*How could she be gone? Gone where? Where was she? How could she go anywhere without saying goodbye?*

Dev understood that she was dead and wouldn't be returning, but despite knowing this, he still felt an overwhelming urge to ask when she would be coming back. He always felt that way when Amina had gone somewhere. Even if he already knew the answer.

Dev was nine years old and knew what *dead* meant. *But dead can't actually mean dead. It must mean something else because what dead means is just too strange. Dead means… lost forever, like… a ripple in the sea, or something,* he thought.

'What can I do?' he asked his father some days later. 'There must be something I can do.'

'No. Everything that can be done has been done,' said Raju, kneeling before Dev and adjusting the black tie around his son's neck.

'That's other people. There must be something *I* can do. I haven't tried anything. There must be something I can try,' pleaded Dev.

'Oh. I see,' said Raju, finally understanding what his son

meant.

'We can't let this happen. We have to stop it, Dad. We can't let this happen to her,' Dev insisted, pulling on Raju's arm.

Raju was empty. He had nothing left that he could say to his son. With his heart and mind in shards, he was running on autopilot to navigate the way through the day. All Raju could do was hug his son tightly as his tears fell on Dev's smart little suit jacket.

'There must be some magic, or, like, a secret code in a cave somewhere that will unlock Amina and bring her back from wherever she's gone.' Raju didn't reply. 'Don't you love her anymore?' asked Dev.

Raju pulled back from Dev and looked him in the eyes. 'Dev, there is nothing I love more than you and Amina, but I can't do anything. I'm not *God*.'

'That's it,' cried Dev excitedly, his eyes suddenly lighting up. 'God! We should go to the temple in Mauritius and see the gods. If we tell them what has happened, they will definitely do something. They just don't know what's happened.'

'Dev, God, can't help,' Raju replied, beginning to lose his patience.

'But you just said –'

'I know what I said,' shouted Raju in frustration. 'They fucking can't do anything. None of them can.'

'Then what was the point of all of it?' Dev eventually asked, shaken, tears in his eyes. 'The orange mumbling man, the offering, the blessing, not turning your back on the goddess?'

Regaining his composure, 'I did tell you they're pranksters,' said Raju apologetically.

'I thought there were rules. I didn't break the rules, Dad, I promise,' replied Dev, ignoring his father's lighthearted response.

'There are no rules to say that God must help, Dev.'

'But, in the temple, I thought they were rules,' insisted Dev.

'They weren't rules. They were rituals.'

'What's the difference?'

'Rituals… just make you feel better,' Raju tried to explain. 'Rituals make you feel better,' he repeated. 'It's okay to want to feel better, but they don't really do anything outside of that. I'm sorry, Dev.' This was when it truly dawned on Dev that his sister was gone.

'There really is nothing we can do, is there?'

Raju hugged his son again, and they both cried.

# 28. A positive mental attitude

It was with Bellyana, Ruth and Tim that Dr. Sharma spent New Year's Eve of 2012. Bell had just been promoted at her law firm. The promotion had meant a move to the London branch. Dev, Bell and their respective friends had already arranged to spend New Year's Eve/Day together, but as it drew closer, Bellyana had begun to grow uneasy about turning down the offer of spending it with her new colleagues.

They were going to see the fireworks at London Bridge and had invited Bellyana to spend time with them away from the office. She had already missed the Christmas party with her move coming too late. If she also missed the new year opportunity to socialise with her new colleagues in the city, when would the next opportunity be? And when it would come, it would be too late. She would have missed her chance to be initiated to the *team* in a social setting.

Having memories to share with others had always been important to Bellyana. She felt it helped anchor her within a given situation and give her a place, especially amongst relatively new people. Additionally, she hoped she could show off the non-work side of her personality.

Being the anxious sort, however, Bellyana had not wanted to feel alone with the group of relative strangers and so had asked, perhaps selfishly, if any of her friends would support her. Her friends were fully aware of what seemed to be Bell's penchant for overestimating the significance of events, so most of them told her the truth: they wanted to stay close to family and celebrate close to home instead of heading for Central London. Dr. Sharma did not have any such problem and agreed to go for the festivities. Tim hadn't kept in touch with Bell over the years, but he surprisingly had no plans for the night and also agreed to make the trip.

At the pub, it was clear that the idea was to drink as much as possible before 23:30. Then everyone would stagger into the street and follow the throng towards the sound of a DJ stationed outdoors, blasting the biggest hits of the year through speakers suspended from mini-cranes, strategically positioned for maximum effect. So at 23:37, that is precisely what they did. Walking along in the cold (it was bitterly cold that year) and having had to endure Bellyana's new colleagues being generally obnoxious throughout the night, Dr. Sharma began to wonder what he was doing there.

Bellyana seemed to sense this. 'Sorry, I dragged you two over here for this.'

'Don't be silly, we're going to see fireworks. Everybody loves fireworks,' replied Tim, who had taken an instant shine to Bellyana's friend, Ruth. Together they continued to shuffle slowly along with the crowd through the streets towards the river like some grand, drunken funeral procession.

*What are any of us doing here?* wondered Dr. Sharma. Under different circumstances, they might be labelled a march. A demonstration. A mob. But those terms imply a common purpose, a shared goal. As Dr. Sharma searched the faces around him, he couldn't help feeling that they had no interest in anyone not part of their group. The people in London to see the fireworks at close quarters were described on the news the following day as "the crowd" and "new year revellers."

The last time Dr. Sharma had been out amongst strangers to celebrate the new year, he had ended up being embraced by more strangers than friends. However, this night, there was a different feeling in the air with people pushing and squirming to get the best view of the fireworks, with the London Eye and Big Ben in the distance. Leaning over each other, they craned their necks for pockets of space through which to watch the coloured lights climb the blank sky and explode before petering out into nothing.

As Big Ben struck midnight and the DJ bellowed 'happy new year, everybody!' over the beat of electronic music from the suspended speakers, like some manic, stimulant-fuelled celestial being. While most people stared at the little coloured lights in the sky, the rest tried to capture them with their cameras. For posterity.

It didn't seem to Dr. Sharma that these people were here to celebrate the dawn of a new year and wish each other the best it might bring. There was no sense of anything having ended or begun. It was just an anti-climactic continuation, which is, of course, entirely accurate. Once the fireworks were done,

Dr. Sharma noticed there was no longer even any pretence that they were at the dawn of a new beginning. Just more.

Walking the streets, after the fireworks, with his friends towards Bellyana's place, Dr. Sharma's mind drifted as they chatted. Through the throng, he spotted an inebriated man engaged in a very one-sided conversation with a lamp post. He passed the man with curly, shoulder-length black hair and wondered how much he had had to drink, how his night might progress…

I'm walking down the street, minding my own business, when someone taps me on the shoulder. I'm rushing to a party and don't really have time for lamp posts. But it's New Year's Eve, so I stop and turn.

You can understand my surprise to find not one, but several lamp posts crowded around on the pavement behind me. All in their typical grey livery, lamps flickering from time to time. I don't remember passing all these lamp posts. *Where have they all come from?* I wonder to myself. Something, maybe a stray spark, draws my attention to the ground. I realise that I did not pass them. They came across me. They have become completely… uprooted and are sliding over the pavement, like snakes over ice. The lamps have no idea how this has happened, but they will soon expire without their electric life source. I struggle to see what I can do for them and mentally kick myself for being the only one out of the crowd of people heading home after the new year countdown to stop and face them. I look up at the lamps and see what is hanging from them, all-weather fairy lights put up a month ago by the local council workers to stimulate an approximation of that thing we call *Christmas spirit*. These weaker lights had already silently perished.

I am due to attend a New Year's party, but the street lights, buzzing and braying, plead with me to stay with them as the crowd disappears in the night. They do not want to burn out alone. They are confident they will die tonight, and I know they are right. Even if I succeed in contacting an engineer, they won't bother at this time on January 1st.

Not having the heart to argue with them, I ask what they would like to do. Their response is unanimous. They want to be amongst people. They want to go to the places they have heard talk about, the places they would see on the side of double-decker buses, the places tourists would point to on maps under the glow of the lamps, but most of all, they want to see as many lights as possible.

The trouble is they don't know what to do, how to get to these places. From as far back as they can remember, they have been rooted to the same piece of ground in the same way. They would greet people on arrival at our beautifully squalid capital. Some would reciprocate, while most would ignore them. They always guided people to wherever they were going by lighting the way, yet they could not see the way themselves. Part of the background of photographs, never the foreground. Never in focus. They don't know what to do with themselves. It is all down to me.

This kind of thing always happens to me. While others are having a good time, I'm involved with something I want no part of. As though sensing my internal debate, the lamp posts assure me that it will not be long before they fade. After this, I could probably still get to the party. Even if I didn't, there would be other parties, but it's not every day that you get asked to babysit a bunch of failing lamp posts. It wouldn't hurt.

I can't think of where to take them to be amongst people. Of course, taking them to the party is an option I consider, but it is a taxi ride away, and they don't have that much time. Besides, it would be selfish of me to force everyone else at the party to put up with dying lamp posts. At this time of year, everyone wants to have fun, not think. The streetlights will be gone soon, but the party people won't forgive me for forcing them to share the party atmosphere with a bunch of dying lamp posts, and I have my standing to consider. People gravitate towards simple fun. They don't want other people's problems. I could take them to a nearby pub or nightclub, but I can't afford New Year's Eve prices for this lot.

It really is quite embarrassing for me. I stand before the posts, pretending I am deep in thought while they squirm all over the pavement, all jagged angles, like gangly teenage elbows and knees. I muse that as they grow dim, they must consider me not very bright.

The glow is fading from the lamps, gradually but noticeably, and I realise action is necessary. Taking charge, I lead them towards Trafalgar Square. It isn't too far from where we are. On the way there, we can feel the gaze of other lamp posts as they stare after our small unit, their glows trained on us, as though actors taking the stage. Conspicuously they lean over to one another and buzz thoughts back and forth. The pavements carry the news far and wide, and the city anticipates our arrival. It knows our destination. As we make our way, police cars and sirens speed towards and away from us in the opposite direction. I wouldn't usually mind this, but their loud, flashing lights, throwing their cool blue tint over surrounding buildings, appear to whet the appetites of my small following, heightening their expectations.

As I walk and the lamps slither behind me, I pray that there will be at least a few pockets of people left. I have no idea what those people will be doing there so long after midnight, maybe still merrymaking. Still, so long as the lamp posts can be amongst them, without bothering anyone, everybody will be content, and my conscience will be clear.

To my extreme disappointment, the place is devoid of any living person. Not even any pigeons. It is extremely cold. I turn to the lamps and try to explain by reminding them what time of the morning it is, but they are not listening.

Instead, they are transfixed by all the different, soft lights that surround them. Here they bask in the glow of lamps and fairy lights, bigger, brighter and further reaching than any others they have experienced. Entranced, they slither from the square and swoon to the neon signs of shops. Some of these signs blink and crackle violently, but this makes no difference to my lamps, seduced as they are by their newfound idols.

Walking around and scanning the horizon, I spy the silhouettes of the lamps who have made their way, awestruck by gigantic backlit digital billboards enveloping the sides of entire buildings. They are wooed by images of soft drinks, technology products and German cars. Humming and gurgling with superiority, they tower over the smitten lamps who have never seen anything like this. Other, smaller neon advertisements also become the focus of attention.

Like small children, the lamps jump around, desperate for attention for the wonders they have discovered. Advertisements for products. Services. Movies. Bright and colourful, they unfailingly exude unquestioning optimism. The sky is clear, but I can't make out the stars with all the extra light. I haven't noticed it before, but the insides of most of the businesses around us also display extra neon signs inside, pressed into wishing everyone: 'A Happy New Year'.

Ironically, I think the green neon cross of a small chemist nearby attracts none of the lamp posts. I wonder why. Were there a church with a big neon crucifix, a Star of David, or some other religious symbol, would the lamps flock to it? Perhaps. Perhaps not. 'Are lamp posts religious?' I ask myself as I watch them snake around, bleeding molten rubber insulation. I have never thought about this.

Shivering as I watch the warm air leave my nostrils against the cold, it is clear to me that the energy of my lamps is fading fast. They move a lot more sluggishly, their braying more high pitched, the light they emit is brighter, as though overheating. Despite this, they seem satisfied. Despite being very near the inevitable, they seem happy enough as they converge on the street corner from where I have been observing them. Thankful and claiming to be content, they are happy to bring their existence to a close. It is now that one of them spots a faint glow emanating from within a plastic bag discarded by the fourth plinth at Trafalgar Square.

The wind blows at the handles of the plastic bag weighed down by its contents. It takes a few seconds for my eyes to focus on what I am looking at in the bag. It is from the corner of my eye that I spot the large paving slabs gradually crawling up the side of The National Gallery, as though trying to get as far away as possible. *They're right*, I think, standing back from the plinth to see the steps leading up to the museum behind it, attempting to grind themselves into the ground, without success. All around me, these once inanimate objects now pursue self-preservation, just like any living being.

'Turning to my lamps, I find them flailing around on the ground, their glow petering out. In the windows of audio/video shops across the city, television sets make sense of the information being transmitted. In the face of destruction, all they can do is follow their programming, their instructions and continue to entertain, despite their fear. They reconstitute information to construct images from *The Italian Job*. Not the remake, the original that remains a mainstay of UK TV programming at this time of year, even if it has been relegated to the small hours. I can see the scene. Zoom in. Explosion. Cut to Caine. Like any peddler of empty promises, I don't need to hear to know what he says. I already know.

'I look up to the sky before we are all engulfed by a brilliant white light, the likes of which none of us has ever seen. No neon advertisement can surpass this. The shockwaves spread, shattering every single window, screen and neon tube in the area. As the burglar alarms are activated, the stars can finally shine through the darkness. As the artificial lights fade, starlight can reassert itself. Faintly at first. Then stronger.'

Fading.
Adjusting.
Glowing.

Stronger.

After Amina.

What next?

Everyone had been understanding. Sympathetic.

Serena and Raju had been offered time away from work.

Dev didn't go to school.

A few weeks after the funeral, when they did persuade him to return, he was despondent and distracted in class. His teacher prepared a daily report that detailed his comportment, attention and consequent school work throughout the day.

Friends and neighbours called to enquire about the family's progress, but they weren't the friends who had been expected. After the funeral, those they had considered their close friends had apparently decided the best way to demonstrate this was to stay well away from them, as though they were contagious. As though there was a *Dead Daughter* infection that could be caught by merely phoning someone to hear how they were.

'I suppose nobody knows what to say,' rationalised Raju.

'You don't say anything. You just phone,' said Serena.

'I know, but… never mind.'

Lately, Raju felt that anything he said on any topic was wrong as far as Serena was concerned. He was learning to keep quiet to keep the peace, sealing his thoughts and feelings in the process. Outside of family, the only friends to contact them were the known gossip-hounds eager to hear of any new developments. Serena didn't suffer their inane chatter, but Raju spoke with them just to have a conversation that didn't end with fear and hostility being bitterly spat across the room at him.

Shortly after Dev returned to school, Raju returned to work, surmising that he couldn't stay at home forever, and the longer he left it, the harder it would be.

Serena's approach was that the longer she left it, the longer she would leave it. 'You know how those women are going to be. I won't be able to stand listening to those simpering bitches without chucking a stapler at their faces.'

'So you're never going back?' Raju asked as the microwave announced dinner with its bouncy beeps.

'I don't know. Maybe not. Maybe I'll just quit and get a new job elsewhere. Somewhere no one knows me. What do you think?'

'I don't know. If you think it's a good idea.'

'I don't know what I think. I don't want to do anything. I don't want to think.'

'No. Me neither,' Raju admitted, staring into the steam coming off the ex-frozen meal.

It was Raju's nature to opt for a gentle approach. When he was at home on the weekends, he would have been the first to cave in and let Amina ditch the textbooks in favour of cartoons. However, his patience had limits. While he liked to think he knew Serena as well as anybody, they were both in uncharted water, dealing with a horror that most cannot imagine enduring.

Nothing they had experienced could have prepared them for this, and neither of them knew how to handle it. Had she been pressed on this, Serena would have said that it was impossible for her because she had no interest in handling it. She had no interest in resuming her life or feeling the pain subside. Raju also carried his pain but concealed it well. So well that Serena began to resent it, disgust at his apparent nonchalance gradually building.

Raju and Serena had taken different approaches to the aftermath. The sympathy and support from others remained, but curiosity and shock from their community, friends and family faded and was replaced. Neighbours tended to avoid them or pretend they hadn't seen them, as though concerned that grief, sadness and desperately unfortunate events were infectious. Or that the family was harbouring some gremlin that could make the leap to their home if they got too close.

Friends began to feel awkward asking the same questions, saying the same things.

'How are you?'

'How are things?'

'You're in our thoughts.'

However, they also feared that those questions would lead to conversations in which they could have only minimal participation. When it comes to conversations, people want to participate and be heard. But Raju's and Serena's friends couldn't possibly contribute to the kind of conversation that would arise from making the type of noises they felt obligated to by social contract. Raju and Serena had family in Canada and France. However, most contact came from Mauritius, where their family deemed it was their duty to continue asking if there was anything they could do, much to Serena's irritation.

'They're 6,000 miles away. What do they think they're going to do?' Serena would complain to Raju.

'They're trying to be nice,' Raju would reply.

‘I wish they would stop.’

‘What else can they do?’

‘Nothing. So they should just shut up.’

Family doesn’t care about repeating the same questions, the same conversations. Family doesn’t need to participate to be seen as knowledgeable and wise. Sometimes family, and genuine friends, are at their best when they just listen.

While the couple bickered about things of no significance, they avoided discussing the source of their grief at all costs. Raju wouldn’t because he feared making Serena’s apparent instinct for isolation more pronounced. Serena couldn’t tell him what she knew. She couldn’t do that. Instead, the truth consumed her from within. Meanwhile, Dev busied himself at school with a need to prove himself.

After the death of a child a family is irrevocably changed. For the Sharmas it was no different. Dev knew that the worsening situation at home was due to Amina, whose loss weighed heavier on him with each passing day. He needed his parents to get back to normal but had no idea how to bring them back. As children do, Dev believed he should have been able to make his parents happy. However, he quickly concluded that his inability to do this was not due to who he was but who he wasn’t.

Dev came to understand that he couldn’t make things better because he simply wasn’t Amina. The yawning maw of sorrow left by Amina was too much for them to bear. It was too much for Dev to withstand. He gave in and let it snap his bones. He let the waves of guilt and remorse cover him until he almost always felt apologetic for the space he took up in the world. Until he constantly felt sorry that he wasn’t Amina.

The only place he didn't feel he needed to apologise was in his dreams. In his imagination. The only place that was entirely his own. His mind.

Serena didn't want anyone's attention. She didn't want any sounds, comforting, supportive, or otherwise. She wanted only to remain where the air was thick, and voices were muffled. For Raju, the pain of losing Amina was like broken glass grinding in his chest. Each time he breathed, it was as though he could feel it shifting, splintering and piercing a little more, never settling enough for comfort.

A natural pleaser, Raju, in contrast to Serena, went out of his way to meet people and present an upbeat attitude. He had soon noticed the growing distance between his family and others. He didn't want to be isolated again, having spent long enough as an unwanted immigrant doing an undesirable job for which relatively few from his adopted country would have the heart. Raju put on a bright smile whenever he met anyone, going out of his way to make everyone feel comfortable, constantly fearing the cold that came from being disregarded.

The way people avoided them felt different from when he was alone and lonely in a foreign country, studying medicine. However, it still pained him. Way back there, behind all his other thoughts, he couldn't help wondering if the death of Amina was a convenient excuse to avoid them.

'We'll not invite them. They must want time to themselves.'

He saw the distance growing incrementally, but he also saw the efforts that were being made. He saw how others had reached out to them and eventually felt that enough time had passed, that they needed to leave the self-imposed isolation and reconnect with their friends and community. Raju couldn't help losing his patience on more than one occasion and snapping at Serena. It was yet another complaint from Serena after a phone call from Mauritius that Raju first snapped at her.

'Serena, it's time to start moving on. Don't you think?'

'I'm trying to. They won't let me.'

'No. It's you. You're still pushing people away. You're the one not letting it go.'

'So you want me to forget? Is that it?'

'That is not what I'm saying, and you know it. How could you say that? No one is going to forget Amina, but we need to try to get back –'

'To normal?' Serena interrupted. 'Do you think anything can ever be normal again? Normal is over. It's finished. Normal is never coming back, Raju.'

He tried on a few more occasions to cajole her into stepping back into the life they used to have, but Raju eventually gave up. He didn't have the voice for it. Instead, Raju watched and waited as Serena got further away from him, baffled at her ability to shut out the world and lose herself. In turn, she was incredulous at Raju laughing and joking with neighbours in the street and resented how easily he did it. Neither genuinely blamed the other for what had happened to Amina. But from time to time, they were consumed by the fantasy of doing just that. It simmered in the background, always there, leaving smears on every surface, clouding the windows with condensation, fogging each room, making it difficult to see.

'I don't see them,' complains Karl, uselessly wiping at the window to dispel the fog.

'You see the balls moving around, don't you?'

'Yeah.'

'Who do you think is kicking them?'

'Not damned ghosts, that's for sure.'

'Don't call them ghosts,' admonishes Werner, 'they don't like that.'

'So what do they want to be called?'

'Former players.'

'And these former players, they now want to be current players again?'

'Yes. There's nothing in the *Bundesliga* rule book prohibiting it.'

'But football is football. It doesn't change for anything. I can't replace real players with ghosts who haven't played in years.'

'They've explained it to me the best way they can. They say they shed blood, sweat, tears of sadness, tears of victory on that pitch as players. They're back exactly as they were when they last played on that pitch.' To this, Karl can offer nothing but silence. He can't even pretend that he understands because he doesn't. 'But that also means they can't travel to other stadiums,' continues Werner.

'So they can only play half the games?' asks Karl.

'That's right.'

'It doesn't matter. I can't bump real, live people from the team-sheet for ghosts. We're all just trying to work with the latest changes, but humanity has to draw the line somewhere with this crisis, and I'm drawing it on the pitch with football.'

'They've met with Yuri.'

'They've met with Yuri? He doesn't speak German.'

'They have translators. They're dead too.'

'Translators shed sweat and tears on the pitch too?'

'No, they can bring anyone they want along.'

'No, they can't. I'm the manager, and I'll say what goes.'

'Yuri feels otherwise, and it's his club. Think of it!' pressed Werner, 'we'll have access to all the best players from any generation. We'll have a huge squad. They'll impart knowledge and the benefit of their experience to the younger players. We don't have to pay them. They won't even get injured.'

'But what about the young, live and literally kicking kids?' asked Karl. 'How will they get to play if their positions are taken up by a bunch of fucking ghosts.'

'They can play the away matches.'

'You and I both know the players thrive on hearing the roar of their home crowd. If being dead is the only way they can get to play, how long do you think it will be before they change themselves for a chance of something greater, for the chance to play for the love of the home crowd? Without that love, they're nothing. Don't you and Yuri see that?'

# 29. Floating in a cellophane brain

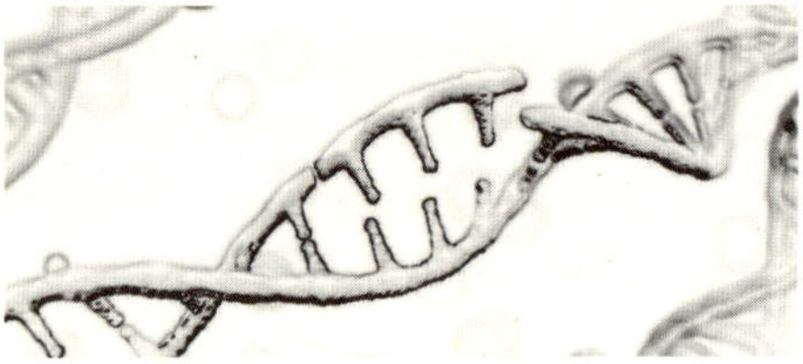

'But I don't see why,' stated Mira as Dr. Sharma took his usual seat on the bed opposite Mira, who resumed her customary opening position by the window. 'Why are you bothering with this lot anyway? What would anyone want to learn from them?' Mira's fingernails were painted black today, and Dr. Sharma could see that the streak of violet in her shoulder-length black hair had been freshly dyed.

He was finding his footing in these meetings with Mira, and his confidence in dealing with her was growing. He was gratified and relieved that his persistence was paying off. From the outset, Dr. Sharma had felt that she wanted to talk but just didn't know how to. Finally, she was finding her way and, he liked to think, was warming to him.

'I explained, I want to figure out how they came by their quirks.'

'How do we know what a quirk is? I mean *quirk* according to who?'

'What do you mean?'

'Well, who knows, maybe missionary position was the first quirk of all? Who decided it was the default position?'

'Exactly. But, I want to consider somewhat newer practices, what might be considered *deviant*, in the true nature of that word.'

'The stuff I do. You sure you're not doing this to work out some of your own quirks?'

'Pretty sure.'

'So you already know what they all are?'

'With the capacity that we all have to absorb new influences and cultures, I don't see how anyone could ever say they definitely know all their quirks. What do you think about your clients? What do you think of the films you make? How did you come to be involved in this?'

'I don't want to talk about all that,' Mira grimaced. 'Look, you've paid, so why don't you come and work on your quirks with me?' a half-hearted attempt to distract him.

'Do you have a problem with it?' he asked deliberately.

'Course not. If I had a problem with any of it, I wouldn't do it.'

'So haven't you ever wondered why there is such demand for this particular niche service you provide?'

'You're still talking like that.'

'Like what?' asked Dr. Sharma.

'Like you're afraid of the words. You say you want to talk, but then you don't know how to talk properly.'

'When you say, "talk properly," do you mean in a way that engages you? Using the correct vernacular?'

'There you go again.'

'Mira, I'm trying here. Work with me on this, please. So

the films you make, they're for a distributor known for making these extreme… films. When they set up a film like this, they will have a list of acts that they will want you to perform when you go to make the film, right?'

'Right.'

'So when these guys crowd around and look to mictur –. Perform a golden shower… routine with you –'

'"Routine!"' exhaled Mira, exasperated, 'you make it sound like they're dancing. It's not ballet. It's a porno.'

'Right. So when they perform this act with you, it's not a spur of the moment thing. You all know what you have to do, and at some point, you get a signal telling you when to do it.'

'Yeah. Something like that.'

'So don't you ever wonder why there is such demand to see this? To see men crowding around and pissing on a woman? Or to see someone dressed from head to toe in rubber? Do you ever wonder what pleasure is derived from that?'

'I bet you've thought of it. Why do you think they do it?'

'I'm trying to ask you. Do they enjoy it? What kind of pleasure do they receive? What's the psychology behind it? You must have thoughts. What do you think?'

'Honestly?' began Mira, exasperated. 'I think it's a bunch of naughty things, all at once. It's dirty. It's rough. It's forgetting all about thinking. You said watersports. It's warm, straight from the body. It has a specific smell. It's normally private, doesn't involve another person. It's not normally soaking the hair of someone you're about to fuck. That's why it's a turn-on for some people. It's different for different people. For some, the turn-on is in… waste. How dirty they think it feels. That's what the films are about. For other people, it's the intimacy of something straight from another person's body.'

'You think people then turn to other things when they get bored with that?'

'Maybe some people do. How am I supposed to know? Some people just stick with what they know they enjoy. Maybe some people get bored, and that's when they invent new things.'

'But we all invent in one way or another. As children, we create stories using our toys. Where does that spark come from?' Dr. Sharma asked no one in particular.

'I think you still are a kid.'

'Why?' Dr. Sharma didn't know whether to feel slighted or amused.

'Because you keep asking: why? where? how? There's no big mystery with children. They just copy what's around them in stories, on telly, what they've seen in the park,' Mira stated.

'But where does that come from? Everything we do, say and think comes from somewhere. For argument's sake, what if we could trace it back, trace it all right back to the start?' asked Dr. Sharma.

'The start of what?' asked Mira, losing patience.

'The start.'

'What, like Jesus times?'

'Well, er, okay, yeah. Why not? What if we could? Wouldn't it be amazing to see the influences, the emotions, the circumstances that led to the Bible and all the different subsequent versions? You ever read the Bible?'

'No. I bet you have.'

'No, but it has to be an amazing text. Think of the very first

Bible, or Torah, or Qur'an that was ever written. They would have been written in a specific way, using very particular words. Never mind the words for the minute, but maybe the style or the tone itself didn't translate properly over the generations and cultures. Even the Vatican has lately had trouble accurately translating documents because they misunderstood an essential element. Maybe the old texts were supposed to be read with a completely different tone that would have led to a different understanding. What if we could trace everything back?'

'How would you do that?'

'I don't know. I'm just interested.'

'But where would you start?' asked Mira, finally forgetting herself for a moment and allowing her interest to show.

'Maybe just pick one person at random?'

'And try to figure out all the stuff that makes them *them*?'

'I suppose you'd take all the information that person received and the circumstances under which they received it, the time and place.'

'But as you look at each person, won't the web just get wider and wider? And don't they say we learn stuff that's passed down in DNA?' Mira asked, leaning on the armrest of her chair towards Dr. Sharma. 'Everybody affects everybody else. My little nephew has my sister and Kevin in his life, but then there's all the stuff he watches on TV, books he reads at school. Oh, *school!* That would mean the teachers, the other kids and everything that has affected them? If you were trying to figure out how someone comes up with a specific idea, you'd have to look at how everything leads them to think of things in a certain way. You'd have to consider everything a person experiences, sees, hears, feels. But maybe not everything. Things only affect us if we let them.'

Dr. Sharma replied tentatively, not wanting to discourage Mira when she was beginning to engage more. 'Things can still affect us and change our way of thinking even if we don't want it to, even if we don't realise it at the time. Bad things that happen, negative stuff that people say.'

'All right,' conceded Mira, 'but how would you tell the difference? How could you know what has influenced someone or not? It'd be impossible to know. I suppose I'd never thought about it before. Well, who does apart from you? But… it's kind of like a… like a virus. Isn't it? Like how it multiplies everything we think and how we put it all out in the world, and it affects other people. They take it and turn it into something else, and it goes around again. Like when you see bacteria and that under a microscope, dividing and multiplying. Here, what's the oldest religion? Is it Buddhism?'

'Maybe. I don't really know.'

'Maybe, back then, if they had a way of getting information around the world fast, maybe we'd all be Buddhists now, and we'd have a slower pace of life and be more peaceful and happier.'

'Maybe, people would create different religions anyway. Like you said, people get bored and invent things. Maybe that's what happened with religion, they got carried away, and that's when they invented taboos in the first place, like not depicting Mohammed, or whatever.'

'Yeah, but if everyone was thinking peaceful thoughts from as far back as possible, they wouldn't have gone around conquering and raping, and pillaging, and enslaving.' Having made her point, Mira sat back in her chair and ran a couple of fingers through her hair, twirling some strands.

Dr. Sharma took a moment to enjoy his first real conversation with Mira. 'Amazingly, we can trace our evolution and estimate that we kicked off as bacteria in a swamp, but I've always been curious about how… well, about how things came about, the massive confluence of our thoughts over generations and generations that lead us to here and now. Doesn't it feel surreal to you that there doesn't exist, somewhere, some permanent evolving record of leaps and connections that we have made using our minds and how they connect and correlate with those of other people? When I was a kid, I couldn't understand there was nothing like that to record all our thoughts.'

'Maybe it's that way for a reason,' answered Mira.

'What if we got to a stage where we could identify all the negative stuff? All the negative influences. Would we choose to get rid of it? As a civilisation, do you think we would choose to get rid of the things that make us worse people?'

'You're asking the wrong woman. I don't even vote. Anyway, they're the ones who would take advantage of that. Politicians. And companies. They'd take away the stuff that makes us bad people.'

'D'you think?'

'Yeah, so we'd be nice and docile. Then they'd give themselves the bad stuff to make themselves more crafty, devious and determined to keep themselves on top. That's why nobody would choose to get rid of their bad side. Maybe we're not on top, but we have a fighting chance. If we were *all* nice, we wouldn't last.'

'Maybe that was the point of religion, to make everyone meek and compliant to be exploited by whatever it was that created it,' speculated Dr. Sharma.

'Assuming that all religion is made up by humans, and none of the stuff in the books actually happened. No blue gods with four arms, no parting the sea, all that stuff.' Dr. Sharma was glad to hear Mira ask him a question for a change, taking the conversation in a lighter direction. 'Has anything miraculous ever happened in your life? Ever feel like you've had a brush with the divine?'

'I don't know, I wouldn't know what to look for,' Dr. Sharma answered.

'Well,' began Mira, 'I've seen a lot of things, and I think I can safely say I have not seen the work of God in any of it. Maybe it's God behind everyone's thoughts,' Mira suggested with a smile.

'Maybe they're between the thoughts. If God is out there,' replied Dr. Sharma thoughtfully.

'Oh God, what have I done here?' Dr. Sharma asks himself as he continues to struggle and sweat on the bed. The memories, the images, sounds, feelings, experiences, emotions continue to sear his mind as his body flails and his hands fight the belt around his neck. From time to time, he is able to pull his mind back to the present moment. The body works to some preprogrammed instinct to struggle against that which is killing it, while the mind takes off to other places, but now that familiar, tinny music from a passing ice cream van brings Dr. Sharma's thoughts back to the present. It's ridiculous to him right now, but the music reminds him that life continues beyond the window, where people are around, going about their lives.

*Perhaps I can attract someone's attention, and they could bring help.*

Unfortunately, before he can formulate a plan, Dr. Sharma's mind begins to drift again.

*Katie's place isn't actually in a bad area. She told me before how she can only afford to rent in a location like this, by the sea, in the winter, when there are no tourists. I think the town mayor lives nearby. Or the former mayor. Jayne… something.*

Yes, that's all well and good. But before we let him fantasise about being rescued by the town mayor, or something, maybe we should give him a little nudge. After all, we are on a schedule here. 'So, Dev, what can you tell me about your surroundings?'

'My surroundings? I'm face down on a bedspread, and you want to know about surroundings? This bedspread. What do you need to know? It's fucking hideous. Who's idea was this? Yellow background with maroon coloured flowers?'

Little Dev traced his fingers over the flowers that made up the design on the carpet that ran up the stairs where he sat. Really there were only three types of flowers. They were just repeated all over the carpet in different ways. He liked to copy Amina in stepping only in the spaces between the flowers as he padded across the carpet. He'd been doing it for years, and his mum had been trying to stop this habit for almost as long. Recently, however, that had stopped being so important. Dev wanted to stay up eavesdropping as his mum and dad chatted, but it was late, and he kept drifting away, bumping his head on the bannister. A bit longer, and he gave up, dragging himself to bed in the room where he tried to remember Amina's stories.

Meanwhile, downstairs in the living room, Serena tried again to see Raju's feelings, but her anger and her hurt proved, as usual, too formidable to let her see anything else in the room. 'We can't carry on like this,' she said from the armchair by the radiator. It was just getting to the end of summer, and the house was being heated a little more often. For now, however, the radiator was cold.

'Why?' asked Raju from another armchair. He knew they were due another talk like this but felt it his role to act surprised each time. He laid out his case: 'I am doing everything I can, but nothing is good enough. Why don't you tell me what you want?'

'I know you're doing everything you can. You're right. It's not enough. We can't carry on like this.'

'What more? What else?' asked Raju.

'I just don't understand you,' admitted Serena after a moment, angling her face slightly more towards him. 'Everything is normal for you. It's like nothing has changed.

Our girl is gone.'

'You think nothing has changed for me? Serena. I don't know how you can think you're the only one affected? Our hearts have been shattered, but we still have our boy to think of.'

'But you don't act like anything has changed. You act like everything is normal. It's not normal. Nothing will ever be normal again.'

'It has been a year. How should I act? We have to continue.'

'We cook the same meals, we see the same people, we buy the same things at the same market each week.'

'What are we supposed to do? You want to make new friends? You want to shop somewhere else?' Raju heard her voice, but her words didn't make sense to him. His own voice rose with frustration.

'Everything has to change. I can't go on living… like this when she's gone. Something. Has. To. Change,' Serena enunciated, anguished that this man she thought she knew apparently refused to see that their life couldn't continue as before. She thought him cruel. Callous. Inwardly she raged at him for discarding the memory of Amina, desecrating it by insisting on getting back to their *normal life* as soon as possible. 'Don't you fucking understand? My girl is dead.' It wasn't like Serena to speak crudely, it wasn't how they were raised in Mauritius, but she needed to get through to him.

'It wasn't our fault.'

'How can you say that?'

'Because it's true. It was an accident.'

'We are the parents, and Amina died. If it wasn't our fault, whose fault could it possibly be? You're not opening your eyes. Whatever has happened is our fault.'

'Serena, I have thought about this a lot. I think about it every day, and I will probably die thinking it. We keep talking about everything. When it happened, it was tempting to blame someone. Other people. The workmen, the council, the drivers, the doctors, the hospital, her friends, ourselves. The truth is there is no one to blame, and it wasn't our fault either. I've been trying to get this through to you for months, but I don't know what I can do or say to help you understand.'

'*Me*? Understand?' Serena was incredulous as she sat forward in the armchair, bolt upright. 'Look, Raju, I don't believe that, and this is just not something where we can agree to disagree.

'I know.'

'This is Amina. She's gone from our lives. She is never going to leave the key in the front door again. She will never ask me to bake a cherry cake and then pick out all the cherries. She is never going to roll around on the grass after you've cut it. I can't just accept that as easily as you. I can't just… Something needs to change.'

'So what do we do, Serena?'

Serena took a moment. 'I'm going to Mauritius.'

'What?' Raju had a shortlist of the things he had expected, but Mauritius had not made it.

'We can't keep doing this.'

'You're leaving us to go to Mauritius? For how long?'

Serena breathed hard before continuing. 'And I'm taking Dev.' She let the words hang in the air for a moment. 'You can't work and look after him as well. If this has taught us anything, it's that we need to keep a closer watch.'

'You've got this all worked out. I'm sure you've got an answer for everything.'

'I've been thinking about it. I need space, even if you don't. I know you don't, but we're different people, and I need… space. And time.'

'What about Dev? Does he need time and space too? For how long?'

'It can't hurt to get away for a while, to think about everything that has happened. From a distance. Under the circumstances… Look, maybe other people can't get away to another country when something like this happens, but I don't care about them. I have that opportunity, and I'm going to take it.' Raju was speechless in the face of this and, despite her staunch tone, Serena began to grow nervous at the silence as he got up and walked into the dining room, where he stared into the garden. 'You and I both know that she would have been safe in Mauritius. There would have been none of this.'

'It's not *England*. This could have happened anywhere. You're *still* blaming me.'

'I need space, Raju.'

'But you don't need space from Dev?'

'Yes. Yes and no. He's my son. I need him. He's all I have.'

'I need him too. I need you.'

'Look, Raju,' began Serena, rising to her feet and following him to the threshold where the living room met the dining room. 'I don't know what to tell you. I need to try… something to move past this because what we're doing is not working. Not for me. So it's your choice. You can make things difficult and add more pain, or you can give us your love and let us go.'

Raju couldn't face her. After everything that had happened, he couldn't believe that it had come to this. He was losing his family to another country, thousands of miles away. He knew that there was nothing further to be gained by arguing with Serena, and he was too tired for the fight. Raju just wanted whatever was next.

# 30. Dear God

Once again, Dr. Sharma's mind has lost interest in the window and his vague thought of drawing attention. Instead, he decides to paint the mental picture of the mayor dealing with the unusual events in her town. Dr. Sharma imagines her breathless conversations with colleagues about the latest goings-on in their town, the wider world, and her sleepless nights as answers continue to elude them…

Jayne would lie awake at night, going over all the recent events that had occurred over the last week that had left the world unable to explain itself.

'Hundreds, thousands of people around the world claiming to be aliens and having taken over the bodies of jailed criminals, all telling the same story, wanting to be heard and let free to explore the world. Thousands of people running to the police, begging to be put behind bars because they had had some odd dreams. The ghosts of dead German footballers returning to taste glory once again. Somehow they think this represents the end of what we know of how the world works. What nonsense! Yes, highly unusual, but it hardly means the rules of the world are changing around us,' she says to herself.

'On the other hand, it is troubling that Belgium is to be shut down. A lot of Belgians suddenly trying to get into other countries. Nothing against Belgians, but they're just not *us*. If they elected better governments they wouldn't be in such trouble. So, really, it's their fault for electing such incompetent representatives. Why is the world turning into such a difficult place? Why is it such a struggle these days to simply live? It seems like things make less sense with each passing day, and that increasingly, the response is, " that's the cost of doing business." What business? The business of living? Raising a family? Who wants to do that in such uncertainty? But then, there has always been uncertainty in the world, and that didn't stop people from living their lives.' Mayor Jayne has a habit of talking to herself, which has only been exacerbated in recent days.

'On yet another hand,' she continues, 'this is not terrorism, or disease, or war. Or a financial crash. This is something we have never faced before. Insanity on a massive scale. They have to be crazy. All of them. The things they say can't be true. I feel like I'm the only sane one left. Even today, the paper is carrying a silly story about a woman who thinks her mother has become a wall or something. An insanity epidemic of epic proportions. Or idiocy. It has to be. Am I the only sane one left? Am I? God?'

God declines to answer.

'If you could give me some signal. Anything. Any kind of

sign showing me the best path to follow, I would go without question. Just tell me the answer, show me the way.'

With that, Jayne lets out a little sigh of resignation, rolls onto her side and sets about dreaming troubled little dreams.

To Jayne, it feels like she has dropped off for mere seconds when she opens her eyes with a start.

She knows.

That is all.

It is that simple.

She knows.

Instinctively Jayne reaches out for the bedside lamp switch. The angle of the light exaggerates her shadow cartoonishly and flings it against the wall behind her, covering the dresser. Turning away from the lamp, Jayne lets out a little gasp, startled by her own moving shadow. As her eyes adjust to the light, she sees the outline of the clay pot. 'There wasn't a clay pot there. Where did it come from?' In fact, as far as she knows, she is not even the owner of a clay pot.

Jayne gets out of bed gingerly and goes over to the dresser. As she does so, she feels something she has not felt in more than fifty years. A child's excitement at Christmas! She hadn't expected to see a pot, or anything at all, yet she isn't surprised. Everything, since she had woken up, feels like a passage from a book she read long ago that she is now reading again and remembering the lines the very instant her eyes alight upon them. That kind of familiarity.

The vessel is roughly forty centimetres tall and twenty centimetres in diameter, with two little handles on either side. Its lid is also made of clay. Jayne usually hates pots like these. It isn't the pots themselves as much as it is the texture of the clay. Jayne would grimace when opening them. The sound and the grind as the clay lid scraped against the rim of the receptacle would send a shiver through her. It would remind her of teachers using chalk on a blackboard or make her imagine etchings in caves, left to be found thousands of years later. 'Imagine if that was the only entertainment you had,' she had once said to a friend in history class. 'Listening to that sound all night. It would drive me *crackers*.' But that was forty-two years ago, and now Jayne places her hand lightly on the lid and leaves it there while she considers the right thing to do.

It's the next day, and Jayne ponders doing what no mayor of her town had ever had to do. A press conference! In her small town, the people had not been called upon to elect her as their mayor or any of her predecessors. Instead, the electorate consists of Jayne and her fellow councillors, who elect a nominee to take on the decorative title, along with the decorative mayoral garb. However, the duties are genuine.

The medallion glints in the early morning sunlight as she stands outside the church being photographed for the local newspaper. For the small-town mayor with an announcement to make, the best that could be mustered at such short notice was a photojournalist from the local newspaper and a skeleton crew of three from local TV news. Local radio stations were also due to broadcast live but have instead been diverted at the last moment by the death of local soap star, and noted cushion collector, Norman Tebby.

As she speaks outside the town hall, those who make up the small assembled group give her as much of their focus as they can under the circumstances. The story Jayne has to tell is undeniably far-fetched, and, as she recounts just how far she has been to fetch it, the rest of the group steal glances at one another from behind microphones, cameras and notepads. The TV people look bemused while the photojournalist seems nervous, but by the time Jayne has finished, they are all slack-jawed with excitement without being entirely sure of the main reason they are excited. There are two choices.

Either: The mayor has just made a veritable fool of herself in her role as representative of this tiny town, and this will make a hilarious story that will travel the world in no time at all.

Or: The mayor really has received a message and is here to deliver it.

The mayor continues:

'Don't ask me how I know. I just do. That's faith.'

Jayne runs this scene through her imagination and admits that she would sound like the crazy old bag-lady that would wander the streets shouting about (and at) everything when she was younger. The old bag-lady was long gone, but in the last few months, she had noticed a middle-aged man who limped along the high street, holding a placard aloft predicting the return of Jesus. The first time Jayne had seen this man with his placard, she had not paid much attention with barely a glance afforded him. However, she paid more attention the second time she noticed him, on a Saturday lunchtime whilst enjoying a tuna and sundried tomato panini in the seating area outside a sandwich shop.

His placard read: "THE RETURN OF JESUS 2!"

Jayne found it confusing.

Either: '2' was supposed to actually represent the figure '2', like the sequel to a Hollywood blockbuster.

Or: '2' was supposed to be short for *too*. In which case, who else did he have returning with him?

Was '2' meant to further emphasise the *RETURN* of Jesus, in case the point had been missed? Or was it simply that this would be his second time returning, marking his third appearance in total?

Jayne considered another possibility, that a figure named Jesus 2 had already been and gone while she had been busy with other things, and that the public was to hotly anticipate his return. Presumably to finish a job he had previously left undone?

Now, in her bedroom with the clay pot in her hands, Jayne realises that her story would be believed by no one. Except perhaps by placard-man. And within moments of her story being released, her standing in the town would equal his. 'Perhaps I could get my own placard, and we could agree to share the high street,' muses Jayne, muttering to herself. Besides, the people would not submit willingly to have some mysterious, unidentified substance applied to them and their children by someone claiming to have received it from God. Mayor or not.

Under normal circumstances, Jayne would have dismissed the whole thing as a strange dream, but she can't deny the existence of this pot in her hands. Also, unlike typical dreams, the more she thought about this experience, the more she remembered. For example, she has not only spoken to God, but God has also replied.

'But why me?' she remembers asking.

'I just liked your name. Jayne Johnson. Straightforward. To

the point. A name that can travel well to other parts of the world with different languages, cultures. Plus, you're the mayor of this town, right? I understand that means you hold some standing in the community.'

'Yes, but I don't know how I will accomplish what you're asking of me,' answered Jayne, all flustered.

'You'll find a way. Don't worry about it.'

'But I *am* worried. If you want people to believe, why don't you just do something that will leave them no option but to believe?'

'I am. This.'

'But this involves me… being involved. Why do you need me?'

'I need a helper.'

'But you have helpers everywhere. Priests, vicars, holy men, imams, rabbis, all the rest.'

'Yeah, but someone like me just *can't* trust people like them.'

'Oh?'

'Yeah, there's something about that level of snivelling commitment that is just… really… *icky*. Besides, you should never give power to anyone who actively seeks it, let alone anyone who begs for it like that bunch.'

'They beg for it?'

'Well… they more or less beg people to see them as an authority, don't they?'

'But you're all-powerful,' persisted Mayor Jayne.

'Who said I was *all-powerful*?'

'Well, that's what they say.'

'Word on the street?'

‘Something like that.’

‘What can I say? It’s good to have boots on the ground, a helper to get the lay of the land. Someone to get things done in a more hands-on, natural way.’

‘But what about you?’ asked Mayor Jayne.

‘They don’t believe anymore. People are largely satisfied. Too satisfied, taking their lives for granted. So maybe they have too much time on their hands.’

‘Not so much recently. People do not know what is going on. The way they have become accustomed to seeing the world is in doubt. People are scared.’

‘Right, so it’s time to consolidate that fear,’ God said firmly.

‘You *want* the people to be afraid?’

‘Of course. All this weird stuff has been great for people forgetting their petty squabbles, but they need to be kept off-balance, so they don’t return to all that.’

‘I don’t mean any offence, but people are more complex than that.’

‘That is why I am to get involved. They need some impetus, and I shall be here to supply it.’

The exchanges that Jayne can remember now rattle around her head as she wonders if she is going insane. ‘Who talks to God?’ she asks herself, ‘and hears him answer back? Maybe everyone has conversations with God, but the insane ones are those who hear back and then go public about their private tête-à-têtes. So which am I?’ wonders Jayne as she arrives the morning after her experience to open a new wing of a residential home.

'And this is Albert, our longest-running resident here. For now,' adds the home manager darkly, as she steers Jayne towards an elderly man in a wheelchair by the aquarium.

'Who are you?' asks Albert abruptly.

'I'm Jayne Johnson.' Albert looks frail, and Jayne wonders if she should subject him to such an experience, as God was suggesting. 'Wouldn't he just have a heart attack and drop dead?' she wonders.

'You from the council? You 'ere inspectin'?' he asks, "cos I've got stuff to say.' Jayne feels herself warming to the task.

'Now now, Albert, the *mayor* is only here for a quick visit, and she wanted to say hello and meet you,' explains the manager, emphasising her words.

Albert's watery eyes dart from the manager's face to Jayne's face, to the face of the fish nibbling hopefully at the glass of the aquarium, as though searching for that ever-elusive passage to a world free from miniature castles and devil-may-care plastic underwater explorers.

'I've got stuff to say about this place,' he finally repeats, 'and I ain't gonna be silenced no more by women. My wife left me and moved to Italy, my daughter put me in 'ere, and now I got this one telling me to shut up, and now I got you in my face. You're the last thing I need, another woman.'

With that, Jayne makes her decision and takes his hand softly.

'Well, I'm sure you won't object when one of the lovely ladies or gents here serves you your lunch, Albert. Have a nice day,' she says, 'God bless.'

'Touch as many people as you can, Jayne,' God had insisted.

‘Through their touch, so it too shall be that they pass it on. And on.’

The morning’s events had left Albert agitated and restless for the rest of the day. Irritable at the best of times, he had been impossible to work with that day, as far as the care staff are concerned. Feeling drained, by the early evening, Albert enjoys a deep, satisfying sleep.

# 31. Domestic silence

The room, and indeed the rest of the tiny flat, was festooned with green houseplants. It was classic Jerome for him to get into something and go entirely overboard. 'Thanks for putting me up, Jerome,' said Dev as he settled under the duvet on the sofa bed in Jerome's living room.

'More like putting up with you. No problem. It's been a while, Dev. Like I said, it's good to see you.' Jerome looked thoughtful as he lingered at the door. 'It's good to catch up.'

'Yeah,' said Dev, expecting him to leave, but then curious at the figure, hovering, unsure of itself in the dim light thrown from the room behind him.

It had been over a year since they had last seen each other, and Dev had thought of taking advantage of a conference in Birmingham to see his old friend. In advance of making the trip by train from their medical school, he had taken a good look at himself in the mirror and tried to identify any changes that might have developed since they had seen each other. *How much can I have changed in a year?* he wondered. Any new creases in his skin, any greying hairs, any dulling of the eyes? Medical school had taken its toll on all of them. The most significant change he could spot by looking at old first-year group photos himself, Lindy, Jerome, Michelle and Richard, was the faint crow's feet reaching from their eyes. That's one of the ageing differences between Caucasians and Asians, Africans. The former tends to collect wrinkles, whereas the latter two don't wrinkle so much, opting instead for liver spots. On meeting Jerome earlier that evening, he found his friend had put on some weight. Healthy weight. And he had more colour in his cheeks.

'Do you still feel like medical school is right for you?' Jerome finally asked, finding a way into the conversation that Dev had been too polite to bring up.

'Yeah. I think so. I mean, I know you just didn't want to do it anymore, right?' asked Dev, rolling onto his side and propping himself up on an elbow.

'Sleep. It was the one thing I just wasn't getting any more. I just couldn't do it. I'm glad I got out. It just wasn't for me in the end. You know that, we talked about it. I had the grades, but I didn't have the… the….'

'Stamina?' suggested Dev playfully.

'I have stamina. What are you insinuating?' smiled Jerome. 'I'm still happy with my decision.'

'Of course, no one suggested otherwise. You don't have to explain anything to me, but you're happier doing what you're doing, right?'

'I think I'm happier doing this,' began Jerome as he approached and lowered himself onto an armrest, 'than if I had stayed on and struggled through medical school. Do you know what it was in the end?'

'You already said. Sleep.'

'No, why I *couldn't* sleep. Responsibility. Getting everything right. I mean *every… single… thing.* There are so many things going on in a body. I don't know why, but the weight of it only hit me when I was trying to explain something simple to my niece, Clara. She was five or six. I don't remember what it was now, but it was something like…

sneezing. I was explaining it to her, and halfway through, she said: *how?* So I had to start explaining something else, and then halfway through that, she asked: *why?* And so on. It was only when my sister came on the phone that I stood back from the whole conversation with Clara and also stood back from what I was doing. I saw medical school with new eyes. That was when I realised what a crazy fucking thing it was that I was doing and that I wasn't made for that kind of responsibility.'

'But you didn't have to practice. You could have done research or something.'

'It doesn't matter. It's all responsibility, people relying on you. Don't you feel it? Anyway, I'm happy now. Definitely getting more sleep. I'm a team manager now.'

'Is that a good thing?' asked Dev, genuinely.

'Well, it is for me.'

'Sure. Yeah. I meant that's, like, a big deal. Or something,' Dev tried to cover.

'Yeah,' agreed Jerome.

'Yeah. So… what is that?'

'Um, nutshell, it means I have to keep track of everyone and write a little report each week.'

'How many people do you have to track?'

'Six.'

'Well, I'm sure you make it look easy.'

'Are you being sarcastic?'

'Nope,' Dev lied.

'I think you are,' smiled Jerome, 'don't you think I'm doing well?' he asked, sitting down with Dev.

It was apparent that Jerome was out for validation, but

now that he had opened up the conversation, Dev couldn't help himself. He wanted to know more, and some vague waffle about sleep and responsibility didn't cut it for him. 'You dropped out. It's been eighteen months.'

'So? What, you think I've had my time off, and now I should just come back like I have no independent decision-making process of my own?'

'No, I mean, it's been eighteen months, and you still measure your happiness by the fact that you dropped out.'

'So?'

'So, shouldn't you have other things about which to be happy? It's like if Spurs fans still gloated that they won the league in the seventies.'

'We do still gloat about that,' Jerome admitted with a rueful rub at his beard. 'Look, I'm happy. I'm a team leader now.'

'You said team manager.'

'Whatever. They're interchangeable terms, apparently.'

'You're working customer service for some electric company.'

'It might not be your thing, but I like it.'

'Don't take it the wrong way. It's not a bad job or anything. I'm saying you're an intelligent person. More than intelligent. You need challenges.'

'Who says? I'm fine.'

'For now, but I'm guessing the work you're doing is simple, and it'll eventually be too simple for you.'

'Why do you care so much?' Jerome huffed.

'We're friends.'

'No, this is more than that.'

'I don't want you to get into trouble. Okay?'

'What, idle hands are the devil's workshop? You speak from experience?'

'I don't know.'

The air around them relaxed as they paid a little attention to the sound of Jerome's neighbour, who was just getting back home. In the dim light, she scrabbled in her handbag to find the keys to her flat before dropping them on the floor. Once she had them in hand again, they listened to the key scratching the metal before finding its target.

'How are things with you? You've hardly spoken about *your* stuff,' said Jerome.

'What stuff?' asked Dev.

'You applying for clinical placements yet?'

'Yeah,' Dev answered vaguely.

'How are your parents?'

'The same as they always are.'

'They still want you to make the trip out to Mauritius? Visit the family?'

'What makes you think I haven't been?'

'Because you would have said already.'

'I don't bother with family. You know that. If my grandfather was still alive, I suppose I would talk with him. Dad always told me he would have been an amazing grandfather. I never knew him.'

'How can anyone compare with a dead guy?'

'No one will, no one from my family.'

'No one from *any* family,' corrected Jerome, before asking, 'what if you did meet him?'

'My *dead* grandfather?' asked Dev, raising his eyebrows.

'Yeah, his ghost, or something. What if you met him? Would he live up to the legend?'

'I suppose we'll never know,' Dev replied vaguely.

'What if ghosts were real –'

'You mean they're not?' joked Dev.

'Seriously, what if they were? I wonder if my dropping out was the influence of some unseen hand. Do you think they might watch over us, look out for us?'

'Don't try to pass it off as some… intervention that you have no responsibility for. Besides, both of those imply they might have the power to change things. Stop bad things from happening, or make our lives better in some way. What if all they could do would be to watch?'

'That would be weird.'

'Why would it be weird for them to just watch? Wouldn't it be just as weird to have ghosts of people, centuries dead, continuing to meddle in your life and change things around?'

'No, it'd be weirder.'

'Why?'

'Because they'd just be… watching. And judging,' added Jerome, narrowing his eyes against some imaginary entity.

'And even if they did have the power to change things in our lives, who is to say that they would actively change our lives for the good?'

'What, you think our ancestors would find it fun to watch their children and descendants struggling through stuff?'

'Yeah. Maybe they need some kind of entertainment,' said Dev, with a smile.

'That's depressing.'

'What if there aren't any children or descendants? Who do

they look over?' The two of them were silent for a little while as they contemplated this possibility. 'My standard reaction to children is annoyance,' admitted Jerome, eventually.

A few moments passed before Dev realised his friend wouldn't elaborate without a nudge. 'Why do you mention that?'

'My sister's children. They're getting to the age where they can sense these things. More to the point, they're beginning to wonder why.'

'What do you mean annoyance?'

'I don't know. I'm not familiar with children. I don't know how to… Aren't children supposed to make you feel younger? When I'm at my sister's house, they just make me feel grumpy. When they make me feel grumpy, they make me feel old, and I'm nowhere near old,' stressed Jerome.

'I think they're supposed to make grandparents feel younger. Doesn't your sister ask you?'

'Yeah, we've talked, but she knows how I am with children, so she knows it's not specifically about hers. On the other hand, Piet doesn't seem to get this. He's been frosty with me for a while, and I think it's about this. How do I get to be one of those cool uncles who brings fun and excitement to the lives of children bored with their parents? Would that make him like me again?'

'Who? Piet?' asked Dev.

'Yeah.'

'Are you saying you want your nephew and niece to find you entertaining so your brother-in-law would like you again?'

'Yeah, does that sound strange?'

'Maybe that's why he's frosty with you,' began Dev. 'Because his children already find you fun and exciting. They're just confused because you also seem grumpy. They can't understand you being all those things at once. If I was a dad, I would want my children to find me fun and exciting. Only me, no one else. Maybe that's why he's frosty. Because when you're due to arrive, it's *uncle this* and *uncle that*, and they forget about him until after you're gone.'

'When did it get to this? That I give a shit what Piet thinks? Or his children? I was here first. He married into my family. He should be trying to be friends with me,' whined Jerome. 'How did it get so difficult for me to just see my sister? It feels like there should be some social infrastructure or unspoken understanding in place for me to just be able to do that without involving myself in… extraneous stuff. Like, like a direct channel, you know what I mean?'

'I think it's called: going for lunch with your sister.'

'We used to be best friends, chat, go to the cinema and stuff. I just want to hang out with my best bud again, but I can't. It's like she has all these other appendages. I want to hang out with her. She wants to hang out with her children. So I go over there to hang out with her children, hoping to also hang out with her. But I'm too busy to hang out with her because I'm hanging out with her children. Meanwhile, she's hanging out with Piet, and I'm left with their kids like some parent-decoy.'

'Do you mean babysitter?'

'Yes!' exclaimed Jerome, his eyes lighting up with the realisation. 'When I go over there, I'm like a glorified, unpaid babysitter.'

'You're the uncle. Uncles don't get paid. That's the glory part.'

'Well, in that case, I'd rather be *un*glorified but remunerated. At least I'd be earning some extra cash for my discomfort.'

'You want your sister to pay you to go over there?'

'If all I'm doing is hanging out with her children, then yeah. It really doesn't matter to me whether I'm babysitting her children or the neighbour's.'

'Don't you have a connection with them?'

'No. I have a question for them. Where's my sister? What have you done with her?'

'But they're your flesh and blood, and all that. Don't you feel that in some way?'

'Maybe I will in the future. Or maybe I'm like you and your extended family.'

'How?'

'You don't feel anything for any of them.'

'No,' agreed Dev.

'But you share DNA.'

'Yeah, we share DNA,' conceded Dev. 'We're not happy about it, but we share it.'

'So it's the same thing.'

'My extended family is a long story. Your nephew and niece aren't even eight yet. It's a little soon to be writing them off.'

'So what happened with yours? It can't just be that they all failed to live up to the standards of a ghost.'

'Well… other stuff.'

'I haven't been sounding really whiny, have I?'

'A bit.'

It's the second time that Dr. Sharma has brought up this idea. The idea that he dispensed with his extended family out of some assumption that they wouldn't live up to the memory of his grandfather. A memory he doesn't even have. He's very keen to put this forward. Indeed he's brought it up twice. He's trying to push us away. What if we take him elsewhere?

The day before Serena and Dev were due to leave, they spent the day with Raju, who had taken the day off from work. Dev had thought his father would have taken more time off in the weeks leading to their departure, but this hadn't proved to be the case. Burying himself in work seemed to be the way for Raju to satisfy everyone's needs. It was difficult for Raju to face reality, far easier to face work.

He took every shift going at the hospital to avoid the reality of his disintegrating home life. Also, to ensure his wife and child would have enough funds for their trip. Despite his pain and hurt at recent events, not least the admission from his wife that she wanted to get away from him, Raju was steadfast in providing for his family.

Unable to get through to Serena, Raju's heart silently came apart as he watched Dev's familiar clothes find their way into the suitcases. Although he knew his family would eventually be back, Raju did not know how long it would be before seeing them again. All he could do was trust. Part of him feared that going to Mauritius and being under the microscope of the family gaze would only make things worse for Serena and Dev.

He wanted them to have everything they needed, the things they had become accustomed to. The toys that would be familiar to Dev and remind him of home. But they were left behind. Brightly painted metal combined with plastic attachments that allowed cars to turn into robots or robots to turn into planes, their heads would pop in and out of chest cavities while arms and legs would become doors or wings. There was no space in their luggage for impractical things.

The next day Dev awoke with butterflies in his tummy. One day left until he and Mum would leave for Mauritius.

'We'll feel better,' Serena explained, sitting on the edge of his bed.

'But what about Dad?' Dev asked, confused.

'It's not as easy as that, Dev. People need different things. We need to get away from here for a while,' said Serena, with the firmness of one who needed to believe their own words.

'Why doesn't Daddy need to get away too?' Dev quietly asked.

'*We* need to get away,' replied his mother.

Raju stood outside Dev's bedroom listening to the two of them and scratched his face. It felt thick, as though the dentist had rendered his jaw numb. These days he was more lackadaisical about his shaving habits. Turning away from his son's bedroom and the conversation, the rationalisation, the soft selling going on within, Raju rubbed at his stubble and made his way to the bathroom.

He wanted his son to remember him at his best when he would think of him in Mauritius. A few moments later, Raju was looking into the mirror on the wall above the bathroom sink as he massaged shaving foam onto his skin. The foam covered his stubble and blended with the unruly rebels that had converted from black to white. Before long, the blade of

Raju's disposable razor was passing over his chin, slicing the hairs, dozens at a time, revealing the skin beneath.

They had decided that the final day before Serena and Dev left would be spent as usual. So in the morning, they all went to the market to buy provisions for the week ahead.

In hindsight, a pathetic attempt at normalcy that achieved the opposite effect. Without true purpose, their actions felt hollow, as though they were puppets going through the motions. Dev's parents seemed to be in a trance as they silently wandered the market, aimless. Usually, his father would have a list. A plan. That day Raju shuffled from stall to stall collecting vegetables in haphazard quantities, no clear idea how he would combine them into meals. It hadn't yet occurred to him that he should buy fewer items since he would be cooking for one. Serena didn't have the heart to point it out to him.

'Two for a pound,' squalled a vendor as Raju gazed blankly at the cucumbers.

'Two,' Raju eventually said, handing the man a pound coin. The man wrapped the cucumbers in a brown paper bag that wasn't quite deep enough for the vegetables before handing Raju the package.

'Thank you,' the man bellowed, announcing another successful sale to anyone within earshot.

Dev watched the different colours filling their shopping bags as they wandered the market. He thought about how he wouldn't be there to eat them next week. He thought about how they would have long ceased to exist by the next time he would be in England.

Raju stopped the car on the way home and picked up

cream cakes to have with tea later that afternoon. He knew Dev's favourite was the apple turnover, and he also knew that he wouldn't see anything like that in Mauritius for a while, despite what Serena might be telling him. In the heat of Mauritius, fresh cream cakes were simply not possible. Back then, supermarkets were still few and far between in Mauritius. Most people bought from small local shops that had little in the way of refrigeration. Those that did have fridges had better uses for them than apple turnovers, although Dev would disagree with this policy.

Later that afternoon, the three of them sat in the kitchen with tea and their cakes. It wasn't the last day in England that Dev had expected. He had thought that at least on this day, his parents would put aside their differences and try to talk as they used to. He needed them, on this last day, to be how they used to be. He needed to remember that it had been real.

Dev brought the apple turnover to his lips and sank his teeth into the flaky pastry. The cream squelched from the sides of the cake, and he had to catch some of it before it fell. He quickly looked up at his parents, expecting his mother to be annoyed at him. They hadn't noticed. Dev took another bite of his cake and pressed the top of it to his nose as he did so, leaving a dusting of white icing sugar on his brown skin. Again he looked up. His father's eyes met his, and they smiled at him.

'I think you have something on your nose,' Raju said, gesturing at his face.

'No, I don't,' replied Dev with a creamy smirk. He had a smile from his father. It was enough for him to continue. 'Mm, this cake is so nice,' he declared theatrically before taking another bite. Serena looked over at him. Dev groaned again, 'mm,' as he rubbed his tummy. 'So nice,' he said before burying his little mouth into the cake's filling of apples and cream.

Serena watched him, a faint smile starting at her lips as Dev slowly took the cake away to reveal the remnants of cream all over his nose, cheeks, lips and chin. 'What?' Dev asked, feigning ignorance. Serena and Raju burst into laughter at their son and the mess.

'Could you be any messier?' Serena asked.

'You're eating like you've never had a cake before,' said Raju.

'Can't help it,' replied Dev, pleased to hear the laughter of his parents again, 'it's just too good.' Dev smiled and imagined the furniture and the house were happy to hear them all laugh again.

# 32. The swindler

He remembers suddenly having to say goodbye to everyone he knew. That luxury is not available to Dr. Sharma, now in Katie's bedroom, but when he was nine, he had said goodbye to Qadir and Jonathan on his last day of junior school in England. Dev told them he would see them again in the future, although, at that young age, he had no idea what the future might look like. Dr. Sharma didn't know if it was to ensure he didn't waste time but he remembers his father hovering a few metres behind him.

Although Dev had been aware of the move, he had not known that a departure date had been set. It had simply been sprung upon him with a week of notice. Thinking back to it years later, Dr. Sharma surmised that his parents had wanted to give him as little opportunity to change his mind or make a fuss. He was soon with his mother on a plane bound for Mauritius.

Strapped into his seat on the plane, Dev thought back to one of the last conversations with his father before leaving.

'Dad?' asked Dev on the top floor of the library. He was standing on a chair to look out of the window over the town sprawling away from them below. It was a tradition of theirs that they had not shared with Serena. Not something from which they had consciously excluded her. It was just their thing.

'Yes, son?' replied Raju, staring out at the city below.

'Do you know about flies?'

'Um. Not really. I know a little,' replied Raju, breaking his focus from the landscape before them, surprised at this topic of conversation from his son, although he knew he shouldn't be. With the impending move to Mauritius, he had expected Dev's thoughts to be more along those lines.

'Imagine a fly gets in a boat while it is docked. It gets trapped on board, and the boat sails out. After a while, the boat is in the middle of the ocean. What happens if the fly gets out?'

'What do you mean?' asked Raju, looking over at his son.

'If it was trapped but then gets out through a window, but it's in the middle of the ocean, how does it find its way back home? Or back to land? They can't land on the water, can they?'

'No, I don't think so,' replied Dev's father thoughtfully. 'Not normal house flies.'

'Can they fly that far? If it got out far at sea, how far can it fly before stopping? How long can they fly before resting or eating? Can they even see in the dark?'

'I think they can see in the dark but, for the rest of it, I don't know.'

'How long would it fly?' asked Dev. 'What if they came

across another boat? Would it be able to recognise it as a boat and land on it to sail back to land? Or would they just ignore it? Would they think it was just part of the water and that they couldn't land on it?'

'I don't know,' confessed Raju.

'Haven't you ever thought about it?'

'No. I don't think so. Maybe, when I was your age.'

'If the fly got out of the boat, would it even know which way to go to find land? Or would it just fly further away from land, not knowing it was flying from safety, just flying further into the middle of nowhere? Do you think it would be like a lost person in the forest, just going round and round in circles until it is exhausted and falls into the water? What about birds?'

'Seagulls would be able to find their way to land.'

'Are you sure? Even way out in the middle of the ocean?'

'I think so. I don't know if they'd be able to fly that far. They pester the fishing trawlers, but that might be when they get closer to land.'

'What about other birds? What about a robin?'

'That's quite a small bird. It wouldn't go out to sea in the first place.'

'But that's not the point, *Dad*,' argued Dev, becoming impatient at the lack of solid answers.

'I don't think it would last very long or be able to tell which way was land.'

'Do you think it would be scared? When it flies off the boat and sees all that water?'

'I don't know if they have emotions.'

'But what if it did? Do you think it would be scared to see

all that water? Do you think it would wonder what had happened to the world? Where all the land and trees had gone? What about animals in the zoo?' continued Dev.

'What about them?'

'Do they know their lives are not the same as other animals? Do you think a red panda in the zoo knows other red pandas are living different lives?'

'What about children?' Raju decided to counter. 'When babies are born, do you think they know there are other babies that are born differently?'

'I don't think so. What do you mean, differently?'

'I mean, some are boys, some are girls. Some are white, black. Some are healthy, and some are born with illnesses. Do you know that a lot of children are born with illnesses or have unkind parents?'

'What kind of illnesses?' queried Dev.

'Some children are born with problems. Like not being able to read or write as easily as others,' explained Raju. 'Some children do not have very strong hearts. You have a heart, don't you?'

'Yes.'

'Where is it?'

'Here,' answered Dev, pointing at his chest and looking for approval from his father.

'What does it do?' tested his father.

'It pumps blood around my body,' explained Dev.

'What do you think would happen if your heart didn't work properly?'

'Hmm, I would be ill.'

'You would be very tired. All the time. That wouldn't be

fun, would it?'

'No.'

'So, do you think babies know that?'

'No.'

'How about your friends at school?'

'No.'

'Why not?'

'Because nobody told us.'

'So if nobody tells you some other children are different, you think they are all like you?'

'I think so.'

'You should remember that there are other people in the world that are not like you. People like to think that everyone else is just like them, but that's not the case. Other children are not as fortunate as you. You have good health, a comfortable life. You also have to remember not everyone is good. You have to be careful. Do you understand?'

'I think so.'

'Is there anything you want to tell me? You can tell me. I won't be cross.'

'I don't think so.'

'I always find out about everything, so you may as well tell me. I'll know about it. Even when you're in Mauritius. I'll know about it all. You can tell me anything.'

There was no longer any point in asking his father why he was not going with them to Mauritius. Instead, Dev sought to reassure his father and avoid another drawn-out conversation along the same lines.

'I don't have anything to say,' he replied. Then, after a while, 'I want to be like you.'

'How do you mean?' asked Raju.

'I want to be like you when I grow up.'

'I want you to be like me too. That's why I say you need to be careful with other people.'

'Do all mummies and daddies want their children to be like them?'

'In some ways, yes,' Raju answered.

'Do other children want to be like their mummies and daddies?'

'Yes, but they don't say it.'

'What do you think happened first?' asked Dev.

'Hm?'

'Do you think mummies and daddies wanted their children to be like them first? Or did children want to be like mummies and daddies? We learnt at school that we used to be bacteria in the water. Then we were fish. Then we were monkeys. Then we became people. Mummies and daddies have children, but mummies and daddies used to be children too. So did children want to be like their mummies and daddies first, or did they want their children to be like them first?'

'I don't know. You'd have to ask your teacher,' replied Raju, looking for a way out of yet another question.

'I read a book before about a boy who finds out that things can learn the things that other things know just by eating them.'

'What have I said about using that word so much? *Things*?'

'Sorry, Dad.'

'Was it a real book?'

'What do you mean?'

'I mean, did it have real facts?'

'It was a storybook.'

'Oh. What happened?' asked Raju, disappointed.

'He and his friends teach insects tricks and then feed them to other insects. Then they find out that it's true. The new insects can do the same tricks that the insects they ate could, without being trained. They just know.'

'Uh-huh.'

'So if they know how to do the tricks, they should know everything else about the insects, shouldn't they? Like they should have their memories and stuff.'

'It's just a story, Dev. It's not real.'

'But, Dad, do you think if a person ate another person, they would be able to do all the stuff that the first person could do?'

'No.'

'But it happened in the book.'

'They ate other people in the book?'

'No, they ate other animals and then they could see in the dark and hear things far away.'

'Well, we eat chickens, don't we? Why aren't you laying eggs yet? I want some eggs. Where are my eggs?' joked Raju with a smile.

'No, we have to eat the right animals. People can't lay eggs, but we can see and hear. We don't eat owls, do we?'

'No.'

'So maybe if we ate owls, we'd be able to see in the dark and hear for miles around.'

'Maybe.'

'So shall we start eating owls?'

'No.'

'Why not?'

'They're tricky to catch, Dev. We'll have to come up with a plan. Maybe tomorrow.'

'Okay, Dad. Will there be owls in Mauritius?'

'Yes, Dev. There are owls in Mauritius. I think.'

# 33. Flight

A few days later, Dev was feeling very sleepy but still helping his mother with their hand luggage as they stood in the aisle alongside the seats they had occupied for the last twelve hours. Dev was tired but excited to see his new surroundings. He had been to Mauritius before, but a lot had happened since then, making this almost an entirely new experience for him.

There were things this time that he paid attention to that he hadn't the last time. One of these things was the chatter of so many Mauritians around him. It was such a shift from hearing nothing but English, and it was already something of a novelty. Dev couldn't remember having been amongst so many of them before in such a small space, although he had.

He listened to them and heard so many words that he didn't recognise. Words he had not heard his parents use, or intonations, inflections that were new to him. In any case, it was chatter in a queue, and that in itself was new to him. In England, queuing is a silent sport, and if there was any chatting to be done, it was done amongst people who knew one another, as far as Dev was aware. Strangers wouldn't begin chatting in England, except maybe to tut and roll their eyes at the wait. That was the first thing Dev noticed this time around.

Mauritians appeared friendlier, seemingly more willing to share a joke with one another, confident of shared understanding, the same way of looking at things. Dev looked up at the adults all around him. Some were Asian. Some were African. He thought he spotted some white people in the throng. In the night, he had asked his mother where all the white people were before she shushed him.

'Don't say things like that! Whisper it!'

So he whispered. 'Where are all the white people, Mummy?'

'It's not their time of year,' explained Serena, unhelpfully.

'What do you mean?' asked Dev. 'Why do they have their own time of year?'

'They normally wait to take their summer holidays, in July and August.'

'What about all these people?'

'They're not going on holiday. They're just going home.'

That was when it hit Dev. It suddenly felt like it was the first time he had heard his mother use the word *home* when talking about Mauritius. It wasn't, but it felt like the first time it had something to do with him.

Mauritius.

*Home.*

Whenever they had talked about moving to live in Mauritius, it had felt as though it wasn't really happening to him. It would be happening to someone else in his place. An alternate Dev. Whenever he had heard his parents speaking about Mauritius as *home*, there had been a divide between what they were calling home and what he called home.

For Dev home had been England. For his parents, home had always been Mauritius. Now the roles would be reversed, and the place he called home would be far away. Either that or he would change to see his new surroundings as home.

For the first time, Dev was part of his mother's picture of *home*.

It was almost 8 am when the queues began to move along the aisles, and the weary travellers filed off the plane that had carried them over the seas, amongst the clouds and through the timezones for the last twelve hours. Dev hadn't slept much through the night, but despite this, his little legs kept pace with his mother's as they made their way along the jet bridge leading from the plane to the airport's main building.

At passport control, Serena chatted quickly in Creole with the official as he flicked through their Mauritian passports. Dev's passport was new, having never been used. They had always used his British passport when travelling in Europe, but his mother explained that using his Mauritian one here would mean getting through passport control quicker. Their official asked a few questions, and Serena answered that they were moving to Mauritius.

It was still early in the day, but the official was already sweating through his shirt while the electric fans, yellowed from age, wobbled from their ceiling fixings and pushed the warm air languidly around the room. Behind Serena and Dev, babies and toddlers cried, tired of not sleeping and irritable from the heat and the journey. Meanwhile, their adults looked jaded and defeated as they tried to rock the children in their arms into a more agreeable frame of mind and stood in the queue waiting for this latest leg of their voyage to be over.

The next booth catered to those with other passports, and there Dev finally spotted an elderly white couple. While the man spoke loudly to their official (the only recourse the man saw available to him to overcome the language barrier), his wife spotted Dev staring at her. Tired, she nonetheless smiled at him wanly as she fanned herself with her passport.

Once he and his mother were past passport control, Dev fetched a trolley for their luggage while a helpful man dragged their cases from the carousel. Their black cases had little rainbow ribbons tied to the handles to allow Serena to quickly identify their luggage from the others, serenely touring the facility like swans on a lake.

Leaving the warm airport and its dingy fittings, the pair was instantly smothered in a fresh blanket of heat, intensified by the direct sunshine that had been warming the tarmac beneath their feet from the early hours of the morning. All around them were people looking to collect family members, friends, clients. It was not long before Dev, and his mother were enveloped in the arms of their own family members and being passed around from one set of lips to another for kisses and greetings.

Once the kissing and greeting were over, they were in the back of the old, brown taxi of a family friend, once again riding along the bumpy streets past palm trees and sugarcane fields. That first day in Mauritius, Dev was surprised at what he had forgotten and delighted in rediscovering so many Mauritian idiosyncrasies.

Before long, Dev was back at the auntie's house with the traditional red floors, waxed and polished to a state so slippery it had been known to break bones. He was back amongst the children with no sense of personal space. Unexpected power cuts in the night meant torches and candles were produced from drawers. Dancing flames and sliding shadows. Annoyed adults and excitable children. The dark oil drums filled with water, ahead of the daily water stoppages, in which Dev could not see his reflection.

At Serena's family house in Rose Hill, they saw Uncle Sachin, who had largely regained his easy-going nature and had forgotten about multiplication tables since the last time Dev had been there.

It has always been difficult for Dr. Sharma to consider with any clarity the years he spent in Mauritius since he didn't pay much attention to his feelings at the time. After all, what are memories shorn of emotions? Just pictures. Ghosts of the mind. He hadn't had time for his feelings, and so they hadn't existed to him. In fact, throughout his time in Mauritius, Dev tried not to think of what he wanted at all. It didn't seem to matter. According to everybody around him, other things were suddenly very important in a way that they hadn't been in England.

Education, exams and success were suddenly the only things that anyone had to talk to him about. Ten-year-old Dev had gone from the relatively relaxed school life of England to the pressure cooker environment of Mauritius within a matter of weeks. Learning to read, write and speak

French fluently was suddenly of utmost importance since it was one of the four main subjects for which he would need to sit an exam.

The CPE. Certificate of Primary Education.

In Mauritius, for the entire year prior to the exams, it is all anyone talks about to those children preparing to sit them, such is the value and importance attached to them.

Upon arriving in Mauritius, Dev had suddenly become a very busy boy with several years of Mauritian schooling to assimilate, a new language to learn and perfect, not to mention after-school tutoring sessions. Family, extended family, distant family, peripheral family were now suddenly part of Dev's daily life, living with his mother's family in Rose Hill.

The Mauritian school year begins in January, fuelled by the blaze of summer. Although he had holidayed there, it had been in Mauritius' relatively cooler winter period. Plucked from an English December and transported to the height of Mauritius' tropical summer, Dev immediately found it a challenge to adjust to the heat, let alone to successfully concentrate and work in the close and claustrophobic heat of the classroom at his new Mauritian school. Living Monday to Friday in the heat of the Mauritian classroom in trousers was quite a change to the Mauritius of shorts at the beach.

His extended family was keen to learn how he was progressing with his new school, with attention that felt near-incessant to Dev. School in Mauritius was certainly different to that in England. French and Environmental Studies were subjects he had not encountered before, and they all came with specific criteria to satisfy that was new to Dev.

Serena dropped Dev off at school and collected him daily, but on one of his first days at his new school, Serena was anxious to not find him waiting at the school gate. She had gone to his classroom to investigate, only to discover that he was not only still taking notes from the blackboard but finding it difficult to concentrate because the other children kept talking to him. There she soon found herself the centre of attention, with the local Mauritian children hanging on her every word. Serena played to her audience and proceeded to make them laugh, making fun of Dev's English-accented Creole. She spoke to them, not entirely as an adult talking to children, but almost as equals, knowing how to ensure they warmed to her.

Serena needed to be liked. She needed to be loved. She already had Dev's love, but it didn't occur to her that in using him to make other children laugh, she was losing his trust. Serena was all Dev had in Mauritius. He depended on her. She was keen to hear the children laugh and used him to make them laugh.

So far from home, and with so much uncertainty and doubt creeping into every thought, he needed Serena more than ever to be there for him. To Dev, it was a betrayal, and from that moment, he found it difficult to trust her, to place his faith in her entirely. The simple fact that his parents clearly had different ideas had already led him to question whether she was right. It was a natural, logical query. If two people have different ideas, usually one idea yields better results than the other. In this case, Dev had to wonder which of his parents had the better idea. Which parent was wrong? It was the first time that he seriously entertained the possibility that his mother or father could be wrong about something.

# 34. Why so urgent?

Whenever Dr. Sharma thought back to this time in Mauritius, most of it came back to his mind in snapshots.

The old orange and white *L'art de Conjuguer* book, handed down by an older cousin.

Picking out French children's books in a dimly lit bookshop near the bus station in Curepipe.

His classmates asking him to teach them English swear words and teaching him Mauritian ones in return. His mother saying they might as well teach him French ones while they were at it.

The playing field at school where the air was always foggy with dust, a polar opposite to rainy England.

The *glaçon râpé* street vendor with the thick block of ice on the back of his bicycle. Scraping the ice into a paper cone, squirting some syrup on top.

The months and months of concentration and focus on the dusty blackboard, through the interminable heat.

The expectation that the *English boy* should do well, despite the slow start.

The Hindu weddings that would last for days. 'Four days. Who was even getting married? Who were those people?' Dev asked his mother. Family friends she didn't know, but it was apparently imperative that they attend.

The long-awaited trip to the seaside that turned into a revision session on the beach.

The shouting, echoing throughout the half-completed house where Uncle Sachin's building work had come to a standstill.

The *du pain Maison*, bought fresh and warm each morning. Sometimes with super salty bits where the salt hadn't been evenly distributed in the mix. Sometimes with unfortunate small insects inadvertently baked into the bread.

The smell of the smoke from burning sugarcane leaves.

Giant pots of food cooked over a wood-burning fire in the back gardens of a house where a *pooja*, a blessing, was taking place.

The much older cousin, with one long pinkie fingernail, who always glared at him.

The nightly comments on the clothes and makeup of the female evening newscaster.

Taking empty glass cola bottles back to the *tabagie* to exchange for full ones.

Walking from the bus stop after school along the long asphalt road, looking like it was melting in the distance.

Small boys scampering up papaya trees to collect the fruit.

The tiny flames from small clay oil lamps along the garden walls for *Diwali*.

His younger cousin using a finger to poke a dot of white chalky paste onto foreheads at the Hindu temple.

New faces all around him, new rules, new people to not understand.

Chewing on raw sugarcane, fresh from the field.

Cyclones bringing sheets of rain that covered the streets.

The last days of Hindu weddings. Adults merry on alcohol. Children drunk on atmosphere. Music pounding, dancing round and round, everybody round and round.

On TV, the Bollywood actors shoot meaningful looks at each other across a field before bounding towards and then prancing away from one another.

Round and round, the Mauritian Sega dancers dance, holding up their garishly patterned, flowing skirts. Holding up their fixed smiles.

Illustrations on the last page of the French exam. Interpreting the images and writing the story in French.

The entire family. Close, extended, distant, peripheral. Watching and waiting to see how he would do in the exams.

So important to do well in these exams. The results determining where he would go to college in Mauritius next year. *Next year?*

Good colleges and bad colleges, in rank order.

Good children and bad children, in rank order.

So important to be *classed.*

Being *classed* means finishing amongst the students with the overall best CPE results in the land, an achievement reserved for the top three thousand out of roughly twenty-two thousand participants. The names of the three thousand are published in national newspapers. Presumably it was once meant to honour the top three thousand. However, it now inadvertently functions as another incentive for parents to pressure their children to do well, knowing that they will be publicly shamed if they do not make it.

So much study, organising. So much to remember and memorise and remember. Dev's fellow 21,999 or so peers all study from 5 am each morning. 'You'll remember more if you study early in the morning.' Memorising everything was the cornerstone of Mauritian education. Understanding was optional.

All of the people. All of the places. No space to think. No time to compute. Just a wall of things. Things and places and people. Pleasing one person after another. Aunts, uncles, cousins, grandparents, family friends, family acquaintances, shopkeepers, teachers, headteachers, private tutors, taxi drivers, bus conductors, ice-cream sellers, corner shop owners, bakers. They all wanted to know how he was doing at school and how he would perform on these exams. They wanted to hear that he was confident. They liked to see the effect of their words reminding these children of their exams. For some, it undoubtedly gave some kind of perverse thrill to see these children squirming under pressure.

'Knowledge is power,' the bus conductor would puff, straightening his back as though he had coined the phrase himself.

'What's happening with the exams, Dev?' his grandfather would ask.

'I don't know. They're six months away.'

'That's not right. You should say: 'I will succeed. I know I will succeed.''

'Okay, Granddad.'

'*Ça va, jeune homme?*' would ask the baker.

'*Oui, ça va,*' would reply Dev.

'*C'est tout?*'

'*Oui.*'

'*Il faut parler plus que ça si tu veut avoir un bon résultat en*

*Francais pour la CPE. Que dîtes-vous, maman?* at which Serena would nod her agreement that he should speak more French to pass the exam.

'*J'arriverai,*' promised Dev.

Mauritius is a small country. Tiny. A small and claustrophobic bubble with a continuously simmering cycle of pressure. For Mauritians, exams end in one of only two ways. You are either judged a success or a failure. Not everyone will succeed at the exams, despite the pressure applied from all sides by the people in their lives. No matter how many extra tuition hours they endure, 19,000 pupils will not reach the top three thousand and will not have their names printed in the national newspaper.

*Why do they even do that?* Dr. Sharma would later wonder. *Why did they start doing it in the first place all those years ago? Was it to congratulate those who made it and bestow pride upon their families, or was it to shame those who failed to make the top three thousand? With Mauritius being such a small country, everyone knows someone or someone's kid who is going through some important exam from one year to another. It's a continuous cycle of applying pressure, checking in with the family periodically to see how the kid is doing, discussing the kid in question with the extended family, who take their turn to visit the kid to apply some pressure of their own. As if they weren't getting enough anger, emotional blackmail and reproach from their immediate family.*

In Dev's case, this all came from his mother, her brother and their father. Having not entirely grown up with this cycle, he occupied the unique position of seeing the whole thing through two lenses. From the perspective of a newcomer, he could watch it all unfolding from a distance, but it didn't remain that way. The blanket of expectation eventually smothered and enveloped him as he found himself at the centre of events, no longer a detached observer. He could almost sense a perverse pleasure being taken from his discomfort.

For over a year, there was no escape from it. From all sides, it was being drilled into Dev's head that the rest of his life would depend upon exams in four subjects.

At his grandparents' home, which they shared with Uncle Sachin and his wife, as well as Serena and Dev, people always unexpectedly dropped in to pry and seek an update on their situation. This was typical of Mauritius. Dev could see how those people sought to chew up one another, depending upon what they wanted. To those who weren't directly involved, the exams were entertainment, while those sitting them were docile, conditioned to take whatever volley of criticism would come their way because it came under the heading: advice and encouragement.

# 35. Something to dance to

It was something neither Dev nor Serena had ever witnessed before. For Serena, it had never been part of her family's background. Her family had only ever done the minimum to qualify as Hindus. *Cavadee* had simply never formed part of her life. Not in the way that it had in Raju's family. They knew all about it and fussed around with their allocated chores. It was late January, and each person sweltered in the midst of the Mauritian summer.

Serena and Dev were at the event to satisfy Raju's family as they bustled about, making sure they were seen by their community peers to be helping. Serena and Dev, not knowing how they could help or what to do, stood in the blazing sunshine amongst the crowd at the side of the road. Dev didn't know what exactly it was all in aid of or what they were waiting for, as people lined the streets on each side, taking care not to take a tumble into the storm drains.

'Mum, what's happening?' asked Dev to his mother.

'Shh, let's see. Look down the road,' Serena replied, as the sound of drums and singing carried on the wind.

Dev followed Serena's gaze as the chants reached his ears more clearly, and the crowd's murmur around them died away. Serena gripped his shoulders with her hands and held her breath as she too craned her neck to get a better view.

Around the corner came the men and women. The women carried pots containing sacred milk while the men appeared, stripped but for the traditional pink and red robes from the waist down. Their skin smeared with paste denoting various symbols, ancient writings. They navigated the route keeping up their half-gyration, half-shuffle as they carried their *Kavadis*, heavy wooden plinths holding elaborate structures, some of which contained food, others contained likenesses of deities surrounded by brightly coloured flowers. All of them were being carried to the temple.

Some devotees chanted while others simply couldn't and jigged under the weight of their *Kavadis* in incongruous silence while the chanting and drumming went on around them. Not due to the weight of their charges or lack of passion, but rather the metal spears – *vels* – that had been pierced through their tongues and cheeks. It symbolised their silence. Their vow. Meditation. Devotion.

Serena whirled, her hand keeping her hair out of her eyes as she took in as much of this as her eyes would allow. The small *vels*, glinting in the sunlight, were pierced not just through tongues and cheeks but through the skin of legs, backs, chests, abdomens, foreheads and beyond. Serena listened to them. They came down the road, swaying, shedding flowers along the way, as well as their repetitive, monotonous chants. The few were soon joined by the many as others caught up. Before long, Serena was caught up too.

She watched, listened and absorbed it all as though in a daze. Her hand was always on Dev, but her heart was already lost to the worshippers, the devotees. They were only a few feet away but Serena could see that they were somewhere else, in a different space entirely. They seemed oblivious to the people on either side of the road. As though they simply didn't exist. Immersed in the pure love and devotion of their sacrifice, the witnesses along the road had vanished as far as the *Kavadi* bearers were concerned.

They danced.

They shuffled.

They chanted.

They trusted.

The devotees surrendered themselves. They surrendered control and offered themselves to *Lord Muruga*, Tamil God of War. In piercing themselves with the spears, they offered more than their flesh. They dedicated their absolute faith and belief to their deity and trusted that he would deliver them from harm.

The weight of the heavy monuments they carried didn't seem to matter. In their fervour, the weight had all but disappeared from their shoulders. In their faith-induced trance, they had formed a connection and looked within to find the best of themselves. Their peace and devotion transmuted into tangible actions for all to see.

Arms holding up the plinths, *vels* through their bodies. Backs sweating from their effort in the heat. Bare feet padding along. The day's heat rising from the tarmac beneath. Nothing mattered. No external elements affected them. It made Serena question the point of doing this for the public gaze if they were then to ignore the people around them. *Because it's the voices and faith of the many Kavadi bearers that induce the fervour, the trance,* she reasoned, answering her own question. *I wonder if it takes them closer to God.*

Round and round, the gyrating worshippers danced. Dozens of them paraded through the streets with dozens more after them, all dancing, all chanting in the street while their minds were clearly elsewhere, in another space. Serena saw they were in a place where love and devotion were the only things that mattered. Amongst these people, the ritualistic dancing and chanting filled her eyes and ears, leaving her intoxicated with the strength of their conviction and belief. They were prepared to pierce their bodies and shoulder heavy wooden plinths in the worship of their lord in sacrifice to purify themselves.

Serena was almost envious as she and Dev watched the last of them gyrate away from them, *vels* through their backs and legs still glinting in the sunlight. She longed for that kind of blind faith, something solid, but she knew she could never have faith in anything as profoundly as they did. As tempting as it was to mock them for such blind devotion, it was humbling to witness such a display, the memory of which would remain with her for the rest of her life.

It was this that ignited the sudden transformation in Serena. Or perhaps it had been there all along, waiting for a spark, waiting for the right set of circumstances. The death of a child is sufficient reason for many people to dismiss any notion of a kind and benevolent God. But Serena had found an outlet, a focal point for her energies that didn't involve testing Dev or checking up to make sure he was studying.

Serena had discovered the simple pleasure, the still and calm of the temple. She would visit a new one each day, sometimes more than one. Temples, Hindu or otherwise, aren't difficult to find in Mauritius. They're everywhere and range in scale and ambition. Some are elaborately decorated with intricate roofs reaching for the sky, while other worship spots are as simple as a small statue within the hewn cavity of a large roadside rock.

Each day, after dropping Dev off at school, or at his after-school tutor's home, Serena toured the island seeking out a new temple to visit. She delighted in the silence that was broken only by the satisfyingly reassuring sound of the bell sounded by each new worshipper. Either that, or it was the *pandit* issuing his prayers in his sonorous voice that bounced from the solid walls and filled the space. If you heard that voice anywhere else, it would be annoying, but here it sounded mellifluous, one with the peaceful atmosphere of the temple.

Every day Serena walked the rows of gods with their smoking incense sticks standing upright before them in metal holders. She took in all the details about everything she saw. The cracks in the pillars that had been painted over. The placid expressions of the statues and their crumbling toes and fingers. From one statue to another, Serena visually compared the fading colours of the material that adorned each likeness. Nothing escaped her attention, and she made sure to speak at each statue.

Quite often, she found time in Dev's schedule to drag him along at weekends. In the beginning, Dev welcomed the distraction and time away from his books. He found relief in having his mother focused on something other than his studies. However, he soon began to resent her devotion to the gods. He watched her lips move. Rapidly and fluidly, her lips insisted, barely allowing for the intake of breath.

She knew everything she wanted to say to them. It came so easily for her when she was talking to them. Each statue would see her pray more ardently, with more fervour than she had at the last until, by the time she had reached the final one, she could barely hold her arms still. Some days after school, on the way home, they stopped by a place of worship. He would watch, and she would pray. She prayed until all the words merged into a stream of syllables. She prayed until nothing made sense anymore. She prayed until she no longer knew what she was praying for.

# 36. Symbols

There was no question that Dev was going through a lot. The death of his sister. Separated from his father. Transplanted to another country. Dealing with another language, another culture. It would be natural for these things to take a toll and the stress to bubble to the surface. Dev hadn't heard of the term *nervous tic*, and he didn't know what it meant to have one. Apparently, neither did Serena, when she heard from her brother, Dev's Uncle Sachin, that he had noticed Dev playing with his hair.

It was true. Dev found himself unconsciously reaching for curls in his hair and winding them around his fingers. Twisting and coiling his hair this way and that, his nervous tic was an unconscious release, something that reassured and calmed him, albeit temporarily, when all he felt was crushing anxiety. Constantly nervous and unsure of himself, this tic was noticeable to everyone who saw him. To his mother and her family, it was unseemly. Fearing that it would become a solid habit, Serena began telling Dev off every time she saw him doing it.

It was due to more than her eagerness to once more fit in with her family, more than her need to garner the approval and love of her father and brother, that Serena allowed them to watch and admonish Dev whenever they saw him reach for his hair. She feared she did not know what else to do as a parent. She feared failure as a mother.

'What is it?'

'Why are you doing that?'

'Why do you play with your hair?'

'It will start falling out.'

Uncle Sachin took it a step further. After consuming more rum than dinner in the evenings, he would turn his hazy, bloodshot gaze to Dev. 'The next time I see you playing with your hair, I swear I'll tie socks over your hands. I'll make you go to school that way. What will your little friends think then?' He would then challenge Dev with an unblinking, glassy stare until, intimidated, Dev would look away, leave the dinner table and busy himself revising, no longer able to placate his nerves the only way he knew how.

Dr Sharma would think back to episodes like that and ponder the contradictory nature of Mauritian culture. Full of colourful idiosyncrasies, yet it rejected any deviation, amongst children, from what was considered normal behaviour. They perceived anything that didn't fit the mould as shameful, undermining their standing within the wider family and community. They fretted over how they would explain any perceived transgressions.

Dev constantly felt eyes on him at home, while at school, he remained the focus of much interest, labelled *Anglais Potis* by his classmates. *Fake English*. Dev felt under surveillance wherever he was. Despite all the attention, he had never felt so lonely. Just as nothing can prepare a parent for the loss of a child, nothing can prepare a child for the loss of a parent.

'What do you think that will accomplish?'

'What are you thinking about when you do that?'

These were questions Dev wanted to ask his mother at the churches and temples.

As the year progressed and the exams drew closer, Dev should have been spending more time at his books, but Serena insisted that they spend more time exploring the temples. Eventually, it came to be that Dev saw the gods every day. Their faces and expressions were no longer tranquil and benign to Dev. Instead, he saw malevolence dancing in their eyes. He felt them leering and jeering. Mockery and barely concealed sarcasm lighting their faces. They looked clownish, as though designed to ridicule anyone gullible or desperate enough to have faith in them. The looks from the faces of Mauritians around him every day, including Serena's, made him feel they knew something he didn't.

Mauritians, such as the builders, Uncle Sachin had finally hired to work on the upper floor in his father's house, which would be his floor. However, they had begun angling for more money to finish the work, making all sorts of excuses, because they thought his sister had come from England with money.

Others began asking Serena if Raju would write them letters of invitation to obtain visas to visit the UK. In effect, making Raju responsible for any violations of their visa terms as far as immigration officials were concerned. The visitors would have guessed that Serena and Raju had separated, but they wouldn't jeopardise their chance to get what they wanted by commenting. They all came under the guise of *encouragement for Dev*. In the midst of it all, Dev didn't think about what he wanted. It didn't seem to matter anymore. Somewhere along the way, the boy had stopped thinking of himself as a real person. With everyone around him telling him everything, he bent to their will. As for his feelings and memories, he let everything pile up and didn't bother processing any of it. There wasn't time.

His mother needing him to succeed.

His father letting go of them.

His sister…

It became a habit, living in every moment as it happened. Reserving his memory only for capturing the pages from his textbooks. To stir pride in those around him. His mother. His father. Dev wondered when his father would come. There had been no talk, between him and Serena, of his father visiting them in Mauritius. It was something that he had silently, unconsciously decided would happen if he did his best at these exams.

Somehow he had come to equate the CPE exam with his father coming to see them. Dev had given himself the impression that his father's arrival hinged on him committing himself to his studies and doing well at them. With this in mind, the eleven-year-old pressed on, somehow convinced that this would bring them all together again.

The snapshots flood back to Dr. Sharma.

The anniversary of Mauritian independence. Flags hanging everywhere. Red, blue, yellow, green. Removing a small flag from its plastic stick and placing it instead on his grandfather's car radio aerial.

The introduction of the shiny new five rupee coin.

Visiting a temple in the middle of nowhere. Statues of Hindu gods everywhere. In rows. In circles. In their unique individual huts and cubicles, like little workers in a call centre. *Why so many? Do they all have different superpowers? Who are they? Why do we have to pray to each one?* Round and round they go until he can no longer remember where he had begun, surrounded by the staring gods.

Tetanus shot at a local clinic after stepping on a rusty nail.

Wondering when Dad was coming.

Opening a drawer, then slamming it in surprise after finding an equally surprised cockroach scurrying about inside.

The energy-sapping heat. Throwing the heavy backpack full of books from his back, onto the asphalt, in exhaustion and frustration.

All at sea in this new country, with its unyielding heat and mosquitoes silently sucking his blood. ('Ugh, why is he so spotty?' asked one disgusted visitor upon seeing Dev. 'Because the mosquitoes have been at him,' replied Serena.)

Serena telling Dev how her headteacher used to say to the class, '*ce n'est pas la mer à boire,*' when confronted with a tricky maths problem. *It's not drinking the sea.*

Fish markets with their bounty of seafood, all different types and colours, freshly caught that morning. Octopus tipped out from a plastic bucket, their alien tentacles and soft flesh incongruous against the counter's hard, smooth white tiles.

Guzzling the water straight from a fresh coconut at the beach.

Pumpkins, calabash, carrots, potatoes, runner beans and greens straight from the garden.

Mauritian rum with the crest of Mauritius printed straight onto the glass bottle.

The smell of cooking carrying on the air from each house at dinnertime.

The neighbours arguing in French before resorting to screeching and cursing at each other in more colourful and cutting Mauritian Creole.

The replica Dodos, constructed from tiny seashells, sold in all the tourist shops.

Parents brimming with hope for their children. 'We only want the best for you.'

The beautiful blue-green of the sea at Mon Choisy beach. Pereybere. Flic en Flac. Belle Mare.

The intense heat in the north of the island married to the bustle of the capital, Port Louis.

# 37. Firewalker

'What?' Dev asked. 'They're going to do what? Why?'

'Because they believe,' replied Serena simply, as she searched the side of the road for a parking space.

'Believe in what?'

Having parked the car Serena and Dev scurried towards the crowd and found a space with a good view. Some people had already had their turn and were receiving medical attention where necessary.

Serena and Dev watched as the next person, pierced with the same little spears that they had seen at the *Cavadee* ceremony, readied himself. Before him, the walkway, replete with glowing embers, made for an impressive sight in the dark of the evening, but that wasn't what the man thought before he began his firewalk. The man took a breath through his mouth, held open by the metal spears, and with the legs of his trousers rolled up, he took his first, purposeful step onto the hot coals.

'What are they doing? Isn't the weather already hot

enough? Do they *need* to walk on fire?' Dev asked, spitting attitude. He was tired after a day at school, and this was another of his mother's tiresome religious excursions that he just didn't understand.

Serena was transfixed by what they were watching. Most of these people believed in a higher purpose to what they were doing. It wasn't simply daring to walk on fire. It wasn't simply pain or withstanding pain. It was purification, as though the heat would burn away all their sins.

Amongst the devotees waiting their turn were also the obvious tourists. The devotees believed they were demonstrating their faith, proving their belief in Hindu values and gods.

The man stepped slowly, deliberately on the coals, step by step. He took normal strides and absorbed each step as the coal cracked and wheezed beneath his heels.

Serena looked down at Dev. He was worrying a tuft of grass with his shoe. She knew Dev was tired of all the studying, the heat, and attention. She knew the novelty of the change, that he had so readily accepted at the beginning of the year, was now wearing very thin.

Serena accepted that the pressure he was facing over these exams was not something he had experienced or witnessed others experiencing whilst growing up. It simply wasn't something for which he had been at all prepared. Not even she and Raju hadn't gone through it. It simply hadn't been that important when they were children. Sometimes he seemed to be doing his best, while at other times, he didn't seem to care at all, talking only of his father, Amina and home in England. Those were things she could not talk about.

Other than his studies, there was little they could speak about.

Serena decided to give Dev the background to what they were witnessing as participants continued to take to the coals. She wanted him to appreciate the beauty of the sacrifice and devotion. Kneeling in the dirt beside Dev, she told him what she had learnt of the origins of Hindu firewalking.

'The *Mahabharata* is the longest epic poem ever. It's written in Sanskrit, and it's one of the two most important ancient Indian epics. I don't know the whole story, but I've learnt a bit. Because it's interesting and beautiful. Apparently, the ritual of the firewalk had come from Draupadi in the *Mahabharata*.'

'What's a *Draupadi*?'

'Draupadi was a young princess who was lost by her five husbands –'

'*Five* husbands?' Dev interrupted, astonished. 'She must have been busy,' he added, picturing all the children.

'Yes. They were five brothers. That's another story. Anyway, they lost her in a game of dice. They lost her to a rival family that was cheating. After gambling away the kingdoms, all their wealth, and then themselves, she was the final asset her husbands gambled away.

'When Draupadi heard what had happened, she was horrified to learn how she had been used and gambled away by her own family and lost to the rival family led by Duryodhana. Duryodhana ordered Dushasana, his younger brother, to bring Draupadi to his court. Draupadi was forced to the court by Dushasana, who dragged her in by her hair.

'At the court, Draupadi asked how her husbands could

gamble her away after they had already lost themselves and had become slaves to Duryodhana. This made Duryodhana angry, and he ordered Dushasana to disrobe Draupadi before the entire court to shame her. Draupadi prayed to Krishna for protection from those men. Krishna took pity and then performed a *miracle.*'

'What miracle?' asked Dev as the next person, a tourist in shorts, planted his foot heavily on the embers before instantly yelling in pain and falling away from the walkway before hopping towards medical attention, to the laughter of all those watching.

If he hadn't begun to resent the hold that her resurgent Hindu beliefs appeared to have on Serena, Dev would have enjoyed the Hindu stories much more. He tried to see things from her point of view, but it just seemed that his mother preferred diving deeper into religion and traditions to spending time with him.

They had once laughed over how silly religious rituals seemed, but he now saw his mother retreating from the world to spend her days in worship at a temple or a church. He found it difficult to watch this rapid change that felt like a rejection of him and a loss of faith in the world around them. He felt her getting further away from him and didn't know how to bring her back.

Serena continued the story.

'Dushasana pulled at Draupadi's sari, which unravelled from her body. He kept pulling and pulling, and the fabric just kept coming. Before long, he had a pile of material at his feet, but Draupadi was still dressed. With Krishna's help, the wraps of her sari became interminable. Dushasana could not remove her clothes, and he stopped pulling, exhausted from the effort.

'Outraged, one of Draupadi's family vowed to cut off Dushasana's arm and drink the blood from his chest. Draupadi herself also vowed not to comb her hair until she could decorate it with Dushasana's blood and make a comb from his femur. After this, a big war takes place.

After the war, Draupadi admits to Krishna that she should have married differently.

'She had married the five strong and brave brothers, but they had all failed her when she had most needed them. Eventually, she proves her purity and loyalty by walking barefoot through a bed of fire.' Serena finished as a woman began her walk over the coals.

Dev considered this before asking: 'Do you wish you had married someone else?'

Behind them, a man had been listening to Serena. 'It is dangerous to walk on fire without faith, little man,' he said. Serena and Dev both turned to look up at him. 'It's not everyone who can do it without hurting themselves. You shouldn't take it lightly. It's not for those without faith. It's only for true believers with pure hearts. God knows the difference.'

'Then why do the tourists do it?' Dev asked.

'They think they're buying an experience, some understanding, but in the end, it's hollow for them,' the man concluded.

That night Dev afforded himself a few moments to contemplate how different things were. Having learned from previous experience that thinking too much of Amina would only lead to a thick, immovable pain that would last days, he tried not to do it too often. Instead, he allowed himself to indulge now and then with a mental trip to her sea. Usually, this would take the form of what about her he missed the most, her stories.

She had given him the taste for stories but not for creating them. Nevertheless, he tried. He imagined Amina in the room with him, speaking across the darkness of the night, entertaining him with outlandish tales. In this spirit, he would try to reclaim a little of Amina for himself. Dev would settle back, pressing his head into his pillow, and letting his thoughts flow.

He imagined this was how Amina made up his stories. On this occasion, Dev recalled a news conference his uncle had been watching on TV. It involved a minister of… something. They had been discussing trade, business, commerce, transport, tax levies on imported goods…

'… the dwindling tourist numbers. The far-right government. The shitty economy,' continues Winston Zha as he reclines in his chair behind the glass conference table in the large airy room. 'How did you think you were going to avoid this?'

'Things are in a state of flux, it's true, but what goes down usually comes up, don't you think?' squirms the Belgian Foreign Minister, Thom Maes, in his chair as he rolls his pen in his hands. He didn't like Zha, but this is what it has come to.

'Sure. If you're talking about bad shrimp. Are you talking about bad shrimp?'

Although it has been a long time coming, it seems that overnight, Zha has become all-powerful, and world leaders are falling over themselves to curry favour with the man, thus ensuring their survival. Maes cannot understand how their nations survived world wars and came through the worst tyranny, only to deal with this. Winston Zha. Who is he anyway? Why does he have to plead to this… despot? If it was a guy with bombs, they'd send in soldiers, but the man with the world's healthiest balance sheet gets total co-operation. He even manages to have his business meetings sponsored by major corporations, like sporting events. 'Can you honestly tell me there are no worse countries out there?'

'I appreciate your dedication to your nation, but this is the first, and we need to make it a reasonable one. Not small enough that nobody notices, but not big enough to upset the world balance too much,' continues Winston Zha.

'But we have Brussels,' argues Maes. 'We're practically the capital of Europe. You cannot just *cancel* us.'

'Actually, we don't feel that Belgium has Brussels,' replies Zha, getting out of his chair demonstratively, as had been suggested to him. 'We feel it's more like Brussels has Belgium, out of necessity. While, admittedly, Belgium is not insignificant, it is not as important as Brussels. Brussels will continue as it is, but Belgium is in line to become a museum.'

'A museum,' echoes Maes in wide-eyed bewilderment.

'A museum,' confirms Winston Zha. 'Belgium is a country… *was* a country… is a country with a lot of history, and we're not indifferent to that. We think the best way to make the nation of Belgium better is to get rid of it and replace it with the *Museum* of Belgium.'

'Museum of Belgium,' echoes the minister again.

'That's right, and don't worry about Belgium's citizens. Wherever there is a museum, there are gift shops, coffee shops, car parks and so on. The people of Belgium will simply become staff catering to tourists who will continue to crave the things, other than history, that you guys are really good at. The waffles, chocolates, frîtes, beer, and that priest who suggested the big bang.'

'And who do you think you are to decide all this?' sputters Maes furiously.

'Oh, and I forgot *Tintin*!' continues Zha, oblivious to Maes' frustration.

'Do you think you're God?'

'No, I'm Winston Zha.'

The Foreign Minister shakes his head. He doesn't want to be there. Maes feels he has been manipulated into this position, a victim of political machinations. *Someone must have known this was coming*, he thinks. *It didn't just come from nowhere, did it? This must have been in the works when I took the position. I've been set up to take the fall. I'll be forever known as the foreign minister who oversaw the negotiations for the cessation of Belgium.*

Maes spots one of the cameras embedded in the wall looking down at them from the corner of the room, and remembers they are being broadcast on a live video feed to the world. Suddenly, he wishes he had worn a different suit. This grey one his wife had picked out for him is smart, but he feels stuffy next to Zha in his customary black jeans and white shirt.

Zha. The star of the show. The one that everyone wants to

trust. He is a celebrity businessman that everyone wants to trust and love and be loved by him in return. Why? Because he leaves a live video feed broadcasting from his boardroom around the clock. Anyone can watch the latest developments at Zha Global. Transparent. Zha feels he is transparent, he doesn't lie to the people, no matter how misguided his views or beliefs are, and they love him even if they do not share those values.

The people allow him the power to influence their lives because they feel he doesn't lie to get it. He tells the truth, but he is wealthy and powerful enough to create a truth that entertains. Different. Anarchic. A truth that suggests nothing matters anymore. Nothing is sacred. That is part of the reason why everyone wants to trust him.

He doesn't try to tell people that things are important. He isn't a leader in that way. He doesn't ever seem to sell things to the people. He isn't a typical businessman in that way. He doesn't try to blame anyone else. He isn't a typical politician in that way. He conducts his affairs in public and invites the world to watch him at work. In return, they love him.

'But why exactly should the world listen to you?' perseveres Maes, even though he can almost hear the teenagers of the world screaming from their bedrooms: 'because he's Winston Zha, the greatest tech visionary who ever lived.'

'Because I'm here to save the world. No nations. Just people. One world. One nation. With my resources, I intend to make that dream a reality.'

'By treating each country... as a TV show? For your entertainment?'

'This is not TV. This is real life, in real-time,' corrects Zha, throwing his hands out as though unveiling real life, in real-time, all around him. 'I don't speak for the people. I speak with the people. How do you think I got here? I know what the people want before they do. Zha Global bought the entire national debt of Belgium, as well as four other countries. Don't worry, it will be a fantastic show. The world will hold its breath in suspense. For the first time in centuries, Belgium will be a star country, in the glare of the spotlight. Out of five contenders, the world's population will vote for their first cancelled country.

'I'm giving you and your government notice so you can begin removing any obstructions. If it is chosen by the people, Belgium will close, after the final show, to reopen a year later for business. Brussels, as the hot seat of Europe, would be part of that. The first cancellation has to be significant, and the weight that Brussels carries would ensure that.'

'This is insane,' concludes Maes, slumping slightly in his chair.

'I like it,' disagrees Zha. 'Europe, and its big, long history, is so fusty and musty. I like the idea that it could essentially be managed via a collection of offices in a ginormous museum. Don't worry. We'll make sure Belgium is seen as a fighter throughout the shows. It will not be a simple case of voting based on what the people know already about these countries.

'Instead, the countries will complete tasks, and they will compete for votes. The people of these competing countries, and the governments, will be encouraged to come together and *work* together. Early research suggests it will be a close-run thing between the UK and Belgium. If the UK loses, it will be turned into a giant shopping mall.'

'A shopping mall?' says the minister.

'Yeah,' said Zha, 'their governments are always fairly malleable. So, we'll probably maintain the government and royal family there because they'll just go along with everything anyway. It'll save bringing in *management*,' reasons Zha.

'But they'll be the royal family… of a shopping mall,' presses the foreign minister.

'A gigantic shopping mall, and yes, the UK is perfect as a shopping mall because who is better placed than royalty to officially endorse products and parade around in the clothes you're trying to sell?'

'Why not make the UK a museum and Belgium a shopping mall?' suggests Maes, thinking of his wife. 'The UK has many cultural attributes, is steeped in history and has many beauty spots.'

'It also has shitty weather,' replies Zha. 'Who wants to be outside in the cold and rain at Stonehenge when you can be inside buying a scaled-down Stonehenge replica constructed from tiny fragments of Welsh slate, or Dover chalk? Get it shipped over to your place in the Hamptons. Think of it. You could use it as a table and stool set. Or get a slightly bigger version with built-in grills and skewers, and you could have the ultimate permanent stone barbecue installation.'

'But, we have shitty weather too?' the minister protests, hopefully.

'Yeah, but you don't have cool celebrities to help sell things. It was Adam Smith in 1776 who first described his compatriots as a nation of shopkeepers, not Napoleon. I like the circularity involved here,' explains Zha, making circles in the air with his index finger. 'Once again, Zha Global will have been instrumental in making real an idea that was once ridiculed,' finishes Winston Zha, clasping his hands together, beaming with benevolence.

'But why? Why do this at all? How will it work? Why will anyone travel from one part of the world to another to do their shopping in the UK?' asks Maes, feeling he has inadvertently stepped into the admin office of a dysfunctional mental asylum.

'Travel, Mr Maes. New technology. New technology from Zha Global will cut travel costs and travel time. Making a trip from Brisbane to Oxford will become the equivalent of walking to a local bus stop. Not a new internet, but an alternative internet.

'Instead of looking up a picture of the tallest skyscraper to go into a school report, your grandkids will just go to Dubai and take their own picture. Instead of seeing things and places on a page or screen, they'll just go there. Because that is what Zha Global is all about, bringing the world together.'

'That sounds lovely, and everything, but does that necessitate this *cancelling* of countries? How does this benefit anyone?'

'You have to understand how *we* are looking at the world. We see it as an exclusive club. To retain your membership rights, there are certain criteria that you must adhere to. If a nation does not meet these criteria, it will find itself disengaged. Disenfranchised. Does that make sense?'

'In what way disenfranchised?'

'Quite simply, it will be cut off.'

'How?'

'In every way imaginable. Economically, politically, simple communication. For all intents and purposes, the country would simply cease to exist.'

'It's.. that's impossible. You can't murder an entire nation.'

'Oh, God no. I'm not a monster. I'm an idealist. What I want is an ideal world. It's time to stop compromising. We need to make what we want happen.'

'So, what are you proposing?'

'I predict the world will be pleased to shed its deadwood. Forget countries. That's how you run *the world* like a business. You cut off the people dragging you down and promote those who can take you to new heights. It's not about nationalism. It's about having the best people on all sides. The flag is just the pretty bow that goes on top. This will be bigger than the Super Bowl, the Olympics, even the World Cup because everyone gets to play. No borders, no rules, nothing matters anymore.

'Countries will compete for the chance to retain power and influence in the world with more points granted to countries that create tangible products and services. The UK, for example, produces a lot of music. On the other hand, its tourism is based mainly on history and past glories, so it loses points for that.

'Losing countries will have their right to exist revoked, and they will no longer be able to communicate with the rest of the world. Countries will have to prove their relevance to remain relevant. Circularity, again,' with another twirl of his finger. 'It will no longer be enough for countries to be in the world. They'll need the world to want them too.'

Thom Maes puts down his pen. He has given up. All he wants is to be at home with his wife and no longer have Winston Zha in his line of sight. He feels humiliated and doesn't want to be watched anymore. Not by Zha, not his cohorts, and not the people staring at him over the internet. It isn't his world anymore, and he wants none of it.

Zha continues. 'I want to put the countries that don't meet the criteria in the shade. I want them cut off from the rest of the world. Temporarily. They'll have the chance to earn back their membership. But until that happens, I want them to turn grey. It's about being the best you can be.

'Do you truly feel that your country is living up to its potential? Do you not think you could do better? How do you think you can be better? How can you be more... attractive? Whatever you're doing, you know you can be doing more to really put yourself out there and say, look at us, world, this is what we're all about!

'Why shouldn't countries strive to be all they can? So many reasons for them all to be the best, but do you want to hear another? Being the best guarantees that you will remain connected to the rest of the world. Engaged.

'How would you feel about the lights going out? How would you feel about ships no longer bringing supplies? Medical supplies. Food. Clothing. How would you feel being forced to live in darkness, with no way to connect with any other part of the world, as though you had been ripped from it and flung into space? Because I will make that happen.'

'You can't do it,' argues Maes. 'People won't stand for it.'

'You'd be surprised. The numbers suggest otherwise. 4

billion people put their trust in me every day. All they want is to be entertained. Distracted from their daily cares that you and your colleagues inflict upon them. They trust me far more than they ever have you guys. They will trust me with this too if it keeps them engaged.'

Putting his papers away into his briefcase, Maes considers the shows, and despite himself, he begins thinking of titles for them. *Cancelling Countries. Not a great title, but it could work*, he thinks. He knows that he should instead be thinking of some argument against Zha's plan, but he knows any argument would be futile. Maes thinks of further names for the show. *Peoples in Peril. When Tech Met Tyranny. The Worldwide Country Cancellation Countdown.* 'But the countries you… grey out. They'll fight back,' Maes finally mutters weakly, undermining his own words.

'Yes, because everybody wants to remain connected. I'm counting on it. I want them to fight to regain their place, fight back by being innovative, creative, constantly seeking the new. That's all that matters anymore.'

'This isn't some talent show.'

'No. It's more than that. Far more. It's about bettering more than just yourself in one area. It's about showing the world your community, your people. I think we'll see the best of humanity.'

'And I think we'll see the worst. What happens when they start pointing fingers, blaming others for bringing them down?'

'They'll lose more points and go down even further.'

'Wars will start, people will die, unspeakable atrocities will take place.'

‘Hey, if they’re incommunicado, we won’t know about it. If we don’t know about it, then did it really happen?’

‘And you don’t have a problem telling me all this in front of the millions of people watching? Or have you stopped broadcasting?’

‘I don’t mind. This is what they want. They want things shaken up. They embrace what’s happening.’

# 38. A healthy outlook

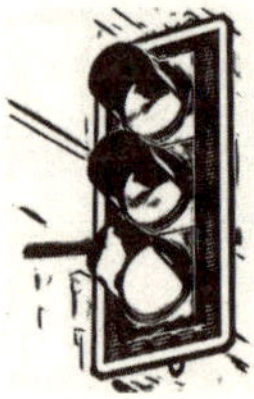

'I don't understand what's happening,' admitted Leona.

'What?' asked Dev as he looked out at the fireworks lighting up the sky. It was Bonfire Night. He had brought her to the display because he knew she loved fireworks, but he hadn't anticipated the argument. It was just the latest in a long series that had intensified as he had begun taking up various regional placements as part of his undergraduate degree in medicine.

'You don't think he's clever?' asked Leona as another explosion lit the sky with multi-coloured sprinkles.

'I didn't say that. I don't know if he's clever or not. He's a kid. I've met him twice. How am I supposed to know if he's clever or not? It's not as if we had any conversations that would reveal that information.'

'Why don't you just say, yes, I think he's clever? Like anybody else would?'

'Because I don't know that. I can't agree with something when I don't know it. Why? What would be the point?' asked Dev.

'But he's my nephew. Can't you take my word that he's a smart kid?'

'Why did you bother asking me if you didn't want an honest answer?'

'He's not stupid.' *BOOM,* went another explosion before the crowd gasped.

'I didn't say he was.'

'He gets excellent school reports,' persisted Leona.

'Okay. I didn't say he was stupid,' defended Dev.

'But if you don't think he's clever, then you must think he's stupid.'

Leona was trying to win the argument – that she had started – at all costs. To Dev, it had become a ridiculous exchange of words. 'All I said was I don't know, I've only met the kid twice. Once we had a kick-about in your brother's back garden, and the other time was at a wedding reception. There's nothing that indicated he was cleverer than the average kid his age. Personally, I think it's weird that you wanted me to form an opinion of your ten-year-old nephew. Why does it matter to you so much what I think of a ten-year-old boy?'

'Because I love him,' said Leona, scrambling. 'He's a sweet boy. I love you too, and I want you both to get on.' Actually, she was just infuriated and wanted Dev to agree with her about her beloved nephew.

'I wish you would stop checking in with me about how I'm getting on with your family.'

'I just want you to fit in with my family.'

'Okay, but it's like you're forcing me to have some spontaneous, immediate connection with a bunch of people

I met a couple of times.'

'What's wrong with that? They're nice people,' said Leona, as the crowd oohed around them.

'I'm sure they are.'

'Our Jack is a clever boy, a sweet boy.'

'I'm sure he is. To you.'

'You see, why did you have to add that?'

'Because it's true. I don't have enough information upon which to accurately base any assessment of sweetness and/or cleverness, but I'm sure you do. So in your opinion, he is both these things.'

'It's like you intentionally put up some kind of disclaimer or waiver around things.'

'What are you talking about?'

'Sometimes it just feels like you watch what you say so much. I wish you could talk and trust people more. That's all.'

'I could probably do that more if people weren't trying to impose stuff on me.'

'Who's imposing? I'm not imposing anything on you. I'm letting you know that my family likes you. I would like it if you liked them.'

'I don't know if you've noticed, Leona, but I am up to my eyeballs in stuff I need to do. A BA in medicine doesn't just happen by accident. I don't have any time to like people.'

'Time to check out,' thinks Dev, 'just a little more waiting and then I'm out of here.'

It's all flitting now. Threads here… snaps there. The air in the room is thick as we watch him. Thick with what? What will he bring out next? What will he decide to focus, linger upon? Can we plant the seed of a little *something* in his mind? Should we? What would happen?

We watch him:

Sprawling
Grabbing
Sweating
Gasping
Coughing
Dying
Doctor

'Doctor?' asked Mr Drake as he stepped into the room.

'Yes. Mr Drake?' asked Dr. Sharma. 'I'm just looking through your notes here.'

Mr Drake cleared his throat. 'The, um… I'm not here about that. I mean, it's not medical, what I'm here about.'

'Oh? What is it then? How can I help you?' Dr. Sharma, not long qualified, was new to this practice.

'I don't know if it says anything about it in there,' began Mr Drake. 'Or whether things like this are even noted there, but my daughter was killed. About eight months ago.'

'I see,' stated Dr. Sharma

'We're still coming to terms with the… I still don't know what to call it. She's my daughter. What do I call it?' Mr Drake asked, with his words, but also his eyes as he peered at Dr. Sharma through his wire frame spectacles. 'My wife doesn't know what to call it either. I've heard her call it all sorts of things over the last eight months. She doesn't seem to have settled on one particular term either. I keep thinking maybe she and I should have a free exchange of ideas, but I think we've left it a bit late now. There's a window where it feels you can still have a conversation like that, but after eight months, it feels like it would be… inappropriate.'

'What have you been calling it so far?' asked Dr. Sharma, not entirely sure of what Mr Drake was talking about.

'Passing. Death. Loss. The thing. I was going to call it *the thing* a moment ago. It depends on whom I'm speaking with.'

'And to me, you were going to say, *the thing*?'

'When talking to friends and family, I say *passing*. With the media, I say *loss*. In correspondence with the military, I use *death*. With you, I suppose I don't owe you any such tokens, facade, formality. Whatever you want to call it.'

'That's fine,' replied Dr. Sharma, eager to move things along, aware of the time. 'How are things?'

'Well, we're still getting over it. Clearly,' replied Mr Drake, who then proceeded to ignore the doctor and play with a loose thread from his jacket.

Dr. Sharma left it a little while, perhaps fifteen seconds or so, before giving him a little push. 'What brings you here today then?'

'It doesn't say anything in there about my daughter's death, does it?'

'Not that I have seen,' answered Dr. Sharma, whose initial instinct had been to turn back to his computer monitor to check, but he resisted the urge at the last moment. 'What was her name?' he asked instead.

'Victoria. Vicky.'

'You mentioned the military?'

'Vicky had completed two tours in Afghanistan. She had

come home. Do you see?' he asked.

'Please, tell me.'

'She had come home. She was finished, and she wasn't going back. She was getting something from them. A medal or something. I'm not an army man myself, and besides, to me, it hardly matters now what she was going to get from them. She had come home. For good. She was back in her old room. Safe. After everything, she was finally back in her old room, just like before. Shall I tell you how it happened?'

'If you want to.'

'It was a few days after she was back. Jet lag was subsiding. She'd gone out for lunch with an old friend of hers.' Mr Drake paused again, lost in thought, needing to rouse himself every so often. 'My wife, Val, she gave Vicky her car keys, but she didn't take them. Val told me Vicky had said that she would end up spending longer looking for a parking space than eating with so much traffic. So, she met this friend for lunch and afterwards they were walking. Along the pavement. Probably laughing, chatting, minding their own business.

'Witnesses say this… person just came out of nowhere,' continued Mr Drake. So fast. People had barely seen him before… he'd moved past them. They remember the sunlight glinting off the metal. They say he shouted, "out of my way, I'm not slowing down for anyone." Like he was so… important. He was on a bicycle, going along the pavement. What's a grown man doing cycling along the pavement?

'He said he wasn't stopping, and he didn't. She must not have seen him. Of all the people there, he had to hit my girl. Hit her so hard he caused internal injuries, head injuries. All sorts. By the time they arrived, it was too late.' Mr Drake paused again and removed his glasses to wipe the lens with a handkerchief. 'We raised her. She went to war and survived all that, only to get run into by some… imbecile on a bicycle. What do you think of that, eh?'

'It's terrible,' replied Dr. Sharma, after a moment. 'Did they catch him?'

'Yeah. They handed him a fine. Two grand.'

'Really? Is that it?'

'Convicted of dangerous cycling. And a fine. That's it. Anyway, I'll not get started on all that. I'm here about something else.'

'Okay,' said Dr. Sharma brightly, glad to be moving onto a new topic.

'That day, after making lunch plans with her friend, Vicky had left her mobile phone behind. The battery was flat, so she left it charging. It's still there. We haven't been able to do anything with her room at all. Tidy it, clean it, clear it out, whatever. It's still there. The phone. Switched on, charging. What would you have done?'

'About the phone? Is it a problem?'

'Well, it's there. Plugged in.'

'Is it that, and I'm only guessing here,' began Dr. Sharma, trying to work out the dilemma, 'is it that the phone is plugged into the electricity, effectively still living while Vicky is gone?'

'What are you babbling about? No, you have it all wrong. This isn't some metaphysical conundrum. The phone rang. The phone rang all the time. What would you have done?' he asked again.

'Couldn't you switch it off?'

'It was too soon. We wanted to just leave everything as it was. You would have gone in and switched off the phone? Unplugged it?' asked Mr Drake.

'I don't know,' Dr. Sharma slowly replied, perplexed.

'People were phoning her anyway. Presumably, they'd heard she was back in the UK. Strangely enough, the calls seemed to increase as the news filtered amongst her friends. I've since learned that it's a relatively new phenomenon. Young people, like you, who have more or less grown up with mobile phones, always connected, when they hear that someone from their group, their close network, has passed away, their initial impulse, as absurd as it may seem, is to phone that person. Have you heard this?'

'No.'

'Well, there it is. The calls increased for a while, but then they gradually subsided. The media took up what, for them, was an unusual story. A *freak* story. My daughter, the victim, being a soldier, fresh from a tour in Afghanistan, gave them an attractive hook. The only way this could have been juicier for them would have been if that idiot on his bike had been an illegal immigrant selling drugs. He wasn't any of those. He's a web designer, I think.'

'So what happened?'

'As I said, the phone calls subsided but didn't go away altogether. The phone would ring at… whenever. That same ringtone once, sometimes twice a day. Thank God she didn't have a song or some novelty ringtone. Just a typical ringing phone sound.'

'I imagine a novelty ringtone would make it more

annoying for you both?'

'More… macabre, I think. With the ringing phone sound, it was initially more startling than anything else. Then with lots of people being around, after the funeral and whatnot, the ringing just blended into the background. With everyone gone, it just interrupted our day, every day. It was impossible to predict what time or how often. Yes, the easy thing would have been to answer or unplug it and let the battery, um… fade, but I had agreed with Val to leave everything as it was.

'We could be doing anything, watching the news, making dinner, chatting, and that phone could ring. We'd both be frozen, silently counting down the rings until it would go to voicemail. I know that's what Val was doing because that's what I was doing. It felt the clocks themselves would hold their breath until those rings would stop. The dust would, you know, loiter in the air, waiting for the call to go to voicemail before continuing its journey, finding somewhere to settle.

'Eventually, it got to the stage where we were sitting almost in silence, every day waiting for that phone to ring from the moment we awoke. It was as if we couldn't do anything until we had heard that phone ring. Or at least it seemed that way to me,' said Mr Drake.

'It went on this way for two, three months. I had to break it. I had to break out of it. It was like a dream world we were living in, where it felt that our lives had come under the sovereign rule of this little plastic box upstairs. One morning I woke up and immediately began thinking about the phone. What I thought was: "what if it never rings again? Will we be trapped like this?"'

'What did you do?'

'I had Val's sister take her out for the day. Val made all sorts of excuses not to go, but I knew it was just because she had to listen for the phone. Eventually, she went. I pulled up a chair outside Vicky's room and waited for the phone to ring. I sat there for hours, waiting and thinking. I thought back to the time six months earlier when we had first heard about Vicky.

'It was a couple of days after that Val let it all out. I think it had taken her that long for the news to sink in and for her to process everything. I don't know what it was. Could have been anything. Maybe one too many people telling her how sorry they were. Maybe she saw someone happy and laughing outside. Maybe she just stubbed her toe. I don't know, but it was the only time she cracked and let anything out. It was good.'

'What do you mean?'

'It felt good. Not to see her crying. I mean, it felt like I was seeing her again for the first time in a long while. Not just the couple of days since Vicky had died, but more than that. I realised then that we'd fallen asleep a long time ago. Our relationship. This was the first time in a long time that we were both awake and looking to each other for something. Some explanation, some truth. I knew it was strange, in the middle of grieving for my daughter, that I was coming to a realisation about my relationship with my wife.'

'Not really. It's in the tough times that we learn a lot about each other and ourselves,' tried Dr. Sharma.

'I find it strange. Anyway, we were drifting into the same kind of fug with the phone where things were happening, but not really. There was nothing we were doing or nothing we weren't doing. It just seemed the natural course of things. Now that I think of it, I wonder if Val was pretending, imagining to herself that Vicky was still in Afghanistan. What do you think?'

'I don't know.'

'Maybe I'm not explaining things properly. It's difficult to put all this into words.' Mr Drake looked down and fidgeted with his fingers.

'Do you want me to… I mean, I can get you some contact details for bereavement counselling if you'd like.'

'What for?'

'So you can talk to someone.'

'That's what I'm doing now.'

'Right,' conceded Dr. Sharma, 'please continue.'

'I… um. Where was I?'

'You were talking about your wife. It was the first time you'd really talked in years,' Dr. Sharma quickly recapped.

'Oh yes. Well, *we* didn't talk. Val did all the talking. I hadn't ever seen her like that. She kept saying how she had been prepared. She had been prepared for what could happen with Vicky joining the armed forces and going over there. "But this happens? What is this? She misses all the landmines, all the missiles, bullets and whatnot. Her plane leaves without being shot down. She changes planes and eventually gets here safely. All that. After all those things that could have hurt her, she arrives back here to her home, our home, and then this happens?" Val couldn't contain herself. I tried to comfort her, calm her down, but it was no use,' continued Mr Drake.

'For over an hour, she kept going around in circles,

repeating the same things until she'd exhausted herself. Fell into an armchair. She kept saying, "I can't accept it. Vicky was finally safe, in her bedroom, in our home, with us. She was supposed to be safe, at last." The thing that stung me most was the questions. As if it was somehow my doing. She'd say: "so you tell me, what is this? She was mine, and now I have nothing. How can I pick up and move on? How am I supposed to let this go?" Anyway, that's what I was thinking of that day I had Val's sister pick her up, take her out.

'I was sitting there outside Vicky's room waiting for that phone to ring. Anyway, eventually, the phone rang, and for the first time in months, I opened *that* door and went into Vicky's room.

'I almost didn't do it,' continued Mr Drake. 'I stopped at the doorknob and had to push myself to turn it and go in. It was strange being in there again, catching her scent again. First, I had to go across the room to open the curtains, let some light in before I could find the phone. It was there on her bedside table, chirping away. I picked it up and pressed the green button.' Here Mr Drake paused.

'And?' pressed Dr. Sharma. 'Who was it?'

'I don't know. A man. Some cold caller in some call centre. You know, they have a list of numbers, and they call them every day until you answer and buy something. Or until they get a new list. I explained the situation, and he thanked me for my time. And then he wished me a nice day. Can you believe that? I told him my little girl had gone, and he told me: "have a good day, Sir."

'It was probably out of habit. Maybe he wasn't expecting that, didn't know what else to say?'

'Maybe.'

A few moments passed until Dr. Sharma, mindful that his appointments were already running over half an hour late, prompted Mr Drake to wrap things up. 'So you had an issue, and you resolved it. That's a positive move, isn't it? How does Mrs Drake feel?'

'Val doesn't know.'

'Sorry, when did this happen? Did I miss something?'

'A couple of months ago. After that, the phone calls stopped. I suppose he did indeed do *the needful* like he said he would.'

'So, did Val come out of her shell, like you hoped?'

'No, she wondered why the calls had stopped. I said I didn't know. The days passed, and things got worse.'

'Worse in what way?'

'Since the phone stopped ringing, I noticed Val was quieter, more introverted. When she did speak up, she was irritable. We still weren't really talking about anything that mattered. What would you have done?'

'Perhaps bereavement counselling?' ventured Dr. Sharma.

'She wouldn't agree to that. I did the only thing that made sense at the time. I began making the calls. I vary them. Different times each day.'

'I see.'

'Obviously, I can't tell her the truth now, and I can't tell anyone else, but I wanted to tell somebody. Thanks for listening.'

'Do you know what you're going to do next?'

'I hold the power, literally in my hands, to either prolong this facade or pull it away and force Val to face herself. What am I going to do? Keep at it for now. Val… she needs it, for now.'

'It's quite a short term solution. I think you should get Val into counselling.'

'I don't know.'

'The sooner she starts working through this… And that goes for you too.'

'I'm fine. What do you mean?'

'Well, if you say Val needs the ringing, then maybe you need it too.'

'I don't see that.'

'Do you feel under stress? Would you like me to prescribe you something?'

'No. I just wanted to tell somebody.'

'I can't help but feel that there is something you want me to do. Look, here are some contact details for the counselling service,' said Dr. Sharma, reaching into a desk drawer.

'Don't you think being on the ground makes too much sense,' asked Mr Drake suddenly. 'I mean *too* much sense. So much sense that it's almost out of focus. Isn't the air supposed to be clean at the bottom while all the exhaust fumes and cigarette smoke rise? Couldn't the filth be the same way? Couldn't the filth and the undesirables, the imperfections, the unbalanced, the retarded, the deformed, the mutilated, the *filth* just lift from the ground and drift away? Wouldn't that be for the best? It would be a lot more satisfying than all the learning to get along stuff. Rehabilitation. Incarceration. Wasting away when you could float away and maybe become something better. Eventually. What do you think?' Mr Drake finally asked, before adding a moment later, 'never mind, don't mind me. Just waffling.'

'Try to talk it over with Val,' counselled Dr. Sharma, 'and see if you can convince her to have a chat. If you need more information, please, come back in. Both of you.'

'Right,' acknowledged Mr Drake, taking the leaflet, before getting up from his chair and adding: 'Thanks.' With that, he left the office.

Once outside in the car park, Mr Drake reached into his coat pocket and felt for his phone. He had yet to make his call for that day. Mr Drake lightly fingered the rounded edges of the device and considered the options.

As Mr Drake ponders, Mayor Jayne drives by, fresh from another outing to carry out her civic engagement. She has been to see her doctor for her flu vaccination, an event covered by local news to encourage all vulnerable persons to also get theirs.

Things are going well for Jayne. Dutifully releasing the *substance* to the public, daily passing it from one person to another, mainly through handshakes, but sometimes through kisses applied to cheeks. Her grandchildren were amongst the first to receive the substance. *How better to spread it,* she rationalised to herself reasonably, *than by releasing it to people who are sure to come into contact with large numbers of the public.*

In getting her flu vaccination, Jayne had been sure to meet all the doctors for a quick chat and a handshake, her ulterior motive for undergoing her flu vaccination. Since God had revealed themself to be not only in existence but also in attendance, Jayne had reconsidered her position on the flu vaccine. She concluded that she would bother with it one last time after all, 'but only because it serves their plan.'

In the future, if they want her to catch a cold, she will catch a cold. 'No point trying to evade their will,' she rationalises aloud to herself as she turns out of the car park and onto the main road. 'Everything is part of a plan, and there is no point believing our actions have any effect,' she persuades herself. 'In fact, with God truly around to oversee everything, maybe there are no more decisions to be made at all by us. Maybe nothing we do matters. Maybe nothing matters.'

Despite these reassuring thoughts, Jayne is left troubled by the whole thing. Since her experience the other night, Jayne has had no more contact with whom she assumed had been God, and a tiny tick of doubt has begun to burrow at her, allowing questions to bleed into the opening.

'Was it God I had heard from? Were the chances not equally good that it was the devil? What exactly is this substance in the clay pot that I am applying to my hands every day? Not to mention those around me. Should I have had it analysed? Who could I have trusted to analyse it? Could the substance be harmful? What is the greater plan? How could any of this help with what is happening around the world?' Jayne allows herself to wonder before silently scolding herself for allowing doubt to whisper to her.

At that moment, a radio advertisement comes on the traffic lights and catches her attention. The songs and advertisements once broadcast via radio waves are now the sole preserve of the traffic lights who would belt out the tunes, sometimes with air guitar, and act out the ads. Yes, this has become a thing.

'In a relationship?' asks the left traffic light to his opposite number in a cheerful male voice.

'Yes,' answers the other lights in a perky female voice.

'No,' answers a lamp post across the intersection in a grumpy male voice. (In addition to ads requiring multiple performers, they sometimes get involved for songs with more than one singer.)

'Maybe,' answers another lamp post in a different female voice.

'Got protection?' returns the cheerful male voice.

'You mean condoms?' asks the male-sounding lamp post.

'You mean IUD?' giggles perky female.

'I mean protection, cover, insurance. Relationship insurance. If, or when, things go wrong, where do *you* go? Where do you stand without relationship insurance? Can you claim back the time, effort, not to mention the financial investment you've made? No? Well, now you can. Prudent4LifeWise.'

'Relationship insurance?' queries perky female.

'Never heard of it. Relationship Insurance?' echoes interested male.

'Relationship Insurance,' repeats cheerful male. 'Only from Prudent4LifeWise. With affordable premiums and packages to meet any eventuality, we have the policy to suit your needs. Date someone who already has a policy with us, and you both get a discount on your premiums. When, or if, things come to an end, you can file a joint claim. Isn't that easy? Take out a policy now and meet matches from our policyholder database. A dating service *and* an insurance service! Don't take a chance. Get serious. Contact Prudent4LifeWise because it's time to add a fourth choice: Marry. Shag. Kill. *Claim.*'

'My God,' thinks Jayne, 'what imbecile comes up with this stuff?'

Jayne is about to pull away when something else catches her attention. The lights blather on while car horns start to sound behind her, but she can't pull away. Someone is still crossing the road in front of her car. Or something. Also, *crossing* might not be the correct term. *Passing*? Or *gliding*, perhaps. Drifting. Definitely *drifting*.

It languidly drifts over the road. Five feet above the tarmac, not following any particular route. Purely by chance, it seems to have sailed on the air at the crossing. At first glance, Jayne thinks it is a kite of some sort, floating in the air, a kite made to look like a heap of clothes. However, as she pays closer attention, she realises that it is not a kite, and the object is not a pile of clothes. It is a person. A man. With brown hair. Caucasian. Just sprawled upon the air. Effortlessly, aimlessly gliding past.

Under normal circumstances, Jayne would have stopped to find out more, but she needs to be at her next engagement and has, like everyone else, become somewhat inured to all the recent episodes and goings-on, not just in the town but around the world. This combination means Jayne pulls away as soon as the body is out of range of her vehicle. No doubt, she would hear about it on the traffic light news later that evening.

Meanwhile, in a car headed in the opposite direction sits Malcolm and Deborah Lockhart with their two children,

Stephanie and Joseph. They all sit in silence while Deborah drives, and before long, they are on the motorway, heading for Dover and then the South of France. They are getting away. A break from it all, which is not to say that they are happy to be going, but with a family member's health on the line, they feel they have no choice.

'We're better off staying where we know what's what,' says Deborah. 'At least we know the area here.'

'We can't take that chance, Deborah,' replies Malcolm. 'With my history, we just can't risk it.'

In the back seats, Stephanie and Joseph exchange glances before returning their attention to their respective windows. Joseph likes to watch the ground speed away past them.

# 39. What if?

On Katie's bed, Dev struggles, as he has been for what seems like hours to him, but has actually been no more than seconds. By now, I understand more, but I also still need more. Unfortunately, he appears to be running out of puff. I need to keep him adequately motivated, so let's talk to him, shall we?

How can we twist him to give the answers we want? Maybe not those we need, but those we want. Why do we want them? Because they'll make sense? They'll fit? What if we wrung from him only answers that fit? What if we ignored everything else? Or, what if we sought only the irrelevance. That which has no bearing on anything at all. Which would you prefer? I can bend him like light. I can make him say what you want.

So far, we've spoken only words into his ears, prompting him this way or that, but perhaps an exchange of thoughts is due.

'Is this what you were talking about? All that time ago. Is

this where you wanted it to lead? Is this what you wanted?'

'Wha- What? Who's there?'

'Doesn't matter. You're here now.'

'Why am I here? Why did I do this?' Dev pleads from the bed to no one in particular as he struggles.

'You wanted to understand people, right?'

'Get me out of this. Whoever you are.'

'I couldn't, even if I wanted to. You got yourself in this mess.'

'I need help. I'm dying.'

'But it's fascinating watching them rattle around trying to help each other, trying to help themselves while you pull apart the little world you constructed for them. They say that's what people really do in times of wide-scale crisis. They help each other.

'I understand that when the aid relief teams arrive at an earthquake site, for example, there are always people on the teams who are surprised that there isn't the looting, the anger, the rioting, the people tearing each other apart, that they see in disaster movies. Dev, may I call you, Dev? Where could we go next? Eh?'

Dev strains his neck in the direction he thinks the voice is coming from to get a look at a person, but he can't make anything out. Just shadows as everything closes in on him, and the belt pulls on his erupting flesh.

# 40. Something else

The year in Mauritius was not without event for little Dev and Serena. Of course, Dev had his seemingly interminable studies to busy himself with, but he also had distractions in the way of his mother's family.

Dev found that both Uncle Sachin and his grandfather were cut from the same cloth and were a lot more alike than either would have liked to admit. Both men were stubborn and excitable, a bad combination. It was challenging to change their minds once they felt they had come to a suitable plan.

Serena and Dev had not been back in Mauritius for long when his grandfather persuaded Serena to drive him to the house of a distant relative. The relative was a young woman who had married her husband four months previously. The young woman's mother was convinced her daughter was physically abused by her husband.

'I'm telling you something is not right over there,' said the mother on the phone one day while Dev was at school.

'Did she tell you?'

'No.'

'Then how do you know?'

'Just a feeling.'

'So, what do you want me to do?' Grandfather asked. 'She should go to the police.'

'You know how it is. We want to avoid all… that,' came the reply.

'So what do you want me to do?' Grandfather repeated.

'Nothing. I'm just telling you what is happening.'

'But why tell me if you don't want me to do anything?'

'We don't want you to do anything.'

'So why are you telling me?'

'We were *hoping* you would help.'

'But you said you didn't want me to do anything.'

Serena looked up from her magazine. The phone conversation seemed to be going around in circles.

'We don't want you to tell you to do anything, but if you were to do something we wouldn't ask you not to.'

'So you're not asking me to do something, and you're not asking me not to do something either?' Grandfather clarified. Serena looked back down to her magazine.

'That's right. We would not dream of asking you to get involved, but if you took a car to her house to fetch her and her things while her husband is at work before he has a chance to lay another finger on her, we wouldn't be able to stop you. Would we?'

'Sounds like I'd better do something,' said Grandfather.

'Do you have a pen? I'll give you the address.'

Although Serena was not keen on getting involved in a

family dispute, she eventually relented for much the same reasons that he had. She wanted to be useful.

Serena had come to Mauritius with her son and without her husband. This was puzzling to the Mauritians, and Serena needed to show that she was in charge and could get things done when necessary. Driving her father to rescue a young woman from an abusive husband seemed an excellent way to achieve this and get into her father's good graces.

Serena's father was an old man who was now seldom consulted for his opinion. This had been the part of growing old that he had found the most difficult to accept. It wasn't the aching knees or the wrinkled hands that no longer resembled his own that he found difficult to bear. It was the way he seemed to have drifted into irrelevance. His counsel was no longer sought as often as it had been, and he no longer felt like the *Gros Bonhomme.* The Big Fella.

That was what they used to call him at Arab Town, the market where he worked before retiring. *Gros Bonhomme.* He was the person you went to see if there was a problem. Grandfather loved nothing more than having his opinion or help sought by a total stranger who had heard of him. He already had the love of his family, but they were *family*, linked by blood. They were supposed to love you and listen to you. What Grandfather always craved was the love of strangers.

He found strangers easier to cope with than family. A stranger would not be motivated by love or sentimentality to show him attention. It was that he could facilitate something for them. If a family member wanted to see him, there was no way for him to know what they truly wanted.

As they set off on the two-hour drive, Serena mused over

the ever-changing relationships between children and their parents. Once upon a time, when she was a little girl, all she had to do was simply exist to stoke feelings of pride in her parents. Now she was driving across the island to investigate spousal abuse based on hearsay a woman had intercepted about her daughter from a friend of the neighbour's niece, who happened to also be friends with her daughter's neighbour.

'You're sure we'll be back in time to pick up Dev?' Serena asked.

'Yes, yes. You fuss too much about that boy. No wonder he's such a girl.'

'I just need to be back for him.'

'I'm telling you, let him find his own way home for a change. He has to become more independent.'

'He's ten.'

'We didn't collect you from school every day. You were fine.'

Two hours later, the car pulled up at the house before the father-daughter duo got out and walked up to the large metal gate. A very furry and very warm, looking alsatian on the other side instantly greeted them by barking and bounding up to the gate, stopped short only by the sturdy metal chain that yanked him back by the neck. The barking echoed around the yard as Serena and her father glanced at one another.

'The windows are open. There must be someone home,' said Grandfather. Sure enough, after a few moments, a young woman opened the door and poked her head around it. 'Lakshmi? Hello, how are you?'

'Oh, *Gros Bonhomme*! Hi! How are you?' Lakshmi greeted them, pulling back on the chain to calm the alsatian and stop him from biting at her latest pop-in guests.

Grandfather drew the bolt across to open the metal gate and stepped gingerly into the yard, followed by Serena. 'Lakshmi, do you know who this is?' he asked, as though playing a game with a child.

'No,' replied Lakshmi, smiling as she kissed the pair on the cheeks. 'Come in,' she beckoned, leading them into the cool, tiled interior. The air was thick with the scent of incense.

'No? You don't recognise her? It's Serena. I don't think you've seen her since you were a child.'

'Oh yeah, I see it now. Yes, Serena. Hi. So nice to see you both,' said Lakshmi.

'We were just in the area. We thought we'd drop by.'

'That's great,' said Lakshmi, as both Grandfather and Serena scanned her face and bare arms for signs of violence. 'Who were you seeing in the area?'

'Oh, just a contractor for the house. You know Sachin has been working by himself on the second floor for ages, and it's going nowhere. He decided to get some labourers to help, but… he's having trouble with them.'

'Oh. I see. That's a shame,' replied Lakshmi. 'Sit down,' she invited, gesturing at the kitchen stools. 'Do you want some cola from the fridge or something?'

'Yeah, I'll have some cola,' replied Grandfather, settling his bulk on a stool.

'Can I have some water?' Serena asked.

While Lakshmi turned her back on them to fetch the drinks, Grandfather seized the opportunity to silently mouth words to Serena. After a few moments of trying to lip-read, Serena gave up. She was annoyed at the long drive. She was annoyed at the traffic and the roadworks, and she was annoyed that there was no way she would be back on time to collect Dev from school at this rate. Instead of getting to the point about why they were there, her father was tiptoeing about it.

'I don't know what you mean,' Serena blurted loudly at her father's silent mouthing.

'What?' Lakshmi asked, turning back to them.

'Nothing,' said Grandfather. 'What has the weather been like here?'

*Weather?* wondered Serena. *It's Mauritius. It's hot. It's always hot.* 'Stop!' she said suddenly. 'Stop beating around the bush. I have a child to get back to!'

'What's going on?' A frown had developed on Lakshmi's face as she returned with a drink in each hand.

'Lakshmi, my father heard that you were in some trouble, that things were not going so well with Rajesh. Is this true?' Serena asked.

'Trouble? What trouble?' Lakshmi asked. 'With Rajesh?'

'Look, we understand that you want to protect your husband, but if he's hurting you…' Grandfather trailed off.

'He's not hurting me,' insisted Lakshmi.

'So you're protecting him.'

'There is nothing to protect.'

'So what are you saying?'

'Rajesh treats me well, and everything is fine. What are *you* saying?'

'We heard that he was…. hurting you,' clarified

Grandfather, lowering his voice slightly.

'From whom? Mum? Don't believe her. She just misses me and wants me at home again.'

'Look,' said Grandfather, feeling the situation slipping away, 'why don't you get your things, and we can decide who did what later.'

'I'm not getting anything. I think it's best if you both leave and don't listen to my mother in the future.'

Moments later, Serena and Grandfather found themselves outside the gates once more.

'Let's just get out of here,' said Serena. 'I have a child to collect.'

'Okay. You'll drop me off at home first, right? I don't want to get stuck in all that school traffic,' he said, getting into the passenger seat. Serena's eyes narrowed as she glowered at him.

Dev had been waiting outside his school for over an hour when he spotted the car pull up. 'Hey, where have you been?' Dev asked, worried as his mum got out of the car.

'Sorry, Dev, are you okay?' Serena asked, hugging him tightly.

'Yes. What happened?'

'Long story.'

Dr. Sharma remembers riding the bus from school one afternoon with Serena, who had collected him. He remembers it because he thinks of it often. He understands now, but it confused him as a child. He remembers sitting next to Serena on the hard, red faux leather. The curved chrome bar atop the seat in front catching the sunlight streaming through, defying the dirty windows.

'Mum?' asked Dev.

'Yeh?'

'Who do you think will die first? Your dad, or your mum?'

He just wanted to connect with her and have something to talk about. Dev had expected his mother to take a moment or two to consider the circumstances for both parents and then submit a carefully crafted answer. He was not prepared for what came instead.

'Why would you ask me for that?' snapped Serena. 'What kind of stupid question is that? Whatever answer I give, it will be like I want them to die.'

Dev remained silent. He felt he had asked a logical question that had nothing to do with an emotional response. He hadn't asked her to pick her favourite parent, just to speculate, based on medical history, age and lifestyle. At that age, he didn't understand her anger, but he assumed that she was right.

Later that night, as he lay in bed in the dark, he thought back to the incident and realised that the question may have upset his mother because of Amina. He mostly believed in his mother, but he realised that her reaction, if it was indeed due to Amina, ran contrary to the talk they had had several times.

Usually, Dev could rely on Serena and Raju to lead by example, but Serena wasn't following these pre-established patterns of behaviour. She wasn't following her own advice. That night, as he lay in bed considering the bus journey, it dawned on young Dev how fallible his parents really were.

Other memories bubble to the surface as Dr. Sharma thinks back to his time in Mauritius.

One weekend Serena and Dev made their way to the south to visit Raju's family, a courtesy visit. With the marital situation between Serena and Raju unclear, the tense atmosphere could have been cut with a wooden spoon. As a gesture, Serena offered to bake them a cake in their oven that had never been used, let alone used for baking sponge cakes. The kind not readily found in Mauritius as the street vendors preferred to stick with the traditional cakes that are either deep-fried or submerged in syrup.

While the cake was baking, some distant family unexpectedly popped in to visit, as was to be expected in Mauritius. Having stayed for a chat and the near-mandatory glass of cold cola, the visitors in the living room began saying their goodbyes to catch their bus on time. At the same time, Serena declared the cake ready and pulled it from the oven.

Having tipped the fresh, moist cake from the small, circular cooking pot standing in as a makeshift baking tin onto a wire rack to cool, Serena turned her back on it and headed to the living room to join in in uttering farewells. Meanwhile, eager to satisfy the Mauritian convention for hospitality, Dev's aunt slipped into the kitchen, gripped the still-hot cake and moved it to a chopping block.

Serena was still working her way around all the cheeks when she heard Dev's aunt cry: 'what kind of *gâteau français* is this, Serena? It's just falling apart. It doesn't look like this in the fancy French cake shops.'

Puzzled by what she was hearing, Serena quickly made her way to the kitchen. *What is she talking about?* Serena wondered as she poked her head around the door to find the aunt brutally hacking at the sponge cake, moments from the hot oven, with a regular cutlery knife.

'What are you doing!' Serena demanded, a thundercrack of horror having descended upon her face.

'Your cake is no good, Serena,' the aunt replied. 'How can you eat this?' she went on as the cake continued to disintegrate under the blunt knife.

'But the cake is still hot.'

'So?'

'So you can't cut it yet.'

'But they're leaving.'

'That doesn't change the fact that it's too hot to cut.'

'Oh, don't worry about my fingers. I used to cook on a wood stove. My fingers don't feel this heat.'

'I'm not worried about your fingers,' snapped Serena in exasperation as the visitors watched on, bemused. 'The cake is still too hot and too soft. When it cools, it will become firmer. You can't cut the cake yet, especially not with that knife.'

'What's wrong with the knife now? Don't blame the knife for your cake falling apart.'

'That knife is far too thick and blunt. There is nothing wrong with the cake. If you had waited for it to cool and used a better knife, it would have been fine.'

'Oh. Well, I didn't know, I'm not used to your fancy French cakes,' said the aunt, putting down the knife and clawing at the chunks of cake with her fingers to transport them to pieces of kitchen foil, which she then wrapped up for the visitors to take away. 'I much prefer my *gâteau piment*.'

She knew it was an accident, but part of Serena couldn't help wondering if it hadn't been more than that. Serena wondered if her sister-in-law's actions had partly been to execute a spiteful culinary snub that, considering the Mauritian regard for food, had been intended to not only bruise Serena's ego but also serve as a rejection of her efforts, in veiled support of Raju, the abandoned husband. As the visitors left, Serena stared forlornly at the defeated cake, crumbling and decimated, like the ruins of an old castle.

Things had changed in Mauritius in the years since Serena had lived there as a full-time citizen. One of the most significant and welcome changes she had noticed was the number of women working there. Women working in Mauritius was no new thing. Serena had always known women to work in Mauritius, fulfilling farming duties, preparing street food for sale, harvesting sugarcane in the fields, and so on. She was heartened to see that as school had become a priority for both boys and girls, it had led to more girls taking up better-paid positions. Not just studying for the sake of family pride, only for all that potential to be forsaken when a future husband demanded they stay at home to be a housewife.

However, when Serena encountered a woman in one of these positions, it was often the case that she was left confused. Whether it was a female shop assistant in a shoe shop or a bank clerk behind a counter, they seemed less than enthused by having to serve. They appeared disinterested, dismissive, lethargic and did everything at a snail's pace, as though they didn't really want to be there. However, whenever Serena met a female family member or friend who worked these types of jobs, they claimed to be proud to earn their own money and not feel beholden. Serena came to the conclusion that they were proud. Possibly too proud to effectively carry out their duties.

One day Serena flagged down a vendor for some *poutou* cakes for Dev. She was surprised to find the vendor's fingers adorned with gold rings. Handing Dev his *poutou* cakes, she relayed what she had observed, surprised that someone in that line of work would place themself at heightened risk. Not of having their cash and *poutou* cakes stolen, but of having their fingers broken for their jewellery.

# 41. Dawning

As far as exams go, in Mauritius, failure does not necessarily mean failing exams. That would be the *ultimate* failure. It can be considered a failure if you fail to meet expectations. Primarily those of family. With the week of the exams drawing ever closer, Dev, anxious at what failure might mean to his mother, wanted nothing more to do with studying or exams of any kind.

Serena was already obsessed with temples and whatever they had come to mean to her. What would Dev's failure mean to her? Somehow she could talk to those macabre statues, made from plaster and moulded crudely by hand, painted in garish colours, but she couldn't talk to him. In a way, the eleven-year-old looked forward to the exams so he could dispense with them and finally let his mind be still.

His mother needed him to do well, in part to justify bringing him to Mauritius, to show everyone that what she was doing was the right thing for her child, that she was a good mother. Dev understood that and, despite having no interest in the school work, he kept at it to please her. Exhausted, he didn't know himself anymore. In a single year, Dev learnt and demonstrated knowledge of things that everyone else sitting the exam had been working on for several years.

Dev knew that Serena and Raju loved him, but he couldn't escape feeling like he had come to mean different things to each of his parents. While he had – albeit unconsciously – tried to fill the void left by Amina, he occasionally felt his mother and father wanted him for purposes other than being a son. Serena, he felt, wanted only to protect him and have him as evidence that she was a good mother. Meanwhile, Dev had begun to confuse his unfounded belief that succeeding at the CPE would make his father happy with the perception that that was all his father wanted of him.

Nervous and fretting, Dev sat each exam over two weeks. After each exam, his classmates would gather and excitedly swap notes on what they had written for each question, as they had done after exams in previous years. With no experience of this, Dev preferred to keep to himself and declined their entreaties to pore over the details. He was simply relieved when each one was over.

Corruption was rife in Mauritius, and bribes were taken everywhere to grease the wheels of bureaucracy. Some would say that they were necessary to get anything done. However, no one would ever dare suggest that exam results could be improved with a sufficient number of rupees pressed into the appropriate palms. It was far too important, far too integral to the structure of Mauritian society. This wasn't an election. These were *exams*!

To cheat in an election would be expected. To cheat at exams would be an unimaginable violation of what Mauritians held most sacred. It went beyond religion because it was universal. Every person was either affected by the exam results or knew someone who would be. Any kind of bribing or cheating would be evidence of a morally bankrupt character. Anyone caught would be shunned by their own family and shamed by their community, the corrosive sin of cheating eroding all other aspects of their entire personality, as far as society was concerned.

With the fervour that surrounded the results of the CPE, the country didn't have to wait long before knowing the outcomes for the 22,000 or so pupils.

A few weeks after the last exam (Environmental Studies), the results arrived, and so did Dev's father, taking advantage of a natural opportunity to visit Serena and Dev in Mauritius. He had wanted to see them but had decided to bide his time and wait for the results, an event that could bring the three of them together without it seeming like he was pushing.

Raju stepped out of the airport and into the blazing light of the day to see Dev running to him. It had been almost a year since the three had been together, and Raju blinked away his tears, squeezing Dev tightly to him as Serena smiled wanly from a couple of feet away.

Reunited a few days later at Dev's school, they discovered results and ranking. Once again, as they scrolled through the names pinned to a large noticeboard in the courtyard, Raju stymied his tears. Dev had not only succeeded in cracking the top three thousand, but he had reached the top half coming in at 1,381 on the list! Not that it meant anything to Dev for himself. He was just relieved to see his parents happy again.

That evening Serena, Dev and Raju visited his family in the south of the island. Serena and Dev hadn't visited much. For Dev, it was the close humidity in that part of the island that put him off. For Serena, it was the unavoidable recriminatory glances that dissuaded her from visiting too often. Raju wanted to spread the news of Dev's achievement, and a simple phone call was deemed insufficient.

Dev was always fascinated by the framed black and white family photos that hung from the walls there. He studied and loved everything about them. He liked the texture of the pictures. He liked that they weren't glossy like the photos he was used to. They were faded but somehow still had a kind of warmth that, despite flat black and white tones, escaped and transcended the severe looks of the subjects.

Raju, his siblings and his father. They stared straight ahead at the camera. The siblings stood behind their father, Dev's grandfather, who sat stiffly on what looked like an exceedingly uncomfortable chair. Raju, almost unrecognisable to Dev, wore flares and a shirt with an oversized collar. His hand gripped the backrest of his father's chair. The ladies in the photos were dressed in sarees with flowers in their hair. They clung tightly to little clutches and stared uncomfortably straight ahead at the camera in the most awkward family portraits Dev had ever seen.

Not one was dressed or standing the way they would in real life, and Dev even loved that about the pictures. Their inhabitants had an otherness about them that hinted at a different world, different possibilities, different rules. The world within those photographs was a fiction made up in a photographer's studio when the family had saved enough money for the privilege.

They had played dress-up for the afternoon. The chairs Grandfather sat on weren't theirs. The tall potted plants on either side weren't natural. The drop-down background depicted the staircase of a grand house that didn't exist. It was how everyone took pictures back then. A show of family togetherness against an illusory background.

The sarees looked so precise, not a fold out of place. Dev imagined the ornate jewellery, usually reserved for weddings, holding their breath, believing they had been taken out in error. Desperate to not be found out, they tried to remain still and be as inconspicuous as possible, going completely against their nature. Dev imagined them praying for a swift return to their little boxes in their respective drawers.

'What, no *pandit*? No smoking fire for the bride and groom to circle seven times?' asked a necklace.

'Well, this has all been a ghastly mistake, I tell you,' added an earring.

A hand on Dev's shoulder shook him out of his reverie. 'Looking up at my dad?' asked Raju. Dev nodded. 'He would have been proud of you, would have loved you. He would have been the best grandfather ever. He was the best father I could have had. The best father ever, the old man did what he could for us.'

Later on in his life, Dr. Sharma would look back on the experience in Mauritius and draw the positives. He would appreciate that he had come through exceptional circumstances with good results and that, while the CPE results themselves might have proved worthless in the world beyond Mauritius, the struggle had taught him something about himself.

As his aunties congratulated him, Dev thought to himself how all those strangers had by now moved on to the next batch of people they knew sitting those exams. He had done well at his, so he was no longer in their thoughts. Much more to dissect amongst those who fail.

'How badly did they fail?'

'What are their options now?'

'Will they repeat?'

'Were they already repeating?'

With Dev having passed his exams, there was no longer anything they could take from Serena and him. For the next batch of children, people they thought they knew would go from being friendly to delighting in seeing these children, and their families, sweat under the weight of expectation and the potential for shame. Subsequently, they would either share in their success or gossip about their failure.

For Dev, it was all, seemingly, for nothing. All the pressure, the tears, the blown self-confidence, the constant babble of strangers. He had tried to make everyone happy. He had thought it would help bring his parents back together permanently, but he had been wrong.

A couple of weeks later, Raju returned to his work in England. Dev thought that he and his mother would also be returning to England with relations breaking down with Uncle Sachin. What Dev hadn't counted on were his mother's sisters.

# 42. What's a cloud like you doing in a sky like this?

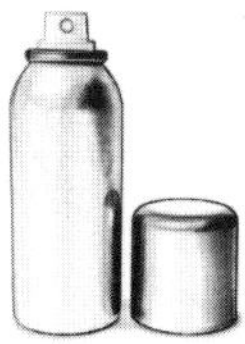

The last memory that occurs to Dev's mind about his time in Mauritius is that which precipitated their sudden departure from the country.

Uncle Sachin had been alluding to something he wanted to discuss with Serena but hadn't yet gotten any further than that. Serena decided to take it up with him one evening after dinner as he wandered the still unfinished top floor of the house after the day at his market stall. There were walls in all places designated for them, and there were holes in the outer walls for windows, but the roof had yet to appear.

Serena climbed the concrete steps running up the side of the house, taking care as she did, instinctively reaching out for a handrail that didn't yet exist. In Mauritius, it was no big deal for a stairway to lack such a rudimentary safety feature that could prevent a nasty fall from the edge of the stairway to the ground below. Serena hated climbing this stairway and rarely went to the upper floor of the house. She was almost thankful that scant progress on the construction meant there was little reason to go up there.

Serena found her brother in one of the rooms earmarked as a bedroom. He was sweeping the dust from the floor.

'Sachin?'

'Yeah.'

'What did you want to talk about? You keep saying you want to talk, and then you disappear.'

'I didn't disappear,' argued Sachin as he set aside the traditional Mauritian broom made from coconut fibres bound together tightly. 'Do you remember when we were children? We were always renting. Look at us now. We've not only bought land and built a house, but now we're building another floor.'

'Slowly,' quantified Serena.

'Don't be negative,' chided Sachin. 'It's happening. I know it doesn't seem like much to you, but it's an important thing to me. You know?'

'Is that what you wanted to talk about?'

'No. I wanted to talk to you about the market stall.'

'The market stall? What about it?'

Uncle Sachin was a stallholder at the same market in Rose Hill where his father, the market's superintendent, had earned his nickname, *Gros Bonhomme*. Affectionately known by locals as Arab Town, the collection of ramshackle stalls sold all sorts. Everything from food containers to deck chairs, to pirated Bollywood movies, to ornamental vases. Sachin and Serena's father had been *The Big Fella*, in charge of the market, allocating stalls to the different vendors, taking payment, dealing with issues and sending non-payers packing.

Many at the market and within the family had thought Sachin would follow in his father's footsteps to become one of the administrators. Indeed he started as a stallholder, like his father, but then didn't progress. Sachin's father was well-liked, respected, and above all, he was known by many people. It was thought that he would eventually arrange some favours for Sachin to climb to management.

It didn't happen, and Sachin remained a stallholder as his sisters came from their various adopted countries for holidays before leaving again. Canada, England, France. They all seemed to be doing well. Until the news of Amina. Until the arrival of Serena and Dev. At first, Sachin, his wife, Grandfather and Grandmother had wanted to help them as they adjusted to life in Mauritius, and Dev adapted to his new school situation.

Now Sachin saw a way that Serena could help him.

'I have one word for you,' Sachin said mysteriously, setting aside his broom. 'Deodorant!'

'Deodorant?' Serena asked.

'Deodorant. There is a lot of money in deodorant.'

'You wanted to talk to me about deodorant?'

'Deodorant. Fragrances. Perfumes. There's a new factory near Curepipe that is churning them out.'

'Okay,' invited Serena, baffled but curious to see where this would lead.

'I have somebody, *on the inside*,' he clarified, whispering as though there were opportunistic enterprising eavesdroppers in the walls. He tells me all the imperfect ones, the cans with tiny dents, the plastic containers with scratches, the bottles with cracked tops, they all get tossed into a giant bin. The bin is filled every week.'

'So?'

'So one of those bins would provide enough stock to fill a stall for a month.'

'What are you saying?'

'I want to open another stall that deals specifically in perfumes and deodorants.'

'So… I'm confused. How do the factory and the bin enter the picture? Also, will you sell enough deodorant –'

'And perfume,' interrupted Sachin.

'And perfume to break even?'

'Well, my guy at the factory will get me the stuff for free. I'll just need to pay him a percentage.'

'But you'll be selling stolen goods.'

'They're not stolen. They were in the bin. But there's nothing wrong with them. They're totally fine.'

'*Their* bin.'

'They just throw it away.'

'Maybe they recycle it.'

'It's not TVs and Hi-Fis. There are no parts they can salvage. It's either perfect and gets exported abroad, or it's not.'

'If your *camarade* gets caught, it'll still be stealing, and he won't hesitate to implicate you. You'll be handling stolen property.'

'You just don't want to help,' accused Sachin, getting agitated.

'Help? How can *I* help?' Serena asked.

'I need help to secure a new stall and to pay someone to work it. You see? I'm not an idiot. I'm not going to jeopardise my old stall over a new one.'

'You want me to fund this?'

'I want you to help me. Be a partner. Just the money. You won't have to do anything except pick up the profit. You keep saying you want to stay. Prove it. Get involved in something. Help me, and earn an income.'

'I… Sachin, I don't have money for this sort of thing. You're building a house. Why don't you use some of that money?'

'Because I don't have it,' Sachin blurted, frustrated and angry at his sister's attitude. 'This isn't England where when they tell you it will cost x amount, that's what it costs. This is Mauritius!' he yelled. 'Here the contractor's price for everything doubles when your sister from England comes to stay.'

'Sachin, what are you talking about?'

'They're not idiots. They just want to get paid like the rest of us. If they think there's more money, of course, they'll go for it. They think because you've come from England, we have lots of money to throw around, so they are charging me extra for everything.' Sachin's anger echoed around the bare grey walls of the building site. 'Now I'm asking you to help me, and you don't want to know. Everything costs more because of you, and you don't want to help. All *you* want to do is visit temples and churches.'

'I… I help with the shopping,' stuttered Serena, shocked at Sachin. 'This is my home too. I'm allowed to come back if I want. They're my parents too, Sachin.'

'But it's affecting *my* life, Serena, and it's not fair. You have everything, and I have nothing. Yes, I'm poor. No, I don't have many prospects. Yes, I need help. Are you happy now?'

'Well, what if *I* needed help? Did you ever think of that?'

'Why do you need help? You live in England.'

'I don't live in England anymore.'

'You can always go back. You have your British passport. You can go back whenever you want. So long as that's the case, you will always live somewhere else. You're not really here.'

There weren't any photographs of Serena and Dev from their time in Mauritius. It just hadn't occurred to them to take any. But every so often, Dev's grandfather would receive a letter from one of his other daughters, and in the envelope, there would be some photographs of his grandchildren. With Dev having completed his exams and the atmosphere at Grandfather's house thick with reproach from Uncle Sachin, it wasn't difficult for Serena to tell Dev: 'We're going to see Auntie Seeva and your cousins.'

'When are they coming?' asked Dev.

'They're not. We're going to Canada. Don't you want to visit Canada? Of course, you do.'

# 43. Lateral thinking

'You want to visit a sex club?' asked Mira, inwardly bemused, twirling some strands of her hair, as was her habit.

Dr. Sharma sighed deeply before: 'I want to see what they see. I want to know what it is like to be in a place like that.'

Seeing Mira at her gangbang had been about understanding how the men would act in pursuit of pure pleasure in… *saltier* circumstances. To see what it meant to these people to pursue only their satisfaction, with no thought for the person providing it, having paid and thus feeling they had the right to her body, as though she were an empty vessel they had hired for a sole purpose.

Dr. Sharma was open-minded, but he had been surprised by how… convivial the event had been. He hadn't expected the gathering to be so chatty and jovial. They had taken care of how they treated her. There had been lust but no imposition of their will from the men. If Mira had asked them to stop, they would have. There was nothing there that he could use to understand the behaviour and actions of, say, those more aggressive about asserting their will over another individual.

He didn't imagine he would find anything of use at a sex club either, but it was an opportunity to observe different genders actively pursuing pleasure.

'Well, you know they're not all the same,' stated Mira.

'In what way?' asked Dr. Sharma.

'There are different… levels,' replied Mira cryptically.

'Levels?'

'All right, I'll be blunt. There are different classes,' clarified Mira. 'The same as, I don't know… hotels. You've got that look again.'

'What look?' defended Dr. Sharma.

'That look like you don't believe me.'

'I believe you. I'm just trying to understand.'

'What's difficult to understand?'

'Surely a sex club is a… *sex club*, right? A place where people congregate anonymously to take part in their personal sexual preferences, and maybe find some new ones, with total strangers.'

'They're not total strangers.'

'Well, no, I suppose you'd go with someone you know.'

'No, I mean the people there know each other from previous nights. Also that everyone involved is there for the same reason. So it's like… a community. There's a kind of trust like everyone's on the same wavelength. It's the one thing they all know about each other, or at least it's the first assumption. You're not about that. You don't belong there.'

'That's why I'll go with you.'

‘That’s why you *won’t* go with me. If you want to go to a sex club to gawp and take notes, that’s your business, but you won’t go with me,’ Mira firmly stated.

‘Why not?’

‘I’d be betraying all the people who go there for the right reasons.’

‘Why do you go?’ asked Dr. Sharma.

‘I’m a different case,’ explained Mira, without really explaining.

‘Why?’ came the inevitable question from Dr. Sharma.

‘Because I’m known. I’m in films. When I go to a sex club, it is just as good for the club as it is for me. When I go somewhere like that, I’m endorsing it.’

‘Do you… do the men pay to have sex with you? I didn’t think that was in keeping with the… spirit of a sex club.’

At this, Mira covered her face with her hands and groaned. ‘Dev, you don’t understand anything. I don’t go to sex clubs to have sex. That would be insane,’ Mira stated, without a hint of irony.

‘Uh, I don’t understand,’ confessed Dr. Sharma.

‘I don’t go for fun. I earn a lot of money from movies and charging people for sex. Don’t you see, if I started doing it just for pleasure, I’d be cheapened!’

‘Funny,’ Dr. Sharma couldn’t help a wry smile.

‘What’s funny?’

‘Most people wouldn’t take that point of view,’ Dev eventually managed, the words stumbling out of his mouth as he scrambled for tact.

‘I’m not most people, and you will not manipulate me into going with you. When I go to a sex club, it’s all about expanding my brand, getting people to buy my films. For the club, they get to say an established adult film star will be appearing, helping to raise its profile as a more credible venue.'

'Well then, you can do that, and I can tag along. If it's all about business, then what's the problem?'

'I still respect them enough as people not to bring someone who isn't there for the right reasons,' stated Mira. You should go somewhere else. That's why I mentioned different classes of sex clubs. Go to a small one where they're used to having people watching from the shadows. The ones I go to are about a lifestyle. People pay a lot just to get in. If you pay that kind of money, you're going to get involved. No reason not to when they pass around complimentary blue pills and poppers. But you're not going to get involved, are you?'

'Maybe, you never know,' teased Dr. Sharma. Mira didn't intimidate him as much as she did at the beginning of their collaboration, and she silently liked that he was loosening up with her. But she found it difficult to contain her resentment at Dr. Sharma's imposition. Mira got up sharply on her high heels from her armchair, leaving Dr. Sharma to follow her movements right out of the room.

She had always bridled at the way he had placed himself in her life and did not understand why he kept persisting with her. But it was his arrogant assumption that he could see things from her point of view, or anybody else's, that truly bothered her.

His project reminded her of a health worker she once knew, with a Christ complex, who thought she could save Mira from the life she had chosen. So far, Dr. Sharma hadn't shown any signs of doing that, but he was trying to understand a world that he wasn't part of, and that sort of behaviour always raised her hackles. After all, how would he like it if she decided to imagine what it was like to be an Asian in British society? British Asian, or not.

Mira could imagine how no matter how much one is welcomed, no matter how *included* in things one is, as a non-white in a society overwhelmingly dominated by Caucasians you are always on the outside. Herself a piece that didn't fit, she could understand how one may not be made to feel the outsider by anyone else.

*It's you. You give yourself the role*, Mira thought. *There's a look when people greet you. Something around the eyes. They don't realise they're doing it. If they're someone you want to like, you try not to see it, but it's there. It says: "Oh, it's you. They brought you. The one that doesn't fit."*

Mira understood what it was to pretend at being in the room. *Acting like you're part of the conversation. You're not real. You're a fantasy*, she thought to herself. In Mira's case, she acted larger than life to make herself solid and real to everyone, including herself. *You can't tell anyone what's going on. You just have to keep feeling it burning from the neck up*, she thought as she rustled through a drawer in the kitchen. *Nobody wants to hear that. We're not supposed to feel that. Not now. We're supposed to be living in a time when we can be who we are, even when we don't know who we are. The truth is, you might be in the room, but you're at a distance. It's like you're watching through crushed glasses. Fractured. Dirty. Light bleeding through the cracks.*

As for myself, I have been around long enough to see how people use their senses to understand the world around them. They don't want it to, but it makes sense. They are happiest when presented with patterns. They try to find them in nature. They find them in mathematics, astronomy, biology, in data from so many other disciplines. They desire patterns. They crave uniformity. They want everything to make sense.

When something, or someone, doesn't fit, it frustrates. It nags at them when they have no choice but to tolerate an irregularity. A blip on the radar. An anomaly. When two people marry who have a significant disparity in skin tone, Mauritians joke to one another, saying *mouche dans du lait*. A fly in the milk. If he could not be seen, Dr. Sharma's English accent would make it impossible to identify him as anything other than British. On the other hand, Mauritians would consider him a typical Mauritian until they heard his voice. If the world was shaken, if the rules that govern instincts and senses no longer applied, would people be more open or closed?

'Look,' began Mira, as she stalked back into the bedroom and thrust a small business card at Dr. Sharma. 'I know a place. You want to know how things work? You want to see what they see? Here. Call and ask for this man. Tell them I…' she struggled for the right word, '*referred* you.' Mira asked herself if it was the right thing to send Dr. Sharma there, but he took the card, and the moment for doubt was gone. 'Only fair to let you know,' continued Mira, 'they cater to some extreme tastes.'

# 44. The one who weighed the world

Back in Katie's bedroom, Dr. Sharma writhes on the bed. He's totally out of it now. He's hearing voices. My voice. I wonder what he makes of it. Me talking to him. I wonder if he would stop me if he could. His eyes are glassy as his head lolls to the side. He's almost defeated now, strung out and spent. I wonder if we can get anything more from him. I wonder what he would think of me.

I am not a man.

Or a woman.

If one were to refer to me, one might use the pronoun *they* rather than *he* or *she*.

I am nameless, although I have often wondered if I should name myself. People and things are ascribed names by other relevant people with their own names. They only get to do this because the person, or the thing, in question has not yet been met, discovered or invented. Or created.

A name forms part of the creation. It's the first thing people ask when meeting for the first time. Without a name, it is almost as if that person does not yet fully exist to them. As though they are a half a person, not yet firmly established in the reality of the person making their acquaintance. Without a name, they can be snatched from existence at any moment, and the person shaking their hand would have forgotten all about them.

I do not have a name, for there is no one to name me. I suppose I have not been met, discovered, invented or created.

I am not known to anyone. There is no one to refer to me by any particular term.

It is easy for me to explain what I do and how I operate. Explaining my *existence* is more… problematic. Considering what I do it seems somewhat hollow to simply echo: "I think therefore I am." But the truth is that I just… am. I exist, so I exist. If I could explain it any more elegantly, I would. I can, at least, say *that* with a high degree of conviction.

It would give me great satisfaction to have the information at hand explaining my being here, being present. To be in a position to set out this information in a logical fashion, and impart it to another, would be good. I think it would be helpful, at least to myself. There is no one I can ask about this. No supervisor. No line manager. No superiors or subordinates of any sort. None that I can perceive, anyway.

I suppose I could take my instincts as being my own set of instructions. Follow my own course, do what comes naturally. That seems to be what a lot of people I observe do. Although, sometimes, they fight it. I have tried to fight it, but not doing what I am presumably supposed to left me with nothing. Rudderless. Drifting through time. So one can understand the difficulty I have in explaining my existence, let alone coming *into* existence.

Watching those around me, observing them. This is me following my instincts. Sometimes I talk to them, the people I watch. I haven't always had language. It was something I absorbed from one person to another. Over time I have observed progress. I have seen people on their journeys. The more they learn about each other, the more I have come to understand and discover. Of course, one could argue that it is useless for me to understand, since I cannot put that knowledge into direct practice.

I talk to people, but it is not always clear that they can understand or even hear me. Nevertheless, it does help my journey, my natural progression and my understanding of what I do. As I observe subjects develop, so too do I. Or is it the other way around?

I am there each time someone comes to realise something about themselves. When connections are made and a new understanding is gained, I am there. I am there for a widening of the eyes, quickening of the pulse. I am there when the connections are made and lead individuals to soar without limits.

I don't know precisely what it has to do with me. Maybe nothing, maybe something. Why am I the one to do this? What is it even? A service? Do I deliver a service? Who do I work for? How do I get from one person to another? From one place to another. All around the world. I don't seem to have any physical parameters to limit me.

I listen, I watch, I pay attention, and then I make my determination. I don't always decide based on what I see and hear. I sometimes make a judgement based on very little. The truth is that I cannot move on to another individual until I have made my decision.

Often I can be with someone for weeks and still not gain any insight to help me with my decision. Unfortunately, I can only go by what I see and hear. I cannot read minds. Admittedly things have become different with new technologies and other distractions. Not that I find myself distracted by such things, but I have had to adapt to pick up the necessary information. Sometimes there are just no indicators whatsoever. So I will just pick something at random for them.

I know I will have caused them a lot of frustration, even pain. But that is the nature of what I do. On the other hand, many other people have absorbed my influence and made it work for them in a way that has brought them joy and fulfilment and those with whom they have shared their insight.

Insight is what I call it, but most people refer to it in other terms. Parents like to say their children are *gifted.* Other people are *talented.* The whole thing refers to an ability they feel some naturally possess to do certain things. I believe the term *insight* is more accurate. It implies a superior grasp of at least the basics necessary for a skill, ability, or quality, to flourish.

I wish they wouldn't call it a gift. Increasingly it seems a gift that is not expressly desired holds less and less value. A gift that did not cost anything is not something most of them seem to remember or hold in very high regard. Like an individual without a name. With that in mind, I wonder whether there is some point to any continued involvement here with Dev. Is there some end in sight, and of what could it consist?

I often fantasise about being one of those people. I imagine that that will be the end of my current existence. I will become flesh, blood and mortal, but I will be packed with the knowledge I have acquired over the millennia as I watched people and gave them insight. Could I be the ultimate human being? What a thing to be! Whatever I would turn my hand to would turn to gold.

Painting, acting, music, applied mathematics, nuclear fusion, linguistics, furniture making, architecture, product design, economics, social work, psychology, magic, forensic science, genetics, chemical biology, basket weaving, plumbing, cocktail making, pharmacology, fashion design, personal training, poetry, event management, theatre management… and on. And on.

My favourite thing is coming across someone I have *treated* before as I have the opportunity to observe their personal progress. I find it fascinating to see how they have taken the insight I have given them and melded it into something else. Usually, if they have decided to work with what I have given them, they have applied it to something definite, something solid that fits within an existing framework, a discipline. Plato. Dali. Jung. These are just a few among my favourites.

One could be forgiven for thinking that I have the ultimate power. Control. If anyone were to meet me or hear my story, they would question how I have been able to do what I do for so long. I don't think I have much control. I give an insight, or a gift, or a talent, if you prefer. What individuals do with their *gift* is impossible for me to predict.

I cannot take responsibility for the actions of others. Undoubtedly there have been some individuals who have used their gift questionably and unexpectedly. On the other hand, I have provided the impetus for so many people who have created so many beautiful things.

I have seen concert halls filled with people whose lives I have touched. There to see musicians I have influenced play pieces of breathtaking beauty. Pieces composed for kings, queens, emperors, lovers, gods, monsters. Music that transcends the banal and affirms that not everything touched by man is wicked and riddled with hatred. Played by those I have touched, such music delivers their fellow men and women to a place where head and heart are overwhelmed with joy.

They forget their bodies. Their physical limitations do not exist. I have seen them. In those moments, when they are roused by crescendo after crescendo, passion rolling through their veins, they can forget everything. It's possible. I've seen it. As the music builds and builds to one thrilling peak after another, amongst the crowd, all that exists is the music and them, and, for a few moments, there are no limits, and everything is possible.

They forget the wars, the debts, the poverty, the failure, the hurt, the cruelty, the disappointment, the world. For that time, nothing matters other than the music crashing over them, the conductor orchestrating a maelstrom of sensory chaos and perfection to rain down on all there to dream and lose themselves, at least momentarily, in a sea of forget.

If what I do can lead to moments such as this, why would I stop?

I can imbue anyone I select with an ability of my choosing. It is not a power. It is a matter of course for me.

All these people. Is there a point at which I will stop? Will there be a natural end to this? Doesn't feel like there will be. I watch them, with no end in sight.

# 45. A human puzzle

'So are we going to do it at some point? Or are we just going to talk about it?' asked Katie, with one of her cheeky smiles.

'Actually, I've decided it would be better to see someone else,' replied Dr. Sharma, hanging his coat on the back of his chair.

'Oh. Does that mean you're done with me?' Katie asked, expertly hiding her concern that this was the case. Aside from finding him interesting, Katie considered Dr. Sharma easy money.

'I still want to talk to you,' assured Dr. Sharma. 'It's just that I wouldn't want the person's thoughts to be affected by prior personal knowledge. I would like to ask them questions afterwards about how they had felt.'

'Is it because you don't fancy me?' Katie playfully asked, mock indignation on her face as she pretended to wipe away tears.

'No,' answered Dr. Sharma without thinking, before

recovering himself. 'I mean… no, that doesn't come into it for me.'

'But you must have fancied me to start talking to me in the first place,' Katie teased, 'otherwise, why did you pick me to talk to?'

'That… has to be true, I suppose,' replied Dr. Sharma, feeling somewhat uncomfortable.

'Right, well, now that's something we both know. Anyway, I wouldn't have sex with you either,' confessed Katie.

'Oh, that's… sweet,' Dr. Sharma teased, 'your need for me to admit to finding you attractive.'

'It's not about that, honey,' said Katie, full of confidence. 'I already know you fancied me. I just wanted to hear you say it, so you know that I know. Now we can continue,' she finished as she brought the coffees over from the kitchen counter and set them on the small kitchen table, putting one in front of Dr. Sharma. They had finished dinner a little while ago. Katie had cooked for them and was warming the dessert he had brought in the oven.

'Thanks,' he said.

'So after all that talking, you're going to go and do it with some other girl?' asked Katie.

'If I decide to do anything myself at all. Is this a problem?' Dr. Sharma smiled openly at her.

'I just felt we were building up to a big performance,' Katie replied with a wink.

'I don't want to complicate my research with any pre-existing… knowledge of the person.'

'So it's not to do with *pre-existing knowledge* of something from my past that I told you about?'

'No, it's not.'

'So you're going to see the same person each time? You don't think *knowledge* will develop between the pair of you if you're going to ask her questions too?'

'I doubt she'll remember me.'

'You'd be surprised. I would.'

In saying they were not victims of abuse Alex and Roisin had become dead ends for Dr. Sharma, but Katie had entrusted him with her story. She had confided in him, but it hadn't resulted in the personal impact he had hoped for. Despite this, he continued seeing her because he enjoyed her company.

'How did you get started doing this in the first place?' asked Dr. Sharma.

'Well, my mum did it. I told you that before, so I suppose it was easy. Don't get me wrong, it's not like I grew up wanting to be just like Mum. It's just... it didn't seem like a big deal. One of my mum's regulars knew that she had a daughter, and he asked her if I could join them for some roleplay.

'I was... old enough, I suppose. I didn't have to do anything naughty myself. This client just wanted me to pretend to come home and catch him having sex with Mum in the living room. *In flagrante delicto*, and that. I had to protest and be angry about it while they ignored me and carried on. That was my initiation.'

'Did your mum... did she want something else for you?' asked Dr. Sharma.

'My mum, she used to say, bless her, she's gone now, but she used to say: "these *doughnuts*, they pay to have sex. They pay *me* for that. Do you know what an ego-boost that is?" I don't know if she was just covering, but I don't think she was.' Katie took a moment before continuing.

'Things were bad, we needed money and I was at the age where I could start making it. All the lads thought I was a prossie anyway, because of Mum, or at least that's what they said. So I thought I may as well make us some money.

'Just hand jobs to start with. Pay some bills. That's how it went,' she said with a little laugh. 'Look at me, eh? I *am* just like my mother. Maybe it really is in the blood.' Katie took a little sip of her coffee, and Dr. Sharma matched her. 'So. Sex club, eh? It's been a while for me,' she said, tucking some hair behind her ear. 'Should be interesting.'

'Yeah, someone I know recommended it,' replied Dr. Sharma, secretly nervous about the whole thing. 'And they gave me a name for someone I should ask for there.'

'Great,' Katie began, without knowing how she was to continue her response. 'The thing you need to remember about sex clubs is that… just like everywhere else, not everyone shares the same aims.'

'What do you mean?' asked Dr. Sharma, confused.

'Everyone is there for the same thing, *but not.* Does that make sense?'

'None.'

'Never mind, pretend I said nothing,' Katie replied, before continuing, 'it's just that, just because everyone is there for the same reason, it doesn't mean that everyone there thinks the same way.'

'Katie, that is what my whole project is about, knowing what people are truly thinking. All people.'

Katie hadn't asked him thus far, she hadn't wanted it to come across negatively, but the question had been nagging at her from the beginning and she finally had to ask. 'But that's an impossible thing, right? You must know that. Dev, why are you bothering trying to do something so fucking impossible?'

Dr. Sharma took a moment to consider his answer and played with placemat edges on the table. 'Because I don't like being told what I can or can't do,' he answered evasively. 'Anyway,' he said, changing the subject, '*you* said you wouldn't have sex with me?'

'So did you.'

'Yeah, but…'

'Yeah, but what?' interrupted Katie playfully.

'What's *your* reason?'

'You're always the one asking,' whined Katie with a smile. 'All right, fine. I wouldn't have sex with you because it wouldn't feel right anymore.'

'Anymore? Since when?' probed Dr. Sharma.

'I don't know. Things have changed. Our dynamic has changed.'

'When?'

'I don't know. In the course of us talking.'

'So let me get this straight. If I had come in on the first day, paid you and not talked to you, that would have been fine.'

'Yes.'

'You would have had sex with me?'

'Yes,' Katie repeated.

'But now we've talked and gotten to know each other, you won't have sex with me?'

'Right.'

'Huh. I'm not sure if I understand, it either makes no sense, or it makes total sense.'

'We kind of know each other now. So it would be weird, like having sex with a friend, or worse, a brother.'

'It's okay. I just wanted to know what it was. Hey, how about this –'

'Oh, what, are you that desperate to have sex with me now?' teased Katie. 'This always happens to me,' she joked, rolling her eyes.

'What if, hypothetically, I wanted to do something unusual that you don't usually do with anyone. Would that not speak to the unique relationship, perhaps the trust, you have with me that you do not enjoy with your other clients?'

'I'm not sure I would use the word *enjoy*,' teased Katie with a wink. 'Something unusual? Like what? It would have to be something where I really could separate you from… you. Like some kind of roleplay thing. Even then… I don't know…' she trailed off.

Dr. Sharma turned his attention back to his coffee for a few moments. 'Have you heard of Zentai?'

'Isn't that like animated porn?'

'I think you're thinking of *Entai*. Zentai, with a Z.'

'Some kind of weird Japanese thing,' guessed Katie with a grimace.

'You're right. It's Japanese. It's a fetish involving dressing up in a skin-tight suit that covers the entire body from head to toe.'

'So, like cosplay?' asked Katie. 'That would certainly be different. Is that what you want to do, then?'

'No,' laughed Dr. Sharma, 'it was a hypothetical. What do

you think of all that? Do you get many people wanting cosplay?'

'No, it's not really what people come to me for.'

'What do you think of it?' Dr. Sharma asked again.

'It's like any other kind of roleplay, except it's a bit more… you know.' It wasn't something that she had thought of before. That was what she found difficult about these chats with Dr. Sharma. He expected her to have considered all this. She was expected to have opinions. She didn't.

In a way, she wished that he would send her a list of questions, like journalists do with celebrities, ahead of their chats. She was always sure to present her most self-assured self to clients, which was easy in most cases. With Dr. Sharma, it was different. As they lost themselves in conversation, Katie found herself dropping the front and weighing her own thoughts for a change.

He was taking the components of what she did and rearranging them in a way that was foreign to her. Sometimes when Dr. Sharma talked about her work, she almost didn't recognise it, such was the unexpected way he re-presented it to her, through her clients' eyes. The inner workings behind their predilections were something she and most others avoided pondering in her line of work. Hence, these were things that she hadn't ever accorded any real thought.

Katie wanted to have answers for Dr. Sharma. Out of everyone he could have gone to, he had chosen her and that was something she appreciated, but she found it impossible to have an opinion on everything. Sometimes she made up an opinion on the spur of the moment. It didn't feel like a lie to Katie, more like a very natural and raw, immediate response, but it still didn't sit well. As an intelligent person, she liked to consider things.

'That's just another reason why trying to figure out what people are thinking is just impossible,' Katie continued. 'People are all pretending. We all have ideas of the ideal thing. We don't know where the ideas come from, but we're all pretending, letting each other pretend, making each other.

'*Zentai*? They've got something for everything. Do you think we're going to end up with all different sexual things compiled in a list, and we're all going to have a go at each thing at least once in our lives?'

Dr. Sharma smiled. He delighted in having Katie join him in toying with these thoughts. 'It feels like people who are inclined to try different things are only limited to what they've heard of. Most people are trying they've heard of, rather than following an urge, a compulsion to do something. It takes some open-minded trailblazers to act upon their kinks, and then they discover other people with the same predilection.'

'It's like one person has an idea for something, maybe they have that urge, then other people find out about it, and it snowballs. No pun intended,' Katie clarified. 'Anyway, it speaks to them. They feel it's something worth trying out because somebody has already tried it,' said Katie.

'Here's a question: Is a kink considered weirder if it's something that was thought out rather than something instinctive?'

'But isn't any urge to do something instinctive?' pointed out Katie.

'What about cosplay? That can't be entirely instinctive,' Dr.

Sharma argued. There has to be a thought process there.'

'Besides, what is *a kink* anymore?' asked Katie. 'Everyone is having a go at everything. Threesomes are normal now. Everyone's doing it. Group sex. Rope play. It's no big deal to try stuff anymore. I don't think there will be any *alternative* because everyone's having a go at everything,' she theorised.

'I suppose it's like a friend telling you about a new band, and you start listening to them. You might like them. You might hate them. They might become your new favourite. I wonder if we're doing things because we've heard of them, not necessarily because it's a natural compulsion,' replied Dr. Sharma.

Katie was dubious about her clients having any protracted thought process. The men who saw her for quickies certainly didn't exhibit much of a thought process for a fetish or a scenario. Unless the quickie was itself a turn-on. Otherwise, they desired only the instant gratification that comes of flesh grabbing flesh. 'Fucking without thinking,' said Katie out loud. 'I wonder if for some blokes that's the ideal thing. Go back to fucking without thinking, like animals.'

'But animals, even sea creatures, have their rituals. Grooming, preening, courtship.'

'Okay then, less than animals. Ghosts. Shadows. Shadows don't think. They seek light. Otherwise, they don't exist.'

'Do you think we need sex to be ourselves?' asked Dr. Sharma.

'Well, do you think we're different people without sex? I don't feel right if I haven't orgasmed for a while. Maybe immediate satisfaction is part of evolution.'

'Many believe autism is to do with evolution. It's a lot more common than people think. I often wonder if it explains a lot about our attitudes.'

'In what way?' asked Katie.

'I mean, like not being able to make sense of all the different thoughts, the different cultures, beliefs, rituals being superimposed over each other, and us being unable to digest it all, absorb it all. Instead of working through it, many reject anything unfamiliar. If we could sort through it, we might find some universal truth and stop hurting each other. Maybe those suicide bombers could finally retire,' Dr. Sharma joked.

'Well, maybe the suicide bombers are more evolved. Maybe they're ahead. How about that for a wacky theory, *doctor*?' asked Katie with a self-satisfied look.

'Evolving… to not give a shit about self-preservation?' asked Dr. Sharma, with the beginnings of a smile.

'No, evolving to prioritise other things.'

'Explain,' invited Dr. Sharma.

'People seem to suicide bomb because they're angry and they have beliefs, whatever they may be. Right? They presumably feel their actions will strike a blow and make things better in the long run. If you were trying to be funny, you might call it a lifestyle choice. A lot of people are deciding not to have children either. A lifestyle choice. Instead, they're getting pets. Lifestyle, right?

'I read somewhere that the world's human population has tripled in the last eighty years or so. So, maybe, we've evolved to not worry too much about preserving the species anymore. We're not evolving physically. Instead, our evolution is making belief our priority,' explained Katie, raising her eyebrows theatrically.

'Suicide bombers must believe in something. They must trust their convictions. Like those *Kamikaze* pilots. They must have believed in… Japan? Or the Emperor, or whatever they had. They believed it was something worth dying for. Regular people have different reasons for killing themselves. Whatever their reason, more people are doing that too.'

'What are you trying to say?' asked Dr. Sharma, looking for the connection.

'Sorry, I got lost,' admitted Katie, 'I suppose what I'm trying to say is that the problems we have now are not the same ones we had hundreds, thousands of years ago, so maybe our brains have become wired differently, or just our whole thought process has changed.

'So, before, when we were wired for self-preservation, we'd be humping each other and then pumping out sprogs as a matter of course. It wouldn't even be a question because everyone was doing it. It was expected. Back then, the struggle was gathering water, finding food, hunting animals, killing predators and keeping your children alive. Then everything became more organised with farms making it easier to get food. Then it all got industrialised, meaning it was even easier for everyone everywhere to feed their family, providing they had the money. Now we just drive over to the supermarket once a week for all our food. We bring it home and shove it in the freezer.

'In that way, finding food and self-preservation are no longer issues, so maybe our brains are no longer wired for just that. Maybe our brains have evolved to prioritise accomplishing longer-term goals based on our beliefs. Goals that won't necessarily be achieved in our lifetime.'

Dr. Sharma took a moment to absorb the theory he thought she was trying to propose. 'So, you think we've evolved to blow ourselves up, to kill ourselves, to achieve goals? Are you insane?'

'Maybe evolved is the wrong word. Maybe self-preservation is just not on our minds as much anymore. It's like parents always say they want their children to have a better life than they did growing up, but whatever hardship or experience those parents went through is part of them and not something they can successfully communicate to their children through just words. They would need to experience it to appreciate it. If they had to struggle to survive and fight to exist in the world, they might appreciate life a lot more. Certainly, they would have less time to think about suicide bombing or exploiting the poor to make even more money for companies their grandfathers founded. Don't you think if the world was thrown into chaos and we all had to resort to gathering firewood and hunting, it would bring everything back into perspective?' asked Katie.

'In Mauritius, when my dad was small, one of his chores was to gather firewood to cook the evening meal.'

'Is that where they're from, then, Mauritius?'

'Yeah.'

You didn't have to do that, did you?'

'No.'

'And are you a better person than him for not having to do that?'

'No, he probably appreciates things more. Besides, parents never say that.'

'What?'

'*I want you to be a better person than me.* They'd be admitting they're not the best person they could be after all. They say, "we want you to do better than us." Progress. My Dad talks a lot about progress.'

The two of them were silent for a while as they each thought of their parents. Katie pondered whether what Dr. Sharma had just said was true. Had her mother been at all bothered about Katie getting further in her life? She had started so simply, relatively innocent, with a roleplay scenario devised by her mother's client. Did she regret that Katie had taken the same route that she did?

'They say, in America, the KKK has more people joining.'

'Oh.' Dr. Sharma wondered where she was going with this comment.

'I mention it because maybe racism should be a factor in your research.'

'Yeah, but that's why your idea of everything going back to zero through some calamity mightn't work.'

'What, you think different races would fight each other?' asked Katie.

'People like to have clear enemies.'

'Explains why sport is so popular.'

'It would have to be something bigger, where the rules were all changed. Otherwise, there's always someone ready to take advantage of a catastrophe.'

'Which rules? Society? Law? Nature?'

'Everything. Rules wouldn't exist. It would have to be that any hope of getting through it would rest upon people clinging to each other.'

Katie brought her hands to her face and rubbed at her tired

eyes before running her hands through her hair. 'What are we talking about?' she asked with a slight shake of her head. 'All this. You do see it's pointless, right? It's just talking into the wind. Y'know, knowing what everyone thinks. It's impossible.'

'Maybe, but don't you think the world would be a better place if we could all understand each other?'

'Of course,' agreed Katie, rolling her eyes at such a pointless question. 'We'd have more sympathy, more empathy.'

'Well, that's what I'm trying to do. I'm just starting with sex.'

'Yes, I get it. It's like you're pressing the back button on a computer to see how the person using it got to the website that they're on.'

'Yeah, but on each previous page, there are links they could have clicked on, and you want to find out which ones they used. They might tell us what else changed their thoughts and ideas along the way.'

'It'd be handy if you could just plug in someone's brain and scan their… thought history, or something. And then delete it. Start fresh again. Total. Mind-wipe. Wouldn't it?' asked Katie.

'But then you'd lose all that they had learnt from their experience of living life. This comes back to what you were saying earlier,' replied Dr. Sharma.

'Yeah, I know,' yawned Katie. 'Maybe they could figure out a way to keep the substance of what they'd learnt but get rid of the experience. Like the program on a device that you can't erase.'

'Firmware.'

'I wouldn't be surprised if they could do that already. I watch a lot of sci-fi. And I love conspiracy theories.'

'Really?' Dr. Sharma raised his eyebrows.

'Yeah, why? What?' asked Katie, amused at his surprise.

'Hadn't occurred to me that you might be into that.'

'You never asked.'

'True,' he admitted before asking, 'why are you laughing?' as Katie chuckled, before draining the remains of her coffee and getting up to check on the pie in the oven.

'What are you talking about?'

'What was that little laugh about?' he asked again.

'All this, Dev, you're looking for some explanation, but it's impossible. It's insane. You'd go mad doing it, if you're not there already. There's too much stuff, too much information. All the things people experience in an entire lifetime, all the outside influences. All the influences passed down from generations, in DNA, or opinions and political beliefs. A lot of people just think and vote the way their family always has,' she stated, glancing at the clock and getting up to the oven across the kitchen.

'Katie, think about all the time, effort and money that is spent on tracing our physical origins, digging up old dinosaur bones, fossils, sending telescopes into space. All this, but the human brain, something we all carry around with us twenty-four-seven, has got to still be one of the greatest mysteries. It's like finding a loaded gun in your pocket. No idea how it got there or how it works, but it holds the power to cause pain, chaos, devastation. Doesn't each of us have a responsibility to learn how it works, how we work?' asked Dr. Sharma.

'But I'm sure there are whole teams of doctors and scientists working on this stuff. Let them do it. It's a huge task. You can't do it alone.'

'I need to know, Katie. I need to know how it looks when they're doing the things they do. I need to see for myself how thoughts flow, disperse, form into ideas, become forgotten, only to resurface years later, along with experiences and acquired knowledge, to form an opinion. We're all people. Fundamentally we all have the same needs. But, somehow, with the other stuff we've piled on top, we've forgotten that each of us is fragile in our own ways. Instead of examining ourselves, we're more comfortable sending rovers out into space. How is it easier to explore space than it is to explore our thoughts? Or do they think we're all thinking the same thoughts?' asked Dr. Sharma rhetorically.

'Is that why it comes as such a shock when people we think we know decide to march for the National Front, or become suicide bombers, or go to fight in Syria?' Dr. Sharma continued. 'How about us? Does the blame lie with us, that in arrogance we assume that someone we share a meal with, or carpool with, reflects our opinion of what's acceptable in another human being? Is it reasonable to take it for granted that others share our sense of reality and understand the fabric of their fantasies? Are we sure they know what the consequences can be for others, should they choose to live out their scenario, their roleplaying, to its utmost conclusion in their search for release? We don't know what they're thinking. We need to know.' He finished with a little shake of his head before running his hands over his face.

It was the first time that Dr. Sharma had shown himself to

anyone like this, purely because this hadn't existed before, as far as he was aware. It was new, but it couldn't have been. These concerns, this pure paranoia, had been pricking at his mind for some time, but this was the moment when it arrived, driving at the surface of his consciousness.

It was here. This was the precise moment that the words presented themselves to his lips in that erratic, blundering order, and once they were there, they had no other place to go. Dr. Sharma was just as surprised as Katie at the words that left his mouth and twirled through the air above them.

It's here, I'm sure of it. This is the moment where things begin to coalesce. This is the fork in the road where Dr. Sharma accepted that his obsessive quest was about more than just understanding all people. It may have started like that, but somewhere along the way, something has changed and driven his need to know into an uncharted, dark and forbidding landscape. Why? What was it?

Although Dr. Sharma's demeanour remained calm and didn't betray anything to Katie that his words hadn't, it was the first time that Katie felt a pang of genuine concern for him as she sensed just how important this project was to him. Watching from across the kitchen, she decided to steer the conversation towards a calmer activity that he could use to recompose his thoughts.

'This is getting a little intense,' said Katie with a light giggle as she sliced the warm fruit pie for them onto two plates. 'Hey, how about you help me with something?' she asked, pulling on one of her cheeky smiles as she set the plates down on the table with cutlery.

'What is it?' asked Dr. Sharma, grateful for a respite from

the flood that had taken him by surprise. He felt he had been ambushed, betrayed by his faculties.

'I've had some new photos taken for my website. Why don't you help me pick the best ones?' she asked, taking the folder of prints from the kitchen counter. 'What do you think of this one?' she asked as he went over and stood next to her.

'Katie, you're practically naked here.'

'That's the point,' she said, nudging his arm. 'Except for the bow. I'm everyone's monthly treat,' she joked, bending to lean her elbows onto the table beside Dr. Sharma. 'Put on a bow and offer me up. Aren't I a gift?' she asked, with a suggestive wiggle.

'I read that if a website uses photos of a person's naked body without consent, and that person wants them removed, that they have to send more pictures of their naked body to verify that the body being shown on the website is actually theirs.'

'That's crazy.'

'You have to prove that you are the owner of your own body to force the website owners to remove the photos. What about all those bodies that aren't claimed? Are all those bodies just ownerless? All those unique characteristics passed through the generations, in the space of a few decades have been copied and published again and again. That collection of features, those entities without anchors, identities. Those photos will continue to exist long after we are dead. These photos of you will keep being used long after you're gone. You'll be dead, but people seeing your photos in the future will still think you look like this.'

'Dev, chill out,' Katie advised firmly. 'Let's take a break and spend a few nice moments looking at my naked photos.'

# 46. O, Canada

Despite the year he had spent in Mauritius, it wasn't difficult for Dev to turn his back on the all-consuming heat as he followed his mother into the airport terminal. Once again, they negotiated passport control, their maroon coloured UK passports paired with their latest dance partners, tickets to Manitoba.

He had been taken to Mauritius, a country that, other than a vacation, he had no real connection with. Dev's cursory knowledge of Mauritius had not set him up to compete with his Mauritian counterparts at school before he was dropped in it and expected to thrive. Every misconjugated verb was an attack upon his confidence and an invitation to second-guess everything he thought, said and did. Still, he had continued because it had seemed so important to his mother, to his father.

*Maybe it would make her happy. Perhaps it would make everything all right again.*

Connecting flights, this time. Unlike the trip from London

to Mauritius, there were no direct flights. A coach journey provided another novelty for Dev as they clambered aboard after collecting their luggage from the carousel. Serena had explained to him that Auntie Seeva couldn't collect them from the airport since she and her husband were working.

By the time they arrived at the coach station, both Auntie Seeva and Uncle Vijay had arrived and were waiting by their estate car or, as they called it, their *station wagon*. The squeeze of another uncle's hand grasping his as he stooped to greet his nephew. Another auntie's kisses. 'How long are you staying?' came the question from Uncle Vijay once mandatory pleasantries had been exchanged.

The shock of the cold after his year on a tropical island was surprisingly reinvigorating and pleasing to Dev, for it reminded him of England. As they made their way through towns en route to the house, the climate, shops and services they passed in Winnipeg surprised Dev by how closely they compared to those in England. After the surprising differences of Mauritius, Dev had been braced for another land replete with idiosyncrasies. One that would contrast as much with England and Mauritius as the latter had with the former. From what he could see through his bleary eyes, this was not the case.

On the plane, Serena had outlined to Dev the skeleton of her plan:

1. They would be guests at the home of Auntie Seeva and Uncle Vijay.
2. Dev would enrol at a local school. Maybe the one his cousins attended.

3. Serena would gather information and explore options.
4. Settled, they would come to some decisions about what to do next.

Dev wouldn't tell his mother this, but he wanted nothing more than to see his father. He didn't miss England or Mauritius, but he did long to hear the unwavering tones of his father's voice. Over a long-distance telephone call, he just sounded small and tinny, a faded version of the father he remembered, like one of Grandfather's worn out, copied *sega* cassettes. A copy of a copy.

'So, young Mr Sharma. You're not a Master anymore, are you?' asked Uncle Vijay as he set a plate of toasted waffles on the counter before Dev in the kitchen that afternoon.

'Aren't I?'

'No, you're twelve, practically a young man now. Young Mr Sharma.' Dev momentarily looked down at his waffles slathered in maple syrup. His uncle had insisted on treating him to one of Canada's most famous products. He could feel the heat coming off the waffles and rising to his face. Dev looked back up to his uncle, wondering if it would be impolite to begin eating while his uncle was trying to chat with him. 'Do you know where your name comes from?' he asked, intently gazing down at his nephew and smiling benevolently.

'Dev?' Dev asked uncertainly.

'Sharma, *Mr Sharma*. Hasn't your father told you? I'm fascinated by all this stuff. Your surname, apparently, goes back to India. It's from the Brahmin caste. One of the upper castes. Have you heard of the Brahmins?'

'No,' answered Dev, lifting his fork.

'Do you know what a caste is?'

'No,' lowering his fork again.

'A caste is... like a class, but the class one belongs to is determined by heritage rather than, um, how wealthy one is. Do you want to know how your caste, the Brahmins, ranks?'

Dev was more interested in his waffles that were rapidly growing soggy, soaking up the syrup. 'Okay.'

'Well,' began his uncle, warming to his topic, 'Sharma is a relatively common surname in India, and it is mainly associated with the Brahmins but also with other castes. The Brahmins were mainly known for becoming priests, teachers.'

'Oh.'

'There is also some evidence that they were warriors.'

'Oh. Who did they fight?'

'Um. I don't know that,' admitted uncle Vijay, suddenly looking downcast. 'They were also farmers,' he added brightly.

Within a few days, it was apparent to both Auntie Seeva and Uncle Vijay why Serena was in Winnipeg. She couldn't bear to go back to England, but she could no longer stay at her brother's house in Mauritius. Meanwhile, Auntie Seeva had been more than happy to play the caring sister from the moment the mother and son combo arrived at the house.

Having taken a few days off from work to hang out with Serena and Dev, Serena's sister pottered around the kitchen, fussing over the breakfasts of her husband and children and preparing their lunches while Serena watched. The familiar life of a Western nuclear family. It was something she hadn't had to contend with, living with her father and brother in Mauritius for the past year. To Serena, the spectacle appealed and disgusted in equal measure.

The easy flow of their family life was something that she recognised from her own life, albeit a bygone era that she couldn't imagine regaining any time soon. And therein lay the source of her disgust. The idea of having that type of easy happiness again, where everything within her little bubble was heart shapes and flowers and perfection, made her feel nauseated.

After what had happened to Amina, Serena could not see how she could ever again trust the world and the people living on it. To Serena, it was inconceivable to her that she could ever have that life again where she believed in the simple certitude of a safe world for her family.

Watching Seeva with her family, the ambience appeared at best jejune, at worst fake, as they effortlessly joshed around with each other. Worthy of a cosy, toothless TV sitcom. Of course, she knew that it was no facade. It was the same seemingly self-satisfied scenario that was being played out in billions of homes around the world. She knew Seeva meant no harm, but it almost seemed she was needling Serena with their casual contentment. With Amina gone, all she and Dev had was a fragmented family and no map back to that simple reality.

Everybody gets lost once in a while, and everybody needs help from time to time. This was Serena. The move to Canada had been the last thing that anybody had expected of her. She was lost but refused to give in and return to England, despite everybody telling her it was the logical thing to do. It didn't seem logical to *her*. As far as she was concerned, it was ridiculous to even contemplate going back to the scene of so much hurt.

Their house there wasn't the place it used to be. Despite living there for another year after Amina's death, it had ceased to be her home. Over two years after Amina's death, Serena still couldn't bring herself to think of anywhere being safe and happy in the same way that their home in England had been. Instead, she had a vague idea of staying on the move. Not stopping, not thinking. Just obeying impulses and moving when it felt right.

For now, it felt right to stay and watch Dev attend school. As she had done in Mauritius, she would watch out for him and meet him after school to ensure he was safe. She had been tricked before into a false sense of security, and she was adamant that it wouldn't happen again, determined that she would keep Dev from harm.

He was to attend a nearby school. That was Serena's plan. She envisioned him making new friends. Until then, he would get to know his cousins.

It was on the first night at his cousin's house that Dev learnt the truth about the CPE exam. He was to share Abigail's bedroom, the younger of the two sisters. Uncle Vijay had pushed Abigail's bed to one side of the room and brought in a rudimentary camping bed. Dev assured his uncle that he didn't need any help setting it up, which is what he did while Jessie and Abigail, in Benetton tops that were in vogue at the time, watched disinterestedly from the bed across the room.

The cousins hadn't seen each other since Jessie and Abigail visited the UK and stayed with Amina, Dev and their parents in England a few years previously. They were two and three years older than him, and with all the subtlety children can muster at that age, they gave him their judgement of the Certificate of Primary Education.

'It doesn't exist anywhere, 'cept in Mauritius,' declared Abigail.

'At least you learnt French. That's cool,' said Jessie, brightly. Usually, she found herself in the position of seeking the approval of her elder sister, but in certain situations, Abigail would allow Jessie to team up with her to pursue an unspoken common goal. Jessie always relished such circumstances and spared no effort in playing her role. 'Why did he come *here*?' asked Jessie to her sister, as though Dev had somehow suddenly disappeared. 'For, like, a vacation?'

'When are you going?' asked Abigail. 'Seriously, what were you and Auntie expecting, that we're happy to see you? With those huge suitcases, it's like you're moving in forever.'

Their cousin didn't know what to say. This hadn't been what he was expecting, and he was at a loss as to how to respond.

Before moving to Mauritius, Dev had learnt about racism in England and had heard some pejoratives, although he hadn't recognised them as such. His father had explained it to him and told him that he should expect some form of racism in his life. Later, as an adolescent, and then an adult, any racist remarks he received from a man would be like water off a duck's back (or, *de l'eau lor brede songe*, as they said in Mauritius), but it was always significantly more difficult for him to hear it from a woman. It was much later as an adult that Dev realised that his first personal experience of racism was from his own cousins.

'Well, aren't you going to say anything?' asked Jessie, once more deigning him worthy of her direct verbal and visual contact.

'You know what's going to happen,' asked Abigail before supplying her own answer. 'He's going to go to our school,' a tired and resigned affectation to her voice, 'and we'll have to show him around. Everyone's going to laugh at us, with our *Mauritian* cousin, in his crappy clothes.'

'I know, not one label. Like children's clothes,' Jessie observed, seemingly oblivious to the fact that he was twelve.

'Don't Mauritians have anything, like, cool, over there?' asked Abigail.

'I'm not Mauritian. I'm from England,' Dev quietly replied.

'No. You're *Mauritian* now. Is there *anything* good about Mauritius?'

'The sun. The beach,' replied Dev, his face growing hot with discomfort under their hard stares.

'So what did you do in Mauritius? What did you do for fun? Where did you go? Where did you hang out? What did you do? What were your friends' names?

'Gopal. Jupin. Tourabally.'

'What kind of names are those?'

'Surnames. That's how we called each other at school there.'

'So what did you do?'

'Um. I went to the beach with Mum, sometimes. I studied lots, like all the time.'

'You study *all* the time? What a loser, you're *so* not fitting in at our school. You and your mum really are helpless here. Just wait and see how much help you'll need to catch up when you join school here.'

It was clear to Dev that they had taken an instant, intense dislike to him, but he didn't understand why. He remembered the family photos from when they visited the Sharmas in England, visited the warfare museum, and played together. Dev, Amina, Jessie and Abigail, climbing tanks, pretending to fire cannons. That was just a few years ago.

Now, in Canada, the only thing Dev could think of that had changed was that he had spent a year and some change in Mauritius. At the time, all he could determine was that he had evidently changed, become less *valid.* With everything that had happened, losing his sister, the withdrawal of his mother, the time in Mauritius, the absence of his father, he could only conclude that, in the eyes of his Canadian cousins, *he* had changed. Their view of him had changed.

They all had Mauritian parents. They all had brown skin. They simply disliked him because he had spent the past year in a country they considered inferior to the one they happened to be in. It didn't sit well. It was a kind of inter-family racism the twelve-year-old couldn't understand.

Throughout his time with the family in Canada, and beyond, he could feel it in his chest, a cold weight that made him feel full, robbing him of any appetite. It was the hurt at being treated that way by people who were supposed to be family, people with whom he was supposed to share something beyond the surface. Some type of kinship. Instead of welcoming a connection, they were angry at him and his mother. They didn't want a connection.

In their belligerence, they arrogantly believed their family had more value. They saw Dev and his Serena, grieving and in pain, as leeches holding nothing that they wanted or valued. The sisters couldn't understand Serena's and Dev's loss and pain. So fragile was their feeling of acceptance they were concerned only with satisfying their own need to fit in and feel comfortable amongst neighbours they had known their entire lives.

They feared Serena and Dev bringing them unwanted attention that would shine a light on how different they were to the rest of their community, undermining their efforts to pass without a hint of foreign heritage. All they wanted was to be what they saw as Canadian. White. The white of the faces they saw around them, that they saw in movies and TV shows.

They saw no value in the colour of their skin, the physical attributes particular to their ethnicity. They didn't connect with Mauritian culture. They didn't want it to be part of them. To them, talk of *Sega* music and dancers, for example, only brought up images from tacky souvenirs. The sisters had spent little time in Mauritius and had no emotional bridge to it.

As an adult, Dev would consider their behaviour towards him and speculate about their mindset. He wondered if they were like some Black Americans who, lacking any cultural connection with Africa, or its people, wished to no longer be referred to as *African* Americans.

To fit in, Amina and Dev had been raised as English. Had they been raised in Mauritius, there is no doubt things would have been different. Having experienced the different sides, Dev felt uniquely positioned to understand with an insight that most of his family would never have. As an adult, he was grateful for this broader-minded worldview. But by then, he also knew the experience that caused it had initiated the erosion of trust in his mother. And father.

Dev thought back to the times they had played together in England and wondered if his cousins had ever liked him or if they had been acting, humouring him and his family, always believing themselves to be better. He would carry it with him for years. It wasn't until he was older, at med school, that he tried again to unpick it, figure it out.

'What was there to figure out? They were stupid little cretins. Morons. Absolute heartless cunts to treat another child, their own cousin, that way. End of!' Alan concluded in the student library that late night when they had the entire floor to themselves.

'I began wondering,' replied Dev, 'if by just being there, my mother and I were unwelcome reminders to them of their heritage and where their family was actually from. With hindsight, I wonder if I reminded them of how they didn't seamlessly fit into their environment. Maybe that's where their frustration came from. They were happy to imagine they had the exact same cultural background as their neighbours and classmates. Maybe the way to do that was to forget that Mauritius was a part of their background. You know? As simple as treating me like an outsider to feel more like insiders.'

'Well, yeah. Racism is just insecurities and small-mindedness. It was them, not you, Dev.'

'Sometimes, I wonder,' said Dev, getting analytical again, 'if having not gone through what your parents went through, does that help or hinder offspring? If you don't have the same appreciation and respect for how they left their country, everything they knew and loved, and worked hard to make a better life for their children? The children reap the supposed benefits of those that went before them, without truly understanding the effort that went into it, without appreciating where they came from.

'Alan…' Dev began, but it was difficult for him to continue. 'When I was thirteen, I tried to stop my parents from speaking in Creole because I wanted to forget about Mauritius. The funny thing was, I tried to stop them speaking their language using a comment from a Mauritian. In Mauritius, Mum and I were buying school books for me to learn French. In one of the bookshops, there was this bookseller who talked to my mum about languages.

'Speaking in Mauritian Creole, he said it has no value in the world since it is spoken almost nowhere else. English and French have value. So, when I was thirteen, I tried to use that argument to stop my parents from speaking Creole. I didn't know… I just wanted to forget that Mauritius had become a part of me.'

'That bookseller was wrong,' replied Alan, 'Creole has value for your parents, for Mauritians. And for you.'

'It was their bit of home. It was their culture, and I tried to change it.'

'You were… how old?' asked Alan.

'Thirteen. Maybe fourteen.'

'You were just a kid. Forget it.'

‘I still feel guilty. I regret trying to change them.’

‘You were a kid. You learned from it. Fucking let it go. We’re adults. We’ve bigger things to deal with now,’ huffed Alan, gesturing to the books on the table. ‘Leave the past where it is.’

# 47. Self-medication

A week after they arrived in Winnipeg, Dev found himself in a school library, sitting at a large square table with two others. The three of them were new starters at the school that was accepting new pupils, and they had been instructed by one of the admin staff to complete the test that lay before them. The sheets of paper covered English, Maths and Science. Dev was working on the maths problems when he sensed movement around him.

He looked up to find the other two half-heartedly leafing through their tests. Dev observed them for a few moments before returning to his attention to the tests. They were the first he had had to face since the CPE in Mauritius and were necessary to determine his abilities and be placed in appropriate classes.

That same week Dev was due to complete his enrollment at the school that Abigail and Jessie attended, but, in the end, Serena had second thoughts about letting him out of her sight. Mauritius had been a different proposition. She had felt safe there in a way that Canada didn't make her feel. After what she had let happen to Amina, she wasn't prepared to risk anything happening to her remaining child.

Serena still had enough self-awareness to recognise she was being unreasonable, but she couldn't help the way she felt. Losing Amina was not something that she would ever overcome, and for now, it resulted in Serena needing Dev close by at all times. It made her feel complete and balanced to know that she was protecting him and maintaining her vigilance.

As time went on, it became more and more important that he was near her when they went out. Looking out for Dev and protecting him against all threats, imagined or otherwise, gave her not only purpose but confidence and a sense of agency.

Each day Serena and Dev rode the buses to visit the churches, temples and synagogues of Winnipeg, sometimes visiting up to four in a single day. Serena didn't discriminate between faiths, and in their places of worship, she found a way to focus her thoughts and slow the rush of recriminations that otherwise assailed her consciousness. They were never bothered by anyone else, and nobody ever tried to talk to them. On her knees, she offered her attention as Dev watched her and waited to head back out into the cold.

Dev looked from Serena's whispering lips to the church statues and their sleepy-eyed middle-distance gazes. So different from the Hindu temples, where the gods' typically fierce eyes were emphasised by their bright primary colours. The differences led Dev to consider the Hindu gods more deeply.

He wondered: *if all those gods could talk, what would they say? What are they thinking? We're supposed to be good, so these gods will look upon us kindly. So that must mean that they're judging us. So what are they thinking? If gods judge, they can punish. Hindu gods are not perfect. They have personalities. They can be vengeful, they can be playful, they can be malicious. We've no idea what they're thinking. If we're supposed to make all these gods happy, with their different personalities, how do we do that when what will please one god will anger another?*

The only time Serena spoke at length was at the feet of the deities. Dev watched his mother's silent lips moving above hands clasped tightly together. She never looked directly at the statues or the paintings. With her eyes shut tight, she would talk urgently and silently while Dev would watch her and wonder what he should be saying. Sometimes Dev would try to speak with his mother to wrest some answers from her.

But Serena was never bothered much with talking to her son, aside from what was essential. This seemed to be what she was comfortable with. It was all she could handle. So, Dev's questioning would be largely fruitless, and he eventually learnt to stop trying. Instead, he tried to analyse what was happening and what they were doing in Winnipeg, a place they had no connection with.

Other than Auntie Seeva and Uncle Vijay, they knew no one there. Dev would watch his mother's lips and their rapid movement, just as he had in Mauritius. Nothing had really changed, just their surroundings. In Mauritius, he had the hope that the CPE exams would precede their return to England, but this hadn't come to pass. Instead, they were in Canada, and he still awaited their return to England.

Return to what?

Still no Amina.

Still a dead girl.

Still an accident.

Still a dead girl.

Still no Amina.

Still searching.

Still other faces, other people.

They had arrived in Winnipeg in November, and it had been two months of the same daily cycle of visiting the churches of the city. The temples. The buses. The grey roads. The grey skies. The driving rain. Serena's silent lips. Her eyes that wouldn't alight from Dev's form until they were safely back at Auntie Seeva's house. Two months had passed, and there was no sign from Serena that she was forming a plan.

Dev, travelling in the car one day, seated in the back with his cousins, shut his eyes against the snowbanks illuminated by the bright sunlight. As the car passed, throwing up slush from its tyres, Dev allowed himself to freefall through his imagination, picking up anything of interest and discarding the rest as he sought an Amina-inspired story, a fix to get him through the day in the company of Jessie and Abigail.

The council of Summerwalk has a long and proud history… of getting rid of their problems. Nothing new about this. For example, many towns and cities shove homeless people on trains bound for elsewhere, with nothing more than a one-way ticket to keep them company. However, Summerwalk is different. For decades it has kept a secret from the rest of the world. That secret being that they have access to the means to transport their *problem citizens* to far reaches, with no hope of ever returning.

The council members haven't ever felt that there is anything wrong with this. After all, they regularly take on the problems that others have given up on. Indeed, many of their population have come from other places to thrive in the town. Where had they come from? Ah, well, that was a different question altogether. Literally, for it is more like *when* than *where*. You see, the citizens they received came from the very spot where the town lies, long ago in the past. They were Summerwalk citizens who had proven themselves to be maladroits, misfits and miscreants in their own time and had been forced through a portal to be dealt with by future Summerwalk councils.

The town received new citizens on an almost daily basis, from all kinds of eras. Once, they had even received a cavewoman who one day must have wandered into the portal by accident whilst foraging. Once she had pinned down the basics of verbal communication, she went on to enjoy a very fulfilling career as a personal trainer. For this reason, the portal (located between the abandoned phone box and the overgrown bush at the end of what once was Wootton Road, but was renamed Kieslowski Crescent, officially in honour of the Polish filmmaker, unofficially after the bus conductor who had discovered the portal back in the eighteen-eighties) had to be manned around the clock.

Previously, new citizens entering via the portal had been left to find their way to the local authorities of their own accord. However, a regrettable incident involving a young woman from 1926, when she mistook a couple of 1984 double-glazed salesmen for gentlemen of high repute, satisfied then council members that modern-day morals had declined to such an extent that no one was safe. Not even flappers.

The frankly surprising outcome that awaits all these outcasts from their own times is that they all thrive in modern-day Summerwalk. The reason for this is difficult to ascertain, and nobody cares to delve too deeply, lest the magic be lost in the process. Suffice it to say that the modern times the newcomers arrive at provides them not only respite from the various injustices they felt had been dealt them in their own time, but also the means to express their true selves without the judgements of their peers.

No one suggests that these people were ahead of their time. It was more that they did not entirely suit the trappings of their original era. For example, once she had put behind her the rotten business of double-glazed sales, the flapper went on to give up the heavy drinking and exuberant partying to become a cherished jazz trumpeter in several London combos. She later hung up her lungs and became a music critic. Her book, *A Mouthful of Jazz*, became a bestseller throughout Europe.

The years intervening their own time and that at which

they arrived had brought a slew of solutions for the troubles that had assailed them. The flapper, for example, collected sobriety tokens at Alcoholics Anonymous, while the cavewoman discovered the fruit and veg aisle at the supermarket. Modern-day services that we take for granted gave the newcomers the confidence and stability to look to the future and make a better life.

The council assumes those it sends to the future find solace, renewed vigour and the opportunity to start their lives over. Win-win! *The past may not be recreated. The future may be anything*, is the town's unofficial motto.

The program's continuing success gives the council members the confidence to carry on sending their *problem-people* through the portal to a time in the future when they will be more… appropriate. The issue the council members face, in the event of the catastrophic changes with which the entire world is dealing, is that fear and panic have set in. The, at best, hazy definition of what constituted a problem-person is being massaged to encompass almost anyone. Meanwhile, others on the council see the world's troubles as a way to publicise and show off the success of their town. They see Summerwalk as not only multicultural but also multi-temporal.

'Most of us would jump at the chance to start again, as new people. As immigrants, we had that chance to work, earn and achieve, and now look at us. We now have the opportunity to give somebody else this gift. Should we deny them, or should we help them?' asks Mo.

'I'm telling you we shouldn't say anything,' Magda persists.

'People have been asking for years,' reasons Iqbal.

'Well, let them continue to ask. Asking doesn't hurt if we don't answer,' replies Magda.

'I agree with Magda,' contributes Anjun, 'for what it's worth.'

'Right now, that is worth nothing. I've made up my mind, I'm going to tell the truth, and we will save the world. Understand?' asks Mo, determinedly.

'No. It was good for our town, but it won't be enough for the whole world, Mo.'

'Don't *Mo* me. Don't you see? What I am doing is bigger than the world. It's about our town.'

'That… makes no sense at all,' says Anjun, 'no sense. You're talking in riddles.'

'I'm not,' replies Mo. 'I'll explain. Summerwalk is mostly made up of immigrants, and we have made it the best town in England. There is no crime, right?'

'Right,' agrees Anjun.

'There is no litter. The roads are clean, right?'

'Yeah,' agrees Magda.

'With all the craziness that is going on, we have managed to avoid all of it, right?'

'Wrong. We didn't avoid it. We just got rid of it all,' Magda counters.

'Right, and it worked. Just like it did with everything else we thought was not to our taste. The population of this town is mainly made up of immigrants. Everyone expects this town to be the lowest of the low, a dumping ground for society's undesirables. A place where the wealthy can buy power and do what they want, while the rest of us keep our mouths shut. We changed all that. Didn't we?'

'Yeah, but – .'

'No *buts*,' interrupts Mo. 'The council was corrupt, and now the bad apples are gone. Police brutality has been eradicated. The prostitutes are gone. The drug addicts, the beggars, the mentally unstable – .'

'Don't forget the street artists,' interrupts Anjun.

'Don't start again with the jugglers, Anjun. We don't have the time,' quibbles Mo.

'I didn't have a problem with the jugglers,' comments Iqbal.

'If a town like this can pull itself together to the point where property prices have increased by two hundred per cent, and be held in such high regard, just think what will happen if we can do that for the whole world,' insists Mo. 'We'd have international recognition. Maybe they'll even put us on the map on the national news when they do the weather!'

'What are you talking about?' pleads Magda. 'We're all happy here. Now! Why are we sharing it? We have this gift. Let's not ruin it.'

'But wouldn't this gift mean even more *if* we shared it… with the world?' asks Mo. 'If a bunch of immigrants can band together and save the world, wouldn't it be an amazing thing that would never be forgotten? No one would ever have a bad thing to say about immigrants after hearing what we have accomplished.'

'Magda, how many times have you heard: "go back to Poland, you east European scum?"' asks Iqbal.

'Lots,' she answers.

'I've lived here for thirty-five years, and kids in the street say more than ever: "go back to Paki-land, you terrorist." Anjun?'

'Yeah,' agrees Anjun.

'Wouldn't it be great to do something immense that we can use as a big shield? For once, immigrants would have some respect in this world. The only reason anyone moves from home is for work, a better life. Why's that so objectionable?'

'But how would we tell them? It's not an easy thing,' says Anjun. 'Plus, how about when they ask questions? We've all turned a blind eye and stopped considering the consequences of our actions, but they must be having an effect elsewhere. Other people will take it a lot more seriously. They will want to know where everyone is going.'

'Who?' asks Mo. 'The people who are no longer themselves? Nobody will care about them if they aren't around anymore and things return to normal.'

'But what is normal? Do we really want things the way they were?' asks Magda.

'Yes, except that we'll be on top,' clarifies Mo, with a glint in his eye.

'On top of what?'

'On top of the… People will think better of us. Don't you see? We won't be at the bottom. They'll want us in their communities, in the pubs, next door. Magda, Anjun, you're both young. You don't know what it was like when I came here.'

'But it's not like that so much now,' protests Anjun.

'Yes, it is, just in different ways. In ways without words. I don't know what to say. You have to experience it to experience it,' Mo attempts to clarify.

'Mo, we can't wipe it away like this. We can't do it for the whole world.'

'Also,' begins Magda, 'when we get rid of these people, we don't know where they are going. We don't even know *when* they are going.'

'Exactly, they're somebody else's problem,' agrees Mo.

'It's not only that they're a problem for another time, but there's the morality of what we've been doing. Can you imagine for an addict what kind of a head-fuck come-down it is to suddenly find yourself two thousand years in the future?'

'Don't worry, Magda, Mo's plan won't work. Who would believe him?' asks Anjun. 'Would you believe someone if they told you they were banishing all the negative elements from their community for future generations to deal with?'

'Yes,' stated Magda, 'because that's what we do. Who knows if there even is a future? Maybe there isn't even a planet left in the future, and we've been sending them into space.'

Mo feels he is losing his colleagues and decides a new approach is necessary. 'We already considered all this. We're sending them to the future, where there will no doubt be top-notch treatments for addicts and criminals. Affordable spas and so forth. Don't begin questioning things because I tried to think big. Don't get spooked. Anjun, you are very excited that we are about to roll out the extraction of character traits from the worst of our neighbours to be sent into the future. This is progress! We will be sending the offending character traits rather than actual people. Isn't that amazing?'

'Yeah. I suppose,' admits Anjun.

'Of course, occasionally, we will still have to send people,' admits Mo.

'Why?' asks Magda.

'Who?' queries Iqbal.

'Well, Abdullah Amann, for example,' answers Mo.

'Why?'

'He ran in the election for local MP.'

'So, he's a politician. We've lots of those. We can't send them all through,' protests Magda.

'He's a failed politician. He had to deliver his concession speech by midday. He brought disgrace upon the area. He will have to go. Clearly, no one will miss him.'

'Poor Abdul.'

'This is such a success we can't stop now, and that's why I think we can use this to bring the world together.'

'There's one thing we haven't pondered,' says Nelson, who has been sitting quietly, absorbing the conversation.

'What's that?'

'What if all this weird shit has been sent from the past, they're just passing it on?' Nelson asks.

The council members all looked around at each other before Mo, rising from the table, gavel in hand, solemnly declared: 'Then it is our duty to do likewise. Let's stick two fingers up to the past and send it all to the future. All those in favour, say aye. Aye.'

'Nay.'

'Abstain.'

'Aye.'

'The *ayes* have it.'

# 48. Fading

'So, Serena, another day of worship?' asked Vijay as they sat around after dinner one night. Dinner that night had been lasagne, and the children had been sent to bed. Vijay lit a cigarette, and the smoke floated up to the light fitting.

'Another day of giving thanks, Vijay. We have to give thanks for all we have and pray for the safety of our loved ones.'

'We understand,' he replied airily.

'Do you?' Serena asked.

Seeva took a deep breath. 'Serena, he's just trying to make conversation with you.' They were tense and apprehensive after the exchange of words the previous night between Serena and Vijay.

'No, he's not,' replied Serena.

'You're taking it the wrong way,' insisted Seeva.

'Seeva, I can speak for myself,' interrupted Vijay. 'Do you think this is fun?' he continued, returning his attention to

Serena. 'I just find it confusing. I just find it confusing, Serena, that you don't just stick with one religion. You go to all of them. You go to temples, the Christian churches, Catholic, Methodist, Presbyterian.'

'The message is still the same. Be good, treat your neighbours with respect, be open to others,' explained Serena pointedly.

'I'm open to you Serena, that's why you and Dev have been here. Our house is your house. I'm just trying to say you might want to give it a break. How long are you going to keep this up? I know it's comforting, but you need to snap out of it and face the world.'

'Really? And what would you know about that?'

'Well, I know Dev has to go to school. How long has it been now that you've been on the run?'

'We're not on the run, and he's fine. I'm looking after him.'

'This isn't looking after him.'

'What do you know about what I've been through? What do you know about me and my children?' Serena asked, her voice rising.

'Serena!' gasped Seeva, disappointed in her sister.

'Yes, well, losing a child doesn't make you holier than us. God won't solve your problems. That's down to you,' snapped Vijay.

'Vijay! Both of you stop before you go too far. Serena, if Vijay says our home is open to you, then he means it, but you have to admit you need to give it a break. You didn't believe in any of this stuff before. We weren't brought up with all that. What happened to Amina wasn't because you didn't go to every church and temple every day. You can't carry on living your life like this.' Seeva didn't like conflict, but she was glad for it in this instance. She was convinced that something had to happen to give Serena the jolt she needed.

'Prayers are beautiful,' explained Serena. 'They're clear. If you read, you'll see it's true. Everything becomes simple. Praying is like,' Serena looked away and thought for a moment. 'Praying is like clear running water. Prayers are a stream.'

'Praying is a stream. Praying is a stream? I don't understand,' admitted Vijay.

'I can see that.'

'When you talk like this, do you think you mean something? What are you trying to prove? Do you think it's healthy?' he asked, pursuing her.

'What do you want her to say, Vijay?' asked Seeva, exasperated.

'It's not healthy. Not healthy for you, not healthy for your child. It's not healthy for us.'

'Vijay!' snapped his wife.

'No, let's be honest. What is happening here? What have you been doing? What will you do? Is there any end to this? What's the plan? What about Raju? He has the right to see his child. You can't just take Dev away from him. What is going through your mind? You need to pull yourself together.'

The barrage of questions was more than Serena could contend with. 'It's simpler this way,' was all she could manage.

'It's hardly simple when you're dragging a small boy across the world with no hint of a plan. He needs school. You can't just drag him from one church to another all day, every day.

Well?' demanded Vijay.

'Well, what, Vijay?' asked Seeva. 'What do you want her to say? Don't keep pushing her.'

'I want her to have answers. She's a mother. She has to act like it. I want her to be a mother to that boy.'

'She *is* being my mother,' said a little voice at the door.

'Oh,' said Vijay, spinning around in his chair.

Having listened for long enough out of sight at the foot of the staircase, Dev finally spoke up at the kitchen door. 'She looks after me. She *is* my mum,' he defended. 'Are you going to change your religion, Mum? Are you going to make me change?'

'Come here,' said Serena quietly, and Dev ran to his mother's open arms without hesitation. The flood of reproach overwhelmed her as she had her face rubbed in how she was failing another of her children.

Vijay was concerned that she wasn't fulfilling her obligations as a mother. He had lost sight that she was also a person who was struggling. As her sister and nephew embraced, Seeva felt vindicated and hoped that having invoked a conflict, a change in Serena's thinking would follow. Serena cried out as she grabbed her boy tightly to her, and the pent up emotions spilt over.

'I didn't see him there,' said Vijay, in lieu of an apology.

'What shall we do, eh?' asked Serena, her chin nuzzled in Dev's hair.

'Maybe we should go and see Dad,' replied Dev, glad for the opportunity to tell his mother what he wanted.

A week later, Serena and Dev took another flight.

By the time Serena announced to Dev that they were to leave Canada, it was clear that her siblings were running out of patience with her. Sachin called to check on her and joined Seeva in urging Serena towards a positive change that would give her life direction. Together they encouraged her to see that Dev needed to get back to school and that she needed to resolve things with Raju, one way or the other. Eventually, Serena took their advice and conceded that she needed to do something different.

At Winnipeg's international airport, Serena and Dev queued silently to check in for their flight. Serena could have rented a small place for them both. In Mauritius, in Canada, wherever. That wasn't the point for her, even if she hadn't known it at the time. Serena wanted to be with family, but she didn't know how to be with them anymore. Serena no longer knew how to accept their love and hadn't been easy to live with. She knew all this, but that didn't make it any easier to change her behaviour.

Still living in the moment of Amina's death, she continued to grow angry at the suggestion of returning to England. Subconsciously she knew she would have to return, but her stubborn streak dictated that if she had to go, it would be on her terms, according to her schedule. This is what prompted Serena to take Dev to visit her other sister, Saarika, in Marseille.

As far as Dev was concerned, they were getting closer and closer to his father the more they travelled, and that was a good thing.

As far as Serena was concerned, they were close enough to England that Raju could visit them and begin laying the groundwork for their return.

As far as Saarika was concerned, Serena would help with the rent due for her apartment.

To Serena, it felt good to be back in France. The cool air there was more polluted, lending it more character than bland Winnipeg. It wasn't as oppressive as it was there and not as claustrophobic as the stifling heat of Mauritius. Despite the near-constant odour of cigarettes that hung over the people, Serena felt she could breathe.

To Dev, Marseille was crowded, busy and noisy, almost the antithesis of Vijay and Seeva's sullen suburban neighbourhood, and he loved it. This vibrant city seemed so full of life and bustle. Later, on a return visit as an adult, Dr. Sharma wondered if it had only seemed that way after the two months with Abigail, who had appeared to suck the life out of everything.

With its fishmongers bellowing at the tops of their lungs and the market stalls resplendent with fresh produce, Dev was reminded of Mauritius, and for the first time since he had left the country, he thought of the various things that made it special. The food; the colours; the smell of burning wood on the air; the filao trees that lined the beaches; the rustling of the sugar cane… The things he had taken for granted or simply hadn't had time to consider while he was there. As much as he loved the port city of Marseille, with its salty sea air, he began to miss Mauritius.

Serena did indeed help with the rent for Saarika's tiny apartment near the university Serena used to attend. It was while visiting Serena here years ago that Saarika had met Manu, the man who would become her husband. Serena had completed her degree in Marseille before marrying Raju and moving to England. Saarika, by then married to Manu, had remained in Marseille, where they lived for some years before concluding that their marriage had run its course.

Saarika lived in a single bedroom apartment where she seethed at her options. Or her perceived lack thereof. Having no formal qualifications, after her divorce Saarika had resorted to making ends meet by doing odd jobs for the university, everything from cleaning work to light admin tasks. Divorced and with her family scattered around the world, Saarika had no one in Marseille to rely upon. She had wanted to empathise with Serena after the loss of Amina, but it was a challenge to see through the mist of her own unhappiness. Instead, it became common for the sisters to bicker and argue in Creole.

From their arguments Dev had managed to gather that Manu had been an abusive husband. Saarika blamed, or wanted to blame, Serena for her marriage to him in the first place.

'You were the smart one,' Saarika would wail. 'You should have known what he was like.'

'You were the one marrying him,' Serena would retort. '*You* should have known.'

The shouting matches didn't bother Dev that much. In fact, he was pleased to see his mother's old fight return as she began to leave the semi-conscious state that had first taken possession of her in Mauritius. What he found tricky was Auntie Saarika's daily-changing attitude.

Each morning after her shower, Saarika would leave the apartment with Serena and Dev before parting ways. She would continue to the Aix-Marseille University, leaving Serena and Dev to explore another part of the large city. Serena and Dev to explore another part of the large city. Unlike the churches near Seeva's home in Canada, constructed from sterile designs with clean lines and finished with smooth walls, Marseille was full of centuries-old churches built from aged, uneven stone. Churches of all denominations were the pillars of this city, and Serena was still keen to explore them all and bask in the solid and reliable silence they offered.

Each evening they would all converge upon the apartment where Serena would prepare dinner for the three of them. Depending on the previous night's words, Auntie Saarika would return contrite for her behaviour or in the mood for another round of recriminations. One day she would be happy to find the pair cooking when she returned from work, glad to return home to company. The next day she would be spoiling for a fight.

'I just don't understand how you could leave. Was it his fault?'

'That's not the point, Saarika.'

'Yes, it is. Raju must be as devastated as you, but he didn't go across the world, did he.'

'He didn't do anything. *That's* the point.'

'What did you want him to do? It was an accident. Did you want him to go out and kill someone? Who? There was no one to blame.'

'You don't understand.'

'All this jetting around, and you're here with me, back here again, where it all started.'

'Where what started?'

'Me, you, Manu and Raju. This city, it's like a magnet that sucks in the desperate. No matter where they are in the world, they end up in Marseille. The desperate.'

'I know where this is going.'

'That's because you know everything. That's why we had to come to visit you while you were at university, to see how well *you* were doing. You didn't know enough to keep me away from Manu.'

'Saarika, you weren't my daughter. You were a grown woman. How could I keep you away from anyone?'

'You should have known, Serena. You're my big sister. You should have looked out for me. You should have cared more.'

This is where Serena would lose all control, and the two sisters would really tear into one another.

Serena and Dev had been in Marseille for a month before Serena finally allowed Raju to visit for another reunion. She finally felt ready to bring her and Dev's self-imposed exile to a close. After a day together as a family again, they left Dev in the care of Auntie Saarika and headed out, just the two of them, to talk privately. Dev had no idea what had been said during their evening out, but it had had an effect on Serena. Perhaps nothing new had been said, but she had been more receptive to his words.

Raju visited for three days, staying at a nearby bed and breakfast, and at the end of that time, he promised Dev that he would be back soon. He watched his mother smile genuinely as she kissed Raju goodbye at the train station.

As an adult reflecting on this episode, Dr. Sharma realised that they had had to reconnect as people before they could reconnect as a married couple, beginning to find a way to address their grief together. With his father leaving on an altogether brighter note, Dev had hope that they would soon be reunited permanently.

But what he hadn't realised at that young age was that things would never be as they were before Amina's passing. The death of a child is something their parents never truly recover from. While they might regroup to live together as a family, each would have lost something that made them who they were. But each parent also gains something else, whether they realise it or not.

For Dev, the self-imposed burden of carrying all the hopes and aspirations they had had for Amina was just beginning.

# 49. Same, but different

Two years away from home is a long time in the life of a thirteen-year-old, and Dev appraised everything with new eyes that found everything familiar yet foreign at the same time. Certainly, the motorway from the airport was typically anonymous, striking him as neither familiar nor strange. However, the neighbourhood around the house was old and new in equal measure.

He thought he could remember number 140 having a different coloured gate. *Wasn't there a letterbox on the end of that road before?* To Dev's delight, nothing much had changed about their house, and as he approached, he saw that the paint on the little red gate was just as faded and flaky as ever. The front garden was still overgrown into a higgledy mess of thorny bushes. He loved it. He was home.

Dev stood at the front door and pushed Raju's key into the lock before twisting it and pushing the door. It took a moment, but it hit him: the scent of home. Inside the house, Amina's absence once again hit Dev in a way that he hadn't felt for some time.

Unlike Dev, Serena had anticipated this and had talked to him about it on the short plane journey. 'Things aren't going to be the same. They'll be different.'

'How?' asked Dev.

'Well, you'll go to a different school, one for older children.'

'But it'll be all of us, at home?'

'The three of us.'

While his parents struggled with luggage, he gingerly stepped into the house and re-acquainted himself with the patterned carpet beneath his feet as he walked through the hall. Dragging his fingertips along the textured wallpaper, with its old-fashioned velvety fuzz that invited contact, Dev was surprised to no longer feel the compulsion to step between the flowers. Once again, he took in the familiar, old scent of home and breathed deeply.

It felt good to have both his parents back together. Despite the last two years, Dev still needed the confidence that having his father could only make things better. He knew his parents weren't sharing a room yet, but that didn't concern him. What did concern him was the return to school the following week. It hadn't been so long since he last underwent a school test to determine at which level he should be placed for different subjects, but here there was no chance that he would be removed at the last minute by his mother.

Raju had been firm that Serena had to let go of Dev. She knew she had to, but that didn't mean it was any less difficult for her. She was silent as Dev came down the stairs on

Monday morning, dressed in his new school uniform. Black trousers. White shirt. The black, green and red tie, purchased directly from the school. Black v-neck jumper. Black shoes.

Serena knew he would be dressed that way when he came down for breakfast but was still startled at seeing him. So much black. So funereal. After two years of wearing whatever he liked at school in Mauritius, it was a shock to see him shorn of colour in a uniform that blended in. He looked grown-up, in a way that she hadn't anticipated, in the same school colours that Amina had worn that day that she had sat on Serena's bed.

Dev and Serena would never really speak to each other about their time together in Mauritius. The time they had spent there had been so different and had changed the way Dev saw his mother so profoundly that he couldn't remember the way he used to be around her, the way she was before Amina's death, the way he used to see her.

Dev observed his mother and tried to compare and contrast the way things used to be, the way his mother used to be before Mauritius. The most immediate change he noticed was that she no longer visited temples or churches. Admittedly there weren't any temples around where they lived, but there were plenty of churches. His mother seemed to have abandoned the entire enterprise overnight.

Back in the UK, Dev realised that finally, away from all her family, she could be his mother again. But then it also dawned on him that she had also been balancing being a mother with being a daughter and a sister for the last few years. Digesting this, Dev came to the logical realisation that she could now focus on being a mother and a wife again, but that she was not only those things.

She was a mother, a wife, a daughter, a sister, an aunt, a cousin, in addition to being a person with spontaneous thoughts, feelings and ideas that weren't always fully thought out and may not go entirely according to plan. He was not a perfect person. Neither was she.

'Do you need me to walk with you?' asked Serena.

'That's okay, Mum.' As Dev finished the last of his cereal, he mulled over what his first day back at school would be like. He mused that it was an opportunity to be anyone he wanted since no one there would know him or about Amina. He could be a classroom troublemaker. He could sign up for all the sports teams. He could be anyone else.

'Okay. Take care and come straight home afterwards. *Straight* home.'

'Okay, Mum. Bye,' he said, his heart feeling heavy in his chest as he gave Serena's soft face a kiss before leaving.

Dev slung his new backpack over his shoulder before setting off through the back door and making his way down the road. The whole while, Serena watched his progress through the window until she could no longer see him, the tears finally rolling.

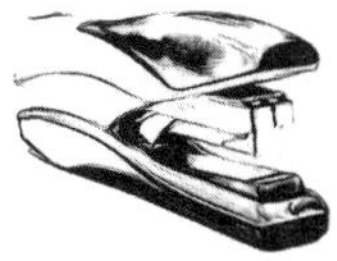

Serena began her job search the same week that Dev returned to school. After her time away from the workplace, she was relegated to seeking more junior positions than she had held. But Raju was pleased for her, eager for her to begin the journey back to being the woman he had married. Raju knew they would never be the people they were before Amina's death, but he didn't want her to continue being the scared and angry stranger she had been before leaving with Dev.

After the events of the past years, Serena knew the return to work would be difficult, particularly when people would inevitably ask what she had been doing for two years. As a woman, they would voice their assumption that she had been pregnant. A thought that would once have left her feeling bitter, but that now only left her hollow. The only consolation was that it would be a fresh start with new colleagues who wouldn't necessarily know her recent history. She hoped that she wouldn't encounter anyone there that she knew.

For both Dev and Serena, the adjustment was difficult. Not only was the change of pace something for them to reckon with, but there was also the unavoidable necessity to meet new people. Serena knew that she would once again be exposed to the petty squabbles and inane chatter that passed for office conversations. Serena and Raju had already had their own little chat on the topic.

'How do I get through this, Raju?'

'I know it's going to be difficult, but….' Here Raju took a pause, for he had learnt from previous incidents that the following words should be handled with care. 'You need to move on with your life. This is a small step in that direction.'

'But I don't know if I can deal with… you know?'

'You've been through a lot. We all have. But we need to keep going and show Dev how to push through the hard times and not give up looking for a better life. That's what we left Mauritius for.'

'I know, but… it just seemed so pointless, all of it. Sometimes it still feels that way. It all seems pointless.'

'The hardest step has got to be the first one. Make a start, and it will get better. It will get easier.'

Serena loathed taking advice from her husband, but these were the words she kept in mind throughout her first few weeks at her new job. As the months went by, Serena and Raju would reconnect with their old friends, and a new type of normality emerged as a routine evolved.

For Dev's first day at school, he was almost as big an oddity to the other children as he had been in Mauritius. There he had piqued everyone's interest as someone who looked like them but didn't sound like them. They found him amusing because he was only just beginning to learn what they had studied for years. They knew more than he did... until he surpassed them.

In England it soon became known to the other children that he had come to them from his last school in a foreign land called *Mor-ee-shuss*. Dev sounded like them but didn't look like them. More importantly, he didn't share their cultural touchstones of the last few years. Just like that time-travelling dog who skips over a minute to arrive at a new point in time, from Dev's favourite film, *Back To The Future*, itself a dated reference that was no longer relevant to the children around him.

Each classroom he went to that day saw him stand with his back to the whiteboard at the front of the class to introduce himself. Some of the children who had already heard his introduction from a previous class preempted him by raucously shouting out: "mor-ee-shuss-mor-ee-shuss-mor-ee-shuss!" to cackles and the general laughter of the room.

'Mauritius,' enunciated Dev. He felt he was telling everyone where he had last gone to school for their amusement, standing to be judged by a roomful of unruly animals. He didn't remember school being like this in England before he had left. Certainly, in Mauritius, it had been very different. The teachers there had complete control over the classroom, and barely a word was spoken without their permission.

Here, at secondary school, there seemed to be no respect at all for anything the teachers had to say. Feeling all their snickering eyes on him, Dev tried to see himself the way they saw him.

'Mauritius?' repeated the teacher distractedly, after half-heartedly shushing the rest of the class. She felt the class would go better if she let them get the ridicule out of their systems. 'What are you doing here? I mean, it's supposed to be paradise. What was the name of the town where you lived there?'

'Rose Hill,' Dev muttered the name of a nearby town, predicting that *Beau Bassin* would only lead to further ridicule. To his surprise, even this elicited big laughs from the children.

Apparently, the idea that a town could be called Rose Hill was absurd to them. Place names such as Bognor, Milton Keynes and Cholmondeley made much more sense. What Dev had not realised was that they would mock any answer he gave to any question. For he was the new outsider. Not only was he one of only a handful of non-white children at the school, but he also came from somewhere entirely different and not somewhere they felt held any value.

As far as they were concerned he *came from* Mauritius, despite Dev's feelings that that was not the case. He had been born in England and had lived there until he was ten. Having spent the two years roaming around, he had returned, expecting it to be relatively easier to slot back into his old life in England than it had been to create a new one in Mauritius.

In Mauritius, Dev looked like everybody else, but he sounded nothing like them, with his English accent, and his life had been nothing like that of the average Mauritian child.

Back in England, Dev may have sounded like the rest of the children, but they couldn't relate to any of his experiences over the last few years. Dev quickly felt marooned, and in that first week of school, he unknowingly sealed the perception that everybody had of him by inevitably giving the wrong answers about the things that apparently mattered most to them.

No, he didn't play football, neither did he support a particular team. No, he couldn't tell them the make and model of their car because they didn't have one. His father had sold the car in his mother's prolonged absence as he didn't like to drive. Yes, he watched TV. No, he didn't know of any of the shows that were popular in the UK. Too late, he learnt the correct answer was: "yeah, I like *Fast Show* and *The Red Dwarf*." Or was it *The Fast Show* and *Red Dwarf*? Still, he did his best to use his skills developed in Mauritius to memorise and regurgitate the right answers.

As an adult, Dr. Sharma could think of nothing that should have mattered less, but at the time, for Dev, as with any child that age, acceptance was everything. During his first few weeks back at school, he often simply couldn't give a genuine answer as to, for example, his favourite music or video games. They were considered frivolities and disregarded in Mauritius, where family, studies and exams were all that mattered. Dev hadn't anticipated how much importance and status these children attached to such things. He hadn't understood these were the cultural foundations they used to find affinity with others.

Such things added up to the final unwritten, unannounced, but universally held assessment of how relevant he was. Their silent judgements lay beneath the surface of what was said, and Dev could sense their feeling of superiority without hearing it.

With these children having had the three years of their lives so different from his, he once again found himself playing catch-up. He had missed a lot of what gave them the thoughts, ideas and values they had, and again he was left to decipher the secret code from the daily trail of evidence he would analyse.

Why was his surname so funny that children would shout it out to break up the boredom of a dull class: 'Sha-rrr-maaah'? Or better yet they would simply answer, "Mauritius" in an affected Indian accent to any question the teacher might ask the class, thus breaking up any momentum the lesson had gathered.

'Michael! Square root of forty-nine?'

'*Mauritius*!'

Passing the wrong bunch of teenagers in the corridor, they would begin shouting his surname at Dev and performing an improvised version of the *Haka*, the Maori war dance that they had seen on TV, performed by the New Zealand rugby team. *That doesn't even make sense*, Dev would think.

Round and round went Dev's mind trying to figure out what he was, according to them. The exaggerated Indian accent, which he didn't have. The Maori war dance, that wasn't Mauritian. The anticipation of his surname being used as a punch-line to a joke that didn't exist, even if it was at the end of the lesson, as they filed out of the room. All these left Dev emotionally exhausted by school. But on the bright side, he at least no longer had so much homework or any after-school tuition.

Weeks turned into months of this claustrophobic atmosphere rippling in the background. To Dev, it was toxic. To his fellow pupils, it was a pastime to break up the boredom of school.

In Mauritius, he had also been treated as the outsider,

sometimes spoken about by family as though he was not there or didn't understand. Some Mauritians mocked him speaking French, or Creole, in his English accent by parodying him, while others simply fixed him with a smirk and called him *Anglais potis*.

Who was he? What was he? What label was his? To whom did he belong? All pressing questions for a thirteen-year-old unsure about their identity.

While these incidents had not occurred often in Mauritius and had usually been meant affectionately, they had been regular enough to make Dev aware that he would never be truly accepted as a Mauritian, and of his consequent insignificance there as a person.

Three months into secondary school in England, the attention Dev endured still showed no signs of abating. One day his French teacher announced that they were taking a deviation from the typical flow of lessons and dedicating the hour to: *Racism in School and the Community*. In fact, it turned out that the entirety of year nine was going through the same topic at the same time with their respective teachers.

Dev couldn't help but feel it was to do with him. It wasn't, but it felt like it as he stared down at the surface of his desk and felt the gaze of the thirty-eight other eyeballs in the room descend upon him. He knew it would only make things worse.

Dev wanted more than anything to have one of Amina's stories to cling to. Desperate to escape to another world for a while, he wanted to conjure up something like she would. However, he was getting older, and his new teachers had told him that he would make better progress if he spent less time daydreaming.

The time had arrived to face his immediate reality without disappearing into stories, daydreams and fantasies. He couldn't conjure up Amina's stories anymore. He had to put her aside and forget about her *Fanciful Tales*. It was clear that his mother was adapting to life in the UK again, leaving behind her need for temples and churches. He also needed to leave things behind. To make progress.

Dev came to lean more heavily on his analytical tendencies once he relinquished Amina's stories.

What he was experiencing wasn't direct, overt racism, but it was somewhere there, seething beneath the surface. At the most benign, one could call it banter. At worst, it was racist bullying. Besides, he had concluded some time ago that it was only five per cent about race. The other ninety-five per cent was about place. These children weren't so much racist as they were *placist*.

The realisation had dawned upon Dev one lunchtime when he had been wandering the edges of the playground. Usually, after his sandwich, he would read a book in the library, but he decided to venture outside for some fresh air on that sunny day. As he munched his apple, Dev spotted the chief perpetrators of his daily challenges across the playground playing basketball on the tarmaced makeshift court (which was also the makeshift tennis court, makeshift hockey surface, makeshift football pitch and so on). Nothing strange about that, except they were playing with Deepak, one of only two other Asians in year nine. They all seemed to be friends on the pitch, working together to score points against opponents. Losing the ball. Attempting ridiculous shots beyond their abilities. Trying. Laughing.

Later that afternoon, during history, Dev analysed this new data he had collected.

Deepak was not at all an academic type, being in pretty much the lowest-ability classes for everything. The one thing at school at which he seemed to excel was lunchtime basketball. Dev, by contrast, was in the top classes, or near the top, for almost everything.

As far as Dev could see, Deepak had grown up amongst these other children and shared their tastes and preferences for different media offerings. He also had an up-to-the-minute cultural framework within which to place these media. Meanwhile, Dev was juggling snapped-off pieces of memories from three years ago, and still wondering what became of *Bros*.

Whilst probably not sharing the exact same kind of home life with the other children with whom he played basketball, Deepak would have a more similar cultural experience by having not spent over two years abroad.

*Therefore*, Dev concluded to himself, *it's not so much about my race. It's about my place. I have been in the wrong place at the wrong time, and now, even though culturally I'm more English than Mauritian, as far as they're concerned, I'm not English enough to be accepted the way Deepak is.*

Or maybe he wasn't sporty enough. Or too bookish. Or all of the above. In any case, it was a swift turnaround to go from being *fake English* in Mauritius to having "mor-ee-shuss!" shouted at him in a hideously exaggerated Indian accent as a slacker version of the *Haka* was performed for his benefit, while others looked on, disapproving but silent. Occasionally Dev wondered who should be more offended, himself or the Maori.

The shouting echoed around corridors lined with grey, metal lockers.

The shouting echoed around the half-built house.

No parent wants to think of their child as the one on the outside looking in. If that turns out to be the case, they reserve the right to believe something else.

Consciously or not, Dev had disregarded the behaviour of his parents over the past three years. But it all hit him at once. All these flags that had lain dormant now sprang up, screaming red. He watched his mother and father silently scramble to tie together the threads of their family life, fixing the stretched fabric with strained, unnatural politeness. But, preoccupied with their own concerns, they didn't see Dev, who decided to keep his thoughts to himself.

They still just saw the small boy that had left for Mauritius. Aged thirteen, Dev wondered how the signs had eluded him. Those red flags signalled they had no idea what Serena and Raju were doing. And that he could no longer trust them because they weren't people he knew anymore.

Even years later, long after the household had regained cohesion, Dev could not bring himself to place his faith once more in Serena and Raju. The lookouts armed, the drawbridge raised, Dev would never trust them enough to let them, or anyone, become close to him again. Anytime he appeared close to someone, it was all surface. An act.

At that young age, he knew there would always be a distance between himself and others. He was aware that a hardness had crept through his veins that would allow him to drop seemingly firm friends in a heartbeat without looking back, if appropriate. Something he had learned before leaving for Mauritius would become second nature to him. Years later, he would become a good friend to others, and they to him, but he would always retain the ability to easily disappear.

Serena and Raju, perhaps they believed, like most parents do, that their child was bound to be liked wherever he went. Able to slip gracefully from one tribe to another, effortlessly adopting mannerisms and foibles that would ease their passage into good graces. Or with enough force of personality to have people seeking them.

Was that how they thought Dev would evolve and make himself part of whatever tribe he found himself in? That location and culture would prove no object? As an informed adult, that is less of an issue. As an anxious ten-year-old with a nervous tic, he had been out of his depth. Even more so as an anxious and awkward thirteen-year-old returning to England from time spent in three other countries, still trying to grieve his sister.

# 50. All I have to do

Cheers of joy and encouragement as the band reaches the stage at the festival.

Dancing

Jumping

Sweating

Gasping

The afternoon. Such a warm day. Inhaling each other, Dev and Rachel fucked in the tent.

Kissing

Smiling

Giggling

Trying not to make any noise. Their friends, outside the tent. Sitting on the ground or on their camping chairs by their tents. Close by Dev and Rachel's.

As he pushed into her, her head over the edge of the inflatable mattress, Dev and Rachel could hear Ffion mocking Jenny about her lunch: a banana dipped into a tin of custard. 'At least I'm getting two of my five-a-day,' they could hear Jenny say.

'How are you getting *two*?' asked someone else.

'Banana,' answered Jenny.

'Yeah.'

'And, think about it. Custard. It's got vanilla in it. Surely vanilla has to be one of your five-a-day, right?' responded Jenny, matter-of-factly. The rest of them laughed. Meanwhile, Nate moaned about having forgotten his hat but was apparently pleased he had brought sunscreen. A few moments later, the plastic top popped off, and the spray went into action.

All the distractions were getting to Dev, who was finding it hard to concentrate. Nate was moaning again that he couldn't angle the bottle correctly to coat the back of his shaved head with the spray. Would someone help?

As usual, Dev made sure to pull out in time and leaned back onto his knees, in doing so displacing the air in the inflatable mattress and making Rachel's breasts bounce about some more. Under the dim light afforded by a wind-up torch in the cramped tent, Dev's semen dripped onto her skin and met Rachel's sweat on the gentle curve of her stomach.

After the overwhelming lust of the moment had been satisfied, to them both, it suddenly felt foolish to have been doing any of this since it wouldn't be until the next day that they would see a shower. Until then, they would be wearing the traces of each other's bodily fluids, despite the wet wipes they had brought. They had planned a bus trip from the festival campsite into the town centre for the next day, where they would shower at the local pool and take a cool dip.

Dev lay back on his side of the mattress and laid his palm on Rachel's bare hip for a few moments before pulling his hand back. It was just far too warm for non-essential bodily contact. Instead, he put his hand under his head as a makeshift pillow and shut his eyes.

The heat is all-consuming, but Dev is too exhausted to move from the tent and seek out the fresh air outside. Instead, he breathes in and out. In and out. Deeper and deeper, he sucks in the oxygen. A strange feeling overcomes him. A physical change is occurring within him. Dev can feel pressure against his ribs. From the inside! He looks over to Rachel, but she has drifted to sleep.

Dev tries to regulate his breathing, but to no avail, his body demands more oxygen, and so he obeys and feeds it, sucking at the air, his lungs straining with the effort, straining at his ribcage! His eyes widening and watering, it isn't long before his lungs outgrow the space afforded by his ribs and force them apart!

On both sides of Dev's body, the bones crack and snap, the jagged shards piercing his skin, forcing slits in his sides, out of which his lungs bubble out, seeking space to roam. Dev's right lung tumbles over the side of the air mattress and balloons against the side of the tent. Meanwhile, his left lung tumbles out onto Rachel, who immediately awakes with a start and tries to scream, but she is engulfed by the giant organ as it smothers her with muscle, tissue and fluids, crushing her under its weight.

It is only seconds before the air inside the tent proves insubstantial to feed the demand and the force generated by Dev's inhalations. Slowly a tiny tear in the tent's material appears, but it soon develops into a gaping hole to the outside world. Dev expects his friends to wonder what is happening inside the bulging tent, but he sees no one. Panicked, Dev calls: 'Hello? Anyone out there? I… I'm in trouble. I'm not feeling well….'

'You're not actually ill,' says one doctor she cannot see.

'So what's wrong with me? I feel scared,' comes the reply. A woman's voice.

'A lot of people are scared, but we can't help that right now. You're just going to have to go home and try to get through this on your own. I'm sorry.'

'There's nothing more you can do?' asks the woman.

'I wish there was. I can give you a prescription, something to relax you.'

'That's it? Can I talk to someone?'

'I know what you mean, but we just don't have the resources.'

'I can't,' the woman persists, fear slipping into her voice.

'Well, you have to,' comes the doctor's reply, firmer this time. 'You can't keep coming in here all the time. There are other people with things seriously wrong with them who actually need treatment. Medical treatment.'

'I have things wrong. I need treatment.'

'I know. I'm sorry, it came out wrong. We don't have anyone left for you to see here at the hospital, but I'm sure you can pay to see someone.'

'You mean a therapist? Do you know how much that would cost?'

'Yeah, and the way things are going, I can't guarantee they wouldn't turn into a pumpkin, or something, halfway through your session.'

'Is that actually happening? This pumpkin thing?'

'No, sorry, that was a bad joke in the circumstances,' replied the doctor.

'This isn't the time for jokes!'

'Sorry, I'm not a counsellor, I'm a doctor, a junior doctor, and they didn't exactly train us for this. I'm trying to get through all these people that I can't help. So I am going to write you a prescription for some pills, hoping they don't explode into woodlice or something and set you on your way so I can continue not giving people what they need.'

'What if things change? What if I get worse?'

'Then call the cops and let them deal with you because we can't help,' replies the doctor, ripping the sheet from her pad and pressing it into the woman's hand. 'Goodbye, good luck. Okay. Next! Popov, Larissa.' The curtain is yanked back harshly to reveal the familiar image of the junior doctor in her dark blue scrubs. 'Didn't expect to see *you* again.'

'You thought I'd be dead by now?' asks Larissa.

'Unlike these others, you seemed fairly stable,' she says, adjusting the curtain behind her for privacy. 'Thought our little chat would have made sense to you. You're still self-harming and still ending up here, but you went upstairs to surgery first. Paramedics initially thought you were a lot worse.'

'They must have made a mistake.'

'Another mistake. With the same patient. Three times in two weeks. I know the health service isn't what it used to be. What is? But that's still extreme.' The doctor takes a moment and leans on the table over the foot of the bed. 'I don't know what's going on with you. You were found on the ground outside the hospital bleeding from an apparently self-inflicted stomach wound.'

'Really?' asks Larissa.

'That's what it says here,' she explains, waving a clipboard in Larissa's face as a lock of blonde hair, lank with sweat, tumbles into her face. 'And that's what it has said the last two times. Each time, by the time they get to work on you, your wound doesn't seem so bad.'

'You should be happy.'

'Oh, I'm thrilled. If this is a new thing, people self-healing, then I couldn't be happier, but how are you ending up with wounds in the first place? Is it self-harm? Stabbing yourself in the stomach is extreme, even for that.'

'What?'

'Look, there's a lot of weird stuff going on and, as far as I'm concerned, the rulebook, the Hippocratic oath, they no longer apply, and I need to save time. So I'll be candid. Are you self-harming and then self-healing? Are you pushing it, trying to see how far you can go before you kill yourself?' asks the doctor.

'No.'

'Then what's going on?'

'I don't know,' admits Larissa.

'I think you need to be studied.'

'I think I ought to be leaving now.'

'Oh, are you all healed up now?'

'I have stuff to do.'

'We can't help you if we don't know what's going on.'

'You can't help me anyway.'

Outside, the air is fresh, and Larissa gorges herself. It makes a refreshing change from the stale, warm atmosphere of the hospital. She feels free again.

The taxi slows to a halt, and Larissa winces a little as she slides into the back seat.

'Where to?' asks the driver through his chewing gum.

'Home,' replies Larissa simply.

The car pulls away from the kerb, leaving the hospital in the rear-view mirror and a flurry of exhaust fumes on the cold air. Before long, they are at some traffic lights faithfully recreating a Rolling Stones classic.

'You want to talk about it?' asks the driver.

'No,' comes the inevitable answer from the back seat.

'We're going to go on like this? For how long?'

'For as long as it takes.'

'What if something goes wrong.'

'It won't.'

'How do you know?'

'I'm still healing.'

The lights change to green as their proponents segue into Vladimir Vysotsky's *Song About A Friend.*

'What would I do if something went wrong?' continues the driver.

'Drive away, live your life. I've paid for your time. You know where to find it.'

'It's not about that. Do you think I would have got into this if you'd told me what we'd be doing?'

'That's why I didn't tell you.'

'So you know it's not about the money.'

'Nothing is about money anymore.'

Larissa is no longer listening. Instead, she examines the dressing on her abdomen.

Later that evening, at her apartment, Larissa sits on her bed and unzips her snug jacket. Wriggling out of the garment, Larissa thinks she can feel stiffness in her joints. *Impossible, she thinks, I haven't felt this good since I played volleyball at college.*

Yet as she removes her vest, she feels the same ache. *Must be psychosomatic. After everything, my brain is expecting pain.* Larissa lies back on her bed and finally allows herself a hint of doubt. *Is this the best way? Could I be doing something else? Boris Sokolov. Irina Vasiliev. Yury Balakin. Kiril Babin. Katya Kozlov. Next, Yury Balakin.*

Four days later, Larissa is in a bar near her apartment, nursing a drink, waiting for the driver. When he eventually arrives, he is twenty minutes late.

'I didn't know whether to show up or not,' he explains, by way of apology.

'Yury Balakin.'

'I was hoping you were going to stop.'

'I've started. I can't stop.'

'Yes, you can. You can always stop. Don't be foolish.'

'They can't just get away with it.'

'It won't make any difference.'

'Yes, it will. It has to.'

'Of course, it has to. For *you*. Otherwise, this will have all been for nothing. Right? Listen, do you think this is the best place for this conversation?'

'Yury Balakin,' persists Larissa. 'He's next.'

'Isn't it getting to you? It's been two people so far. That's how many people you've….'

'They had it coming.'

'Okay, but this isn't you. You're not built for this.'

'Apparently, I am.'

'When do you want to do it?'

'As soon as possible. I have a list to get through.'

'You don't need to.'

'This list is the reason I can do what I do. Nothing else matters.'

'You don't remember anything else. There's a difference.'

'I'm not meant for anything else. Someone, or something, willed me into being. This is what I am here for. I know it.'

'And when you get to the end of your list? What will happen to you?'

'Just be ready,' says Larissa, closing the subject.

It is coming up to 7 pm when the driver pulls up outside the apartment block the following evening. Leaving the engine running, he switches off the headlights and waits for Larissa. She is in her now customary position in the back of the car behind the passenger seat, wearing dark blue jeans with her slim-fitting black jacket. She wears her hair tied back in a loose ponytail, topped with a navy blue baseball cap.

This is their third time sitting together like this. Ready. It is the second time the driver has not thought much of her superhero costume. But then, she isn't a superhero. Superheroes don't do this.

A few moments later, Larissa closes the car door behind her, and seemingly in one fluid motion, she moves up the steps leading up to the main entrance. Apartment 21 is a few flights up. Once there, Larissa wastes no time. With a small but sturdy metal chisel produced from inside her jacket, she grinds into the wood and crowbars against the frame. Before long, she is inside the apartment. Yury Balakin's apartment.

The man himself is across town in a small Italian restaurant with his mother. Yury is taking her out for a birthday treat.

'What do you think you'll have?' he asks.

'There are so many different things. What will you have?' asks Mum, looking at him over her reading glasses.

'Paté sounds nice for a starter.'

'Paté? I thought this was an Italian restaurant.'

'It is,' replies Yury.

'Why do they have paté? That's French, isn't it?'

'Maybe they want to diversify.'

'Which paté?' asks Mum.

'What do you mean? There's only one paté.'

'Where is it on the page?'

'Under the starters.'

'I know that.'

'Fourth one down, Mum,' directs Yury.

'Oh, yes.'

Larissa ignores the light switches, opting instead for her pocket torch with a narrow beam. In the cramped hallway, she looks through the mail. Sure enough, it's all addressed to Yury Balakin.

*Definitely, his place* thinks Larissa. *Where he eats. Where he sleeps.* A blur of motion, she silently moves into the bedroom. *Where he washes.* Larissa puts the pocket torch down on the edge of the window sill next to a glass holding a toothbrush. She pulls off a glove and picks up the toothbrush.

Slowly she presses her thumb against the bristles. The brush is still wet. Larissa replaces the toothbrush and rubs away the moisture left behind between her thumb and index finger before replacing her glove. In the dim light, she looks up and catches a glimpse of herself in the bathroom mirror above the sink. It's only a moment, then Larissa snatches up the torch and moves on to the next room.

Thankfully for Larissa, it is a small, one-bedroom apartment and the things she needs are easy to locate. In the bedroom, Larissa finds the laundry hamper with clothes. Yury Balakin's scent. Her gloved hands pull a dark coloured T-shirt, with an orange dragon motif on the front, from the tumble of fabrics.

The design is unfamiliar to Larissa, but that isn't a surprise. Everything is new to her. Holding the fabric close to her nose, she breathes in deeply, drawing in the scent, focusing all her attention on it, trying not to compare this to any other. Having satisfied herself that this step is completed, Larissa moves on to the bed behind her.

Across the bed, a digital alarm clock sits upon a nightstand casting a brown-red hue upon the wrinkled bed sheets, giving them the appearance of sand dunes. Gingerly, Larissa sits upon the mattress before swinging her legs up onto it, resting her head on the pillow. She clicks off her pocket torch and opens her eyes to what Yury Balakin sees every night before sleep and after waking.

The light from the digital alarm clock.

The peeling paint on the ceiling above.

Suitcase above the wardrobe.

The moon reflected in the wardrobe mirror.

Through the windowpane, the stars outside.

She lies still a while before clicking the torch back on and moving through to the living room, the torchlight fondling the items there. Expressionless, she scans the room before putting the torch away again. The orange glow from a street lamp throws a dim light from a distance through the window.

On a small table in the corner of the room, Larissa finds the answering machine next to the telephone. Her hand hovers for a few moments above the device before she presses the button.

'Hi. This is Yury. Leave your name, number and I'll get back to you.'

Larissa runs it through her mind before pressing the button and listening again.

'Hi. This is Yury. Leave your name, number and I'll get back to you.'

Facing the wall is a desk and a swivel chair that Larissa sits on next. She turns to face the rest of the room. The sofa. The TV. The faux wood floor. The pattern in the net curtain. The light through the window.

Larissa feels her heartbeat quicken.

'Tiramisu?' asks Yury.

'Sounds right. Italian restaurant. Got to have Tiramisu, don't you?' smiles his mum.

'You don't *have* to have it. It's an option. There's also gelato.'

'Is there?'

'Yeah. Can you see, Mum?'

'Of course, I can see! Yes. Ice cream,' replies Mum.

'Seriously. Mum, if you're having trouble with your eyes, we have to look into it.'

'Are you trying to be funny?'

'No, I didn't mean to be funny. It just came out that way. Sorry, Mum.'

Yury feels a pang of guilt as he watches his mother fiddle with the frayed corner of the menu. Whatever will be said next will be difficult to hear. With this, Yury's pulse races.

'Mum, I'm here for you.'

'It doesn't matter, Yury, whatever it is. There is no magic that will be enough.'

'I can help. You're not alone. Your life doesn't have to get worse. We can do things to raise your quality of life.'

'Yury, let's just give it a rest, eh?'

'Okay, Mum.'

Yury looks down to the dessert menu on the table, but he can no longer read it either. His mind focuses on his mother, while his heart beats in fear that this is where he has forever lost her as she was.

He wants to cry.

He wants to be sick.

He feels a lump in his throat, pain in his chest.

A pain in his stomach.

A sudden, sharp attack.

'Aarrgh!' screams Yury. Around the room, cutlery freezes mid-journey, and the murmur of conversation dies away as fellow diners turn to stare at Yury, who grabs at his stomach.

'Yury! Are you okay? What's wrong?' demands Mum.

'Mum, I…' is all Yury manages to get out before the pool of blood that has suddenly formed in his mouth begins to drool from his lips.

'Oh my God!' screams a woman at the next table. 'Can't you see he needs help? Is there a doctor? Somebody get him a doctor. What did he eat? Did I have it?'

The driver listens for the end. It's usually three stabs to her abdomen. Sometimes four. Despite self-healing Larissa still experiences pain upon wounding herself. However, she has opted for a fifth stab on this occasion, surprising the driver, who can only guess why.

Maybe she hadn't wounded herself in the right place and needs that fifth one to finish. Perhaps, whatever he'd done, he deserves one extra. Larissa lets the six-inch blade drop to the plastic covering that the driver has applied to the back seat in her absence.

'You ready?' asks the driver.

'Take me to the hospital, the other one this time,' replies Larissa.

The driver pulls away gently so as not to rock his bleeding passenger in the back seat. After a few moments, he looks in the mirror. 'You okay?'

'Maybe.'

The driver can't stand these silences. Thankfully they come across some traffic lights.

'That was Jackson Gafferty's new one. First new song in, well, who knows how long,' blathered one set of lights.

'Didn't know he was still alive. What did you think of it?' asked the set on the other side of the street.

'First new material in a long time. Anything new from Jackson is welcome, and we will be welcoming the man himself on next week's show. Remember that we want fans to call in and take part in a special fan quiz. Stay tuned for more details after these messages.'

'For the best of yesterday's tunes today, stay tuned.'

'In a relationship? Not in a relationship? Want to be in a

relationship? Just ended a relationship? Either way, our lives are ruled by them. It's good to have certainty, assurance. Get in touch and let our advisors strengthen *all* your connections. Relationship insurance. Because you know that relationships are easier, and dysfunctional relationships are less upsetting if you have something you can trust and hold on to. Contact us for more.'

'How can I succeed?' Larissa asks herself, lying on the gurney. 'Is this what it's going to be like? What I'm going to be like? For how much longer? How long can I go on?'

All around her in the unit, doctors and nurses scurry from one patient to another. The chaos is taking its toll, and hospitals worldwide are struggling to cope with the demands being made upon time and resources. It isn't that the people are busy hurting each other, at least no more than usual, but they are convinced that they are ill and need attention. Larissa can hear the explanations being given to the patients. As a patient herself, she can understand their confusion and suspicion.

As for Dev, all he has is confusion and exhaustion. He is beyond fear, eager for it to end. He is in no mood for visitors. Especially unexpected ones. With the belt around his neck and his continuing struggle against his self-imposed predicament, Dev sweats and lolls. 'Why did you do it?' asks Rooble as he gazes down at Dev, who is still at a loss. He has no idea who is speaking with him and doesn't care what they want. He is in no position to care about anything anymore. 'So, it was your idea of a joke?' continues Rooble.

'What?' Dev finally manages.

'The *stress* you caused. Meanwhile, you're here, doing… whatever you're doing.'

'It wasn't my fault,' comes the croak, finally.

'Then whose?' asks Rooble. 'Why couldn't you just find her for me?'

'I don't know. That's just how it happened.'

'So you have no control at all then?'

'It's just my brain,' answers Dev.

'It's not good enough. Do you understand me? If you want to have a good life, don't you think you should try harder?'

'What?' asks Dev.

'If you don't try your best, how will you get anywhere in life?'

'I'm dying here!' cries Dev.

'That's my point.'

Dev can't take much more of this. He rolls over and Rooble disappears from his field of vision.

# 51. Weapons

It is never an easy decision for a family to take. The institutionalisation of one of their own. Serena had been diagnosed with cancer. It hadn't been identified soon enough, and she had deteriorated quickly.

The mundane conversation about whether to hastily begin treatment, or live a shorter but better quality of life, held little interest for me. It was a typical debate. Dev already knew what lay ahead for Serena, and as a retired medical professional, Raju didn't need him to explain anything. He knew the prognosis. The conversation did not last long.

'Do you understand?' asked Dev, locking eyes with his father as he rotated his coffee mug around and around.

'Yeah. It's just… shock. It's all happened so quickly.' Raju sat on the edge of his armchair, his back having recently become estranged from the backrest. 'A couple of months ago… she was fine. Now we're talking about a hospice.'

'It's for the best, Dad.'

'I know. It's still difficult to reconcile. All the logic is there, it all adds up, but it's a hard thing to….'

'I got her a spot at the best place in the county, Dad.'

'That's good.'

'I… we can't look after her.'

'I know.'

'She's going to need more than we can give her,' continued Dev. Raju nodded slowly at him, pulling on a weak smile he hoped would make Dev stop rationalising. 'I'm sorry, Dad.'

The next day the two men silently began packing Serena's things.

'All this time, Dev,' said his mother. 'All these years, and this is what I have to deal with. Even now, here, I feel I'm slipping away from myself. And still, there's more. More disappointment.'

'It's no one's intention to disappoint you, Mum,' replied Dev, as he looked around the room that Serena was moving into. Each magnolia-painted wall was adorned with at least one print of a landscape, sealed within a pine wood frame. Bland but inoffensive. The home's manager wasn't there, but her assistant had been on hand, as she always was, to ensure the smooth transition of incoming residents.

'Intentions don't matter. Anyone can have intentions. It's what actually happens that matters. Everyone disappoints me. Do I deserve this? A nursing home, at my age?'

'I don't think there's a set age for hospices,' answered Dev falteringly. He and Raju could not give Serena the care she needed, and they had reluctantly decided to get her professional attention. She was mostly lucid, but occasionally she was lost to them. 'Besides Mum,' continued Dev, 'it's not a nursing home. It's a hospice.'

Serena ignored him. 'I left Mauritius for a good education. I had a scholarship to study in France. I was supposed to go back to Mauritius. Instead, I met your father and came to England for his work, but there wasn't a day that I didn't regret not being in Mauritius. Do you know how difficult it was to move completely to another country, permanently?'

'Yeah, Mum, I know,' replied Dev. He hadn't ever

anticipated that things would go like this. Dev wished he could do better and hated seeing his mother like this. He felt helpless watching the decline of his mother, whose inner workings still remained a mystery to him after all these years.

'Oh, you. You had me looking after you. When your father and I moved, we had no one here to look in on us. It was more difficult for us. You were a child. It was easy for you. Anyway, you moved to Mauritius. Who doesn't want to move there? Mauritius is like you've died and gone to heaven. Compared to this.'

'How… exactly did you look after me?' Dev queried, focussing on the muscles around her once proud mouth as she spoke. Her mouth was still proud and obstinate, but the skin around it was tired. It no longer occurred to her to dye her silver hair black.

'I made sure you ate. I sent you to school. You had a place to live. I was your mum. I was there. You had things a lot better than a lot of other children.'

'Mum, you weren't there,' Dev replied gently. He didn't want to argue with his mum, but he couldn't let her twist the truth either.

'If I wasn't, then who was? If I wasn't there, where was I?'

'Mum,' pressed Dev, 'you were lost. You took me away from Dad, from England. And then it was like you didn't know what to do with me.'

'That's not true.'

'Yes, it is. You couldn't talk to me.' He knew he shouldn't have been arguing with her, but the day's emotions were getting to him.

'Why are we talking about this now, like this?'

‘Because we never talked about it before,’ replied Dev. ‘We never talked about Mauritius. About Canada, or Marseille. It was like we had an unspoken agreement to just brush it all away and pretend it never happened.’

Serena fidgeted with her hands. She was seated in her armchair from home that had been brought over with her belongings, but somehow it just didn’t feel right. It was going to take her a while to get comfy in it again. ‘Look, Dev. After Mina, I wanted to make sure you were safe. *I* needed that. *I* needed you with me. You were *my* responsibility.’

‘Moving from country to country? No,’ argued Dev. ‘It was like you just wanted to get away from Amina. Did you feel guilty about her?’

‘What do you think?’ answered Serena scornfully. ‘Of course, I felt guilty. If I didn’t, I’d be a monster. Your father too. He felt guilty. If we weren’t in England, it wouldn’t have happened.’

‘It was an accident. Accidents happen everywhere.’

‘Yes, but accidents don’t just happen. Your father should have been watching. We should have been watching out for her. That’s what they do in Mauritius. Everyone watches, and they tell you if something is amiss.’

‘Mum,’ replied Dev, ‘I know you’ve carried guilt around all these years, but it *was* an accident. It’s time to let go.’

‘If we paid more attention, she’d still be alive. She wouldn’t have been with… those people,’ Serena insisted, her hands growing more agitated in her lap.

Dev let a break open up in the conversation, and for a few moments, he and his mother listened to the sound of birdsong outside the window. However, Dev was only allowing some space for Serena's emotions to simmer down. 'What people, Mum?'

'Her *friends*. Never mind, it doesn't matter anymore.'

'So what if she had friends, Mum? They were probably the last ones with her when she had her accident.'

'What?' Serena asked sharply.

'She was with friends when she had her accident, wasn't she? She wouldn't have been there alone.'

'Her *friends*?'

'Yeah, she was with friends. That's what you and Dad told me. She was with friends.'

'Stop saying that! Don't you see yet? There are no friends? You can't trust anyone.'

'Amina had friends. She was with them when the accident happened.'

'Ha! Friends!' Serena dismissed bitterly. 'Do friends let you get used?'

'Used?' asked Dev. 'Wha… What are you talking about?'

'She started something she was too young to handle,' began Serena, before looking up from her hands to Dev's open, enquiring eyes. 'Oh, never mind all that now. Change the subject.'

'Mum, what are you saying? What happened to Amina?'

'Dev, there are things that a mother never wants to hear. The day Mina died, she told me what those… What they'd done to her.'

'Mum. Why didn't you tell me?' asked Dev, still unclear about what exactly she was talking about.

'What good would it have done? What good is it doing now? What's the use of talking?'

'No, but you *never* talked,' pressed Dev. 'After Amina, we never had a normal relationship. Why did you take me with you from England to Mauritius to Canada to France if you weren't going to talk to me.'

'I needed you, I told you. You're my child. I brought you *back* to England, didn't I? Back to your father in the end,' Serena justified. Her eyes searched his, silently imploring him to abandon the topic, but she could see he wasn't going to let it go.

'Everything about you reminded me of her. Have you ever been scared of something you love? I didn't know how I could talk to you. I was afraid… I was afraid of the pain if we talked. If I heard Mina in you. Are you satisfied?' demanded Serena. 'This isn't about you, Dev. I'm the one who's ill. This is about me. Not you. Not Amina. You have no idea what me and your father went through. We came to England with nothing, and we worked damn hard for what we have, so don't you dare judge me. Or him. Now get out, so I can settle in this waiting area they call a bedroom.'

Dev didn't need to be asked twice. 'I'll take a walk. I'll be back,' he said as he collected his jacket. As much as he wanted to continue the conversation, he couldn't. He had been suddenly transported back to his childhood, where he was both afraid of and for his mother.

*Ridiculous,* he thought, a *grown man being afraid of his mother,* but he was scared of her judgements. He always had been. Judgements don't discriminate according to age. No matter how old you are, the opinions of others can hold the power to cut deep. The only difference is that as you grow older, the knives of those you care not for grow smaller. While those of people you do love take on imaginative new shapes.

*What was that about Amina?* he wondered as he wandered the grounds, waiting for enough time to elapse before he could go back. *What did she mean?*

Half an hour later, Dev knocked softly at Serena's door, as he always had been since Amina's death. There was no answer, so he let himself in. In the armchair, his mother was very still. He wasn't sure that she had moved at all since he left her, but she had been waiting for him. Serena opened her eyes and gazed at him with her tired eyes.

'You think I don't see her?' she asked, striking first. 'Every day. Every day I see her sitting on that bed. Every day I hear what she told me. I don't hear her reciting her lines from the school play. I don't see her learning to read. I don't hear her laughing. Instead, I hear only what she told me that day. I can't help it. What can I do? What could I have done? It was already done,' blurted Serena.

'What are you talking about, Mum?' asked Dev.

'Amina. I can hear her now. Word for word,' said Serena.

'What?' he persisted.

'That day. I should have listened more. Or talked more. Something different that I should have done. She'd still be here.'

'It was an accident.'

'I wanted to believe that, Dev. I really tried. For a year, I tried.'

'What, Mum? What are you saying?' Dev demanded, his face a mess of questions.

'Because it's true. I know it. I should have been better. It was just a moment. And I failed.'

'Failed what?'

Serena had endured the last quarter-century keeping Amina to herself, never even considering telling Raju or Dev the truth about what had happened. But it had all taken its toll on her, her mind, and she was no longer strong enough. She was too weary to keep it to herself. Pulled apart from the lack of sleep. Worn down by the years of silence, and the course of action the thirteen-year-old girl had chosen. Serena had let everyone believe it had been an accident, despite knowing in her bones that it had been otherwise. Serena had taken the reality and buried it deep within, refusing to reveal the genuine reasons for her hurt, anger, regret, disappointment, self-loathing, and everything in between that had eaten at her over the years. For Raju and Dev, she kept her silence, choosing not to pull apart the fiction.

The pain the truth would have caused Raju would have torn him apart. Of this, Serena was certain. She knew the pain of imagining the way her daughter had been manipulated. Cajoled. Forced. Used. She had spared Raju the same pain.

Now in her room at the hospice, surrounded by neutral decor under soft lighting, Serena knew the end was not far. Looking up at her son, she questioned the wisdom of having kept it all to herself. What had she achieved? All these years, she had protected her husband and son from the truth, allowing them to live a fiction while the truth perpetually ran through the fraying synapses of her brain. The bitterness of knowing the truth and being unable to do anything had consumed her over the years.

Between the pain enveloping her mind and the illness

attacking her body, Serena felt there was nothing left to her but death.

Would it have been easier if she had shared the truth? Or would they have found ways to transfer different versions of their recriminations, hurt and anger to each other over the last twenty-five years as their feelings gathered in strength? Like light through a lens. Would Raju have been able to forgive her? He would have never forgiven himself.

As these thoughts tumbled through Serena's mind, her son looked expectantly to her to finish what she had begun.

But what had she begun? Could she continue? Should she remain silent? Could she take the truth with her? If she did, would Amina's death have meant anything? Would it have meant anything anyway? If the truth about Amina went with Serena to her death, would that mean it hadn't happened? As the only person holding the truth, would Serena's death mean only the fiction would stand? The only possible story. A closed matter as far as reality was concerned. What about Dev? Did he not deserve to know the truth? What had happened to his sister? His mother?

In explaining to Dev the secret she had carried all these years, could she redeem herself a little in his eyes, open the door and allow him to understand her? Even if he didn't immediately understand her and her actions, he could, in time, with the truth at hand.

In Serena's eyes, it came down to an elderly woman choosing to protect her husband and son from pain or her desire for her child's love and wanting him to understand her before she died.

'Dev. Sit down. On the bed. I have… I have to tell you this.'

# 52. Flesh and blood

Amina sat on the bed beside her mother and dreaded what was to come. Her feet fidgeted while she squirmed with anxiety.

It was a sunny afternoon. It was *that* afternoon.

Dev played outside in the garden while Raju, pretending to read the newspaper, watched him through the French windows. Like most parents, Raju enjoyed watching his children play, but Amina didn't play anymore, at least not when she could be watched. She was upstairs in Raju and Serena's bedroom, having the chat he and Serena had discussed.

To keep Dev from becoming curious and interrupting them, Raju had encouraged him to play outside in the autumn sunshine. He watched Dev create games for himself. From them, he grew worlds engaging their own peculiar logic. Raju watched, wondering how *the chat* was progressing in the bedroom upstairs.

Amina felt, like the coloured earth in Raju's jar from Chamarel that Dev had shaken up, her insides had been displaced, leaving nothing in the right place. *Maybe this is what they mean when they say, "my heart was in my mouth,"* thought Amina.

'It's okay. You don't have to look so worried,' smiled Serena. 'Go on, give me a smile.'

Amina could not, and while Serena's own smile remained on her lips, it slipped from her eyes. 'Amina, what's going on?

I know you, and you're not yourself. You're very quiet.'

Amina shook her head and looked down at the patterned duvet cover. 'Nothing,' she mumbled.

'What do you mean, "nothing"?' Serena pressed, eager for them to get past the stilted conversation part so they could really get talking as she thought a mother and daughter should. 'We haven't had Ayesha and Sadie over for dinner in a while. Do you see them at that youth club now?'

'Sometimes.'

'They used to come for dinner all the time. Why don't you ask them over some time?'

'No,' replied Amina.

'Why not? What's happened? Aren't you friends anymore?' Serena probed.

'It's… it's not… I don't know.'

'Is this why you've been so quiet? Have they upset you? Come on, my love, what have they done?'

'It's…' began Amina before falling silent once more.

'Is it a boy?' Serena asked. 'You can tell me, I won't be cross. I'll understand. I can help.' At this, Amina finally looked up at her mother. 'There you are. Now I can see your pretty little face,' gushed Serena, unintentionally making Amina feel worse. 'It's always better when you talk about it. You'll see. Tell me.'

'You promise you won't be angry?' Amina asked.

'I promise.'

Amina gathered herself and took a deep breath. 'You know how me, Ayesha and Sadie have been friends for a long time?' she began, looking down at her thumb as it ground into the duvet cover.

'Of course I know. You were all at playschool together.'

'We've all been friends in infant school and junior school, but when we started secondary school, it changed,' Amina managed before stopping.

'Go on. How did it change?' encouraged Serena.

'They started leaving me out of things.'

'Oh. Well, sometimes these things happen. People change and switch friends, and then switch back again.

'In the start, that was all.'

'Then what happened?'

'In the summer, we went to Mauritius. I came back, and they'd had a summer without me. I didn't know what I'd done, but I must have done something wrong. Right?'

'No, Amina, things aren't always your fault. Why do you think like that?'

'But it feels like that.'

'Why, Amina?'

'I don't know.'

'So are they still friends, or have they found other people?' asked Serena.

'They're still friends. I found out they had started going to the youth club. That's why I wanted to go. I thought they… we would be friends again. But Ayesha just ignored me. She was talking to me before, but at the youth club, she ignored me. I don't know why. Sadie just does whatever Ayesha does. But, I thought I'd just keep going anyway.'

'So all this time, they didn't want to be friends with you, but you carried on going to that place?' Serena asked, annoyance now creeping into her voice, despite her earlier promise.

'Yes. Sort of.'

'What does that mean?'

'I met a boy there.'

'What boy?'

'That first time, Ayesha and Sadie went as soon as I got there. I was upset because they didn't want to be friends anymore. There was a boy. He started talking to me. We played table football. He's the one I've been seeing at the youth club.'

'Is he…' began Serena, but he didn't want to use the word. She didn't think she'd be using the word *boyfriend* so soon. 'What is he?'

'I… no,' stuttered Amina. 'He talked to me. He was nice. I felt like I knew he wouldn't say anything nasty.'

'Nasty? What have those girls said to you?'

'After, like, a month Ayesha and Sadie started saying things about me at the youth club and at school. Calling me things….' Here Amina stopped again.

'What things?' Serena asked with a new hardness to her voice.

'They said…' It was the first time Amina was repeating what they had said aloud. It felt difficult to even physically form the words. She took a deep breath. 'They said I smelled like… leftover Indian takeaways. They said I stuff my bra with chapatis. They said the only boys that would like me would be ones who could find no one better. Stuff like that. We don't even eat chapatis. That's Indian food.'

'Amina, why didn't you say anything? It's bullying. Did you tell the teachers?'

'No.'

‘Why not?’ demanded Serena.

‘That just makes things worse.’

‘No, it doesn’t.’

‘Yes, it would. You don’t know. There’s no one at school to say it was true that Ayesha had been bullying me. Everyone would say I was making up stories. They’ve made it so there’s no one there for me.’

A moment passed as Serena took this in. ‘God, Amina, I wish you’d said something sooner,’ exhaled Serena. This wasn’t the conversation she thought she would be having, but she was glad she had gotten to the bottom of things.

‘I’m sorry, Mum, I’m really sorry,’ said Amina with tears in her eyes.

‘It’s not your fault, baby girl. Come here for a hug.’

Amina leant over to her mum and buried her face in Serena’s shoulder. A few moments passed.

‘So this boy. Is he in your year at school?’

‘No.’

‘So he’s… older than you?’

‘Yes.’

‘But he goes to your school.’

‘No.’

‘So, where does he go to school?’

Amina pulled away from her mother’s embrace and looked her in the face. A couple of tears had trickled from Amina’s eyes, but Serena could see they were truly reddening as her daughter struggled to hold them back. Despite the cascading emotions within her, Amina had a look of determination on her face. She needed to tell her mother everything, and she didn't want the sound of her words to be muffled by sobs. She had to get this out of her and didn't want to repeat herself or answer additional questions. Amina just wanted to be heard and hugged.

'He told me he went to another school,' she finally managed, having gotten her breathing under control. 'He told me he was fifteen. We were just friends. I'd been seeing him for a month at the youth club when I heard the things they'd been saying about me.

'I told him they'd been saying horrible things, that nobody wanted to be friends with me because of them. He hugged me and invited me to his for dinner. He said he didn't live far away, so I went with him. He lived in a flat. When we got there, I was surprised his parents weren't there. I thought we'd meet his parents and they'd be nice like him.

'He put something in the microwave. I kept asking where his parents were, but he didn't say. After we ate, he took me to his bedroom to talk. I told him I had to get home, but he said he wanted me to know how important I was before I left.

'When I went in his bedroom, there wasn't a bed. There was just a mattress on the floor and sheets. He didn't have a desk or school books or anything. I didn't see his school tie. He closed the door, and that's when I saw a uniform on a hook, but it wasn't like a school one. It was like the ones they wear at the supermarket.

'I said something, and that's when he told me he wasn't fifteen. That he was nineteen. He told me not to worry and that he knew what he was doing. I told him I wanted to go, but he said he wanted to talk to me first. He made me sit on the mattress, and he sat with me.

'He held my hand and kept telling me I was important and special and that I didn't have to worry about people at school because he was there for me. Then he kissed my hand. Then my cheek. Then he kissed my mouth.

'I tried to say no, but he kept saying how much time he'd spent with me and that he'd always been nice to me. He started putting his hands on my legs. It happened so fast. I didn't feel I could say no, Mum. I don't remember, but he must have taken my trousers off. Mum, I tried to stop it!

'I just remember it hurting. He was on top of me. It… it hurt so much. I started crying, and I think I tried to push him off, but he had his hand on my face, Mum… Mum, I was so scared. I thought he was nice, but he wasn't. I know that now. I know that now, Mum.

'Afterwards, he said it was normal. It was what everyone did if they were important and special. Every time, he said what we did was normal because I was important and special.' These last words managed to stagger out of Amina before she finally lost control and began sobbing.

Serena sat silent for a while, dumbfounded at what had come from Amina's mouth. 'Are you saying you kept going there?' Serena finally asked through a dry throat, stunned and sickened by what her daughter had had to say.

'He made me feel…' Amina managed, between sobs. 'He… I was confused. He was nice again afterwards, but it hurt so much. It hurt every time, but he made me feel like I was being silly. Like I was making a fuss about nothing.'

'My God! Amina! I don't understand. What have *you* done?' Serena eventually managed to blurt. 'I don't know what else to say.'

Nothing in Serena's life had prepared her for this. No parenting advice passed down from previous generations had ever covered topics such as this, that she knew of. Deep down, Serena wanted to do better for her daughter, but the necessary response simply wasn't there.

'He told me it was normal,' continued Amina, breathing hard, 'like it was my fault if I was making a fuss. The last time I went there… he had a friend there… I… I didn't want to do any of it,' finished Amina as she began sobbing again with her face in her hands. 'I know. I've been stupid. I'm sorry.'

'I don't know what to say, Amina. We… come here,' she finally said. Serena hugged her daughter tightly. 'We have to tell the police what has happened.'

'No,' said Amina, shaking her head against her mother's shoulder.

'We have to, Amina. You've been hurt. They need to find him and lock him up.'

'No, then everyone will know. I don't want everyone to know.'

'I have to tell Raju. We have to tell the police. How can this be happening? I have no idea how I'm going to tell Raju this. It'll break his heart. My God, what are we going to do?' Serena said, her eyes closed to her daughter as she began busying herself with thoughts of what was to come.

# 53. Liquid skin

Dev had kept himself together as he made his way from Serena's room at the hospice to the exit, operating without thinking, going through the motions like he had switched to an autopilot setting, even nodding and smiling warmly to a nurse on the way out.

Once in the car park, beyond the threshold of the hospice lobby, past the need to maintain appearances for any onlookers, his knees buckled but didn't give way altogether. He wanted to kneel on the ground to steady his nerves, but he couldn't. His subconscious did not allow him to damage his suit trousers on the rough surface. Surprisingly his mind somehow still had the capacity to care about his suit. As though, despite Serena's news, his mind wanted to preserve the veneer of *business as usual.*

Serena had shattered him with the words she had spoken. Fear. Anger. Sorrow. They filled his veins and raced around his head and heart as the memories of life with Amina and his family flooded his senses and brought him to the ground.

Finally, on his knees, hands gripping the wet tarmac, his mind gave in, and his body threw up, vomiting on the ground before him.

Dev could barely keep his hand from trembling as he slotted his key into the lock to open the door to his flat. In no shape to drive, he had opted for the bus but had continued to feel queasy. He felt out of place on the bus, at the back, sitting across from an overweight grey-haired, middle-aged man with a side parting and wearing a too-tight jacket.

Dev had no idea how he had made it home from the hospice car park. He didn't remember the walk from the bus stop to his front door. He didn't remember pressing the little red *stop* button. He certainly didn't remember buying a ticket from the bus driver. Mind splintered, thoughts scattered, he sat on the chair by his desk, hunched over, as he tried to regroup his faculties, and come to terms with all that he had heard.

Adolescent Dev had supposed the origins of his interest in the thoughts of others lay in a combination of learning of MacDougall's twenty-one grams experiment and the copy of *ICE* at the barbershop. As an adult, he had reluctantly delved deeper to conclude that his interest was borne of his childhood after Amina. Moving from one place to another, attempting to deduce the right thing to say, do, and think. Wondering what others were thinking, whether they liked him or only pretended to. This was what he had thought of as the genuine foundations of his interest before Serena's revelations, shocking enough in and of themselves, not only revealed more to himself about Amina, they revealed more about himself.

This realisation was one of the new pieces of information Dev struggled to reconcile. He had thought his interest had occurred from his own experiences, but he was wrong. It came from Amina. She had unknowingly given him the impetus. He just hadn't realised it. Now that he knew more, he could see a link between his interest in thought and what had happened to her. Something that had driven her to leave everything behind.

The maelstrom of emotions he felt for Amina crashed over him again and again, but, prompted by Serena, he thought back to that night Amina had scared him with her unusual behaviour. He thought of her and now saw how Amina had left a parasite, a foreign object that had lodged itself within him all those years ago and had lain undetected, influencing him.

Serena's words had devastated Dev, but they were now compounded by the sad realisation that something Amina had said, in her terrible and lonely state of hurt confusion, had profoundly shaped his life. That night he tried to encourage Amina to talk to him. It all came back flooding back. There was the familiar fear of not knowing how to be around his own sister anymore. There was the confusion over the things she was saying and the way she was acting. However, now mixed in with all that was pure anguish as the further recollection of that night flooded his eyes and ears.

'Amina. You can talk to me,' tried Dev.

'No, I can't,' replied Amina, struggling to hold in her emotions.

'Why not? We used to talk about everything.'

'Because I shouldn't be talking to anyone.'

'Why not?'

Here she paused, not knowing how to go on or if she should. She'd been told not to, but she wanted to let it out, but without needing to put it into words. She was feeling so much, things beyond the capacity of her words, things she could not give voice to. 'I'm… not good, Dev.'

'Yes, you are.'

'I'm not. I'm bad.'

'But Mum says there aren't *really* any bad children. That's why we all get Christmas presents.'

'She's wrong.'

'But Mummy's never wrong. You know that.'

'I don't know anything. I'm a bad girl.'

'No, you're not. Bad girls are the ones that don't pray. That's what they told us in Mauritius. Bad girls don't do their homework. Oh! is it homework? I don't have homework yet.'

'It's not homework. I'm bad because of a boy.'

'Oh.' Dev didn't know what to say next, he didn't know enough about the topic, but he was curious how a boy be bad for a girl. He and Amina used to do lots of things together, but that didn't make either of them bad. He wondered what else there could be.

'Do you know what I'm talking about?' asked Amina, knowing that he didn't, but needing to unburden herself of at least a little.

'No,' admitted Dev.

After a moment or two passed before she quietly said, 'I kissed a boy.'

Dev considered this before saying, 'that's not so bad.'

'Yes. It is,' came the reply from across the room.

Dev was confused. They always kissed each other's cheeks to say goodnight. 'You mean on the lips?'

'Yes. But it's more than kissing.'

Dev was even more confused. He wasn't aware there was anything beyond kissing.

'What was it like?' he asked.

'Dev. Do you know what sex is?' Dev didn't and didn't know what to say in response either. 'Oh, never mind. Just go to sleep,' Amina snapped. 'Let's all just go to sleep,' she pleaded into her pillow, no longer able to contain the tremors in her voice.

With her face crushed into the pillow, Amina prayed for sleep to come easily and instantly, prayed to leave her body for a little while at least. She no longer felt any of it belonged to her.

The skin she wore felt like paint. Crumbling, offering what lay underneath no protection. Her hair was a kite that would blow away with the wind. Her bones were sticks and twigs for bird nests. Those lungs she used to breathe, the red blood cells, the white blood cells, the oxygen, the carbon dioxide, the heart, the entire engine of her body, was something she could disregard.

She had learnt to look at it from another place, and it didn't matter anymore. This body she thought she knew was now alien to her, and in her mind she had already severed her connection to it. As far as she was concerned, her body was nothing more than a vessel.

Upset and afraid of Amina's uncharacteristically sharp tone, Dev quickly slid back into bed, hoping this would stop her crying. Listening to Amina, he rolled over and with his face turned away from his sister, he reconsidered the story she had just told him.

A building that could think and help people to leave behind their feelings. He wondered if it was true that going to a building could make people feel better. Like when their auntie in Mauritius told them it made her feel better every Friday when she visited her temple. Amina wasn't in the habit of visiting temples or churches, so he couldn't see how that could help her.

Dev had been trying to reconnect with her, and in her own way, she too had been trying. He hadn't understood that at the time. He was too young. Too sleepy. Instead, Dev wondered how a building could think, assuming it could think because Amina had described it as sensing people. That night he fell asleep wondering about buildings and Amina.

Later, whenever he had thought of the building in Amina's story, he had dismissed it as just a story, with nothing more to be read into it. As an adult, he didn't consider it, reluctant to examine too closely that which would reopen old wounds. After talking with Serena at the hospice and remembering the night he had been scared and upset by Amina, Dev came to understand the building in Amina's story was more than it appeared, but it was not a place of worship. In his mixed up state of shock and grief, Dr. Sharma came to believe that her child's mind had subconsciously created a conscious building, an entity needing caring attention but unable to ask for it. In his anguish, he came to believe the building in Amina's story *was* Amina.

Dev's head swam with Serena's revelations and the memory of that night with Amina in their bedroom, as well as overwhelming anguish and remorse. Remorse that he hadn't told his parents about her crying. They might have helped her sooner. Anguish because her final weeks had been so full of torment and loneliness that the little girl had apparently wanted nothing more than to be free of it.

She had come to no longer value herself as a person, instead, considering herself as worthless as a dead leaf on the air, drifting into a road. All of this coalesced into a stark need for Dr. Sharma. The more he thought of his sister, the stronger the need to know her became, to know what she had gone through. He needed to understand her. He needed to connect with her.

This was where things changed for Dev.

In a way, it felt natural, as though he had come full circle. Amina had inspired him to consider thought. Now, for Dev, there was no choice but to weigh hers. At his desk, Dev lifted his head from his hunched-over position and looked over to a new notebook Bellyana had given him as a birthday present. It had since lain on a shelf, awaiting purpose.

Dev rose unsteadily to his feet and snatched it hungrily before ripping away the flimsy clear plastic wrapping and flipping the front cover. To bring order to his thought, he began writing. Let's read a little of what he wrote.

*How did Amina find herself in a sexual... relationship? is that what to call it? A relationship? From what Mum said, it was ongoing. Amina told her she'd had sex with him on more than one occasion. Was it her choice? How could she choose at that young age? Was she manipulated? She must have been. She was coerced!*

*Mum hinted at something more, but she didn't say it. i couldn't ask her. After everything she'd told me, i couldn't ask for more. i didn't want to. Mum's on many medications, but she's mostly lucid. She wouldn't be making this up. Like, for attention, or something. i have to assume that what she said is true.*

*With hindsight, it... that night, talking with Amina... what was she thinking? She was a child. How did they let this happen? How did they not know? And then... How did she get so desperate? Why didn't i see? Why didn't she talk? How could they do it? How can anyone hurt a child like that? How could anyone hurt Amina that way? She was my sister, a sweet girl. She'd gone there several times, so what was her thought process? i need to understand her.*

At this point, Dev got up from his chair and paced. Vaguely aware of the furniture and the walls but not paying them any mind, he walked around with his eyes on the floor. He wanted to look out of the window, but he also feared becoming distracted and losing his train of thought if he did.

Like many, Dev is unable or reluctant to think clearly when in a state of emotional turbulence. Had he taken a break and come back to all this the next day, or even just spent a few more moments, he may have come to a different conclusion. However, in his arrogance, or his loss, Dev came up with a simple but ill-conceived plan to satisfy his immediate natural impulse to take action.

In a way, I can understand him. In light of the news he received, he felt... impotent. It was impossible for Dev to reconcile what had happened to his sister. As a child, he had known that he would never again see Amina alive. But the fresh revelation that she had killed herself made that knowledge all the more jarring.

He had been unable to control her death. And what came after it. Now, knowing the truth about Amina, he relived her death, this time seeing himself unable to seek justice, unable to track down her rapists and bring them to account. He wouldn't know where to begin. He didn't even know the whole story.

Instead of turning to the window, he returned to his desk and the notebook.

*All this time, i had no idea that this had happened to her. Now that i do know, how do i get past it? it's like mourning her all over again. Or maybe it's mourning her for the first time. i was so young, i'm not sure that i did it back then. How do i do it now? How do i understand her? Can i understand what went through her mind without knowing what the people who did it to her were thinking? What are any of us thinking?*

His long-held fascination about how people thought had lain dormant as Dev busied himself with life, his career. Now, in light of his mother's revelations and his own returning memories, it returned with a pulsing vengeance. He needed to know more about his sister. He needed to understand how they thought, the people that had hurt her. What was it that could push them to hurt a child?

Wracked with unanchored guilt over Amina, his mind bounded from one possibility to another. Still, the one he kept coming back to was the need to take his fascination with thought and apply it to understand what his sister had gone through. The lens of his analytical nature focused his need to understand how those who could use another for pure sexual gratification thought. As odious as it appeared to him, the only recourse he felt he had available was to see the world through their eyes. This way, he might understand more about his sister.

Dev looked up from his notebook. He had written a word he never thought he would use about anyone he was close to. He looked back down.

*Paedophile.*

Dev took a breath to regain his composure and apply his analytical mind before pushing through.

> *Amina was abused by paedophiles. Or Hebephiles. Paedophilia is not a sexual orientation. Not a fetish. It is currently termed a mental disorder where an adult or older adolescent has a sexual predilection for children up to the age of thirteen. How do they think? i've always been curious about thoughts. Amina apparently gave me that curiosity. Now i need to know how someone could be compelled to hurt someone else for sex.*

Needing to take action, this was the first plan Dev came up with, at least the first one that struck him as most satisfying in the moment. Dev, consumed by his pain, needed resolution.

In the weeks and months that followed, he dove headfirst into all the most recent studies on human sexuality he could find from around the world, from all different cultures. He read up on as many of them as he could find. He read all the studies available to him on the motivation of these predators, how they saw their victims, how they saw themselves. Each other.

It wasn't enough for Dev. They were just words on a page. Words that could be taken apart and rearranged. He needed to talk to people who could give him an insight into sexual gratification. People with first-hand knowledge, for whom sex was a daily constant. Dev needed an insight into the underlying thoughts. He wanted authentic voices, real people, people who had gone through what Amina had endured.

Sexual abuse.

He wanted to hear it in their own words, immediate, raw and visceral. Dev could have reached out to professionals in medicine and psychoanalysis. Instead, he reached out to professionals in the sex industry. People who weren't intending to talk about their experiences, people who would be caught off guard, unprepared, thus yielding the most candid insights.

A week later, looking to understand the drive to subjugate another for sexual pleasure, Dr. Sharma booked a place at Mira's gangbang. He had expected a victim.

# 54. Host

Not the most exotic of locations, but the family has to get away, and this is as far as their meagre savings would allow them. Having booked the cottage for an entire month, their people-carrier is fully loaded with as many clothes, supplies, and necessary possessions as it will carry.

While they largely deny it to themselves, and each other, deep down each of them knows the truth. That they have acquiesced and travelled to the South of France without protest attests to how they have ceased fighting their fate. The family simply tries to expect the worst and dodge the rest.

In this case, with everything they know caving in on itself, they have decided to retreat to a house in the French countryside. Entirely self-sufficient and off the grid, the house is in a remote area with the nearest neighbour a ten-minute drive away. Even the postman only visits a few times a week.

With everything happening, particularly in his condition, Malcolm is understandably concerned… with the dead rising from the graves. Or mutants. Or something. In any case, he feels it is better to stay away from other people altogether and, at its formulation, his plan had seemed entirely logical.

It is the middle of the night when they arrive in their dusty, maroon-coloured vehicle and, as prearranged, find the keys to the house taped to the inside of the letterbox just below the narrow opening. Twelve-year-old Joseph, the youngest of the family, slips his fingers through the slot to retrieve the keys with ease.

'Good job Joe!' beams Malcolm to his son.

In the dead of night, the family slips into the house, taking from their vehicle only the essentials they need for now.

Stephanie and Deborah wander upstairs to inspect the bedrooms and wait for Malcolm and Joseph to locate the stopcock and get the water running so they can shower. The whole trip had been Malcolm's idea, necessitated, he felt, by his condition. As usual, he feels entirely deserving of his family's resentment. He is, after all, one of the world's unluckiest men. That being said, he is yet to hear any resentment directly from the rest. In fact, Joseph seems to be enjoying himself and doesn't appear to mind being away from home. Malcolm knows Stephanie will be missing her friends.

'But did we all have to come? Really? It's just Dad that has this thing,' sulks Stephanie upstairs to her mother.

'I've explained it already. sweetie, don't give your father a hard time. Can we try to have a quiet life? For once?' pleads Deborah.

'Have you seen where we are? I don't think having a quiet life around here will be a problem.'

'Well, there'll be problems if you keep moaning,' says

Deborah, pulling bed sheets from the drawers. She tosses a sheet to Stephanie. 'Help me, will you?'

They work around the bed in the master bedroom.

'I love your father. You should be happy about that. I can't leave him like this, in this condition. You and Joseph are too young to stay behind,' continues Deborah.

'We wouldn't be alone. We'd be with friends,' protests Stephanie.

'That's what I'm worried about. Anyway, nobody knows what's going on. At least here we're safe from other people.'

'Not everyone out there wants to hurt us.'

'We're stronger together, Steph.'

'I think we're stronger apart. Surely we'd be better off as four separate failures instead of one big failure-family, watching each other suffer, taking out our disappointment on each other.'

They sit on the freshly made-up bed and move on to pillowcases.

'What was the plan when you and Dad got together?' continues Stephanie. 'That you'd have unlucky children and then unlucky grandchildren? Like a disease?'

'They say you make your own luck in life,' replies Deborah neutrally.

'Then why don't you? Do we always need to hide?'

'This is different.'

'What about Joe? He doesn't need to grow up like this. He can be more positive.'

'He is positive.'

'Then why aren't I?' Stephanie wondered aloud.

'Because you're a teenager!'

'Deb?' comes Malcolm's voice from downstairs. 'I think we've got the water flowing. Is it working upstairs?'

'Hold on, I'll check.'

Deborah gets up, leaving Steph sitting on the edge of the bed. Eventually, she hears the sound of running water from the sink.

'Water's running, Dad,' Stephanie shouts.

'Okay,' Malcolm shouts back. 'Well, that's a little victory,' he says to Joseph. 'Still early. Shall we empty the car?'

'Maybe we should leave it for now, Dad. You don't want to overdo it.'

'Yeah. Okay.'

'Hey, let's see if we can get the TV working.'

'Good idea, kiddo. Tell you what, you figure out how the TV works, I'll figure out how the sofa works. Deal?'

'Deal.'

'Great.' With that, the father and son team move to the living room.

Joseph quickly finds the remote controls in a drawer, and Malcolm finds a comfy position on the three-seater. From there, he watches his son, crossed-legged on the floor, hunched over the remote control, getting the TV to scan for channels.

When the attack comes, it is sudden.

It doesn't begin with a sensation.

There is no warning.

Malcolm senses the pain is everywhere all at once. With his blood-curdling scream Joseph whips round to find his father suddenly contorted on the sofa, struggling to breathe!

'Dad! Mum! Mum, come quick,' screams Joseph, wringing

his hands, at a loss. 'There's something wrong with Dad. It's happening again.'

Careening down the stairs, Deborah slips before the last few steps and crashes down to the wooden floor, crushing her knee in the process. Paying no attention to her own pain, Deborah quickly gets up and scrambles to the living room. The scene she finds there freezes her blood in her veins. Malcolm is laid on the sofa gasping, his mouth contorted in silent agony while her son is on his knees by his father's side, crying and softly slapping at his father's chest with both hands.

'What do we do, Mummy?'

'We beat him.'

'What?' shouts Joseph, tears streaming from his eyes. 'I don't want to. Daddy!'

'We'll beat it out of him. Like the doctors said,' encourages Deborah, a look of steely determination coming over her face.

'This is fucking nuts,' concludes Stephanie, approaching slowly from the stairway, fear and revulsion clouding her features. 'I'm not doing it.'

Deborah turns from Malcolm and grabs Stephanie tightly by the shoulders, pulling her face close. 'If you love your father, young lady, you'll hit him as hard as you can and keep on hitting him!' orders Deborah.

Meanwhile, Joseph has taken a few steps back to get a good run-up, which he now takes with both hands clamped together above his head.

'Aaargh,' comes the little boy's high-pitched scream as he runs at his father. Deborah spins around at the commotion just in time to see Joseph leaping in the air to throw all his might behind his little fists, driving them into his father's chest.

Stephanie and Deborah step closer as Joseph rolls off his father, sobbing. Malcolm appears to have recovered a little. Regaining control of his facial muscles, he seems to have experienced some relief at Joseph's fists. Stephanie and Deborah exchange shocked glances as this realisation sinks in. It doesn't take long to figure out their next move.

Poor Malcolm has nowhere to escape as his family pile in on him, pinning him to the sofa.

Throwing fists, Deborah screams, 'don't stop punching,' her hair flying into her mouth in the process.

As the TV continues scanning and logging channels, the family punch, hit and kick Malcolm in his face, chest and stomach until he looks as though he will vomit.

'Get a bucket or something,' cries Deborah.

Sobbing, Joseph runs to the kitchen for a bucket he had seen by the stopcock under the kitchen sink. Behind him, he can still hear the screams and shouts. He can't believe that this is happening to his father, to his family, but there is no time to ponder. Joseph grabs the bucket and scampers back to the living room. Once again, he freezes as he arrives at the sight of his father, on all fours and coughing over the floor.

'Quickly Joe! The bucket!' screams his mother, her face a mess of tears, sweat and saliva from her exertions, her words jolting Joseph back into action. Joseph places the bucket beneath his father's face while Deborah continues to kick Malcolm in the stomach. 'Stephanie, grab the grate from the fireplace and a couple of those logs.'

'Okay,' pants Stephanie, glad for an opportunity to turn away.

'Be ready Joseph! Be ready!'

'What is it? What's coming out?' asks Joseph, holding the bucket in place beneath his father's sweat-drenched head.

'It's the attack. We have to catch it,' replies Deborah. 'Come on Malcolm! Let's go, let's get this out, come on, you can do this! Do it for us!'

Stephanie returns and kneels beside Joseph, ready with a grate and the biggest log she can find. Seemingly on cue, the heart attack begins to make its appearance. Three tentacles swing over Malcolm's bottom lip and grip his chin. With a shriek, Stephanie jumps back in fright, and Joseph instinctively draws the bucket closer to shield himself.

'Don't move, be ready,' barks Deborah, her voice now hoarse from screaming, her sweaty clothes plastered to her body.

The pink tentacles suck onto Malcolm's chin, hauling the rest of itself through his mouth. Further tentacles spread over his top lip as Deborah stops kicking him to join her children and offer encouragement.

'Come on, Malcolm, cough that fucker up!'

Malcolm, grunting throughout, now gives one final phlegmy retch, blowing the heart attack into the bucket with a sound like lumpy custard dropping into a bowl.

'Quick Steph,' exhorts Deborah, needlessly since Stephanie has the grate in place within milliseconds and slams the heavy log over it.

The family has caught a heart attack, fresh from the source. The source, now laid on his back, panting into the air, receives tearful embraces from Deborah and Stephanie while Joseph stares through the slits of the grate at the little being in the bucket.

*If it could talk, what would it say?* wonders Joseph. *Would it explain itself? Is it dying?* Joseph looks up at his family. 'What should we do with it?' he asks.

'Come here. We'll worry about that later,' replies Deborah. Joseph gets up and joins his family, taking his dad's hand.

'Let's look on the bright side,' says Stephanie.

'Yeah,' agrees Deborah, 'at least we can go home now. I mean, nothing the rest of the world has to throw at us can be as bad as that. Right?' she asks Malcolm.

Still drenched in his sweat, he rolls over and faces the being.

'Okay,' struggles Dev through a dry, inflamed throat, 'what do you want? Who are you?' he asks me.

I see them. I see them all. The simplicity. The chaos. Their ability to extract clarity from chaos, and vice versa. I have no judgments. Only wonder. Only questions. The taste for adventure courses within me.

How many of them go through their life, the world, content to remain caged within a body? How can they reconcile themselves to such beautiful simplicity, such an uncomplicated existence? Minds and thoughts contained safely within bodies, each with a limited lifespan. All minds, all thoughts formed and shaped by the physical world around them. If a physical world did not exist? What then? What would those minds be? What would they think of?

'Are you Death?' Dev asks, to which I laugh. 'If you're not going to help me, what do you want? Why are you putting me through all this? Can't you see I'm dying!'

# 55. Access all areas

'This place is ages away,' moaned Dr. Sharma from the driver's seat.

'It's *your friend* who recommended it to you,' Katie reminded him, absolving herself. 'On the bright side, you won't run into any of your patients,' reasoned Katie, as she air-drummed to the tune on the radio. 'That could be awkward,' she sang playfully.

'Yeah, but what if they had the same idea? They didn't want to run into anyone they know?' asked Dr. Sharma. 'Their doctor, their kid's teacher.'

'We'll just have to hope they went somewhere else.'

'Are you worried you might run into anyone?'

'Are you joking? I'm not worried about people knowing what I do. But I wouldn't want to see any clients. They might feel weird, uncomfortable, especially if they're with their wife or something.'

'I'd have thought it would be an opportunity for you to network. What do you normally do when you see a client outside of work? You must see one or two around town from time to time.'

'It happens, but I don't do anything. If they're with someone, I just ignore them.'

'What if they're alone.'

'Still nothing, unless they come over to me.'

'I see. What if you saw me?'

'I… I don't know. We're not having sex, but if you were with someone, you might not want them to know we're friends.'

'Are we friends?'

'Sort of.'

'So you would hang out with me even if I wasn't paying for your time?'

'Yeah, I think so.' The two of them let that hang in the air for a few moments before Katie continued. 'Just so we're clear, I'm not having sex with anyone there.'

'Just so we're clear, I'm not having sex with anyone there either,' confirmed Dr. Sharma as he took the exit from the motorway.

'I know that,' smiled Katie.

'What do you mean?'

'I'd be very surprised if anyone gave you the signal to come and play on your first time there. There's… a kind of trust that gets built up by the regulars. They usually don't want to play with men who are there for the first time.'

Fifty minutes later, Katie and Dr. Sharma got out of the car and smoothed down their clothes as they made their way across the courtyard. In the car park, Dr. Sharma's sky blue hatchback looked incongruous, nestled amongst the imposing, shiny, two-door German cars that looked as though they were doing eighty miles per hour just sitting there on the gravel.

As they approached the elegant, stone-built country manor, it looked smaller from the outside than it actually was. Pretending to be a couple, Dr. Sharma reached out and took Katie's hand in his. Katie squeezed his in return, both nervous and excited at what they would walk into.

Dr. Sharma once again assessed her outfit. High heels. Hold-up stockings. Short black skirt. She held a small black clutch in front of her tight, sparkly top with a light black jacket draped casually over her shoulders. Her maroon lipstick and mascara constituted the only makeup she had applied to her face. She didn't need anything else. Her hair, freshly washed that afternoon, gave off a fruity fragrance. He mused over how easy it must have been for her to pick something out. Dr. Sharma felt lost when deciding what to wear earlier that day. After all, what does one wear to a sex party? And does it matter, since the idea is to undress once you're there?

In the end, after texting Katie to collaborate and learn what she would be wearing, he had settled on a simple combination of black trousers with a smart white shirt and a black blazer. Having set eyes on the venue, he was glad of their choices.

Together, Katie and Dr. Sharma ascended the steps that led to the large doors where a doorman waited to greet them.

'Good evening, sir, madam.'

'Hi, good evening,' replied Dr. Sharma. 'Er, we're here for the… the *thing*. Um, the evening?' he staggered, struggling for the correct nomenclature in the circumstances.

'Have you been here before? Sir?' asked the doorman.

'No.'

'Not a problem. Has the lady?'

'Yes,' answered Katie, with a smile, prompting Dr. Sharma to turn to her, surprised.

'I see, so you can show the gentleman around. I'll have my colleague, Sandra, greet you and take your payment,' smiled the doorman, ushering them through the front door and into the lobby, illuminated by soft, forgiving lights that flattered rather than deceived.

'Please wait here, and Sandra will be along in just a moment,' they were assured by the doorman before he stepped back outside to man his post in his warm overcoat, pressing an orange button on a walkie talkie that he had produced from within. 'Sandra,' they could hear him say into the device, 'another couple here. Thank you.'

'You've been here before?' asked Dr. Sharma, surprised that Katie hadn't divulged this earlier.

'Only once before. Client brought me here. I thought the area on the way looked familiar. This all definitely looks familiar,' she said as they both eyed the black and white ceramic tiles that covered the lobby floor. An ostentatious chandelier threw soft light down on an impressive collection of waist-high potted floor plants bunched together inside the front door and along the walls. Their playful green leaves invited visitors to leave their cares and inhibitions, along with their clothes.

'Through there are the changing rooms,' directed Katie, pointing at a door in the wall to their right. 'Up that staircase are the private rooms,' she continued, gesturing to their left. Ahead of them were a pair of frosted glass panes framed by wood doors that appeared to lead to the bowels of the building. 'There's a sauna, a bunch of jacuzzis here and there, and, um, there's a bar,' recalled Katie, struggling to come up with more intel from her earlier excursion. 'Um, what else? Oh, I think they had canapés out last time I was here. Finger food,' she explained, helpfully.

'Yeah, I know what canapés are, Katie.'

'All right, sorry, I'm just nervous.'

'*You're* nervous?'

'Yeah, I'm allowed, aren't I?'

'Of course, I just....' Dr. Sharma trailed off.

'Just what?'

'I don't know. I thought you'd be at ease.'

'Why? Are you?'

'No. Not at all.'

'Then why should I be?'

'You're right. I assumed. I'm sorry.'

Just then, the doorknob on one of the doors containing the frosted glass rattled into life as it was pushed and twisted from the other side. Dr. Sharma had expected Sandra, but instead, a woman and a man emerged, snug in fluffy robes. Both wore bright smiles, their faces flushed with excitement as they scurried along towards Katie and Dr. Sharma, arm in arm.

As they approached, the man, leading the way, grinned broadly at them and nodded politely, while the woman smiled genuinely to them, holding eye contact with Katie as she slipped past in bare feet, following the man up the stairs. Dr. Sharma and Katie followed their progress, but they didn't look back down as they followed the right angle of the stairs and continued climbing.

'Think we're in the right place?' joked Dr. Sharma before turning back to catch Katie's amused smile.

'Oh, hello there,' said a slim woman with short, brown hair cut into a bob, who had just emerged through the frosted glass doors. 'I'm Sandra. Sorry for keeping you waiting. Are you here together?' she asked, striding towards them in her black and white trouser suit, holding a wireless device to receive Dr. Sharma's payment.

'Yes,' answered Dr. Sharma, 'we're here, as a couple.'

'I see. For couples, the entrance fee for tonight's event is £1,200. What name is your booking under?'

'Oh, yeah, I didn't book. I told them on the phone that Mira Cassavetes suggested this place. She gave me a card, and they told me to just bring it along on the night.'

'Oh, Ms Cassavetes?' asked Sandra, unconsciously standing a little straighter at the name. 'Yes, do you have her card?' Dr. Sharma did, and he produced it from his jacket pocket for Sandra's inspection. 'Ah, in that case, no payment is necessary. We are honoured to have you as our special guests for the evening.'

'Oh, okay,' replied Dr. Sharma. 'I suppose Mira did some promotional work for this place at some point?'

'No, we've not had Ms Cassavetes here in a… commercial capacity. The exclusivity of this venue feeds its popularity. We do not pay performers to bring others here. Ms Cassavetes and Mr Grealish are old friends.'

'Oh.'

'I have some gowns for you here. If there is anything else

you need, please let us know.'

Moments later, Dr. Sharma found himself in the men's changing room, negotiating with a locker that refused to relinquish its key, despite the coin he had sunk into the plastic opening to activate the mechanism. Each time, instead of the expected *plink*, he heard a disappointing *thunk* as the coin was rejected and ejected.

'Here,' said a pot-bellied man with greying hair, 'you have to give the door a *whack* sometimes, he explained with a chuckle before slamming his palm against the faux wood locker. Sure enough, they both heard the satisfying *plink* of the coin before the key was released from the lock to Dr. Sharma's hand.

'Thanks,' said Dr. Sharma, surprised at the help from a stranger but realising a greater level of openness was to be expected. After all, these people were here to have sex with strangers, so what was a little assistance with a locker?

'No problem, see you on the other side,' said the man with another chuckle before he waddled off to the far end of the changing room and disappeared around a corner.

Pocketing the key, and its wrist strap, within his robe Dr. Sharma followed the man out through the exit and found himself walking a short passageway. White painted walls illuminated by tiny blue LED lights embedded in the ceiling lead to a heavy wooden door at the end of the passageway. Dr. Sharma reached for the black handle, then stopped.

He could hear beyond the door the repetitive thump of dance music but nothing else. He pressed his palm flat against the wood and felt the vibrations through the door. With a quick twist of the handle and a light push, the heavy door swung open with surprisingly little effort, due to a powered mechanism.

Dr. Sharma's eyes took a moment to adjust to the light before surveying the surroundings as he stepped through the doorway, and his feet found the tiled surface that ran around the outer edges of the pool, a few feet away.

'Dev,' shouted a voice, but the lights flitting and bouncing in time with the music impeded the progress his eyes were making in adjusting. 'Dev!' came the voice again, pulling Dr. Sharma to his left where he spotted Katie, enrobed and waiting for him, standing a dozen metres away.

'Hey!'

'Hey, what took you so long?'

'Locker trouble.'

'Ah. Wanna take a look around?'

'We're here, may as well.'

Everywhere they looked, guests were deep in conversation with one another. Throwing their heads back with laughter, little touches to forearms. Couples, locked in conversation, occupied every corner and crevice of the space, sitting on couches, wicker chairs, bar stools, even deck chairs. Some sat side by side, dangling feet into the pool.

The jacuzzis seemed to be the optimal place for groups to recount stories while sipping drinks. The pool was apparently not the venue of choice for those who wished to chat in a group. The jacuzzis penned everyone into a close and intimate space, while the pool offered inhibition-dissolving freedom where couples, familiar and strange, could take things further.

Men and women swam nude amongst kissing couples

whose hands roamed ever-downwards. In one corner, a man and a woman took turns to duck under the water to perform cunnilingus on another woman, laughing upon coming up for air.

For Dr. Sharma, it brought to mind something that he hadn't thought of since school.

He thought to himself: *Civis Romanus Sum.*

I am a Roman citizen.

*A Roman had only to utter those three words to expect safe passage throughout the world, on any continent*, he thought to himself. *By virtue of simply being Roman, they expected, as their right, to pass unmolested. They expected to be helped merely due to where they happened to have been born. Those three words gave them that expectation, the assertion, that they were above all others in the world. That they had been chosen to thrive. They were Romans. They apparently had every advantage anyone could possibly need to succeed. The history of humankind at that point seemingly having led to the creation of the ultimate civilisation.*

Dr. Sharma thought: *If I was a well-to-do traveller from Ancient Rome, confidently uttering Civis Romanus Sum, I would probably believe that some kind of deity had favoured me with a blessed life, especially when compared with all the poverty around me. What would it be to feel that confident, so sure of your place in the world?* Dr. Sharma asked himself. *What is it to be white, a white man, able to walk into, say, a country pub, receiving not a second glance? What would it be to move through a white community and not feel those looks linger on your person, the question dancing behind their eyes? What would it be to speak Creole with a Mauritian accent, to blend in completely?*

Dr. Sharma continued surveying the crowd with Katie. *It's fascinating to watch those people who are so sure of themselves, so confident of their right to be present. To belong. To exist. Seems almost outrageous that anyone should be so self-assured, able to forget where they are, what they look like, what they sound like. For them, their sense of belonging is not arrogant. There is no belligerence in it. It just is. They don't even consider it. Maybe I just want to forget myself and be in the moment when I am at the bar in that country pub or ordering a pair of dholl puris in Mauritius. Feel at home in my own skin. But then it wouldn't feel that way. It would just feel like a normal day. It wouldn't feel like the confidence of belonging. It wouldn't feel like nonchalance either. It would just be part of the background noise, barely perceptible static that is only picked up when something, or someone, presents a contrast.*

As Katie and Dr. Sharma moved away from the pool towards the bar, they spotted a lot more activity lining the room, where the darkness hugged the walls, offering revellers the best of both worlds. Intimacy with others, titillatingly aware that they were vulnerable to the gaze of onlookers.

Lining the walls were couches occupied by couples and groups eager to please one another, experience one another, lose themselves in the darkness as the music beat the walls and their audience bore witness to their performance.

This was them revealing their other, private selves. The versions that most people reserve for the bedroom. Instead, these people were open and free. In control. Revelling in their acts were being watched, witnessed and registered. They felt real. Being watched made their acts real.

The cunnilingus, the fellatio, the spit-roasting, the

rimming, the pegging, the same-sex play… Dr. Sharma saw it all through their eyes and understood how highly they valued their sexuality. To them, their sexual selves were just as big a part of who they were as the people they portrayed outside of this building, but here they could exhibit that in a way that made it so much more.

Each surface vibrated with the basslines while the coloured, flashing lights beat upon each being. For some, having strangers looking on as they engaged one another physically made the experience more intense and intimate. Intimate activity within a public space made their connection stronger, more real. The intimacy intensified with their awareness that others were watching. The nexus created by their consciousnesses was stronger here, strong enough to overcome the reality of their physical circumstances and create a new reality where onlookers were on the periphery of their imaginations, rather than a focal element of their immediate surroundings.

For these moments, they lost themselves to another existence.

Among people who shared their predilections, experiences and reasons, they could satisfy their desires with confidence in themselves and trust in each other.

Under normal circumstances, no one would be here who wasn't confident they wanted to be. There would be no ulterior motives, no aim other than enjoying the human body, so-called *pleasures of the flesh*. There exist perhaps few other events where people would gather with the same basic thought, where the impulse for each individual would be the same. Here Dr. Sharma knew what they were all thinking, and they sought nothing other than pleasure and contentment.

The bartender, nude, save for his black leather apron, quickly served Dr. Sharma and Katie. Soft drinks in hand, Katie pointed out a jacuzzi that had become vacant, from where they could observe. Dr. Sharma nodded in agreement, and they made their way, continuing to register the carnal activity unfolding around them.

Reaching the jacuzzi, Katie casually discarded her robe, setting it down on a chair as the breath momentarily caught in Dr. Sharma's throat. It was the first time he had seen Katie naked. Sure, he had seen her photos, but there she was a two-dimensional image, an idea separate from reality. Of course, he knew that she had a sensitive, responsive body radiating warmth under her clothes, but it wasn't something he actively considered in their meetings.

Dr. Sharma's hesitation was just for a moment as he also quickly disrobed and followed Katie up the steps and then down again into the water. He didn't know why, but he had expected Katie to tactfully avert her gaze as he stepped down into the jacuzzi. Instead, she cocked her head slightly to one side and openly took in his attributes. Unnervingly she remained silent after he had settled in the water, foam swirling around them.

'Well?' he finally asked, feeling like a teenager again, eager for validation, 'everything you dreamed of, and more?' he joked.

'Very nice, Dev,' she replied from across the water. 'You'd do nicely.'

They hadn't been in the water long before another couple

joined them, politely nodding and smiling their greetings, pushing Dr. Sharma and Katie closer together on the slippery bench beneath the bubbles. As their new jacuzzi-mates chatted, their tentative physical interactions made it clear that they were relatively new to one another.

Leaning closer to one another as they talked, the man grew ever-confident, moving from touching her forearms and shoulders to pushing auburn hair from her face with his wet hand before pressing his lips to hers. Her hand finally came up to his shoulder, and her painted nails brushed the skin.

Katie and Dr. Sharma furtively exchanged glances, guessing where this was leading but unsure how far it would go in the jacuzzi with them in it. The woman turned slowly in the still water, the system having inopportunely chosen that moment to quell its noisy jets and replenish its energies ahead of another assault of bubbles. Clasping her nape, the man's other hand guided his penis as anticipation grew between them.

At this point, it was clear to Dr. Sharma that he should leave. But how? The couple had by now blocked access to the steps! He hadn't ever been quite this close to the sexual activities of others. At Mira's gangbang he had observed from his distant royal box. Yes, he had wanted to see what these people see, to understand their thoughts and predilections, but was this too close for comfort? Desperate to distract himself, he turned to Katie in the hope of finding a conversational topic.

'These people here, they're all about pleasure,' Dr. Sharma observed to Katie, unnecessarily.

'Yeah.'

'But it's not just physical pleasure. There's something deeper than that. We all want to think of sex in the most basic terms possible, but it's not that simple, at least not for humans.'

'I suppose not.'

'So why do we try to boil it down to basic, common elements and remove individuality?'

'It's just easier.'

'It strikes me that sex is one of the only things where the brain and the body are inexorably linked. They're both dependent upon one another for genuine stimulation. For most other things in life, one can work without the other.'

'You mean like how the body can continue living while the brain's dead, and the brain can continue working while a body's paralysed?'

'Yeah,' said Dr. Sharma as he thought of something. 'Have you heard of this case in Spain? *La Manada*? The wolfpack?'

'No.'

'Apparently, these guys lured this teenage girl into a basement. They surrounded and attacked her. One of them filmed it, and it was shown during their rape trial. The video showed her eyes closed for the whole ordeal. She didn't fight. She didn't protest.

'The judge said the video showed her *passively suffering*. Like her mind had checked out, leaving her body to take it. The trial concluded that it wasn't rape because she didn't fight them. They said there was no obvious violence or intimidation from the men but that it *was* abuse because they had used her position of weakness to avoid gaining consent.

'Essentially the judges gave the men the benefit of the

doubt, assuming that had she protested, they would have let her go. But if your mind has checked out, how can you fight? The court needed her to engage her mind and body in protest to deliver a verdict of rape. They couldn't account for someone freezing in the moment. Her lack of reaction initially saved this *wolfpack* from a rape verdict. What drives people to want to exert power over another, or what drives someone to kill themself?'

'I don't know, Dev. These are difficult questions. It's difficult. For me,' answered Katie, trying not to observe the couple in the jacuzzi with them.

'Oh. I'm sorry,' Dr. Sharma sincerely apologised. 'Oh, that was *really* insensitive. I'm so sorry, I didn't mean to....'

'I know you didn't. It's fine, but you're asking questions that only awful people who do those things can answer. But *you're* trying to answer it. To do that, you'll need to think like them. Why, love? It's not who you are.' Katie paused a moment before asking, 'what happened, Dev?'

Attending Mira's gangbang had been about understanding the men but more about seeing a flicker of something from Mira. Something that Dev could connect with what Amina might have felt. However, it hadn't been the case. As he had said to Tim, Mira had been one of them, part of the team.

Dev had not wanted to imagine his sister distressed, but he had wanted to understand something of her, to carry the load for her, in some way. Having then failed to equate anything from Mira's outward appearance with what he had presumed for Amina, Dev had applied himself to understanding the thoughts and feelings of the victims like Amina.

Knowing the statistics indicated many workers, including

porn stars, experience sexual assault before entering the sex industry, he had hoped that talking with them would lead to a raw, visceral and emotional first-hand account of their experience of sexual assault.

Such was the grip of Serena's revelations on his mind that his own manipulation and violation of trust was of little consequence to him.

Since childhood, his desire to understand human thought had always been genuine. However, using it to better understand humanity was, since speaking with Alex, Roisin, Mira and Katie, only a cover for his true motivation: having a victim show him the pain and loneliness Amina had gone through.

Dr. Sharma and Katie's conversation was cut short by the conversation on the other side of the jacuzzi. 'It's no use, mate. I'm just too tight, or you're too big. That thing's not going anywhere,' said the woman.

'Nah, you'll be alright. The water's gonna lube you up,' the man assured her.

Dr. Sharma and Katie were dubious about this. So was the woman, who decided to turn around and fellate him, at least for a little while. Sitting back, the man's erect penis protruded from the water, periscope-like, before the woman leant in, her wet tongue sliding over his glans until he tipped his head back, enjoying the motion and textures of her soft mouth.

Before long, the woman administered a final lick, signalling the end of this segment and the beginning of a new one as she moved away from the steps and took a seat on another side of the jacuzzi. Leaning back, she lifted herself from the water and parted her legs slightly.

‘Now you,’ she said, with a smile, inviting him to reciprocate, which he did, following her away from the jacuzzi steps and affording Dr. Sharma and Katie their escape route. They scurried up out of the water and then down the steps and recovered their robes.

‘I’m going to find the loo,’ announced Katie once they had their robes back on. ‘Get me another juice?’

‘Sure.’

‘Listen, Dev. Don’t take it the wrong way, and I know I’ve said this before, but be careful. Just because they’re open-minded enough to screw strangers in hot tubs in front of each other, it doesn’t mean they won’t beat up gays, or think abortion is a sin, or think this should be whites only. This isn’t some sixties love-in.’

‘Agreed,’ replied Dr. Sharma, ‘meet you at the bar,’ he added before they headed in opposite directions.

Waiting his turn, as there was now a queue at the bar, he had time for a better look at the barman’s area. It had been done up like a little plastic beach shack, palm tree fronds decorated the frame, redolent of the beach theme of the venue. On the far side of the shack, Dr. Sharma this time spotted a man, stocky, bald-headed and entirely clothed. Clearly, he was a bouncer or a minder of some sort. With his drinks, Dr. Sharma decided to find out more.

‘All right?’ he asked, in greeting as he set the two orange juices down on the bar and sat on a stool.

‘All right,’ the man responded airily, barely glancing at Dr. Sharma before returning his gaze to a distant point in the room.

‘Can’t help but notice you’re fully clothed,’ stated Dr.

Sharma. 'Are you like a bouncer, or something, in case someone gets out of hand?'

'Something like that. I keep an eye.' Then after a few moments, 'first time here, isn't it?'

'Yeah.'

'You don't know where to start, do you?'

'Oh, well, I'm not really here for that.'

'Really?' asked the man with a smirk. 'What're you here for then?'

'You could say I just like to watch.'

'That's a lot to pay to just watch.'

A few moments passed before Dr. Sharma asked, 'you do this regularly, at these parties?'

'It's my job. One of them.'

'So you get to see all sorts of people who come here.'

'Yeah.'

'What do you make of them? Why do they come here?'

'Well... began the man. 'It's all about people, innit?' he continued after a few moments. 'I mean, it'd be a lot cheaper in the long run to buy a sex sleeve or a dildo. They come here for spontaneity, being in the moment.'

'But it's not spontaneous, everyone is here for the same thing, and everyone else knows that,' countered Dr. Sharma.

'They say the brain's the most erogenous zone. It's a turn on when you can't predict who you're going to meet, what they're going to do. Yeah, everyone's here for the same thing, something different. *Someone* different. Right body's easy to find. It's finding the right mind. The right words it says or doesn't say. Right timing. Right sounds. Does it cry? Does it scream? Does it make the body push against you because you're in too deep? Does it make the body grind against you to go harder?'

'*It*?' asked Dr. Sharma.

'Yeah. *It*. I reckon when they come here, it doesn't matter what the person they're fucking looks like, just what they do. It's all about pleasure, and other people become food for their needs, so only the senses matter, and the minds. That's just my fucked up view,' he added with a wry smile.

'So you think they cease to be people?' asked Dr. Sharma, somewhere between fascination and disgust. 'They're just *its*?'

'Mate, in that moment, they're there to perform a function. Do the right thing to get you off. Natural is better, but by design is also good. I mean, a fantasy only really becomes real if it happens naturally. You've only fucked your secretary over her desk when she's your actual secretary. It's no good getting your wife to pretend unless you can really make yourself believe your wife is your secretary.

'I'm only speculating here,' he continued, 'but take paedophiles. They could get a teenage prostitute to dress up like a schoolgirl, pretend to be even younger, but it's not the same. I reckon they crave that fear. Maybe they want to see that confusion and be the cause of it. To scare the shit out of someone, who better than a kid who has no idea what to do and is completely vulnerable?

'You could get an adult to pretend, but it wouldn't be the same. You could go beyond that, string 'em up, torture 'em, make 'em really fucking beg for their lives, but they would be too… aware. But for someone doing that, fear wouldn't be enough. They would want fear and confusion, having it dawn on them that something very wrong is happening, something they are totally unprepared for because they didn't know it existed.

'That's what I think about paedophiles, anyway. Rape's a weapon of war. Maybe the paedophile's war is fear and confusion. We should call *them* terrorists instead. Hearts and minds, and all that. They fuck both up, don't they?' the man finished with a dark chuckle.

'Bloody hell!' exclaimed Dr. Sharma, appalled at the turn this conversation was taking but unable to drag himself away. 'What are you talking about?'

'That if you come to a place like this, it's not just about bodies, it's about minds. We're all trying to put things in each other, one way or another. Dicks, cum, nipples, infections, words, beliefs, drugs,' replied the man. 'A lot of sex happens around me at these things. I don't watch, but sometimes I can't help seeing the looks on their faces. I listen to what they're saying when they're fucking. In the beginning, it feels weird, but then over time, you notice patterns.

'There was this one bloke who used to go upstairs to a room,' the man continued. 'The rooms don't lock so we can keep an eye on things. He'd always have the woman on top, and you could always tell he was about to finish because he would spit on his fingers and slip one or two up her backside, lay back on the bed, pull her down close and tight.

'Then he'd start whispering in her ear, as if it was only then that he would be making a connection with her, only then that he could get those words out of his head and into hers.' It was then that the man caught sight of Dr. Sharma's face, a mixture of consternation and revulsion. 'Hey, you asked about it,' said the man, absolving himself.

'No. I really didn't,' insisted Dr. Sharma.

'You really think this place is just about people fucking in pools? Strangers meeting to give each other nothing but pleasure, like some kind of utopia?' he scoffed. 'This place ain't for you. How did you get here, mate?'

'I was invited,' answered Dr. Sharma, recovering himself.

'Oh yeah, by who?'

'Mira. Cassavetes. The pornstar?'

'Oh yeah, that's interesting.'

'She said to ask for Grealish. I'm his… special guest? Apparently.'

'I know. They described you. I've been keeping an eye open for you. And that's *Mr* Grealish to you. Come with me, then. Let's see if he's free.'

The minder righted himself from his position leaning against the bar and casually sauntered past some more jacuzzis, sofas, tables and chairs, across the space to the wood doors with the frosted glass. Dr. Sharma left his drinks on a table and followed as the man opened and went through the doors, leading him to another door beneath the staircase where he and Katie had been waiting.

He hadn't noticed a door there before and had assumed that it was all solid wood panelling. This was the first point at which Dr. Sharma began to feel worried.

He had not wanted to enter any private rooms, at least not alone and not without Katie. But it turned out not to be a room as he followed the minder through the small door. Instead, it opened onto a spiral stairway. And went down.

# 56. The crawling of skin

'Watch your step,' cautioned the minder, and Dr. Sharma did. The top of the stairway was dimly lit, as though to discourage anyone who just happened upon the stairway from going down it. But they descended nonetheless. Dr. Sharma was well aware that they hadn't gone very far, just down a level, but it instantly felt like he was being led through a labyrinth of stairways and passageways.

'This way,' the man beckoned when Dr. Sharma reached the foot of the stairs in his robe, and they continued along a passageway. Like the passageway from the changing room to the swimming pool, this was painted and well illuminated. However, it didn't smell of chlorine.

The long spiral staircase had left him disoriented, so Dr. Sharma could no longer be sure of which part of the main building they were below. He followed the minder who never bothered to turn and check he was still there. A dozen metres or so, and they came to another wood panel door with a small inset window.

To Dr. Sharma, it looked like an office door with frosted glass, but he had no idea why anyone would have an office down here. The underground passageway was surprisingly warm and he thought he could spot condensation on the painted walls. The minder rapped on the door, and to Dr. Sharma's surprise, a little steam escaped from the opening when the minder's knock was answered after a moment.

*Oh! It's a sauna*, thought Dr. Sharma as he stood back and minded his own business while his guide exchanged words with whoever was inside the sauna. Eventually, the minder let the door shut and looked to Dr. Sharma before gesturing with his head towards the handle. Apprehension devouring his chest, Dr. Sharma moved cautiously towards it and reached for the handle.

'Uh-huh,' grunted the minder. 'You'll have to leave that on the hook,' he continued, gesturing at a row of hooks on the wall beside the door. On one of the hooks hung another robe. Royal blue. Dr. Sharma presumed it belonged to the man in the sauna and felt awkward pointing out that he wasn't wearing anything else.

'Neither is he,' the minder replied. 'It's a subtle way of making sure you've no recording devices. Although I don't know what recorder would work in all that steam.'

'Oh,' replied Dr. Sharma before he removed his robe and hung it on a hook.

'Just come back the way we came when you're finished,' advised the minder, as he turned back towards the spiral stairway.

For a second, Dr. Sharma considered retaking his robe and making his way back, but something enticed him to keep reaching. Gingerly, Dr. Sharma tugged the door handle and peered in through the steam. Inside was a nude, rotund man, in his fifties, sitting with his penis and testicles hanging over the edge of the middle-level bench. The man used his fingers to wipe away a layer of condensation from his lenses before he placed them back on his large, pitted nose.

'Hello there,' said the man amiably. 'Grealish. Neil Grealish. He put out his hand, and Dr. Sharma shook it.'

'Tim,' lied Dr. Sharma.

'Pleased to meet you, Tim. Please, sit down.' Dr. Sharma took a seat on the middle tier bench opposite Grealish. 'Our friend thinks we share a common interest,' he continued.

'Actually, it was Mira Cassavetes who said I should ask for you,' replied Dr. Sharma.

'Oh! Right! You're the one with the card!' Grealish smiled broadly and openly to him as if they were old friends, and Dr. Sharma couldn't help feeling somewhat charmed by his inviting manner. He didn't feel afraid of the man or the situation. A little intimidated but mostly intrigued by what would happen next. Like it was a scene from a play, Dr. Sharma felt he should be in the audience, watching from a distance rather than having to respond to Grealish and actively participate to keep things moving along.

'Yes, I'd heard from Sandra that she'd encouraged someone to seek my counsel. How is the lovely Mira. Did you bring her with you?'

'No.'

Grealish misread his brief response as reticence and decided to take the lead in the conversation. 'I like to have a little chat first, so we know each other before taking any next steps.'

Dr. Sharma still had no idea why he was there or what Grealish might represent and thought a well-placed question might shed light. 'What would be the next step?'

'Well, we first need to find out what you're looking for and then see if I can help. So we need to have a chat.'

'Okay,' assented Dr. Sharma.

'So, how are you enjoying my place?'

'It's nice.'

'Your first time here?'

'Yes.'

'Did you come alone?'

'No. I came with… another woman.'

'Not your wife,' Grealish calculated. 'Girlfriend?'

'*Friend*-friend.'

'Ah. *You* share a common interest?'

'Something like that.'

'Have you gotten to know some of the other people here?'

'A little,' answered Dr. Sharma, recalling the disturbing conversation with the minder.

'How about your friend?'

'A little. She's more used to… this. She has been to places like this before.'

'So, she's guiding you. You're new to this. Have you had any fun and or games with anyone upstairs?' he smiled.

'No.'

'How about your friend? Do you enjoy watching her with other people?'

'We're just observing, for now, soaking up the atmosphere.'

'The first time you attend a new venue, it's about showing your face, getting to know the regulars, gaining their trust, confidence, common ground. You understand. It's a nice place here. I bought it five years ago. We only completed all the renovations last year. I'm sure you'll enjoy it. Are you sure it's just about settling in tonight? Especially you, I'd have thought you'd want to be more active, your first visit to a party. Maybe no one here really catches your imagination. What do you think?'

Dr. Sharma genuinely didn't know what Grealish was getting at. 'I took a holiday in Croatia earlier this year,' continued Grealish. 'You ever been to Croatia?'

'No.'

'I went just after the peak of the summer season. Things were cooling down a bit. Just as hot as Spain at its peak. Hotter. Do you like hot climates?'

'I'm amenable. I like cold climates too.'

'We live in England. No choice, have we?' he laughed. 'I love the heat. That's probably why I spend a lot of time in here. I don't spend the entire party here. I have a comfy little room next door where I can watch in peace, without all that noise. As you know, if you've been waiting for one, I only have these parties once every three or four months. That's what keeps it exclusive, accessible only to select friends. And invitees.

'In your case,' continued Grealish, 'the delightful Miss Mira Cassavetes vouched for you. The parties are an excellent way to meet new people. People like you. Mira knows enough to only send me people who are… serious, so I have to believe that you are a serious man. That's why you're our guest this evening.

'I suppose the reason I mentioned Spain is that what I got

up to in Croatia reminded me of a time when I lived in Barcelona. I worked there at a news agency about thirty-three, thirty-four years ago. My dad's old school friend set me up with a job at a newspaper he owned there.

'My boss was a Spaniard, of course, a fair bit older than me. I was still a bit green when I got there, and he took me under his wing, often had me over to his house for dinner. That's when I met his family, his daughter. Mm, his daughter.' Grealish paused for a moment. 'She was like nothing I had seen before. She was… well, to be honest, I can't describe what it was about her that set her apart. All I knew was I wanted to fuck her. She knew. She must have known. She knew she had my attention.

'One day she came into the office, her mum used to leave her at the office a lot to see Dad during the school holidays, while she went shopping. One of the photographers was fiddling about with a new camera. He asked to take her picture in different lighting conditions to try out the camera, calibrate it and such. She was full of life and laughter, just having fun. Mimicking poses she'd seen on TV or in magazines. Each pose, whatever it was, blowing a kiss to the camera or running her fingers through her hair, she made me want to fuck her more and more.

'She was tanned, her skin glowing from the heat. I wanted to lick the crease in the skin at her neck. I wanted to put my hands around her little chest. I wanted what was between her legs. It felt like she must have known I was watching her. I didn't make it obvious, I tried to conceal it, but I just felt this… connection. You know what I mean? Of course you do. Like she was playing it up, but just for me. She was playing *with* me.'

Grealish fixed Dr. Sharma with his gaze. 'I fancied she enjoyed my eyes on her, and I knew she wanted more. She was eleven, no way I would have done that. At the time. I hadn't even considered it a possibility. I'd just imagine how good it would be. That and... well, I respected her father too much to do anything about it. Like I said, I was young, hadn't figured things out yet.

'As I was saying, earlier this year I was in Croatia, beautiful beaches, by the way, you really have to go. I was in a... relevant establishment, and I saw her again.'

'Really?' breathed Dr. Sharma, desperate for this to turn into a harmless story about adults.

'Well, no. Not her,' replied Grealish, once again locking eyes with Dr. Sharma. 'But another girl who looked exactly like my boss' daughter all those years ago. Except, this time, there was nothing to stop me. I took what I wanted, Tim. It was there. Available. Waiting to be plucked from the vine. For an hour, I satisfied myself that she was my old boss' girl. I convinced myself she knew exactly what she was doing. That she wanted me to bend her little body every which way. That she wanted my fingers in her mouth.

'It's a great thing to be able to lose yourself so thoroughly. That one in Croatia, the best yet, and I'm not a small chap. I don't know how she took me, but she did because she was still alive and gasping when I left, honest, guv,' he chortled, holding up his hands in mock surrender. 'But then you get what you pay for, right, Tim? Quality. She is a prime cut. The sort we should all have in our lives, whatever our taste. Tim, no one's going to just give you anything. You know that. We deserve what we want. Whatever we want, we should get.'

'You paid for her,' clarified Dr. Sharma, repulsed by what he was hearing but in no position to remonstrate. After all, he surmised, there was no telling what could happen to him there, should he voice dissent.

'We always pay, Tim, one way or another. She was already a real *go-getter*, fulfilling the fantasies of dreamers everywhere.'

'What was her story? How did she get there?' asked Dr. Sharma, struggling to contain the tremor of anger in his voice.

'Don't know, don't care,' stated Grealish. 'I wasn't there to hear her story, was I? It wasn't like I wanted to talk to her. Even if I wanted to, I don't speak Croatian, and she probably doesn't understand much English beyond *fuck* and *suck*. God, when I think of that sweet little mouth, wet little lips... Who wants to know about them? That's the whole point. They're... blank. Empty. That's how you've got to think about them. No thoughts, no personality, no story. Nothing except what you give 'em. They don't know any better. You know that. They think that's the way it's supposed to be, for them at least. Their parents, relatives, whoever's supposed to be looking after them, they know the score, and they've got them toeing the line, got them believing this is what it's supposed to be. So they just want to please. Because that's what they believe.

'There's so many of them now as well, don't ask me why,' Grealish continued. 'A lot of them are messed up, but that's neither here nor there. As long as they get treated right, they're happy to please. In the end, that's all we want. We want their little faces that can fit the palm of our hand. We want to make them into somethin' else, just for an hour or two.'

Grealish paused for a sip from his water bottle before continuing. 'Some people want it just the once. Just to satisfy their curiosity. They try it. Decide the lifestyle isn't for them after all. And that's fine. They think it's something they want, but they're mistaken. But they don't know until they try.' Smiling again, Grealish continued. 'Now, Tim. All we need to do is find out what you like. So, what's your pleasure?'

The doctor was taken aback by this. Despite sitting only a few feet away, he felt far from Grealish, powerless to stop his words from making their way to his ears through the steam. The heat of the sauna was disorienting him, but it was the pally, jokey arrogance of this repulsive human being that nauseated Dr. Sharma and made him want to bring up his orange juice over the white, tiled floor.

Air issued from a vent as details of the room swam in and out of focus while his blood pounded in Dr. Sharma's ears.

As for Grealish's question, he had been completely blindsided. While he should have seen it coming, his frame of mind meant that he was in no position to do anything other than follow Grealish's lead. However, still reeling from every single thing Grealish had uttered, Dr. Sharma's thoughts had barely kept pace with the conversation so far.

There he was, in an underground sauna, talking to a man who had just told him a story about paying to use a child for sex, although Grealish had been careful not to state any specifics. Dr. Sharma had no idea how to answer him.

'Well, I don't know. I haven't really thought about that,' stalled Dr. Sharma.

'Can't help if I don't know what you're a-hankering,' came the jaunty reply from Grealish, through the endearing smile.

'Okay,' said Dr. Sharma, despising himself for playing along. 'What if I want a UK girl? Born and raised?'

'East European is safer,' divulged Grealish, leaning forward, 'but I can get you a UK one. Higher risk, higher price.'

'Thirteen.'

'Ooh, now that's really difficult. That age, you can't know what they're going to do or say. They can't keep their mouths shut. If you want one that age, we really need to go foreign, like Hungarian. Honestly, only amateurs deal with UK girls that age. Younger is better.'

'Asian.'

'Now you're on the right track, but I don't work in the Asian market. Central Europe, East Europe, North Africa. That's me.'

'What would the story be for a girl like that? A thirteen-year-old British-Asian girl. What would the price be?' asked Dr. Sharma, his voice growing harder, despite himself. 'In your *experience*, do thirteen-year-old British-Asian girls turn up a lot in these… circles? Is that something a lot of men want?'

'Tim, you're looking at this the wrong way,' replied Grealish. 'Consider the phrase *dream girl* or *fantasy girl*. See a good looking woman in a magazine, and she's called a *dream girl*. You know why, don't you? Because she doesn't matter. She's not real. She's not really there because she's not meant to be.

'Tim, this is all real, my son, what I'm offering you. I'm

telling you that you matter. You are important. If you are real, you matter. Your feelings exist. You can continue to live in the dream world where you don't matter, or you can reach out and take what you want. Pain is real. Pleasure is real. These are things we can hold on to, depend on to anchor us when dreaming's not enough. Otherwise, the real world will drift away from us.

Grealish continued. 'You want to enter the real world, don't you, where you matter? The real world is the only place where pleasure and pain make sense. The real world is the only place discord works perfectly, where chaos is perfectly logical. It's unhealthy to doubt your desires.

'If you desire something, it must be natural, right? If it's natural, why fight it? That makes sense, doesn't it?' asked Grealish pleasantly. 'Look, some people feel like they need to make up a story, and that's different. I know someone who pretends he's saving them. Serving a higher purpose. He imagines he does that by turning these special, *golden* girls into women. He's been saving them for decades. It's a pity he can't brag about his heroics,' scoffed Grealish. 'Every couple of years, they get too old, and he chooses a new one to make him a hero.

'Tim, I meet fellas like you all the time. Let me save you the time and energy and give you the benefit of my years.' With that, Grealish reached out with his wet hand and grasped Dr. Sharma's. 'It's okay, son,' he nodded. 'It's *okay*, now. You're with us. We're your brothers and sisters. We understand you and your struggle, but it doesn't have to be a struggle,' he emphasised before withdrawing his hand. 'Tim, I'm going to give you something. Stay there,' he said before getting up from the bench and crossing the wet tiles to the door.

Dr. Sharma pictured him slipping on the tiles and cracking his skull open on the edge of the bench as he disappeared behind a heavy glass door that opened into another room. Presumably, the room where he did all his watching while the party went on above him.

He wasn't gone long. When he returned, Grealish held a memory drive between his puckered fingers, which he proffered to Dr. Sharma as he shakily got up from the bench.

'You imagine a world where you can have what's on this,' began Grealish. 'You can have this at your fingertips. That's the world you can be living in. Tim, a journey is full of steps, and this chat with me is your first one. You take a look, and when you're ready to stop dreaming, stop apologising and claim your place in the world, you get in touch with me. Just tell them to tell me you're Tim from the sauna, I'll know who you are. I never forget a name, and I never forget a face. I'm good like that.'

# 57. Project manager in charge of closure

Katie was put out that Dr. Sharma had left her alone for so long but understood once he explained to her his difficult predicament that stemmed from his being a guest at the request of Mira Cassavetes. Although she understood his not having a choice, it didn't mean she was any less bothered and had declared that she would be sleeping the entire journey home.

So it was, with Katie asleep under his blazer on the back seat, that Dr. Sharma sped home in the small hours of the morning. He didn't tell her about the memory drive. Or the details of his conversation with Grealish. Instead, he ran everything through his mind again and raged internally at what he had come into contact with. His anger fuelled by his impotence in the face of evil. An evil that had been so charming, disarming and ingratiating.

*The skeletal structure, the muscle, the tissue, the layers and layers of epidermis falling into place, all to create some truly horrific person,* rambled Dr. Sharma's mind as it took off in multiple directions at once. *All of this natural selection, natural engineering, the evolution of humankind, the sum of all biology's achievements of design, form and function that give a physical enclosure to thoughts as sickening as Grealish's.*

*A one in 400 trillion chance of being born and Grealish's barbarity is the result?* he asked rhetorically. *The ability to compute so much information, see millions of colours, discern so many sounds, create such beauty, and yet they wilfully choose their sexual desires over a child's need for safety. We're not all working to the same threshold of what is acceptable in the world, in life. We're pieces of jagged, broken glass that do not fit together.*

Dr. Sharma's mind spiralled, asking and answering its own questions. *Who are these people who can rape and see it as a personal achievement? A victory? What kind of mindset allows one person to hurt another for pleasure? For power. For gain. For control. Sex is used in different ways. To express love, for creation, recreation, to destroy innocent people caught up in war, and everything in between.*

*Suicide, too, can be visceral but also ruthlessly premeditated with meticulous precision and used in different ways. As the means to end an unhappy life, as a way to end physical pain, to end illness, political protest, removing oneself from the world... For those who abhor the idea, suicide probably represents the ultimate symbol of nihilism. To others, it might represent the ultimate act of devotion.*

*Surely, for some, there is validity to the assertion that suicide is an exertion of control over one's existence, to bring an end to that existence. Suicide isn't just about helplessness, is it?* asked Dr. Sharma. *It has to be a choice. Otherwise, it's not suicide. It's murder, like that teenager who encouraged another to kill themself.*

*If Amina killed herself, was it because she had nowhere to turn? Did she feel she had no one in her corner? Or was it an act of defiance? Can I see her suicide as her protest?*

# 58. Destroyed room

It was still dark outside when Dr. Sharma left Katie at her place, the car skirting the bends through the darkness of the night to carry him home, but it wouldn't be long before his part of the world would once again turn towards the sun. Dr. Sharma knew he needed to get some sleep before his day at work, but he couldn't put it off.

The memory drive had been growling and gnawing at him through the pocket where he had placed it. Now that he was home, he had to see what was on it. He had to know what had been passed to him. He had to know how they saw Amina. How she had felt.

Once inside, Dr. Sharma kicked away his shoes and threw off his jacket before palming the memory drive that, to him, almost seemed like a living entity in his breast pocket, pulsing and breathing, leaving his skin clammy. He strode purposefully through the living room to the second bedroom that he used as a study, where he came to a stop, hovering before the laptop computer, weighing up his options.

Unable to make sense of his thoughts, he threw the drive down onto the desk. It clattered upon the hard surface and ricocheted off the side of the machine. He had no idea what would be on the drive. Considering where it had come from, he imagined pictures. Video. Considering where it had come from, he didn't want to find out.

He felt he would be giving in to the likes of Grealish if he watched it, as though vindicating their *lifestyle*, as Grealish had put it. He didn't want to, but, he argued to himself, it might give him some insight into how Amina had felt.

After what his mother had told him all those months ago, Amina's torment was all that mattered to him anymore. All the conversations he had had with the likes of Mira, Katie, Alex and Roisin, his research, had been building to something.

This wasn't necessarily it, perhaps just another stepping stone along the way. *On the way to what?* On the way to some kind of resolution, some closure. *Resolution? Is that even possible?*

His mother's revelations had changed everything for him. Gone from him were the thoughts of Amina as a happy little girl who suffered a terrible accident. That wasn't her anymore. That person had been taken from him. Instead, Amina had been manipulated by a paedophile for their pleasure.

That evening he had sat with a paedophile who had tried to sell him a lifestyle.

Dr. Sharma's skin crawled as he recalled the conversation with Grealish. Filled with self-loathing, he was ashamed of his cowardice.

*Why didn't I stand up for what was right? Why didn't I stand up for Amina? Far too late to make any difference to Amina, but it would have felt good to watch Grealish's blood drip into the gutter, mixing with the piss and shit of the sewers.*

Other than that, what resolution could he possibly hope for? The secret that Serena had kept for so long had suddenly been transferred to him, and now he was expected to maintain the same secret, keep it from his father.

Too late. Too much time had passed for Dr. Sharma to mount any kind of battle against one specific person. Who could he fight? How could he seek justice for his sister? It would be impossible to track down whichever individuals had been responsible for this monstrous violation. The violation of trust, the trust of a child, a small child who barely knew herself.

A typical man in this way, Dr. Sharma chose to busy himself with an impossible task rather than face the emotions bound up with the failure, he presumed, of being unable to track down, after all this time, the perpetrator of Amina's repeated rape.

*Rape.*

It was the first time he had allowed himself to think that word in connection with Amina. She had been raped. His sister had been raped. As a child. Repeatedly. He didn't know at the time, but now he did, and he could no longer let her go through it alone.

Could he consciously, deliberately effect an instance of transference, here and now? Whatever child appeared on this memory drive, could he use them as a proxy, use them to get closer to his sister, get close to what she had seen, heard and thought? Or would he be doing precisely as Grealish had encouraged? Using a child as a blank slate, imposing what he wanted that child to reflect. Albeit for entirely different reasons. But still…

In handing him the unsolicited memory drive, Grealish had provided an unexpected voice, a conduit, that he had not sought but that may have also provided the means to understand the final weeks of Amina's life. Could he watch it happen to someone else to see things from the body, the brain, the thoughts, the eyes of his sister?

Dr. Sharma thought he might find some feeling, emotion, memory, idea or truth. With that, he might also draw a line beneath all this and finally grieve for his sister.

Since Serena had revealed her truth, Dr. Sharma realised he had never really grieved for Amina. As a child, he had neither the tools to mourn nor the vocabulary to frame his thoughts. With the move to Mauritius and beyond, he had learnt to memorise information but process very little in the way of emotions. He didn't know how to grieve. He was aware of the relevant feelings but not how to connect them for the desired outcome. The ability to put everything away again.

There was a blocked ventricle. There was water in the lungs. Excess fluid in the brain. Something was haemorrhaging. He needed to exhale again.

Whatever Dr. Sharma would view could not be unviewed and would probably remain with him for the rest of his days. If he learnt anything from the memory drive, would it be enough to afford him some release?

For hour after hour, Dr. Sharma turned it all over in his mind as he wandered the small flat, sweating through his shirt, struggling with all the memories, struggling with the guilt, the stench that he felt had come off the memory drive and had applied itself to his hands, his clothes, his skin.

Dr. Sharma mumbled and rambled to himself as he roamed each room, seeking an escape from his own selfish need to regain some kind of equilibrium. But nothing had been normal for him since Amina's death. He no longer knew what *normal* would be. Everything he had been, said and done in aid of feeling normal had been an imitation of what he saw around him.

*Who am I, really? Who would Amina be right now?*

The first orange glows of sunlight were just becoming visible through the window of Dr. Sharma's study as he crouched on the floor, leaning against the cheap, wooden door that he had meant to paint since he moved in. The air outside would be nice and cool on his burning head. Nice, fresh air. Renewed and pristine, awaiting the day's opening exhaust fumes.

Getting up from the floor with resolve, he snatched up the small rectangle of plastic from where it had landed hours ago and sat before his computer before plugging the memory drive into the relevant port. Having not viewed anything like this before, Dr. Sharma was frightened of what he might find, but his frame of mind was such that he just needed to know. Mentally and physically exhausted, he needed to see what she had been through.

The screen illuminated his physicality, that of a person who had hours ago ceased to operate their body with any deliberate thought. All available energies were being redirected to his mind as his brain braced for impact and ran through the various possibilities for what might lie on the memory drive.

Pornography, of some sort.

Photographs. Or video.

A child. A girl. Being molested. Being raped.

A conscious child. A drugged child.

Adult hands. Adult genitalia. Men. Women. With children.

No adult faces. Just children.

Maybe no faces. Body parts.

A green field. Blue sky. Fluffy clouds.

Hideously incongruous, given the circumstances. The forced sentiments of tranquil safety greeted him as the operating system went through its various processes. Automatically executing preprogrammed commands. Allocating various resources.

Dr. Sharma was sure he was to view child pornography.

In consuming pornography, the viewer traditionally experiences the presented sexual act vicariously. Dr. Sharma's goal was to understand what Amina might have encountered, absorb the experience vicariously through the unfortunate child on the screen. Having argued with himself all night, he decided he had no choice but to seek more information and complete Amina's story in his mind.

Dr. Sharma looked to the computer screen. The screen glowered at him in return. He imagined the machine vehemently disapproving of what it was being compelled to do, but despite this, his fingers coerced it into complying.

*Here goes*, he thought as he clicked on the tiny graphic representing the drive.

It opened to reveal a single file.

A video file.

# 59. Run your eyes

Inhaling deeply, Dr. Sharma manipulated the cursor, dragging the file to a video player. He had half expected or hoped that the file would be password protected or corrupted, stopping him from viewing the video. He was surprised as the solid black beginning of the video expanded to take up the entire screen. Dr. Sharma held his breath as the seconds ticked by, and the screen continued to show black.

By the timecode at the bottom of the screen, thirty-six long seconds had passed before Dr. Sharma's face was suddenly lit by the bright image on the screen. Surprised by the sudden light blinding him after the darkness, his eyes took a few moments to adjust.

When they did, what he saw wasn't an actual video but a static image.

The image showed a girl. About ten. Not in any state of undress. Instead, she wore her school uniform.

No tie. Just the skirt, shirt, knee socks and black shoes.

Shiny, blue eyes and shoulder-length blonde hair.

Sitting on a kitchen stool, she smiled openly and genuinely with her entire face.

On the counter next to her was a mug of tea. On the wall behind her was a partially open kitchen cupboard. Past the cupboard door, Dr. Sharma could make out the branding belonging to familiar breakfast cereals.

It wasn't a pornographic image.

It was simply a picture of a girl sitting on a stool in a kitchen with a mug of tea.

For the ten seconds that the image was on Dr. Sharma's screen, there hadn't been any sound, but here the image was suddenly joined by the voice of a man. The sound quality was scratchy, captured by a basic microphone on a household video capture device. A child could be heard faintly in the background.

Whimpering.

'Look at yourself. In the mirror. Look at yourself while you do it. Look at yourself. How do you look? Eh?' The male voice asked before the sound crackled away, and the image abruptly vanished, retreating to its file, leaving only a black screen.

There was no multitude of images. Just one girl sitting with her mug of tea in a kitchen. An old image. (He could tell, from the cereals that had since been rebranded to shed their unhealthy image that appealed to children but had concerned parents.) Although not obviously pornographic, it was, in a way, worse than what Dr. Sharma had already braced himself for. It was not what he was expecting.

A typical memory a parent can bring up from any school morning. The hideous incongruity of the sound projecting anything but a wholesome image. Could the sound of whimpering be pornographic? It hardly mattered. Both items had seared themselves into his memory, and he thought of Amina whimpering in fear, quietly begging for them to stop.

Losing herself.

Getting closer to the end.

The pain, the fear. Being pushed to do things.

The loneliness she had endured, unable to tell anyone.

The desperation and shame, combined with the belief that her life was worthless.

Dr. Sharma felt he understood more about what had happened to his sister, but it wasn't enough to explain her decision to end her life. He was unable to think of her in such a way. Unable to think of her as someone who, at the age of thirteen and no matter what had happened, would see death as the most appealing solution.

'How could she decide to do such a thing?' he asked himself out loud. 'Was it even her decision? Yes, she did it but maybe she didn't decide. She wouldn't have been in the right state of mind. She wasn't even ending things, as far as she was concerned. She was seeking,' he concluded.

*What was she seeking?*

'She was seeking something better. She has to be somewhere better. Amina was too beautiful for this place.'

*What was she seeking?*

'She was seeking… I suppose she was seeking what she thought was something beautiful. God? Yes. In her way, she was looking for God!'

*But you don't believe in God.*

'But she did, then, I think. It can't have just been grief. I can't let that be the truth. I won't let her be so crushed and used that death was her only escape. She was seeking God. That was it.

'How could she leave certainty? How could anyone leave the absolute, unchanging certainty of the world? People hope they'll go to God upon death, but what if this world is as close as they get?

'How can you check out like that? Leave everything behind? Lots of people believe without seeing. At least while alive, one can choose to believe in the munificence, the safety of God's embrace, the hands of God, whatever it is they believe in. God's whisper that puts everything in its proper place. How can one so young take steps to remove doubt about the existence of God? How does anyone do that? Surely it's too large a step to take? It's too final. What if they're wrong? What if there's nothing?

'There can't be nothing. Amina has to be out there, connecting with me. She has to be… because I don't want to be alone anymore.'

In the aftermath, Dr. Sharma drifted aimlessly from room to room of his flat, as though once more becoming familiar with everything in the context of this new event. To him, the words continued to seep from the bare walls at him.

*Look at yourself.*

*How do you look?*

*Eh?*

Dr. Sharma's mind was full of Amina. No space for anything non-Amina-related. A search for God made beautiful sense. It fitted a narrative he could accept. He could reconcile her state of mind before her death. *A search for God.*

Dr. Sharma could reconcile his own state of mind after his mother's revelations. *She was searching for God.* In those moments after watching the video, to Dr. Sharma, everything suddenly made complete, glorious, beautiful sense.

'Ever since that day at Mum's hospice, some days feel like a dream while others have had the sharp laser of some ultra-focussed hyper-reality,' he said to himself.

'I feel, at the click of my fingers, I could forget all the feelings and emotions I ever felt. All people would disappear from my mind, like a dream. Like none of them ever mattered.

'Is that why she would kill herself? Is that what she was doing? She thought she was getting closer to God? Is that what she was looking for? Then where is God? Where are they and when are they coming? I want them to see us, all this, what we have become. Have we lived up to expectations? Do we deserve them? I want them to see us. They need to see this world.'

*Look at yourself.*

'I don't believe God exists,' he continued. 'I believe Amina exists. I should be a different person. Whom should I have been? Who should Amina have been?

'Like my father, all those years ago, I'm empty. Nothing left. I am at that place where letters, symbols, numbers, fears, dreams, beliefs and facts, come together and disappear. That place where none of it matters anymore, as it all comes apart with the destruction wrought by our most outrageous desires.

'With the terrible thunder of explosions and roaring jets, did those first men who sought to break orbit and leave the planet really only believe in science and physics, mathematics, astronomy, cosmology?' Dr. Sharma asked himself. 'Part of them must have contemplated meeting God up there.

'What if they came upon some being that announced themself as God, creator and destroyer of all things? What would they say? Did the space agencies prepare their ambassadors for any potential meeting with God? Or other beings? A *Do* List and a *Don't* List?

'How about Laika, the first canine cosmonaut? Did she have any religious convictions? Did she believe in God, or only in other animals? And things she could see and sniff. What about Ham, the chimp?

'In the vastness of space would you become completely free, unburdened of everything you thought you knew. Mightn't your mind unravel to accept all ideas and notions without the limits imposed upon us by what we can sense? Faced with such ever-reaching emptiness, would everything come apart, leaving ordered reality a distant dream?

'Meanwhile, on Earth, the pursuit of knowledge goes on. In all sorts of fields, our honours assume the knowledge and skills we accumulate will continue being relevant. If everything we know is declared invalid in a world collapsing on itself, will anything continue to mean anything?' Dr. Sharma asked.

'Does being human matter as much as we think it does? Is it all we truly have? Is it essential to go on being humans with reason and logic? Courage in the face of adversity? Why is that important? Extremes of pleasure and pain alter our view of what we are capable of. A chemical reaction in the brain.

'What if our lives were suddenly nothing but extremes?

Would we forget who we were? What if all the things we had once achieved were declared as no longer possible? That time your kid scored a freekick from a seemingly impossible angle. What if geometry and the laws of physics no longer worked in the same way as before? Would it erase what she had done that day? The way the ref's whistle fell from his lips. The way all her friends hugged her as if they had already won the trophy. What if things like that were not possible anymore?'

Dr. Sharma wandered his flat and continued. 'Would you want to continue living under such conditions? All those physical parameters that make us humans and make the world the way we know it. If they all changed to form something totally unrecognisable, would you want to continue? If your family was no longer recognisable as such… if you could no longer recognise yourself, would anything matter to you anymore?

'Evolution, a painfully slow process, but what if evolution could happen overnight and you could suddenly sprout wings? I can imagine and accept that everything that we know is solid and true about science, biology, astronomy, cosmology, physics, maths, and everything. But suppose all that can be completely changed at any moment by some vengeful God or some other being. Then, it must be possible that everything we know and accept as solid and true is ultimately insignificant fiction.

'A simple fiction with no real consequences for anybody involved. Is that what thirteen-year-old Amina figured out before taking steps? Tangled masses of half-baked philosophies, part-dreamed impulses, arbitrarily concocted values we impose and standards by which we judge. If everything suddenly changed, nothing would matter anymore.'

Rambling, Dr. Sharma collapsed on his bed, his head hot, his clothes damp with sweat. At last, he finally slept, unaware that he had been rambling like this through the morning, consequently missing his surgery hours. Instead of being aware, he slept and dreamt.

# 60. Electric sleep

Exhausted, Dr. Sharma slept on his stomach, still in his clothes, bedraggled from the hours he had spent up and stumbling around his flat, speaking dissonance to himself. He slept long, plunging deep into a pit of night, the unyielding dark of space.

In that space, he inevitably dreamt. He dreamt many things that night, mainly images, unconnected spits, bubbles and crackles. Here and there. Nothing that made any kind of sense. Nothing that he would remember later on. The only dream that was half coherent was this:

Dr. Sharma dreamt he was back at the hospital. A trainee surgeon. He was operating on a patient. He was taking up surgery, as his father had advised. The scalpel in his hand. The blood on his gloves. The others, his mentors, watched him. Expectantly. Eyes above surgical masks. All watching and waiting.

Dr. Sharma was exhausted from a night of study in preparation for this operation. He fought sleep from his eyes, but he was losing. The cavity below yawned at him, reflecting the yawn behind his mask, while the machines monitored the patient's numbers. Everything was stable. Everything was fine. All he had to do was stay awake through the next steps and finish.

And finish.

He couldn't. It was all too much. The weight of sleep was too much to carry. He finally allowed it to wrap around him, consume him. Like a boa constrictor, its powerful muscles clenched tightly and forced his head down, down into the cavity. Organs pushed against his face as blood flooded his nostrils. He was vaguely aware of his ears filling with a viscous substance before his shoulders followed him past the clamped folds of flesh.

Dr. Sharma's arms, waist, knees and feet soon disappeared amongst the red, pulsing organs.

The next thing he knew, he was outside, rising from the slime in a wasteland. He could hear cries, but he saw nothing. His eyes were caked over with ooze. He brought his hands to his face and wiped the slime away.

Looking down at his hands and the rest of his body Dr. Sharma saw he was covered in a slimy substance, a burnt sienna colour in the dying light. He guessed it was dusk. Unable to make things out clearly, he appeared to be in a swamp of this sludge. It took him a few moments to locate the smell, and when he did, he realised it was blood.

Oozing, gelatinous, congealing blood.

The shock of this was quickly surpassed by the realisation that it wasn't mud under his feet.

Organs.

Body parts.

He could feel them with his feetd as he moved around, crushing them. Lungs, livers, eyeballs, kidneys, brains. Immediately Dr. Sharma panicked and began slapping the pieces of human remains off himself. The sound of the flesh echoed around his thoughts. He clawed at the blood, trying to strip it from his skin with his fingers, but to no avail. He couldn't see in the fading sunlight, couldn't identify his skin from the remains.

He heard the cries again, above him. They were human cries. He looked up and saw people. Naked.

Instinctively, Dr. Sharma backed away to the bank behind him. He hid by a tree, trying to meld himself to the trunk. There he watched these people.

Wave after wave, they ran to the cliff where they overpowered those already there. At first, Dr. Sharma couldn't make out what those people were doing there in the first place. He gradually realised that they were gratifying themselves with the bodies of the fallen, dead and alive.

They used bones. Human bones. All shapes, lengths, sizes. The men and the women. Their bare bodies slick with blood and other fluids. Each wave set upon the previous. Each time, the last wave failed to anticipate the attack, consumed with their pleasure.

The next group grabbed at them, bit into them, drew more blood. They bit, and pulled, and clawed, and tore the flesh from one another. They plunged their hands deep into the gashes they made and ripped out the organs they found. On these, they gorged themselves, tearing at the tissue with their teeth, chewing the muscle.

Once one appetite was satiated, they set about satisfying the other, finding a suitable bone, texture, or orifice, natural or otherwise, with which to gratify themselves. Then, the cycle began again.

In a state of complete shock, Dr. Sharma realised he needed to hide. He decided to climb the tree to hide amongst the branches. But as he began climbing, he saw there were animals already there, also hiding. In the dim light, he could see their eyes. Somehow, he sensed they didn't want him there with them. They were afraid of him. He had no choice. He had to go back down to the swamp. There he reached down into the sludge and pulled up a bloody heart. He hesitated, but just for a moment before baring his teeth and tearing into it for sustenance.

And then… he woke up.

'Hey! Wake up!' I shout out to him as he nears the end.

His eyes dribbling water, he no longer struggles against the belt. He has accepted the allergic reaction that has transformed the skin around his neck. He has accepted that it distracted him. He has accepted that the belt is not loosening. He's going to die, but I'm not finished with him yet.

'Why do you need to know what everyone's thinking?' I ask him. 'If you are so worried about what other people think, why not just tell everyone what to think? Do you think this is how religions got started? One group of people, so concerned with what another group was thinking, they decided to tell them what to think. All the time. Around the clock. Through the calendar. Maybe that's really what religious festivals, holy days, and observations were originally about. An opportunity to, if you will, top-up the thoughts of the people. Make sure they were still thinking the *right* thoughts.'

'I don't know. I'm not starting a religion.'

'Aren't you?' I goad him. 'You want to know the things that go on behind closed doors. You want to explain the things people do to each other. That's what you told Tim and your parents. You wanted everyone to accept everything.'

'No. Just to accept that we're not so different. Humans don't need to live in the dark... scrabbling for truth... wilfully turning eyes to ignorance because it's closer than the truth... It just takes a little more effort to get there. People approaching different races, faiths, cultures, religions, histories with new eyes... new perspectives.'

'Sounds like you're preaching to me,' I cajole him, looking for a reaction.

'Think what you want.'

Like clouds casting shadows over valleys, the contours of my shadowy being seem to change to him as the light in the room shifts, and dark outlines meld from one thing into another. Dev slowly blinks again to find his focus.

Instead, he finds...

'Mira?' he asks, his eyes widening as she looks down at him. Wrinkling her nose at his sweaty stench of oncoming death, her eyes hold no pity for him.

'Mira... help me... please,' Dr. Sharma whispers. At this point, his energies are so depleted, his acceptance of death so complete, that he may as well add: 'if you feel like it.'

Mira is in no mood for him today. 'Why should I... want

to understand people and their sick thoughts?' Under normal circumstances, Dev would be taken aback but try not to show it. Here, though, he is too tired for any reaction. 'Who are you, some sick fuck, like them?'

'No, Mira… I'm not.'

'You don't know what you are, but I do. You're no better than them scumbags. You're just another man who wants a piece of me,' Mira states.

'That's not… no.'

'You're not going to take advantage of me,' she mutters, tears rolling down her cheeks as she leans over him, her long hair brushing his wet shirt as the tears drop from her face to combine with his sweat before she screams at him. 'No man takes advantage of me!'

Terrified of her, confused as to why she is so angry, Dev tries to put up his hands in defence, but he's too weak. Mira's long nails easily pierce and plunge into his skin. She beats and beats on him so hard that her arms come clean away from her body!

They're not her arms anymore, and yet they still beat down on him all around his head. The fingers scratch at his face. Dev cries out in pain, but she is too far gone to hear. Such is the uncontrollable rage within her that she screams herself out of existence.

The screeches of a trapped individual fill his ears, thicker than the pounding blood. Dev tries to turn his head away, crying out at the pain that dissipates almost as suddenly as it arrived. The fists and arms, having slid away from Dev's head, invite him to cautiously look up.

He turns weakly back to find Mira gone and I am here once more.

# 61. Venture

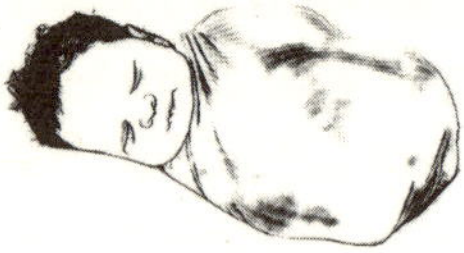

Ah, but I see we've stimulated our *good doctor* a little too vigorously. He no longer knows where he is, barely knows what he is. Like a baby, he just wants discomfort to end, to feel better. This is no fun. There is nothing to be gained while he is like this. Nothing to be learnt. Let's dial this back a little, slow down his rate of degeneration. After all, without the relevant information, I cannot decide.

'Decide what?' he asks. 'What do you want from me?'

'Oh good, you can hear me. Well, I need to decide what to give you, although it is a shame to give you something you will never use.'

'Who are you?'

'I don't know. Who are you?'

'Huh?'

'You have been taking us on some kind of journey. Although I understand more than I did a couple of minutes ago, you are too erratic. Your thoughts, memories, needs, imaginings… I cannot discern a pattern. So, where will you take us next?'

'Help me. Please. You can help me.'

'What if I say the word, *family*? What does that bring up?'

Dr. Sharma finds himself in his office. He is at the surgery. He isn't a locum in a strange room. This is his own. His familiar shelf of books is on the wall behind him. Mainly for show and primarily consisting of the latest copies of *MIMS*. His house plant stands guard on the corner of his desk, next to his computer screen.

Facing him was Charlotte Newbury. In her forties, with blue eyes and brown hair, she sat on the armless chair, across the desk from Dr. Sharma, with her hands in her lap, fumbling with the buckle of her handbag.

'I don't want to be here,' she began, 'talking about this, but I've tried talking to them, and I'm not getting anywhere.'

'So things are still the same?'

'Worse.'

'Worse? In what way?' asked Dr. Sharma, leaning forward.

'They don't talk to each other. At all. Sometimes, they don't even talk to me. It feels like I'm the only one trying, and then neither of them talk to me. I think: "what is that about?"'

'Why don't they talk to you?'

'They both think that I'm helping the other. I'm just trying to help my family. I feel like everything is out of my control. How can I get them both to understand each other? They are father and son, and they can't stand each other. It shouldn't be like this. At least when they were both talking to me, I could pretend things were part-way normal. Andy just completely shuts down. I don't know what is going through his mind. I know Jeff is in pain, but Andy doesn't give me anything. He's so cold. I wonder what I did to make him that way. I didn't raise him like that. Somewhere along the way....' She didn't finish the sentence.

'I'm sure he's just going through his own process,' replied Dr. Sharma. 'He's working things out in his way. It's a new situation for both of them. You too. You're all working it out separately.'

'It feels like he goes from being one person to another every other day. When I get home, I don't know what I'm going to walk into. When I leave your office, I don't know if I'll find Andy friendly or sullen, or silent, or angry. I don't know how to predict it.

'I wish I had a chart to work it out. I could say: *it's been cloudy today, but City won at the weekend, and we're closer to payday, so that should make him, let me see...*' she said, consulting an imaginary chart, '*silent.* I'd like to know what the parameters are. The variables. That would be good,' she finished with a nod.

'I know. I wish it was that simple,' empathised Dr. Sharma.

'I could do with things being level for a while. I don't need peaks and valleys. Just a smooth road with some consistency.'

'Charlotte. Do you want another prescription?'

'I don't know,' she answered, eyeing the printer on the side as she imagined the conversation that lay ahead of her.

At the family-friendly pub that overlooked the sea, Dr. Sharma and Tim ignored the large TV on the wall, with its images of international unrest. He cradled his habitual black coffee and stared at Dr. Sharma, who benevolently divided his attention between his friend and the stony-faced newscaster.

'So… yeah. It looks like we're separating,' said Tim, from across their usual table. Had Tim not been so wrapped up in his own matters, he would have spotted the change in his old friend. He might even have been so moved as to bring up his uncharacteristically distracted demeanour.

'I know the whole thing is a touchy topic. I was trying to be…' the doctor trailed off.

'Yeah, well, don't,' interrupted Tim. 'Let's just talk straight if we're going to talk. Otherwise, let's just sit, drink our drinks and watch the news.'

'Okay,' said Dr. Sharma, accepting that there was no way he could avoid this. He turned his face away from the TV and focused all his attention on his friend. 'It's not what you want?' he asked.

'No,' replied Tim.

'What *do* you want?'

'I want a normal marriage like our parents had.'

'Right, so you want monogamy. Nuclear family. Kids' birthday parties. Barbecues in the summer. That sort of thing?'

'Yes, you know I do. Why are you pretending like you don't know?'

'Then is there any way to salvage it, your marriage?'

'I love her,' tried Tim.

'Is that enough? Does she love you?'

'We're married. It must have been there. It's not like we got married by accident.'

'People do. Do you want to stay married?' Dr. Sharma

asked his friend.

'I don't know.'

'Tim, you wanted me to talk straight. This is what we're dealing with.'

'It's my fault, isn't it?' asked Tim, rhetorically, going off-topic. 'If I'd dealt with it earlier… this wouldn't be happening,' he admitted. It was a rare moment of introspection for Tim. 'I thought I was being… that that was what she wanted. An open marriage. I thought I'd give it a go, you know? I thought I was being adventurous, forward-thinking, open to new ideas. I don't know what we are anymore. We don't… we've stopped talking about anything that matters. I think she craves excitement. I just want to know what I'm coming home to after work. Look, Dev, aside from all that, let's face it, it was never going to work. Me and her,' reasoned Tim.

'Why?'

'She's a top solicitor, and I deliver flowers. How did I convince myself that that was ever going to work?'

'People are more than their jobs, Tim.'

'That's what I thought. I'm not so sure anymore. Too much disparity between what we do for a living.'

'There's a big difference between what you and I do, but we're still friends.'

'That's different. I'd think of you the same way whatever you did. When I met Ruth, I think I was so impressed by her that I dismissed all the negative stuff.'

'Negative stuff about her, or –'

'In general. I just kept asking myself: "could I do what she does?" Not just becoming qualified, but imagine that I already had all that knowledge and those qualifications. Could I then argue cases, think on my feet, remember all that stuff? I couldn't. It's not me. I'm not her. So, I was in awe of her. I suppose that made it even more amazing that she would give me a second look.' Tim took a sip of his coffee.

'What are you saying, Tim?' asked Dev, confused. 'Do you want her job?'

'No. She is always working her job. My job ends when I park the van. Other than dodging cyclists, my job is no to low-stress. She can never switch off.'

'So you think you mistook being impressed for being in love?' asked Dr. Sharma.

'It's not as simple as that. Dev, I was always the loser at college, right? In our group, I was always the one who couldn't concentrate… no discipline.'

'No –' began Dr. Sharma.

'It's okay,' Tim interrupted. 'I've always been the one who did things on a whim because they seemed like fun. And it was. When I was a kid, everything felt so stale, boring. I promised myself that when I could do what I wanted, it would always involve fun. No plans. So, job-wise, I've ended up being, what my family would call, the loser. Because I drive a van delivering flowers for a living, I'm the loser in my family.'

'I don't think you're a loser, Tim,' Dev assured him genuinely.

'Yeah, you do, and my parents definitely think I am. They think it makes them losers, by extension. Maybe I thought a little of her star-shine would rub off on me if I married Ruth, and I wouldn't look so bad anymore. Maybe they would think: *there must be something good about him if someone like her wants him.* I don't know. It's a pretty shit reason for marrying someone, huh? Maybe that's what I was thinking. Or maybe I just loved her. Or maybe it was both. It's all so confused now. I just don't know anymore. If I loved her, why say it's okay for her to fuck another man? Why *did* I fuck someone else? What was I thinking?'

'Maybe, because you thought it would make her happy?'

'I don't know if that's good or bad, being so desperate for her to be happy and not leave that I agreed to sex with other people.'

'Well, why do you think she married you?'

'Maybe she loved me. Maybe she thought she was marrying someone else.'

'Like who?'

'Someone more fun?' suggested Tim.

'But you're all about fun and doing things on a whim. You just said –'

'Yeah, but I didn't want to be that person anymore. I was in a bad place when I met her. You knew it. And I knew it too. I thought Ruth was someone safe and stable. Dev, I feel like I've been acting… all my adult life. I told you when I was a kid I thought my life was fucking boring. I never moved around like you. Our family always lived in the same house. My parents never did anything fun, we never went on holiday anywhere. They would always say no to any invitations that came our way. They were boring. They made me feel boring. Do you know what it's like to actually feel boring? Like, if you met yourself at a party, you would edge slowly away?

'Our lives were dreary and dull. Safe. When I got old

enough, I decided to accept every invitation. I met a lot of people, Dev. I've been to a lot of places on the spur of the moment. That's how I met Ruth in the first place.'

'I know. I was there.'

'Hm? Oh, yeah, right. I got wasted at a lot of gigs, went travelling with total strangers, found myself in some crazy places at four o'clock in the morning, no idea how to get home. Stranded in a field.' Tim chuckled at a memory. 'I already have more amazing memories than my parents will ever have, but it wasn't me. The whole time... I was just fighting myself. Instead of being somewhere in the middle, this extreme version just took over. But now it feels that it was never really me,' explained Tim.

'I was just trying to block out the boring me with all this other stuff that now has no real value for me. I didn't want to be that version of myself anymore, but it was difficult to stop. Difficult to be me with other people. It would be like admitting defeat, like finally being what everyone had wanted me to be all along.'

'And you think that impulsive person is who Ruth thought she was marrying?' asked Dr. Sharma.

'I'm not the person she thought she was getting,' concluded Tim.

'You wanted certainty, stability, and ended up with an open marriage. Ruth isn't the safe option you thought she'd be, either.'

'She and I need to talk. Clearly.'

'Good idea,' agreed Dev, glad that the conversation had found a natural end so he could stop thinking.

'Anything you want to tell me?'

'What do you mean?' asked Dev tiredly.

'About this thing you're doing. Talking to these prostitutes and stuff.'

'I already explained,' exhaled Dr. Sharma, exasperated. 'I thought you understood. I need to feel what they feel,' stressed Dr. Sharma as he rubbed his hands over his face, a futile attempt to wipe the exhaustion from his head.

'Why's it so important to you?'

'Tim, how can you imagine what they're thinking if you can't see their actions the way they see them, their feelings? Do they feel power? Do they feel vulnerable? Do they feel pain? Do they feel free? Do they feel dehumanised? Do they feel like completely different people? Do they feel they have no control?' This part, at least, was true, although Dr. Sharma had chosen not to tell Tim the new focus his interest in thought had taken.

He hadn't explained that he was seeking only to understand Amina's mind and what she had gone through. As far as Tim was concerned, his friend was still pursuing his pet project and the theory that the origins of all thoughts could be tracked to determine how people think about everything.

'But why is it special to you? All this because you think you might be able to read minds by the end?'

'Not read minds, trace what they were thinking, stop people doing the things they do,' replied Dr. Sharma, maintaining the pretence.

'Yes, but you'd need to know who they were in the first place to remove the influence, or whatever, wouldn't you? Plus, everyone is different. Not everyone is susceptible to the same things, the same events in their lives. It's a personality thing. Some people are more up than down,' observed Tim.

'Then, are people born with personalities, ready-formed from the womb? Is it nature or nurture?' Dr. Sharma asked rhetorically.

'It's like asking if people are born gay or just decide on it. People develop personalities, skills, interests. Otherwise, what's the point of reading to babies in the womb? Anyway, there are too many variables. To prove anything, you'd need to start with, well… babies. And raise them under observation, like animals in captivity or something. Otherwise, how do you track them?'

'Babies already carry some psychological traits of their parents. Besides, we both agree sexuality isn't dependent upon personality,' Dr. Sharma said flatly.

'It's such a wide-open thing. Human thought, people firing ideas all over the place. Different ages, races, cultures, religions, beliefs, backgrounds, DNA, genders, sexuality, or asexuality.'

'I know,' Dr. Sharma stated. He no longer wanted to talk about it.

The memory drive had brought everything crashing in on his mind. His mother's secret, the need to understand Amina, the encounter with Grealish. It had all coalesced and congealed, leading his interest in the thoughts of others to a different turn. It was no longer a curiosity borne of his childhood.

Instead, recent events had transformed it into an obsession that had come to consume Dr. Sharma's every thought, waking or otherwise. He ached for the comfort of knowledge, but the only thing he knew for sure was that the safety of certainty would forever elude him. He was fighting the need to understand what had happened to his sister, but he was losing.

Whenever he closed his eyes, he imagined the worst and saw his failure, his guilt that he could never hope to resolve. The doctor wanted to close his eyes to Tim, stop him from talking. Exhausted, he no longer had the energy to argue, not even to divert him to another topic.

'What if you did get a group of babies, or several groups?' asked Tim. 'Fuck it. Call it a thousand kids. Even if you had a thousand kids, it wouldn't be enough to study all the different types of people in the world and the different kinds of lives that people lead all over this planet.'

'I know,' answered Dr. Sharma.

'It seems easier to just hypnotise everyone into not doing bad things. Why don't they just do that? They could throw in some subliminal advertising while they're at it.'

'You'd be eliminating free will.'

'How's your thing different? You'd want to identify negative influences and eliminate them before they happen.'

'That was just an idea, Tim. But, what parent wouldn't want to ensure their child made life choices that they approve of? Become their best self, not the mess they would have been. Isn't that what they're all trying to do anyway?'

'Well, yeah.'

'When people wind up bombing, and murdering, and raping, something must have gone wrong somewhere. Unless… that's something those particular parents approve of… like, social domination.'

'What about genetic manipulation? Before long, they'll

probably be able to boil out stuff like… bipolar disorder. Stuff like that.'

'How about a honeymoon, Tim?' asked Dr. Sharma, desperately trying to change the subject, his scrambling mind finally alighting upon a solid distraction.

'Well, I'm flattered, obviously,' joked Tim, 'but we're not married. Plus, while I am bisexual, I'm pretty sure that you're straight. Mostly. Nevertheless –'

'You and Ruth didn't go on a honeymoon,' said Dr. Sharma, cutting Tim off. 'Maybe you should do that? Leave behind the phones and computers.'

'Dev, it was never a good time for her to go. It was always one more important thing after another. I actually think she enjoys telling people her work stopped her from going on honeymoon. Or, maybe it just feels that way to me.'

'But would now be a good time?'

'It's never a good time.'

'How about a little city break over the weekend?'

'She doesn't have weekends.'

'Work with me, Tim. How about the pair of you spontaneously jump on a ferry to Rotterdam or somewhere? Three days away, have chats, sort it out.'

'Yeah. Maybe. I'll suggest it, see what happens.' Tim paused before abruptly asking: 'You want to talk to her?' At this Dr. Sharma looked up from his pint. 'If I could engineer some kind of way where the two of you would be alone together, you could ask her what's going on?'

'Right, yeah. That's not such a good idea, for me. This is between you and Ruth. I have a lot going on.'

'Dev, you can't make things any worse, and besides, people

talk to you. She might open up.'

Dr. Sharma shook his head ever so slightly, almost to himself, and turned back to the TV, its glow illuminating his face as the image of the newscaster gave way to the bouncing lights and music accompanying a man's progress as he took to a white stage.

Dressed in a simple pair of blue jeans paired with an open-collar white shirt, the man, in his fifties with greying hair, makes a show of clenching a raised fist in triumph. This only encourages the already enthusiastic crowd. Eventually, the lights and music dissipate, and the man on his stage is simply lit. As the cheers and applause abate, the tech company CEO finally finds the space in which to begin his presentation.

'Here at QualChem,' he begins, 'we are known for togetherness, for family. Your family. We live in an age where the fabric of our relationships is increasingly held together by the technology at our fingertips. Relationships that once would have stagnated and faded for lack of time to visit, or an opportune moment to call, are now kept alive through our technology. Our devices. And that's a great thing, right? No question. I love the technology we have today. I love how my devices let me connect with the people dear to me in ways that my parents could never have dreamed.

'What I don't love?' he continues, answering his own question, 'when they dry out. When they run out of juice.

'How about you?' he asks the crowd. 'How about your electric vehicle? Love it, right?' The crowd cheers. 'It's good to know you're doing the right thing. Gets you where you're going. It's affordable and good for the planet. Except sometimes, it just needs a little top-up to get you where you want to go.

'What do we know about the human body? Other than it's amazing, often attractive. Occasionally, even amazingly attractive,' he adds, pausing for the crowd to snicker. 'What is true of all human bodies? That we all know without any medical training? We all breathe in oxygen. We all expel carbon dioxide. We have blood coursing through our veins and arteries, pumped around our body by our hearts. We consume food, digest and convert it into fuel. Our bodies are made up of masses of atoms. We can generate electricity.

'Electricity,' he repeats. 'Electricity changes everything. Look back through history, and we'll see that finding a practical method of generating and using electricity is what set us on the road to living our lives the way we do today. Our ancestors spent so long figuring out how to harness this tremendous power, looking up at the sky and the lightning it threw down, but they never thought to look down to their bodies.

'Our bodies, the complete package, right? They allow us to interact with one another, share emotions, understanding, experiences. Our bodies can self-heal and regenerate. And now, QualChem has unlocked the secret that will take us to the next level. We have designed the technology. We have created the tools. We have made real the ability for our bodies, your body, my body, any body, to generate and distribute electricity in quantities and voltages that can be used in our daily lives.

'Yes, that's right,' he said to the whoops and cheers from the crowd. 'We have finally learned, not how to harness the electricity from the sky but to extract it from within. Your initial reaction may be: *why?* If that's true, then my answer is to ask that you reserve judgement and consider the implications of such revolutionary technology.

'QualChem is rolling out the infrastructure to all relevant participating medical centres. Before long, you, your family, your friends, your loved ones will be blessed with the ability to store the energy they produce and distribute it to devices on the go.

He waits for the latest roar of excitement to die down. 'As if that isn't enough, you can alternatively even transfer surplus energy to a storage device at your home. You can even share it with others unable to generate enough power for their needs.

'Just think of powering your entire home using your body and those of your family members. You really will be making your home your own with clean energy for where you eat, sleep, raise your children and look after your loved ones. Clean energy for your home, your life, your community. You will be creating something from nothing every single day. And so, it gives us great pride to be here today and to unveil: UniBody.

'UniBody. Elegantly engineered. Elegantly constructed. Now elegantly perfected. UniBody. Upgrade. Rediscover your body. And then power up.'

# 62. Some power

It was an accident.

It had begun as an accident.

It had continued because Dr. Sharma wished it to. He wanted to see what would happen.

He wanted to watch from a distance, observe the outcome.

It *had* begun as an accident.

It happens all the time. Files. Notes. Prescriptions. Patients. Tags. They become confused. It could be careless filing. An overworked clerk entering incorrect details for a patient. Details that should have been used for another. It happens. A recent incident was Dr. Jackson's patient who had been supplied dozens of repeat prescriptions for co-codamol. Accidents happen.

On this occasion, the man who had originally been prescribed the co-codamol for back pain happily sold the surplus to his son, who in turn sold it to mums at the park. Having had his mind and thoughts shattered by the conversation with Grealish and his memory drive, Dr. Sharma made a mistake with a prescription at work. He had rectified it before the patient returned to collect it. However, it wouldn't have resulted in significant discomfort for the patient even if he hadn't. Just one inhaler for another. But it did set Dr. Sharma thinking about the potential.

Not the potential for harm, but change and observing it. The incident started him thinking about prescribing medication purely to observe the side effects, direct and indirect. (Or perhaps it was an idea he had retained from his conversation with Ken Stanton, all those years ago, and forgotten until he had cause to explore it further.)

His mother's revelations had shattered his certainty of what had happened to his sister. Having accepted from childhood that Amina had fallen from Hayden Overbridge, Dr. Sharma had not ever considered other possibilities. As an adult, he had continued to believe it had been a tragic accident until his mother's confession forced him to see things differently.

Amina was more than he had imagined. Something had happened to change her mental state. Some apparent logic had formed in her mind, persuading her that the unfinished bridge was not simply a course of action but also an appealing one. However, before that, some influence, some spark, must have taken root to transform her from the happy little child she used to be to one who put herself in harm's way to feel wanted.

Since the chat with his mother, all the memories had been flooding back to him. But the one that he always woke up with was the sound of Amina crying in the night. He asked himself why he had remained silent? Why he hadn't done something? The guilt assailed Dr. Sharma every waking moment. It was there. The sign was there that something was wrong. Anyone else would have realised. They would have read the unspoken thoughts being manifested in physical behaviour. How could her thinking have changed to allow these men to use her?

Dr. Sharma needed to understand the change that had come about. He needed to. He needed to be able to reconcile how she could have come apart.

*I was her brother. What had I missed? What had we all missed? Was it one thing, or was it a confluence? Had Dad been involved? Uncles? Friends of the family? Did they do something that set her on this course?*

It sickened him to think like this, especially of his father, but he had to entertain the possibility in the absence of any solid data.

*Could people I knew have manipulated Amina? Did Mum know more than she said? But she made me promise not to tell Dad. Is that why she kept quiet? How about me? Could something have happened to me as a child that I blocked out? Was that why Mum took me to Mauritius, to Canada, to France? She always said it was so she could keep an eye on me, keep me safe. I remember wondering what she was keeping me safe from if Amina's death had been an accident.*

Dr. Sharma's eyes had been opened. He knew men were involved but were they strangers? The ones at the end may have been, but had there been anything before that? When she was younger still? A thirteen-year-old girl doesn't kill herself without some catastrophic incident.

*She dropped from the overbridge to the dual carriageway below*, Dr. Sharma would think to himself. *How about the fall? The fall killed her too. Or maybe just injured her. The cars killed her. Travelling at least sixty miles per hour. The first would have been enough, but then the second and the third before they came screeching to a halt. Her little body shattering windscreens, creating dents in the metal bodies of these hulks of machinery, before landing on the tarmac. Hit, smashed, flung, crushed. Broken bones, broken skin, open eyes, bleeding chest. Her skin, a sack for pulped internal organs.*

After Serena's revelation, Dr. Sharma knew Amina didn't simply fall. She wasn't playing at the overbridge construction site. She made a decision. From her high perch on the barrier overlooking the overbridge, Amina looked out over the roads, the cars. She looked out over the tall trees that lined the dual carriageway below, the green fields beyond, and decided she didn't want them anymore.

She no longer wanted the world. In that moment, she was stronger than anyone. In that moment, she was the most powerful girl in the world, more powerful than any God, for she held the power to change the world. Her world.

Unfortunately for Dr. Sharma, this was something that he could not see, something he could not reconcile. Not just yet. His own acceptance would come via a different route, and his understanding would be different too. For now, he needed to understand what could change a person so much. It would not suffice to simply read about it. Dr. Sharma wanted to watch the change for himself.

He needed to hear first-hand how the change was occurring inside that individual. He needed to at least glimpse the beast within as it changed a person. To do that, he would need to induce a spark. He would need to alter someone's life so drastically that it would shatter the fundamental assumptions that individuals held about themselves, the rest of the world and how that world viewed them.

Dr. Sharma carefully selected patients with as little family as possible to question his treatment. Patients who would make it to regular appointments at his practice every two or three days. He selected patients who were willing to believe in the treatment as the drugs altered their mental state and wrought changes to their physiology they had never before experienced.

The treatment they did not need would give Dr. Sharma the answers he sought. Or so he thought. He would begin by engineering a physical and emotional change in his patients, entertaining the vague possibility that an illness they didn't have, and the side effects of the medication they didn't need, might turn them to suicide. He would chart their thought process, appointment by appointment. In this way, he would understand more about his sister's thought process and how she had found her way to Hayden Overbridge after her own physical and emotional trauma.

'That's what I'm doing, Mum,' Dr. Sharma confessed to his mother. 'Betraying the trust vulnerable people have placed in me. Breaking the oath that most doctors work by. I have to know what Amina felt. You understand,' he whispered. Serena didn't respond. Her wet eyes instead stared blankly at the window.

She hardly responded to anything anymore as the illness took greater hold of her, but Dr. Sharma continued to visit her almost daily at the hospice. Raju also visited, despite the sadness of seeing his wife reduced to such a state. Unfeeling. Unresponsive. He found it increasingly difficult to talk to her, a woman who was no longer his Serena, a person who wasn't really there.

# 63. All change

Her body straddled his. That was how he liked her, sometimes, so he could lay back and appreciate her. His hands on her thighs, he felt her muscles tensing as she rocked back and forth. When he felt he was about to climax, he slowed her movement, and raised himself, bringing her face close to his. He felt her breath on his skin before moving to suck her nipples, his fingers caressing the small of her back. She enjoyed his lips softly squeezing her and liked it more when he reached up, gently grabbed a fistful of her hair and held it firmly.

A few moments later, he released her hair and looked up from her chest. First, their lips met. Then their tongues. Greedily, they tasted each other. His hand moved to her neck, where he stroked her delicately, delighting in the feminine grace and elegance of her slender neck.

Her mouth tasted sweet, but he wanted to taste more and gently lifted her thighs. The woman rose from him and he stood beside the bed, stimulating himself. He liked to sense the traces of her body on his. He silently watched her move on to all fours, putting her feet over the edge of the bed, inviting him to kneel behind her.

Delicately sliding his hand between her legs, he briefly massaged her, enjoying her warmth, before squeezing the smooth flesh of her backside with both hands. Gently moving his face between her legs, he kissed her vulva affectionately before lapping at her vagina, tasting her, making her gasp in delight at the sensation.

His tongue against her warmth, slowly at first but gradually gaining intensity, he licked at her before moving down to her clitoris, eliciting from her a deeper gasp of pleasure and the anticipation of more. Again, with his tongue, he played with her as she closed her eyes and lost herself.

He pulled away from her briefly, and she began to move away from the edge of the bed, not anticipating him grabbing her hips tighter before he once again pushed his tongue into her. His fingers massaged her clitoris. Increased persistence. Stronger, faster. Her breasts gently swayed in time with his movements, her nipples grazing the bedsheets before he lifted his mouth away again she rolled onto her back.

He could feel the pleasure rippling through her body. He could hear her impending gratification. Breathing hard, she urged him on as he hungrily returned his tongue to her engorged clitoris. The tiny circles there drove her closer to climax as she concentrated, focussing on driving everything else from her mind.

The woman cried softly. Her thighs and arms shuddered with the escalating waves as she climaxed.

Getting up from the floor and moving on top of her, he

pushed into her as her hands unclenched the edge of the mattress behind her and grasped his shoulders. He grunted as he drove his motions faster. Her hair fanned out around her head as he pushed into her again and again.

He continued, slowing until he eventually collapsed on top of her naked form. He breathed, open mouthed, into her hair, the air around them sweaty with sex.

That was Scott's favourite sexual experience, and he liked to fill his head with her pleasure, to relive the moment of her satisfaction. At least, when he could consolidate the mental capacity for it. What Scott is facing now is certainly not what he had ever thought possible for himself, and, in the beginning, he was understandably perplexed.

*You would be too*, he thinks as the doctors finally let him go, and they *are* perplexed, but more from the point of view of medical professionals confronted with a condition they had never before encountered. Scott cannot explain it, and apparently, neither can the doctors because they are giving up on him. They are sending him out on his way.

The world is being pulled apart, and they have neither the time nor patience for him. From what he can gather, they are no longer working on treatments for new medical conditions unless a significant number of people present displaying the same symptoms. In a time since gone, Scott, and many others, would have been outraged at this. But these are new times, and he is a new person. He has had a lot of time to think about things.

Scott is let out at the supply bay at the back of the hospital. Fewer witnesses that way. Passing through the double doors, just before they shut and lock behind him, Scott hears one of the porters. 'This is fucked up. We really just gonna leave him?'

SLAM!

The doors are closed.

He is free.

Free to roam.

Scott can't explain what is propelling him, what force determines his trajectory. He has no inkling of a clue as to an idea about why this is happening to him, but Scott tries to be philosophical. How could he not under the circumstances? Scott has nothing left, but what does he need? He has the air. He has the rain. He has the sun. And he has a lot of time to think.

The things about which he thinks would have surprised him a month ago, but now everything is different. He has the world at his feet and no idea where he will go next. The thing Scott wonders most is: *why me?* Don't get the wrong idea. Initially, Scott was appalled. *You would be too*, he reasons again, to no one in particular. Well, maybe not, but this is Scott we're talking about, not *you*.

Why him? *Why me?* Why has he been granted this privilege? Sure, at times, it isn't glamorous, but it is exhilarating. He feels refreshed by the rain, warmed under the sun, transported by the wind. In the beginning, however, Scott did not see it that way. In fact, Scott didn't see anything at all. He could not open his eyes. He still can't, but Scott has matured a lot in an incredibly short space of time. *My parents would be so proud of me*, he thinks as he hangs around, close to a couple who are locked in an argument in a car parked on the third floor of the hospital car park.

‘Who did you get it from then?’ she screams at her partner.

‘I don’t know, I swear,’ he swears.

‘They can’t fucking help me. Do you understand? The best I can hope for is… I remain like this. Worst case scenario, I’m going to complete my… *transformation* into a whole fucking swan!’ she yells, flapping a wing at him. ‘Pretentious doctor, arsehole, kept waffling about women having graceful, elegant fucking necks.’

‘I know, I’m so sorry, but what can I do?’

‘Stop fucking people, stop spreading it around, you stupid fuck.’

‘I’m as freaked out as you are. Look, I’ll be straight with you. This time last month, I was a Capybara.’

‘A… what? What the fuck is that?’

‘I know, we’re, apparently, one of the least popular animals, which hurts a little, but, hey, it could be worse. You could have turned into a completely different person.’

‘Well, that’s still better than being a fucking swan. Why a fucking swan? You were a Capy…’

‘Capybara.’

‘And you turned into a person. I’m turning into a fucking swan here. How does that work?’

‘Look, I’m sorry, I knew I had an infection when I slept with you, but I was hoping maybe you had it too, and I’d turn into something else.’

‘You are such a fucking cunt.’

‘Well, the thing is that we both have it now. So, maybe, if we have sex again, we’ll both turn into different things. Maybe I’ll turn back into a Capybara, and you’ll turn back into a human?’

'Are you seriously saying you want to have sex? After the damage you've done already?'

'Well, it couldn't hurt, could it? And it might work.'

'Okay. I suppose there's logic in that. Somewhere. But I'm not shaving anything. With all these feathers, it'd take forever.'

They don't notice Scott, who drifts away and out of the open car park, floating down to ground level. He can no longer keep track of how long he has been like this. He had, in the beginning, but it just doesn't matter anymore. Why should it? Why should anything matter when it is possible and acceptable, for there to be no medical explanation for never waking up again after going to sleep and instead taking off on the air.

Under normal circumstances, the authorities would have found it unacceptable to not have a diagnosis, but they would have found a bed somewhere for him to live out his coma. These, however, are not normal circumstances. Scott's body is floating. He has heard one of the doctors use the word *levitating*, but Scott feels that implies some sort of control.

He prefers *floating*. He feels it inspires more whimsy. Whilst whimsy is not in short supply these days, it has not played a part in Scott's waking adult life of late. He has been afforded the time and space to float free across land, sea and continents, entirely at the pleasure of the natural weather patterns and according to the dictates of gravity. And maybe even the moon.

Scott can sense everything around him, but he cannot respond. He is asleep. Whilst asleep he has had a lot of time to consider why he has been granted this opportunity, for he sees it as such. A chance to wander the world and listen to voices, accents, stories, prayers, songs, discussions, poetry, arguments…

Before this happened to him, sounds and images would ricochet from his senses, leaving him absorbing nothing but the essential information necessary to carry out his day of work, and evening of interaction with those he thought he was close to. It turns out that they weren't so close to him since they had left him at the mercy of the hospital.

On the other hand, he doesn't resent them. The world is coming apart, and everyone has to deal with things the way they see fit. Just as his family has decided to let him go, he has decided to accept his situation, shut his eyes and drift away.

Now, the people he comes across constitute more than the fleeting images and sounds they did when he was awake. Each person passes through him, leaving an indelible impression. He hears and absorbs them. He senses them and feels them. Scott poses no threat and expresses no opinion, leaving him roundly ignored by the people making sense of a new world no longer theirs.

Their lack of interest in Scott leaves him to wonder how billions of people are capable of such an array of emotions by their very nature. The excitement, the happiness, the sorrow, pain, loss, grief, love, affection, anger, desperation, fear, exhaustion… Something that is a natural, in-built impulse. Something that we are all born with. All of us. Truly universal. Something that money cannot buy, privilege cannot acquire. Available to most, whether they like it or not, from birth to death. Emotion, order, chaos, oxygen, blood, sex, the sky, sun, moon…

*All those beautiful things belong to everyone*, he thinks, *and I'm the only one with the time to appreciate it.*

Scott continues. He floats over lakes, seas, gardens, parks, swimming pools. Through shopping centres, offices, petrol stations, transport hubs. Sometimes people try to wake him, but without success.

Scott continues to sleep.

Scott continues to drift.

Scott continues.

Dev continues to take us from memory to memory, sprinkling his little fantasies here and there.

The group sat around the rectangle of sticky wood on legs called a table by the proprietors of this pub. The worst pub on the face of the planet, of this the group was sure. But it was also the pub where they had all destroyed Christmas songs. On a karaoke night. In the middle of August. It was the pub where Jerome had had to have his long hair held back by Michelle as he vomited his drinks into a toilet bowl the night before he quit medical school.

Why has Dev brought us here? Probably because this was

the pub where, after they left, they continued to gather every so often, at least for the first few years until they all became too busy. Here they caught up with one another, celebrated one another's successes and commiserated over failures.

This group was important to Dev. It allowed him to observe the changes in his friends as new priorities presented themselves. It had been some years since they had all last been here together, but here they gathered once again, about a month after Dev's cosy chat with Grealish.

'So what happened this time?' asked Michelle, ready to sympathise.

'It's not *this time*,' replied Jerome, already baulking at the implied judgement.

'What do you mean?' asked Michelle.

'Yes, Jerome, yes, just what do you mean?' asked Lindsay in mock exasperation.

'Well, I *will* tell you if you give me a chance,' he replied.

'I was only joking, Jerome,' apologised Michelle.

'I know, but I'm not. I'm losing my job here.'

'You know, it's not true about gays. It's *not* all drama with them,' teased Lindsay sarcastically. 'So go on, tell us, what happened?'

'I think this all started about two months ago,' Jerome admitted.

'Jerome, is this one of those stories where it is everybody else's fault? That you had nothing to do with why you got fired?' asked Dev.

'No, but yes,' Jerome said, the advance warning giving the others adequate time to prepare themselves.

'Okay then, go on, tell us,' invited Richard.

'No, does it matter why he got fired? Just that he got fired. Again. Jerome, you've got to pull yourself together. You have children to impress now. You need to sort it out,' admonished Lindsay.

'That's how I got in trouble this time.'

'Your sister's kids?'

'No, my boss' kid.'

'How did you come into contact with your boss' kid, or should we not ask?' asked Lindsay.

'There's always something with you, Jerome. The year has only just begun, and you're already out of a job,' goaded Richard, taking some delight in Jerome's difficulty. 'It doesn't bode well for the rest, does it?'

'Thanks, Richard. Thanks for your support,' Jerome sarcastically reproached.

'That's right, it *is* support. It's tough love.

'We do love you, Jerome,' Michelle cooed soothingly.

'Yeah, we do,' agreed Richard. 'You should have come out with us to see in the new year.'

'I didn't feel like it. There's not much to *see in* when you've lost your job.'

'You still had a job at that point.'

'I was on gardening duty. I knew I was going to be fired.'

'What's gardening duty?' asked Dev.

'I think it's when they have you working on nothing at all. Is that right?' asked Michelle.

'Yeah, it's when they know it's highly likely that you'll be *leaving*, so they don't want to trust you with anything that matters,' clarified Jerome.

'That must have been humiliating,' Richard pointed out.

'I didn't care about that. They could have kept me on gardening duty as long as they wanted, as long as they kept paying me.'

'Well, still, you should have come out with us instead of staying at home.'

'Richard, do you know how much a babysitter costs? On New Year's Eve?'

'Oh yeah, how are the little tykes, anyway? Can't believe your sister literally left you holding two babies. What a wake-up call.'

'Not literally, because they're not babies. And she left Piet holding them, not me. Mum and I take them on weekends. Besides, even if I could afford a sitter, do you know how expensive it is to go out for New Year's?'

'Yeah, we do, because we did,' reminded Lindsay. 'We went to see fireworks. Took our own booze. Wasn't so expensive in the end.'

'It was fun,' commented Dev.

'It was romantic,' added Michelle.

'Except for those couples dancing cheek to cheek in the middle of the crowd like no one else was there,' said Lindsay.

'That was the romantic part,' Michelle pointed out.

'They were in the way,' argued Lindsay.

'You're incorrigible.'

'Didn't realise you were trying to.'

'Always, dear.'

'Always failing too.'

'About fifty-fifty.'

'I think you're being kind to yourself.'

'I think you're being a tit.'

‘I can’t tell if you two are fighting or flirting,’ admitted Jerome.

‘A little from column A.’

‘A little from column B.’

‘No, it’s worse than that. You’ve become siblings,’ teased Richard.

‘Very funny. So what happened?’ asked Lindsay.

‘Yeah, you said it started a couple of months ago,’ reminded Dev.

‘It was around the middle of November,’ continued Jerome, ‘All the Christmas shit was out in the shops. The fairy lights were on the lamp posts and all that stuff.’

‘Okay, yeah, we get the picture,’ pressured Richard.

‘I’m explaining. It’s important.’

‘Never mind him, go on,’ encouraged Dev.

‘So, my boss has a young daughter. She’s about eleven, and she’s one of these Girl Scouts, or Guides, or whatever.’

‘Right.’

‘He told us one morning that she and one, or two, of her scout buddies would be coming in to collect money for charity because Christmas was coming. In Poland, we don’t do this so much. So when he said they were coming to collect money, I thought they would be like the people in the street, just shaking a tin, but at Daddy’s place of work. Right?’

‘Okay,’ encouraged Michelle.

‘It wasn’t that?’ asked Lindsay.

‘No. They got stuck in traffic after school and didn’t get to the office until about 17:20. I was going home that day at 17:00. I stayed late to be a good guy and show my boss that I am all for these community things. Team building and all that crap. That's the thing. If I'd just fucked off home, I'd still have a job right now. Anyway, I stayed and eventually, the girls turned up. But they didn't have those collection tins. Instead, they had trays.'

'Trays?' echoed Richard.

'Trays of brownies. And cookies and muffins. There were three girls, and each had a different thing. It was a Friday, and it was late. Man, I just wanted to go and pick the kids up from Piet and take them to my mother's for the weekend. My desk was the first one in my row by the door. Each girl took on a different row of desks.

'My row of desks got brownie girl, and her brownies looked *really* good. They were selling these baked goods they say they made themselves and giving the money to charity. So I asked her how much for a brownie. She said thirty pence. "Thirty pence?" I said, "okay, I'll have all of it." She had twenty pieces. I bought the whole tray for six pounds.'

'You bought the whole tray?' asked Dev, with raised eyebrows.

'What were you going to do with a whole tray of brownies?' asked Richard.

'Take them to my mother's, with the kids. Twenty chunks of brownie disappear real quick when she's around.'

'Thirty pence per brownie is really… *reasonable*, Jerome,' commented Michelle pointedly.

'Right? So I jumped all over it. It was a bargain. I thought: they must know what they're doing. She must have been told by a grown-up that that was the right price. So I gave her the money, bagged the brownies and quickly left. I was late to pick up the kids. We had a great weekend. We went swimming and took the brownies. They're always really hungry after swimming. My mum joined us, and we had a nice walk after.'

'Then?' asked Dev.

'Then I went back to work on Monday. When I walked in, everyone went quiet. Then, my boss called me into his office. So, it turns out, after I gave the little girl the money on Friday night and took her brownies, she went to compare with her friends. The little girl had six pounds. But her buddies had forty, fifty pounds.'

'What?'

'Yeah, the girl had sold all her brownies to me for six pounds. When she realised what she'd done, she burst into tears and stayed that way all weekend. She was inconsolable that a big meany man had tricked her into selling him all her brownies for six quid,' explained Jerome.

'But, you didn't. That was the price,' confirmed Richard.

'No, that wasn't the price,' said Jerome.

'That was the price the girl said to you, so that was the price,' argued Richard.

'It was for charity. He was supposed to give more,' clarified Michelle.

'Then she should have asked for more,' insisted Richard.

'They don't want it to seem like a shakedown,' pointed out Lindsay.

'But it *is* a shake-down! It is a shake-down fronted by girl scouts, and it backfired on them,' explained Richard. 'They deserve it, trying to use their little munchkin faces to extract hard cash. This guy, Jerome's boss, used his position to fling these girls at a captive target.'

‘If I’d known I was supposed to give more money, I would have given more money,’ insisted Jerome, ‘but I didn’t know. I gave what I thought she wanted. I thought she’d be happy she sold all her brownies.’

‘Thirty pence per brownie must have been the price just to breakeven,’ explained Michelle. ‘They wanted money for charity. You were supposed to give more than just thirty pence per brownie.’

‘Well, I didn’t know that at the time. It’s no use telling me now. Where were you when I was being accosted by scout girls?’

‘How does all this result in you losing your job?’

‘So, after I left, the little girl was crying and crying. Her friends refused to share their money with her, so everyone else tried to give her money but she wouldn’t take it. The entire office came to a standstill because of this screaming little shit.

‘They could hear her on the next floor. Everybody had to come off the phones. My manager told all the other managers it was my fault. It’s a place of business, not a school, not a playground. It’s like no one knew what to do with this kid. She wouldn’t shut the hell up.’

‘They can’t fire you for that.’

‘No, but it was my manager’s idea to bring the girls in, and he looked a total idiot in front of all the other managers. So he decided to audit all my work. They looked for every little mistake, late arrival, every upset customer they could find. There was a hearing. That’s it,’ he finished, theatrically dusting off his hands.

‘So you got fired because of your own mistakes?’ clarified Lindsay.

'I got fired because of a privileged little bitch.'

'No, you said you got fired because they found a load of mistakes.'

'They found a few little mistakes.'

'Plus your timekeeping,' pointed out Richard.

'And customer complaints,' reminded Lindsay.

'But no one would have focussed on all that without the girl,' insisted Jerome.

'This is typical you, trying to blame someone else.'

'Look, we all make little mistakes at work. We just do. No one goes through them with a comb.'

'Er, excuse me, you're talking to a bunch of doctors. When things go wrong, there's plenty of blame,' pointed out Lindsay. 'That's why we have insurance.'

'That's also why we learn to cover our mistakes and accidents,' explained Michelle. 'What? Don't look at me like that, Lindsay. You know it's true.'

'I'm not trying to avoid responsibility,' Jerome insisted, 'but it's been a witch-hunt from start to finish because of that spoilt brat, and now I don't have a job.'

'I don't have a job either,' Dev suddenly disclosed.

'What?' asked Richard.

'I quit,' he explained.

'What? No!'

'It's true.'

'Why?' asked Michelle.

'I wanted to.'

'What are you going to do?'

'I don't know.'

'You just quit?' asked Lindsay, with a hint of suspicion.

'Yeah,' confirmed Dev.

'Why?'

'I don't know. It's difficult to say,' he lied.

'What did your family say?'

'They don't know yet.'

'You didn't tell them?' asked Richard.

'I'll have that conversation with them. Soon.'

'Is this like a sabbatical or something? Or have you quit for good?' asked Michelle.

'Yeah, maybe I need to take a break for a bit. Stuff I need to do.'

'What else could you possibly need to do? This is the point in your life that… you find the point to your life. This is where the direction of your career becomes… solid. You're checking out right when it's getting serious,' argued Lindsay.

'That's what he's doing, changing the course of his career,' encouraged Jerome positively, giving Dev a clap on the back.

'By going on holiday for a year? Priorities? Hello?'

'He's not going on holiday. It's a sabbatical. He has other stuff to do,' said Richard, echoing Dev, inwardly pleased at the apparent burnout of another from their group.

'What are you going to do then?' asked Lindsay.

'Er, research. Maybe I'll take on a research project. Or something. I don't know. I'm going to visit Mauritius for a little while too. My uncle died. He was a widower. No children. He left his property to my mum and her sisters. I'm standing in for Mum to sign papers and sort it out.'

'Well, when you get back, you need to get serious, Dev. Get a plan in place, or you'll end up like Jerome here.'

'Hey!' protested Jerome.

'Hey, what?' continued Lindsay. 'You left med school, you didn't have a plan and look at you now, getting fired from a call centre over brownies.'

'People with plans fuck up too, you know,' Jerome answered back.

'Not as much as people without plans. People need blueprints to follow, patterns, solid plans with little room for uncertainty. Before maps, they navigated by looking up at the constellations. You ever tried doing that? It's really fucking difficult. Shows you how desperate people are for any kind of pattern they can follow. Without that, what do people do? They follow their emotions, become slaves to their own whims.'

'See, that's what we like about you, Lindsay. No need to wonder what you're *really* thinking because you're always *really* telling us,' said Jerome sarcastically.

'Uncertainty, no plan, no direction,' continued Lindsay, pretending to ignore Jerome. 'Who wants that? Losers, that's who, and most of them can't help it. They're like Jerome. They're just wired that way. It's not even their fault. Right, Jerome?'

'Shut up,' Jerome spat at her.

'You, on the other hand, Dev, already did all that stuff. You did what most of us here did. The studying, the planning, the revising, the exams, the case studies, and then several years as an actual doctor. You're going to give up this net of interconnected things and just float free with nothing?'

'Oh my God,' interjected Michelle, 'I've just realised you and Jerome remind me of the other night.'

'What other night?' asked Jerome, glad to hear from

someone other than Lindsay.

'The other night,' insisted Michelle, tugging on Richard's arm.

'What?' asked Richard.

'At Sam and Kevin's. That couple arguing.'

'Oh yeah,' Richard's face brightened at the recollection.

'What happened?' asked Dev.

'Well, we were at Sam and Kevin's, our neighbours, for dinner, and there were some other people there that we didn't know. Sam and Kevin said: "why don't we play a party game?" So we played one of those games where you answer fake questions.'

'Or you answer hypothetical questions, even.'

'Be quiet, Richard. I'm telling the story. Anyway, we get to one of the couples in the game. I've forgotten their names, but anyway –'

'Peter and Janet,' supplied Richard.

'Peter and Janet got asked the next question.'

'What were *you* asked?' queried Dev.

'Oh, I don't remember, it was a dinner party game, something stupid.'

'I remember,' said Richard.

'Of course you do, shut up. So Peter and Janet got their question. Janet has a sister and the sister –'

'Liz.'

'And Liz has a husband –'

'Anthony.'

'And they have four kids. Peter and Janet don't have any children. They're not married, don't even live together yet. They've only been going out for a few months.'

'Get to the question, Michelle,' pressed Richard.

'I will. I was just giving context. The question came, and it was this… What was the question?'

'Terrorists put bombs around a primary school, and they say the player must make a choice. The choice the player has to make is between their partner and their sister or brother in law. The terrorists will kill one of them. Either the player chooses, or if they refuse to choose, they will blow up the school with the children inside.'

'Right!' squealed Michelle. 'So, in Janet's case, she had to decide between saving her boyfriend, Peter, or her sister's husband, Anthony.' For a few moments, the entire group was silent. A rare occurrence.

'What kind of terrorists are you?' asked Jerome's best Takagi impression.

'What kind of game is this, is more relevant,' commented Dev.

'That's what I thought,' Richard agreed.

'That doesn't matter,' replied Michelle.

'It doesn't make sense.'

'It doesn't have to. That's not the point.'

'What was the point then?'

'There was no *point*. It was just a stupid game, a stupid question.'

'You got that right.'

'So what did she answer?' asked Lindsay.

'Her answer was, Anthony. The brother-in-law.'

'Oh. So what happened?' asked Dev.

'Her boyfriend went nuts! He was livid! He kept saying: "how can you pick him over me?"'

'Well, how *did* she pick him over him?'

'Well, Anthony has a wife, three children, parents still alive. They want to encourage their children to be sociable, so they always have people around the house. Peter doesn't have so many people around. Also, Janet has known Anthony for a lot longer than Peter. Of course, it was completely reasonable, but it still probably wasn't the answer Peter was expecting. Especially in front of a bunch of strangers. He was really put out that his girlfriend would pick her brother-in-law instead of him. So what should have been a pointless party game descended into bickering and then all-out fighting. It was simultaneously hilarious, awkward and bizarre,' squeaked Michelle before descending into cackles of laughter.

Richard took up the story. 'Of course, everyone else was too polite to get involved, so we just let them go at it in the other room while we listened. We pretended to get on with the game and prayed for the evening to just come to an end. She was saying how not as many people would miss him if he were dead, and he was arguing that her brother-in-law had hit his peak, whereas he still had unfulfilled potential when it came to accruing, well… people.'

'See, Dev, that's what I'm talking about,' said Lindsay. 'If you give up the things in your life, there's no longer any plan, any stability holding the elements in place. Aren't you scared of that? The fewer normal things you have in your life, the less people want to be around you. Before long, you'll be like Anthony, getting his brains blown out by terrorists.'

'Peter,' corrected Richard.

'Whatever.'

'Anyway, she wasn't his girlfriend by the end of the evening,' concluded Michelle. 'So he had one fewer person in his life.'

'Like Jerome,' badgered Lindsay.

'Lindsay, I didn't come here to take shit from you.'

'I'm sorry, Jerome,' she said, reaching over to and cuddling his arm, 'I just want to mobilise you into some kind of action.'

'But I didn't come here for action. I didn't know it was going to be tough love I'd be receiving. I was hoping for some understanding from you lot.'

'Jerome, maybe you don't deserve our understanding,' joked Michelle mischievously.

'Oh, hey, d'you know what Tommy wanted to do the other day? He wanted to go to Farport Bridge to find our padlock.'

'What padlock?' asked Richard.

'Padlocks they put on fences to consolidate everlasting love, or whatever. Why did we do that? Why do people do that? Are you supposed to visit the padlock once you snap it on? Have we been negligent?'

'Maybe that's the whole point,' wondered Michelle aloud. 'You don't visit it. You just have to know it's out there. No matter what's happening in your life, no matter where you are, there's a physical place where your feelings for each other were at their highest peak.'

'Nah, it's not about feelings,' argued Lindsay, 'it's memory. I think the lock is supposed to represent a memory locked in place forever, or at least until a sweaty caretaker comes along and lops them all off. Like skin tags.'

'Always so delicate, Lindsay,' muttered Jerome sarcastically.

'The two people who placed it know it is always there, a physical point they can go back to and find that feeling again if they ever lose it. That's what he's trying to tell me. I know it. You didn't have to say anything. What do I do?'

'Go visit the padlock?' suggested Lindsay.

'Take it some muffins,' sniped Richard.

'Brownies!'

'Shut up, Lindsay, it's still not funny!'

'Oh, *I* know,' said Dev, 'take the key to the padlock so you can unlock it, and then lock it again.'

'Who keeps the key?' asked Jerome. 'Isn't the point that you don't keep the key, symbolically ending the possibility of unlocking the padlock, leaving each other?'

'That's romantic,' simpered Michelle.

'That's retarded,' stated Jerome, 'I don't want to start a thing. Visit the padlock once and then, every so often, it will be like: *we don't visit the padlock anymore, why don't we visit the padlock?*'

# 64. Go back where you came from

Since Dev had last visited Mauritius, the airport had expanded. With the extra space was an additional duty-free shop for those entering the country. Arrivals had expanded, and the process of getting through Passport Control seemed to move a lot more quickly. With the queue rapidly shrinking, Dev soon found himself standing before Passport Control Officer Gopal.

'Passport,' Gopal barked from behind his desk, stony-faced as Dev placed his maroon coloured UK passport on the counter. Gopal quickly leafed through the pages until he reached Dev's headshot. He glanced back and forth a few times between Dev and the photo before satisfying himself that the latter was indeed derived from the former.

'What is the purpose of your visit?' Gopal demanded. 'Vacation?'

'No,' replied Dev distractedly.

'Business.'

'Not really. I'm just... here.'

'Here for what?' pressed Gopal in his sing-song accent. Dev was hearing it for the first time in a long time from a full-time inhabitant of the island.

'Uh, just here to see family,' Dev lied.

'You have a return ticket?'

'Yes.' Dev showed him evidence of his booking, and Gopal noted the date in a folder.

'Where will you be staying?'

'A hotel in Flic en Flac.' Dev produced his reservation, and Gopal noted the address. With that, Gopal's mood seemed to instantly brighten, and his stamp came down on Dev's passport with an unexpected flourish.

'Okay. You may go.'

'Thanks,' muttered Dev.

After the luggage carousel, Dev pushed his trolley towards the exit, where there was the usual throng of people expecting the arrival of other people.

Taxi drivers waited with cardboard signs.

Tour operators waited with clipboards.

Hotel pick-up services waited with impatience.

Relatives waited with bated breath.

Everyone there waited for people from abroad. Nobody waited for Dev. Nobody there knew he was arriving. Wheeling his trolley gingerly between the clumps of excited relatives embracing with abandon, Dev soon found himself once more stepping from the air-conditioned arrivals hall and into the thick heat of the Mauritian daytime. The wind ruffled his hair as his eyes adjusted to the brightness, and he scanned his surroundings for changes since the last time he'd been there.

White stone benches were now dotted around the area outside the automatic doors. Beyond that, the clean, asphalted road led to the outer perimeter of the airport grounds and the rest of the country. Above, watching over everything, was the perfect blue sky, marred only by a few grey clouds just passing overhead.

At that moment, it suddenly dawned on Dev that that might be why some Hindu gods are blue. All-seeing, part of the scenery, blending in with the heavens. Camouflaged. He hadn't considered it before. There may have been some other explanation within the mythology, but he wasn't familiar with any of it. Dev took advantage of the shade afforded by a passing cloud to break cover and quickly make his way to the taxis.

Moments later, Dev's luggage was in the back of a new, silver Mercedes sedan while he sat in the passenger seat with the window wound down. The driver kept his eyes on the road as he chewed gum. Chit chat was in short supply, Dev was relieved. On the radio, the latest modern hip-hop tinged Bollywood hits reigned the airwaves until a break for the noon news.

Another killing of an unarmed black man in the US by police officers.

Another Black Lives Matter march.

Another press conference where someone tried to defend the officers, explaining that it was perfectly legitimate to kneel on a person's neck to subdue them. The news unsettled Dev and only added to his agitated state of mind. After decades away, the return to Mauritius was disturbing enough to Dev.

His phone had been switched off for the flight, and Dev turned it back on in the car. As the updates and notifications pinged through, a comment caught Dev's eye. Someone he had counted as a friend had commented: "if a black man finds himself with a white knee on his neck it's cos of natural selection."

Repulsed, Dev despaired at narrow-mindedness and those who would apparently allow themselves to be manipulated into believing and regurgitating such a thing. Inwardly raging, he thought to himself:

*They only care about what feels good. Take what feels good and rationalise it until it feels right. Strip away all the rhetoric, and it is just about destroying what they hate and what they hate is anything that doesn't affirm their way of life. It's not blackness. It's what is associated with blackness. Or any other minority. Bigots consider them inferior, the worst of society, simple-minded, less than human, with a culture they are unwilling to believe is equal to their own.*

*But what is American culture?* Dev asked himself. *Doesn't it steal from black cultures, as well as that of minorities? Isn't its rampant commercialisation, commodification and global proliferation its only originality? Was it a narcissistic need to affirm their faith in themselves that led them to have their culture reflected back to them in their media, which they then aggressively exported worldwide, boosting the magnitude of that reflection, its success serving to vindicate their sense of self?*

*A reflection shorn of the complexities that constitute a nation, that speaks to how it treats its inhabitants. Like Grandfather's old Sega tapes, a copy of a copy, with the subtleties disappearing over time. Do we take away from that reflection only the most pronounced elements? Key amongst those, nationalism, a desperate celebration of its own ideals and weaknesses, repackaged as strengths.*

*Instead of addressing that which is fundamentally broken, they choose to paint over cracks, effectively seducing themselves into believing their own marketing as the greatest nation, the land of the free, welcoming that luxuriant fog, that complacent conviction that theirs is the only culture that matters, the only culture worthy of consideration, the one to continue unchanged for eternity.*

*An unwillingness to accept that change occurs and that ways of life evolve inspires hatred of the unfamiliar,* Dev theorised. *Shifting baseline syndrome. A generation's experience of the world is different to those that came before. Those who hate do so out of fear of change threatening their view of themselves and their self-appointed position as a dominant race with a culture that belligerently throttles, usurps and crushes all others with its persistence.*

*What is it they are so determined to protect against change? Is their true culture the automatic presumption that one race is superior to all others and should naturally dominate? Is it the belief that any vestige of original culture retained by an indigenous people is due to the benevolence of a seemingly dominant race that is happy to give things, certain freedoms and trinkets, as long as they aren't expected and aren't demanded as legal entitlements?* Dev asked himself.

*Is its belief in its superiority only reaffirmed through post-aggression selective benevolence? Does that post-cruelty kindness delude the aggressor into feeling they are doing the right thing in the sense of satisfying a higher calling?*

Dev's thoughts continued to brew. *Do they now feel that their benevolence has been taken for granted with inferior races and cultures expecting to be treated as equals with rights now enshrined in law, better educated and holding better jobs that were once the preserve of any straight white men who do not want change? We can't forget that there are plenty who do.*

*All in such a short space of time. Gay couples, interracial couples are commonplace. Increasingly women are at least equal to men in more areas of society. Is the makeup of Western family life changing and threatening the position of white men who feel challenged by the prevalence of other cultures, the increasing appointment of individuals from other races to higher positions, and the growing assertiveness of women who seek equal recognition, equal pay, and refuse to be undermined and be seen as less than human, due to their gender?*

As the palm trees whizzed by, Dev's thoughts took on new dimensions. *With homosexuality being legal and part of mainstream culture, and gender questions that challenge traditional social structures, the lifestyle and attitude changes wrought by climate change will only add to this metaphorical fire, threatening the once simple world and identity of some straight white men.*

*A society made equal by word of law does not make them feel special, with a glow of superiority. That has vanished in a relatively short space of time, and they want it back. I can see that for certain white men, not all, it could be a time of great unease.*

*The unlawful killing of a black man by police is not just about black lives. It is about all lives that have not been valued as they should have.*

The anger from Dev's friend's flippant response combined with his unease at being back in Mauritius to fuel Dev's thoughts.

*The significance of this killing, and others like it, should be felt by those who are misunderstood, marginalised, or victimised by the powers that be, the powers that weaken women's rights. The right to not just recognition for what they do, equal pay, the right to appropriate support, the right to choose for their own bodies, but also the right to be safe amongst men, regardless of whether those men are powerful or just want to feel powerful for a few moments. The powers that do not regard gays, those questioning their gender identity, and the wider LGBTQ+ community as individuals, human beings and valuable members of society.*

*This is a fire whose tinder was merely frustration at a clash of two different ways of life, but it should have wider ramifications regarding change. The changes we all need to make now to navigate climate change and survive its consequences. Clinging to ideals from bygone eras will hamper us when we all need to come together and bring our most positive attributes for a sea change in our thinking and ways of life.*

It had been easy enough for Dev to board the plane, but it was a different feeling now that he was back in the country, back amongst the people. Affected by being back in Mauritius, anxiety had gripped him once again, influencing and charging his thoughts.

However, he was sufficiently self-aware enough to wonder: 'Is what *I* just thought actually racist? Am I mistaken? If Richard or Lindsay were to hear this, would they be offended?'

Dev occasionally glanced at the fingers of the taxi driver as he allowed the steering wheel to right itself after turning a corner, slipping smoothly against the palms of his hands. The fingers of one hand were adorned with gold rings while a gold bracelet slid around a wrist. Dev thought of his time there as a child when his mother had met the *poutou* cake vendor rolling around town on his bicycle wearing his gold rings. It was something that adult Dev would notice everywhere he went where he tried to get things done. The men would wear gold bracelets, rings and necklaces, while the women would be dismissive in their attitude and lethargic about their work. In the evening, after a day of getting nothing done fast, Dev would ponder this and conclude that it was some kind of subconscious passive-aggressive reaction to a sense of inadequacy or inferiority.

Mauritians disliked serving other Mauritians they thought were better-off than them or whom they assumed would have an attitude of superiority. This was most prevalent when dealing with Mauritians who lived abroad, for whom they seemed to have a sixth sense. Dev surmised that the men nonchalantly displayed large amounts of jewellery to show how well they were doing. As for the ladies, he guessed that they worked to say that they worked and weren't housewives, like their mothers and grandmothers, a position that apparently commanded no more respect there than anywhere else in the world. However, they didn't like the actual work that went with the job title and salary, work that usually involved serving the public. They had taken a job to prove that they were better than others, as well as earn money for their families, but had ended up feeling demeaned as serving others only fed their own perceived sense of inferiority.

Dev closed his eyes, hoping this trip would be a break to give him some respite from thoughts of Amina, his mother, Grealish, the memory drive, and his quest. He let the taxi carry him along smooth, freshly asphalted roads lined with expensive new European cars. Through cities with tall bank office blocks, ostentatiously designed to make a statement about the financial institution that owned them. Past villages, still with those homes made from repurposed metal sheets, with those wiggly metal roofs.

# 65. Come back to what you (don't) know

Exhausted as Dev is, I cannot let my visit to him end just yet. Instead, I watch over him. All he wants is for things to end. I know it. In a way, that's what he's always wanted.

After his two weeks in Mauritius, Dev was back in England, in Raju's kitchen, to report on his trip and the process regarding the transfer of the property, which Seeva and Saarika had decided to sell. On Serena's behalf, Dev had agreed and placed the property on the market for them.

Dev had anticipated that his time in Mauritius would distract him from Serena's confession, the truth of Amina's death, her rape, Katie and Mira, the sex club, Grealish and his memory drive. The prescriptions. However, that had not been the case.

The heat had only exacerbated Dev's insomnia, and he had laid awake most nights running everything through his mind. Instead of calming his thoughts, the two weeks in Mauritius had left him isolated and, with no outlet he had returned, a pressure cooker of impulses.

Raju had been cooking them dinner while they chatted about the house, but Dev had soon steered the conversation to the subject of Amina. The onions went into the hot pan, where they fizzed in the oil as Raju quickly and roughly moved them around, manipulating the pan back and forth.

Raju waited for the sizzle to die down before turning around and answering his son.

'Well, I'm listening now, aren't I?'

'Yeah, Dad,' Dev replied sharply in frustration, 'and maybe if you had been listening in the first place, Amina would still be alive!'

Dev expected a slap from his father. In fact, he still expected a slap from his father whenever they exchanged harsh words, although his father had only ever struck him once when Raju had visited Dev and Serena in Mauritius.

The day after the slap little Dev had admitted to himself that he had been insolent and had deserved it. He still didn't know why he had pushed his father on that day in Mauritius. Had he been pushing for a reaction? Some evidence of love. As he got older and Dev thought back to the incident, he realised that his father had been under a lot of pressure. The son he was trying to get back was being spiteful, acting up and making the event more difficult, more painful than it already was. He understood that the slap in Mauritius had probably pained his father more than him.

Dev had been pushing his father's patience in front of other Mauritian family members.

People, always watching to see how the family could have lost Amina.

*How could Raju have lost his family like this? Having to scurry around the world, hoping Serena would see him.* He could imagine them asking one another. Raju had to prove himself. Hence, the slap, on that day, during his brief visit to his wife and son. A show of control.

Dev would have understood if his father had slapped him

now, but that understanding wouldn't mean he regretted his words that still hung in the air. Dev felt his words had been too abrupt. But had they? In the circumstances, it was difficult. Everything was so much more difficult now for him. Acceptance of the circumstances surrounding Amina's death was still not at hand. The boundaries of what was appropriate no longer made sense to him.

'How can you say that?' Raju eventually managed to get out. 'How can you say that to me?'

'I don't know,' admitted Dev. 'Maybe because we never talk about it. In fact, we never talked about it, ever.'

'That's not true,' argued Raju, leaving the spatula in the pan, 'We talked about it when it happened. How long do you want to keep talking about it?'

'No. We didn't. You and Mum told me what had happened like you were talking about the weather.'

'What do you want us to do? It was over thirty years ago. Your mother's in a hospice. There's someone for everything now, but there weren't all these counsellors and therapists when you were small. You just got on with it, muddled your way through. There was no one to tell us what to do. There wasn't a book to tell you what to do when your little girl dies. Do you think we weren't in pieces? That our hearts weren't ripped out? But there's only so much you can put yourself through. It was an accident.'

'Dad, I've seen the medical report. I know it *says* it was an accidental death….' Dev grappled for his words. He had promised his mother that he would say nothing to his father about it, but he couldn't live alone with what Serena had told him. If he could bring his father to understand it for himself, he could still keep his promise. '... but it doesn't look that way.'

'She was playing, Dev. It was an accident.'

'Thirteen-year-old girls don't *play*, Dad.'

'Well, Amina still did. She was messing around at that fly-over they were building. She did something… she fell. It was a terrible accident.'

'She was messing around at the fly-over, on her own?'

'She wasn't on her own. There were other kids there, but they ran away.'

'If it was an accident, why would they run away?'

'Because they were kids. They were scared. Why are we on this? Why are we talking about this?'

'Because we never talked about it before.'

'Yes, we did. You just don't remember.'

'Dad, why do you think Mum took me to Mauritius?'

'I know why she went back to Mauritius.'

'She wanted to get her grief out in her own words, in her own language with her own people. You were her own people, but you were too wrapped up in yourself,' pressed Dev.

'If I was so selfish, why didn't I just stay in England? Why did I keep coming to Mauritius, to France? To persuade your mother to come back with you.'

'Because you were worried about what everyone was saying about you.'

'What would they say about me? I don't care what they say. My home is England. This is where I earned my living. This is where I live. If I was so worried about what other people thought, why did I wait? Why did I give your mother space?' argued Raju.

'Why did you wait a year to come for me?

'Dev…'

'I was your child too, Dad. Do you know how difficult it was?'

'You seemed okay,' was the only response Raju could come up with at short notice.

'Dad, what happened to Amina?'

'I told you, it was an accident. If you're thinking of something else… I don't know what else you think could have happened.' They both fell silent as Raju turned back to his onions. A few moments passed before he continued. 'When I came to Mauritius, I talked, Dev. I talked about our beautiful Amina. Our girl had an accident, and she's gone, but she is still our beautiful girl. I did talk about her. I keep her, always, inside.'

'You didn't, Dad. You didn't talk about Amina,' argued Dev, hot tears rising to his eyes and threatening to escape. 'You talked about some girl. It wasn't Amina.'

'What is this now?' asked Raju, turning back to him with another look of incredulity.

'I nodded and went along, but it wasn't her.'

'I'm tired,' replied Raju, who could no longer track the accusations Dev was levelling at him.

'I didn't remember those stories you told about her. You didn't keep her alive. You didn't keep her personality alive. Just images, reflections, shadows. It was a topsy turvy, fiction version of her.'

'You were very young, Dev, and for your mother and I, many of the memories we have of Amina are from when you were younger still. It might be easy to forget, but she was older than you. You just don't have all the memories that we have of her. Is that what you have been thinking all this time, about your mum and me? You had it wrong,' stated Raju.

'I don't know. You changed her. You and Mum. Every time you talked about her, you changed her.'

'I don't know how you mean. I'm tired.'

'Every time I heard you talking about her, it changed the picture I had,' persisted Dev.

'Well, I'm sorry about that. We didn't do it on purpose.'

'That doesn't alter the fact that you changed her for me,' Dev went on, tears pricking his eyes. 'She was dead, she was gone, but she was still changing, every time I heard of her. This other person that I didn't recognise. I just wanted to get back to Mina, the way I remembered her, before everything. How do I get that back, Dad?'

'I don't know, Dev. Look, I don't know what you think you're going to accomplish, after all these years, bringing it all up? Hm? Do you think you're the only one that feels things?'

'No.'

'Then why? What will it get you?'

'Because I want to know.' Dev looked past his father and over to the stove. The onions were blackened and smoking in the pan. 'Those onions are no good anymore.'

'Oh,' Raju sighed. 'Can you peel and chop two onions for me? That'd be a big help, Dev. I need to go… and sit down.'

Sitting with her thoughts, Jayne realises that this is not what she had envisioned when she began this process.

The *process* being: alerting the general public to not only the existence of God but their words.

When she thinks of it like that, she feels it sounds a little silly. Even sillier is how she feels now that the word of God has finally come.

As per the plan, she had dutifully distributed what she was calling *ointment* – although *elixir* was still under consideration, despite her feeling it was a little pretentious. *On the other hand, we're talking about God. God!* she would think to herself. *Not a topic customarily associated with subtlety. Just look at all the cultures across the world and the opulent shrines. Or gaudy, depending on your perspective.*

Anyway, she has done as she was bid and had gone about pressing the *elixir* (yes, she prefers that) into the palms of anyone she met. Jayne paid particular attention to people travelling abroad since they would redistribute it, aiding its proliferation worldwide, speeding up the connection. Of course, they had no idea what they were taking away with them, the power or influence their travels would eventually have upon one another.

Of course, Jayne can be entirely forgiven for not having entertained even the shadow of the thought that when God would eventually communicate to everyone, it would be met with such a reception.

*Somehow, everyone just knew. Well, how everyone knew was obviously something to do with them. I mean, it's God. All-knowing, all-powerful, all possible God! What other explanation is necessary?*

Somehow everyone knew they had been spoken to by God. That is, everyone who had become part of this vast network of people who had received the elixir by touch. Touch zero, of course, being Jayne's.

Sure, in the aftermath of the *happening*, far more people say they have experienced it than had actually been touched in the first place. It is also perhaps inevitable that some people simply do not believe it is God that has spoken. Others who do believe do so so fervently that they imagine God has said more than they actually have, or that they have delivered a special message tailored just for them.

Ultimately, when God spoke, they did so to the entire network, all at once. Their presence breathed through all senses, softly, like the rustle of autumnal leaves on the wind. The network did not hear their words so much as experience them.

'I am with you. Look to yourself.'

After the event, many tried to describe the voice of God, but they couldn't, leading to the broad assumption that it was some kind of a hoax being perpetrated on a world gone weird. Surely, if God has indeed spoken, their voice would be ingrained in the consciousness. Was it deep? Was it hoarse? Was it that of a male? Female? A child? With a lack of consensus, it seems to have been a different experience for each person. Despite that, the overwhelming majority of people agree that they are generally underwhelmed.

Before long, the excitement and fervour that had built up around the event of God's words were being recanted.

"I am with you. Look to yourself." *What was that? What did it even mean?*

In the absence of logic, those who want to believe in signs, religious or otherwise, have been expecting something. Something other than how it seems, for the world as everyone knows it is coming apart. It is time for a sign, feel the believers. They think it is time for something that will crush even the faintest molecule of disbelief or cynicism, time for something that will give the disbelievers nowhere to hide, eroding the foundations of all their arguments that support their cynicism.

"I am with you. Look to yourself," is not what had been expected. Yes, the world is on fire with talk of God. No, it wasn't the comeback it might have been. It was more like a band approaching that tricky third album, having focussed all their first-album energies on stripped-back urgency, opted for stadium fillers on the second, and were subsequently at a loss as to how to consolidate the two approaches for their third album. You know, *that* band.

*"I am with you? Look to yourself?" I mean, who was he kidding?* thinks Jayne, right before she says it. '"I am with you? Look to yourself?" I mean, all due respect, but what are you saying?' Jayne asks.

'What are *you* saying?' replies God.

Jayne kicks her heel a little and throws her hands out in exasperation, replying, 'what do you mean, "what are you saying?" What are *you* saying?'

'What do you mean?' asks God.

'Oh, wait, is this like a riddle? Or… the seeds of an allegory?'

'Mm, I don't think so. Just tell me. What are you getting at?'

'People need more. People are expecting more. From you.'

'People? Look at them. They're so beautiful. So ugly. Stubborn. Fragile. Fucked up.'

'You can't say that,' reprimanded Jayne.

‘What?’ asked God.

‘You can’t use *that* word,’ then, screwing up her face, she repeated: *“fucked.”*

‘Why? They *are* fucked up. It’s true. All of them. Every single one of them in their way. No two are the same. They’re all beautiful. And ugly.’

‘I know it’s true. Everyone knows it’s true, but *you* can’t use that word. It’s a terrible word for something that should be emotional and full of feeling,’ clarifies Jayne. ‘A reflection of the love two people are supposed to feel for each other.’

‘If it’s terrible, then why does it exist?’

‘How the… *fuck* should I know?’ she explodes, frustrated.

‘There! Ha! *You* said it! There, see?’ God points out, delighted.

‘I said it because I was angry. That is when my generation uses it. Moments of anger, frustration, or shock. Now people just use it for anything.’

‘But why are you angry?’

‘Because you’re supposed to… be better than this. Everything is supposed to be better. But it’s not, it’s shit, it’s just shit. Everything is just fucking shit.’ Jayne is now screaming and spitting out her words.

‘Like?’ enquires God.

‘Well, like *fucking*. It’s supposed to be love. It’s supposed to be intimate relations. Procreation. Between a man and a woman.’

‘So that’s it? You object to words?’

‘No, I object to what people have done. I object to them turning something that should always have been a pure form of expression and turning it every way to satisfy their agenda.

The people, the doctors and scientists compelled to dissect, prod and poke and weigh and measure to search for the science, taking away the romance, the mystery of something we don't fully understand. And on the other end, there are all the others and their horrible things.'

'You'll have to fill me in. I'm a little hazy on specific details.'

'People who force themselves on others, manipulate, trick, betray and degrade each other in the most unnatural way possible, taking pictures as they dehumanise. What about the warlords?'

'What *about* the warlords?'

'They use rape to control the people. They use soldiers to rape women, children, men, everyone. How many children are born from rape? How many people in the world have their genitals mutilated for no good reason? Just because tradition and beliefs dictate it.

'How could you let something that brings such intimacy and happiness, the spark that galvanises life and creation, also bring such cruel pain and devastation? How could you have made things that way? The people who do these things, what do they have faith in that allows them to be so vicious? What do they believe in that lets them sleep at night? Where is their compassion?'

The tears dry on her cheeks. The anger subsides from her chest. Jayne falls asleep again, her fingers tightly interlocked over her chest. Sometimes she needs the anger. It makes her feel alive, and as long as she is alive, she feels the glow of faith within.

I watch him, Dev, and I consider all these people. People, people everywhere. Always more where they came from. Flesh. Flesh everywhere. Flesh wanting other flesh. Rubbing, snorting, sweating, craving, pressing, pushing. Flesh pushed to consider or to disregard the value of other flesh. Because, in the end, it's all just flesh, and there is always plenty more where it comes from.

# 66. Nothing important happened today

'So, how was it? You been yet?' asked Mira as she assumed her now customary position in the armchair by the window and crossed one leg over the other as Dev made himself comfortable at the foot of her bed. This time she wore a light cashmere top and black jeans. She had taken the day off and wasn't seeing clients. Her only visitor would be Dev.

'It was… informative,' commented Dev, not wishing to expand upon his disturbing encounter with Grealish.

'What?' burst Mira, surprised. She uncrossed her legs and leaned forward. 'You mean you actually went? I didn't think you would.'

'I actually went,' confirmed Dev.

'On your own?'

'No, I took someone.'

'A girl?'

'Yeah.'

'What did she make of it?'

'She'd been there before.'

'Oh, right. So, what was it like? Tell me all your innermost thoughts and feelings,' she said, playfully mimicking his voice, clearly relishing the role reversal.

The night had been overshadowed by his conversation with Grealish, the memory drive and Dev's subsequent morning of turmoil as he tried to overcome the fallout from the video file. Two months later, he was still dealing with it. In the immediate aftermath, Dev hadn't paid much mind to any thoughts or feelings about his time at the actual party.

'It was,' he began, 'completely different to anything I've ever experienced. Watching people really throwing off their inhibitions, being open, confident about their place in the world, themselves. That's what came across.'

'It's not just confidence, but maybe that is all you see from the outside.'

'Grealish,' Dev started hesitantly.

'Oh. Yeah,' responded Mira, simply, her smile momentarily slipping. She had given Dev the card, told him to mention her name and ask for Grealish, out of frustration at his badgering, immediately regretting it. 'So, did you partake?' she asked, wanting to feel in control again, asking *him* the questions.

'No.'

'Think you'll go back?'

'I don't think so.'

'Why not? You just said everyone was really open. Didn't you want to be like that?'

'Um, I don't know.'

'Wouldn't you like to know how it feels? To do something different? Wouldn't it make you feel alive to do something different?' Desperate for Dev to not change the subject, Mira uncharacteristically pressed on. 'I mean… sex makes you feel alive. Pain makes you feel alive. Pleasure. Pain. Tears. Touch. Smell. Taste. Sight. Sound. It all reminds us that we are alive. It's up to us to enjoy being alive.'

Silhouetted by the light from the window behind her, Mira paused to look Dev in the eyes. 'People concentrate on life instead of *being alive*. Most people I know are shit at life, but most of us have what we need to be great at *being alive*. We all go through life looking for that thing that we are truly great at. That thing that tells us who we are. I think we overthink it. I mean, we have senses. That *is* the thing we are *all* good at, naturally.'

'You don't think we should strive for more?'

'Look. All the information we get about the world around us is from our senses. Why do we deny that simplicity and look for more? We're so preoccupied with making ourselves different that we don't see how much fucking fun we can have,' she said with a smile.

'We can all sense the same things, just the way we handle it is different. Anticipation of the unknown, that's where the turn-on is. Not knowing. Being in control, or not. Being alive is so exciting. It's not just sex. Earthquakes, hurricanes, volcanoes, riots, forest fires, tsunamis, meteors, nuclear disasters, serial killers, mass murderers. When will the fuckers pop up? The circumstances, how many will be affected?

'Isn't it exciting to see what happens next? There is so much that is exciting and beautiful about the world. It's not all bad. Really, it's all beautiful. If you were watching the world and weren't in it, wouldn't it be beautiful? Not like a TV show with cuts and edits and action all over the place, but imagine you were watching things happen in the world a lot more slowly. Imagine if you could watch it all without participating. How beautiful would it be? Seamless. Continuous. Like one of those big icebergs bumbling through the sea.'

Dev was at a loss for words, astonished as to how forthcoming Mira was being. He wanted to point it out to her and ask what had prompted this flow of thoughts from her. His chats with her were usually so stultifying until he found a hook to stimulate her. Here, she was expansive from the outset. What had changed between them? Was it the sex party? Was it Grealish?

'Do you ever give up control? Control of yourself,' asked Mira.

'Hm, sometimes,' admitted Dev. 'Why? What's the attraction when you do it?'

'It's exciting, isn't it? It's like something that is out of place, unusual and dangerous. Like blood.'

'Blood?'

'Yeah. Have you ever really looked at blood and enjoyed it? The way it feels, on your fingers, on your body, the way it smells? You're a doctor. You're around blood, but have you ever looked at it, in a way that was nothing to do with a medical thing?'

'Well, then what else is there? That's what blood is all about.'

'No,' said Mira with a little shake of her head as she leaned forward, resting her elbow on the armrest of the chair. 'Blood is being alive. We need blood. When you look at it outside of medicine, just as this life-giving force, it turns into something else, something magical, full of wonder.

'People don't like seeing blood because it's supposed to be inside, only otherwise acceptable in syringes or transfusion bags. They don't want to see it glistening under a lamp post at night or dried up on a wall. It scares them.'

'Yeah. Violence,' agreed Dev.

'What if you saw blood, and it didn't mean violence or pain? What if it meant trust? Faith? That's what giving up control is like. Whether it's tying you down, or hurting you, or choking you, it's like letting someone use a blade on you, expose your blood, letting it trickle down your arm, across your palm, and along your finger, to drip onto the floor. It's putting your life on the blade of their knife and trusting them not to go too far. It's delicious. It's the best fucking meal you've never had. Trust me.'

'How do you know that I've never?' asked Dev.

'You're not the type,' she judged, leaning back again. 'If you gave up control, you'd implode. With people like you, it's not that you like control, so much as you need it.'

'I don't think so.'

'I do. You're not going to put yourself at risk,' Mira said, looking up at the ceiling and putting her fingers together contemplatively, revelling in her moment of insight as Dev looked down, absorbing her words.

'Giving up control means handing it to someone else. Submission. Not knowing what the person with the blade might do, what's behind their eyes. The excitement of uncertainty. What will happen? How will it feel? Will they do it slowly? Will they linger? Will you be the same afterwards, or will you be different? You know, in a way, giving up control is kind of taking control as well.'

With all the soul-searching Dev had been doing about Amina, he couldn't listen to any more of Mira's talk about control. 'You know, Sir Walter Raleigh, right?' asked Dev.

'The potato guy?'

'Yeah, potato guy. He had this idea for weighing smoke.'

'Weighing smoke?'

'I've forgotten exactly how it was, but basically, it was something like, he had an audience with the queen. I suppose he had just returned from somewhere and was recounting his exploits. There was all the well-to-do, the wealthy, and the famous from society there. He asked if they knew how to weigh smoke and then had tobacco, scales and a pipe brought in. Raleigh weighed the tobacco before smoking it, carefully tipping the ash onto the scales when he was done. The difference, he called the weight of smoke.

'Yeah, I think I remember that story from school. Why?'

'What if knowing someone's mind could be as easy as something like that? The difference between one state and another. All you had to do was burn away the excess to reveal the secrets. You say that blood is magical. That's how I see thoughts. Maybe there's some easy way, like Walter and his smoke, that we can measure intentions, feelings, the weight of someone's absence when they're gone.'

'You see thoughts as words, but most of them would be feelings, emotions, colours, music, smells, things we can sense. That's the language of thoughts, personality.'

'Don't we always think in words?'

'My cousin, Donna,' began Mira, preparing to launch into a story, 'she's a hot-head, even more than me,' she smiled. 'We always say she should think before reacting. Maybe she feels more than she thinks. You don't feel in words, do you? What about people who don't have words? People with serious learning problems. They still think. They just seem to think in emotions, impulses. Natural instinct.'

A few moments passed in silence before Mira grew restless. 'Dev, I don't get the point of *this* anymore. We're not even talking about sex now. Aren't you interested in that anymore? One day maybe you'll want something riskier than talking. Maybe you'll do all the dangerous shit people do. Bungee jumping? Skydiving? Or be an army medic, dodge landmines trying to save people. Or does your religion stop you going to war? Are you a lover, not a fighter, Dev? What is your religion?'

'Not really anything.'

'What were you born with?'

'Kind of Hindu, I suppose.'

'Kind of? You weren't raised religious then?'

'It's complicated. How about you?'

'I was born Church of England,' she replied quickly before continuing with her next question. 'What do you think about Muslim women and the whole Burqa thing? You think it should be banned? Do Hindus wear Burqas, or is it just Muslims?'

'No, Hindus don't. I don't know. I haven't really thought about it. It must be strange for them to be out in public, without wearing it anymore.'

'Yeah, but they should be free, not following whatever someone came up with ages ago. We live in the here and now. Why do people stick with traditions to stay in touch with the past? Do they think they're better than everyone else, closer to some solid truth? I mean, who cares about tradition when you can feel the sun on your face?' asked Mira, unconsciously kicking out her feet at the mention of the sun, as though imagining she was on a lounger somewhere warm.

'*They* might care. They might not want to lose a tradition that they think connects them to their parents, their ancestors.'

'But things have changed. Now we think different. There are revolutions all over the place.' Mira paused, puzzling over how to approach this: 'I tried to get back into it. Christianity.'

'Really? When?' asked Dev, nonplussed by her admission of religious affinity.

'Well, I'm always trying to get back into it. But I really tried after 9-11. That was *my* reaction. I suppose I wanted to defy, show them they weren't winning anything by doing that. Or something. I never left Christianity, but I don't go to church. Back then, I tried to get into… the *community*, I suppose,' she added awkwardly.

'I was eighteen when it happened, so maybe I was nineteen when I tried going back to church. Ages before doing films, but I was working, doing what I do. I thought it would be fun, or something, to belong and share something with other people. So, I started going to a church group, and I made friends with someone there, someone my age. Eventually, I told her what I did. She was fine with it. In fact, she was really nice. She was… like you, but less of a dick.'

'Oh. Good,' deadpanned Dev.

'She wanted to know all about it, how I got into it. I just told her what I told you. She didn't try to make me quit. She just seemed to accept it as my way of life. A couple of weeks later, I went out with her and some of her other Christian friends. She knew I was there. It's like she said it, just to hurt me or shame me.'

'What did she say?'

'We were all talking about marriage because one of them was getting married. Out of nowhere, my friend said: "anyone who has sex before marriage deserves to get AIDS. They deserve to die from an STD."

'I just thought: "who would say something like that?" I thought we were friends. I suppose she weighed it up and decided the role of being in with them was more… beneficial than… me.' A moment or two passed before she asked: 'What's your role, Dev?'

Dev hesitated a moment. 'Maybe… a watcher.'

'You like to watch, do you? I knew it,' Mira said with a playful smile.

'As a doctor, I feel like I'm watching all the time, not always able to do something when people are truly looking for help. Sometimes it's out of their control. Sometimes they go looking for trouble.'

'And now you want to be the one looking for it in sex clubs,' said Mira, forgetting herself.. 'What will it be, when you find it?'

'What do you suggest?'

'We're humans. Surely the worst we can do to each other is our imaginations. That's our only limit, right? So what's the worst you can think of?'

Something made Dev reluctant to bring up the sex party again with Mira but calculated that she had touched on it for a reason. He replied: 'Grealish.'

Mira's sly smile vanished instantly from her lips, and she sank back into her armchair a little at his mention. 'I thought you were done talking about the party. You didn't seem up for it earlier.'

'That's the worst I can think of. You asked me.'

'Look,' Mira said, rising from her chair, 'you like talking about sex, don't you? Come here,' she said before stepping towards Dev. Undoing the buttons of her jeans, she gyrated her hips a little and revealed her delicate underwear.

'Why?'

'Come here,' she invited again, ignoring his question, as she climbed and straddled him, her hand snaking down, between his legs.

'Are you going to try to have sex with me again?' asked Dev.

'I'm not trying anymore. I just am,' Mira breathed. 'I know you want to fuck me,' she insisted, looking down at him.

'Really, that's what you think?' he asked.

'It's what you wanted all along. It's alright if you need a story to justify it, Dev. I've heard all sorts. My wife's in a coma. My girlfriend's working abroad.' She leaned her face close to Dev's, whispering, 'one bloke, before sticking his cock in my mouth, said he wanted to help the local economy. Like he was at a fucking farmers' market.' She paused before continuing.

'Now… is this good?' she asked, stroking his penis over his clothes. 'I know it is. I can feel you. Just relax. Let Mira take care of you. In the end, you all want what you don't get at home. But if you get it at home, it's not a fantasy, is it? You all need it, don't you? Don't pull away. Don't think. Just relax. Do you want me to be quiet now? Hm, what could make me be quiet? What do you think?' she asked, biting her lip, fully in character.

'You sent me to Grealish,' stated Dev, looking up at her.

'Mira, you knew I'd find out. You want to talk.'

'Stop talking about him. Stop talking, Dev, just concentrate on what *I'm* doing to you.'

'Mira. You're working with him. You send him clients.'

Instantly dropping out of character again, her soft body tensing around him, Mira sharply shot back at him: 'I'm not working with him! I'm in charge of myself now. I do what I want,' she continued, needing him to believe. 'Why aren't you getting hard?' she asked, her voice growing higher with her need to stop thinking, to stop feeling.

'Don't,' he said softly.

'Get hard for me,' she pleaded before adding, 'please,' undoing his trousers and forcing her hand through the opening.

'Stop,' he said, a little more firmly, his hands on her shoulders, willing her to understand that she had more value to him than simple sexual gratification.

'No!' she shouted back at him, pulling away from his grasp before gripping his arms and using her strength to push him down on the bed before pinning him with her weight. The light from the lamp above them glinted in her eyes. 'I can't! I need it, Dev, I fucking need it. Because I'm fucked up! They fucked me up. Is that what you want? You happy now? They fucked me up!' she screamed at him, spots of saliva flying from her mouth.

There it was. What Dev had been seeking. A first-hand, candid reaction from a real victim. Uncensored. Shorn of the distanced, sterile veneer of research papers, case studies and professional guidelines. This is what he thought he had wanted. A visceral view of a real victim, brought to the edge of their composure, made to confront what had happened to them. Dev had come close with Katie, but she had long ago achieved her own kind of peace that he wouldn't undo. Katie couldn't be pushed. She wasn't pretending.

'Do you think I fuck bareback with strangers because I really fucking love myself?' Mira continued. 'I fucking hate myself, you cunt, ever since I was a kid.'

'You know what he does, don't you?' pushed Dev, needing her to acknowledge it.

'Same thing he's always done,' cried Mira, 'but it's not happening to me anymore. So I'm not a victim, all right?'

Dev had always known Mira was a fuse, ready to ignite. There she was, tears in her red eyes. Her voice trembled. A bunched fist. The pain stretched over her face. Mira could hide it no longer. She swallowed hard, fighting the urge to break, fighting to keep herself together in front of him.

He had pushed and made her confront demons that she ordinarily wouldn't or had only ever faced in private. As she pushed herself off Dev's shoulders and kneeled back, still straddling him, the raw emotions stretched over every sinew. Ready to snap and curl back.

'But you're still doing what they taught you,' replied Dev, tentatively, as he pushed himself back up again, slowly coming face to face with her.

It was everything Dev had craved as he watched and took her in. It was what he had thought would give him even the slimmest glimmer of what Amina might have been like. The emotions she held down. The naked vulnerability in her eyes that had been there, but that he had been blind to as a child.

'You should have been someone else.' He breathed in

deeply and then exhaled hard. 'My sister should have been someone else,' he continued, a tremble creeping into his voice.

'Your sister?' Mira asked, her voice softening almost imperceptibly.

'It was a long time ago.'

'Your sister… why didn't you say something?'

'I wanted to understand.'

'What? What is there to understand? They're scumbags, Dev. They're not even human. There's nothing to understand there,' Mira explained with a little shake of her head.

At that moment, watching Mira, Dev realised there was a fundamental difference between the two. Amina would have been a hurt and confused girl. A part of Mira was still a girl, frozen in time. Hurt and confused from her own abuse. Despite this, the rest of her had grown and matured. She had forged her own path, but it had not spared her any of the bitterness, rage and frustration that had accumulated and congealed over time. Mira was less like his sister, Dev realised, and more like his mother.

'Understand? Why? So you can forgive them? And then what?' she demanded angrily. 'Forget? You'll never forget. Your sister will never forget.'

'My sister's dead, Mira. When she was thirteen. I only just found out what she went through. My mother…' he started explaining before he paused. 'Now, I don't know anything. Understanding is all I have left.' Dev finally allowed his face to crumple as the tears dropped from his stinging eyes.

He had lost Amina all over again. Just as on the day of her funeral, all those years ago, he was once again in a bedroom, facing up to the loss, oncc again sharing his loss with someone who understood the pain, but Mira understood in ways that he never would, no matter how hard he tried.

As Dev's eyes locked with Mira's, a prick of regret reached him. He had wanted her to admit that she had been abused, to tell him everything that had happened to her. For catharsis. For him. For her. For Amina. But he couldn't do it. If she wanted to talk and heal, she would, but Dev couldn't bring himself to push her any further.

Mira may have worn a mask, but it had been a very effective one, and in seeing her stripped of it, Dev realised he had exposed her and brought her down. He had pulled down her pride and her defences. He had made her face her vulnerability in a way that she only ever did privately. All to better understand his sister's state of mind.

Dev couldn't undo what he had done, just as he couldn't continue to take what he thought he needed from Mira. Suddenly, all Dev could think of was his mother and the sadness she had held within, hidden from her husband and son for all those years as it ate her from the inside.

Seeing only Serena's anguish on Mira's face, Dev was instantly transported back to any one of the countless temples in Mauritius, where he watched from a distance as his mother mouthed silent words to the gods.

With the knowledge he now had, but seeing his mother once again through those child's eyes, he found renewed empathy and a more profound love for her than he had felt for many years. Dev wanted to reach out and comfort her. As all adults do at one time or another, he wanted to be that small child again. For his mother. This time a child who understood more.

Therein, Dev realised, lay his true motivation for persisting with Mira, pushing for mutual understanding. He needed to understand her, and her him. He needed them both to accept each other. She had only revealed hints of herself, and so Mira remained a mystery to Dev. However, any facts gleaned would have only paled in comparison, for him, to the moment she finally opened the door and let him see her pain.

# 67. Nothing really matters

Tim was officially worried about his friend. Dev had been due to meet him at the pub but hadn't turned up. Usually, Tim would think nothing of it and just go home, but these were no longer normal circumstances. He had called Dev, who had failed to answer his phone. Now, standing in Dev's living room, he stood in open-mouthed astonishment as he surveyed the carnage around him.

Every surface was covered in A4 pages, writing pad pages, notepad pages. They were scrawled all over with notes, what looked like calculations, diagrams, mathematical equations, quotes, all sorts of memories. Stooping to pick up a sheet or two from the floor, Tim found that almost everything written linked to Amina.

The moment with Mira had led to a catharsis of sorts for them both. However, for Dev, it had also delivered a realisation. He had once again taken a wrong turn. This experience with Mira had not delivered the desired resolution because, yet again, he concluded, that wasn't what he had needed.

The conversation with Mira and his emotional collapse had brought him an insight, that insight being that he was just as preoccupied with Amina's actual death as he was with her mental state in the weeks and months that led to it.

Once again, he had set about understanding her through the only framework that he found familiar. His last conversation with Mira had brought him some sense of resolution, but that had also set free within him a torrent of emotions that he did not have the capacity to control.

Navigating the fallout of his mother's revelations and thinking analytically to execute plans designed to bring relief had only been possible because he had tried to stem the flow of his feelings. Instead of allowing himself to fully face the horror that his sister had endured, he had cowered behind statistics. Data. The careful language of case studies that Mira had picked up on in their first one on one meeting.

She had been right about his circuitous self-censorship but wrong about whom he was protecting. He hadn't been selective about his words out of sensitivity to her as a potential victim, only to protect himself. The emotional collapse and connection that they had finally experienced had only been possible for either of them because it had occurred with the right person there to prompt it, a person they trusted.

Now the floodgates were open, allowing his thoughts free rein to assail Dev with unceasing enmity. He had experienced hints of this in the aftermath of viewing Grealish's video, but Dev now dropped into uncharted depths of obsession.

Tim found him sprawled in bed, mumbling in his sleep, as though trapped deep within a labyrinthine nightmare. It had taken a few shakes and shouts for Tim to successfully rouse his friend from his sleep. Now they stood in Dev's living room, surveying the chaos that surrounded them. For the first time since they had known each other, Tim was the one who was concerned for Dev as he moved around the room, a blur of activity.

'Dev, you're seeing stuff that isn't there. Mate, I'm worried about you.'

Dev continued, ignoring his friend. 'I'm talking about an emotional connection to the act. What feelings does it create? Can we feel anything close to what they do? Can we see what they see, not just in reality, but in their *minds*?' he rambled as he darted around his flat. Dev collected and re-arranged sheets of paper in some kind of order that made sense to him but looked like a maelstrom of unconnected ideas, thoughts and memories to Tim. 'Can we truly experience what they are experiencing?'

Outrage flashed across Tim's face as he remembered what he had wanted to discuss with Dev at the pub in the first place. 'Is that why you changed up the medication on your patients? We all know about it. We all know what happened. Someone from your surgery leaked it to the local press. Why did you keep it a secret? *How* did you keep it a secret?' Tim asked.

'That… it doesn't matter,' dodged Dev.

'No, it does matter, Mate. You need to be straight with me here.'

'Nobody wanted any bad publicity. I agreed to leave quietly,' said Dev, careful not to look Tim in the eyes, busying himself instead with the handwritten notes in his hands.

'How could you do something like that? Was it an accident? Was it deliberate? How could you be so reckless?' Tim was shocked, his disgust at his friend rivalling his concern. 'You didn't want to help your patients. You were just looking for a thrill. But then watching wasn't enough. You had to fuck up lives as well, giving drugs they didn't need, changing their meds. You're fucked up,' he concluded as Dev continued to dash around, shuffling notes and pinning them to new notice boards as he unwrapped the plastic packaging from each one.

'What if I could change someone's personality. Would their loved ones leave, or would they make allowances and compensate because the person in front of them looks and sounds like the person they know, everything the same except the machine that makes the words come out has been recalibrated.' The words spilt from Dev's mouth as his brain whirled.

'This isn't you, Dev. How can you do this? I don't understand you.'

'You're right,' admitted Dev, turning back to face Tim, sweat beading his brow. 'I want uncertainty, I don't want control, I don't want to know what will happen, I need to *see* what will happen. What if the change was only physical? What if someone put on weight? A disgusting amount of weight. The kind of weight where small children in the supermarket pull their parent's clothes and say, *look, look at the fatty.* Would they become depressed? How would that play out?

'I wanted to watch what would happen, to see that person change and watch what words and actions would result when it met the thoughts and experiences accumulated over the years, wisdom and prejudices passed down from generations. I wanted to follow the ripples from my actions and see what would drive that person to end it all.'

Tim could see that his friend was slipping away from him. Tim knew that it was only Dev's words that appeared determined and defiant. He knew that behind all that, it was Dev's desperation and fear that were fuelling his search for answers, for understanding. Just like himself, all those years ago, when Tim had revealed his homosexuality to Dev. This vulnerability Tim now recognised in his friend.

'So you wanted to play God?'

'God is supposed to be all-knowing. I didn't know what would happen. I wanted to see. I grew up with uncertainty, and I tried to live my entire adult life without any risks or danger, but that's not me. You showed me that. Adults generally don't seek danger like children do. I wanted to see the consequences of my actions. To touch it. Taste it. See if it's real, because what if it's all wrong? If it's all made up, imaginary? All a lie?' The words left Dev's brain like machine-gun fire.

'So? What if it is?' asked Tim, confused.

'Then none of it means anything,' explained Dev. 'All the things everyone is told and taught. How to live, how not to live, what is important in life, what is not, what to believe, what exists, what is true, what to think. It all falls away. Dissolves. Like a web falling from a spider's clutches.

'If all this burden were lifted from us, maybe we would grow light. So light the Earth would simply fall away, leaving us passing through the air, the clouds, the sky, the stratosphere. We'd all break orbit and float into space. The planets would lose their alignment and slide around the galaxy. Nothing would matter anymore.

Dev continued. 'We would just be souls floating through space, equally blessed and damned to the trajectory our physical bodies took. Every so often, we might pass by another, but there'd be nothing to say or do. Just recognition of another spinning soul from planet Earth, in the same situation. Too dizzy and confused, no longer able to put one logical thought in front of another. No family. No friends. No feelings. No prejudice. No us and them. No others. Just a blank space where all that used to be.

'I remember the newsreaders from when I was a kid. The local news on two different channels, they used two different phrases. One said: "a girl fell from the Hayden Overbridge." The other said: "a girl fell off Hayden Overbridge." I was only nine, but I wondered if they both meant the same thing or if one hinted at something happening to send her from the bridge, and the other simply meant there was no further explanation. She just fell.'

'Are you talking about Amina?' asked Tim, as Dev returned to unwrapping his notice boards.

'I don't know anymore. I want to know what she was feeling. Don't we need to know why? Doesn't it matter? What are suicides looking for? Are they looking for themselves? What could be so strong that could induce someone to end their life? It's not something you would do on a whim. Surely you would consider all the points and make an informed decision. I want some kind of glimpse of what drives people to take such a final decision about *everything*.'

'Dev, what you need to do is slow down. You're talking a mile a minute. Have you taken something? I'll talk you down,' Tim reassured Dev as he continued roaming the room, attaching papers to papers, detaching and reattaching them elsewhere, a continual flurry of activity.

'That's impossible. You can't measure talk in miles, you know that, Tim. They're entirely different, as different as one person is from the next, despite our bodies being so similar.

The differences are relatively negligible, a drop in the ocean really, compared to how many things are the same. How can our bodies be so similar, but our brains, thoughts and reactions so different?

'All the crazy, dangerous, pointless stuff we do to ourselves, to each other, what compels us? Sex, murder, torture, war crimes, suicide. Who brings a child into all this? What kind of selfish fucking monster brings more children into a world like this?'

'Well, I thought you just said you like uncertainty now,' replied Tim.

'I need it. For myself. I wouldn't want it for anyone else. I wouldn't want it for *my* children. Is there some deeply embedded drive to keep the bloodline going, keep our own DNA around? Procreate, protect and perpetuate our lineage, traditions, family tree?' asked Dev.

'If you had no roots, wouldn't you feel disenfranchised? Rather than belonging to a single place, would you not feel you were split up all over, like pieces of yourself were everywhere. I feel like the best parts of me were taken away when I was a child, and I don't deserve anything. My life doesn't mean anything to me anymore, Tim.'

'Don't say shit like that,' replied Tim. 'Come on, stop moving and breathe with me. Slow, deep breathing, come on.'

'Do you know I can barely remember her as she really was? Nothing is anchored. Nothing is fixed. Everything is always moving, changing. How many times can I change, Tim? I can't lie anymore and pretend everything is dependable.'

'Dev, you're losing yourself.'

'I haven't lost myself. I've just stopped pretending to be someone else.'

'I don't know who I'm talking to anymore. Dev, we love you, and you've clearly had a breakdown of some sort, but you have to snap out of this.'

Ignoring Tim, Dev continued ranting: 'So easy to die and drop out of life, out of the world. Seemingly so easy to end up alive. What did he say? Born out of a whisky bottle on a Saturday night? How can one take life so seriously? As if it means anything at all. A one in 400 trillion chance of existing. All just pure luck that we have evolved and developed the ability to make more of life than there actually is.

'If it is so easy to die, how can life be so serious? Life should be fantasy. What if suddenly none of it made any sense? What if everything we thought we knew as solid facts about biology, life, the world, the universe all ceased to hold true? What if everything began coming apart? What if nothing mattered anymore? What if the fictions we create to make sense of life came apart? What if we've been waiting for God all this time, and when they finally come, they tell us that everything we thought we had figured out was all wrong?

'Everything, I mean *everything*,' emphasised Dev. 'Like we don't actually breathe oxygen, that we breathe dust. Dust is what we need to survive. All the instruments we made to measure things and see things, they were all wrong. Like, instead of using lenses in microscopes, we should have been using… spiderwebs.'

'Dude, seriously, you're going to have a heart attack. Breathe and slow down. Everything's going to be okay.'

Dev finished unwrapping another notice board and

instantly began plucking sheets of paper from the sofa and spiking them to the soft, blue surface. 'My life doesn't mean anything to me anymore. I don't want family. I don't want friends. Success. A job. Responsibility. Standing. Status. Walls. Roofs. I want the sky. I want the soil. I want the sea. Family is fantasy.

'How can I have happiness when I know Amina suffered? I have to understand how it can happen, how someone can change so radically. Doing these *family things* fits into boxes. Boxes of acceptance. Nice, cosy little families in nice, cosy little houses. I don't want to fit in like everything is fine, and everything is the way it is supposed to be because nothing is normal anymore, and nothing matters anymore. People. Their welfare. What they do. What they look like.'

Dev continued. 'With all the crimes that happen and the perpetrators that are never caught, surely what it means is that nothing actually matters. Society doesn't mean anything. Laws do not mean anything. Anything is possible. We like to think laws protect the innocent and punish the guilty. Laws, family, friends are the frameworks we use to build our lives, but they are fragile, *fragile* frames.

'We like to think that everything has meaning and matters, but it doesn't, Tim. If terrible things can be perpetrated, affect the people we love, and go unpunished, then why does anything matter? Why do we matter to each other? We are all outraged by immoral things that happen to other people. Why? Is it simply because we don't want it to happen to us? We don't want to be illegally invaded. We don't want to be murdered. We don't want to be raped. We don't want to be bombed with chemical weapons.

'Despite all the terrible things that happen, people affected by them go on with their lives, they get up and adapt and go on. They know it should not have happened and that their lives should be different, but they live with it anyway, adapting to their situation because their lives matter to them. Because they believe they have value. Even though, proportionally, their lives do not matter much to many others. The people who go to supermarkets. The people who catch buses. The people who accept lifts late at night. The people living in fear of warlords. The strung out. The glassy-eyed, living only as an alternative to death.'

'Dev,' began Tim, completely bewildered by his friend, 'you're not making any sense, you're spiralling. What's happened? I'm getting that someone's been hurt. Who? Who's been hurt?'

'I feel everything,' explained Dev, crouching to collect more of his scrawlings from the floor. 'It all bleeds into my line of sight. I feel it all coursing through me. Electrons, atoms, particles. You don't believe me, but I'm *vibrating* with energy. My body pulses with electricity, elements, fluids, sinew, muscle. I can feel every single atom. You don't believe me,' Dev stated again.

'I do. I know.'

'What do you know? You're not even real.'

'Dev, what's happening?'

'*Amina* Tim!' Dev snapped as if the answer should have been self-evident from the beginning.

'Dev, Amina's dead. I'm sorry but –'

'Amina was raped. Again and again. Mum told me, Tim!'

'What?'

‘She killed herself. It wasn’t an accident. She jumped, Tim! From the bridge they were building!’

Finally, Dev had got it out of himself. He had shared it with someone else, but he didn’t feel any better. Instead, slowly, Dev continued picking paper from the ground. Putting his fingers to them, he came to a halt. And froze. His incessant jabbering and dashing around had been stopped, like a switch had been flicked, shutting off the flow of instructions from his brain to his body. Seemingly unable to go on. Unable to stand. As frozen physically as he was suspended psychologically.

At his side, Tim tentatively moved closer, reaching out to his friend’s shoulder. The moments ticked away, but despite Tim’s efforts to rouse him from his state, Dev didn’t respond.

‘Dev?’ he asked, desperate to find some way to reach him, some way to jolt him, for his motionless silence and dead-eyed stare were just as unnerving as his manic babbling. ‘Ruth’s pregnant. I’m… I’m going to be a dad. It doesn’t matter. None of what happened before. We’re going to start over. We’re going to be all right.’ But Dev didn’t hear him.

# 68. Something everyone can enjoy

Instead, he hears the voice of a woman.

'Today, I'm going to tell you something that will change your life forever.'

Tinny, as though from a TV.

'In fact, not only will it change your life, but it will transform the lives of your loved ones.'

A presenter.

'Perhaps revealing themselves in a completely different light.'

On one of those shopping channels…

'A revolutionary new technology.'

The audience applauds.

'Let me ask you this,' she continues. 'How many of you have loved ones in the hospital? I know many of you are sitting at home and thinking: yes, I have someone I love in the hospital. They've been there for a while, and I hate it. I wish they were at home with me having a nice dinner. I wish I could feel them, hold their hand, feel their heartbeat next to mine.

'Perhaps you have grandparents, parents in nursing homes. Wouldn't you like them close by instead of drifting away amongst strangers? How much time do they have, and what is it worth to you? Impossible to answer, right? You can't put a price on time, feelings, family or love. You cannot put a price on the memories and experiences you are missing out on as we speak. You can't. You just can't.

'Right now, if you have loved ones in, what the doctors call, a *persistent vegetative state*, you are missing out on having those you love on vacations, trips, family meals. All because they need the care and medical know-how that only trained professionals can provide. Isn't that right?' she asks the camera.

'Well, today I am pleased to announce that we have the means to bridge the gap. We have the technology, and it works. No need for your loved ones to remain on hospital ventilators. No need for them to remain cooped up in hospices and residential homes, being pumped with drugs under the supervision of the professionals.

'Your loved ones can remain with you, and at this point, their presence means more to you than yours does to them. Knowing they were present at your graduation, at the birth of your first child, or on the holiday of a lifetime that you all planned to take together,' continued the woman.

'I can almost hear you all shouting at your TV sets. *How does this work? Tell me now!* I can't go into specifics. This works on a case by case basis. Our team takes you and your family by the hand and, with a dedicated service, we will comb through the medical history and quality of life needs of your loved one. Based on that information, we remove the affected organs and replace them with alternatives that do the same job, or even better! With the relevant augmentations, your loved ones will have the appropriate medication and preservatives distributed throughout their body.

'Using the latest communications technology,' she went on, 'your family member will upload up-to-the-minute medical data that shall be transmitted via satellite to our comprehensive medical database. Whatever the body needs, the body shall get via embedded microchips. Before taking your loved one away, they will be fully loaded with the necessary components to synthesise their own medication. How about *that*?

'Don't go without them any longer. Cherish the time you have. Just think, no more hospital visits, no one missing from your life anymore.

'This will revolutionise your relationship with your loved one and change the world, all for a bargain price. Order now, and we'll throw in the maintenance fees, free, for twelve months!'

When Dev snaps back, he is with me again, in Katie's room. A few seconds have ticked by. He still sweats through his clothes, the lesions around his neck still angry, pulsating.

Another female voice.

'Why did you have to change them?' The voice of an older woman.

'What? Who the fuck now?' croaks Dev.

'Don't use that word, please. Why would you choose to do that to my God?' asks the voice again as Dev's eyes loll in his head, seeking something upon which to rest.

'You say, "*my* God", like they're your personal assistant.'

'My view of God is different to that of the next person along the pulpit, so yes, my God is personal, unique to me. They're my piece of the world that doesn't change, not for me. Why did you have to change them and involve me in it? Did we all have to be so scared? Do you know no remorse? Did it feel good, using your will to crush the vulnerable, just because you could?'

Dev's eyes finally focus through the sweat dripping into them, and he sees her sitting on the edge of the bed. 'Jayne! Mayor, please, help me!'

'I can't. Not until you answer.'

'*They* didn't answer. We're all their children. We all deserve answers. If they won't show up, I'll make of them what I want.'

'Who says they're absent? You think you're so clever, but you ignore the basics that even a child can grasp and accept as true. God is everywhere. Can't you see? Without God, you would be nothing.'

'Without science –'

'Science didn't paint the Sistine Chapel, Dr. Sharma. *Dev.* Science didn't compose sonnets and concertos. God is always in the details that make things beautiful. And ugly. When some medical breakthrough occurs, it's a marvel of modern science, but when an earthquake destroys a city, they call it an *Act of God.* How do you know there isn't the work of God in science? Why are the two mutually exclusive?'

'Can you hear yourself?' laughs Dev.

'Yes, and I have faith, the same faith that inspires millions of people each day to overcome.'

'No, you have faith in faith. That alone does not save. Those people must also want to save themselves. Otherwise, they have nothing.'

'Whether we believe or not, we have all heard of them,' assumes Jayne, 'and therefore, we have an attitude towards and a relationship with God. You think thinking is what all people have in common. I say it's God. Whether we believe or not, God is in the background of our thoughts, from the moment that they are brought to our attention as a possibility. They are always there in the back of our minds, casting their shadow, casting their light. You can't escape them.'

'I don't believe in God as some third party, the way you do.'

'How so?' asks Jayne.

'We constructed different cultures, civilisations, tribes, *and gods*.' Dev struggles and croaks. 'If we have constructed God and they're in the back of our minds, then their love is not the only thing back there. We're humans, so we also created their hate. That shadow and light validate all the things, right and wrong, that we do because we want to.

'You're right,' continues Dev, 'they're back there, and we might not all call them God, but they allow us to disregard our feelings and carry on with what we're doing, whether it's good or bad, whether we're hurting, or hurting someone. There is love back there, but also guilt. You can call it God if you want. I just call it thought.'

'But if they are a construction of our imagination, then they do not exist, and neither does their love. Their guilt,' argues Mayor Jayne.

'Don't you see that none of it matters? None of it is real. If I can believe in something so arbitrary… then I can just as easily believe none of it exists. Anything I imagine can be real. It's *my* new religion. There is no God to worship or fear… only ourselves and each other.'

'You're not making any sense,' mutters Mayor Jayne.

'Prerogative of the dying, Jayne. No ghosts watch over us. Watching us do terrible things to each other, trying to stop us or encouraging us. No all-seeing God watches to keep us safe, thinking about us. We're alone. We're fragile beings, and we need to look after each other. Because there is absolutely nothing else out there.'

'What about your mother? When she was going from church, to temple, to mosque. Praying. Didn't that mean anything to you? Your mother's faith?' asks Jayne. 'Doesn't that still touch you in some way?'

'No. Because I know the truth now. She wasn't trying to talk to God. I know she was talking to Amina.'

'Ridiculous,' sputtered Jayne. 'Your mother would talk to a ghost before she talked to the Lord Almighty? What utter tripe,' she scoffed, enraging Dev. This is good. This is a good reaction.

'Where is God, then?' he croaks. 'When are they coming? I want them to see us, what we have become. Have we lived up to expectations? Do we deserve them? I want them to see us, this world, and honour us with their benevolence.'

'Why? You don't even believe.'

'I want to believe she went somewhere better. Better than all this. Amina was too good, too beautiful to be amongst all this, to be in this world.'

With that, Dev feels himself suddenly shooting upwards as Mayor Jayne watches from the bed. The belt still tightening around his neck, he crashes through the ceiling of the bedroom, upwards through the living room of the flat above, through the roof and up through the sky. Dev's eyes water as he passes through clouds and continues towards the stratosphere. The G force yanks at his head as he continues to climb through the atmosphere. He struggles to breathe as he makes for the dark reaches of space.

But what else is new?

# 69. Who are you?

His eyelids pull themselves open again, and his eyes marble around their sockets, locating Dev in the familiar surroundings of Katie's room. Fresh from his sojourn in space, he sees that something is different. A light. Muted. Soft light. It throws its glow in his face. He can hear something. It sounds far away. Faint. Electrical hum. Dev's eyes gaze down to the severed electrical wires that snake from his latest visitor.

Forgetting his fight against the belt for a few moments, Dev reaches his hand out for the familiarity of the cold, smooth metal at the bed. The humming grows louder, pleading with Dev, beseeching. For life? For death? 'Shh,' soothes Dev, 'just let it happen. Not long now.' The lamp post lets out a final hum. Of protest? Of acquiescence? Dev's jaded eyes simply stare, unblinking, betraying no feelings. The lamppost staring back, questioning.

We're almost full circle. Nearly caught up. It has been a difficult slog. At times drearily trivial. At others, confusing and infuriating. I think I understand a little more, certainly enough to finally bestow upon Dev his gift. Talent. Insight. Whatever you want to call it.

To those of you who have joined me for this merry little joyride, this vaguely amusing jaunt through one man's fleeing subconscious, I thank you for your commitment. That you made it this far is a testament to your persistence and that you had absolutely nothing better to do with your time.

But let's put aside your empty dance card woes and focus on the final events from earlier this evening in Katie's bedroom…

'We can change our physical features to attain what we want or be who we want,' rambled Dev, sitting on Katie's bed but talking at speed again, thoughts pulsing through his mind as Katie tried to get a word in to express her anger at him. 'Does the way we see our physical selves influence the way we think?

'The way we appear to others can affect our experience of the world in terms of how we are treated. What if you could assemble the perfect personality? Inquisitive, productive, insusceptible to negative influences. A personality that will not be changed or swayed from fulfilling its true potential. What if we could identify the ultimate keys to unlocking all the potential of each human brain.'

'Yes yes,' pressed Katie, 'like reading Shakespeare to babies in the womb,' she stated distractedly. She knew all was not well with Dev, and she paced around the room, only half listening to him as she waited for an opportunity in his near consistent monologue to bring the conversation back to the terrible truth with which Dev had opened this visit.

'Yeah. Or if you could take a brain and rewire it to place memories, influences, ideas, thoughts in the right place at the right time. Paste everything in place. The layers and layers of information that go into making a person and lead them to do the things that they do,' Dev bumbled on, 'what if we could identify them exactly and recreate them to fit exact specifications? Isn't that what parents try to do?'

'I think parents try to help their children to find their own personalities, Dev. The same parents you prescribed medication they didn't need. Let's talk about that, shall we?' pushed Katie.

'One day,' philosophised Dev, looking up to the stained ceiling above their heads, 'there'll cease to be any *right* or *wrong*. *Good deeds* and *bad*. There'll just be human behaviour. The kind of behaviour society found unacceptable a hundred years ago is now commonplace. Who's to say that what we baulk at today won't be typical in decades to come?

'Katie, there is no *good* and *bad*. It's all bleeding at the edges, becoming seamless. They're fraying, the memories of Amina. The threads coming undone, being woven with others into a new pattern. Nothing is what it once was. Everything is simultaneously old and new. Like blood from a cut. Do you see? The blood is fresh to your eyes but not to your veins. It's one thing, but also another.'

'But there's no point talking about that, Dev, we can only talk about what's real, like those people you hurt,' Katie pressed. She angrily sat herself down on the bed, away from Dev, burying her face in her hands in frustration, the spring mattress undulating beneath her. 'No mind is perfect, to create a perfect mind, you'd have to start it like you were designing a product. No memories. No traits from previous generations leftover to get snagged and broken on. But no one is that way. You can't create that for yourself. Is that what you want? What is it you are searching for, Dev?' Katie asked.

'I know you're searching for something. Everyone is searching for something beyond themselves that they *know* will complete their lives. Sometimes they look for it in others and need to take something from someone else, but they don't treat them like lab mice. What you did is unforgivable. I know something has happened to you, but I just… I don't know who you are.'

'Not the person I should have been. So don't ask me because I can't help you,' muttered Dev.

'Well, if you can't tell me, no one can.'

'I can't help you. Because so much of me is Amina, and I don't know what happened to her. Not really. And if Amina is gone, and I don't trust my memories of her, then I don't know who I am. All the children we once were, we'll never be them again. Our lives will never be that simple again.'

'Dev, who's Amina?' asked Katie.

'Amina is… incomplete. I'm trying to piece her together, trying to make her make sense. Sex, family, children, religion, work. These are the basic things that frame our lives and make our worlds whole, aren't they? So that's what I was using to know her. I wanted to understand what she went through, to share it, carry the weight for her.

'The weight of being used by others for their pleasure. As if the life of another is worth nothing at all. Then I tried to understand her mindset when she let go. I used my patients to engineer a way to see what it was to have their world be turned inside-out and push them to suicide.

'After finding out from Mum… I was trying to know her, and my mum too, it turns out,' Dev slowly admitted to Katie. In engaging him, she had succeeded, at least momentarily, in curbing his manic chatter.

'But I can't know her, what she went through, what she thought. Do you understand? Now I just want… I need to know that she was… at peace. You've made your peace with what happened to you. I need Mina to have made hers. Does that make sense?'

'I don't know, Dev,' Katie admitted, her tone softening.

'I can understand her not caring for her body anymore, not feeling it was hers anymore. Deliberately attacking it. I get that. But she could have been calm, in her mind, the part of herself she still loved, that I loved. Purposeful. No hesitation, no fear, no hate. I don't want to imagine her afraid, Katie. But she's blank to me now. Everything's confused. I don't remember what was real about her anymore.'

'If she's blank, she can be anybody,' reasoned Katie, leaning into Dev's logic, still hoping to talk him down. 'She can be anybody you want. She can be as strong as you need her to be.'

'All I can do is guess or watch other people to look for any sparks in them that match what my sister was like, some trait that I can track to understand how Amina could have reached that place. Everywhere I look, everyone I meet, I'm looking for her. If I can give it a story, if I can give a reason to what happened, then I can accept it and move on. I can let it go.'

'Whoever she was then, you can make of her what you like now. She is part of you. Who would you like her to be?' asked Katie. 'Just make her that person, create that memory and lock that image in place.'

'I just need to have a connection to hold on to,' answered Dev. 'That's why I'm doing this.'

'But wrapping a belt around your neck is not going to help with that!' snapped Katie in frustration.

It was all too much for her. With no idea what else Dev

may have been involved in and convinced that he needed psychiatric help, she could no longer be around him. 'You're trying to see her point of view, but you can't do that!' she cried, her voice filling the room. 'It's not enough. It's too simple. You need a bigger… hit each time. It won't ever be enough, Dev. You're better off stopping yourself before you go too far. Before you hurt yourself. Or someone you care about.'

'I'm not going to hurt myself, Katie. I'm a doctor. I know what I am doing,' Dev replied, leaning to the floor to collect the package he had dropped there. He began opening it. 'I ordered this, it's designed for auto-erotic asphyxiation, but I'm going to use it for just the asphyxiation part. It's the safest way to take myself to the brink, to feel how she felt, without actually killing myself. It has these special natural fibres that contract and close around your neck. There's a strap you pull on to stimulate the fibres to loosen naturally.'

'You're not yourself right now, Dev. I don't think you should do this,' Katie paused before adding: 'Not here.'

'You said you'd help me. They say you're not supposed to do it alone. Just in case.'

'I can't, Dev. I can't watch you do this,' she said, her eyes filling with tears. 'You're not well. You need help.' Katie paused again. 'Dev,' she began before breathing in deeply. 'You're an addict.' She stopped again for a reaction from Dev. He simply stared at her, nonplussed by her statement. 'Watching you would be like watching myself. It's too much. I can't. I'll step out for a cigarette or two.'

'Step out? The whole point of doing this here was for you to keep an eye on me, so nothing goes wrong. You agreed.'

‘That was before. Things have changed. Then, I thought it was research. Now it’s… something else, some… addiction. You may as well be strapping up and doing heroin. I can’t be around addicts. Don’t make me watch.’

‘Fine then,’ huffed Dev, ‘step out and give me ten minutes.’

Katie turned to leave and was almost at the door when she realised she’d left her cigarettes behind. Dev was already unwrapping the belt from its packaging when she turned back. Picking up the carton, she couldn’t help asking him. ‘Dev, I know you’re in pain, and you’re not yourself right now. But you violated those people. You know that, right? You didn’t respect them or their bodies.’

Dev began undoing the packaging, ripping a tear in the plastic and setting free a fat sachet of Dimethyl Fumarate, which landed on the bedsheet with a thud. ‘I want to go back to our little house, and for this all to have been a really terrible dream,’ he admitted. ‘I want to wake up as a nine-year-old again. Can we do that, d’you think? Is that a service you provide, Katie?’

‘No, darling, I’m sorry.’

‘No. I didn’t think so. All you can do is open your legs for the right price!’ he suddenly snapped, cruelly.

‘Hey! Dev, I understand that you’re upset, but that doesn’t mean you can lash out at me.’

‘Actually, Katie, yes it does, because I’m paying you to listen. We’re not friends. I have always paid you for your time.’

Shocked and hurt, somehow Katie maintained her composure, ‘Dev, I’m being really patient because I know that this isn’t you.’

'Really? How do you know? I don't know who I am. I wasn't supposed to be in this room with you. I was supposed to have a sister. Instead, I'm being dragged through places and experiences that I should never have been involved with. So, I'm angry, Katie. I'm *really* fucking angry and tired,' he cried, the tears running down his face.

'I get that,' said Katie, neutrally, her hands holding her cigarettes and lighter, backing away towards the door. 'I'll… I'll leave you,' muttered Katie, edging out of the door and closing it behind her after a final look at Dev sitting on her bed.

And that brings us to the here and now.

# 70. Who I am

Here, being Katie's room. *Now,* being roughly three and a half minutes after, she, fearing for his sanity, closed the door on Dev to place a call to the emergency services, who dispatched officers, requesting that Katie stay on the phone until they arrived. The irony is that if the emergency services Katie had phoned to save Dev's mind hadn't insisted that she remain on the phone with them, she literally would have saved his life.

Unfortunately, I have to step in and go through this whole tedious process to do my little bit. Now, after what seems like hours of struggling, everyone he has brought up, the different voices, faces, accents, sounds, colours, countries... everything. They all rush at him, assailing him with their various issues, needs, desires. In this moment, he finally accepts that he understands none of them.

'Tsk, tsk,' I utter to announce my presence and gain Dev's attention.

'Who are you?' he asks, his brow wet with sweat, eyes bulging.

'You don't know me,' I reply. 'I assign everyone I meet a particular... gift or insight, and I imbue them with it. You don't just dream up your ideas out of nowhere. You all need a helping hand, and that is where I come in. I mean, what are you if you don't have ideas? Just a bunch of animals following impulses. I give you all that which makes each of you different from the other.'

‘What’s mine then?’ he asks.

‘I haven’t gotten to deciding yours yet. So, tell me, succinctly, in your own words, how did you end up here? Here, let me loosen that for you a little,’ I offer, helpfully reaching out to the belt around his neck. He’s going to die, so it seems like poor form to allow him to suffer. I suppose I could have done that some time ago. Ah, well.

‘If you give talent to everyone… thank you, that’s kind,’ he says as the belt loosens a little, ‘why don’t you give yourself the talent to know everything?’

‘How do you know I haven’t? We’ve been floating through your memories and I don’t understand that last argument you had with your friend.’

‘Katie?’

‘No, Tim. He was excited about having a child. What was so wrong with that?’

‘I don’t know. Why does it matter?’ asks Dev.

‘Because I need to assign you some insight, and I need to know more.’

‘Tim doesn’t know the first thing about children.’

‘And you do?’

‘No, I never said that.’

‘So how can you know Tim would be no good?’

‘I didn’t say that either,’ Dev croaks. ‘He just doesn’t take anything seriously. Children are a serious thing. Everything needs to be in place from the beginning. If you can’t take care of yourself, how can you take care of anyone else?’

‘Can’t he take care of himself?’

‘But, the whole thing has to be planned. You can’t have stuff just happening all the time. You have to plan the next eighteen years. You have to have the answers to all the questions. They need to have confidence in their world and the certainty of their situation. If I had children, I'd need to be able to give them that. So… that means I'm not having children.'

'That, and the fact that you're dying. Your distrust of people meant you wanted to know what everyone was truly thinking, which led you to this. Dying, face down, on a prostitute's filthy mattress?'

'That's not true. Her mattress is not filthy.'

I laugh at this. 'Look at yourself. You don't realise how ridiculous you are. This is your personal meaning to life? Finding what people are like behind closed doors, seeing what's behind their eyes, these people you refuse to trust. I don't understand people like you, Dev. What did you ever think you'd find? Some pure truth that explains everyone? Makes everyone equal?'

'I wanted to know I could go back to the beginning.'

'What do you mean?'

'I want to explain.'

'So explain,' I press.

'No, I wanted to explain it *all*. If I can put together a story that explains it all, it might stop feeling so bad. Then I can forget about it. If I can get the story straight about what happened, I can stop thinking about it, and the whole thing can disappear like it never happened. Because of Amina, I always knew there was no safety, no matter what. If Amina hadn't gone, everything would be different. I hadn't realised it… it was her death.'

'Yes,' I push.

'It was her sudden death…' he croaks, 'that first made me mistrust the world. I couldn't reconcile how she could suddenly be gone… I would remember that night she scared me with her crying… that night she told me the story of the building that could think… which made me wonder how thoughts work… my mistrust made me wonder what everyone was thinking… led me to consider researching it… then Mum told me the truth… and I needed to understand Mina… her death… her death that first taught me that life cannot be trusted… before everything else confirmed the world is subject to change… without warning.' Dev allows his body to slump. With the tension gone, the muscles finally relax.

'Maybe she knew it too,' I suggest, 'that there's no safety, no certainty in anything. You're all so much more fragile than you'd like to admit. Maybe she freed herself from any need for safety. You're doing the same. It is your body that limits you. It is your body that is dying. You can *choose* to be happy about your exodus from this tiny enclosure. Allow your thoughts to scatter free. Let those feelings grow and evolve to meld with millions, billions of others. Let your body die. It is my gift to you.'

'That's your gift! Are you serious?' Dev asks, his eyes lighting with incredulity.

I take a different approach. 'There are so many things in nature that aren't what they appear to be. Do you know why the sky is blue?'

'Not really.'

'It isn't. Do you know this place, Paulding? Somewhere there, under the right conditions, strange lights regularly appear, hovering in the night sky. People go from all over to see these peculiar hovering lights. Inevitably they think they see UFOs. But the lights have been identified, and they are not from flying objects. They are the headlights from oncoming vehicles far away. Atmospheric conditions in the area converge to make it look like the lights are in the sky, far higher than they actually are.

'Despite the explanation, some people convince themselves they really are seeing spaceships. Use your mind, your imagination. There you can live and thrive. Tell yourself you can breathe. Stop struggling. Breathe, so you no longer have to. Everything has disappeared. The past no longer matters. Is that what you want?'

'Yes.'

'I cannot do that for you. Do you want to die?'

'I don't know.'

Dev
Son
Doctor
Grandson
Boyfriend
Nephew
Friend
Brother

Whatever you call him, to me, he is a sample. Another human. Another physical body. For humans, their bodies are unchangeable, but their minds can be influenced. Shaped. Despite that, they need their bodies to function practically in the world. They depend upon being seen, acknowledged, and recognised.

With each birth, a physical body is a non-negotiable clause in the contract. The only question being, what it will look like, its possibilities and limitations. All bodies are preprogrammed with unchangeable physical needs and instructions, yet thoughts and beliefs can be stimulated. Manipulated. Humans possess the capacity to persuade themselves, rationalise and justify to themselves the suffering they deal one another, whether it is for power, pleasure, or profit.

To deliver a more convincing performance, actors can convince themselves that they possess a physical impediment. They can temporarily believe fully in their character's justifications for their monstrous acts. Often little more than vessels propelled by their emotions, humans can, at times, choose how they feel. They can choose hope. They can choose optimism. They can choose to think with positivity, but they cannot spontaneously alter their physicality.

They marvel at physical feats, yet I marvel at the inherent flexibility of human thought. They can numb themselves to the rules of the world around them to make their own inner world come to life. For all the horrors that they dream up to inflict upon one another, there lies incalculable beauty in how the fertile human mind can bring itself to hypothesise, create and believe so many things that have no foundations in what they call the *real world*.

I never tire of watching it happen, but I am consistently astonished at how they unwaveringly place their trust in thoughts every waking second. Thoughts. Intangible streams that cannot be weighed or quantified in any way that has meaning for the average person. A neuroscientist may monitor a brain for patterns but cannot yet delve far into specific impulses. Human thought is limitless in a way that the physical world is not.

Dev had convinced himself he had wanted so many other things throughout this journey and the various travails he has put himself and others through. Finally, he accepted that all he had wanted to know was how Amina felt in those moments as she placed her body on the cusp of death. To this end, Dev had passed the belt over his head and felt it instantly tighten around his neck.

He wanted to see what she faced, even if it was only a glimpse of a glance. Had he been in his right mind, he wouldn't have ever considered this, any of it. Or, if he had, he would have considered it absurd in the extreme. But I suppose that is what a completely devastating event can do. It devastates completely, affecting people we think we know in ways we cannot anticipate.

All strapped up with nowhere to go, Dev is finally free to face Amina. No more hiding behind statistics and the arid language of research papers. No more ill-conceived plans for knowledge and understanding. No more charging away on a quest in lieu of a meaningful connection or of processing his emotions. Finally, he is caught.

Unable to move far, shorn of the tiresome preoccupation of keeping his body alive, Dev can focus on facing Amina. Instead of mourning what he has lost, calling forth a memory, he is finally connecting with the person, with what he has left of her.

What humans choose to perceive as the real world, which can be deconstructed into subatomic particles, serves only to limit them. Yet, thoughts – fleeting, transient, ephemeral – evade capture and quantification, offering so much more. Humans can choose, and now Dev chooses hope. Dev chooses to breathe.

'Stop struggling, breathe and get up.'

'I can't.'

'It's my gift to you, Dev Sharma. Engage your thoughts. Breathe.'

With that, I leave Dev to his thoughts.

# 71. The beginning

With that, they leave me to my thoughts.

Immediately the belt tightens once more around my neck, and I'm struggling again, but it's in real-time now, not slowed down like before. The oxygen is not getting through. Not enough. Won't be long before my brain pops, leaving that tell-tale stain on the inside of my skull. *Breathe*. What the fuck? Gift? Some gift! Were they joking? I can't really be dying like this, can I?

*Engage your thoughts*. What did they fucking mean? Do they believe I can think my way out of this? This is a belt around my fucking neck, not some kid's story with magic and trolls or something. How can I think my way out of this? I'm killing myself. This is it. It's happening. I didn't think it would, but it is. I'm killing myself.

I'm almost there. I'm almost with Amina. I'll see what she saw… that day… when she did it. What did she see? Did she see concrete? Did she see tarmac? Cars? Street lamps? Headlights? What did she see?

Do those who kill themselves do so out of devastation at their life caving in? Or is it that they no longer accept a world that they cannot love. For some, could it not be that they choose not to live in a world that refused to be as beautiful as its potential? For those, is their love they feel for the world, its inhabitants, possibilities and permutations, too strong to allow them to accept the corruption of that ideal?

That's how I choose to think of Amina, that she chose not to see her world tarnished. Her love for the world was too great to allow her to reconcile the world she saw with the world she saw in her mind.

My mind screams. My eyes bulge, and my pupils dilate, letting in more and more light. Too much, as though I'm gazing at a star going supernova. The light obliterates the room, and for a moment, I see nothing.

What did *she* see?

# 72. To be free

Amina looks out over the back garden from her bedroom window.

Perhaps.

Perhaps she thinks of leaving a note, but how could she give words to such a thing?

Amina dresses simply for a spring day. Jeans. Sweater. Hair tied back, she leaves her room for the last time. She makes her way down the stairs for the last time. Perhaps she looks in on her mum and dad in the kitchen. They would be bickering, as usual, busy getting in one another's way, except Mum would be different. Quieter than usual. Or louder. A weight on her mind. Filtering thoughts and feelings.

She hadn't considered Amina's. Not really. She had considered her, physically. Mum had hugged and consoled, as an automatic response, horrified at what had happened to her daughter's body. But she hadn't reached the stage where she could connect it with Amina's mind, her emotions. She would have to process her own first. That was just Mum.

Amina would go through the dining room on her way to the French doors leading to the back garden. Although it was spring, there would still be a chill in the air, meaning the door would be closed. Amina would slide it open and walk along the concrete path along the side of the grass to where I am crouching by the strawberries growing by the hedge. Amina leans over me, blocking out the sunlight.

'What are you up to?' she asks.

Remaining crouched at the strawberries, I twist my body to look up at her. She's a silhouette, the buoyant sun revelling in its freedom and strength, shorn of the winter clouds, like Samson pulling down those pillars. Every autumn, it is like the clouds have shaved the sun's hair, putting it at their mercy.

Despite squinting, I can't make out her features with the bright sunlight behind her. Later, I would wish I had made more effort to see her face that day and lock it in my memory. Instead, that silhouette is all I could call to mind as a child whenever I thought of her on that day.

'Keeping an eye on the strawberries,' I say. 'Mum always says they're no good by the time they are ripe because the birds and bugs have already gotten to them.'

'Only you would have the patience to sit here and watch out for bugs.'

'I just want us to be able to eat the strawberries this year. Are you going out again? You're going out a lot,' I reproach.

'Yeah.'

'And you haven't told me a story in ages. I mean a real story.'

'Yeah, I'm sorry.'

'Tell me one now.'

'Okay,' she agrees, 'why not? Which one shall I tell you?'

'Make up a new one.'

Amina sits cross-legged on the concrete path next to me as I continue monitoring insect activity around the strawberry patch.

'Where shall I start?'

I like the familiarity of these redundant questions. 'At the beginning.'

'And how shall I start?'

'With *once upon a time*,' I say, smiling.

'All right, once upon a time, there was a man. No. Yes, yes, once upon a time, there was a man who had one child, a son. Eventually, the man grew old and the son grew up and became a man. On his deathbed, the old man told his son that to have a life free of stress he should have a good accountant, a good doctor and a good mechanic.'

'Why those things?' I query.

'Doesn't need to be people with those jobs exactly,' replies Amina, as she brushes a few unruly strands of hair out of her face.

'Does it need to be three?'

'It can be more. It can be fewer.'

'Can it be one?' I ask.

'Er no. It can't be one. Doesn't work with just one.'

'Okay. Three.'

'All right. The old man dies, and the son is very sad.'

'Why does he die?'

'Just because he's old. The son gets married, and his wife has… triplets! When they get older, their father pushes each child to be one of the things his father said he needed. And they all hate him for it.'

'Why?' I ask.

They didn't want to do those things.'

'Couldn't they do something else?'

'No.'

'Why not?'

'Well, because they have to pay to go to school, and their father wouldn't pay for them to study anything else.'

'What happened?'

'They went far away to their different schools to learn their different jobs. When they finish studying and pass all their exams, they go back home. By this time, they are grown-ups, but they are still angry with their father, and they go to see him. When they get to his house, they find him dying.'

'Why was he dying?' I ask.

'He was ill. Before he dies, the children want to tell their father how angry he made them.'

'But he was ill. When you're ill, people have to be nice to you. That's how it works,' I say with conviction.

'It doesn't matter. They have to do it. They finally tell him how they feel.'

'What do they say?'

'They say that the only reason he made them study those things was for his own benefit because that was what his father had told him. Their lives had been controlled by a dead man.'

'What does he say?'

'It is difficult for him to speak. They are his last moments, and he is in pain, but he tells them that he loves them and only wants the best for them. The old man tells them that the knowledge and skills he pushed them to learn were never for his benefit. He tells them that they were always meant to help each other.

'Each of them has skills in things that can help the others. The man says he is happy with what he has done because he has ensured they are stronger together. The sons realise he is right. Although he is going to die, the children have each other. They have each other's love, and they live happily ever after,' finished Amina. 'Good story?'

'It was okay.'

'Dev. Whatever happens, you know that Mum and Dad are always thinking of us. They want the best for us, right?'

'What do you mean?'

'Nothing. Just that. Okay?'

'Okay,' I agree, suddenly remembering my strawberries and turning back to them.

'I'm going out. 'Bye.'

Amina touches my shoulder as she gets up from the path.

'Where are you going?'

'To see friends.'

'Okay, 'bye 'bye.'

Amina leaves through the garden gate and doesn't look back.

Amina ambles. And the world is silent.

Before long, Amina strolls under the overgrown tree that hangs over the pavement. In autumn, the pavement there is slimy and slippery from the rain mixing with the droppings from birds in the overhanging branches and their dead leaves that would flutter to the ground.

Passing Larissa Lane, Amina sees a familiar sight there, Mr Michaels' navy blue Sierra. With the hood of the vehicle up, Amina cannot see him, but she assumes he is working on it, as usual, while his two children, whom she can see through the rear window, toil within the vehicle. Working together, they clean the interior with their little cloths.

On the back of the car, just above the tail light, Amina has always noticed a strange decal. The outline of a fish. She has always wondered about its significance, but not today. Today

Amina continues.

In the opposite direction comes a minibus. As it glides past her, she recognises the emblem on the side but has never been able to discern the animal pictured within. A beaver? A capybara? The emblem belongs to a local amateur football team. From the corner of her eye, she spots a player snoozing, his head against the window. She recognises the name on their cap. *Dortmund.* A club from Germany's football league.

Amina takes a shortcut through the park, avoiding the civic building where the mayor was pictured recently on the first day of the construction work to improve the building. There works a Somalian builder, seemingly with a passion for *Abba*, always singing one of their songs.

A light breeze blows the fragrance of lavender across her path as Amina exits the park, a lamp post flickering in the daylight. She wonders why some of them do that. Aren't they all supposed to come to life together at a pre-programmed time?

Amina is startled by a butterfly, seemingly out of nowhere, beating its wings about her before fluttering away. Amina tracks its progress across the road where she sees a man at the bus stop.

He is not waiting for a bus. He is a worker taking down the old poster from the shelter and putting up a new one. She knows the one he is taking down. A movie poster for a forthcoming blockbuster. "Coming This Summer: *Walk,*" the poster says. "Enter The Portal. Begin Again."

The worker has left the engine of their van running. The music fades as the presenter returns to debating with his guests the latest news about Brussels, insisting the EU's member states take in traumatised refugees from war-torn countries, despite protests.

Before long, she is at the metal fences, haphazardly stationed, supposedly to stop trespassers accessing the site where the bridge awaits its finishing touches. She squeezes through a gap between two of the temporary fences and wanders to the barrier, where she looks out over the traffic below.

She wonders where they are all going, whether they would get there without incident, without breaking down. How many of them had just joined the road? How many were just passing through? Before long, her thoughts are interrupted by a rumble more intense than that of the traffic below.

Amina looks up to see the silhouette of a plane passing overhead, probably on its way to Heathrow, which is close by. Or perhaps it had left Heathrow and is on its way elsewhere. Amina thinks of the different places the plane could be headed. Paris. New York. Hong Kong. Cape Town. Naples. Sydney. Quebec. Or maybe just somewhere else in the UK.

Amina imagines a man on the plane. A whiskey glass on the tray in front of him. His head asleep against the window. What would he dream of? Would he dream of the plane he was on? Would he see all the people, the stewards, the passengers? Maybe he dreams the side of his head has melted into the window. The glass has become soft and claggy, melding with the skin and forming part of him, gaining access to his circulation… his organs…

> The machine is part of him, and he is part of the
> machine. He can feel himself becoming forever

connected to the craft, never to be extricated, drained
by the machine functions...

Lights, landing gears, propulsion, heating, electrics,
dials, signals, radios...

Maybe it will be fine. He can live like this forever.
What happens to planes when they get too old?
Recycled, dismantled, turned into millions of pens?
Wouldn't that be a thing, to be taken apart into a
million pieces and sent here, there and everywhere...

Would people like that? Little pens made from fingers,
microwave buttons made from fingernails and
corneas...

Is that my retirement plan?

Could be a tourist attraction for this plane... People
would buy a flight just to sit next to me and have their
photos taken. I could discuss politics and current
affairs. They'd be amazed that I could think so clearly,
unconcerned at the jumbo jet attached to my brain...

Maybe I could continue working. I'd just need my
briefcase. I could get another lobe to help so I could
also work on aircraft systems, keeping everything in
check...

I could get that built and installed. Might need

planning permission. You need planning permission for everything. Why shouldn't I get planning permission for my brain. It's my brain. It's inside me, not some listed building...

Light, light everywhere and not a drop to drink. Being light would be like being those millions of pens everywhere in all those places, all those hands, behind all those ears, handbags, falling out of pockets...

I'd like to be light travelling so far through space. If I could come back as something, it would be light. Always there in one form or another.

Look up and see light shining down on them. Flashlights on survivors, candles in churches, desk lamps on secrets...

That's it! I want to be part of everything everywhere in the world.

To be an essential atom, proton, quark in the working of everything living or otherwise.

Wouldn't that be beautiful? Wouldn't that feel like purpose? A perfect existence...

How would it feel to come apart? Implode. Naked to the microscopic eye. Or something...

What if I got up, stopped dreaming, sleeping, sitting, got up, walked past the stewards with their drinks trolley?

Past sleeping passengers with earphones stuffed in their heads. I'll walk over, flip the levers and fling open the doors...

It'll be alright. The cabin won't decompress or whatever. The attendants will simply smile benignly. As though I was slipping off the bus at my stop.

I'll step out along the wing.

And at the end of the wing, I'll jump away.

Unafraid...

Drop down. Atmosphere whipping past. Terminal velocity. Screeching. Ears, arms pinned back. Frozen face. Can't breathe.

Wind stripping skin away. Layer by layer. Particle by particle. Until I dissolve and break apart completely.

Into nothing...

Particle by particle by particle. Through the clouds. Through the smog, Through the mist. Through the rain. Through the fog. Through the snow.

All over the world. Swept around and around. Scattered
by wind, blizzards, tornadoes, hurricanes and butterfly
wings...

Carried on the air by bees and insects. Blown around
by car exhausts and ventilation systems. I shower down
on everything particle by particle...

I'm part of the chess game in the park.

The dying flowers on the window sill.

Attack in a dark alleyway.

The stairwell with a sleeping homeless man.

Cream on a cat's whiskers.

Rain on a classroom window.

Dust behind a wardrobe.

The seat of a taxi where a woman bleeds.

Fragments of a torn page.

The mattress in the cell at a prison where prisoners
protest.

Hand sanitiser at a residential home.

The prescription pad at a clinic.

The new recording equipment a musician refuses to use.

A room where a door argues with its paint.

The light in the room that bends, changes, refracts.

Travelling the distance from space through the atmosphere.

Changing along the way.

Magnifying. Spreading bioluminescence. Infrared diffraction...

Finally feeling like something other than the person on the plane. Feeling I am where I am supposed to be...

Dust particles spinning aimlessly in the sunlight coming in through a window between partly drawn curtains. I'm part of everything. Part of light. Part of water in the air that is breathed...

In the emotions that are felt. The love. The fear. The hate.

Want to calm. Want to make everything all right for everyone. No one has to be afraid.

There is purpose. Everything is working towards something. Something comes from nothing...

Stories about nothing. Nothing can hurt us. Everything flows. Bends. Shapes. Light in a room.

Dust particles spinning in the air over a man strangling himself. Struggling against it.

Wanting to get out of this moment, to convince himself this will end differently...

Separate the body from the mind. One dies while the other tells stories. Will it continue living through stories and memories?

In a hospital. Assisting fibre optic endoscopy procedures. Pushing through intense light. Illuminating a living, bleeding, pulsing human body from within.

Presenting organs, functioning, gulping and gasping...

What if it came apart? What if the fibres came apart one by one? And formed part of the body.

What if they carried on, no longer controlled, disappearing into the body. Amongst veins, arteries, organs, wriggling away beyond reach...

Amongst the sensitive network of pink and red

rhythmic pulsating organs working together to keep this body and mind alive.

For the sole purpose of surviving, maintaining this living state for as long as possible...

Nothing else matters to the organs. The muscles. Epidermis. Bones. Joints. Arteries.

Veins throbbing with blood. Carrying oxygen, carbon dioxide, iron, haemoglobin, proteins, sugars, fats, salts, nutrients. Throbbing, pulsing, beating red and red everywhere...

Red and red everywhere. At a Hindu wedding. The bride wears red and gold. Covered with jewellery. The last of the four days. Everyone is drunk. Alcohol swilling. In the blood. Through the body. Up to the brain. Heart pumping pumping pumping...

The people shouting, clapping, stamping feet to the music pounding pounding pounding.

Does the body control the brain, or does the brain control the body?

Every body jumping to the music in celebration. To be happy. Happy to be celebrating. Or celebrating to be happy...

Convinced this is important. Right here and now. Making it a moment to remember. Bring us back to be part of the network.

Notting Hill Carnival dancers. Multicoloured. Banging drums. Marching. Swaying. Floating past...

Women on trucks. Dancing atop giant speakers sweating sound. Topless men on stilts. Dancers with elaborate costumes.

Representing something of their country. Their culture, heritage, pride. Something part of everything. Interconnected, interwoven, inextricable...

Absence would leave a gap that doesn't make sense.

At a music festival now. Pounding pounding pounding. The lights strobing across the mass of bodies. Writhing with the rhythm. Red lights wash over them all. Nothing else matters. The music is everything...

Music is a stimulant in the system, hearing something you know, altered by the musician, flowing through the system. Blood sloshing through the heart. Heart pounding, squeezing, clenching, red everywhere, throbbing faces, joy, dancing, sliding, sweat sodden, dripping cotton, it's everywhere...

It's everywhere, arms in the air, heads thrown back, legs

jumping, eyes squinting, torsos, limbs, fingers, elbows. Flowing, crashing, flooding, flesh.

She is somewhere...

Somewhere she knows what she was thinking. I have to know what she was thinking. To do that. So sad. So desperate. So alone. She was trying to talk. I didn't understand...

Can't be that easy to just slip away, no no no no no, I just want to be light, I want to be light from the point of view of light, light sees everything touches everything...

Passes through, changes form, what is it like to pass through glass, to feel everything, to pass over everything? The light seeping over everything, knowing everything...

Light passing through a prism, refracting, constantly changing, passing through different things, becoming something else, light is always there even when it is pitch black, it is still there, the light seeps over everything, pours over everything...

I want to be light. Can I be light? I am the light that passes through. I light the cracks and weaknesses. I am a part of everything. I am light. I am everywhere. I am everything. I change everything before me as I leak and pool and drip...

*Engage your thoughts.*

Oh, but what is this now? I open my eyes to the room again, and they turn to the window just in time.

Just in time…

… to see the saltwater that comes without warning, washing away all dirt, dragging all human life under, covering heads and brains and washing away all thoughts.

All computer files are wiped, all records are destroyed.

Magnetic fields, tides, the moon all work together to ensure everything is decimated by the majesty of the oceans, ground down into nothing.

A thousand oceans descend upon the planet, turning it into a blue ball of water, spinning in the universe under the vacant gaze of gassy stars, doing whatever it is that they do.

Perhaps waiting to help the next series of sailors and explorers navigate towards whatever it is that they are looking for. Big blue ball spinning in the nothingness.

Lifeless, useless human bodies submerged underwater in what were once offices, bedrooms, restaurants, taxis, becoming entwined with time and tide.

Strangers occupy each other's personal space, the bodies
jostling one another, consent no longer necessary once dead.

They are just male bodies and female bodies. Different
races and colours. Wearing different fabrics and
garments, silently going about their business of ebbing
and flowing with the water that goes on and on.

Bodies that no longer hold any meaning, deteriorating
a little more with each cycle of sun, moon and tide.

Dissipating, dispersing and dissolving in the water,
passing through other creatures more suited to the new
environment.

Creatures that have managed to avoid becoming
beached upon piles of toppled skyscrapers and
collapsed office blocks.

What does anything mean? The thoughts and beliefs
that we cling to?

The perceptions, positive and negative that help us
define ourselves in relation to others?

The religions, the fucking, the jobs, the qualifications,
the achievements, the failures.

Against a thousand oceans of water, nothing matters
anymore.

There is no time for screaming, no time for help, no time to make a single sound before a wave that blocks out the sun comes crashing down, obliterating skulls, ripping flesh, causing internal injuries that no car ever could.

The sheer pressure from the force of the water sends bodies crashing into each other, into brick walls, vehicles, through tree branches.

Forced, ground through metal railings, flung through window frames, whipped through the air to fall back to the water from height, shattering every bone.

Bodies unrecognisable, leaking their various liquids from orifices, gashes and wounds. Nothing survives. No person is left alive. No thought is left intact.

I know now. I know now what they meant. *Breathe*. All I have to do is *Engage your thoughts* and *Breathe*.

I know that now. And so, that's what I do.

My eyes turn to the window, and I imagine myself breathing, breathing sweet lungfuls of air.

Even if it's stale air, it's still oxygen, the life-giving force that bypasses my lungs, making its way directly into my brain.

No need for anything else.

I breathe because I see myself breathing.

The belt falls away. Defeated.

Why should this be the end of my life? I turn my head and look to the window. The trees blow about outside under the bullying wind.

Rising from the bed, I approach the bay window. It is open just an inch.

Greedy for clean, fresh air, I reach for the glass to push it out further, but the wind gets to it first and pulls it away from me.

The salty sea air fills the room, engulfing me. I can imagine no more wondrous feeling than this cool sea air blowing against me and billowing around me.

I breathe in the air, the room, the world… and cry tears of joy.

The window ceases to be as I move towards it. Instead, I suddenly find myself on the beach beyond the bedroom, pebbles underfoot, yet I have no idea how I got here.

For an all too brief moment, the reality shimmers

before me, and I feel more real than I ever have.

All the nonsense is cast aside, and like having a gentle hand upon my shoulder, I suddenly feel unburdened, as though I'm seeing colours and hearing sounds for the first time.

I feel outside of my own body but more in control than ever. I can make everything fit together, so it makes sense, so everything is in focus all at once.

No trade-offs. No compromises. Everything is there, in its proper place, and now that it's all there, I know that none of it matters.

It's all suddenly so light and delicate, like fog around a street lamp or a blade of grass showing off that drop of dew. Again, as though it were the littlest trophy in the world.

Such moments are delicate and fleeting, quickly forgotten as my mind reaches once more.

I stare out at the immense, thick, impenetrable waters of the dirty sea and recall my mother telling me about her headmaster when she was a schoolgirl in Mauritius.

Of their studies, he would say, "*ce n'est pas la mer à boire.*"

*It's not drinking the sea.*

Life is so fragile. But the compulsion to keep living is so strong.

THE END